THE
LUCILLA
ANDREWS
OMNIBUS

THE LUCILLA ANDREWS OMNIBUS

My Friend the Professor

Highland Interlude

Ring O'Roses

Harrap  London

My Friend the Professor first published in Great Britain 1960
by George G. Harrap & Co. Ltd

Highland Interlude first published in Great Britain 1968
by George G. Harrap & Co. Ltd

Ring o' Roses first published in Great Britain 1972
by George G. Harrap & Co. Ltd

This edition first published in Great Britain 1979
by George G. Harrap & Co. Ltd
182 High Holborn, London WC1V 7AX

ISBN 0 245 53461 X

*Printed in Great Britain by offset lithography by
Billing & Sons Limited, Guildford, London and Worcester*

CONTENTS

LUCILLA ANDREWS

My Friend the Professor

For
Veronica Lucilla

1. Three Young Ladies for St Martha's

The country annexe of St Martha's Hospital, London, was ninety miles from my father's turkey farm.

'It's as off the map as we are, Frances.' My father gave me my railway ticket. 'So don't forget you've to change three times. Here comes the first.' He kissed me briskly. 'Good luck, darling. Don't forget to write to your mother. Nervous?'

I swallowed. 'Very.'

He said he didn't blame me, and slammed the carriage door. The small local train lurched forward, he waved, and I was alone.

No one seemed to be travelling that day. I had a carriage to myself in all three trains. They ambled through miles of hop gardens, apple- and cherry-orchards, as if they had all eternity in which to carry me to my destination, while I practised calling myself 'Nurse' aloud. By the time I was in the third train 'Nurse Dorland' sounded quite unexceptional.

There was a corridor on that train. The ticket-collector came in as I was chatting to myself. 'Did you say something, miss?'

I pretended I had asked if he knew anything of St Martha's annexe. 'Is it near Pine Halt?'

He pushed back his cap with the stub of a pencil. 'It'll be around seven miles to the hospital, I reckon. You'll have been working in the London branch, I take it? I know you young ladies all change over now and then. Make a nice break to get a bit of country air, eh?'

'Very nice, thank you.' I tried to sound nonchalant and experienced. I felt very pleased with myself as he offered to get down my cases from the rack. He said he always liked lending nurses a hand, because he had been in hospital and he knew. He did not explain this knowledge as he obviously took me for an old hand, and I could not question him without spoiling my act. I wondered what he meant when I was alone again; then the elderly train rattled and groaned to another stop. Pine Halt was written in large letters on a sign just by my carriage window. My nonchalance dropped like an old coat from my shoulders. I thought, Oh, no! I'm there.

I clutched at my cases for support, and left the train reluctantly wondering what had ever made me think I wanted to be a nurse. Surely I should be far wiser to jump straight back into the carriage and meander with the train round the branch-line stations of southern England?

The train moved on, deciding my future for me. I put down my cases and looked around, uncertainly. There were two other young women waiting on the platform. They looked at me with equal uncertainty.

The girl nearest to me was fair, attractive, very well-groomed, and wearing a suit that could only have been cut in Paris. Her pale, pointed shoes had stiletto heels; her hat looked as expensive as her suit. I was on the verge of smiling hopefully, when I took in her appearance. Her clothes made me dismiss her from the possibility of being an embryo student nurse. She was obviously just a passing traveller. I turned towards the second girl. Her clothes could have come out of my wardrobe; her handbag had come from the same chain-store as the one I was carrying. I risked a smile.

She rushed up to me. 'Would you by any chance be bound for the Preliminary Training School of St Martha's?'

'Yes. You? Oh, good. I'm Frances Dorland.'

She beamed. 'I'm Hannah More. I'm so glad I've met some one. I was feeling lost. How about'—she jerked her head at the fair girl who was studying a timetable by the booking office—'her? Do you suppose she's one of us? She doesn't look like it.'

The station-master came out of his office and answered her. 'Would you three young ladies be for St Martha's?'

The fair girl looked round. 'I am, please.'

We joined her. 'So are we.'

The station-master said he was glad we were all present and correct. 'You'll just have to wait six minutes, ladies. The Sister from the hospital said there'd be two more nurses coming on the up train. The hospital's sending a conveyance to collect the five of you.' He walked round the booking-office, and looked over the low fence that separated the minute station from the road. 'That's one of the hospital cars coming along now. The porter'll look after you.'

The hospital porter was a fatherly young man. He checked our names and luggage, then sat us in the back of his station-wagon while he met the up train. When the two other girls joined us in the wagon he told us to keep an eye out for the view as he drove, and to send home immediately for our bicycles, if we possessed them. 'The P.T.S. and the hospital are a tidy step from the bus route, Nurses. No buses run up our hill, see, it being private, like. So if you've got bikes you get your mums to pack 'em off sharpish.'

The fair girl had not spoken a word since Hannah More and I joined her. 'Would I be allowed to have my car?' she asked quietly.

Hannah More had very dark hair and eyebrows. Her brows shot up.

The porter glanced round momentarily. 'I can't say as I know the answer to that, Nurse, seeing as you're the first nurse I've known to ask it. You'd better have a word with the Sister about that.'

One of the new girls had sandy hair and thin lips. Her companion was a rather pretty brunette with a lovely complexion. They stared with open hostility at the fair girl. She looked at her hands, and relapsed into her former silence.

'Obviously,' I said, 'a car or bike is a must if buses are out.'

Hannah agreed, introduced herself and me. 'What are your names, girls?'

Sandy hair was Fay Kinsley. Her friend, Agatha Carter. I looked expectantly at the fair girl. I had not heard what she said when she gave the porter her name. 'I'm Estelle Dexter.' She smiled, a polite and strangely anxious little smile. I smiled back, wondering if she was really anxious or only shy. Then I noticed Hannah's eyebrows were on the move again, and Fay was visibly nudging Agatha Carter. The atmosphere in the back of the station-wagon had not been particularly amicable, but at that moment it was positively and—to me—unaccountably electric with disapproval.

I had never been able to tolerate atmospheres. I had to say something. 'Any of you girls done any nursing?'

'Have you, Frances?' queried Hannah.

'No. The only time I've been inside a hospital was when I went up to Martha's for my interview with Matron. The prospect before us scares the daylights out of me.'

Estelle glanced at me in silence. Agatha Carter and Fay Kinsley exchanged smug smiles.

Fay said, 'I suppose it must be rather frightening for you. Personally, all I feel is that starting again is going to be the most awful bore. Agatha and I were discussing it on the way down to-day. We've come together. We worked in the same hospital in our home town.'

'You've done another training?' I asked. 'Children? T.B.? Fevers? Mental?'

She gave us the impression that, although they had no specific qualifications, there were few branches of the nursing profession in which they were not highly experienced. 'Of course, it's going to make all the difference to us at Martha's. Frankly, I simply can't wait to get back into a ward.'

Agatha nodded. 'It'll be like old times.'

'Honest to God,' murmured Hannah, 'is that so? It must be nice to be an old hand.'

'You'll feel like that a year from now,' Fay promised.

Hannah caught my eye. 'Maybe. Mind you, it took me more than a year to feel at home when I was doing my children's.'

'Children?' demanded Fay. 'Have you done that training? Where?'

Hannah named the most famous hospital for sick children in the British Isles.

Fay was speechless. I asked, 'Why do a general training on top of that? And if you're qualified for kids why do you have to come to the P.T.S.? Can't you start off as a second-year?'

'In most hospitals. Not Martha's. If I want a Martha's certificate as well as an S.R.N., which I do, I've got to go through the whole works again—only I don't take Prelim. State twice, naturally. I want a Martha's certificate because—frankly—it's a key to any hospital anywhere in the world. Even in places where an English S.R.N. doesn't carry much weight a Martha's certificate can tip the balance. It's well worth an extra year to get that.' She looked at Estelle Dexter. 'I don't suppose you've done much nursing?' she asked not unkindly, but as if she knew what she was talking about.

Estelle shook her head. 'No.'

'I'm glad some one else is green,' I said, as the station-wagon began to climb an apparently endless and very steep hill. 'I've been wondering how I'd make out amongst all you experienced characters.'

Hannah said Estelle and I would probably get on far better for being green. 'No two hospitals agree even on bed-making. I expect I'll have to forget a lot of what I've learnt and keep quiet about the things I can't forget.' She glanced at Fay. 'It doesn't pay to know anything in a P.T.S.'

The porter joined in. 'You've got something there, Nurse. That Sister P.T.S. is a one for learning the nurses in her way and not no other. Got a proper name for that, she has.' He jerked a thumb to the left. 'Take a look between them pines, Nurses. There's the hospital.'

The trees beyond the fringe alongside the road had been cleared; the long, low, white-painted buildings were sprawled all over the clearing, and connected by a long covered ramp. We passed quite close to one of these buildings. Two nurses were pushing a patient in bed out of one of the open french windows of the ward. They were laughing as we drove by. Their laughter surprised me. I thought the most hospital nurses were permitted was a gentle smile.

Hannah asked about the land. 'Does it belong to the hospital?'

'That's right, Nurse. It did belong to one of our gentlemen. He used to live in the P.T.S. house when he was a lad—see? He give the lot to the hospital when it was bombed bad in the War. That was afore me time, but me dad told me about it. Me dad was Head Porter in London for twenty-three years.' He swung the wagon round a hair-pin bend and then into a wide drive. 'Here you are, Nurses. Your house. I'll give you a hand with them bags, then I'll have to get off.' He turned, grinned at us, and raised a thumb. 'Best of luck, all.'

Sister Preliminary Training School was waiting with her Staff Nurse, in the open front doorway. Sister P.T.S. was tall, youngish , with straight hair parted in the centre and draped severely over her ears, then drawn back into a Jane Eyre bun. Her eyes were small and keen; her back was like a ramrod.

Her appearance momentarily made us into a band of sisters. 'Heavens, what a battleaxe!' muttered Fay. 'Thank goodness that Staff Nurse looks human. She's got a sweet smile. I'm sure she'll be a dear.'

Hannah recovered first. She took another good look at the pair in the doorway, called 'Good afternoon, Sister,' politely, as she jumped out and helped the porter unstow our luggage.

Fay and Agatha went in first. In the shelter of the wagon back doors, Hannah murmured, 'Don't be too shaken, girls. Looking a battleaxe is part of the stock in trade of any Sister P.T.S. Take my tip and reserve judgment and—be as meek as two little lambs. The old girl may be human underneath.'

I found it hard to believe her then. I did, later. Sister's formidable exterior hid an acute sense of humour and a very kind nature. Staff Nurse Naylor's sweet smile and gentle voice were soothing at first meeting, but her smile meant only that she was showing her very good teeth. She smiled all the time; she often laughed at us; she never laughed with us.

We were the last arrivals in our set. Sister shook our hands, and told us tea was ready. 'You will be shown your rooms after tea, Nurses. Go and wash in the downstairs cloakroom.'

Tea was perfectly dreadful. Sister and her Staff Nurse sat at each end of the long table; polite conversation was made only at the ends of that table; no one else said a word. I sat between Estelle and Fay, and thought how lucky Miss Nightingale had been. P.T.S.'s had not been invented until long after she returned from the Crimea. If she had had to go through this, even she might have had second thoughts.

After tea Sister gave us an introductory lecture on ethics, then showed us how to make up an ordinary bed in the approved Martha's manner. When she finished she handed us over to Nurse Naylor. 'Nurse will show you how to make up your caps and wear your uniform correctly. Then you may go to your rooms, unpack, and get into uniform. I shall expect you to have finished your unpacking and have your empty suitcases ready for removal when the first supper gong sounds.'

Naylor surveyed us as if we were so many angel-children, and in the softest voice tore our attempts at cap-making to shreds. 'That is supposed to be a cap, Nurse Dorland. Not a pancake! I don't know what you think you are doing, Nurse Kinsley. You are certainly not making up a St Martha's cap.'

She sounded really saddened by Estelle. 'We'll have to do better than that, won't we, Nurse?' She ripped out the cap-wire Estelle had painstakingly inserted. 'And something must be done about your aprons. They're nearly two inches longer than your dresses. Surely you could have had them attended to?'

I wondered why she stressed the 'you,' and why Hannah, Fay, and Agatha looked so knowing. I felt very sorry for Estelle, who was staring fixedly at the floor. This was all so reminiscent of my first day in boarding-school that it had stopped bothering me, but possibly she had been to a day school, and was unaware of the unwritten institutional law that insists all newcomers must be made to feel as stupid as possible.

Eventually Naylor dismissed us to our rooms. We dispersed in obedient silence. In the middle of my unpacking I found one suitcase was missing. I went out on the landing and saw it sitting outside a room two doors away. Estelle's room was next to mine, as we had the same surname initial. Her door was open. She was standing surrounded by unopened suitcases, gazing blankly at them. I looked at her as I went by the first time. On my return I stopped. I had wanted to talk to her since we arrived in the house. She seemed so lost. But every attempt I had made at conversation had met with either a monosyllabic reply or a polite smile. I watched her unnoticed for a moment, and was reasonably sure I recognized what was wrong. I had three sisters. My second sister Pauline was often petrified by shyness. People thought that she was a problem-child or a square, depending on their age group, when she was only dumb with nervousness.

I tapped on her open door. 'Can you manage? Anything I can do?'

She looked up slowly. 'No, thank you.'

She did not move. Nor did I. She was reminding me too much of Pauline. 'Nearly finished?' It was an absurd question, as she had obviously not started.

'No. Not yet.'

'Shouldn't you get on? Supper's at eight. It's nearly half-past seven.' I went into her room. 'Sure I can't help? Maybe you don't like unpacking? Lots of people don't. My mum says the sight of a filled suitcase unnerves her.'

For some reason this made her blush. 'I—don't—know. I've never done any unpacking.'

'First time away from home? That's tough. I know. I felt like you do now, when I first went to boarding-school. How I loathed it!'

She did not answer for a few seconds. From her expression she was making up her mind about something. She must have reached a decision.

'I know this'll sound crazy,' she said quietly, 'but although I've often been away from home, I've never done much for myself.' She folded one hand in the other. She had beautiful hands. 'Snag is, I don't quite know where to start. I suppose that's inevitable, as some one's always packed and unpacked for me.'

'I suppose so.' I tried not to sound surprised. 'Don't give it another thought.' I shut her door, left my case on her mat, lifted one of hers on to the bed. 'Behold an expert. I'm the oldest of four girls, and as our mum's allergic to suitcases, I've had to learn the form. Got the keys?'

She gave them to me without more argument. 'What can I do?'

'Pull open all those drawers and your wardrobe door.'

She did this in silence. She went on being silent. Pauline would have behaved like that, so I behaved as if she was Pauline, and talked about the P.T.S., the hospital, the Dorland family, and turkeys.

She thawed slowly. She told me she was an only child. 'My mother loves travelling. I've lived with my grandfather. I can't remember my father. He died when I was four.'

I was no longer surprised she looked lost. 'Did your mother nurse?'

'No,' she murmured, and froze again.

I changed the subject to Hannah. 'She looks fun. Kinsley looks—well, as if she'll be taking over from Sister, very very shortly.' I noticed the label on the dress in my hands. 'Blow me! No wonder it looks good!'

She smiled slightly. 'I like their cut.'

'Like?' I held up the dress. 'Isn't that the understatement of the year? It's perfect. Do you get all your clothes there?' I suddenly remembered the time. 'We'll have to get on. Can I look at these later?'

'If you like.' She smiled properly for the first time in our acquaintance. 'Do. Any time.'

We were in my room, when Hannah came to say Estelle was wanted to take a phone call in Sister's office.

She looked worried. 'It'll be my grandfather. He said he'd ring. Will Sister mind?'

'Shouldn't think so. Better hurry.'

She looked from Hannah to me. 'What do I do? Walk in?'

Her ignorance of the most elementary facts of normal living surprised me yet again. 'Knock first, then go in.'

'Thanks.'

Hannah looked after her. 'She bringing out your maternal instinct, Frances?'

I had liked Hannah at sight. 'She needs some one to take her over,' I said openly. 'The poor girl doesn't seem to know what time it is. I can't make her out.'

'Why should she bother to know what time it is, when she doesn't have to? All I can't make out is, what is she doing here?'

'Why shouldn't she be here? If she wants to train?'

'Honest to God! You mean you don't know who she is?'

'Should I?'

She shrugged. 'Don't you read newspapers on your turkey farm? Listen to the wireless? Watch TV?'

'Very often. Why?'

'Then have you never read, heard, or seen anything about Sir Hamilton Dexter, the aeroplane king? Girl, he's one of the richest men in the country! The multi-multi-type—although how he manages that with the income tax he must pay, God only knows. But he's got the lolly, all right. And one heir. His granddaughter. Name of Estelle. She was deb. of the year—they had 'em still when she came out—and she had the lot. The Sunday papers were marrying her off weekly. Who wouldn't want to marry her. And here she is with us. Just a lowly P.T.S. pro.'

'Wow!' I sat down on my bed. 'That explains those Dior labels—also her car and her helplessness. Poor girl.'

'To inherit the odd million?' she asked drily.

'A fraction would be fine. The lot—no. It would be crippling—and look what it's done to her. She must want to nurse pretty seriously to be here—she's in for a hell of a time. She doesn't know how to unpack, how to mix, has obviously never made a bed in her life. She's probably had a wildly expensive education, but it clearly has not taught her one thing about the life of a working girl.'

'Fay Kinsley was holding forth about her bed-making in the sitting-room just now. Maybe it's as well you've decided to hold her hand, Frances. The Fay Kinsleys in Martha's will go to town on her mistakes. You, my child, have got yourself a full-time job.'

Hannah was right and wrong. Estelle needed a great deal of help during our first days in the P.T.S., since everything we did was new to her. I knew nothing about nursing, but I had made beds, used dusters, swept floors, before. She genuinely did not know one end of a broom from another. As we were both 'D's, generally we worked as a pair, which suited us both. I got into the habit of keeping one eye on my own work, the other on hers, and whenever she ran into trouble she rushed to me. 'Frances, what does Sister mean about my bath having a rim? How can I take it off? Isn't it the edge of the bath?' 'How do I high-dust? Do I stand on tip-toe?' 'What does Naylor mean by my corners being ragged?'

I translated or helped, and when in doubt, asked Hannah. Between us we managed to carry Estelle through those early days. And then, slowly but very definitely, she realized what she had to do and how to do it.

Once she grasped any fact, she never forgot it; she was quick on the uptake, and in her movements. Hannah and I were delighted. Fay Kinsley was infuriated. 'Of course this is just a passing phase for Dexter! She won't last out at her present pace. She'll be bored and leave long before half-term.'

The term settled in and Estelle showed no sign of being bored by the regular routine of early cleaning, the lectures from nine until one, afternoons off duty, and the evening practical nursing classes. We rolled countless bandages, bandaged each other and the life-sized dolls on whom we practised all forms of nursing; we washed each others' heads in bed; chanted the names of the muscles and bones over meals, discussed the central nervous system, the lymphatic system, drainage systems, and how to manage when there were no drains at all; gave innumerable injections of water into the sawdust pillow in the classroom until its weight trebled and it had to be put out in the sun to dry.

There were twenty-five girls in our set. After a while, although most of us got on well together, the set split into little groups. Estelle, Hannah, and I became a fixed three some. With the exception of Fay and Agatha, the girls accepted as shyness Estelle's habitual reserve with every one but Hannah and myself. Fay and Agatha insisted she was being upstage. The sight or mere mention of her irritated them, and they never lost an opportunity to rub in the poor-little-rich-girl-slumming angle. Estelle ignored them outwardly, which inevitably irritated them still further.

One evening I found her in floods of tears in her room. For once we had attended different classes. I had been at Sister's practical nursing demonstration; she had been summoned to Naylor's extra sewing class. She had not been able to sew at all, when she first arrived. Hannah and I had turned up her aprons for her when she explained that she did not know how to hem. She could now hem fairly well.

'Hey—what goes on?' I closed the door behind me. 'What's wrong, honey?'

She mopped her eyes with an unfinished many-tailed bandage. 'I'm just being a little woman.'

I removed the bandage and gave her a handkerchief. 'My dear, you mustn't weep on that, whatever you're being. It's your test piece.'

'I know.' She sniffed. 'That's what's so maddening. I can't do it right. I'll fail the exam. because of it—and my mother and every one'll say, I told you so. I shouldn't have come—I'll never get through.'

She wept on my shoulder for a few minutes. I did not say anything. She had told me a great deal about her mother. The more I heard, the less I liked the sound of Mrs Dexter.

Eventually she calmed down. 'It's all that damned bandage's fault.

Naylor said herring-bone. I didn't know what she was talking about and
asked Kinsley. She was sitting next to me. She said I could use my eyes
and watch her, but she wasn't going to do any for me, as these are our
test-pieces.'

'Didn't Naylor show you?'

'I didn't ask her. She'd only have made some crack if I had. I
pretended I knew what I was doing. Look at it! It's a complete wreck.'

'No, it isn't.' I pulled out my scissors and unpicked her sewing.
'Where's a needle and more thread? Oh, thanks. Now, watch ...' I sat
by her. 'Herring-boning's dead easy once you know how. You go over
here—over there. See? Sort of criss-cross. Now you do it.'

She dried her eyes. 'It looks easy. But should you be sewing my
test-piece?'

'Forget that rubbish. Try it.'

She tried and, as always, after a couple of false starts succeeded very
well. 'This bandage is filthy. Will that matter?'

''No. We'll just wash and iron it.'

Afterwards I told Hannah what had happened. 'That miserable
Kinsley and snake-in-the-grass Naylor! They really got her down! They
only had to show her.'

'Frances, don't be dumb. Kinsley loathes Estelle's guts. She wouldn't
help out. And Naylor, we all know, is a two-faced so-and-so who wants
to be known as the dear, sweet staff nurse who is not impressed by all
that lovely lolly.'

'She's so hellish impressed, she never lets the poor girl forget it for
one moment. She's foul to Estelle. Thank goodness Sister's got more
sense.'

'Problem there,' said Hannah thoughtfully, 'is that Naylor has Sister's
ear. And Naylor's a trouble-maker. Her type in hospital is the type to
avoid. Beware the curves, smiles, soft voices, Frances. Beware the girls
who can hardly bear to put down their lamps to eat. Beware any one
who makes such a song and dance about being dedicated to their
profession. People who really are dedicated—like Sister—never make
any fuss about it. It's just as natural to them as breathing. There's not
one thing about Naylor that's natural. And she resents Estelle quite as
much as Kinsley. Naylor would like to see her chucked out.'

'But that's up to Sister.'

She hesitated. 'Don't forget Naylor makes a report on us too. She's
caught on to how much you do for Estelle. I actually heard her telling
Sister that Nurse Dexter should be grateful for Nurse Dorland's guiding
hand. Sister didn't look peeved, but no one can tell what Sister thinks.
You watch out. Because I don't trust Naylor. Honest to God, I don't.'

'I gathered that.' I smiled faintly. 'I'll be careful. Thank goodness it's cooking to-morrow. No one can say I guide any one at cooking. I'm a lousy cook.'

The next day was Wednesday, our half-day. The cookery class occupied most of the morning. In the afternoon Hannah wanted to visit a hair-dresser. Sister had given Estelle permission to keep her car in our drive, so she suggested driving us to the nearest town, fifteen miles away. 'Hannah can get her hair done; we can all have tea somewhere and go to a movie.'

We accepted willingly. 'After cooking,' I added, 'I'll be ready for a little escapism.'

I was ready to escape when 1 P.M. came, but not free. My egg-custard had curdled into an unattractive lump; my bone jellies refused to jell; my creamed chicken, according to Naylor, would have given acute dyspepsia to any patient unfortunate enough to eat it. 'An eight-year-old child could do better, Nurse Dorland! I refuse to pass such work. Come back this afternoon, and really work on your cooking.'

'Will some one please tell me,' I demanded at lunch, 'how I really work on a custard, jelly, or creamed chicken? And anyway, who would want to eat such nauseating food?'

The girls tried to explain, and said they would wait until I was finished. 'You shouldn't be more than an hour.'

'Two'll be more like it. I know me in a kitchen. You girls go without me. I'll have my escapism next week. Naylor's determined to have her pound of flesh from me. Let's not give her the satisfaction of having yours as well!'

They were reluctant to leave me behind, but as the last thing any of us wanted to do was to give Naylor any satisfaction, they did as I suggested. I went back to the kitchen when they had gone, feeling like Cinderella, with no Buttons or Fairy Godmother to cheer me. Naylor's quite natural displeasure at having to cut short her own half-day did not make the atmosphere any more cheerful.

'I cannot conceive why you do not take more pains over your cooking, Nurse,' she remarked later as she gingerly tasted my creamed chicken. 'You seem quite content to take endless pains over matters of interest to you.'

I was too concerned by the gritty texture of the cream, and the fact that my new custard had also curdled, to pay much attention to what she was saying. 'Yes, Nurse. I'm sorry, Nurse. Shall I make another custard?'

'Indeed you must. In your own time, and at your own expense. You have wasted quite enough of my afternoon and the hospital stores. Perhaps,' she smiled sweetly, 'Nurse Dexter may care to repay a little of your very willing assistance to her and help you out?'

There was a possibility she was only referring to Estelle's natural ability to cook. Knowing her and realizing now what lay behind her previous remark, I did not think it a probability. I did not want to show how annoyed I was, so I assumed my best Idiot Pro expression. 'Yes, Nurse. Thank you, Nurse.'

'Then you may clear up and get off to what remains of your half-day.' She sighed. 'I'm afraid Sister is not going to be pleased about this waste of food. I'll have to report it.'

'Yes, Nurse. I'm sorry.'

'So am I, Nurse,' she murmured sadly, and walked off shaking her head. She came back when I had finished washing-up. 'Sister would like to see you now, please, Nurse.'

I dried my hands gloomily. I wanted to be a nurse, not a cook, yet it seemed my nursing career might end before it had really begun, because I could not bake a custard. It was my curdled custard that had really infuriated Naylor. I did not blame her for that; it had infuriated me. If she had not made that crack about Estelle I should have been genuinely sorry to have spoilt her half-day.

Sister P.T.S. was at the desk in her office. My anatomy note-book was open in front of her. She was comparing my book with another open in her hand. I recognized Estelle's handwriting upside down, and wondered what else Naylor had reported.

'Nurse Dorland, did you do both these illustrations?'

'Yes, Sister.'

She lowered Estelle's book. 'Do you consider that fair, Nurse? How am I to judge Nurse Dexter's capabilities, if you do her work for her?'

I had an answer. I was afraid she would not like it much, but could see no alternative to giving it.

'I did both drawings, Sister, but—well, Nurse Dexter wrote the basis of the notes we both used.'

Her lips tightened. 'A combined operation?'

'Yes, Sister. Does it matter as it was not a test?'

She considered me reflectively. 'It would not matter if this was an isolated occasion. I like my nurses to help each other. I am pleased to know that some of this work has been done by Nurse Dexter. I would feel happier if it was all her own work. I can appreciate your concern for a new friend,' she went on slowly, 'but I think you would be well-advised to be a little less solicitous over her. I will say no more about these illustrations now, but in future I do not want to be able to trace your guiding hand in any work of Nurse Dexter's. You may go, Nurse.'

I went up to my room feeling worried and disgusted. I could hardly wait to get Hannah to myself and tell her how right she had been to warn me. Sister even used Naylor's wording. 'Guiding hand.' Bah.

Looking at it bluntly, I thought as I changed out of uniform, What good could Estelle's cash do me? I had no brothers with whom I could persuade her to elope. Our homes were at opposite ends of England, so I could scarcely entertain hopes of her introducing me to her wealthy friends, if she had any. There would be no point in my borrowing large sums of money from her, even if she were foolish enough to lend them to me, since we had no time or opportunity to spend money in the P.T.S. and, according to Naylor, would have still less time once we worked in the wards. Naylor adored chilling our spines with tales of the footsore years ahead.

I decided I was growing introspective and bitter, and must get out of the house, if only for a walk. I wandered aimlessly out of the front gate, crossed the lane, and climbed the hill beyond, forgetting that on an early summer afternoon in England it is seldom wise to go out of doors without first having a look at the weather. I had climbed some distance before I realized the sun had gone in.

I looked at the sky. It was heavy with purple-black thunder clouds. I had on a sweater and skirt. I stopped on the hill, wondering whether to go back. I did not mind getting wet, but I did mind the prospect of being caught in a thunderstorm. Thunder had terrified me when I was small, and it still did. I turned, then turned again. To go back would mean an afternoon spent avoiding Naylor and Sister. I had another look at the sky. The clouds were fairly high. They might move over. It was worth taking a chance.

There was a small plateau above tree-level on top of that hill. A squat, three-sided, roofed stone shelter had been built on that plateau as a memorial to some one who died in 1853. The name had worn off, but the date was still clear. I had often been up to the top and regarded the shelter as my private property, since I had not been able to persuade any of my set to make that climb, or seen anyone up there during the various half-hours I had spent sitting on the crumbling wooden seat against the back wall, looking out over the miles of open country below. The lane did not go over the hill. It ran round about half a mile from the plateau. The crest above tree-level was covered with bracken; the gradient so steep that even in fine weather it was often necessary to use both hands as well as feet to keep balanced. I was scrambling quickly about two hundred yards from the top, when the rain began in slow, heavy drops. It was followed immediately by a sharp crack of thunder. The sky split with lightning. A second and louder crack shook the hill.

I tried to ignore the noise. I told myself it was just harmless noise. There was nothing to worry about. It was raining. Some one had told me thunderstorms were perfectly safe, so long as it kept on raining.

The rain stopped like a tap being turned off. I hurled myself over the edge of the plateau as the full violence of a dry thunderstorm broke directly overhead. Panic gave me wings. I had done those last two hundred yards at the double. I literally leapt across the plateau and into the shelter, intending to drop safely on to the wooden seat and wait while the storm rolled on. Instead of dropping on to the seat, I missed my footing after the final leap, stumbled, and went down backwards. It was mainly surprise that made me stumble. The shelter had always been empty. It belonged to me.

It was not empty that afternoon. A man in a grey suit had got there before me. It was as well he had. The shelter floor was made of stone. He caught me as I went over and saved me from a nasty crack on the back of the head.

'I think,' he said calmly, 'you had better sit down.' He pushed me not ungently on to the seat, put his hands in his pockets, and looked at me thoughtfully. 'Forgive my being trite, but next time you go mountaineering in a thunderstorm it might be an idea to look before you leap. You might have knocked yourself out just now. If you had been alone the consequences could have been quite serious.'

2. A Storm and a Stranger

The thunder paused, and the rain returned. It hammered like machine-gun fire on the flat roof, turned the plateau into a shallow lake, then spilled over the hillside, sweeping away twigs, stones, and bracken.

My companion had fair hair. He stood in the opening watching the curtain of water. 'This plateau gets larger every time it rains. If it were not for those pines the whole hill would erode. It's certainly coming down now. You got here just in time.' He turned. 'Getting your breath back? Here'—he handed me a clean handkerchief—'use this as a face towel. It's larger than yours.'

'Thank you very much.' I mopped my face and hair. 'And thank you for breaking my fall. I'm afraid I must have given you a shock, leaping in as I did. I didn't expect anyone to be here. I've always had this shelter to myself before.'

'So have I. It's fortunate that this afternoon has proved the exception to our rule.' His smile was only polite. 'You're pretty wet.' He took off his jacket. 'As we've no means of drying you, you had better put this on.'

'Oh, no, thank you. I don't need that. It's very kind of you, but I'm not at all cold.'

'You will be, when you cool down.' He held the jacket by the shoulders. 'You put it on.'

I accepted reluctantly. 'Thank you. But what about you? Won't you be cold?'

'I doubt it, thanks.' He sat at the other end of the long seat. 'Tell me, are you in training for a four-minute-mile-up-hill? You should make it, if you can keep up the speed you produced over the last fifty-odd yards.'

'How could you see me? I came up from that side.' I nodded at the wall on his left. 'I couldn't see you.'

'I was watching you through glasses.' He produced a small pair of binoculars from the corner of the seat. 'And through this crack in the wall. Here. I was actually watching a pair of falcons. They've taken over an old crow's nest in one of those trees down there. Your scarlet jersey came in my line of vision, and I followed you.'

'Falcons? Up here? Hobbys? Aren't they rare here?'

He had treated me with polite detachment. He looked really interested in the habits of the hobby. 'Yes. Very. That's why I came up here this afternoon. I saw them yesterday, tried to get some photos, but the light wasn't good enough. Are you keen on birds?'

'Fairly. My father's a passionate amateur ornithologist. I've been out with him a lot, and picked up all I know about them from him. He's got masses of photos, but his main interest is more bird-song than birds. I don't think there's a dyke on the Romney Marsh in which he and I have not sat with a tape-recorder.'

He smiled. 'He must have a good collection.'

I nodded. The thunder had come back, and the shelter vibrated after a tremendous crack. I winced involuntarily.

'Worried?' he asked kindly.

If he had been a young man of my own age, nothing would have made me admit my complex about thunder. I could not guess his age exactly, but although there was no visible grey in his thick fair hair, the lines of his thin, intelligent face, and his generally assured air made me place him automatically in my parents' generation.

'Yes. I know it's absurd, but it scares me.'

'I shouldn't worry about feeling absurd.' His long, slender hands played with the straps of his glasses. 'Every one's scared of something. Not every one has the courage to admit it.' He bent forward to look up at the ominous sky. 'This is too violent to last.' He had to wait until the next peal faded before going on. 'Violence in any form is generally short-lived.'

I said I was sure he was right and wished I could believe he was. The lightning was brilliant, forked and constant. It seemed to me to be aiming for our shelter.

He glanced at me. 'I shouldn't watch it. Do you smoke?'

I dragged my eyes from the sky. 'No, thank you.'

'Mind if I do? Then would you feel in that right pocket for my pipe, pouch, and—I hope—matches. Thanks.' He filled his pipe, and watched me over the flame of his match. 'Where do you work in the hospital?'

'How did you guess that?' Then I smiled. 'I suppose it's a fair guess to make about anyone on this hill. We all work here.'

He smiled back. 'I don't.' He did not enlarge on that, and as I did not care to question him I told him about the P.T.S. 'It's in the large house'—the lightning made me blink—'just higher up the hill than the hospital.'

'How are you getting on? Like nursing?'

'We haven't done any real nursing yet. We practise on dolls. I like all we do—apart from cooking.'

He looked amused. 'You can't cook?'

'No. I'm the world's worst cook. I know what I should do in theory, but it never works out right. Either I produce charcoal or my food comes out of the oven raw. Our Staff Nurse says an eight-year-old child could do better.' I told him about my afternoon. 'I've only to look at an egg custard to make it curdle.'

'What happens'—he raised his voice slightly to be heard over the uproar around us—'to all the food you cook in your classes?'

'We eat the successes. The failures go in the pig-bucket. Some one, somewhere, is raising some fine little piglets on my cooking.' I knew none of this could interest him, and he was only keeping me talking to keep my mind off the storm. It seemed only fair to meet him half-way and keep on talking. 'There's no doubt, good cooks are born, not made. Estelle—one of the girls—had never cracked an egg before our term started, but all her things turn out well. Imagine—she never even curdled her first custard.'

'Just imagine,' he echoed soberly, and we both laughed.

'Possibly,' he said a minute or so later, 'you use too much heat. Do you use gas or electricity?'

'Gas.'

'Then I should say you want something that resembles a candle flame. And perhaps you try and work too quickly?'

I guessed he had picked up these tips from his wife. 'It might be that. Our Staff Nurse is always fussing about my being in too much of a rush. Can you cook?'

He smiled. 'No.' His next words confirmed my guess. 'I've only acquired this knowledge second-hand. Try it out in your next class.'

'I will. Thanks.' I thought it over. 'Hannah told me I should go slow.' And I explained whom she was, and why she was training.

He knocked out his pipe, looked at the sky, refilled it slowly. 'And what are your plans when you finish training?'

This time I had to wait to be heard. 'Haven't any, yet. Four years is a long time to go.'

'You'll probably be surprised how quickly it does go. Time speeds up as one gets older. Or haven't you noticed that, yet?'

I discovered I had. 'Through my youngest sister, Judy. She's ten. A week is an eternity to her.'

The walls of the shelter were positively rattling with the noise. 'Have you a large family?'

'Three sisters.' I looked at the lightning and then away. 'I'm the oldest.'

'Where do you live?' he demanded civilly.

I had to give him my attention or seem rude. 'In Kent. My father's a farmer.'

'What does he farm?'

'He grows turkeys.'

'Many?'

'Six thousand—roughly.' If violence was short-lived, it was time this particular spell of violence died.

'Does he breed them?'

'No. He says that's too tricky. He gets them as chicks. Day-old, generally.'

'Tricky? In what way?'

I did not intend talking turkeys, but he seemed so genuinely interested that soon I was telling him not only all the problems of turkey-growing, but all about my family and the farm.

'It's actually on the Romney Marsh? No wonder your father knows about birds.'

I nodded. 'In all weathers and seasons it's a birdwatcher's paradise. Good shooting, too, if you like shooting.'

'You don't?'

'Afraid not. I prefer people who go after birds with a camera instead of a gun.'

He did not comment on this. 'The Romney Marsh is pretty big. Is your home very isolated?'

'Not really. Only three miles from our village.' I told him the name. 'It's a small village, but when Daddy was a boy it was quite famous for a while, because some one found the ruins of a Mithraic temple just beyond our church.'

'I think I remember that.' He watched the rain through half-closed eyes. 'Let's hope this is the finale.'

'I hope so. I've never known such a long storm.'

'It'll pass. Tell me, do you miss your home much? Or are you too busy in your new life?'

'I miss the family a bit—but we are very busy.'

'Are your fellow nurses pleasant?'

'Very'—I remembered Fay and Agatha—'on the whole.'

'Only on the whole? Where's the rub? Your Staff Nurse?'

I smiled slightly. 'She's a rub to us all. We've a problem pair in our set.'

'Why's that?'

I had no more intention of telling him about Fay and Agatha, than I had had of talking turkeys. I not only told him about our problem pair, I threw in Estelle, Naylor, and Sister P.T.S. 'Have you ever heard anything so stupid? What if she has lots of lolly? It's no good to me or anyone else in our set. I just like her. But I don't like the idea of Sister having these dark thoughts about me.'

'Apart from Sister—do you mind about the others?' he asked curiously.

'Not really. Their opinions aren't worth anything. They can think what they like.'

'I don't imagine your Sister really does entertain dark thoughts on this matter. She must have a great deal of experience in dealing with young women to hold her particular job. With experience you learn to recognize certain qualities when you meet them. I should say all she meant this afternoon, was that this girl must stand or fall on her own. Which is fair enough.'

A hideous thought struck me with the violence of the storm. 'Are you a psychiatrist? One of our medical staff?'

'I'm not a psychiatrist. I don't work or live down here. Didn't I tell you?'

'You did. I'm so sorry. I forgot.' I was infinitely relieved I had not been pouring out my life's history to some one I might one day meet in a white coat in one of the wards. 'Are you on holiday?'

'Just down for a couple of days. I live and work in London.'

I would like to have asked what work he did; about his family; if they were down with him. But the obvious difference in our ages, the fact that he reminded me vaguely of my parents' friends, and the austere lines of his face in repose prevented me asking personal questions, even though none of these had prevented my talking to him as if we had been friends for years.

Our conversation drifted back to birds. It was some time later that I realized the storm was over.

He stood up. 'I hadn't noticed, either. Come outside. I'll show you the tree in which those hobbys are nesting.'

We strolled over the muddy plateau. The air was clean and fresh as it always is after a storm, the light stronger than it had been all afternoon. I discovered he was much taller than I had previously thought, but he did not look at all strong. His face was too thin and drawn. My mother would be horrified if my father looked as he did. I wondered why his wife did not do something about it. And again, I wondered what he was. He was reassuringly unlike any doctor I had ever seen. His grey suit was of good material and well-cut, but it was far from new. His shirt was white, his tie sober. He looked, I thought slowly, very like some one I knew. Whom?

I placed that likeness a few seconds later when I watched how he walked. He walked exactly like my mother's older brother. My Uncle Joe was a Fellow of a Cambridge college. My companion had the same academic air. He would look absolutely at home wandering round the streets of any university town with his thin shoulders slightly hunched under a long, flapping Senior Member's gown.

I returned his jacket, thanked him again for saving me a cracked head, and for helping me sit out the storm. 'I'm afraid I've talked far too much. I always do. I'm so sorry.'

His lips twisted in a crooked and very attractive smile. 'I've enjoyed listening. Please don't apologize.' He looked round suddenly. 'Quick— see—there's one of them.'

A small bluish-grey bird with pointed wings rose from one of the trees. 'Isn't that the male? I never realized their beaks were so like a hawk's.'

He nodded. 'That's him. I wish I did not have to get back to town this evening. This light's quite good. I'd like to try for at least one photo.'

'I don't know if this light'll last. Are those clouds over there coming, or going?'

'Coming, I'm afraid. You had better go back.' He looked round nostalgically. 'I must go too, more's the pity.'

'Did you know this hill before it had a hospital?'

He answered my question with another. 'Do you see that church down there? The tower's just visible? The man who was Vicar there up to— let's see—twenty-odd years ago was my godfather. I used to spend a lot of time with him when I was a boy. So I know most of this part of the world very well.'

We said good-bye then. I looked back once as I slithered and skidded downwards. He was standing where I had left him. He noticed my pause and raised a hand. I waved back.

Hannah and Estelle were enchanted to hear about my storm. 'What was his name? What does he do?'

'I dunno. Watches birds. Saves young women from cracking open their heads. Keeps up their morales in storms.'

'Didn't he ask your name?' demanded Hannah.

'No. It was about the only think he didn't ask. It was a long storm. He kept me talking.'

That, they said, was not difficult. Estelle asked why I had not tried to find out anything about him.

'It would have been like cross-examining one's father or uncle. It didn't seem to matter. He was nice, polite, and sensible. I liked him.'

Hannah said he sounded deadly dull. 'He must be aged to have good manners. Modern young men have to be angry, and that means plain rude. Now you take my cousin Bart,' she went on eagerly. 'Remember, Frances? I told you Bart was a Martha's student? Estelle and I met him in the high street this afternoon, just before we went in to the movie.'

'It was quite a while before we went to the movie,' corrected Estelle. 'We had just come out of the car park.'

'Well, we met him, anyway! And he just adores being an angry young man. He's for ever flying off at a tangent about something! He is good fun, but can be impossibly rude when he wants to be. I was so pleased we met him this afternoon. I did write and tell him we were here, but thought he must still be in London as he hadn't rung me. He never writes letters.'

I was not sure that I liked the sound of Bart More, but as Hannah was so clearly delighted about him, I said I thought it all very splendid.

She slapped me on the back. 'You'll love Bart! He's just your cup of tea. Am I not right, Estelle?'

'Quite right, Hannah,' echoed Estelle politely.

I looked at her curiously. I was coming to know her well, and somehow her words did not ring true.

Hannah's mind could go off at tangents, too. 'Do you mean to say, Frances, he didn't make so much as a pass?'

'Not one. Why worry? We've agreed he's aged.'

Hannah said age never stopped any man making a pass. 'Maybe he's queer?'

'Not with his voice, dear.' I jerked a thumb downwards. 'It came up from way down there. Deep and quiet. Like—like—gentle thunder.'

'You might be describing Bart's voice—eh, Estelle?'

Estelle said she was afraid she was not very good at noticing voices, and changed the subject to the mid-term test we were due to have at the end of the week. 'We've an hour before lights out. Shall we do some bandaging? I cannot get my ascending spirals right. Frances, be an angel and model, then Hannah can criticize.'

Hannah was our private bandaging expert. 'You do me, then I'll do you. I'm very shaky on fingers,' I said, 'and can never remember which side you tie the sling.'

'Over the injured side,' chanted Hannah, 'over the injured side. let's go and borrow the wherewithal from Naylor.'

With Nurse Naylor's permission we loaded ourselves with crêpe bandages, and retired to Hannah's room. As first victim I lay on the bed while Estelle bandaged me under Hannah's instructions. She dropped the bandage twice. Hannah caught it both times, handing it back imitating Naylor's agonized protest, 'Ten little marks gone, Nurse Dexter.'

'That's not right, Hannah,' I said, after the second occasion. 'Dear Naylor does it this way.' I sat up, simpered, and flapped my eyelashes. 'Ten teeny weeny marks gone, dear Nurse Dexter,' I purred revoltingly. 'You naughty little nurse, you! What will Matron say! Ouch!' I yelped normally. 'Watch you, Estelle! You've cut off my circulation!'

'Sorry,' muttered Estelle, dropping the bandage again.

I picked it up for her. 'You are in a dither to-night.'

She said she was suffering from an acute attack of pre-mid-term-test nerves. 'It would be grim to be chucked out half-way, and it can happen! Remember Sister warning us about it, in our opening lecture?'

The thought sobered us all so much that for the rest of that hour we concentrated only on bandaging.

When the test day arrived, our whole set was jittering with nerves. When the written work was over, we gathered in our sitting-room to wait for lunch, and commiserate with each other's mistakes.

'Will somebody please tell me'—I searched through a surgery text-book—'how many bones there are in the foot? I could not remember and had to blur my illustration with some very arty-crafty shading to hide my ignorance.'

Fay Kinsley said she had found the anatomy paper quite straight-forward, but had been aghast by the nursing paper. 'We might have been taking State Finals! Really, Sister expects far too much—setting a paper like that!'

'I don't think Sister honestly expects us to know the answers,' said Estelle. 'When I met her in the hall just now she said she knew the nursing paper had been stiff, but had set it intentionally to give us some idea of the questions we might get in our Final P.T.S. exam. She actually told me not to worry too much, and I'm sure she meant that for us all.'

Fay snapped immediately. 'We all know you don't have to worry about anything, Estelle! You needn't shove it down our throats.'

I looked up from my book. 'She wasn't shoving anything down our throats. She was boosting our morales. Do stop making cracks, Fay. My nerves won't stand them. I've simply got to find out how many bones there are in the foot. Oh, no!' I suddenly found the illustration I had been looking for. 'That does it! I drew a hand instead of a foot! Sister'll take off!'

The others crowded round. 'Look up the knee joint, Frances. I'm sure I got the capsule wrong.'

The sitting-room resounded with groans as our post-mortem continued. 'Thank God, there's the lunch gong,' said Hannah piously. 'If it hadn't sounded we'd all have nervous breakdowns.'

'One thing—we can't go very wrong this afternoon.' I replaced the text-book. 'Sister always says practical nursing is mainly common sense.'

An hour later I discovered my mistake. Sister walked over from her desk as I blanket-bathed a life-sized doll called Mrs Brown. 'I presume your patient is having a full course of penicillin, Nurse Dorland?'

I gazed at her blankly, 'I'm—er—afraid I don't know, Sister.' I looked at the doll's serene face. 'Should she be on penicillin?'

She removed two blankets from the neat pile I had arranged on the chair at the foot of the bed, and laid them carefully over Mrs Brown. 'Indeed she should, Nurse. She will need all the help medical science can give her to counteract the acute attack of pneumonia she will inevitably suffer after your ministrations. Do you realize you are bathing a patient in front of an open window, and have only covered her with one thin blanket? Shut the window, make the bed, change your water, and start all over again. And then kindly do as you have been taught. Use your eyes, consider the temperature of the room, and always close near-by windows before washing so much as the face and hands.'

I said weakly, 'Yes, Sister. I am so sorry.'

'And I am equally sorry for any patient unlucky enough to be nursed by you at this juncture, Nurse Dorland,' replied Sister calmly, looking beyond me to something on the far side of the room. 'Nurse Franks—one moment, please!' She gave me a brief nod—'Carry on, Nurse Dorland'— then sailed across to Sylvia Franks. I heard her ask Sylvia whether she had ever had the misfortune to break a bone. 'No? Then allow me to inform you that fractures are painful, Nurse. Mrs Smith [Sylvia's doll] has a newly pinned fractured right femur. I saw you place your heavy hand directly over your patient's injury. You may not consider your hand heavy, Nurse? You must believe me when I say that under certain conditions even the weight of a light sheet can be an intolerable burden.'

A few minutes after Sylvia joined me in the improvised sluice-room that had once been a housemaid's cupboard. 'The old girl's going to town this afternoon,' she whispered. 'She's got me so on edge that when I got soap in Mrs Smith's eye just now I apologized aloud even though Sister was behind the screen with Fay.'

I refilled my washing bowl. 'She's given me such a conscience about

Mrs Brown's pneumonia that I feel you may as well call me Sarah Gamp and have done!'

'Where's the gin bottle, duckie?'

'In my bib pocket ...' I broke off as Fay Kinsley flew past the sluice door looking very pink. Half a minute later she hurtled back, lugging a heavy oxygen cylinder behind her. 'What ails you, Fay?' I asked, opening the classroom door for her.

'I dropped George in the bath,' she muttered furiously, 'and Sister insists I give the wretch artificial respiration and fix up an oxygen tent. It's too crazy! He might be a real baby—not just rubber!'

Sylvia looked at me as Fay rattled on. 'Do you suppose the old battle-axe has a sense of humour—or just knows her stuff—or both?'

I did not dare answer as Sister was watching us. I had no doubts about Sister knowing her stuff, but was not sure about Sylvia's first point. We now knew how we all stood with Naylor, but Sister P.T.S. was still very much of an unknown quantity.

When Mrs Brown had been bathed to her satisfaction she sent me next door to Naylor who was presiding over the bandaging and poultice-making tests. A girl called Alice Linton was temporarily acting as model.

'Nurse Linton has fractured her right scapula and left os calcis, Nurse Dorland. Will you apply the requisite bandages.'

Thanks to Hannah, bandaging was one of my strong points. Nurse Naylor gave my bandages an approving nod. 'You have a little time to spare since your bandages are right first time, so will you set for, then give a hypodermic injection into the sawdust pillow.'

I felt quite pleased with life, and myself, as I scrubbed-up. My spirits rose still higher when Naylor passed my setting with a sweet smile. I fitted the hypodermic syringe together, and decided we had been most unjust to Naylor. Her gentle manner and soft voice made her really pleasant to work for.

She smiled so gently as I gave the injection. 'Nurse Dorland,' she breathed the words, 'would you be good enough to remember you are supposedly giving a patient—a human being—that injection, and are not digging up your father's garden? Please wash and do it again.'

My second attempt was no more successful. She merely used different words. 'Nurse, you are holding a hypodermic syringe, not brandishing a harpoon. And look what you've done to that needle! Possibly you might be able to use it as a crochet-hook—you can certainly never use it again for an injection. Put it all away now and make a linseed poultice. You have just time to get one made before the test ends.'

I began my poultice hopefully. Perhaps I could make a beauty and cancel the bad marks my injections must have earned. I lost hope very soon. The linseed refused to allow itself to reach the right consistency. I stirred feverishly with the official wooden spoon, then in desperation used my scissors and fingers in my attempt to spread it correctly. Consequently, instead of a smooth brown poultice, the result was something like a miniature mountain range.

Nurse Naylor considered this with an angelic smile. 'How very odd that looks! Just what is it supposed to be, Nurse Dorland?'

'A linseed poultice, Nurse.'

She widened her eyes. 'I would never have thought it. Does your father keep horses?'

'Er—no, Nurse.'

'What a pity. Never mind. Perhaps you know some horse to whom you could present it? And meanwhile, I think you had better make me another.'

I made another; then a third. When five o'clock and the official end of the test arrived, I was still struggling with soggy squares of brown paper, and covered in sticky linseed. Naylor told me to remove my mess from the classroom, and my person, and go to tea. 'You had better practise your poultices on your own, Nurse. Matron may well ask you to make a linseed in your Final test, and if she should,' she asked brokenly, 'what will you do?'

'I know exactly what I'll do,' I told the girls at tea, 'if Matron so much as murmurs "Linseed"! I'll burst into loud tears and hand in my lamp.'

'At least your bandaging went well, Frances,' called Alice Linton from the end of our long table. 'Mine was a nightmare. Naylor told me to fix a right tib. and fib. on Sylvia. I got in a state and began on the right radius and ulna. Good old Sylvia kept mumbling 'Tib. and fib., tib. and fib.,' out of the corner of her mouth—but Naylor heard.'

'What happened?' we chorused.

Alice grinned. 'Naylor told Sylvia to recollect she had been knocked unconscious and wouldn't be round for hours. For good measure she threw in a fractured skull. That was sheer murder as Sylvia's hair's so thick!' She waved her tea-cup at me. 'My only consolation was that I hadn't got you, Frances. Your curls would have been the end!' She set down her cup with a cheerful crash, the tea slopped over, staining the clean white cloth. 'Blimey! I'm still in a state! I can't even drink tea this afternoon. What will Sister say?'

I stood up and smoothed imaginary cuffs as Sister always smoothed her cuffs at the start of each lecture. 'That you are sadly failing in one of the most important attributes of a nurse, Nurse Linton. Every nurse worthy of the name,' I announced, in a copy of Sister's voice, 'should have at her finger-tips the correct method of drinking tea. Prepare to make a note, Nurses. Ready?'

'Yes, Sister—please, Sister,' they chanted obediently.

'Very good. Now. A nurse may only drink tea in the following circumstances; (a) when she has a cup, (b) a saucer, (c) a teaspoon. No St Martha's nurse may consider drinking tea without a teaspoon. And the position of the hands should be—so.' I picked up my cup and saucer. 'Note the elbows, Nurses. No flapping ducks on the nursing staff of St Martha's Hospital, if you please. Any questions?'

Sylvia Franks choked and had to be slapped on the back by Alice. 'You've got her voice exactly, Frances!'

'She's better at Naylor,' said Hannah. 'Frances, let Naylor take over.'

I was too cheered by the discovery that I had not been the only person to make a hash of the test to feel self-conscious. I relaxed my ramrod posture and beamed at their upturned faces. 'Lecturing is Sister's province, Nurses. I'm just going to have a teeny weeny little cosy chat with you. It won't take more than four or five hours, and we'll put our heads together and really get down to working on this question of tea-drinking! It may seem only a simple point, but, a good nurse is known by her simple ...'

'Mind?' suggested Alice gravely.

'Nurse Linton! Naughty, naughty! Not worthy of you! What would Sister say if ...' my voice faded as the room rose to its feet.

The girls facing the door—which was behind me—were staring dumbly over my shoulder. I turned very slowly. Sister and Naylor were just inside the door. Sister's face was expressionless. Naylor was looking at the floor; her cheeks were tinged with pink.

Sister cleared her throat. 'We have come to tell you that you may all be excused extra duty this evening, Nurses. You may go off-duty after tea.' She looked deliberately at me. 'When you have finished your tea, will you please come to my study, Nurse Dorland. Thank you. That will be all, Nurses. Sit down and enjoy your tea.'

No one said a word for the few seconds after Sister and Naylor left us. Fay Kinsley broke the silence as she alone obeyed Sister and went on with her tea. 'I tried to catch your eye, Frances, directly I saw the door open. I'm afraid,' she added primly, helping herself to a slice of currant cake, 'I was not surprised to see her looking so cross.'

I got up. 'I've lost my appetite, so may as well get this over. Write and tell me how you all made out in the test, girls.'

Estelle touched my arm. 'I'm sure she won't be too annoyed. She's too intelligent not to know we were all letting off steam through you, and I'm sure she's got a terrific sense of humour.'

Fay shrugged. 'I don't see how she can possibly overlook being publicly ridiculed, but I suppose I'm very dense.'

'Stick around and I'll tell you. If I'm not sent up to my room.' I straightened my cap. 'Am I tidy?' I shot out of the dining-room, across the hall, and knocked gingerly on the closed door of Sister's office.

She was sitting at a small table in the bay window sharing a tea-tray with Naylor, who was pouring out tea.

'There you are, Nurse Dorland. Good!' Sister smiled pleasantly, stood up, and flicked back the neatly folded corners of her apron. 'Now, where did I put it? Yes—here.' She handed me a smallish registered envelope. 'This arrived by the afternoon's post. Mrs Mallinson signed for it, as you were occupied in the test. Just add your name under hers in my book, to show you have collected it in person.' She pushed a red-ruled exercise book towards me. 'And add the date and time.'

I thrust the envelope in my apron bib, signed mechanically, then waited with my hands behind me for the real reason for her summons.

She sat down, helped herself to a cucumber sandwich and smiled again. 'That's all, Nurse. You may go.'

I looked at her uncertainly, wondering if she expected me to apologize before she said anything. Perhaps her smile was only for Naylor. 'Excuse me, Sister, I—er—think—I mean—know—I ought to apologize. ...'

'For wasting a quantity of excellent linseed?' she queried smoothly without giving me time to finish. 'I'm sure it was not really wasted. You have no doubt learnt from your failures. Go back to your friends, and have a pleasant evening relaxing after the strain of to-day. Unless,' her eyes danced, 'you plan to continue your most instructive course of lectures?'

I felt my face turn scarlet. 'Yes, Sister—that is, no, Sister. Thank you very much,' I mumbled and fled back to the dining-room.

'What did she say? Is she going to send you to Matron?' demanded the girls directly I opened the door.

I closed it, leant back, and smiled widely. 'Relax! Panic over! What do you know, girls! She's actually human!' And I repeated Sister's words. 'Isn't she a honey?'

Estelle came up to me. 'My God, Frances—I've just aged ten years. I thought she'd be all right, but I only had instinct to go on.'

Hannah said her nerves could not stand any more of anything. 'Let's change and go out, before I go into a decline.' She led the way to our rooms, and, as usual, we went into hers as it was on the floor beneath Estelle's and mine. 'Did she just send for you to set your mind at rest?'

'Actually, no.' In my relief I had forgotten the registered letter. I pulled it from my bib. 'She wanted me to sign for this. It must be something special from the family,' I said glancing casually at the postmark. The postmark was London. I turned it over now curiously. 'It's not from the family. It's from a J. S. Slane. Slane? Whoever? I don't known any Slanes.'

'Perhaps it isn't for you after all?' Hannah peered over my shoulder. 'Yes—Miss Frances Dorland. Do open up, Frances. This is fascinating.'

I slit the envelope with one blade of my scissors, and shook the contents into one hand. 'Streuth! Photos.'

Hannah seized them. 'Am I seeing things? Birds.'

I took them from her. 'Let me see. Why, they're the hobby babies in that old crow's nest—and look—there's Mum coming in on the wing. They are good. They must have been taken with a cine.'

'Most peculiar little objects I've ever seen.' Hannah gazed entranced. 'How do you know that's Mum? And what's a hobby when it's at home?'

'A small falcon. I know it's Mum because it looks like a hobby Mum. It's got the right markings. It must have taken him ages to get them. How cute of him to send them.' I looked at the envelope again. 'So he's J. S. Slane.'

'Your bird-watching man?' asked Estelle.

'Must be.' I was extraordinarily pleased, and took the photographs from Estelle. 'Let me see them again.'

Hannah removed the envelope from me. 'Isn't there a letter? There's nothing on the backs of these snaps. Yes, here you are, jammed inside.' She drew it out, and handed it to me. 'What's he say?'

I smiled, 'Not much. Listen:

'DEAR MISS DORLAND,
    I thought the enclosed might be of interest to you and your father. I hope you are having a good term, and that the egg custards no longer curdle.
                                        Yours sincerely
                                        J. S. SLANE.'

3. My Friend the Professor

'I've met a good many opening gambits,' said Hannah, 'but this is a new one on me.'

'I suppose it is an opening gambit?' Estelle looked at me. 'Why else should he send them?'

'I don't think it is.' I re-read the letter. 'This is civil, but hardly forthcoming.'

Hannah asked me to be my age. 'Men don't go round sending strange young women pretty pictures of birds for no good reason.'

'Amateur ornithologists do. Daddy corresponds and exchanges bird snaps with total strangers all over the world. Male and female. This'll probably start an interminable correspondence on falcons large and small between him and this man Slane. I'll send them on home, which is obviously what he wants me to do.' I replaced the photographs and letter in their envelope. 'I'm glad I know his name. I detest not knowing people's names. Wonder what the J. S. stands for?'

'How did he know yours?' asked Hannah. 'I thought you didn't tell him?'

'I didn't. I had forgotten that detail. How peculiar. How do you imagine he found it out?'

Hannah smiled. 'A strategically dropped handkerchief with your name tape on it? Or maybe your scissors?'

'There was the father and mother of all storms going on. I wasn't in uniform—didn't have a handbag. My skirt had no pockets, my handkerchiefs are only marked with initials, and I certainly did not drop one that day, as I only had one with me and used it when I got back to get the mud off my shoes before coming into the house. Nor did it occur to me that there would be any point in giving him my name, discreetly or otherwise. Honestly. he just wasn't the type.'

'He couldn't have conjured your name out of thin air,' she protested reasonably, 'so he must have got it from some one. Whom?'

Estelle said thoughtfully, 'Are you positive he wasn't one of our men, Frances?'

'For Pete's sake, don't suggest that! Not after Mrs Brown's pneumonia, my linseed, and then tea to-day! If I seriously thought I had unburdened to a senior member of Martha's I'd walk out here and now! And he'd have to be a senior member to be on our staff at his age.'

'What was he wearing?'

I relaxed. 'Estelle, thank heavens you've got brains. Of course, there's our answer. He couldn't be a pundit because Naylor says they all wear black jackets and pin-striped trousers. He was just in ordinary grey.'

'Sure it wasn't just a dirty white coat?' suggested Hannah.

'It was a suit he had on, neither a long nor a short white coat.'

'Which rules out Senior Residents, registrars, and housemen,' agreed Estelle.

'Unless he was off-duty?' put in Hannah.

Estelle remembered Naylor's lecture on form far better than Hannah and I. 'He would still have been in a white coat. Naylor told us it's a Martha's private rule that all residents must wear their white coats in the hospital grounds, even when off duty. That hill belongs to the hospital, so is part of the annexe grounds.'

Hannah was determined to be difficult. 'Maybe he was a student?'

'He was far too old—and not wearing tweeds or corduroys.'

Estelle looked amused. 'We're whittling him down. What's left? Naval, military, law, divinity—medicine's out—City, art?'

I thought this over. 'He couldn't work in the open—he was the wrong colour. And he certainly couldn't work with his hands. He might be a lawyer—' I told them about Uncle Joe. 'But I got the impression he was something academic. He had that kind of scholarly—pardon me while I just turn Einstein's theory of relativity over in my mind—air, some dons have.'

Hannah said she was sure I had something there. Estelle was doubtful. 'Why wasn't he up? The term's on at present. And he told you he worked in London.'

'What about London University?' demanded Hannah. 'We're close enough for him to get down in a couple of hours to look at his falcons. Perhaps he's a Professor there? His own boss? Then he could nip off and bird-watch at will. What do you guess he's a Professor of, Frances?'

I laughed. 'I don't even know he's one. He was old—but not that old. He did not look Professor-ish—he hadn't even a beard. We've a splendid Professor of Zoology at home who has the most magnificent beard.'

Hannah said beards were not at all essential. 'There were two Professors at my children's hospital. One did have a tiny goatee, which was purely an affectation, we all thought. The other might have been a retired sailor. He was fat, tanned, clean shaven, and didn't walk the wards—he rolled round them.'

'Did your Professor show any signs of a roll?' asked Estelle cheerfully.

'No. Nor was he fat or tanned.'

Hannah flopped on her bed, and removed her shoes. 'He's probably got a gastric ulcer. But we still don't know how he got your name, even if we think we've got him taped. Ask him when you write to acknowledge these.'

I sat down, and took off my own shoes. 'I suppose I must do that. I don't see how I can ask how he traced me.' I half closed my eyes and reflected on the face in my mind. 'No. I haven't the nerve. Anyway—can I write back? Where's that envelope? Pull out the letter, Estelle, and read the address. I didn't look at it properly.'

She did as I asked, while Hannah peered forward. 'Is that how you pronounce that name?'

I looked up. 'What is it? A house?'

'A club,' explained Estelle, 'rather like the Athenaeum. Grandpa stays there when he's in town.'

'Your Professor must have a good job to move in the same circles as Estelle's grandpapa,' said Hannah bluntly. 'Is the subscription very heavy, Estelle?'

Her expression tightened as it always did when her money was mentioned directly or indirectly, but as Hannah and I had previously agreed privately that the kindest way to deal with Estelle would be to treat her wealth as a normal subject of conversation, we ignored her expression. 'Is it?' I asked.

'Fairly. It's—well, rather more exclusive. My great-grandfather was a member, then Grandpapa—and so on.'

I said, 'It's very handy having you here to educate us, Estelle. I like knowing things like this. One thing—my Professor knows how to bake custards. Maybe he is in the cookery line, if they have such things? I haven't curdled one since I took his advice on slow motion.'

'Tell him that when you write—and ask if he has any hints on linseed,' insisted Hannah. 'Who knows? He may have the answer to all a pro's little problems. We can use him, if he has.'

'I'll do that,' I agreed lightly, intending to do nothing of the sort.

Later that evening I wrote my weekly letter home, and enclosed the bird photographs in their own envelope to prevent their being crushed. I explained how I had come by them, and added, 'I've really no idea who he is, but Hannah's name seems to have stuck.'

My words were more true than I guessed. From that afternoon J. S. Slane was 'the Professor' to Hannah, Estelle and me; and before the term ended our whole set called him 'Frances' Professor.'

When I had sealed my parents' envelope, I re-read the Professor's short note. I decided to answer it at once, in case I forgot later, which was only too probable, as I was for ever forgetting to write letters. I modelled my answer on his brevity. But where he seemed to me to have succeeded in being brief without being curt, my own effort seemed abrupt to the point of rudeness. I tried again; tore that page too. I write the third attempt without any fixed plan. The result covered a page and a half. I read it through doubtfully, wondering how to shorten it, and why I had allowed my pen to meander from thanking him to Mrs Brown and the linseed.

Sister P.T.S.'s head appeared round my door and prevented me writing a fourth letter. 'Ten minutes after lights out, Nurse Dorland. You should have finished your letters by now.' She waited while I tidied away my writing things. 'If you care to give me those, I will see the postman takes them early in the morning.'

I hesitated momentarily, then feeling Sister's impatience was growing, slipped the Professor's letter into the envelope I had already stamped and

addressed to encourage myself, and gave it and my parents' letter to her.
'Thank you, Sister. Good night.'

'Good night, Nurse. And in future please see your lights are out on
time.'

Next day we heard the results of our test. To every one's astonishment
Estelle came easily first in the written work.

Fay Kinsley took this as a personal insult. 'You never told us you had
brains, Estelle!'

For the first time Estelle hit back. 'You never asked me, Fay.'

Hannah and I were jubilant for Estelle. Hannah had done very well in
the practical test, was fourth from the top in the written. My name came
in the middle of both sets of marks.

'I'm only too thankful I wasn't lower down,' I said as we surveyed the
results on the hall notice-board for the twentieth time that night. 'I wrote
reams on everything, but most of what I wrote was wrong.'

Sister was behind us. 'I'm happy you realize your weakness, Nurse
Dorland,' she said not unkindly. 'You must not let your pen or tongue
run away with you, in future. You merely have to conquer your habit of
answering all round a question and go straight for the main point. You
wrote essays yesterday, where you need only have tabulated facts.'

'Copy your Professor,' murmured Estelle after Sister walked on, 'he
seems a model of brevity.'

I slapped my forehead. 'Don't mention him. I tried it last night—and
from what I remember ended by writing him an essay on linseed.'

They laughed, and Hannah told me not to worry. 'He can't be horse-y
as well as bird-y. The two things don't go together. Probably he's never
heard of linseed. Only horses and P.T.S. pros have any use for the stuff.'

Apparently the Professor did know about horses. A few days later I
had another letter covering barely half a page. 'I believe an old groom
told me when I was a boy that the technique with linseed is to warm all
the utensils first to prevent the seeds coagulating.'

I shared this information with Hannah and Estelle. At the next
poultice practice we produced three fine linseed poultices. Naylor was
reluctantly pleased. 'You are coming along at last, Nurse Dorland.'

'I feel an awful fraud,' I told the others, 'but I could hardly say,
"Don't congratulate me; congratulate my Professor." '

A couple of days later we had a very complicated lecture on the
formation of the blood. Sister P.T.S. was a good teacher, and normally I
was able to follow her very well, but a faint thunder-storm was going on
during her lecture. It did not frighten me, being too far off, it merely
reminded me vividly of the last storm on that hill. My mind kept drifting
from reticulocytes and normoblasts, to fair men in grey suits, and, above
all, to the still unsolved problem of how my specific fair man in grey had

discovered my name. When the lecture ended I was in a complete but oddly contented daze. I remembered every detail about the Professor, but not one word Sister had spoken. I had to write up the lecture and illustrate it with reasonable accuracy, so I borrowed one of Estelle's many medical text-books and spent my next free 'two-to-five' poring over the highly technical words.

Estelle looked in to my room from time to time to see how I was getting on. 'All straight?'

'Uh-huh. I'm way out of my depth. What's a lymphocyte? Or a basophil? I didn't get either down.' I showed her my rough notes. 'Only those four.'

'She did mention them. See here—it's like this—' and she tried to explain. It was no good. Her brain worked far too quickly for mine, and although she was very patient, she could not teach.

Hannah came in to help; so did two-thirds of our set. 'It's really quite simple,' they all said kindly. The trouble was, I did not find it simple. In desperation I learnt by heart a chunk from Estelle's book, wrote an essay on what I had learnt; illustrated my essay with what I considered was almost impressive chart.

The chart earned me a visit to Sister's office. 'What exactly does this represent, Nurse Dorland?'

I took a deep breath. 'It is a diagram to illustrate the formation of the blood, Sister.'

'It does nothing of the kind, Nurse. As you would know,' added Sister sternly, 'had you paid any attention to the drawing I made on the board in my lecture. I noticed your mind was wandering, which is why I am not going to repeat my lecture to you now. If you cannot take the trouble to attend in class you must find this out for yourself. Let me have it back as soon as you have got it right.'

I returned to the girls, sunk in gloom. 'How am I going to get this right?'

'Why not send your Professor an SOS?' suggested Estelle thoughtfully.

'He couldn't know the answer to a thing like this. Besides, I can't keep on badgering him. I'll just have to find out for myself, as Sister said.' I borrowed all her textbooks. 'I'm going to bed with the lot. Maybe my subconscious'll dream up the answer in my sleep.'

My subconscious seemed otherwise occupied. I dreamt about my Professor all night. In the morning I felt very cheered by my dreams, but very worried about the formation of the blood. Fay Kinsley and I were paired as bed-makers in the practical nursing class that day. Sister told us to put Mrs Brown in a rheumatic bed; Mrs Smith into an orthopaedic bed; and then to make up the empty bed in the class-room to receive a patient returning from the theatre after an amputation. 'Collect all necessary equipment before you start, Nurses. When you are ready wait by your beds until I return to inspect your work.'

We loaded ourselves with fracture-boards, bed-cradles, extra mackintoshes, extra personal blankets, mackintosh pillow-cases, and bed-blocks.

I closed the store-room door with my shoulder as my hands were full. 'I'm sure we've forgotten something—apart from the kitchen sink.'

Fay looked down her nose. 'I don't know why you think you always have to joke, Frances. Nursing is not a joke.'

I let that pass. 'There's something else we'll need. What?' I stopped Estelle as she hurried by to Naylor's First-Aid class. 'We're doing rheumatic, orthopaedic, and amputation beds. Do we need anything else?'

Fay's lips tightened, but she said nothing, knowing, as we now all did, Estelle's memory for detail was the best in the set.

Estelle glanced swiftly over our collection. 'Tourniquet to tie at the foot of the amputation bed. Lower rail. Maybe a transfusion stand, just to be on the safe side. Sorry, girls—I must fly. Naylor's waiting.'

'Fly, dear. Heaven'll reward you even if I don't.' I put down my load and took a rubber tourniquet from one of the shelves. 'We'll have to come back for the transfusion stand. Bless that girl! She's the brightest person I've ever met.'

Fay smiled unpleasantly. 'She's certainly brighter than you were. Now she's got the hang of things, she's not lending out her brains, even if you did cosset her when she was so green.'

'What are you talking about? Hasn't she just done that?' I heaved my load higher. 'Let's get on with those beds.'

'I wasn't talking about just now,' she said as we stripped the empty bed. 'I was talking about the rocket Sister gave you on that chart. If Estelle had any decency, she could have saved you that rocket. She's got the facts all right, but is keeping them to herself. I suppose she inherited that tendency along with everything else from her precious grandpapa. I suppose you have to be grasping to get rich and stay rich. Personally, I think it's a pretty rotten way to act.'

'Personally, so do I—about the way you're acting. She hasn't inherited from her grandfather yet, he's still alive. I've never heard such nonsense in my life.'

I had to stop speaking then as Sister had come back to watch us, even though I was bursting to tell her just how much Estelle had tried to help me over that wretched chart. Later, when we were alone again, I changed my mind. It was useless trying to persuade Fay about anything concerning Estelle, but unless I got my facts right about that last lecture, she would probably spread her nasty little ideas round the whole set. That night, in desperation, I wrote a really short, urgent letter to the Professor.

He answered by return of post. This time his letter actually covered the whole of one side of a page. Accompanying it was a spare typewritten sheet of paper on which was given a very simple account of the formation of the blood; on the reverse was a clear diagram illustrating the account.

'I called in the assistance of one of my fellow-members here,' he wrote. 'A pathologist. He recommends the enclosed as being successful with his students. I hope it may be of some use. If not, drop me a line and I'll tackle him again.'

I was enchanted by his helpfulness; doubly enchanted to be able to understand his enclosures.

The following Friday evening Sister summoned me once more. 'Explain this diagram to me in detail, please, Nurse Dorland.'

When my somewhat nervous explanation ended, she nodded approvingly. 'I see you have taken pains with this, Nurse. Good. Did you manage alone?'

'No, Sister. I consulted—one of my friends.'

She smiled. 'I thought as much. Well, Nurse, you may tell Nurse Dexter that I consider she has the makings of an excellent teacher.'

This time it was Estelle who felt a fraud. 'I can't take the credit, Frances!'

'Nonsense! You must. The Professor wouldn't mind, and Sister would have a stroke if she thought I was writing to him about it.'

My set never knew the Professor had helped me over that particular problem, but his existence was now common knowledge. When anyone had a problem, I was besieged immediately. 'Frances, is it your turn to write or the Professor's? Then will you ask him—this—that—or the other? Thanks.'

I mentioned this to him in one of my letters, without telling him of his nickname.

In his reply he seemed amused:

I find myself much enjoying this novel situation. I have never been an oracle before. I only hope I will be able to come up with the right answers. I must admit your questions lack neither variety nor entertainment value, and are infinitely preferable to crossword puzzles.

I always enjoyed getting his letters; I loved getting that one. I wondered, as I did constantly, about his background; if his wife was attractive; if he had any daughters. His tolerant attitude reminded me a great deal of my father, so I suspected he had at least two growing daughters. Perhaps he had more than two; perhaps a vast family? Estelle said Professors were reasonably well-paid, but a family can eat money, as I knew from my parents' food bills. I got quite upset at the thought of the Professor having to over-work, and do without to support his many children, and wondered if I ought to bother such a busy man with my letters. I also wondered whether his wife minded his writing, if she knew. I could not decide if I preferred her to know or not; he was older than me, but—well—not all that much older. If I were his wife, I thought finally, I would not like it at all. Yet that was sheer folly, because as he had admitted, my letters took the place of crossword puzzles and meant no more to him than that. I was a little disturbed to discover how much they were beginning to mean to me.

The second half of the term was now well under way. Our Final Test was no longer a vague date, but merely a matter of days ahead. Hannah lost interest in her hair-dressing appointments; Estelle's shining car stood silent in the drive; my bicycle developed two flats, but there was no time to mend either. Every spare moment we had off duty we devoted to working through test-papers, nursing each other in bed, chanting the muscles and bones, and finishing our many-tailed bandages.

One afternoon Estelle and Hannah were in my room for a change. We had had a very busy morning of practical nursing, and our legs were weary. I massaged my calves then drifted round the room barefoot and on tip-toe as Naylor had advised. 'I can't say this makes much difference. What's this chap here?' I slapped my leg. 'Some name like a Rider Haggard character. Gastroc—something?'

Estelle was reading the anæmias. 'Gastroc nemis—I think. And not from Haggard—it's pure Martian.'

'I'm not all that up in space fiction.' I leant out of my window and watched a bright blue dot appear on the winding white lane running up the hill. As it came closer the dot turned into a motor-scooter ridden by a man in a white crash helmet. 'Talking of Martians—come here, girls! There's a very muscular Martian getting off a blue scooter at our front gate.'

Estelle looked up quickly, but showed no other sign of interest as Hannah bounded to the window.

'It's Bart! Good! I thought he had forgotten his promise to call.' Hannah scrambled for her shoes. 'Come and meet him, Frances. You too, Estelle. You remember Bart? We met him in the town.'

'Bart?' murmured Estelle vaguely. 'Did we? Oh, yes, I remember. He was charming.' She hesitated, then added politely, 'Will you mind if I don't come down? I'm whacked, and must get these anæmias taped. But you go, Frances. You'll like Hannah's cousin.' Her eyes met mine for a fraction of a minute.

The expression in her eyes silenced the protest I had been about to make over her absurd statement that she needed to get the anæmias taped. She had reeled them off to us only a few minutes ago, and once she learnt anything, she never forgot it. I glanced at her curiously, put on my own shoes, and said I would love to meet Hannah's cousin.

Hannah looked hurt as we went downstairs. 'I'm afraid Estelle didn't like Bart. She was fearfully standoffish when I introduced him.'

'She was probably only stricken dumb with shyness. Remember how she first was with us? I'll bet that's why she's staying upstairs.'

She brightened. 'I expect you're right. You really know her even better than I do.'

I agreed heartily, but inwardly was not so sanguine. I knew Estelle well enough now to know something was wrong. I did not understand what that something could be, and when I met Bartholomew More, I understood even less.

Hannah's description of him had been quite wrong. He was no Angry Young Man; he was exceedingly gay, had pleasant manners and exceptional good looks. He had Hannah's dark hair and eyes, but his features were far more regular, the lilt in his voice far more noticeable— I suspected intentionally so.

Sister gave Hannah the choice of entertaining in the sitting-room or garden. Hannah chose the garden. It was a lovely afternoon and we sat on the lawn by the summer-house, while the bees hummed over the lupins and columbines in the flowerbeds, and Hannah scolded her cousin for not visiting us sooner.

'Darling Hannah,' he said plaintively, 'do you appreciate the risk Luigi and I have just run? The chaps below told me I'd need a signed pass from Matron to get beyond your front gate. This place is out of bounds to one and all. And I risked it,' he laid a hand on his heart, 'for you, and you, Frances!'

I said, 'I'm deeply touched. Is Luigi your scooter?'

'And who else would he be?' He looked round the lawn. 'Where's the third member of the trio? You did say you were a trio, Hannah? That afternoon we met? Wasn't that blonde the third? Esther Something or Other?'

Hannah looked worried. 'Estelle. Yes. She's—working.'

I said, 'Up yon.' I waved at the house. 'With her head in a medical book. You mightn't guess it from her fair and fragile appearance, but Estelle is the brains of our set. She's not just plain clever, she's staggeringly bright.'

'Is that so?' he asked eagerly. 'Maybe, now I come to think of it, there was something unusual about her.' He suddenly noticed I was watching him and promptly altered his manner. 'Unlike Junior,' he drawled. 'No brains—not even keen—just the slack type.'

Hannah laughed. 'Your years in Martha's haven't changed you, Bart. You always were daft.'

'She mocks me,' he said sadly, 'mocks me. Let's ignore her, Frances. You, I know, will understand me. We must get together. When do you girls join the old firm in town?'

I smiled. I did understand him—as much as any young woman can ever understand any young man, or vice versa. I had met too many other young men of his type not to recognize it at sight. Our village at home was very social place, oddly lacking in young women. I had never been more than mildly in love with any of them, but had been on dancing and going to Point-to-Point and Hunt Ball terms with several Bart Mores since I left school. 'We don't mention the old firm yet. We still have to get over our Finals. All is dark beyond that date.'

He said he knew just how it was. 'Is your fair friend jittery, too?' He glanced at the house. 'Is that really why she's flogging the books? It seems too bad to have to stay in in this weather. Who knows? To-day may be the summer.'

Hannah said Estelle would not let a little thing like sunshine deter her once she had made up her mind to stay in.

'Strong-minded as well as bright?' asked her cousin.

'Inevitably. Or she wouldn't be here at all.'

'And why wouldn't she?'

'Bart. You surely realize she's Estelle Dexter?'

He stared at her, momentarily. 'That—Dexter?'

She nodded. 'The only one.'

He looked at the house for several seconds before making any comment. 'So she's the lass with all that lovely lolly,' he said at last. 'Well, well, well. Useful stuff, lolly.' He turned slowly to me, as if it took him a tremendous physical effort. I expected him to ask what Estelle was doing at Martha's, since that was the first question every one asked on discovering her identity. He said only, 'You in the money, too, Frances?'

'Not me. My father's a farmer with four daughters. I have what I earn.'

He smiled faintly. 'My old man's a parson. I'm the oldest of five. And I don't even earn.' He glanced back at the house. 'How does she fit in?'

Hannah said, 'Frances can answer that. She's Estelle's closest pal.'

I said, 'It was tricky at first. She seemed utterly helpless. But once that Dexter brain catches on to a fact, it really catches. She's streaking ahead of us all, and fitting in very well.'

'That's just great.' He stood up. 'And it's been just great seeing you girls, but it's time I made tracks. Be seeing you both, in town. Take care of yourselves.'

We walked with him to the gate. Hannah watched his scooter vanish down the hill. 'I hoped he'd spend longer with us. Never mind. We'll see him in town.' She smiled at me. 'Wasn't I right about him? Isn't he exactly your cup of tea? I knew you two would click. You can't conceive how differently he behaved to Estelle. He barely opened his mouth to her.'

I was on the point of remarking that despite that original reticence he had managed to say quite a few words about Estelle, when she came out of the house and joined us.

Hannah hailed her cheerfully. 'Bart quite understood you wanted to work. He had a fine time with Frances. They might have known each other years.'

'How very pleasant for all of you. Will he be up in town when we get there?'

'I'll bet he'll be there when Frances gets there, if I know my cousin Bart,' replied Hannah, who was patently in a match-making, and highly imaginative mood.

Estelle smiled politely. 'That should be fun, Frances.'

'Sure. Great fun.' I noticed her smile did not reach her eyes. 'How did you get on with the muscles? All taped?'

'I think so. That's why I came out.'

'This sun is too good to waste,' I said, and went to shut the gate which had just swung open. I did not remind her that she had officially stayed in to read up on anæmia. 'Let's go back on the lawn. Hannah's cousin was right. To-day may be all the summer we have.'

Bartholomew More was not right. The weather remained settled and brilliant. He did not visit us again during the rest of our term, which annoyed Hannah irrationally, since he had only mentioned seeing us again in town. I heard twice from the Professor during those final weeks, and then there was no time left in which to open another text-book, roll another bandage, practise another bed, or write another urgent letter.

On our last evening I persuaded the two others to climb the hill. I would have preferred to go up alone, but knew they would be hurt if I vanished in the middle of our post-examination celebrations, so I insisted the exercise was what we all needed.

They said they were glad I had insisted when we reached the top. The evening was warm and golden; the sun only half-way down the sky. We lay out on the bracken, removing prickles and burrs from our hair, wishing we had brought a rug. Below us the hospital was white in the pine-trees, and on the cement ramps the scarlet blankets covering the patients lying in beds made vivid splashes of colour against the green and white.

We talked over the term, then the future. Estelle and I were going to a ward called Josephine in London. Hannah was to work in Arthur.

'I wish we could start in the annexe,' said Estelle drowsily, 'it's such heaven here now.' She shielded her eyes with one hand. 'What's that bird, Frances?'

'Flying east? That's a hobby. One of the Professor's babies. A honey, isn't he.'

Hannah sat up. 'Which way?'

'Thataway. East, girl. Blue-grey with pointed wings—see?'

'Think so.' She lay back. 'You know, we ought all to write and thank your Professor. He's given us a packet of help. Wasn't it a good thing you messed up your cooking that morning? You'd have come out with us if you hadn't, and never met him. Of course, you would then have met Bart earlier, and we might have seen more of him, but there's masses of time ahead.'

'That's true,' I agreed casually, glancing at Estelle. She was still watching the fast-vanishing hobby, and apparently ignoring our conversation. She had never mentioned Bart to me, but whenever Hannah talked about him, which she did frequently, Estelle made a point of not paying attention. This was odd, because Estelle was normally very good about paying attention.

Hannah twisted her head round and surveyed the stone shelter. 'So that's where you nearly cracked your head? You were mighty lucky, Frances. You'd have had a fractured base almost for sure on that floor.' She relaxed again. 'I wonder if you'll ever come across the Professor again? Does he ever mention a date?'

'No.' I said no more, hoping she would drop the subject.

'Then why on earth does he go on writing to you? The man must be nuts. No passes; no attempts to date you.' She looked me over. 'You did say he wasn't a queer?'

'He wasn't. Why does he have to be one to write? Maybe he just likes writing letters? Maybe he's just plain kind.'

Hannah snorted. 'You're no raving beauty, duckie, but you're a good-looking wench with a smashing figure and the best legs in our set.' She extended her own complacently. 'And we've got some pretty good legs among us. I won't say that men can't be kind, but kindness is seldom the motive that inspires any man to pursue an acquaintance with a young woman.' She turned to Estelle. 'Aren't I right?'

Estelle hesitated. 'Grandpapa says there is no such thing as a platonic friendship between a normal man and woman. Grandpapa's generally right.'

'It's hardly a friendship,' I protested. 'We only met in that storm. I
expect it's amused him to write as he has, but he'll probably get bored
with it soon.'

'You can't let him get bored before you find out how he managed to
get hold of your name. You don't know that yet, do you? Or, really,
anything about him?'

I was very fond of her, but I could willingly have choked her. 'No.'

She said she thought I had been disgracefully unenterprising. 'Can
you even remember what he looks like?'

'Sure,' I said, 'sure. It's engraved on my heart. Haven't you guessed?'

She laughed. 'I'll bet. Since the poor old Professor's been such a boon
and a blessing to us, I only hope he doesn't feel the same.'

Estelle asked quietly, 'Why?'

'Quite obviously he's married—decent men of his age always are. He
must be decent, not to have made any passes or dates. Maybe he's at the
dangerous age. Was he?'

'He wasn't dangerous, whatever his age.'

Hannah said I was very young and innocent and she was very old and
cynical. 'You wouldn't recognize danger if you saw it.'

Estelle nodded. 'It's probably just as well there's not much chance of
your meeting him again. Those snaps might not have been an opening
gambit, but if you hadn't made some impression on him, you'd never
have got that second letter. Hannah's right. Your friend the Professor
sounds charming, and has been extremely helpful, but has obviously
decided to stay at the end of a letter—and just as well if there's a Mrs
Professor and lots of little Professors.'

I had been first embarrassed, then annoyed, now I was honestly
amused. 'Girls, you are a pair! Poor man! You aren't giving him a
chance. And you don't know what you are talking about, for all your
worldly wisdom—though you ought to! You've seen his letters. They
couldn't be more impersonal or discreet. You talk as if they were Sunday
paper love-letters.'

Hannah said she would have thought it all far more natural if they
were.

'For Pete's sake! Why? He's not in love with me!'

Estelle came over to my side. 'He's certainly not acting as if he is.'

Hannah rolled over and looked up at me. 'Maybe he isn't. All the
same—watch out, Frances. I'll tell Bart to watch out for you, too. When
I was doing children,' she went on dreamily, 'we were always getting
kids in with measles. We shouldn't have had them, but they developed it
once they were in. Some one on the staff always caught it. Love, my
dear little Frances, is like the measles. The older in life you get it, the

worse it hits you. So I hope for Mrs Professor's sake, that for once Estelle's grandpapa is wrong. You'll forgive me, I hope, Estelle?'

'Even Homer sometimes nods,' agreed Estelle. 'But—I've never known Grandpapa wrong.'

I shivered although the sun was still there. 'I'm cold. Let's move.'

There was a party going on when we returned to our sitting-room. Earlier I had decided to leave the party discreetly to write a last letter telling the Professor about our results. I wanted to write to him as never before. I did not. Hannah and Estelle had forced me to face all the questions I had previously refused to face. I stayed in the party until Sister sent us to bed.

4. Bart asks me out

The sun shone on Josephine Ward balcony that Monday morning, the river was the colour of polished pewter. A small, dirty, red tug ambled lazily past the hospital. A seaman holding a rope on the narrow deck waved at us, and the two patients in beds on the balcony waved back. The tug's funnel tilted back as it approached the bridge, a trail of black smoke floated up to us. In a few seconds, young Mrs Ellis' face, hands, and clean white bedspread were spotted with soot.

'Oh, dear,' I dropped my wet string duster. 'I am sorry, Mrs Ellis. Did any get in your eyes?' I took her face flannel from the back rail of her locker and removed the soot from her person. 'Sure your eyes are all right?'

'I'm all right, duck.' She smiled. 'A bit of dirt don't hurt. Makes me feel I'm back home along of the Power House. My Mum,' she gasped, in the way Sister Josephine had told us was typical in acute cardiac disease, 'reckons we all thrive on a peck o' dirt. But you'd best do something about me quilt, Nurse. Staff Nurse won't half create, if she catches it in this state.' She paused for a longer breath. 'We did really ought to have them red covers over our quilts, duck. You nip along and fetch 'em to us afore that Nurse Garret sees us out here without 'em.' She looked across the balcony to her companion, Mrs Astor. 'See what that tug done to me quilt, Gran?'

'Dear, dear, dear,' clucked Mrs Astor anxiously. 'Poor Nurse. What a worry we are for you.'

They were great friends despite the sixty years between their ages. They were so obviously fond of each other that at first Estelle and I had thought them actually related. Mrs Ellis had been longer in the ward than any of our women, but both of them had been in and out of Josephine several times before.

Sister Josephine had given us a diagnosis class on our second day in her ward. She had said Mrs Ellis was very ill. I knew she had to be right, but found that difficult to remember and believe when I was with Lily Ellis. She was two months older than I was, very attractive, gay, and good-natured. It seemed impossible to associate her with my previous notions of illness.

She had scattered those notions and adopted me as 'my Nurse Dorland' from the moment when, on our third morning in Josephine, I had spilt tomato soup all over the clean turn-down of her top sheet. She not only consoled me; she even soothed our Staff Nurse. 'I'll bet I look real classy with ketchup on my best bib and tucker, Nurse Garret! Talk about clumsy! I always was a shocker and no mistake! There was this poor little new nurse trying'—gasp—'to feed me real lovely, and I gives her a shove and bungs the tray clean out of her hands.'

When Nurse Garret had helped me change the sheet and left me with a new bowl of soup to feed her, I had attempted to thank Mrs Ellis.

She lowered one eyelid slowly. 'Shush, duck. Don't say no more. If I say it was me own fault, it was me own fault, see. The patient is always right—eh? Hasn't that Sister Tutor told you that yet? She will.'

She was perfectly right. Sister Tutor gave us this maxim in her opening lecture a day or so later. By then I had discovered that Mrs Ellis was a mine of hospital information. She knew all that went on in Josephine; a great deal about nursing; and exactly how to manage Sister Josephine and Staff Nurse Garret.

I did not hesitate when she said I needed to get two red-check covers. 'Do I just help myself from the linen-room?'

'Half a tick, duck! Hey—Gran! Is it all clear?'

Mrs Astor was allowed to move freely in bed. She sat forward and peered into the ward through the open balcony doors. 'The Staff Nurse is just going into the lift, dear,' she whispered conspiratorially. 'You're safe.'

Mrs Ellis agreed. 'She'll be off to the dispensary. She won't be back afore eight-thirty. Get weaving, duck.'

'Bless you both—I will. Thanks.' I shot down the ward that even after two weeks seemed four miles long and to contain four hundred and not forty beds. The linen-room lay at the opposite end to the balcony. Sister's office, and the changing-room were on the same side of the small ward corridor outside the main ward and called 'the flat'; the kitchen and clinical-room were on the other side.

Estelle gave me a faintly harassed smile as I passed the open kitchen door. I waved back, then dropped my hand like a stone as Sister Josephine came out of her office.

'Nurse Dorland, is one of my patients hæmorrhaging?'

I swallowed, knowing what was coming. 'No, Sister.'

'Then I can only presume my ward is on fire?'

'Er—no, Sister.'

'Then what do you mean by racing in this fashion? This is the fifth occasion upon which I have had to speak to you about running on duty, Nurse. Kindly spare my having to do so again. Carry on with your work decorously.'

I collected the red-check covers, and walked with what I hoped was suitable decorum back to the balcony. The women nodded at me amicably. 'Always on the go, these young nurses. Shame. But, there. Got so much to learn they have.'

On the balcony Mrs Astor sat forward to help me arrange her cover. 'Lil, dear, has Nurse done the end right?'

Mrs Ellis was watching carefully. 'Only sort of. Look, duck, tuck down them sides—see—' she breathed deeply—'not like it was a quilt. Then get to the bottom and pull up the end from the middle, like you was making an envelope. That's it, duck. Now, bung the lot under neat. There. You catch on quick.' She glanced round the balcony. 'Better give that wet linen bin a shove against the wall—Nurse Garret'll create if she sees it sticking out. And don't forget your wheel-chair with your rubbish. Nurse Garret won't be shutting her eyes to nothing now you been here two weeks.'

If Nurse Garret had shut her eyes to anything during our first fortnight, neither Estelle nor I had noticed it. Garret was a slim, brisk, dark-haired young woman with a fine complexion and dark-rimmed slanting spectacles. Those winged frames added to the impression she gave of being constantly on the point of taking off from the ground. She moved like silent lightning, yet never seemed to distress Sister by her speed, possibly because she was so quiet. She came into the sluice as I was drying the last washing bowl. 'Nurse Dorland, did you do the feet of your trolleys this morning?'

'Yes, Nurse.'

'You turned them upside down and scraped the wheels with your scissors?'

'Yes, Nurse.'

'Then you must have done them most carelessly. They're all over fluff. Do them again when the sluice is finished.'

'Yes, Nurse,' I said meekly, feeling like a gramophone record stuck in a rut.

Nurse Player, our Senior Pro, arrived in the sluice directly Garret vanished. Monica Player was in her second year—and our guardian angel. She hovered maternally over us, helping when we were lost beneath mountains of mackintoshes needing scrubbing, plates that needed heating, linen that had to be sorted, sterilizers that had to be cleaned, bed-tables that required polishing. She seemed capable of being in three places at once, and appeared to possess six hands. She came to my rescue now.

'I'll do those trolleys for you, Dorland. You get straight in here.' She paused on one foot. 'Have you been very careful about your locker backs? Garret's in one of her Monday morning moods. She always gets worked up about trolley wheels and locker backs on Mondays.' She glanced out of the window towards the balcony. 'Have the balcony girls got their checks on—oh, yes! Good girl. I forgot to remind you when we were pushing their beds out.'

'Actually, Nurse, Mrs Ellis reminded me.'

'Thank God for Mrs Ellis,' she said sincerely. 'I don't know how we'd cope without her. And the others. They're a nice bunch.'

Estelle said much the same when we did the flowers together at ten to nine. 'They were heaven at breakfast. Garret told me to manage second cups alone. I was terribly slow without Player and the tea got more and more stewed. Sister noticed the colour when she was doing the pulses, and asked Miss Ronson if it was too strong. Dear old Miss Ronson adores weak China tea, but she swore blind the foul stuff she was drinking was just how she liked it! I could have hugged her.'

Player sailed into the clinical-room in which the flowers were stacked at night. 'Come on, girls, or we'll be late. All these vases must be in before I take down the screen across the door at the first stroke of nine.'

Thanks to Player we were done by nine. She removed the screen that showed whether the ward was open or closed for medical rounds, and marshalled us up to the centre table. Sister dismissed Estelle for the morning; gave Player a list of treatments; told me I was to do 'morning routine' on my own. 'You've been with us long enough to be able to manage, Nurse Dorland.'

Player gave me a slight nod. I took the hint and smiled weakly. 'Yes, Sister; thank you, Sister.'

'Don't look so rattled, Dorland,' she whispered as we retired to the kitchen. 'It's quite simple. Errands first, then temps., charts, drinks, treatments, set for lunch, close the ward, round; open the ward; help serve lunches.'

I felt even weaker. 'Yes, Nurse. Thanks.'

'Don't forget you mustn't start the four-hourly temps. before ten to ten. The four-hourly book lives on Sister's desk. Ask her for it if she's sitting there, if not, help yourself. Don't forget to put it back when you've done the charting, or Sister'll go through the roof.'

Maggie, the ward-maid, considered me grimly. 'So I've to have another of you new nurses getting under me feet all morning, have I? Then you listen to me, Nurse Dorland. I'll have no milk spilt on me clean stove, nor drips on me floor, so don't you forget it. All right—all right,' she grumbled, although neither of us had said a word, 'I'll put your milk on and see to the urn. And you mind you fetch all the used crocks back to me by eleven. I'll want me kitchen to meself to get straightened up before I goes down for the dinners at a quarter to.'

I had been nodding like a mandarin. 'Yes, Maggie; no, Maggie; right, Maggie. Nurse Player, do I go to Sister for the errands?'

'Dorland, Sister takes round the S.M.O. immediately after nine.' Player spoke slowly as she would have done perhaps to a backward child. 'Nothing must interrupt the S.M.O.'s round. He may not be a pundit, but he is the senior resident.'

'What about the S.S.O., Nurse?'

'I've told you, physicians take precedence over surgeons. Do get that into your head. And do get off to Garret for those errands. She won't like being kept waiting.'

Garret did not like it. 'What have you been doing, Nurse Dorland? Why weren't you here five minutes ago? Now, take this'—she handed me a test-tube—'and keep it warm. Not in your pocket, child! It'll spill and you'll be drenched in bugs! In your hand. It must stay at blood heat. Take it to the Path. Lab., before you do anything else. It's labelled—this is the request form. These notes'—she pushed a file under my arm—'are for the in-patient Lady Almoner. Leave this bed-ticket'—my other arm was needed—'at the dispensary. Tell them the digitalis can come up in the basket as I've enough until the after-lunch round. That's all for now, but hurry. I may have more errands when you get back.'

'Yes, Nurse; thank you, Nurse.' I rushed off to look for Player, and met her coming out of the kitchen. 'Please, Nurse, which floor was the Path. Lab. on?'

'Which Lab? We've got four.' She tilted her head to read the label on the tube I was clutching. 'For Sir Marcus. Top Lab.—top floor over the Admin. block. Not the Lab. I took you to—that was the Central slap opposite to Arthur. Know how to get to the Admin. block?'

'Is that where Matron's office is? I think so.'

'Yes. It's quite simple. Go along to Matron's office, turn right past the Dean's office, and take the lift marked "Private, Pathological Department Only." That tube lets you use it. Come down the same way and make for the Almoners. You know here they live. I took you only last week.'

I felt breathless already. 'Beyond Casualty?'

'That's them. Ask the Almoners to direct you from there. They'll do it. They're good girls.'

'That's a mercy,' I murmured feelingly.

She grinned. 'Don't worry. Pathologists don't bite.'

'Just one thing, what do I do when I reach this Top Lab.? Do I ask for Sir Whatwashisname?'

'I wouldn't, if I were you. He's the Director. He doesn't deal with anyone under the rank of Ass. Mat. You won't have any snags up there. If there isn't an assistant pathologist around there'll be a label. Our Labs. are stiff with labels. It must be something to do with pathology or maybe the back-room boys are just allergic to being disturbed. Do get going, or you'll not be done in time to get your temps. taken by ten.'

I walked as quickly as I dared along the main corridor that connected all the hospital blocks. I knew the way to Matron's office, and did not anticipate any difficulty in finding the Dean's, until I reached the Admin. block and found I was quite lost. Matron's office was there all right, but I could see no sign of anything leading to the Dean. On my right was an opaque glass door marked 'Private.' I turned left. The notice on the only door in sight ran, 'Medical Reading-room.'

I hesitated and was promptly engulfed by a crowd of students who must have been following me down the corridor. The sea of tweeds and heads hid both doors momentarily, then swept by as if I was invisible and without substance. I gazed after them wondering if I had enough courage to call one back to ask the way, when I recognized one of the heads.

'Bart More,' I called quietly, 'can you help me?'

He glanced round incuriously, then smiled. 'Hi, there, Frances Dorland. I didn't see you. So you made it? How about the rest of the trio?'

'Fine, thanks.' I had no time to waste in civilities. 'Where's the Dean's office?'

He had joined me. 'Taking up medicine?'

'I've got to get this'—I held up the test-tube—'to the Top Lab., and I'm lost.'

'Not now you aren't, angel. Come with uncle. Out of the way, chaps. The lady wants to rise to the upper regions.' He thrust his colleagues aside, and opened the glass door marked 'Private.' 'This way. The Dean's yon'—he jerked a thumb—'and there's your lift. I'll see you in.'

'Thanks.' I waited as he opened the gates. 'You don't know how relieved I was to see you.'

'You can do the same for me sometime. Where are you working?'

'Josephine.'

He closed the gates very slowly. 'Cousin Hannah?'

'Arthur. Bart, I'll have to go.'

'That's right.' But he had not yet closed the gates completely. 'How about your other pal?'

'Estelle is in Josephine, too.'

He let go then. 'Just press that button, angel, and it'll take you right the way up. Take care of yourself.'

I stepped out into another long white corridor. I had not been up there before, but, as Player had said, there was no question of anyone visiting the Lab. being in any doubt. The door directly opposite to the lift-well was marked Pathological Research Department. Beneath that was a smaller notice: 'Will all nurses walk in without knocking.'

I obeyed rather timidly. I expected to find a room filled with intelligent-looking youngish men in long white coats absently eating dusty sandwiches. I was alone in a large tiled room lined with china shelves on which stood hundreds of empty test-tubes of various sizes. A line of white sinks with long-handled taps occupied the centre of the floor; four long zinc-covered tables were in a row by the outside wall that was almost entirely of plate-glass. The room was full of light and silence; the whole of London seemed spread before me and I wished I had the time and courage to linger and look out.

As I had neither I looked round, wondering what to do next. I felt exactly like Alice when I read an obliging label. 'Will nurses please put any specimens to be kept at blood heat in the incubator under this notice.'

'Thank you,' I murmured automatically, opening the incubator. Directly I opened it, a bell rang. It went on ringing until a door at the far end of the long room opened. A middle-aged man in a long white coat, with rimless spectacles, and thinning grey hair, stood in the doorway. 'I don't think you can have closed that properly, Nurse. Turn the handle right up. That's better.' He came forward. 'Where are you from?'

'Josephine.' The bell had unnerved me, and I forgot to add, 'Doctor.'

'Good. I was expecting you. You've brought Miss Yates' specimen for culture? I may as well take it now. I want to get on with it.' He removed the tube I had just left in the incubator and showed me how to close the door to cut off the bell. 'Right, Nurse. We'll send the report down later.'

'Thank you, Doctor.' I made for the door, then wondered if I should have said 'Thank you, Sir Marcus.' I decided I should have used his title as Player did, but he did not seem to have noticed my mistake. He was shaking his head over the request form and muttering something about the last Van den Bergh showing a positive indirect reaction.

I wondered what or whom a Van den Bergh might be and if Player would be able to tell me. If not I might find it in one of Estelle's medical books.

In the P.T.S., I thought as the lift carried me down, I would have written to ask the Professor. I had not written or heard from him since we left. Although we had only left the School a couple of weeks, that term and the Professor now seemed to belong in another liftetime to another person. I thought over the man I had just seen. He was a genuine Professor—and looked it. Mine was—I did not really know what he was. As the girls said, he was obviously married: as I had said, he had obviously grown bored with our correspondence. The girls were right. It was just as well he had faded out of my life as he had. I had spent far too much time thinking about him in those last few weeks in the P.T.S. I would have more than enough to occupy my mind and time in the next four years. I wanted to make a success of my training and the only way to make a success of anything was to have a one-track mind. I was really grateful to the girls for making me look the facts in the face. From now on, men were out, as far as I was concerned. I was absolutely determined on that point. And then a strange man with fair hair walked by. He looked nothing like the Professor, but the faint similarity in their hair-colouring made me wander into Casualty without realizing it.

A bellow from Sister Casualty brought me back to earth. 'And where do you think you are going, Nurse? Yes! You! You with the untidy hair!'

I swallowed. 'To the in-patient Lady Almoner, Sister.'

'Then will you oblige me by using the main corridor, and not using my department as a short cut? This is Casualty. Not Oxford Circus.'

I apologized, backed to the door through which I had come, and lectured myself on the obvious necessity for that one-track mind. Player had warned me never to set foot in Casualty if there was a possibility of Sister Cas. being on duty. 'She may be young and pretty. She can be as tough as old Sister O.P.'s—and being younger, moves faster.'

The Almoners' office was a haven of peace. They gave me one of the maps reserved for patients. 'It's so easy to get lost here when you are new. The dispensary's marked on it and most other places you'll need. Every one should have either a map or a guide dog. Martha's covers over half a mile of London.'

'I feel as if it covers all London.' I deposited the file of notes, thanked them for the map, hurried on to the dispensary and then back to Josephine.

I had not hurried sufficiently. 'You must not dawdle in this fashion, Nurse,' said Garret sternly. 'You don't seem to realize that you have work to do. Get on with those four-hourly temperatures.'

The ward was very quiet when I took the four-hourly book off Sister's desk. A cardiologist called Dr Curtis was lecturing to a group of about thirty students at the far end of the ward. His words were inaudible to me, but his voice hummed deeply like the hum of a sleepy bee.

I looked at him curiously. Sister said he was one of the coming men of modern medicine. He was wearing professional clothes, but he looked more like a farmer than a doctor. He was large, plump, and—at a guess—forty. The Professor looked around that age. My father was forty-eight, so that put them in the same generation.

'Nurse Dorland.' Garret was hissing at my elbow. 'You're shaking down a thermometer, not shaking out a salad. You're been maltreating that bit of glass for the past two minutes. What are you trying to do? Dislodge the mercury for all time?'

Ten minutes later Player appeared at my other elbow. 'Are you going to sleep over those charts, Dorland? For Heaven's sake, get on! The drinks should have been in by now!'

Sister frowned hideously as the cups rattled on my tray. 'Less noise, please, Nurse,' she murmured as I scurried past the round.

Maggie looked closer to exploding each time I returned to the kitchen. Her flash-point arrived when, in my too violent attempt to dislodge one cube of ice, I sent the entire contents of the ice-tray on to her floor.

'You young nurses! Think I've nothing better to do than clear up after you, you do! Look at me floor—and all that ice-wasted!' She ignored my immediate offer to dry the mess and wielded her floor-cloth like a weapon. 'And now I suppose you'll want to borrow more from Margaret as that second tray hasn't set?'

I mopped my forehead with the back of one hand. 'Maggie—can you do that? I was just wondering what to do as Mrs Jenkins will only take iced milk. I thought I'd have to ask Nurse Garret.'

She rinsed and wrung the cloth, tipped the ice into the tea-bucket, washed and dried her hands. 'What do you want to go running to Nurse Garret for? Isn't this me kitchen?'

'Oh, yes, Maggie.'

'Then don't you go forgetting it again. I don't let nobody forget it,' she added sternly, 'and if anyone tried it on, I'd go to Sister and ask for me cards.'

I did not then know that Maggie had threatened to ask for her cards throughout the eighteen years in which she had ruled the kitchen in Josephine. I must have looked suitably shocked, because she grew more mollified. 'I'll see to that Mrs Jenkins' milk. If they ask why it ain't in yet, you tell 'em as Maggie says her fridge ain't frozen and you can't have no ice. They won't say no more.'

'Maggie, you're wonderful! Thank you so much.'

When I had collected the empty cups, Garret sent me down to the dispensary with another bed-ticket. 'It can come up in the basket too.'

The dispenser on duty at the staff counter was a solid-looking young Scot. 'Josephine again, Nurse? Aye. It would be. Let's have it.'

I passed the bed-ticket over. 'Nurse Garret said it could come up in the basket, so there's no hurry.'

He looked meaningly at the clock. 'Your basket goes up in ten minutes, Nurse. It'll take all of twenty to decipher Dr Curtis' script.'

I apologized automatically. I seemed to have done little else all morning.

He smiled dourly. 'I doubt it's your fault, Nurse. You wouldn't have been born when he was here as a houseman, so you had no hand in guiding him through his first scripts. When you get to being a Staff Nurse, give a thought to it. A doctor may be too busy to write clearly, but we happen to be busy, too. We waste an awful lot of time this way— and I had best not waste any more of yours or mine. Good morning.'

Directly I returned to Josephine, Sister called me to her desk. 'Just run along to the Physiotherapy Department with this request, please, Nurse.'

I waited to consult the Almoners' map until I was out of the ward. I stopped ten yards from Josephine and drew it from my apron bib.

'Where do you want now?' asked Bart's voice.

He was sitting on one of the broad windowsills a few feet ahead. He slid off and came up to me. 'And what are you doing? A private tour of Martha's?'

'Seems like it. Next time I'm on in mid-morning, so help me, I'm bringing roller-skates. I want the Physiotherapy Department. Know the way?'

He tucked the pile of books he had left on the sill under one arm. 'I ought to. I've been nigh on six years in the old firm. You go in the opposite direction this time.' He jerked a thumb downwards. 'Via the basement. Come—I'll show you the nearest stairs.'

'Thanks.' I studied the map. 'I expect I can manage from there.'

'Not with that, you can't. It doesn't show the basement. That's for patients. They aren't allowed to wander down there, but it's much the quickest way. Now, get this'—we had reached the basement stairs, 'turn right at the bottom and carry on until you pass the Blood Bank. You can't miss that. It has a dirty great notice. Then you go left—left—past Repairs and Works. Left again and you come to the physios gym. Up the first stairs and you're there.'

'Bless you again. What would I have done without you this morning, I hate to think. I've no bump of whatsit like Estelle. She seems to take the right turning by instinct.'

'Too bad she wasn't sent on tour in your place.'

'She couldn't be. She's off. On to-morrow morning.'

'Is that so?' He glanced at his watch. 'I may as well take you along to the physios myself. Time I was shifting.'

I accepted gratefully. 'What were you doing on that sill?' I asked as we went down.

'Damn it, girl. A man must sit somewhere. This walking the wards racket is hellishly hard on the feet.'

I smiled absently, being too interested in the basement to pay much attention to him. I had not been along there before. It was a new and most—to me—unhospital-like world. The apparently endless corridor was neon-lit, lined with huge tubes and pipes, and inhabited by men in boiler suits, and women in laundresses overalls. 'This is very Orwell-ish.'

'A little too matey for Big Brother. I like it down here, and the fact that it's technically out-of-bounds lends it added piquancy.'

'It's what?' I demanded.

'Relax, angel. Not to you, to me. So what? Authority never walks this way.'

I stood still. 'Home Sister does. I saw her in the laundry as we went by. I'm sure she saw us. Will she mind?'

He grimaced. 'I don't suppose she'll give three loud cheers. She probably didn't recognize you. She's pretty short-sighted. If she did— well, I'm only escorting you with the most honourable of intentions. Stop dithering, angel.'

'Sorry.' We walked on. 'It's hard not to. Our Senior Pro in Josephine gave us the most tremendous pep-talk on the folly of having anything to do with the medical staff in our present junior plus state.'

He laughed. 'I'm not medical staff. Just a student man. And for the record, that's less than the dust.'

I thought about Home Sister. 'I hope you're right.'

'And why wouldn't I be? After all the years I've been here? Look—I tell you what we'll do. We'll show the old girl this isn't just a pick-up and you and I are old pals from the P.T.S.'

'We will?' I looked at him curiously. 'How?'

He answered my question with another. 'When are you off, to-day?'

'This evening.'

'Care to join me for coffee and a hamburger on a park bench this evening? We could look at the ducks. Supposing I call for you at six-thirty? Any good?'

His invitation surprised me considerably. I could not conceive why he wanted to take me out. I knew very well it was not for the pleasure of my company. I had had a great many doubts about my Professor, but none at all about Bart More. He was no more interested in me than I was in him, yet I could see he wanted me to accept his invitation. Curiosity made me do so. 'Yes, thank you.'

'Thank you.' He smiled. 'Jolly good.'

He left me almost immediately after that, explaining that the physiotherapist students were nice girls who could not keep their big mouths shut. 'They'll all be standing on their heads in their gym at this hour. They never stop keeping fit. Most exhausting. We'd better not tempt Big Brother too much. See you later.'

It was a reasonable explanation, but it rang no more true than his invitation. Curiouser and curiouser, I thought, and finished my errand alone.

When Estelle arrived on duty at one I told her I had seen Bart. 'Not once, but twice.'

She smiled her polite smile. 'Hannah'll be pleased. How long is he up for?'

'I don't know.' Her expression gave nothing away. 'I didn't ask.'

Monica Player bustled in to the changing-room. 'Girls, do stop nattering. Sister's ready for us to report.'

Hannah was at lunch. I told her I had seen her cousin, but said nothing about my date. I wanted to tell Estelle first, and there had been no time before lunch. I did tell Hannah about the basement and Home Sister.

She twisted her head to look at the Sister's table. 'She generally comes to one o'clock lunch. I'll keep an eye out when she gets in and see if she gives you any dirty looks.'

Fay Kinsley joined us. 'Did you say something about Home Sister, Hannah? Surely you've realized Monday is her half-day? What do you want her for?'

Hannah kicked me. 'Frances has a laundry problem. How's Florence?'

Fay promptly lost interest in Home Sister, and for the remainder of our lunch half-hour gave us a lecture on just how Florence Ward should be run. Hannah was off until five; I had to return to Josephine; and as Fay left the dining-room with us, we were unable to continue our former conversation.

Bart drifted into Josephine directly the ward opened to students at 2 P.M., and spent the entire afternoon reading patients' notes at the students' table at the far end of the ward. I had no opportunity to see what effect, if any, his presence had on Estelle, as she was hidden in the bathrooms doing extra cleaning until four, then vanished behind varying sets of drawn curtains to help Nurse Garret with the heavy washings. We attended different teas and only met eventually when she reported to Sister Josephine for her evening's work-list, and I reported off duty.

I made my third daily trip to Matron's office to look for any post before returning to the Home. There were two letters in the 'D' pigeon-hole; neither was for me. I strolled on wearily feeling irrationally disappointed, and wondering how I was going to raise the necessary energy to change and go out. My legs seemed on fire. A pain shot down each calf and round each ankle, then split into wicked little white-hot tentacles that accumulated in the balls of my feet. I thought longingly of a hot bath and supper in bed, and wished I had refused this date.

The portress leaned out of her lodge as I limped into our hall. 'Home Sister's been asking for you, Nurse Dorland. Will you please go straight to her before going to your room?'

I damned all medical students. 'I thought Sister was off, Mrs Higgs?'

'She is, dear. She's going out later. She's been waiting to see you.'

'Thanks,' I said grimly. 'I'd better hurry.'

Home Sister was wearing an uncharacteristically gay blue mohair coat. Her manner was iron grey and bristling with starch. By the time she had finished with me I wondered why the Wolfenden report had overlooked hospital basements.

Mrs Higgs hailed me again when I reappeared. 'I've been holding a call for you, Nurse Dorland. Go into Box three and I'll put the gentleman through.'

Bart having second thoughts, I decided, shutting myself in the third of the four telephone booths at the end of the hall. He wasn't the only person. 'Frances Dorland, I said, between my teeth, and waited for Bart to say he had been held up on a case in Josephine.

' 'Evening, Miss Dorland. Slane, here. How,' asked the Professor, as if he had been in the habit of telephoning me for years, 'is the hospital?'

Home Sister's rocket, Bart, and the pain in my legs and feet, vanished from my conscious mind. So did my power of speech.

'Are you there?' he prompted.

'Yes. Yes. I'm here.' I took a deep breath. 'Sorry.'

I expect you needed a couple of moments to place me.' He sounded amused. 'It's some time since we met. I hope you don't object to my ringing you like this, but as I was down at your home yesterday, I thought you might like first-hand news of your family. They are all very well and your young sister Judy is engaged in finding names for six thousand turkeys.'

That second shock jolted me back to normal. There was no question now of my wondering if I was awake. Never in my wildest dreams could I have visualized the Professor talking turkeys with Judy. 'You were at the farm? I didn't realize you knew my parents.'

'I only met them yesterday. Your mother was kind enough to ask me to lunch and I'm afraid I stayed on until the evening, listening to your father's tape-recordings. Luke Anderson said they were unique when he took me round to have a before-lunch drink with your parents. He's absolutely right.'

I should have guessed, I thought, smiling weakly at my reflection in the mirror behind the instrument, I should have guessed, having been brought up by a passionate ornithologist. Dr Anderson, our local G.P., was almost as enthusiastic as my father. But I could not have guessed the Professor knew Dr Anderson. 'Were you spending the week-end with the Andersons?'

'Saturday night.'

'I didn't realize you knew them, either.'

'How could you? I didn't mention it. Luke Anderson was at Cambridge with me. We hadn't met for some years, then ran into each other a few weeks ago and he asked me to go down to Kent this past week-end. You know how it is when you meet very old friends; you pick up where you left off, and then run out of conversation. I suspect,' he added good-humouredly, 'he was as grateful to your parents as I was. Sunday afternoon invariably seems to me to be the great argument against week-ends with old friends, and yesterday the exception to prove my rule.'

'My mother would agree with you.' I wondered why he had not apparently taken his wife to the Andersons and how I could bring her into the conversation. 'She says that when she has visitors from Friday to Monday, she reaches screaming point after lunch on Sunday. If the lunch has been a success, every one is in a coma, so she has to refuse offers to help with the washing-up; if it's been a failure she feels like hurling a plate at anyone who dares come in the kitchen.'

He laughed. 'She permitted me to help her yesterday. Into which category does that put me?'

'Neither. You were only there for the day. She loves people to drop in like that. Does your wife? Or does she prefer to have warning?'

'I'm afraid I'm not married. I remember my mother used to insist on having ample warning. She didn't encourage stray lunch guests.'

I was no longer smiling weakly at my reflection; I was grinning like the Cheshire Cat. 'It can't be very easy—unless you live on a farm. Catering, I mean.'

'That's so.' He paused momentarily, then asked, 'I've given you all my news. How are you getting on?'

'Fairly well, thanks.'

'Only fairly? Why's that? Work very hard?'

'It is, but it's not that that worries me.'

'Then what does?'

His tone was so in line with the tone of his letters that I answered with the truth I had used in my letters to him. 'I've put up a major black to-day. According to Home Sister—five minutes ago—I'm a disgrace to the entire nursing profession and inevitably bound for the gallows.'

'Are you indeed?' he queried mildly. 'Specifically, why?'

I told him. 'If Home Sister had stopped to draw breath once I might have been able to explain. She didn't give me a chance.'

He said he thought that was probably just as well. 'Explanations seldom do much good. Friends don't need them; enemies don't believe them.'

'I never thought of that.' I could hardly wait to pass this on to Hannah and Estelle. So much for Mrs Professor and all the little Professors! 'And I certainly never thought she'd wait in specially to take me apart. I'm going to do a little of that myself, this evening. That wretch Bart More said she was short-sighted. I've got news for him. She isn't.'

'Bart More? I thought her name was Hannah. Or did you say 'him'? I couldn't quite hear you.'

'Him. It's a hideous abbreviation, I agree, but Bartholomew is too much of a mouthful. He's Hannah's cousin.'

'The student in question this morning?'

'Yes. He's in his last year.'

'And what are you doing with him this evening? Film? Dance?' he asked casually.

'Not with my feet! We're going to drink coffee and look at ducks in some park.'

'Well, don't be too hard on the poor youth. He was only indulging in wishful thinking. A not uncommon failing. I hope you have a good evening, and that I haven't delayed you too long.'

'Oh, no.' I thanked him for ringing, and, to keep him talking just a little longer, for all the help he had given me in the P.T.S. 'That diagram was superb. Even Sister P.T.S. was impressed.'

'Good.' His voice sounded as if he was smiling. 'I'll pass that on to the right quarter. And now I think I had better get down to doing some of the work that I should have done on Saturday morning.'

I could ignore his civil hint momentarily, but not that opportunity. 'What is your work, Mr Slane?'

'I'm one of the many variant types of Civil Servants. That mayn't sound interesting, but in point of fact I find it extremely interesting. However I could wish there was not quite so much paper work. I am always trying to cut it down, so far without success.'

So much for his being a Professor, I thought, and said I was sure his work was most interesting.

'I like it. Good night. I'm glad I was able to find you in.'

'It was very kind of you to bother to ring.'

'Not at all,' he said politely, and rang off.

5. Red stands for Danger

I remained in the telephone booth for a couple of minutes after I put
down the receiver, wondering whether to ring my mother. I had no
money with me, but she would not mind my reversing the charges. I was
agog to hear what my parents thought of the Professor. So agog, that I
did not make that call. I knew my mother would be able to guess what
was in my mind from the sound of my voice. I had never before had any
inhibitions about telling either of my parents anything. They knew all
about my first meeting with him, roughly, the number of letters he had
written and the general contents of those letters. We were a matey
family. There was, I now realized, a limit to how matey any family could
be. I loved them all, but the Professor was no longer some one I wanted
to discuss with them. I would wait until the next letter from home
arrived with their version of his news.

As Bart was not due to call for me for half an hour, I took off my
shoes and cap and relaxed on my bed directly I reached my room. It
would not take long to change. I could spare ten minutes. I beamed
idiotically at the ceiling and wished I had not got a date. I should be
more than happy to spend the entire evening thinking about my
Professor. I thought my father exceedingly clever to be so keen on birds;
Dr Anderson just as clever to go to Cambridge and not Oxford, and
quite brilliant in his choice of week-end guests. There was nothing like a
hobby to keep a man happy. Nothing. I thought up a series of appalling
puns on a hobby and the hobby and was delighted by my wit. Dear
hobbys, I thought dreamily. Dear bird-songs—tape-recorders—thunderstorms. Dear every one.

Estelle woke me three hours later. No one had called me to say I had
a visitor. Bart had obviously stood me up.

I blinked at her. 'Off, already? I've missed three suppers.'

'I wondered where you were.' She sat down and removed her shoes. 'I
thought you must be out.'

'I was, dear. Cold. Nice evening?'

It was an automatic question we all asked each other. It only required
an automatic answer. Apparently she had to give it considerable thought.

'Quite. I spent most of it chaperoning. We've got a new bunch of clerks in Josephine.'

I thought about my date. 'Bart More's set?'

She studied her hands. 'Must be. He's one of ours.'

'You been chaperoning for him?'

'Yes. God, he's slow. He held me up for ages. I thought I'd never get my routine done.'

And I thought, so that's why I've been stood up. The thought only amused me.

Hannah came in with a tea-tray. 'Frances, have you had any food?'

'No. I've been snoozing. It doesn't matter. Think of the good to my waist-line.'

Estelle said she was. 'If it gets much smaller it'll snap in two. I've got a cake and some chocolate in my room. Just the job.'

Hannah smiled as Estelle left us. 'She's even beginning to talk like you. Remember how upstage she was? Doesn't seem possible anyone could thaw as she has. Mind you, it's only with us. I met Bart on my way over. He was very low in spirits. He told me he had spent the evening being chaperoned by her. I gather she handed him the frozen mitt.'

'Hannah dear, one can scarcely be matey in the middle of a ward.'

She said there were ways and ways of chaperoning. 'Bart isn't used to the frozen mitt. He generally gets knocked over in the rush if he lifts a little finger. By the way—he asked me to offer you his humble apologies. He didn't have time to explain for what, because Sister Tutor suddenly came out of her office. I suppose he meant about this morning? Did Home Sister say anything?'

'She did.' I told her about it and wondered if to mention my date.

Hannah was very upset. 'He is naughty! He never thinks one inch ahead!'

'Never mind. He saved my life this morning. I'd still be looking for the Top Lab. and that man Marcus would still be waiting for his little tube, but for Bart.'

'That man—? Frances, what is all this?'

I explained. 'You don't know the morning I had,' I added. 'I covered Martha's.'

She waved that aside. 'You mean you actually spoke to him? You've made hospital history? He never speaks to nurses. No one is allowed to disturb him.'

'Sorry about that. He didn't seem to mind.' I smiled. 'Why? Player says pathologists don't bite.'

Estelle had come back with the cake and chocolate. Hannah said she was the girl to answer my question. 'Just tell her what you told me about this Marcus Everly, Estelle.'

She hesitated. I recognized her expression and demanded openly, 'Is he due to come in to a packet too?'

She relaxed. 'You've got the wrong tense there. Frances, you must have heard of him!'

'I've never heard of anyone. Remember, I told you—not even you.'

'So you did. But your father's a farmer. Or doesn't he need a tractor for his turkeys?'

'He's got some land as well as the turkeys. Of course he has a tractor. So what?'

'What make is it?'

'An Everly—blow me down! His?' They nodded. 'Then what's he doing in our Path. Lab.? Why isn't he turning out more tractors? He ought to be. English agriculture is the most mechanized in the world. Why is he neglecting the home market for the bugs?'

'Honest to God! Will you just listen to her, Estelle!' Hannah exclaimed indignantly. 'The man has his Membership, an M.D., and is the only man in Martha's to have collected a gold medal for medicine and another for pathology—and she says he ought to be turning out the tractors.'

'Well, who does turn them out for him?' I asked.

'My dear,' said Estelle, 'it's a huge concern.'

'Large as Grandpapa's?'

'Almost. Same sort of thing. A man called Bryce Macindoe runs it. I don't believe our Everly has ever had much to do with it. He gravitated straight to medicine. There are a couple of other Everlys—second cousins, I think—on the Board.'

'Our man,' said Hannah, 'has only one passion in life. Bugs. Right, Estelle?'

'Dead right. He's allergic to all else. He's so keen on his privacy that not even Matron walks uninvited into his lab. He's got the reputation of dealing in short order with anyone who strays up there to look at the view.'

'The view's worth seeing. He isn't. I'm glad I didn't know all this this morning. If I had, I'd have been out of that lab. like a bat out of hell when that bell went off.'

'Did he deal with you in short order?' queried Hannah.

'No. He was perfectly civil in a dreary sort of way. How old is he, Estelle? Fifty? Sixty?'

'I would have said he was younger. I'm not sure. Grandpapa knows him. I've never met him. Grandpapa was at school with his father, he was—hang on—Sir Claud.'

'So he's inherited a title with all the rest?'

'It's been going some time. He's the fourth—or it could be fifth.'

'Wow!' I took a chocolate. 'All that and he spends his life on our top floor peering down a microscope. Or has he a wife and kids, somewhere?'

'We've told you,' said Hannah, 'he's allergic to humanity. He only loves his bugs.'

'But, why? Crossed in love? Too much cash? Or just plain bats?'

Estelle said she had never heard of his having a love-life. 'People have been trying to marry him for years. No one's even got to first base. No man with his brain could be bats.'

'Must be his cash. Don't you go that way, Estelle. No good'll come of it. It's agin nature.'

'God,' groaned Hannah, 'she's on a soap-box. Come down off, Frances, and have some more cake.'

Bart came into the clinical-room early next morning. I was doing the flowers alone, having for once finished my cleaning ahead of schedule. He gave me a wary smile.

'Are we on speaking terms? I hoped Hannah had given you my message, but you cut me dead when you came out of breakfast.'

'I certainly did, and will do so again whenever there's a dark blue dress around. Don't you ever speak one word to me in the hospital—or mention basements. Home Sister,' I snipped stalks as I talked, 'took me into little pieces last evening. But all will be forgiven and forgotten if you'll just go right away—now. I know Garret's having a day off, but Sister Josephine'll finish her pulses any minute now.'

He squinted into the clinical-room microscope. 'I'm officially here with her blessing. I asked last night if I could come in early to use this chap'—he fixed in a slide—'and she said yes, indeed, provided I understood that at this hour the nurses had to come in here to do the flowers.' He looked at me anxiously. 'I'm really sorry about Home Sister and feel a perfect heel over last night. Did you get very mad at having to wait?'

'No.' I explained why. 'Then, when Estelle woke me, she told me she had been chaperoning for you and I guessed what had kept you.'

'You did?' He looked up again. 'Didn't she think it odd I was here when I had a date with you?'

I shook my head. 'She didn't know you had dated me.'

'You didn't tell her? I thought you girls told each other everything.'

The Professor's phone call flashed through my mind. I quoted him out of context. 'There has to be an exception to prove every rule. No. I didn't tell anyone.' I picked up two vases and made for the door. 'So that's one more weight off your mind.'

He straightened. 'Just what,' he demanded curtly, 'are you getting at?'

'Why, Bart—that you don't have to worry about feeling a heel for standing me up because I didn't mind.' I flapped my eyelashes idiotically, but he was too on edge to notice. 'I'm glad you came in this morning to straighten things up. To-morrow's my day off. Estelle'll be doing the flowers alone and you'd have had to go on worrying. I wouldn't want that to happen,' I added quickly, and sailed into the ward before he could answer. When I returned the clinical-room was empty.

Estelle did not tell me if Bart had used my information. I heard it from Nurse Player. 'We've got the keenest bunch of students I've ever known. One of them was actually in the clinical-room by a quarter-past eight yesterday morning. Long before Dexter could get to the flowers.'

Bart continued to haunt not only the clinical-room but the ward. He could do this legitimately as he was one of our clerks. Whenever the ward was open, he was a permanent fixture on one of the locker-seats, talking to his patients, writing endless notes.

Lily Ellis was one of his patients. 'That young Mr More's real cool, duck! Ever so nice-looking, too. He ought to be on the telly. And the way he works! Cor! Proper keen he is! All that writing an' all!'

Bart did not only write notes in Josephine. When he had to leave the ward because it was closed to men, and the clinical-room booked by some other clerk, he either sat on one of the main corridor windowsills a few yards from the ward entrance or on the steps of the statue of Miss Nightingale that overlooked the door to our dining-room, and went on with his note-writing.

In a very short time our whole set knew that Hannah's cousin had taken root in Josephine. Hannah was very bucked by her insight. 'I knew you were his type, Frances.'

I heard nothing from the Professor for several days after his telephone call. When my mother's weekly letter arrived her comments on him were disappointingly brief.

We were most amused to discover Luke Anderson's friend was your Professor. We liked him. Daddy says he really knows about birds, and gathered he works for some Ministry. We agree he should have been a don. He is very like Joe. We hope he will come down again, some time.

Time in Josephine passed even more quickly than it had in the P.T.S. The weeks flashed by, partly because we were so busy in the ward, and partly because every other week I heard from the Professor. His letters were as pleasant and impersonal as they had been in the P.T.S. Now I knew he was single, that impersonality really puzzled me. He never suggested meeting me, barely mentioned himself or signed his name with anything but the initials of his Christian names. If he had not enough interest in me to make one date why bother to keep on writing? Yet he did. And because I loved getting his letters—I would have been grateful even for a typed postcard from him—I wrote back regularly on the alternate weeks.

My set asked about him occasionally. 'What's happened to your P.T.S. Professor, Frances? Ever met him?'

I answered no, quite truthfully; they assumed he had faded from my life and stopped asking questions. If Estelle noticed his handwriting on a letter addressed to me in the 'D' pigeon-hole she never mentioned it. She was obviously having her own problems, and because I disliked being questioned about the Professor, I did not question her about Bart. He continued to behave in the most absurd fashion; haunting both Josephine and Estelle, and doing nothing but look haunted. One of these fine days I knew I would have to do something about those two, the difficulty was going to be finding the time. Josephine was hectic; we had started regular thrice-weekly lectures; I always had at least two back lectures to write up—and every other week I used a good two evenings on my letter to the Professor.

I decided to have a splendidly casual chat with my mother about him. I went home for a day off. I had chosen the wrong day. They had started de-beaking the day before; both my parents were in the turkey-houses all day. They refused my offer to help. 'You're having a day off, darling. Why not go and look up some one in the village? Take the car.'

At lunch I talked about Luke Anderson, hoping to get the conversation round to the Professor.

'Luke's on holiday. We've got a locum.' Father handed me a plate. 'Seen anything of that man he brought round?'

'We haven't met. He writes, occasionally.'

He nodded absently. 'He must like writing letters. Wish I did. Meg, how many have we done so far?'

'Three hundred and eighty.' My mother passed him the vegetable dish. 'We should make the eight hundred by to-night,' she added, and we went back to talking turkeys.

Josephine was a different ward next day. Lily Ellis had had a heart attack in the night. Her bed was back in the ward and hidden behind curtains. The women were strangely subdued. 'Shame poor Lily Ellis is so poorly, dear. How is she? Better? Give her my love when you go in to her, Nurse.'

I was far too junior to be allowed near her that day. I felt lost without her and very anxious. She had become more than just a cheerful patient to me; she was one of my great friends. The balcony was vast and empty without her, and old Mrs Astor embroidered diligently as if she dared not keep herself unoccupied.

It was several days before Lily showed any sign of improvement, but at last her curtains were drawn back. I was delighted to be allowed to help nurse her again, not only because I wanted to be with her, but because the fact I was there showed how much better she must be. The sense of strain faded from the ward. The other women waved and smiled at her. 'Better, dear? That's lovely. Your old lady on the balcony will be pleased to have you back.'

Mrs Astor often talked to me about Lily. 'She's a good girl, dear. I've never known her grumble. I do miss her.'

I plaited her long white hair. 'She'll soon be back with you. She's looking almost herself to-day.'

She gave me a long, queer look. 'Yes, dear. That's good.' She was silent until her hair was finished. 'That nice young Mr More has been such a comfort to me. He sat out here for over an hour yesterday, keeping me company. Isn't he a friend of yours, dear?'

'Yes. His cousin is in my set.' I put away her brush and comb, thinking how pathetically easy it was to give gentle old ladies the wrong impression.

Mrs Astor promptly taught me how easy it was to get the wrong impression about gentle old ladies. 'I've seen him smile at you, dear. Is he Nurse Dexter's young man? I've noticed how he's always looking for her—and at her. Have they had a little tiff? Is that why Nurse Dexter pretends not to see him? She's such a sweet girl to us—so kind. But she never smiles at him. I haven't been able to avoid noticing the difference.'

I said, 'Mrs Astor, is there anything you haven't noticed?'

'I don't mean to spy, dear, but I get so interested watching all you busy young people. I like to watch and think about you all. I love young people. Youth has so much courage and gaiety; it does me good to have you around me.' She took one of my hands. 'I hope you don't mind my mentioning this to you, dear, but I know Nurse Dexter is your great friend. She seems to me to look very sad in repose. Has she had a hard life, or is she troubled by this little tiff? Such things seem so important when one is young—and youth should not be sad. Wouldn't that nice boy be only too willing to make it up? I think he would. As you are their friend—couldn't you help them?'

'I wish I could, Mrs Astor. It's not quite as simple as it sounds.'

Sister appeared on the balcony before we could say any more. 'Come and help me with Mrs Ellis now, Nurse.'

Lily looked unbearably frail and ill, despite the report I had given Mrs Astor. Her pulse was fibrillating badly; her respirations agony to watch; her spirits were higher than ever. 'See them lovely roses my Bert fetched me up this morning, Sister?' she gasped. 'From me own garden.'

Sister admired them. 'Beautiful, Mrs Ellis.'

'You ought to see me garden, Sister. Two yards by four—and six inches of solid soot.'

Sister talked a great deal about roses, I guessed to save Mrs Ellis having to talk. Later that morning she came into the kitchen as I was collecting Mrs Ellis's lunch tray. 'Mind you sit down and let her take as long as she wishes over her meal, Nurse.'

'Yes, Sister.' I wondered why she had come to tell me this. I would not have dared sit down when feeding a patient in Josephine, since that was one of her strictest rules.

She frowned at the wafers of sliced chicken and small bowl of strawberries. 'Where is the cream, Nurse?'

I hesitated. 'Mrs Ellis doesn't care for cream, Sister. Had I better try and persuade her to take some?'

'No.' Her expression suddenly reminded me of Mrs Astor's when I had said Lily would soon be with her on the balcony. 'She may have what she fancies and as much as she fancies. If she does not want to eat, you may just sit and talk to her for a while. I have observed that she enjoys a little gossip with you. A chat cannot harm her now. Take that in.'

I settled down by Lily, and we had a glorious chat about life, roses, turkeys, Bert Ellis's promotion to charge-hand in his bottle factory, and Mrs Ellis Senior's passion for shopping in super-markets.

She talked eagerly, and ate hardly anything. I did not attempt to coax her after what Sister had said, even though I could not follow why she had said it when she was normally so insistent that we persuaded our patients to eat well.

'No more, ta, duck,' said Lily wearily.

I put down the spoon. 'A little drink? Lemon? Would you like iced milk? No? All right, love.'

'I wish,' she whispered, 'every one could take the hint same as you, duck. That poor Nurse Dexter tried so hard with me dinner yesterday. I was really sorry not to be able to take it for her. Weren't no use. It wouldn't go down.' Her eyes followed Estelle, who was clearing plates on the other side of the ward. 'What's come over her, duck? Why she looking so down in the mouth? She had words with that young Mr More what's courting her?'

'Lily. How do you do it? Second sight?'

She chuckled. 'I got eyes in me head. I can spot a bloke what's courting when I sees one. It don't take much savvy to see Mr More thinks the world of your pal. Mind, he acts proper, what with his writing notes and taking histories. Cor! Does he write them notes. He must have a ruddy book by now, duck! And always trying to catch her eye, he is, but she won't have nothing to do with him! Have they had bad words?'

'My dear, they hardly know each other.'

'Then what you waiting for, duck? You wants to give them a shove, like. Or have you got your own troubles with your own young man?'

I smiled. 'I haven't one. No time. And besides, my feet hurt too much.'

She laughed out loud. 'Your feet! Nurse Dorland! You are a one!'

Sister's head jerked up. She looked at once at Lily and I expected a quick frown in reprimand. She merely smiled. 'You sound merry, my dear,' she called. 'I am pleased.'

Estelle and I discussed Sister's attitude to Lily when we went off that night. 'I can't understand her,' I said reflectively. 'I wish we knew more medicine. Maybe then it would make sense.'

'Player was talking about it when we did the sluice to-night. She was just telling me Lily's heart had gone into failure ages ago, when Sister called her to tidy beds. I'll look it up when we get over.'

'Hang on.' I recognized the inevitable figure on a windowsill twenty yards off. I looked round quickly. The corridor was empty. I beckoned to Bart. 'He ought to be able to explain.'

Her expression froze as he came towards us, uncertainly. I ignored both their attitudes. 'We want to know some medicine. What exactly is meant by a heart going into failure?'

He glanced at Estelle. She gave him one of her best 'Miss Dexter' nods. Not surprisingly, he stiffened, then smiled affectedly. 'I'm flattered, ladies, but, alas, a mere student man.'

I could willingly have shaken him. 'Bart, be serious. We want help, not a good laugh. We're worried.'

'Oh.' His manner altered instantly. 'What's up? Not Lily Ellis again?'

Estelle looked at him sharply as if taken aback by this reaction, but said nothing.

I said, 'Yes and no. She hasn't had another attack—Thank God—but we want to know. What's gone wrong? Why?'

He looked at his feet. 'Just about everything.'

Estelle said, 'What's her prognosis? She has got a prognosis?'

I think they were the first words she had ever addressed to him of her own accord. He raised his eyes to her face. 'I'm sorry, Nurse Dexter. She hasn't. She's booked.'

I said, 'I'm sorry, but you're both above my head. What's a prognosis? And what's booked?'

'The forecast of the course of a disease,' he said quietly. 'Booked is—well, our word for—the finish.' He flattened one hand in the air and tilted it slightly. 'She's been'—he tilted it again from side to side—'like that for months. According to Curtis, all that's keeping her alive is guts. She doesn't want to die, poor kid.'

I simply did not believe him. I might have done so had we been talking about Mrs Astor, or any of the older women in the ward. Lily was our youngest patient. I could not associate her with death; she was too full of life, too young, too much fun. Death was for the old and tired, not for people like Lily.

Then I had to believe him. When we arrived on duty three mornings after that conversation with him, we found the small ward was in use. The small ward was the single room off the main ward that was only used for very ill patients who were not expected to recover. It had never been used during our stay in Josephine.

The door was open, the interior hidden by a red screen. Red in hospital, as elsewhere, is a sign of danger.

The senior night nurse looked grey with fatigue when we reported to her. 'Dexter, will you do all the early routine. Player will help you. Dorland, Sister wants you to take over from my relief. She's with Mrs Ellis in the small ward.'

It was a warm August morning and I felt very cold. 'I'm to special her, Nurse?'

She nodded. 'Yes. She's been asking for you. Sister says you are to stay with her. Don't leave her at all. If you want anything ring. Sister's gone to early breakfast. She'll be back in a few minutes, and will come in to see her.'

It was very quiet in the small ward. Lily was sleeping heavily, and when the night relief nurse handed over, I sat with one hand on her left wrist, feeling as if I had stepped into a nightmare. The fact that I was sitting doing nothing at that, perhaps the busiest hour of the hospital day, only added to the nightmare. I was frightened of my inexperience, frightened of the hours ahead, and above all frightened I might show my fear.

She woke up briefly after Sister's third visit. 'I'm glad you're here, duck.'

I sat and held her hand for most of that day. Sister, Nurse Garret, Dr Curtis, the Senior Medical Officer, his registrar and houseman were in and out constantly. We were seldom alone for more than a few minutes. No one said anything; did anything. They looked only at her and then went away, avoiding each other's eyes. I gave her little sips of glucose and lemonade, at first through a straw, then with a teaspoon. 'Ta, duck,' she sighed heavily, 'ta. No more now.'

Sister took my place when I went to lunch, and during the afternoon sent me off duty for one hour. 'Sister will make up this off duty to you another day, Dorland,' explained Garret in an unusually pleasant tone. 'She wants you to stay with Mrs Ellis to-day. You've been her great friend. All we can now do for her is let her have a friend hold her hand.' I was supposed to have tea in that hour. I could not face the dining-room. I walked round and round the hospital until I could go back.

She seemed to have rallied a little when I returned and my wavering hopes soared. Her husband and mother-in-law smiled at me, pathetically pleased by this change. 'Lil's looking more herself. She'll be pleased you're back again, Nurse. We've heard so much about Lil's Nurse Dorland.'

A long, long time later, Sister told me to close the door and remove the red screen. 'Then go straight off, Nurse. Home Sister knows you have been kept on duty late. You need not report in. Just go to your room and your friends. Good night, Nurse, and thank you.'

I walked very slowly down the main corridor. It was empty and silent, and somewhere a clock was striking a quarter to ten. My eyes felt as if they had been rubbed in sandpaper, but I had not wept one tear. I was too sad for weeping.

I walked on without realizing where I was going. Only when I passed Casualty did I notice I had missed the exit we always used on our way to the Home. I hesitated, wondering if to take a short-cut through Casualty; it would be quite safe as Sister Cas. would not be on at this hour, but I might meet some one. I did not want to meet anyone. There must be another side exit into the grounds. The corridor was full of doors. I walked on again.

I had gone another fifteen yards or so when I saw a small alcove I had not noticed previously. At the end of the alcove was a door obviously leading to the outside. I tried it; it was unlocked. I closed it behind me and found I was at the top of a narrow flight of steps leading down to the car park. It was quite dark; I had not been in that part of the grounds before; so I stopped at the top to get my bearings. I did not even see the man in the light mackintosh coming up the steps until he stopped a couple of steps from me.

'What are you doing here, Nurse? You shouldn't be using this door. It doesn't matter this once, but don't do it again.'

I recognized his voice instantly, but was beyond surprise. Nothing could have touched me at that moment. I just looked at him. 'It's you, Mr Slane. I'm going off. I saw this door and came through it.'

He stayed poised on that second step for perhaps twenty seconds. Then he was beside me. He bent slightly to look at my face. 'Frances Dorland. What's up? Is something wrong?'

I said, 'Yes.'

6. The Professor takes over

I found myself sitting on the front seat of a car, with no clear idea of how I had arrived there.

'Wait here,' said the Professor. 'I'll be back, directly.'

I waited, without thought or feeling.

A new wing of wards was being built at the far end of the car park. Its darkened outline was splinted with scaffolding. There were no lights yet in the new wing. The scaffolding was strung at intervals with red workmen's lamps serving as warnings, not illuminations.

I was grateful for the darkness; grateful the car had its back to the well-lit hospital roughly fifty yards off; grateful the sky was low and moonless.

He was back before I started wondering where he had gone. Vaguely I recollected his original explanation about calling on one of our residents. He had mentioned a name. I could not remember which name now, nor had I recognized it at the time. We had dozens of residents, but I knew only the names of the three who worked in Josephine.

He got into the driving seat. 'Your Home Sister says you may stay out until eleven-fifteen.'

'Home Sister?' I looked at him dully. He had not switched on any light inside the car, his face was in shadow. 'You did say Home Sister?'

'Yes.' He started the engine, backed in a half-circle, and drove us into the road. 'I've just been across to see her. The Casualty porter told me which was the Nurses Home. I introduced myself, explained I was acquainted with you and your parents and the circumstances of our meeting to-night. I asked her permission to do what I believe your father would under these circumstances. I'm going to take you for a drive right away from the hospital.'

Surprise, even interest, were still beyond me. 'Thank you.' I rested my head against the back of the seat, closed my eyes, and relaxed. I could not remain relaxed; every pin in my cap was sticking into my head. I sat forward.

He glanced sideways. 'Why not take it off? You can put it on when we get back.'

We drove in silence. After a while I opened my eyes and saw we had crossed the river. The long line of light that marked the hospital on the far bank was disappearing behind us.

'Where are we going?'

'Chiswick. We haven't much time and there are odd places down there that could be a hundred miles from Oxford Street. Do you know London?'

'No.'

'We're on the Chelsea Embankment.'

'Thank you,' I said, and he was quiet again.

He seemed to know London like a taxi-driver. We left the main traffic, meandered through side streets, old crumbling Georgian squares, along what looked like cul-de-sacs but were not, until we reached a quiet terrace of Queen Anne and Regency houses overlooking the river. The trees outside the houses were heavy with late summer leaves; there was a cluster of trailing willows by the water; an empty rowing-boat swung placidly on the end of a rope.

He stopped the car by the willows, switched off the engine, sat sideways to look at me. 'Did you have any supper to-night?'

'Sister Josephine sent me to early supper.'

'That,' he said quietly, 'doesn't answer my question. Did you eat anything? Or just spin out time?'

'How could you know that?'

He did not answer. He turned on the interior light and reached for the mackintosh he had at some time thrown on the rear seat. I watched him, dazed not merely by the light. I could not even remember his taking off that mackintosh.

He produced a flat packet from one of the pockets, a large bar of chocolate from the dashboard shelf. 'I know you aren't hungry, but you'll feel better if you eat something. Have these'—he opened the packet, laid it on my lap, and snapped the chocolate—'and this.'

The packet contained sandwiches. 'Thank you—I'd rather not.'

'I realize that. All the same, have some.' He took out a cigarette-case. 'Will smoke put you off?'

'No, no. Please smoke.' I looked at the food in my lap. I felt it would choke me, but did not want to refuse again in the face of his kindness. I ate one ham sandwich, and the chocolate. Both tasted as if made of sawdust and were as difficult to swallow as sawdust.

He did not ask questions or talk at all. He sat smoking, watching the river occasionally, mainly watching me. There was nothing to disturb me in his scrutiny, no strain in our silence. It was only inexpressibly comforting to have him there.

'Have one more sandwich,' he said at last; 'then I'm going to give you a drink.' He took a leather-covered flask from the same shelf as the chocolate. 'It's neat, which is why I didn't give it to you first. I doubt it would have gone to your head, but it might have made you feel sick.'

'Is it brandy? I'm awfully sorry I really can't tolerate——'

'Whisky.' He put the cup in my hand. 'If you don't like the taste, eat some chocolate to take it away. But you drink it.'

A few minutes later he removed the empty cup, remaining sandwiches, and chocolate paper from my lap, brushing aside the crumbs as if I was a small child.

I apologized for the crumbs. 'I'm afraid they'll mess your car.'

'It doesn't signify if they do.' He opened his cigarette-case again. 'You don't smoke, I believe?'

'No, thanks.' I realized he was chain-smoking. 'Have you given up your pipe?'

'I prefer cigarettes on occasions.' He shifted his position, and looked at the river. 'Would you like to talk? I'll understand if you wouldn't. But it might help.'

I said bitterly, 'I'm not the person who needs help. She needed it. But no one could help her.'

He nodded slowly. 'Tell me about her.'

I had given him only the briefest explanation when we recognized each other at the top of those narrow stairs. I would not have believed then, that I could share with anyone the thoughts I had had in the small ward all that long, agonizing day, while I watched the dragging hands of the clock, the defeat in the eyes of every member of the staff who came into the room, and the shadow of Death falling over Lily's bed.

Suddenly I was talking. I talked and talked, my words tumbling out on top of each other.

'Sister said, "Turn off that oxygen, Nurse," but I couldn't. Lily was still hanging on to my hand. Her fingers were so tight that Sister had to help me to get my own free.'

The muscles in his face tightened as he stared at the river, smoking constantly. He did not interrupt, or murmur soothing words. No words could have soothed me just then.

'Bert—her husband—was there all the time. He didn't speak from tea-time onwards. At the end he just patted her arm, then walked out of the room without saying a word. He's twenty-three. He looked like an old man.' I shuddered. 'He really loved her. If I feel like this—what must it be for him?'

He said, 'To-night the poor boy's in hell.'

I turned on him. 'Mr Slane, why? I know one shouldn't ask that if one works in a hospital, but I can't help it. Why did she have to die? Why does Bert have to be in hell? There are so many unhappy married couples. They were so happy. So—why?'

He threw away a half-smoked cigarette, and folded one arm on the other. 'I can't agree that one should not ask why.' He twisted back to face me. 'I think one should.'

'What's the point of asking questions that can't be answered?' I demanded wildly.

'I distrust generalizations, but I'm going to make one. All questions can be answered, if one is prepared to take the trouble to find out what they are. You ask if there's any point, because you think you already know the answer. And that thought inevitably disturbs you. Doubt does take one by the throat. It's as suffocating as ignorance, and indeed, often synonymous with ignorance. You've asked me why she had to die? I don't know. I intend to find out.'

'You're going to ask some one at Martha's?'

He nodded. 'You. Now. Tell me, how did she come to have a bad heart?'

I shrugged. 'It's been weak for years.'

'Why?'

'I—I think, because she had bad rheumatic fever as a child.'

'Why?'

'I don't know.'

'Think,' he said gently. 'How do you get rheumatic fever? Do you catch it like measles?'

'No. It's—oh—from damp. Conditions. Clothes. Houses. Things like that.'

'Who allowed a child to live in a damp house? Wear damp clothes?'

'Her parents, I suppose. Or whoever brought her up.'

'So what finished this evening began years ago when, through ignorance or carelessness, some supposedly responsible human being neglected Lily Ellis as a child? Right?'

Slowly, I realized what he was doing. 'Yes.'

'Which makes her death not the cruel and inexplicable act of Providence as you've been fearing, but the logical if none the less tragic follow-on from a human error. Understand?'

'Yes.'

He lit yet another cigarette, and watched me over the flame of a match. 'I'm sorry, Frances.' His voice was very gentle. 'Truth may resolve doubt, but it never has been an analgesic.'

I said, 'I'm never going to let myself get so fond of a patient again. It hurts too much.'

'You had her friendship—obviously affection. Wasn't that worth having?'

'Of course, but ...'

'Everything that's worth having in life hurts like the devil. There's no way round that.'

'Yet it seems such a waste.'

'No.' He studied the lighted end of his cigarette as if it was the first he had ever seen. 'Sympathy, love, the rest of that ilk, are only wasted when one gives them to oneself.'

Without any warning I began to cry. I did not stop until I had soaked both my handkerchiefs and one of his. 'I'm so sorry.' I mopped my face, eventually. 'I really am. I didn't mean to do that.'

He did not say a good cry was just what I needed to make me feel better, offer me a shoulder, or any sympathy beyond his handkerchief, and silent presence. I was grateful. I had not wanted to weep in front of him, and I did not feel any better. I felt physically ill and exhausted.

He handed me another drink and more chocolate. 'I don't think you need apologize. I wish I had some water to add to this. Take it'—he removed his ruined handkerchief from my hand and gave me another— 'and this.'

A little later he put away the flask and glanced at the dashboard clock. 'I believe we should be moving if I'm to get you back on time.'

'Did Home Sister mind my going out with you? Didn't she think it very odd?'

He fiddled with the ignition key. 'She didn't appear to do so. Remember, something like this happened to her once.'

'I never thought of that.' Another thought occurred to me. 'What about your friend? I forget his name. Will he have been waiting all this time? I've ruined your evening. I'm terribly sorry.'

'Don't be. I was only going to play chess with a man called George Aspinall. We had not fixed it specifically. I merely said I'd look in to-night if I was free. He'll take my non-appearance as a sign that I couldn't get over.'

'I see. Aspinall? Physician or surgeon?'

'Physician. You don't know him?'

'I don't really know anyone on our medical staff.' We had stopped at some traffic lights. 'Or anything about Martha's outside of Josephine. I had no idea I should not have used that door. Who's is it?'

He frowned briefly at the lorry directly in front of us. 'If he backs another inch he'll sit on my bonnet. What was that—? That door? It's the Dean's private door.'

'Oh, no.' The second drink had made me feel strong enough to smile. 'No wonder it's out of bounds. Do you often come to Martha's? Is that how you know that?'

He nodded at the lorry as it began to move off. 'Aspinall's brother was once a colleague of mine. We've been playing chess together for some years. How often I get to Martha's depends on how much work I have to do. I haven't had much time for chess lately.'

When we were on the Embankment he reminded me to put on my cap. 'Can you reach over? It's on the back seat. I dropped it out of range when I gave you the sandwiches.'

'I never noticed. Thanks.'

He said no more until he stopped his car at the foot of the steps to our Home. 'Will you forgive me if I don't get out? I daren't park here. I've just seen three policemen.'

'Please do keep the engine going.' I jumped out, then paused momentarily, with one hand on the open window. 'I don't know how to thank you.'

'I'd much rather you didn't attempt it.' He reached across and reclosed the door properly. 'Would you go in? I'd like to see you in the house before I leave. I can be having engine trouble for the next thirty seconds.'

'I will. Good night.'

He raised a hand. 'Good night.'

I heard his car move away as I closed the front door behind me. Home Sister came out of her office. 'I saw you drive up, Nurse. I'm glad you met a friend to-night.' Her expression was curious as well as sympathetic. 'Go up quietly as the lights are out.'   .

I dreaded breakfast and the inevitable questions from my set next morning. To my surprise and infinite relief, no one mentioned Lily Ellis, or my late return to the Home.

Later Hannah told me Estelle was responsible for this. 'She went round all our rooms that night and bullied us all—Fay included—into silence. She really went to town, Frances! I expect you were pretty relieved not to talk about it. What time did you eventually get over? After eleven?'

Something like that.' I had not yet told her of the Professor's phone call, and had no intention of telling her how I had met him. She was a pleasant girl, but quite incapable of keeping anything to herself. She had made him public property in the P.T.S. and would have no hesitation in doing so again. She would willingly promise not to breathe a word to a soul; past experience had taught me that from Hannah that meant not telling more than five people in strict confidence. I had not minded at all in the P.T.S. I would now. 'I've seen her in her chip-off-the-old-Dexter-block moods in Josephine. She can produce the most fantastic drive when she wants to. Often I wouldn't get done at all if she didn't rustle round and help. She's quick as Player already.'

Hannah looked thoughtful. 'Dear Naylor'll be shaken if she collects a gold medal when we finish. We won't.' She sighed. 'Ah me. They say you can't have everything. I look at Estelle and think—no? Looks, brains, cash. She's got the lot.'

'Not quite.'

'Frances, duckie, please—no corn! Don't tell me she lacks the love of a good man. If she wanted a man—any man—she'd have him. Estelle gets what she wants. Besides, is the man yet born who wouldn't break his neck in the rush if Estelle Dexter showed willing? Even if she looked like the back of a bus? Which she doesn't.'

I did not argue with her since I knew I would never persuade her to my view, and have never seen that you gained anything but a headache from ramming your head against a brick wall. Now we had left the isolated and idealistic atmosphere of the P.T.S., Hannah's character was either altering or returning to normal. I was not yet clear which. She seemed to like Estelle as much as ever, but where in the P.T.S. she had never seemed in awe of her money, now possibly because she was assimilating the comments of nurses-in-training as a whole and not merely those of our one set, she seemed obsessed by it.

I thought over Hannah's new attitude during the next few days and, at the same time, Lily's and Mrs Astor's advice. I wondered if Bart saw things as Hannah did. I watched him and Estelle covertly but constantly. This was not hard, as he was part of the furniture in Josephine. He always treated me as his oldest and closest of friends—until Estelle appeared in the clinical room to do the flowers, or the bathroom to scrub mackintoshes. The temperature would then freeze, despite the late summer weather that was breaking records for sunshine, if Estelle looked at him at all, she used the expression most people reserve for a tedious child, while he was content to look and behave as if made of solid wood.

There were occasions, particularly as the real temperature rose, when I could gladly have banged their heads together. They seemed to be making themselves intentionally miserable and after Lily's death I was in no mood for tolerance. I missed her dreadfully; came near to resenting the other women for being alive when she was dead; had to nerve myself to go on the balcony or into the small ward; and still winced at the sight of one special red screen.

The Professor rang me about a week after Lily's death. It was quite late. I was about to have a bath when Estelle bellowed through the door. 'Outside phone for you, Frances!'

He said he knew it was late and would not keep me long, but wanted to know how I was. 'The world the right way up again?'

I hesitated. 'Not really. You see, being still in Josephine, it's not very easy to forget her.'

'I can understand that. All the same'—he hesitated too—'although grief is agony, it's the agony of a moment. The indulgence of grief can be the blunder of a lifetime.'

'You—you think I ought to snap out of it?'

'I wasn't going to put it quite like that—but—yes.'

'I see.' I sighed. 'Oh dear. I've been wallowing.'

'It's hard not to. Tell me—are you by chance free next Saturday evening?'

I stiffened hopefully. 'Yes. I'm off from five-thirty.'

'Do you care for ballet? I find I've two tickets which I can't use myself. Would you care to use them for me?'

I tried not to sound too hollow as I thanked him.

'Good. I'll put them in the post to-morrow. Good-night.'

Estelle looked out of her room as I walked by to the bathroom. 'Family?'

'Friend of,' I stretched the truth without qualm as Hannah was sitting on her bed, 'with two tickets for the ballet on Saturday evening. I suppose you can't get off as I am. How about you, Hannah?'

Hannah said she would get off if she had to bribe Sister Arthur herself. 'It'll be something to look forward to. Arthur's a furnace these days. You girls don't know how lucky you are to be in Josephine. Facing the river it must have some air.'

'Air?' queried Estelle. 'Now what would that be? Any idea, Frances?'

'Not me. I work in Josephine.'

Josephine grew more airless with every passing day, despite the wide open windows and balcony doors. The medical staff shed their jackets and waist-coats; their white coats were limp and more grey than white. The students rolled up their shirt-sleeves, and slung their jackets from their hands, donning them only for ward rounds, removing them before they passed the row of fire buckets at the end of Josephine corridor.

In the grounds the yellowing plane-trees were motionless as if too hot to risk exhaustion by moving a single leaf. The women in our ward lay as still as those leaves, covered only by their top sheets, too warm even to wear their wireless headphones. They propped these on their pillows a few inches from their ears; and the faint chattering and music that filtered constantly through the ward seemed to add to the pressure of the atmosphere.

Sister Josephine's invariably quiet manner grew even quieter, until she seemed as ominously silent as the air before thunder. Garret's speed was unaltered, but her temper became razor-edged. Nurse Player's amiable nature seemed impervious to the heat; not so her cap and apron. The starch wilted in her uniform as rapidly as in Estelle's and mine, since being the three most junior members of the nursing staff our work was seldom sedentary. We took two clean aprons on duty with us instead of the normal one and always needed to change before the ward opened at nine. Estelle's hair clung damply to her head like an extra yellow cap; while the heat had the reverse effect on my hair. 'For God's sake,

Dorland,' stormed Garret at least three times a day, 'do something about your hair. You look as if you've been pulled through a bush backwards with all those curls on end. Cut it, if all else fails.'

At lunch on Saturday Hannah swept into the dining-room in a fury. 'I could kill Sister Arthur,' she announced, helping herself to a glass of water, 'here and now! I can't make to-night. I've been changed to off this afternoon! I told her I was going out, and all she said was "what a pity!" Pity! Bah!'

'Hannah, how miserable. I am sorry.' I looked round the table. 'Any of you girls off this evening?'

No one was, but Alice Linton said Sylvia Franks had a day off, was not going home, and would almost certainly be in her room when I got over late. 'She'll love to go with you, Frances.'

'That'll be fine—if I survive an afternoon of extra cleaning in this temperature. Who do you suppose was the jolly soul who ordained that all the major extra cleaning should be done by juniors on Saturday afternoon, when the rest of the world is setting forth to play?'

Hannah looked a little more cheerful at the realization of what else her changed off-duty was causing her to miss. 'Rub up your lamp, duckie. It's flickering.'

'Huh. By the time I've scrubbed forty bed macks it'll have been out for hours. We change the lot on Saturdays.'

Bart was sitting on one of the wooden benches under a plane-tree when I eventually limped off-duty. He got slowly to his feet. He was very sun-burnt, the tan suited him, making him look quite outrageously good-looking. 'You walk like I feel, angel.'

I looked round automatically. Home Sister was being unusually nice to me these days, but I did not want to run risks. There was no visible signs of authority, so I stopped. 'How do you expect me to walk after running up and down Josephine all day?'

He apologized and asked obviously, 'Off?'

I nodded. It was less exhausting than speech.

'Booked? Or can I take up that rain-check on our last date?'

'Did you take a rain-check on it?'

'Of course. And since we're still on speaking terms I gathered you understood that. Well? Care to spend a quiet evening with uncle?'

I was too hot and weary to be civilized. I had not forgotten the ballet, but I was still very curious about him. 'Why?'

He raised his eyebrows. 'Why not? I'd like to have you join me.'

'So I gather. But why?'

'See here,' he said impatiently, 'if you've another date, say so. Maybe you want to go out with the girls? Is—what's her name—Estelle—off?'

'She was off this morning,' I retorted with equal impatience, 'as you must have noticed since you've been in Josephine most of to-day.'

He shrugged. 'Can't say I did.'

'Oh, yes you did!' I had reached flash-point. 'You always do notice her. So why bother to date me? Why not ask her? Not just this evening—other times?'

'And why would I want to do that? God! You are the most impossible girl! Why can't you accept an invitation without a man having to make a Federal case out of it?'

'Hunch.'

'Oh, no! Not that! Spare me the womanly intuition!'

'Gladly. If you and Estelle'll spare me having to watch you act like a couple of refugees from Freud. Seriously,' I added more calmly, 'I'd like to help.'

'Just a Girl Scout?' he jeered.

'That's me.'

He grinned briefly. 'So long as I know. Well, now,' he had calmed too, 'can we go back to square one? Find a park bench? Look at some ducks? Soothing birds, ducks. Nothing like a soothing background for a full meeting of the Lonely Hearts Club.'

I had a better idea and said so.

He shook his head. 'It's good of you, angel, but, frankly, no.'

'Don't you like ballet?'

'Very much. But the More finances don't rise to it,' he explained with a refreshing lack of pretence.

'This is for free.' I told him how I had come by the tickets, using the official version I had first used on Estelle and Hannah. 'Sylvia may be out. In any case, I haven't yet asked her. If I couldn't find her I was going to have to waste one and go alone. You may as well come. It doesn't start until seven-thirty, so we can sit on a bench first.'

He winced extravagantly. 'Ouch. These coals of fire are burning.'

I took that as an acceptance. 'Give me half an hour to change.'

He was waiting in the front hall of our Home when I left the lift thirty-five minutes later. We strolled to the nearest public park, chose a bench by the lake, watched the ducks, drank coffee from thick china mugs, ate even thicker hamburgers, and talked Estelle.

'Just date her, you say! It's so simple! Angel, the More finances just stretch to coffee and hamburgers on a park bench. I can't offer you a proper dinner. As for her—I don't even own a ruddy dress suit.'

'If she wanted the bright lights and expensive meals she could have them any time. Why can't you forget her cash and treat her as a human being?'

'That is so easy,' he replied drily. 'Do I also overlook the minor detail that she can't tolerate me?'

'Would it make any difference if she liked you?'

'It would be a pleasant thought—it wouldn't help otherwise. How could it? I've nothing to offer her. I don't even earn a living.'

'You will.'

'And since when has a medical qualification been a short cut to wealth? It'll be years before I'm able to support some one like you as a wife. It would never work with her. Her only hope is to marry some well-heeled character.'

'Do you have to talk marriage from the start?'

'Surprisingly enough'—he sounded surprised—'I do—with her. I happen to love her. I never intended, or wanted, to love anyone yet. I saw her—and it was all over. I thought; that's her. I didn't twig who she was, which was why I came up to call on you girls in the P.T.S. Once I heard the score I realized all I could do was get back on Luigi and beat it like a bat of hell. I meant to steer clear of her.' He looked at me. 'Like hell I've been able to do that now I know I've only to walk into a ward to see her. I've not been the only man to do that. I doubt there's a character in the Medical School who hasn't taken a look and opted out. There's only one man in Martha's in the position to do otherwise.'

'There is?' I asked absently, wishing I did not see his point of view so well.

'Old Marcus. But he retired to his ivory tower years ago.'

'Him? He's far too old.'

'Oh, I dunno.' He stretched his legs and leant his head against the back of the seat. 'He's not such a bad chap. What if he does keep himself to himself? It's his life. Now I've run up against Estelle, I feel mighty sorry for the man.He's stiff with brains as well as lolly. A man with his brains wouldn't be able to delude himself that any woman would be able to see him for his lolly. He probably took to his microscope in self-defence. It's the same with her.' His voice softened. 'That must be why she hands out the frozen mitt to one and all?'

I nodded. 'Once I thought her reserve was just shyness. It isn't. She's never shy with the patients.'

'Think I haven't noticed that while writing those reams in Josephine?' His smile was self-derisive. 'Have I made notes! I've also noticed how you're the only person to whom she lets down the barrier. Which was why I tried to date you last time—and to-night. Now call me a heel and have done!'

'I knew you weren't asking me for me.'

'How so?'

I smiled smugly. 'Womanly intuition, dear.'

He grinned. 'I deserved that.'

'Want me to pull a string?'

'I did. Even this evening. Not now.'

'What's made you change?'

He said that while he had been waiting for me to change he had walked round the car park. 'I made myself take a good look at that car of hers. It would take my first year's salary as houseman to keep that machine in petrol—if she went slow on using it. So there's no dice. Like me to opt out of the ballet?'

'Of course not!' We ought to move soon.

'Before we do—mind if we make a deal? I've opened my big mouth far too wide this evening. You won't let it go any farther?'

I hesitated. The Professor had been in my mind throughout our conversation. I was not sure that he could advise me on this, but I very much wanted to discuss it with him, if only to help me to get it in proportion.

He misunderstood my hesitation. 'Frances,' he caught both my hands, 'don't you dare wonder how you can put in the right word to her. Or ask Hannah or anyone else to do likewise. You're not to breathe a word about how I feel about her. Get me?'

'I won't tell anyone you're in love with Estelle,' I promised obediently, adding the mental reservation; so long as I keep Estelle's name out of it, I can ask the Professor.

He kissed my cheek lightly. 'Good girl. Hey'—he held me against his shoulder—'don't look round as it'll be too obvious—but there goes old Marcus on his way back to the old firm.'

I waited a few moments before releasing myself from his hands. 'Which way?'

'He's gone behind the island.' He stood up, held out a hand, and pulled me to my feet. 'Let's move or we'll be late. And for a break, let's talk about you. How's your love-life?'

'Haven't got one.'

He smiled. 'Too bad. Hey—how about that aged bird-watching character? Hannah told me something about him. All those avuncular letters sound mighty fishy to me.'

'Maybe.' I had to smile as he was watching me. 'Not if you knew the Professor. There was nothing like that about him.'

'With due respects, angel,' said Bart, 'there's something like that about every man. Let's run. We want that bus.'

The ballet was good, but not as superb as I made out in my next letter to the Professor. Once it was posted, I had the inevitable doubts and wished I had not been so enthusiastic. He would probably think I was begging for more tickets; be nauseated by such pure saccharine; never write to me again.

'Has your mother changed her letter-writing day?' Estelle asked as we hurried to a medical lecture the following Thursday morning, and despite our rush, I insisted on going via Matron's office. 'I thought she wrote on Mondays?'

'She does. I was just hoping one of my sisters has remembered my existence. They're all home on holiday. I love getting letters. Don't you?'

'Depends whom they're from, dear.' She reached the pigeon-holes first, sorted through the 'D's', handed me an envelope. 'Frances, you can't stop to read it now! We're late. Think of Sister Tutor's blood-pressure.'

'Sure.' I grinned idiotically as if I found the thought of Sister Tutor's blood-pressure exquisitely funny. 'Mustn't give the old girl a stroke.'

If I had been alone I would not have given the time or Sister Tutor one thought until I read the Professor's letter. As I had to leave it unopened, it occupied nine-tenths of my thought during Dr Higgs' lecture on Graves' Disease. I fixed my eyes on the round little physician who kept dropping his chalk; fingered the envelope in my pocket while his words flowed over my head and my colleagues wrote pages of notes on exophthalmic goitre, hyperthyroidism, toxic adenoma, and thyrotoxicosis.

Dr Higgs did not approve of too many notes being taken. He stopped by my desk on his way out. 'Interested in medicine, Nurse? Eh? Thought you must be. Wise girl. Fascinatin' subject. And you'll learn it better if you carry on keeping your eyes and ears open and hands still. Good morning.'

Sister Tutor beckoned me as he left the room. 'One moment, Nurse Dorland. What did Dr Higgs have to say to you?'

When I gave her a shortened version of this she clicked her tongue against her teeth impatiently.

'Dr Higgs is far too conscientious a man for it to occur to him that you were gazing at him to cover your lack of attention. I hope you feel ashamed of yourself! If I see you going to sleep with your eyes open in a lecture again, I shall send you to Matron. I strongly advise you to do something to conquer that childish habit before you begin work in Out-Patients. Sister Out-Patients will not tolerate absent-mindedness in her nurses.'

I apologized meekly, and automatically, then realized what she had said. 'Out-Patients, Sister?'

She smoothed her cuffs primly. 'That was what I said, Nurse. You should be aware of the fact. I pinned the change list to the board outside

Matron's Office earlier this morning. You have eyes, Nurse. May I suggest you use them for the purpose for which they were intended.'

I was as surprised to think Estelle had missed that notice as I was by her news. Estelle was the most observant person I had ever met. I had spent some time in the lecture wondering if she had recognized the Professor's handwriting, decided she must have done, but had had the good sense—and good manners—not to mention it as I had not done so.

Sister Tutor gave me another little homily on the disasters that must inevitably attend any nurse who lacked observation, then dismissed me. Estelle was waiting anxiously in the corridor. 'What was all that about? Rocket?'

'I nodded. 'That's not all. We're changing.' I told her about the list. 'Did you see it?'

'No. Let's go and look now.'

We walked as quickly as we dared back to the Office, because we were already bound to be late when we returned to Josephine. We discovered our whole set was changing wards as the new P.T.S. set was due to start in the hospital in a couple of days. Estelle was going to the General Theatre; Hannah to Josephine.

'I'm sorry we're splitting,' she said as we walked on. 'Of course, it was bound to happen.' Her expression suddenly froze. 'I expect,' she drawled, 'I'll find it quite amusing to spend the next three months hiding behind a yashmak.'

'Maybe you will,' I replied absently, looking round. I was sure Bart was somewhere near, although I had not yet seen him. When Estelle switched into that dreadful Top Deb. voice he was always close at hand.

He was there all right. He was leaning against the bust of Lord Lister about ten yards from us, talking to three other students. He waved casually in our direction as we went by. The look he gave Estelle was not at all casual. She ignored him and drawled on about the theatre until we had left him well behind. 'Do you think you'll like O.P.?' she asked in her normal voice. 'I've heard Sister O.P. is an absolute old devil.'

Garret was waiting for us in Josephine. She looked very annoyed. 'Nurse Dorland, did you scrub the linen-room shelves last evening?'

'Yes, Nurse.'

'Come with me.' She nodded curtly at Estelle. 'You get on with the routine. Now, Nurse Dorland'—she swept towards the linen-room and threw open the door dramatically. 'Look at the chaos you have left behind you! Three of those pillow-cases—two hand towels—are facing the wrong way! And you have put thirteen sheets on a pile, not twelve! I've never seen such a shambles! Get this straight before you do anything else!'

I said, 'Yes, Nurse, I'm sorry, Nurse,' and tried not to look as delighted as I felt. I had thought the Professor's letter would have to wait until I went to lunch, but she had given me the perfect refuge in which I could read in private.

I tidied the pillow-cases and towels quickly, then heaved forward the steps, climbed to the sheet shelf, sat on the top step by the shelf, and read my letter.

He wrote his now usual page and a half. He was happy I had enjoyed the ballet; pleased I had been able to take one of my friends ...

'Nurse Dorland!' Garret stood at the foot of the steps looking about to explode. 'What do you think you are doing up there?'

I said, 'Reading a letter, Nurse.'

'Do you suppose I have no eyes in my head? Put it away at once! What do you suppose would happen to the patients if we all retired to linen-rooms and sat on the top of ladders when we wanted to read our post? Have you no conscience at all? If you think you will be permitted to get away with this behaviour in Out-Patients you had better think again! Sister Out-Patients will know how to deal with you!'

Estelle overheard Garret's strictures as she set the patients' lunch-trolley in the kitchen. She was really upset. 'Frances, do be careful. Two in a day is two too many,' she warned me at lunch.

I promised to be careful, and promptly dropped the plate of Irish stew I was carrying.

Sister Dining-room was quite as angry as Garret had been. Hannah, who had overheard about my morning, shook her head unhappily. 'This can't go on, Frances! For God's sake, girl, take a grip. Sister O.P.'ll go round the bend if she hears about things like this.'

I felt a miserable failure, a disgrace to my set, inevitably bound to bring sorrow to my aged parents, until I remembered my parents were not yet aged—and the Professor's letter.

I had to talk to some one, so I wrote to him that evening:

The shadow of the gallows looms large, as Home Sister forecast. And after the appalling build-up every one's given Sister O.P. I am not sure it would be a happy release. Of course, there's always the river, but I can swim quite well. I believe it's hard to drown if you can swim? Still, it seems I have got to be sensible,, so I have decided to turn over a new leaf.

Estelle looked round the door as I signed my name. 'So there you are! You were so quiet I thought you must be in Hannah's room with the others.'

'I'm feeling very virtuous, attending to my correspondence. Notice my halo? Well over the ears?'

She smiled. 'It had better stay there, Nurse Dorland. Remember Sister O.P.'

I groaned. 'Must I?'

'I'm going to miss not having patients.' She wandered aimlessly round my room. 'It'll make a change.'

'Need a change?' I asked carefully.

'It's always a good thing to get around. More experience.'

Shock tactics had worked with Bart. I decided to try them on her. 'No medical clerks in the theatre, either.'

'Just what,' she drawled, 'do you mean by that?'

'You won't have to keep ignoring Bart More.'

'Bart More?' she asked icily. 'Why would I do that? He's a friend of yours—not mine.'

'Bart More.' I ignored her final remark. 'Don't ask me why you avoid him. That's something I wouldn't know. Just as I wouldn't know why he watches you when you aren't watching him and vice versa.'

'Frances, you do talk the most ghastly rubbish at times.'

'Could be. But I'm not at this moment—as you know. So, why? I won't spread it about, but I'd like to know. I think you like him one hell of a lot.'

She sat on my bed. 'I'm really not interested.'

I sat by her. 'Come off it, Estelle. I haven't your brains, but I've three sisters. I know when a girl's interested and when she's not. You are. So why?'

Her manner thawed visibly. 'You must see why. It's impossible from every angle.'

'Because of your cash?'

She hesitated. 'More than that. Grandpapa.'

'He surely didn't say you were to take the veil because you've taken up nursing?'

'No,' she agreed slowly. 'But when he gave me permission to come here he said he only gave it because he could trust me to be sensible.'

'He's dead right. You are. Surely he wouldn't object to your just getting to be friends with a student?'

'He would. He doesn't hold with platonic friendships—as I've told you. Particularly when the female half is me.'

'I suppose I can see his point. You're his one and only ewe lamb, due to inherit no small fortune, and very good-looking. You aren't as other women and it's no use pretending you are.'

She said reflectively, 'I've never met anyone like you. You've no inhibitions about saying the sort of things most people leave unsaid. But where their silence embarrasses, your talk doesn't.'

'Couldn't you shed a few inhibitions with Grandpapa?'

'Uh-huh. You don't know Grandpapa! If he suspected a Martha's student was giving me the green light—and that I thought he looked pretty nice—hell, yes, I do—well, he'd have me out of Martha's and back home before I had time to pack. I'm under age, remember.'

I was very pleased to have this admission from her, even though it was not apparently going to do anyone any good.

'Estelle. He couldn't object to Bart. Bart's no fortune-hunter.'

She smiled with humour. 'According to Grandpapa, every man who's ever looked my way has been one—and I'm afraid he's right. Heavens, Frances—you don't know what it's like—I know it sounds a piece of cake to be me—it isn't. Grandpapa says he trusts few women and no men where I'm concerned. We had a long chat the night before our P.T.S. term began. He made me promise I would not so much as accept a date with any man who was not personally known to him, or who had not first asked his permission. I know that sounds Victorian. ...' She broke off apologetically.

'How old's Grandpapa?'

'Seventy-nine.'

'Then he was raised under Victoria. Can't blame him for running true to form.'

She smiled properly. 'You two ought to meet. He'd like you, and you wouldn't be frightened of him. But, Frances—can you see any of these boys asking Grandpapa if they can take me to the movies?'

'N-no.' I sighed. 'There must be an answer, though. The Professor,' I added unthinkingly, 'says there's an answer to everything.'

She looked at me keenly. 'When did he say that? Seen him lately?'

This was Truth Night in the Nurses Home, so I had to be honest. 'Once. He's telephoned a couple of times.'

'And sent you those ballet tickets?'

'How on earth did you guess that?'

She laughed. 'I've no sisters, dear, but a few brains. Found out any more about him?'

I nodded and told all I knew.

'He visited your family?'

'All bird-watchers together, as I forecast.'

She seemed about to say more when Hannah swept in and asked why we were looking so gloomy. 'The tea's stewing, girls. Do come along, or it'll be too bitter to drink.'

7. *Afternoon in the Sun*

The senior nurse-in-training in the Out-Patient Department was called Simpson. She was tall, dark-haired, with very blue eyes. She wore a fourth-year belt and spoke to the tip of my cap. 'O.P. Four'll show you what to do, Dorland.'

It was my first morning in the department. I had no idea who, or even what, O.P. Four was. I looked hopefully at the four other girls in the changing-room. Three wore the same fourth-year belts as Simpson; the fourth was a second-year nurse. No one took any notice of me or bothered to explain what was obviously an elementary fact of O.P. life.

The department was a new world to me. The conversation in that changing-room taught me that in this world a new language was spoken. 'The S.O.P.O. was so right,' insisted Simpson. 'That B.I.D. belonged in Cas. We can't admit stiffs with all our follow-ups. The S.M.O. was furious about it. He went along to Cas. to speak to the S.C.O., himself.'

'Why should a B.I.D. come in at all?' asked another girl. 'We're a hospital. Not a flipping morgue.'

A third girl said she could understand about B.I.D.'s because of our P.M. room, but what really got her was Sister Mary's creating to her because an infant was B.B.A. 'You would have thought I induced the poor little creature when I had to escort him to Mary. The S.G.H.P. said both should have gone to Christian. I ask you!'

She was not asking me, for which I was grateful, being utterly dazed by all these letters. She did not so much as glance my way, nor after that first remark did Nurse Simpson or any of the others. They wandered off, leaving me waiting for the second-year to finish rearranging her hair.

At last she was satisfied with her appearance. She spun round in a burst of efficiency, smoothed her apron, and produced two tin boxes from beneath one of the shelves. She thrust one at me. 'O.P. Five's cleaning things. Will you start on the children's room?'

She was a plump, moderately pretty girl with light brown hair and a faintly disgruntled air. She did not explain further or offer to show me to the children's room. Fortunately, on my way in I had noticed a large spotted rocking horse in one of the many rooms off the long corridor dividing the department, so when she shot off in one direction I hurried in the other in search of the rocking-horse.

It had a friendly face and looked lonely and out of place in its aseptic surroundings. I patted it as I set it in motion while dusting. 'You and me, pal, both,' I murmured aloud.

The second-year nurse looked in about five minutes later. 'You ought to have finished, Dorland. We've all the other rooms to do—five medical, fifteen assorted surgical, plus this. The room cleaning is all done by O.P. Four and Five. I'm Four. You're Five.'

'Yes, Nurse.' I tried to sound briskly efficient. 'Is there a Six?'

'Obviously not, as you're Five! Every new nurse in O.P. starts as Five, regardless of her actual hospital seniority, as the work here is so specialized. Simpson's Head Nurse, Carver O.P. One. Simpson's due to move in about a month. When she goes we'll all shift up one. You'll be Four then,' she added a little unnecessarily, but with patent doubts on the subject. 'It's a bit unusual, our having anyone as new as you here. I suppose Matron must know what she's doing.'

I made no comment. I could scarcely say no and feared that if I said yes she would look even more disapproving.

'Oh, well. I suppose I'll have to take you round. Come on. Incidentally,' she added over her shoulder, 'I'm Vickers. Monica Player's in my set.'

The piece of information cheered me. Hospital sets in some strange manner tend to have a form of family resemblance within their numbers. Monica Player had been a pleasant and very helpful senior. I beamed at Vickers's back. She glanced round, noticed my expression, but did not return my beam. I switched it off quickly.

'Twenty-one rooms in all,' she announced half-way through our tour. 'Those over there'—she gesticulated vaguely—'belong to the S.M.O., S.S.O., S.O.P.O., and S.G.H.P., so they don't concern us as they are only offices. No patients are allowed in the offices. We do only the patients' rooms. The rest get cleaned by the lay staff.'

I had to stop her. 'I'm sorry, Nurse. I can't work out those letters.'

She tapped her foot impatiently. 'I simply can't waste time explaining. You'll have to have one of Sister's printed lists. I'll just tell you now— the S.O.P.O. is the Senior Out-Patient's Officer and our permanent resident. The S.G.H.P. is more or less permanent too—when he's not in Cas.—he's the Senior Gynæcological House Physician. There are dozens more. Wait here. I'll get a list.'

The list momentarily added to my confusion. There were approximately sixty men on the resident medical staff; the majority appeared to work in Out-Patients during some period of the day; each man being known by the initial letters of his specific appointment.

Vickers ran rapidly through our routine as we scampered on. 'After cleaning, we stock and test. We report to Sister at a quarter to nine

every morning. Although O.P. never shuts, we open officially at nine
each morning and all the rooms remain open until eight P.M. Only the
acute rooms are open at night, unless there's a major crisis. Then they
can open the lot. Sister,' she went on as we reached the last room, 'is
very particular about none of the patients' rooms being left unattended
by the staff in the day.'

I looked again at the list and counted the O.P. nursing staff. 'How do
we manage that, Nurse? Twenty-one rooms—eight on the staff counting
Sister and her Staff Nurse.'

'If I were you, Dorland,' she retorted sharply, 'I wouldn't try to be
funny! You may think you're quite important, having important friends
and so on, but we simply aren't interested in your private life here. The
dressers and clerks help, naturally! They're perfectly capable.'

Her reaction astounded me. She looked genuinely annoyed. I could
not conceive why she should have taken such umbrage over Estelle—and
she could only have been referring to Estelle, since, with the exception of
Bart, I had no friends, important or otherwise, in the hospital. She was
clearly waiting for me to make some answer, so I fell back on some
advice Player gave us in Josephine. 'When in doubt, agree, apologize,
and keep quiet.'

If I had any real doubts, she dispelled them when, with the four
seniors, we waited outside the door of Sister's office at sixteen minutes to
nine. She gazed pensively round the steadily filling department. 'I
believe I can guess why Matron sent you to us so soon, Dorland. It'll
prevent your having delusions of grandeur—do you good to be reminded
how the other half live. The half who don't drive around in expensive
Continental cars,' she added triumphantly, as if she had brought off a
magnificent witticism.

Estelle's car was French. I longed to retort that I had only been in
that car twice since we left the P.T.S. I very nearly did. Again Monica
Player saved me. 'Never hit back at a senior, even if she is in the wrong.
It doesn't pay. Act dumb and pretend the crack's gone over your head.
That'll annoy her more than anything you can say'.

I assumed the Idiot Pro expression I had not used since I left the
P.T.S. and Staff Nurse Naylor. 'Yes, Nurse.'

She looked at me sharply. The seniors looked amused. I widened my
eyes a little farther. They felt about to drop out.

The Staff Nurse opened the door. 'Come in, Nurses.'

The immediate prospect of Sister O.P. prevented my brooding on the
long-term prospect of working with a tiresome colleague. I had never
seen Sister before. Her appearance in every way lived up to her
reputation.

She was a square, solid, elderly lady with iron-grey hair and light grey eyes. She did not talk; she barked. 'So you're Nurse Dorland, hey?'

'Yes, Sister.'

'Don't slouch, child! God gave you a back-bone. Use it!'

'Yes, Sister.'

'You've worked in Josephine Ward?'

'Yes, Sister.'

'You've done no departmental work?'

'No, Sister.'

'You'll have a great deal to learn, won't you, Nurse?'

'Yes, Sister.'

She looked as dubious as Vickers had done earlier. 'Sister Tutor tells me you are apt to be absent-minded. A sad fault, Nurse. Conquer it.'

I swallowed. 'Yes, Sister.' And since she had not dismissed me, I waited as Sister Josephine always insisted we waited in front of her desk with our hands behind our backs until she said the actual words, 'That will be all, Nurses.'

Sister O.P. peered over the top of her desk, and glared at my feet. 'Glue under your shoes, Nurse? Short of breath?'

I stepped back as if the floor was red-hot. 'No, Sister.'

'You have relieved my mind, Nurse. And why do you still wait? Can you not see that my Staff Nurse is waiting to show you your morning's work? Do you consider my Staff Nurse is free to await you in your own good time?'

I crossed to the Staff Nurse who was standing by the door, feeling as if I had walked into my father's bulldozer.

The Staff Nurse gave me a charming smile. 'We'll begin in Room One, Nurse Dorland.'

Nurse Vickers had made me wary, and I reserved judgment as to whether our exceptionally attractive Staff Nurse was as charming as her smile. It did not take me long to shed that wariness. Staff Nurse Neal was a genuinely friendly person; she treated me as an equal, chatted as if we had known each other years. She was unlike any other staff nurse I had yet met in Martha's; she behaved like a normal human being who knew more than I did because of her years of hospital experience, but took no credit for those years. She was obviously very popular with the patients. Every few minutes during that morning some man or woman advanced on us, seized her hand, said it was real good to see her again it was, and how was the Doctor keeping?

I had noticed her wedding ring directly we left Sister's office. As I listened to and watched her wondered if marriage had given her her human touch and, if so, whether something could be done to marry off Naylor in the P.T.S. and Garret in Josephine. I wondered about her husband too. If Vickers had been less hostile I would have gone straight to her for information, but that was clearly out of the question. Then Neal gave it to me unasked. "My husband was S.O.P.O. here last year— before he decided to specialize in pathology,' she remarked after one of her many reunions with old patients. 'They've got wonderful memories. They never forget a thing.'

'I wish I could say the same, Nurse.'

'Don't worry about that,' she said cheerfully. 'No one remembers anything about the workings of O.P.'s during their first week here. It'll suddenly all fall into place.' She looked at the corridor clock. 'That skin clinic's running over-time as usual. We can't help out in there as it's time we went back to Sister. I'm not sure which lunch she wants you to go to, or when you'll be off. Wait outside her office. I won't be long.'

The office door had been half-open all morning. Neal did not close it when she left me in the doorway. I waited, watched the coming and going of patients, long white coats, short white coats, nurses and students, and wondered, not for the first time in Martha's, how any of the medical staff ever had time to do any real work, because they were always hurrying from one point to another, staring at the floor, and clutching huge sheafs of notes. And surely rubber-wheeled roller skates would be ideal for nurses? They would be so much quicker and far more graceful than the swaying jog-trot used by all my fellow O.P. girls.

A quiet discussion on off-duty had been going on in the room behind me. I paid no attention until something Neal said made me listen instinctively. 'Is that the child you were telling me about, Sister? The Dorland Sister Tutor mentioned?' I could not catch Sister's answer, but Neal's next words told me more than I wanted to know about Sister Tutor's comments.

'Then do you suppose we'll keep her long, Sister? I don't.'

I had no wish to hear Sister's confirmation of this view. I moved a few feet from the doorway, stared at the waiting patients and thought bleakly about my future.

'Nurse—here.' An elderly lady, in a red hat sitting three chairs away beckoned me urgently. 'Is that young doctor over there trying to get your attention? That dark-haired young doctor—over by the wheel-chairs, dear.'

I looked round vaguely. Every other physician and surgeon in O.P. appeared to have dark hair. 'I don't think he can be, thanks'—and then I saw Bart.

He caught my eye at once, spread his hands dramatically, and came towards me.

I scowled to keep him off. He ignored my scowl and climbed on over the wheel-chairs. The lady in the red hat smiled archly. 'I thought he must be your young man, dear. I watched him trying to get your attention for ever so long.'

I thanked her again as Bart reached me. 'Go away,' I said between my teeth, 'far, far away. Sister and Neal are both in the office.'

'In a minute. Where is she? And what are you doing here? Why aren't you in Josephine? I've combed Martha's.'

'We've all changed. She's in the General Theatre. For Heaven's sake—go away!'

He obeyed this time and just in time. Neal came out of the office as he walked by at the double, correctly gazing at the floor. 'You are to go to one-thirty lunch, and be off this afternoon, Nurse Dorland.' She smiled. 'I expect you'll be glad to have an extra afternoon off?'

I could not see any genuine reason for preferring to be free from two to five, instead of from five-thirty onwards, but since she had been so pleasant and seemed to expect me to be delighted, I beamed and said I was most happy to have an extra free afternoon.

Vickers came into the changing-room a little later when I was tidying my cap before going to lunch. 'Is Bart More another of your friends?'

I cursed all itinerant students mentally. 'His cousin's in my set, Nurse.'

She smiled unpleasantly. 'Quite a famous set, what with this and that. All the same, I think I ought to warn you—that cuts no ice here. No one—just no one—impresses Sister Out-Patients.'

'That I can well believe, Nurse,' I said drily, and went to lunch.

No member of my set was at that meal. When I returned to the Home afterwards our floor was empty. The heat-wave had finally broken, but the afternoon was far too fine to waste indoors, even though my conscience insisted I should stay in and write up Dr Higgs' lecture on Graves' Disease. I squashed my conscience by reminding it that Sister P.T.S. was the fount of all Martha's nursing wisdom, and she had always told us that every nurse needed a brisk walk in the open air every day. 'It is your duty to care for your health, Nurses. A healthy nurse is a happy nurse; a happy nurse makes happy patients.'

I had no real patients in O.P. but it was obviously my duty to spread happiness among our drifting follow-ups. I changed out of uniform, and strolled back to the hospital to care for my health on the stone-flagged terrace that ran the length of the building on the river side. My feet refused to be brisk after their morning in O.P., and the terrace was the ideal spot for getting the maximum of air with the minimum of energy. It was away from the noise and smell of traffic, quiet, and after two in the afternoon generally empty. The students had all gone in to rounds or lectures when I reached it, apart from a man in a boiler suit at the far end, I had the terrace to myself.

I leant against the embankment wall contentedly, too soothed by lunch and the sunshine to think of anything in particular as I watched the river and the traffic on the opposite bank. I had been there perhaps five minutes when I first had that odd sensation you get when some one is watching you. I turned slowly, looked up and down. Even the man in the boiler suit had disappeared. I was quite alone.

I looked towards the ward blocks which lay on my right. I had intentionally not stopped in front of any of the wards in case some Sister might see me, disapprove, and remember my face if I ever worked in her ward. The Admin. block was directly behind me; Matron's office was in that block, but faced on to the small courtyard between the blocks; the Dean's offices, the Hospital Secretary's, and, I believed, a board-room lay under the top-floor Lab. I looked up at each floor, then for some time at the great plate-glass window. It stared down at me, as unwinking as a glass eye. There was no one at any window, nor was it likely that any of the occupants of those floors would be taking time off to watch me, but the sensation persisted so strongly that I moved away.

There was a door in the embankment wall just beyond the Admin. block. It was labelled 'Members of St Martha's Hospital only.' I had not used it previously, but as I was a member of Martha's I could not see how even the Dean could object to my using it now. I crossed the bridge, and in a few minutes reached the public park we all regarded as an extension of the hospital, remembering the last occasion when I had used a side-door for the first time. I wished I could have told Lily about that; she would have been so pleased for me. And then I wished I had not been born with a photographic memory, and winced mentally.

The Professor would say I was indulging in grief, I thought suddenly and dragged my thoughts away from that small ward. I did not attempt or want to drag them from him. I strolled on aimlessly, wondering if I was really in love with him, in love with the thought of being in love, or merely fascinated by a man who was so unlike any man I had had as a friend or acquaintance previously.

There was a wooden bridge over the lake in the park. I leant on one rail for some time, watching the water, the many small children playing on the grass in dresses and suits that had been faded by the abnormally long summer. An endless stream of couples ambled by. I watched them too, and was a little surprised to find that they did not make me feel lonely. Like most young women alone—and possibly young men— couples generally had that effect on me, yet, although I would have loved to amble with my Professor, that afternoon I did not feel alone. Perhaps there was something to be said for a photographic memory, I decided, leaving the bridge. He did not have to be with me for me to see his face, and being alone I was free to carry on a splendid mental conversation with him; a conversation which was wordless, and yet allowed me to be brilliant and clever.

My feet reminded me I was on duty at five. Perhaps I ought to go back and do that lecture. Perhaps.

It was too late. I had noticed an empty bench close to the lake. I forgot all about the thyroid gland. I even forgot that I had shared that particular bench with Bart, until the ducks rolled out of the water and up to my feet. They waited expectantly as they had done that evening before the ballet. 'Sorry, ducks,' I said aloud. 'No hamburger crumbs, to-day.'

'Do you think,' asked a voice directly over my head, 'they'd care for an egg sandwich, Frances?'

His presence had been so vivid in my imagination, that for one moment, I thought I could only be imagining his voice. I looked round very slowly. He was there. He smiled, and I felt as if the sun had risen twice in the same day.

'Don't look so startled,' he said. 'I'm no ghost.'

'I'm so sorry. I was miles away.'

'I saw that from the other side of the lake. I tried to get your attention. You looked straight through me.' He moved round the bench, but did not sit down. 'Do you often come here in the afternoon? I've not seen you before.'

'Not often.' I folded my hands primly. I had to be prim until I recovered my mental breath. It would shake him rigid if I gave him the welcome I wanted to give. 'Do you?'

'Fairly frequently. My office is quite near'—he jerked his head at the long grey line of Government buildings on our left—'just a couple of minutes from here to be accurate.'

I made a mental note to haunt that part of the park on every free two-to-five I was given in future. 'Isn't it a wonderful afternoon?'

He agreed the afternoon was perfect and looked at the still waiting ducks. 'Do you want to feed them?'

I looked up at him, and stayed looking because he was apparently fascinated by the birds. I had not seen him in such a strong light previously. The sun exposed the lines under his eyes, making him seem older and thinner than I remembered, and yet more attractive than any man I had ever seen.

'Have you really got some food on you?'

'Yes. Here.' He pulled a paper packet from one of his jacket pockets. 'They'll be a shade stale. They won't mind.'

I unwrapped the packet. 'Do you always carry sandwiches around with you?'

He turned to me, grinned, and shed about ten years. 'One can scarcely blame you for having that impression.' He glanced at the bench. 'Expecting anyone? Or on your own?'

'On my own.'

'Mind if I join you?' he asked politely.

Equally politely I said I would like him to join me. I sounded exactly like Estelle in her Miss Dexter mood, I thought savagely. I had to let off steam somehow, so I chucked over half the sandwiches to the ducks.

He sat by me in silence. I had to say something. I talked about sandwiches. They made a change from the weather. 'Do you eat a lot of them?'

'I usually have them for lunch.'

'Is this your lunch?' I asked quickly.

He smiled. 'Not to-day's. I had ham to-day.'

'You have them every day? Truly?'

'They're convenient.'

We seemed to be having two conversations. The important one was unspoken. 'If you eat them.'

'I meant to,' he said apologetically, 'and forgot. My secretary's very good about having them sent up and worries if I leave them lying about. To save a great deal of unnecessary fuss I push the packets out of sight as soon as they arrive. I use a drawer in my desk—a pocket—or the car. The man at the place where I leave my car at night is used to unloading spare food from the dashboard. I believe he keeps chickens or something. Don't know where. He leaves the whisky.'

I was no longer surprised he looked thin, and too concerned for him to pay attention any longer to the laws of civilized behaviour which had had me by the throat since I turned and found him standing behind me. 'Just what do you have for lunch?'

'Coffee. Tobacco.'

'How long have you been living on that?'

'God knows. Years. Hasn't done me any harm.'

'Nonsense,' I said firmly; 'it must have. That kind of food's no good for a man. No food value in it. My mum would have a stroke if my father started skipping meals.'

He considered me thoughtfully. 'Your father must have a certain amount of physical work. My job's sedentary.'

'That's got nothing to do with it all. Honestly, I do know what I'm talking about. I know I'm new to hospital, but anyone in Martha's would say the same. You don't know the risks you're running with your health. Why can't you go out to lunch?'

'It's such a waste of time. That's why I gave it up.'

'You really ought to start it again. Or, if you can arrange it, have a proper meal sent up.'

He smiled faintly. 'You seem to have very strong views.'

'I have. Because, as I've said, I do know what can happen. You wouldn't think of running a machine without fuel—so why try to run a human body without proper food? It's asking for trouble. If you keep on, you'll crack. Hasn't your secretary or some one told you this?'

'No.' He took out his pipe, pouch, and matches. 'Which makes me most grateful for your kind—if somewhat stern—warning.'

'Have I been rude? I'm very sorry. I didn't mean to be.'

'You haven't been at all rude.' He slapped his pockets absently. 'I don't believe you could be.'

The sun rose a third time at that. 'Are you looking for your matches? They're under your pouch.'

'They are? Oh. Yes. Thanks.' He filled his pipe. 'I've no business to be sitting here. I should be working.'

'I should be writing notes on the thyroid gland.' We smiled at each other. 'It would be wicked to waste this sun.'

'Criminal. Do you get any in your room?'.

'Actually, yes. It faces south. Does your office?'

He shook his head, but he was still smiling. 'It's a typical small back room.'

'Are you what used to be called a boffin?' I asked curiously.

'Used to be? Now, that'—he said—'dates me. I thought boffins were still called boffins?'

'I thought it went out with the war. The Second World War.'

'Believe it or not, that's the war I call the war. The Crimean campaign was a little before my time. Not much. Just a little.'

I laughed. 'You weren't even at Mafeking?'

'Alas, no. Tell me,' he went on more seriously, 'do you remember my war?'

'Only vaguely. I was five when it ended.'

He nodded to himself as if he had expected that answer.

'Were you in it?'

'Inevitably. Every one of my generation was involved.'

'I mean—did you fight? Were you a soldier?'

His eyes were amused. 'I spent six years in the Army. I wouldn't care to claim that made me a soldier.'

I tried to visualize him in uniform. I could not do it. 'Six years. That's a terrific slice out of your life.'

'It seemed more like six hundred at the time.' He looked at me meditatively, and I had the impression he was not seeing me at all. 'I was twenty-two when I went in. I feel now as if it only lasted a couple of weeks.'

I wished he had not said that. Knowing his age made no difference to me, but his talking so openly showed that he was quite content to underline the fact that we belonged to different generations. He obviously thought of me as a pleasant, perhaps amusing child. And nothing more. Two of the suns went down fast.

'Daddy was in the Navy. He didn't enjoy it much. He used to get seasick, poor darling.'

'What happened to the turkeys?'

'We didn't have any then.'

He shifted his position slightly. 'This reminiscing must be very boring for you. Let's have your news. How's the new job? Gallows still looming large?'

'Larger than ever, even though I've only been in O.P. one morning.' I threw the last crumbs on to the yellow, patchy grass and folded the sandwich paper. 'My lamp's so dim, it's good as out.'

'What happened this morning?' He crossed his legs and settled into a more comfortable position at the far end of the bench. 'Sister live up to her reputation?'

'She did. I wasn't merely that.' I told him of Sister Tutor's report, and the one-sided conversation I had overheard. 'There's just one bright spot about that. If I get chucked out of O.P. I won't have to work with Vickers.'

'Vickers? Hold on—I'm lost. Nurse? Student? Doctor?'

'Nurse. She's O.P. Four. I'm Five. We get called by our numbers like the cards in Alice's garden.' I smiled briefly. 'It's all rather absurd. She's only in her second year, but oh, so senior. And the others, so help me, are all fourth-years.'

'And oh, so senior?'

'Heavens, yes. They don't speak to me or even see me. When the head girl has to talk to me she talks to the tip of my cap. Shook me a little at first, but I'll get used to being invisible. I don't mind that sort of thing from genuine seniors, which, to be fair to them, is what they are. Fourth-years in the wards have a lot of responsibility. They act-Staff Nurse and so on. It must affect their attitude.'

'Possibly.' His eyes smiled. 'Some people grow with responsibility; others just swell.'

'Vickers swells while you watch. She's in the same set as Monica Player in Josephine, but she's totally different. Player never made a single crack.'

'From which I gather Nurse Vickers does?'

'She does.' I explained her fixation about Estelle. 'Do you remember my telling you I ran into something like this in the P.T.S.?'

'Very well. What's this girl's name? Estelle—?'

'Dexter. That's right,' I added, as he obviously placed her instantly. 'Hamilton Dexter's only grandchild. Honestly, that moron Vickers behaves as if Estelle's cash is a personal insult to her. Have you ever heard such rubbish as that bit about my having important friends? Friends, my foot! Apart from my set I only know one person in Martha's, and he's an impoverished student. He had to turn up this morning, too.'

He glanced at me. 'Surely, you were quite pleased to see a friendly face?'

'There's a time and place for everything, Mr Slane. O.P. in mid-morning is no place for any one's love-life. But he was just a minor detail. What's really eating her is Estelle. Imagine my having to be reminded how the other half live. Me. A working-farmer's daughter. Daddy isn't broke, but he doesn't make all that much out of his turkeys yet. People only eat turkeys at Christmas, unfortunately. If they had the sense to eat 'em all the year round, maybe we'd have enough to run to two elderly cars instead of one. We certainly can't at the present, and, frankly,' I went on warmly, 'I'm not sure that isn't a good thing. The little I've seen of people really in the lolly has made me quite content that I haven't a wealthy papa.'

He refilled his pipe leisurely. 'Money isn't everything, eh?'

I smiled. 'I wasn't going to be quite so corny. But much wealth and many snags do seem to me to go together.'

He watched me over the flame of his match. 'You seem to have given this a lot of thought.'

'Only since I arrived at Martha's. There must be something about our hospital; we go in for millionaires. Not only Estelle—one of our men. But you must have heard about him? Our head pathologist?'

He lit another match. 'Should I have heard about him?'

'Maybe not, if you don't have anything to do with agriculture. His name's Everly. Farm machinery.'

He nodded over a third match. 'I know his name. So he's at Martha's, too?'

'Very much so. He's one of the brains. And do you know what the poor man has to do?'

'Tell me.'

'He hides behind microscopes on our top floor with a variety of deadly bugs rather than come down and meet his fellow men—and women—in case some one wants to up and marry him for his money. From what Estelle's told me of her angle, I no longer blame him.'

'You consider it inevitable that he could only be married for his money?' he asked mildly.

'Having seen him, I'm afraid I do. He may be pleasant underneath, but he's not particularly attractive.'

'Indeed? How did you see him for the microscopes?'

I smiled. 'Quite legitimately. I was sent up with a specimen for him when I was in Josephine. He's reputed to scare the living daylights out of every one from Matron downward, but he was perfectly civil if a shade whoffly.' I paused momentarily, recollecting that encounter. 'Maybe he was not so unattractive as a young man. Of course, with his cash, brains, and a title thrown in, he must have been one of the most eligible men in England. I wonder why some enterprising deb. didn't snap him up.'

'Why necessarily a deb.? Why not a nurse?'

I thought this over too. 'From the little I've seen of hospital life—because nurses don't have enough time for a successful social life—and their feet hurt too much. Laugh if you like, but it's true! If you run round a ward or department all day some one else must do any running that has to be done when a nurse is off duty.'

'Nevertheless wouldn't you consider that in this case an extra output of energy might have paid dividends?'

'Obviously the man's a piece of cake in some ways—if you want that kind of cake.'

'It doesn't tempt you?' he asked quizzically.

'Me? Having seen him? Oh, dear me, no!'

'Leaving personalities out of it, talking academically, wouldn't you be tempted?'

I said slowly, 'I suppose every one has their price. I don't know if that's really true. No one's ever tried to buy me. Naturally it would be every nice never to have to worry about cash, but I think you probably have to be used to having a lot of it, to feel it's the be-all and end-all. If you aren't used to it, it's easier to see the snags. And look what it can do to people. Take Estelle'—I waved her name at him—'she's got one big complex about it. And old Sir Whatsit above stairs—what sort of a life is that for a man who could probably buy Martha's outright? He may have fun raising his little colonies of streps. and staphs., but he'd have far more fun raising grandchildren—which he ought to be doing by now. No. I honestly don't think wealth on that scale does tempt me. I'd like to have enough, but life is quite problematical enough without Estelle's crippling complex, or the state of mind of that poor old man—even if he does have a whale of a time among his bugs.'

He was having a bad time with that pipe. He had given up trying to light it, and was knocking it out against the back of the bench. 'Why is life quite so problematical? Would the problem be male?' He smiled crookedly. 'Please, don't answer unless you want to.'

I looked at him and then away. 'Actually there's something I've been wanting to ask you about a male problem.' I felt quite pleased with myself; with a little care I could switch the subject easily to Bart and Estelle.

He said he could not pretend he was surprised; was not sure if he would be able to assist; but was at my service.

'It's about Bart More.'

'I thought it might be,' he murmured. 'Go on.'

I did not go on immediately. I had to choose my words if I was to keep my promise to Bart. 'He's in love with a friend of mine.'

'Your set?'

'Year,' I corrected—I hoped diplomatically. 'He's pretty serious. He wants to marry her eventually.'

'A reasonable desire for a man in love,' he remarked drily. 'Is your friend equally fond of this youth?'

'He's not all that young. He's twenty-four.'

'I apologize.' He continued to maltreat his unfortunate if unsatis-factory pipe. 'You haven't answered. Is she?'

I nodded.

'Forgive me—but where's the problem?'

I hesitated again. 'I know this'll sound daft—but she doesn't want him to know how she feels.'

'Why not?'

'Mainly, because of her family's attitude. She doesn't feel they'll approve of him, she is under age, and doesn't want to have an affair behind their back.'

He frowned briefly. 'Why won't they approve?'

'He isn't qualified yet. He's broke.'

'Surely time'll remedy that?'

'In a way—yes.'

He asked, 'Why only in a way? Because for some years More will inevitably have little money with which to support a wife? Do your friend's parents take the view that she'll be throwing herself away on a struggling young doctor, when, conceivably she might do very much better for herself materially in another direction?'

This was not what I had been trying to explain, but as it roughly fitted Estelle's position, I agreed.

'One can appreciate her parents' point of view. She's consulted them about More?'

'Not yet. She knows their views on students. She hasn't told anyone but me, or let anyone else even guess.'

'And More?'

'Oh, I guessed about him, even before he told me. He's been so obvious. Even the patients noticed what was up.'

'They say there are only two things a man can't hide. When he's drunk; when he's in love.'

' "They" are right. I was certain about Bart long before that evening we went to the ballet. You don't mind? I took him with your tickets, not one of the girls.'

'My dear child, why should I mind?' He smiled properly to prove his words. 'I was delighted to have them used as you pleased. Glad you had a good evening,' he added, and gave his pipe what became its final whang against the seat. The stem cracked in two and the bowl flew towards me.

I caught it in mid-air. 'Bad luck! Have you another?'

'Not with me. It's immaterial.' He pushed both parts in a pocket. 'I'll have to be moving directly. Let's get back to these friends of yours. This business of its being a problem obviously distresses you and for that I'm sorry. But I'm not convinced there is any occasion for distress. I can well understand your friend's impatience and yours. You're all very young. Youth is always impatient, even though, ironically, youth alone has time for patience.'

'Time'll sort things out? They'll get over it?'

'Not necessarily. I hope they will merely succeed in getting over the parental opposition. Parents generally come round in the long run.'

'I hope you're right.' I remembered Estelle's description of her grandfather. 'I don't know.'

'I do.' He stood up. 'We are discussing my generation now. I may not be able to follow how the minds of your contemporaries work; I know my own. Give them a little time; use not deception but discretion; they'll see things as you do, if they love their daughter—which I'm sure they do.'

It was too late to say we were talking of the generation before his. I smiled weakly. 'Oh, yes. They love her.'

'Then I assure you you've nothing to worry about. Tell your friend to be honest with More. I'm sure he's only too anxious to be honest with her. And then all they'll have to do is wait a year or two for something some people wait for all their lives in vain, or find too late.' He held out his hand. 'I must get back to work now, or get the sack. I came out for ten minutes and have been away a good hour. Good-bye, Frances. I'm so glad I met you.'

His hand was the normal temperature, but his words were so final that I felt as if I was touching ice.

I thanked him for his advice. He said I had been very good to listen to him so patiently. 'I hope the sun goes on shining for you. I'll remember your advice on proper meals. Thanks again for it. Good-bye.'

He walked away and did not look back. I watched his fair head vanish in the crowd beyond the far gates, then stood up slowly. I looked round and felt quite unbearably lonely. I left the park at once, went back to my room, and spent the rest of my off duty working on Graves' Disease. That soothed my conscience, if nothing else.

8. Top Secrets and Scarlet

Four clinics were still in progress when I returned to Out-Patients at five. The broad corridor running the length of the department was as crowded with waiting patients as when I went off duty at one.

Nurse Neal considered the crowd anxiously. 'Poor dears, they're getting mutinous. They should all have been seen by now. It's no one's fault—but there they are.'

Once again I was her official shadow. 'Don't we have an appointments system, Nurse?'

'Oh yes. A very high-powered one. Only snag is, it doesn't work.'

I asked why not?

'Mainly, because—like all general hospitals—we're running a twenty-four-hour service with what is actually a twelve-hour medical staff. As the men have to keep going and work the kind of hours that would send any trade unionist screaming to his union for a strike, the staff tend to slow down, if only to eat. They also have to drop everything when a crisis crops up, and that's happening all the time. With every interruption the clinic gets held up; the queue piles up; the fixed appointments have to be scrapped, and we have to go round soothing irate taxpayers who think all we need is a little efficiency.' She surveyed the muttering patients. 'Those post-op. gastrics'll develop new ulcers if we don't do something. Come along.'

It took her ten minutes to reassure the gastrics. The fracture follow-ups, rheumatics, and cardiacs needed only half that time. We went back to the office doorway.

'There's nothing like a peptic ulcer for producing an acute attack of hæmademention,' she murmured.

'What's hæmademention, please, Nurse?'

She smiled enchantingly at the middle-aged bus driver who had been particularly irate. 'The literal translation, I believe, is a bloody mind. You'll see it written on notes.'

'I will? Oh. I see.' I smiled. 'Thanks, Nurse.'

'Don't think I blame them. I'd be hæmadementic with an ulcer. They are maddening, but that's part of our job here. If you ever get annoyed—don't show it. Remember, in places like O.P. and Casualty, the patients will judge the hospital by the staff they meet—so you represent Martha's. The technique always is to smile.' She glanced at me. 'I'm not advising that because I want you girls to be little rays of sunshine, but because it'll make life so much easier for you or any nurse. There are few women and—in my experience—no men who don't feel soothed when a pretty girl in a nurse's uniform smiles at them.'

I told the girls about Neal when we discussed our new jobs over tea in Hannah's room that night. 'She's so normal, she's unnerving.'

Hannah groaned. 'I wish some one would marry Garret. Does she always pull out the lockers and run her finger along the rim at the back?'

'Always,' said Estelle and I together.

'That woman's got a mania for cleaning,' Estelle went on. 'She must have enjoyed herself in the theatre. You can't conceive how we clean in the General, Frances. We scrub everything every day; cleaning the clean as well as the dirty.I don't think I've put down my little scrubbing-brush once to-day, except to go to meals.'

Hannah helped herself to more tea. 'I thought you had a long abdominal list this afternoon? You couldn't have scrubbed during the acute abdos?'

'Hannah, dear, you ought to know better.' Estelle smiled at me. 'Get this. I was Extra Dirty Nurse, which meant dogsbody. We had eleven cases on the list, used an average of six large and four small macks per case. Who do you think was Mack queen?'

'Oh, dear! You always detested the macks in Josephine.'

'Eleven abdos?' Hannah whistled. 'Bart told me he had been dressing for the S.S.O.'s marathon. I thought he was exaggerating the way he always does.'

'Is Bart on the surgical side now?' I asked evenly.

Hannah answered for Estelle. 'As from this afternoon, he told me when I met him on my way over to-night. He was surprised to hear we've changed. Of course he could scarcely recognize you behind a yashmak in the theatre, Estelle.' She peered into the teapot. 'This wants more water.'

I did not waste any time when Hannah vanished. 'Bart came into the O.P. in a panic this morning. Don't ask me why—he did. I told him you were in the General.'

She coloured slightly. 'Frances, you ought to sit on your imagination. The man can't pull strings like that. And anyway, he didn't recognize me according to Hannah.'

'Didn't he?' I wished more than ever, that I had not made that rash promise to Bart. 'And what makes you think that acting dumb is your prerogative?'

'Frances, I wish you'd stop suggesting ...'

'I wasn't suggesting one thing. I was just asking a question. I know it's none of my business and Grandpapa wouldn't approve and so on, but if I were you, I'd have a little chat with Bart More.'

'What good would that do?'

'It might,' I said, 'stop you both from being somewhat hæmademen-tic.'

'I'm not—am I?'

I shrugged.

She said soberly, 'I'd hate to hurt him.'

I decided that enforced promises could be treated with ever increasing reservations. 'I've a hunch he might feel the same about you. For two people who don't want to hurt each other,' I added quickly as we heard Hannah's returning footsteps, 'you're both doing a pretty bad job.'

Hannah apologized for being so long. 'Some one swiped my kettle for her hottie.'

'A hottie? To-night? It's far too warm,' I protested.

She said I only thought that because I had been racing round O.P. 'The temperature's been falling all evening. The summer's gone on much too long. It probably ended this afternoon.'

Hannah was right. The summer did end that day. And so, apparently, did my friendship with the Professor. He did not write or telephone, or appear in the park, car park, or hospital grounds, on any of the innumerable occasions when I haunted all three places. I even risked using the Dean's private exit. That got me nothing but a ricked ankle, and torn nylons, when I slipped on the steps in my anxiety to get away before any hospital authority discovered what I was doing. The days turned to weeks, the weeks to one month—then another. I used every kind of excuse for him. He was very busy, on holiday, had been transferred to some other city, ill, had an accident, abroad on business. I tried to persuade myself that my instincts were wrong. He had not been saying good-bye properly that day in the park. He only meant he was glad we had met that afternoon. One of these fine days he would get bored with crossword puzzles, remember me, and I would get another letter—perhaps more tickets—or bird photographs.

I received nothing at all from him, and as the second month of silence ended, I forced myself to face the truth. I had always expected that one day he would be bored by our relationship. That day had arrived, and there was nothing I could do about it.

Those first two months in O.P. were the most unhappy months of my life, in or out of hospital. I found departmental nursing quite interesting, but totally lacking in the human side of nursing that you get in the wards. Our patients were all strangers to me; the endless clinics reminded me more of a factory than a hospital; and because I was the only member of my set in O.P., I was very much on my own on duty, and almost as much off duty, since my free time seldom coincided with the ward nurses. Estelle in the theatre was in much the same state where off-duty was concerned, but she had taken to the theatre, and seemed happier than I had ever known her, when we met occasionally at meals or for tea at night. Bart wandered through O.P. roughly once a week, waved at me as amicably as ever, but apart from that vanished from my life almost as completely as the Professor had done. In a hospital as large as Martha's it was far easier not to see than to see a given person, if you worked in separate departments. Each ward and department was its own private world. Out-Patients was notoriously a difficult world.

Oddly enough I got on far better with Sister than I would ever have dared to hope. She was very exacting, but she was also fair. She never expected me to know anything during my first month; never left me in any doubt about what she wanted me to do; and so long as I obeyed her in every detail, not only made no complaint, but sometimes even smiled at me. 'You're learning, child. You're putting your mind to your work. That's what I like to see.'

There was one great disadvantage about her approval, it accentuated Vickers' original disapproval of my presence in O.P. I had hoped she would grow out of this, but the reverse was what actually happened. 'I simply cannot understand why Sister bothers over you, Dorland,' she protested one morning after Sister had checked my setting of the S.M.O.'s clinic-room. 'It's such a waste of every one's time.'

I had never attempted to query her comments until then, as I had been afraid if I did I might lose my temper. I was feeling quite bucked about that clinic that particular morning and genuinely puzzled by her remarks, so I dropped my rule. 'Presumably, Sister feels she has to train me, Nurse?'

She looked me over. 'You do think you're so clever with your meek little pro act, don't you? Personally, I like people to be honest!'

I stared after her as she swept out. 'What the devil did she mean by that?' I demanded of the heart-trolley.

Neal appeared in the doorway. 'Did you say something, Dorland?'

'Just thinking aloud, Nurse.'

She smiled. 'Careful. Can be dangerous,' and walked on.

I smiled after her. She was the one person who made O.P.'s tolerable. She treated us all in the same pleasant manner, and often chatted as if we were the same set when we were alone. But, being a staff nurse, she was inevitably far too senior for me to chat to her or run to when I wanted a good laugh, wild grumble, or the odd furious tear, all of which I had shared with Estelle in Josephine. The four senior girls had never relaxed their original frigid attitude towards me, but this never upset me as their behaviour was only to be expected from fourth-years. Probably, not even Vickers would have upset me if I had heard from the Professor, but his silence and what lay behind that silence nagged me like a toothache.

I could not get him out of my mind no matter how hard I tried. And I did try. The early mornings and late evenings in O.P.'s were the blackest periods. From nine A.M. until seven P.M. we were occupied with clinics; in my off-duty there was always a lecture to attend or write-up; on my days off at home, the turkey season was working up for Christmas and no one sits around day-dreaming on a busy turkey farm when plucking-time is drawing near; at night I was too tired to stay awake. But during those cleaning hours in the department when my hands were occupied, but my mind free, I came close to wishing I had never gone up that hill. If this was love I did not want it. It hurt too much.

One Saturday evening around eight-thirty I was checking and dusting the cylinders in the oxygen cupboard when I heard Vickers calling for me.

'What do you want Dorland for?' asked Nurse Simpson from the stock-room next door. Simpson had not been transferred as we all expected, and was acting Staff Nurse for the week-end.

'To help me finish the linen-room, Nurse.'

'Finish it yourself,' said Simpson sharply. 'It's Four's job, not Five's. Let the poor girl get on with her own work, and you get on with yours. And while you're here, Vickers, I may as well say what I've been meaning to say for ages. You're being much too tough with Dorland, and very dense. She's not a bad kid and never steps out of line. We thought she might at first, but she's shown us her private life is her affair, which it is. You ought to have enough sense to realize you're playing with fire, narking at her as you do. If Sister heard you, she'd be furious. None of us are supposed to know anything—and we wouldn't know anything if Tom Neal hadn't told his wife. I promised Neal it wouldn't go any farther.'

'It hasn't gone any farther, Nurse,' muttered Vickers sullenly.

'I should ruddy well think not! It's the top secret of Martha's. Don't you forget it. And don't forget that if Dorland felt bitchy—and I wouldn't blame her after your cracks—she could pull a string that would land you in Matron's office just like that! Now go and get on with your linen, and leave that kid alone.'

I leant against the nearest cylinder, and dropped my duster. I did not attempt to pick it up for at least two minutes. And when I did recover my mental and physical breath it took all the self-control I possessed to make me go on with my checking and dusting, and not burst into the stock-room to ask Simpson what on earth she was talking about. What strings could I pull? Why? And what was all this about Tom Neal? I knew Neal's husband was called Tom—but had never seen him.

When nine o'clock came I was a living question mark. I had to find some one who could explain this to me, and the obvious person was Bart. If he could not answer me at once, he could find out, being free to roam the hospital, and from what I gathered on chatting terms with the entire staff.

I went straight to Estelle's room when I reached the Home, intending to ask if he was on theatre call for the week-end or at his digs. If he was on-call I could ring him; if not, the porters would know his address. I would write and ask him to ring me.

Estelle's room was empty. She must have gone out in a great hurry because her cap and apron were lying on the floor. She was far too tidy a person to leave anything lying about without good reason. I picked them up absently, dropped them in her laundry basket, and wondered if she had a date with Bart. It must have been suddenly arranged because she was at second supper, and had not said anything about going out. Perhaps she was treating her promise to Grandpapa with reservations too. If so, though I could see her grandfather's point, I was all for it.

I went along to Hannah's room and was surprised to find her in bed. 'Hallo? Did you get off early?'

'No.' She smiled, but did not sit up. 'I thought I'd give my poor feet a rest.'

I sat on the end of her bed and looked at her anxiously. 'Are you all right? You never want to rest.'

She said she had a cold coming. 'I've had a wretched head all evening. My throat's sore-ish. I'll be fine after a good sleep.'

'You look a bit pink. Think you've a temp.?'

'Doubt it. I never have a temp. Stop flapping, girl.' She moved her wrist out of range as I reached for her pulse. 'I was hoping you'd come in. I've got some terrific news. Where do you think our Estelle is?'

'I was just going to ask you. Date?'

She grinned. 'She has. With Matron. Poor old girl, she was in such a dither. I've never known her like it, before. I think that's what made her open up. She said I could tell you, but no one else.'

'Tell what? And why Matron? At this hour? What's she done?'

'Honest to God, girl! Will you give me a chance? She hasn't done anything. It's about the new block. Guess what?'

'What?'

'Matron wants to see her about the opening date. Her grandpapa has donated it—can you imagine that! Apparently he's always wanted it to be anonymous, then something's made him change his mind. She had a letter this morning from him saying he's going to allow us to call it the Dexter Wing, and is coming along here for the opening, and the reception.'

My brain gave an almost audible click. 'That's what Simpson was getting at! Tom Neal must have heard it somehow—' and I explained.

'Neal? He works in the Central Lab. He would know. That Lab.'s shifting to the new block.' She beamed at me. 'The Dexter Block. Can't you just see us all basking in its reflected glory! And poor old Estelle looked utterly crushed—you'd think Grandpapa had done something shameful. She made me swear blind I'd only tell you. She's scared stiff of it getting round before the last possible moment.'

'It's round O.P. already.'

'Then don't tell her. You know what she's like about her cash.'

I nodded. 'Grandpapa can't be too grim if he goes round donating new blocks to hospitals.'

'People can have generous sides as well as tough sides. Take Marcus Everly. You know what a so-and-so he's supposed to be? Well, did you know he gave not only the P.T.S. house, but that whole hill to the hospital?'

'Did he now? How did you hear that?'

She laughed. 'Dear Fay heard Sister Robert saying something about it to Sister Arthur.'

'What would we do without our Fay to tell us what's going on! I should have gone to her at once when I overheard Simpson! But, Hannah, aren't they crazy? As if I'd run to Estelle, or she'd run to Grandpapa, because Vickers is being foul to me! Bats. All of them.' I stretched lazily. 'So old Marcus gave us the hospital? Maybe that's why Hamilton Dexter bunged in the new block? Must be fun to be like that. Take this mountain, chum—and how about a new hospital? Two million? Why not?'

She laughed again, then sat forward, and rubbed her neck. 'Ouch. That hurt. My glands are getting worse.'

I considered her seriously. 'I'm not sure I like the look of you, duckie. Relax. Nurse is going to get a thermometer.'

I met Sylvia Franks in the corridor. She was looking worried. 'Frances, have you got a thermometer?'

I stopped. 'I was just going to find one for Hannah. Some one else feeling ill?'

'Alice has a wicked throat. It's her day off, and she's been lying down most of the day. I think she ought to report it. What's up with Hannah?'

I explained. 'There must be some mighty queer bugs around this corridor. Wonder who'll be the third?'

Estelle stepped out of the lift. 'Hallo, girls.' Her smile was weary as she came slowly towards us. 'Any tea going? I'm dehydrated plus. I don't know what the temperature was in the theatre to-night, I do know I've never known it so hot.' She fingered her forehead. 'It's given me a splitting head.'

Sylvia and I exchanged glances. I asked. 'Got a sore throat? Any aches and pains?'

'How did you guess? My throat isn't too bad—my back's ready to break in two.'

We told her about the others. I touched her arm experimentally. 'You're even warmer than Hannah. You get to bed fast. I was on my way to borrow your thermometer. Can I get it and take your temp. too?'

She was obviously too ill to argue. 'If you say so.'

Sylvia borrowed the thermometer for Alice Linton while I helped Estelle into bed. 'I wonder what bug you girls have picked up.'

' 'Flu or something. Did Hannah get a chance to tell you about Matron?'

'Yes. Estelle, I really am thrilled! I'd adore to have a Dorland Block. Was Matron nice?'

'Very,' she replied flatly.

I hung her cloak in her cupboard then turned to look at her properly. She was clearly sickening for something, but she sounded very much more ill than she looked. 'Is this honestly being hell for you?'

She closed her eyes. 'Grandpapa's timing always was perfect.'

'His timing? What's that got to do with—' I broke off, suddenly understanding. 'Bart? Have you told Grandpapa about Bart?'

'No.' She opened her eyes. 'I've just told Bart about Grandpapa. Right now—when I came out of Matron's office.'

I sat on her bed. 'So you're on speaking terms at last?'

'Have been for some time.' A smile flickered through her eyes. 'Since your pep-talk. It's been quite fun in the theatre. Sister Theatre says she's never known such a keen dresser.'

'Sister Josephine could say the same. You must be doing that lad a power of good, Estelle.'

The little smile vanished. 'If you could have seen him ten minutes ago, you wouldn't have said that. For the record, the Dexter Block is the last straw.'

'But why?'

'If you can think of a better way of reminding him who I am, I can't. He said so himself.'

'My dear, he'll get over it.'

She patted my hand. 'You're a nice soul, dear, but you still believe in fairies. I don't.'

Her touch reminded me belatedly of her temperature. 'We can't go into this properly now; we'll work something out later. Don't get too gloomy, it'll send up your temp. I'll go and see where Sylvia's got to with that thermometer.'

Sylvia came out of Hannah's room as I walked into the corridor. 'Hannah's just over a hundred. Alice is a hundred and two.' She returned with me to Estelle. 'You do look muzzy, Estelle. You must be higher than Alice.'

Estelle said she felt muzzy, but her temperature was not as high as Alice's. Sylvia shook down her thermometer. 'You go for Home Sister, Frances. She likes you. I'll stay.'

Home Sister was perturbed. 'All three, Nurse? I'll come up now.' She was even more perturbed when Dr Spence, the S.M.O., diagnosed scarlet fever. 'Dear, dear, dear,' we heard her cluck as she and the S.M.O. walked slowly towards the lift at the end of our corridor, 'how unfortunate! I hope these are not the first batch of a scarlet fever epidemic.'

Sylvia and I exchanged another of the many glances we had been exchanging for the past half-hour as the S.M.O. said he hoped not, too. 'Most sincerely. But I doubt we'll escape one. Where do those three nurses work?'

'Nurse Dexter in the General Theatre; Nurse Linton in Arthur Ward; Nurse More in Josephine Ward.'

'Two wards and one department, plus all the nurses on this floor, and the dining-room staff are already close contacts.' He sounded resigned. 'The infection's over half the hospital already. I wish I knew where they picked it up.'

'You've had no patients develop it?'

'No.' Through the crack in my slightly open door we watched him smooth his prematurely thinning hair thoughtfully. 'I only hope they picked it up outside, and we haven't a carrier in our midst. Are they particular friends? Do they go out together? It's hard to see the connexion between the general theatre, a male orthopædic and female medical.'

Sister said Nurse Dorland was Nurse Dexter's great friend and she was sure I could answer his question.

'Nurse Dorland? Could I see her, Sister?'

Sylvia murmured, 'This I must watch. I'll have to copy your technique, Frances ...' then stepped back behind the door as Home Sister knocked. 'Are you there, Nurse? Come along.'

The S.M.O. asked me immediately if I had had scarlet.

'Yes, Doctor.'

'That's something.' He smiled briefly. 'Now about your three friends. Have you any ideas where they could have met the same contact?'

Home Sister gave me an encouraging nod, as if I was a small child about to repeat a lesson. 'Think hard, Nurse.'

At which my mind inevitably went blank. 'I can't remember ...' I broke off. 'Oh, yes. They went to a film together on Wednesday morning. The Press showing of that new children's film. They said, apart from the critics, they were the only adults in the audience.'

Dr Spence looked relieved. 'The ideal place to pick up any of the infectious diseases. Wednesday would be right for scarlet. Good.' He nodded at Sister. 'Let's hope that's the answer, Sister. I'll ring up the M.O.H.'s office later and find if any school cases have been notified. I'm pretty certain the answer'll be yes. There's always the isolated case about. Well—thank you, Nurse. Good night, Sister. I'll fix up about the ambulance. Expect it in forty minutes.'

Sister waited until the lift carried him downward, then returned to me. 'Nurse Franks may help you pack for your three friends, Nurse. I shall be going with the nurses in the ambulance. When we have gone I want you both to have baths, wash your hair, leave all the clothes you are wearing now soaking in disinfectant in the first bathroom, and then label the bathroom 'out of bounds.' You'll see to that, Nurse? Good girl.'

Sylvia bounced out of my room when Sister vanished. 'The old girl eats out of your hand, Frances! Why?'

'Search me. Maybe she wants a turkey for Christmas.'

An Office Sister arrived on our floor a few minutes later. When the porters arrived for the three girls, she helped Sylvia and I to strip their beds. 'The bedding will have to be stoved. Put it in the first bathroom for now. I'll lock these doors for to-night. The fumigating can wait until morning. Good night, Nurses. Thank you for your help.'

Sylvia said I could have the bath first as she wanted to wash her hair in the hand-basin. 'I can't bear shampoo dripping down my back.'

I turned on the bath and shed my uniform. 'What do we do with our halos? Soak 'em in carbolic, too?'

'No. They'd tarnish.' She grinned. 'Do tell me—since when have you had this magic touch with blue dresses? I don't remember Sister P.T.S. oozing charm at every pore when you were around, but now you're obviously the Sister's pin-up. Do you suppose they all want turkeys for Christmas?'

'Expect so.' I tested the water, absently thinking of the three girls. 'I hope they aren't going to be ill.'

'No one's ill with scarlet these days.' She plunged her head into the basin. 'All the same, Estelle looked pretty ill, even though her temp. was only a hundred and one.'

'She did.' I relaxed, and let the warm water soak up the back of my head; that is, I relaxed physically, not mentally. I was too genuinely worried about Estelle to do that. I had not had much nursing experience, but I had had enough in Josephine to recognize how people look when they are, or are about to be, very ill. Estelle had worn that look when she was wheeled to the lift. The little she had been able to tell me about her conversation with Bart might have accounted for some of the wretchedness in her appearance, but surely not for all? 'I wish I knew some medicine.'

'Don't panic, Frances. Leave that to the S.M.O.' She reached for a towel, and scattered shampoo suds all over the floor. 'They haven't got the plague—though no one would guess they hadn't after all the fun and games we've had up here to-night.'

Some one banged violently on the door. 'Frances, are you in there?' demanded Agatha Carter's voice.

'In the bath and washing my hair. Why?'

'Bart More's on the internal phone. He wants you.'

'Oh, no! Tell him he can't have me—no ...' I suddenly realized I wanted to talk to Bart very much. I would have preferred knocking his well-shaped head against the nearest stone wall, but since he was larger than I was, I realized I should have little hope of doing that. 'Agatha, explain I'm all wet. Ask him to hang on. Say I want to talk to him, too.'

'I will.'

Sylvia wound the towel round her dripping hair. 'I suppose he's heard about Hannah?'

'Probably,' I agreed untruthfully to save argument. 'Chuck me that other towel, please.'

'Frances!' Agatha was at the door again. 'Are you out?'

'Yes?'

'You can get back in. He can't wait. He's got to get a train that leaves in fifteen minutes. He said he just called to let you know he was making tracks. He'll let you know when he gets back.'

'Blast the man!' I opened the door furiously. 'He might either have let me bath in peace or at least waited to hear about Hannah and the others.'

'What about Hannah?' Fay Kinsley appeared behind Agatha. They were both in mufti. 'And what are you two doing in there? Turning the place into a Turkish bath?'

Sylvia looked at me and began to laugh. I was very cross with Bart and worried about Estelle, but I had to laugh with her. For the first time in our hospital career, Fay had to come to us for news. 'Keep back,' we spluttered, 'we're unclean—we've been in contact with the plague.'

Fay looked gloriously prim. 'What is all this nonsense?'

We told her. 'You should have been in, Fay,' added Sylvia. 'It was some party. Dr Spence, Home Sister, an Office Sister, porters, ambulance men—the lot. It's too bad you missed it.'

Fay said she considered us utterly cold-blooded and adolescent. 'I thought Estelle and Hannah were your friends, Frances. You might at least pretend to be upset instead of just standing there draped like a French movie star laughing your head off.'

'I might,' I agreed, 'if I wasn't so cold-blooded. I'm not just cold, I'm iced. Come in if you must, but forgive me. I'm getting back into the bath.'

One of them slammed the door at that. Sylvia leant against it, laughing weakly. 'There's only one thing for you to do. Don't wait until Christmas. Send her a turkey right now.'

9. *Text-books can be Wrong*

Dr Spence was right. By the end of the next week Martha's was hit by what every one hoped would be a minor epidemic. Half-way through the following week a major staff crisis developed. As the incubation period for scarlet fever was short, a steady trickle of nurses, students, and housemen vanished in ambulances to the fever hospital on the other side of London, and in their absence a general post went on among the remaining hospital staff.

We remained unaffected in Out-Patients until the middle of that second week. Simpson, our head nurse, was sent on night-duty in Alberta; Wade, O.P. Two, was removed to the orthopædic theatre. Sister O.P. rearranged all the work among the four of us left to her, and that evening Vickers went down with scarlet.

Next morning Nurse Carver, head nurse and O.P. One, actually smiled at me. 'As you alone have had it, Dorland, you'll probably find yourself coping with the lot in O.P.'

Nurse Stevens, O.P. Two and Three, who had never addressed an unnecessary word to me before, asked, 'Think you'll enjoy being kin to the Ancient Mariner, Dorland?'

I had barely time to recover from this double shock when I had a third, and far more shattering one. Sister O.P. appeared in the changing-room. It was half-past seven in the morning; she was not due on duty for another hour; I had never seen her with her cuffs off.

She came in rolling her sleeves high. 'Let me have Nurse Vickers' cleaning tin, Nurse. Now then—I'll clean the fracture and skin room. You get on with your routine. Nurse Neal has just started stocking and testing.'

Carver noticed my expression, and lowered one eyelid. A little later she stopped in the children's room doorway. 'Sister's always like this in a crisis. She can be murder when all's going well ...'

'And when she finds her nurses gossiping at this hour of the morning!' Sister's awesome figure suddenly loomed behind Carver. 'Get on with your work at once, Nurse Carver!'

Carver apologized and vanished. Sister came a couple of steps into the room, and watched me scrubbing a glass trolley. 'That's cloudy, child!'

'I'm sorry, Sister.' I put down my brush, and took up the soft cloth I used for polishing glass. The cloth was damp with much use; the glass remained cloudy.

Sister watched me impassively. 'How many more trolleys have you to do?'

'Seven, Sister.' I rubbed violently, and waited for the inevitable lecture on the inefficiency of junior nurses.

'I presume Sister P.T.S. taught you to scrub and polish glass trolleys as you are doing, Nurse?'

'Yes, Sister.' I was still waiting.

'You must always do as you were taught in the P.T.S., Nurse. You carry on with your work. I will do these two for you. Will you kindly find me some clean newspaper and methylated spirit?'

I gaped at her momentarily, then rushed to collect her requests.

She received the newspaper and spirit with a brisk nod. 'Carry on with your work, Nurse.' She poured the spirit on the first glass shelf, crumpled the newspaper, rubbed the shelf briskly, then held it to the light. It was spotless. 'An aseptic and quick, if unorthodox method, Nurse,' she barked. She dealt with the second shelf, then the second trolley. 'Finish the others, quickly, Nurse.' She glanced at the bottle of spirit, nodded to me and swept out.

I did not hesitate. I put down my soft rag, and never scrubbed another glass trolley in O.P.

Vickers' absence, and the scarlet epidemic transformed life in Out-Patients. Instead of being a strained department, it became positively hilarious. Sister's temper improved hourly, her bark was almost jovial. Neal was pleasant as ever. Carver and Stevens treated me

as if I was one of their set. I found myself looking forward to going on
duty instead of dreading it, as previously, and genuinely regretting going
off at the end of each day. Our corridor seemed so empty without Estelle
and Hannah, and the seven others of my set who had scarlet; the nights
were far too long and too quiet.

Possibly because we really were over-working in O.P., for the first
time in my life I was suffering from insomnia. And so I had time to
think and think about the Professor. And think I did as I stared at the
black ceiling, and my thoughts were far blacker than the darkness
around me.

It was fairly easy to be sensible about him by day; there was no time
to be anything else. Every morning I faced the fact that I was never
going to hear from him again; every night that fact made me twist and
turn until my pillow felt heavy as lead and my well-sprung mattress
stuffed with sawdust.

I dreaded the nights so much that I began looking forward to Bart's
return from wherever it was he had gone. It was too cold for sitting on
park benches now, but he could have stood me a cup of coffee in some
dockside café. Once I even went along to the Casualty porters to ask if
they had his address.

Sam the head porter scratched his head. 'Mr More's gone on his
holidays, Nurse. He didn't leave no address with us, but the Dean'll have
one if you wants to reach him.'

I thought this over for twenty-four hours then decided I did not want
to reach him. I wrote a short letter telling him about the girls.

> According to Home Sister, they're doing nicely. I miss them a lot,
> and want to see you. Ring me when you can, but make it after eight
> P.M. I'm seldom off before then any day, these days.

I added a P.S.

> Sam says you're on holiday. What on earth are you doing having a
> holiday so close to Finals? If Galahad's big-game hunting in darkest
> Africa to forget, wouldn't he be more sensible to come back and
> qualify?

I called in at Home Sister's office on my way out to the post that
night. Nurse Charles, the assistant Home Sister, was at the desk. 'Sister
is over at the fever hospital, Nurse Dorland'—she seemed very grave—
'so I'm afraid I can give you no report on the nurses until she gets back.'

I could not understand why she should look so serious; we had all
heard our girls and the various men were doing reasonably well. But she
was a sober person who took life grimly so I thought no more of it,
thanked her and crossed the road to post my letter.

Sister O.P. looked grim when she joined us for cleaning next morning. I caught her looking at me a couple of times, and wondered what I had done wrong. She was a very much more human person these days, but she was still Sister O.P. and Sister O.P. never lets anything pass.

At ten-past-nine a strange second-year came into the fracture-room. 'Are you Dorland? Will you go to Sister? I'm from Cas. I'm to take over from you with this clinic.'

'Right, Nurse. I say—do you know why?'

She shrugged. 'No one tells me anything.'

Sister was in her office. 'Come in, Nurse.' She looked me over. 'You are very white, child. Do you feel well?'

'Yes, thank you, Sister.'

'I don't believe you, Nurse. You are much too pale. Go off for two hours and have some fresh air. Walk by the river. Come back at eleven with some colour in your cheeks. Off you go!'

I did not feel at all like going off or taking a walk by the river. It was a dull grey morning, raining fitfully and a sharp east wind was blowing up from the docks. But no one disobeyed Sister O.P., even if the hospital was in the middle of a scarlet epidemic. I went back to the home to leave my cap and fetch a mackintosh.

As I opened our front door Mrs Higgs leant out of her lodge. 'There you are, Nurse Dorland! Good. I've just been ringing your floor. Call for you. Go into Three and I'll put the gentleman through.'

My immediate thought was that Bart had got my letter. I picked up the receiver in Three and realized he could not have had time, unless he was back in the hospital. 'Bart, you're back. I'm so glad. Did you get my letter?' I asked without waiting for him to announce himself. I had no doubts about my caller's identity. Bart was the only man who had telephoned me in months.

'I'm sorry, Frances,' said the Professor's voice as calmly as if we had met five minutes and not two months ago; 'it's me—Slane.'

I thought myself too shaken for speech; I had not realized how deep my training had already gone. I heard my voice say equally calmly, 'It's my fault for jumping to conclusions. I was expecting Bart More to ring me—or rather I hoped he'd ring me. How are you?'

He said he was very well and had been out of town for a while. 'And you?'.

'Oh, fine, thanks.'

'And the hospital?'

I said the hospital was not so good and explained why.

'Scarlet fever? Sounds most unpleasant.'

I leant against the glass wall and blinked to see if I was awake. Nurse Charles scuttled across the hall carrying a vase of flowers. I was awake. I should never dream about poor old Nurse Charles. 'Luckily, it's not very serious these days with the sulfa drugs and what not,' I said, quoting all I had heard from my fellow nurses during the past two weeks. 'Estelle and Hannah should be coming out soon. They were in the first batch.'

'Indeed? I saw Hamilton Dexter having breakfast at my club this morning. I suppose,' he asked casually, 'he's in town because of his granddaughter's illness?'

'I shouldn't think she's ill enough for that. Perhaps he's up on business.'

'Possibly.' He was silent momentarily; then he added in a rather odd tone, 'Is one quite out of danger from complication by the end of the second week? I had it when I was sixteen—I seem to remember there being some fuss about the second and third week.'

'Really?' It seemed so natural to be chatting to him again, and he was chatting so naturally, that the long empty weeks that had filled the endless two months since our last meeting faded like last night's dream. 'I honestly don't even know my fevers. We haven't had our lectures on them yet.'

'Couldn't More give you the details?'

'He should be able to—if I knew where he was. He's taken a holiday of all crazy things. Just vanished. He doesn't even know anyone's got scarlet for all I know.'

There was another small silence. 'Vanished? How's that?'

I told him the truth, if not all the truth.

'So after hearing what you describe as an overwhelming bit of news, he took himself off? I follow his reasoning.'

I looked across at Mrs Higgs and wondered why I had never realized she had such a pleasant face before. 'I can't. He ought to realize he's hurting her badly.'

'But does he?'

I had to be fair. 'I rather doubt it. That's why I want to see him.'

'So you wrote care of the Dean? That was intelligent.'

'Not really. Sam, our head porter, gave me that tip. Our porters,' I added cheerfully, as happiness broke through properly and I realized I was actually talking to him again, 'are incurably sentimental. They see themselves as so many blue-jacketed cupids.'

He said he was sure they must be exceedingly helpful under certain circumstances. 'And now I must tell you why I've bothered you with this call.'

I stiffened. He was obviously married; going abroad for years; emigrating. 'I'm afraid I've been talking too much, as usual.'

'No. No. In point of fact I thought I'd give you a ring to ask how you were getting on. It's a long while since I heard from you, and, being back again, I thought it might be an idea to find out if all was well with you. Is it?'

I hesitated. I could not conceivably tell him the truth or remind him that he had been the person to write, since the last letter in our correspondence had been written by me. 'I—I think so, thank you.'

'You don't sound very sure.'

'Life,' I said tritely, 'is always full of problems.'

'I know. You think everything's splendid, turn a corner, and there's life waiting for you with a sandbag.' He paused, then asked with strange abruptness, 'Have you got a good memory?'

'It's sort of photographic. I remember things as pictures.'

He did not tell me, as anyone else would have done, that I was repeating myself unnecessarily. He merely said, 'That's convenient. Then can you recollect one letter I wrote you in your P.T.S.? In the days when we were dealing with curdled custards? In case you've forgotten—which is only too probable, since you must have many other things to remember—it was a letter in which I said I'd be happy to help out with any problems. You've obviously been too busy to take me up on that recently, but if you should'—he paused again—'need help, let me know.'

I had often read about people's hearts bounding against their ribs in moments of emotional stress. I never believed it actually happened. It happened, all right. 'It's very kind of you. I haven't liked to keep on bothering you.'

'Frances,' he said slowly, 'I'm going to tell you something. When a man gets to my age he seldom says and never writes anything he doesn't mean. So don't forget what I've said. I'm glad you are well. I hope young More returns soon. I'm pretty sure he will. Good-bye—but remember, if you want to get in touch with me you know where to find me.' And before I could even thank him for phoning he had rung off.

Sister O.P. gave me an approving nod when I returned at eleven. 'The fresh air has done you good, Nurse. You look a different child. Go along and help Nurse Neal with the skins.'

I had only spent one hour in the skin-clinic when Sister summoned me once more. 'You are making up your lost off-duty to-day, Nurse. Matron wishes you to go on night-duty in William MacPherson to-night. And for the next hour you are to go to Casualty. Go along there now.'

Sister Casualty looked doubtfully at my first-year belt. 'You've not worked here before, Nurse? Oh, well. We're lucky to have you. Go and help with the dressings in Room 15. The senior dressers are in there. They'll be very useful to you.'

The masked dressers, with sleeves rolled high and ties buttoned in their shirts, greeted me like old friends. It took me a few minutes to realize they were old friends. They had been clerks in Josephine. 'Have you heard John Jones has been smitten with the plague?' one asked.

'The Jones in Josephine? Our houseman?'

'That's our John! What with old Curtis having been called over, the entire cardiac firm seems to be moving across to fevers.'

'Dr Curtis called over? Who for?'

None of them knew. They shook their heads, I shook mine. We agreed that whoever needed Dr Curtis had had his—or her—chips. There was no slur on Dr Curtis in that reflection. He was considered one of the best cardiologists in England by outsiders; at Martha's we considered him far away the best; but the fact that another hospital had sent for him automatically meant that the medical staff of that hospital were very worried. Hospitals seldom call in consultants from other hospitals, except, it was generally accepted, as a last hope.

I looked round the dressing-room. It was filled to capacity with men with minor injuries. 'Who's the houseman?'

At that moment Dr Perry the Senior Out-Patients Officer walked in. 'Sorry I'm late, gentlemen.' He nodded my way, then recognized me. 'You an exile too, Nurse? Let's get on. Forgive the delay'—he washed his hands—'but I've had to do a round in place of Dr Jones. I suppose you've heard he has it?'

'Yes. I'm so sorry.' I handed him a towel.

'Thanks.' He dried his fingers carefully. 'It's tough all round. The S.M.O. looks fit to drop this morning. You've heard about Dr Curtis? Rough, that. Well—who's first?' He glanced through the pile of admission cards on the standing desk. 'Who's Mr J. A. Holloway?'

A man in a wheel-chair by the far sink held up one hand. 'Here, Doctor.'

Dr Perry walked over to him. 'What've you been doing to this foot, man? Dropping bricks on it?'

Mr Holloway grinned. 'That's right, sir.'

'Were you wearing this?' Dr Perry picked up a discarded boot and examined it. 'Stout. Good. Let's hope it's saved you a fracture.' He wrote rapidly on a card. 'Nurse. X-Ray in a chair, please. Wet plates back here. Next?'

It seemed only five minutes later that Sister Casualty was beckoning me from the door. 'Thank you for your help, Nurse. You must go to lunch. I'll take over in here.'

I went back to Out-Patients for my cloak, walked out of the department into the main corridor, and Bart.

I jumped back. 'The very man I want to see. When did you get back? I suppose you've had no chance of getting my letter?'

He looked at me in a peculiar fashion. He seemed dazed. 'Letter? I haven't had any letter from you.'

'I've just said—you haven't had time. I only posted it last night. It was to tell you about Estelle.'

He said dully, 'So you know?'

'Of course, I know she's got scarlet. She was in the original batch. But, Bart—why did you have to vanish?'

He looked up and down the corridor. 'I've got to talk to you, Frances. When are you off?'

'I'm on my way to lunch now. I want to talk to you too. It'll have to keep until afterwards.'

'What I have to say can't keep. Come to the canteen.'

'I can't—'

'You've got to,' he said simply. 'Come.'

I looked at him momentarily, then did as he said. I did not know what was wrong; I only knew from his expression that, whatever it was, it was very wrong. I went with him to the canteen. We chose a table against the far wall. We did not bother to eat or drink anything.

He sat down stiffly as if he was very old. 'I don't believe you can know about Estelle.'

I sat very still. 'What about her?'

He avoided my eyes. 'Curtis has been called in. He saw her last night—again this morning.'

'Curtis? For scarlet?' My voice cracked. 'Why?'

'According to Nigel Curtis'—his voice was without emotion—'she's got suppurative pericarditis. Understand?'

'From scarlet?' He nodded. 'No. At least, I know roughly what it means, but not how she could get it.'

He turned on me savagely, 'God, woman! Don't you know anything? It isn't common—according to the books it occurs, quote, in a small percentage of cases. And she's had to get it. Curtis was hauled in—he hauled in Marcus Everly—they both spent most of last night there. Hamilton Dexter went over with Curtis last night. They sent for him during the evening. You know what that means?'

I said very carefully. 'She's on the D.I.L.?'

'And what the devil else would she be on?' he snapped, with the petulance of extreme anxiety.

I had been so happy since the Professor's phone. Now I was in a nightmare. I had to wake up out of it. I had to discover we were not talking about Estelle. But I was awake—and we were.

'Bart. What's the prognosis?'

He shook his head.

'Bart. There has to be one.'

'All right,' he said bitterly, 'all right. Maybe there is a good one. Maybe I missed it this morning. Maybe I looked in all the wrong books. God, Frances! I looked in the lot. I've been reading up on it since I got back to town just after eight. There's not a ruddy word on it in our library I haven't read. I'm a bloody mine of information on suppurative pericarditis as a rare complication of scarlet fever. And I can't give you a damned answer because I daren't.'

And I dared not think we were talking about Estelle. Women are not supposed to make good friends to each other. I did not know if that was true or not. I only knew I was as saddened as I would have been had she been one of my sisters.

'How did you hear?'

He explained he had been on a walking tour with Nigel Curtis. 'He's in my year. We were in Salisbury last night. Nigel rang his mother just to say hallo. Mrs Curtis gave him the news of the old firm, and said his old man had been called over to see one of the nurses. Since the nurse was Hamilton Dexter's granddaughter, she obviously made news. Nigel passed it on to me.' He lit a cigarette. 'I came up by the first train. Not that there's anything I can do. I just had to be up.'

I was too distressed for coherent thought yet. 'Why has Curtis called in Marcus Everly?'

'Frances, do you have to be so bloody dumb? It's suppurative. That means pus. Pus means bugs. Who's the bug king here?'

I was quite glad to have him storm at me. It acted as a safety valve for him and did not touch me at all.

'What can he do about the bugs?'

'Am I a bleeding pathologist?' He stubbed out his cigarette. 'Frances, I'm sorry. I really am. I shouldn't give you hell like this.'

'That's all right. You're in it—why shouldn't I share it. I like her, too.'

He touched my hand. 'I know.'

We sat in silence. At last I said, 'You had better write to her.'

'Sure.' His lips twisted. 'And maybe send her a lock of my hair?'

'Bart. I'm serious.'

'And what do you think I am?' He pushed his hand through his hair. 'You're a good kid. You mean to be kind. You don't know what she's up against. She's on the D.I., and the mortality rate, for your information, is—'

'I don't want to know it.' I slapped the table with the flat of my hand. 'I refuse to believe Estelle's booked. And I refuse to listen to any more of the nonsense I've listened to before from you about her.' I met his eyes. 'You must write to her. You won't be allowed to see her—but you can write.'

'It's too damn late. She'd be too ill to read. You don't understand.'

'Maybe I don't understand much medicine. Or men. But I know a packet about women, particularly young women. And I have nursed very ill women. The most irrational things can make a power of difference to a very ill woman; I've seen it happen. I'm just talking about what I've seen—get that—and not what I've read up in the books! I haven't read any books. But I've seen things—things like an indigestible cake cooked by some miserable husband who has never done so much as the washing-up before, or a bunch of withered dandelions, or a get-well card in smudged capitals with finger-marks all over it. I've seen these things sway the balance with the women in Josephine. I remember three women'—I had to stop for breath—'three D.I. women, who were too weak to hold an envelope or read, but not too weak to read the writing on that envelope, smiling when they should have been dead. We used to read them their letters, then prop their envelopes on their bed-tables so that they could lie and look at them. Don't tell me what the books say! I don't give a damn! I'm telling you what actually happens in real life!'

'But—but—it wouldn't make any difference to her.'

I turned on him quite as furiously as he had on me. 'Do you have to be so bloody dumb? Can't you tell when a girl's in love with you?'

He just looked at me, then slowly tapped his chest.

I nodded.

He stood up carefully, as if he had been ill and was not sure his legs would support him. A group of students at the next table watched us openly. We ignored them. We might have been the only two people in the world.

I got on my feet. 'I must go to lunch. I'm on nights to-night.'

'Where?' His voice did not seem to belong to him.

'William MacPherson.'

We walked out of the canteen. In the corridor he stood still. 'I'll be taking a letter over to her this afternoon. If I've any news of her I'll bring it up to Willie Mac. to-night.'

I was breathing as if I had been running hard. 'Good. But what about Night Sister?'

'To hell with her. I'll get up somehow.'

I was very late for lunch. Sister Dining-room was very annoyed. 'It is most inconsiderate of you to be so unpunctual, Nurse Dorland.'

I apologized mechanically, helped myself to a plate of food, and carried it over to the half-empty first-year table.

Sylvia pulled out the chair beside her. 'I'm so glad you've made this meal.'

'Thanks.' I sat down.

She looked at me. 'Frances, what's up? You look queer.'

I said that was how I felt and told her why.

The whole of our table was listening before I had finished; my news spread quickly to the other tables; a strange, strained silence settled over the normally lively dining-room. The silence was in the Home all that afternoon and evening when I lay in bed unable to sleep, watched the sun go down, and thought of Estelle dying.

The hospital smelt different by night. The air was heavy with a mixture of cooking, coal, ether, and iodoform. I wondered how anyone could sleep or work in that atmosphere and if it really was as intolerable as it seemed to me or if acute anxiety had put an edge on my senses. The main corridor was probably no more deserted than was usual for that hour of the night, but as I walked to the dining-room it seemed to be a desolate place. I had asked Nurse Charles for news of Estelle before leaving our Home. She had told me Matron and Home Sister had gone over to the fever hospital; 'I'm afraid,' she added, with the typical hospital understatement that so infuriates the outside world, 'Nurse Dexter is not very well.' I had not been infuriated; I had been frozen with fear. 'Not very well' when translated meant desperately ill.

She need not have said any more after telling me about Matron. Matrons do not leave large general hospitals at eight at night to visit sick members of their staff in other hospitals without good reason. I glanced at her office as I went by. An Office Sister was pinning a notice to the board over the letter pigeon-holes. The lights were on in the outer office, but Matron's private room beyond was in darkness. I could see this because her door was half open—all the office doors in Martha's were left open when their occupants were elsewhere. That darkened room made me wince mentally. I was as scared of Matron as we all were, but because she was out of the hospital I felt as I used to when I was a child, and my mother was out.

At Martha's the night staff took supper in the evening, dinner in the middle of the night, breakfast in the morning. Tea and coffee were provided at all meals. The girl sitting next to me at the junior table told me that some hospitals served breakfast at night and supper in the morning. 'We much prefer it our way round. I expect you will too.' She looked at my belt. 'First-year. First nights?'

'Yes.'

'Poor thing.' She smiled pleasantly. 'I'm Ames. In Henry. Where are you going?'

'William MacPherson.'

She looked at me keenly. 'Are you Dorland?'

'Yes.' I braced myself.

'Isn't Estelle Dexter in your set?'

'Yes.'

'Is it true she's on the D.I.L.?'

'Yes.'

A girl on my other side turned to us. 'Matron's been over there all evening.'

'Oh, God!' said Ames. 'Are you sure, Polly?'

The girl called Polly nodded. 'Poor girl must be on her way out.'

I said nothing. I caught Ames looking at me and then frowning at Polly. 'Dexter's in Dorland's set,' she said simply, and for the rest of that meal no one at our table spoke at all. I thought they were quiet because they were night nurses. It was not until nights later that I discovered that night nurses' meals were hilarious affairs, and permitted to be far more noisy than any in the day-time.

The night senior in William MacPherson was named Nixon. She was a tall, very slim young woman with a cool voice and prim manner. William MacPherson was a male general surgical ward. When the day report was over Nurse Nixon took me into the kitchen. 'Your first night duty, Dorland?'

'Yes, Nurse.'

She handed me a work-list. 'I wrote this out this morning. You had better read it through while the milk's heating for the men's drinks. I'll take you round and give you a quick diagnosis class directly I've got my evening drugs out.'

Her work-list covered both sides of four large sheets of writing-paper. I read it through twice and wondered how any one night would be long enough for me to do all the work listed. I knew I had no hope of remembering it yet, so, as the kitchen was apparently my domain at night, I clipped the pages to a spare bed-ticket and propped it on the dresser. I consulted that list roughly every ten minutes throughout the night. When I did this a little after midnight I found an extra sheet had been added. 'Sorry, no change. B.M.,' was scribbled in pencil across that sheet. I looked at the words for a few seconds, then removed the page and pushed it into my apron bib. I had no feelings at all at that moment. I was not a person; I was a machine in a starched uniform. And because I was a machine I was able to keep up with that work-list.

Once, like the echo of a forgotten song, I remembered how happy I had been after the Profesor's phone call that morning. And then, just as he had said, life had waited for me round the corner with a sandbag. One day, I thought, I'll tell him how prophetic his words have proved. One day. But I did not really believe that day would come. The night was too dark; the ward too dim; and even the patients were shadows.

Nixon came into the kitchen after Night Sister's two A.M. round. 'I didn't realize Dexter was a friend of yours and in your set, Dorland.'

I was cutting bread. I put down the knife. 'Was, Nurse?'

'Sorry—I mean—is.'

I took up the knife carefully as if it was hot. 'Did Night Sister mention how she is, Nurse?'

She hesitated. 'No change yet, I'm afraid. Night Sister met Sir Marcus downstairs just before she came up here. He's on his way over to Dexter now.'

My ignorance brought me close to tears. 'Is that good or bad, Nurse?'

She had been standing in the doorway. She stepped out into the corridor momentarily, looked down towards the quiet ward, came back again. 'I'm no physician, Dorland. I can't honestly answer that. But I am an S.R.N., and I do know that if I was Dexter now there are no two men in the world I'd rather have had by my bedside than John Curtis and Marcus Everly. If she can be hauled back from the gates those two men'll haul her.'

Her expression was so sympathetic, her voice so gentle, I wondered I had ever thought her prim and cool.

'Some one told me this morning—there's no prognosis.'

She came up to the table, and began buttering the bread I had cut. 'Some one might be right, theoretically. In actual fact that's never true. I've spent four years here. I've seen people who were booked walk out of here cured. Not once—dozens of times. I've seen the dying become the living—pass me that empty plate—for no good reason at all on paper. And I've seen other people die, for as little reason. Dexter's in a bad way, but she's young, strong, and must have a tremendous will or she would never have come to work here. Nursing's no sinecure—no gentle art—no soft hands on fevered brows'—she buttered efficiently, stacking as she went—'it's just plain damned hard and badly paid work, with long hours and no glamour. You have to be tough to take it—and tough people don't die easily. You'll be surprised how much it takes to kill a strong human being. Dexter may be facing the last enemy right now as the small hours are on us, but she's strong all right. I don't need to know her, to know that.'

I said, 'She's tough, Nurse.'

'So are John Curtis and Marcus Everly. They won't give up easily, either. They wouldn't for any patient, but they'll hang on just that much longer because she's what she is.'

'Hamilton Dexter's granddaughter?'

'Not that. One of our pros.' She laid a clean, dampened tea-towel over the first filled plate of bread and butter, put it on top of the fridge, and began filling a second plate. 'That's what's hit the hospital. She's one of our girls, and there's not a member of Martha's to-night who isn't thinking, There but for the grace of God go I.' She glanced at me. 'We get used to seeing the patients ill; even used to them dying. When they do we get upset if we know them. We can't get upset for those we don't know. We have to forget them. We'd all have nervous breakdowns if we didn't.' She took another look at the ward, then came back. 'We haven't any D.I.'s up here, but there'll be some in Martha's to-night. There are names on the list every night. They may cast a shadow over their respective wards, but that's as far as it'll go. Yet because one of our first-year pro's may be on the way out, to-night there's a shadow over all Martha's.'

'I thought it would just be over my set.' I reached into the bread-bin for another loaf. 'And her friends and family.'

'She's one of our girls,' Nixon said again. 'So we're all part of the family. That's why Matron, Home Sister, John Curtis, and Marcus Everly are all up and over there with her. And there's not one pundit on our staff who wouldn't be out of his bed to-night at the drop of a hat, if he was called in. Good hospitals look after their own. This is a very good hospital.' She had finished buttering. She covered the last plate and washed her hands. 'When you've cleared up in here, come into the ward. There's something I have to show you.'

'About Dexter, Nurse?' I asked urgently.

'Take a grip, Dorland,' she said not unkindly. 'I know you aren't with us at all just now—all the same, take a grip. We've got work to do. Even if we feel like weeping we've no time for tears. Get rid of those bread-crumbs and join me in the ward. I've got to show you how to write a night report. Night Sister insists all juniors learn that during their first night on.'

I apologized. 'Yes, Nurse. Thank you.'

10. A Man with a Microscope

There was a weighing machine in one of the ward bathrooms. It was an old-fashioned machine, a cross between a wheel-barrow and an armchair. The bathroom had white tiles on the walls, green tiles on the floor, and was the room in which the night junior in William MacPherson folded, counted, and listed the soiled linen used in the past twenty-four hours at half-past four every morning. The soiled linen was the final routine item on the list Nixon had made for me. At five we officially started work.

I finished with ten minutes to spare. I spent those minutes sitting on the weighing machine, too weary for anxiety or even coherent thought.

To keep awake I counted the floor tiles, then the walls, one at a time. 'Eighteen—nineteen—Estelle's nineteen and perhaps she's dead, so she was nineteen—I won't think of that now—twenty—twenty-one—the Professor's forty-two—I wish he was here—I'll write ...'

'Dorland! What are you talking about?' Nixon came in. 'And just what do you think you're doing in that machine? Don't you know you never sit down on duty?'

I stood up stiffly. 'Sorry, Nurse.' I yawned. 'I forgot.'

'Don't forget again,' she said sternly. 'I don't mind your sitting down—you can lie down for all I care—but if you or any other night junior sits at this hour you'll inevitably go clean off to sleep. Martha's night nurses do not drop asleep on duty—and that I do care about. If you feel exhausted lean against something—never sit. If you pass out standing you'll wake up when you hit the floor. So keep on your feet in future. Now come on. It's time we did some work.'

Home Sister looked as tired as I felt when I knocked at her office after breakfast. 'I'm sorry, Nurse Dorland. I'm afraid Nurse Dexter is not very well this morning.'

Nurse Charles had used those words last night without infuriating me; this morning I knew exactly how the general public felt. Why couldn't Sister be honest and say the poor girl was booked, I thought savagely, as the lift took me upwards. How could it help to talk as if Estelle had a cold in the head?

I rang Bart on the internal phone at the end of our corridor before going to my room. It was not yet nine, and there was just a chance I might catch him in Casualty before the morning rounds and lectures started.

The porter I spoke to had never heard of Mr More. I asked for Sam. Sam was sympathetic but unable to help.

'Like me to ask him to give you a ring if I see him come in, Nurse?'

'I don't think so, thanks. I've got to go to bed.'

He cleared his throat. 'I'm—sorry about that Nurse Dexter, Nurse. Pal of yours, ain't she? They say as she's what you might call poorly.'

'Yes,' I said, 'you might. Thanks, Sam.'

I stormed back to my room and sat down to write to the Professor. Writing was the next best thing to talking to him, and I had to talk to some one. My head dropped forward before I finished one paragraph. I tried to hold it up; it was too heavy; it went on dropping forward until the back of my neck ached. I left that letter unfinished and lay on my bed, meaning to take a short nap and then go on writing. I fell asleep as if I had been pole-axed. Some time in the afternoon I woke to find I was very cold, had ruined a cap, and left streaks of black shoe-polish on my white bedspread, since I had forgotten to take off my shoes.

It seemed only five minutes later that Sylvia Franks was shaking me. 'Frances, your first supper bell's gone. Get up!' She gave me another shake. 'Awake? Good. Listen. I've only got a couple of minutes—Sister Margaret sent me over for a clean apron. Estelle's as she was this morning according to Home Sister at tea-time, and I've just been stopped by Bart More. He asked me to say he's sorry he missed your call this morning and hopes you got his message in Willie Mac.'

'I did. Thanks. Anything else?'

She shook her head. 'Should there be?'

'I hoped so. Maybe he'll ring later.'

'I don't suppose he will or he wouldn't have stopped me,' she pointed out reasonably. 'I'd adore to ask leading questions, but I simply haven't time. Just tell me quickly—how did you get on in Willie Mac.? Senior decent?'

'Not too bad. Thanks for coming in.'

Home Sister was in our hall when I raced downstairs a few minutes later. The lift was in use, and I could not afford to waste time waiting.

Home Sister disapproved of racing, and I expected a stern warning when I leapt round the final turning on the stairs, then slowed—obviously only because she was there. She merely smiled kindly. 'Oversleep, Nurse? Poor child. This must be an anxious period for you in every way.'

I thanked her mechanically. While I cut the bread in William MacPherson kitchen a couple of hours after, I thought about Home Sister. She was a nice old thing, and I was growing quite fond of her, but I could not understand at all why she should be so indulgent with me.

Nixon's head came round the door. 'Leave the bread. Those post-ops. have come round. Come and help me sit them up.'

One of the four men who had been operated on that afternoon was having a blood-transfusion. Nixon altered the speed of the drops of blood falling through the glass drip-connexion. 'He's got to have one more pint of whole blood after this, then switch to glucose-saline. This'—she illuminated the vacolitre on the stand with her pocket torch—'will take about twenty minutes to run through. Ever changed blood before? Then I'll show you how. Join me in fifteen minutes.'

We were changing the vacolitres when Night Sister arrived for her first round. She looked up the ward, saw what we were doing, and drifted to the centre table.

'I'll have to go,' muttered Nixon, altering the rate again. 'This is running all right. Dump that empty in the sluice for the moment—rinse it later. You must stay in the ward while I'm held up with Night Sister, so you may as well begin my four-hourly temps. The book's on the desk.'

A few of our men had not yet gone to sleep. 'You going to be our regular night, Nurse?' one asked.

'I believe so.' I offered him a thermometer. 'Under your tongue, please.'

His name was Doughty, and to-night he had a face. I knew his name because Nixon had made me learn all their names by heart last night. 'Night Sister'll test you on the names any time after and including your second night.'

The other men had faces as well as names, but they were not yet people to me. They were not really patients, either. As I had only nursed women previously, patients were still always female in my mind. I knew how to treat sick women; I had no conception of how to treat sick men; nor had I realized how heavy men were in comparison with women.

I did not talk to any of our men that night, but as I did not wish to seem unpleasant, took Neal's advice on smiling. Much to my surprise, her advice worked excellently.

Nixon beckoned me to the centre table when Night Sister's long, slow round of all the men was over. 'You've gone down well with our men, Dorland.'

'Me, Nurse? But I don't know them—or they me.'

'Don't kid yourself they don't know you. Patients know all there is to know about a new nurse after she's been five minutes in a ward. They watch everything. They think'—she smiled slightly—'you're ever such a nice little nurse. Ever so quiet with a real lovely smile. Now, sit down.' She drew out the chair by her. 'I've news for you. Night Sister said I could pass it on as she knew you'd want to hear it. It's all right. It's quite good.'

The table was shielded by two red screens. The ends of the screens were left open to allow anyone at the table a clear view of both ends of the ward. The overhead light directly over the table was pulled down to the full length of its flex. It hung only a few inches over our heads, and, being swathed in a red shade cover, threw a pool of rose-coloured light on the table.

I sat down quickly and folded my hands in my lap. My apron looked pink. 'Good? About Dexter?'

She nodded. Her cap was also pink. 'She's beginning to respond.'

'To what? I thought there was no treatment? I looked it up yesterday—'

'What did you look it up in?'

I named a standard text-book of medicine.

'When was that written?'

'I don't know, Nurse.' I wished she would get on and stop this futile cross-examination.

'I do. Before the last war. Practically before the sulfa drugs, certainly before penicillin and the mycins. So just forget all you read and listen to me. See here.' She took a clean case-history sheet from Sister William MacPherson's file and drew a rough diagram of the heart. 'Here's the pericardium. She's got a purulent effusion here.' She shaded an area. 'Right? Well, she had a paracentesis this morning.'

I had to stop her. 'What's that, Nurse?'

'I keep forgetting how little you know. They drew off some fluid.'

I looked at the drawing, then at her. 'Direct? Isn't it a moving target?'

'Of course. It's fairly simple if you know how. I've seen John Curtis do it—oh, half a dozen times. He sticks in a long, wide needle first—the needle moves with the beats—then fixes on the syringe. Roughly'—more shading—'it goes in here. Between the fourth and fifth left interspaces.' She put down her pencil, and tapped my chest with one finger. 'About an inch from the sternum.'

'Simple,' I echoed, feeling torn between concern for Estelle and academic interest. 'How much is taken off?'

'Can be a few hundred c.c.'s. I'm not sure how much they took off Dexter. Point is this—shifting the fluid gives the patient a lot of relief and the Path. Lab. something tangible to work on.'

'Isolating the bugs?'

'That's right. Until they know what they're dealing with they can't know what weapons to use.' She turned her head sharply to the left. 'That's either Chalmers coughing in his sleep or Davis about to be sick. Go and see.'

I returned a few seconds later. 'Chalmers coughing. Davis is asleep, too.'

'Good.' She looked up and down the ward. 'Then we can go on. They're all right for the moment and far quieter than I expected us to be to-night. Of course, we've still one empty bed.'

I sat down again. 'Think we'll have an admission?'

'We haven't had one for three nights. We're due for one.' She frowned at her drawing. 'What was I saying?'

I told her. 'Just what is she responding to, Nurse?'

'Chemotherapy. Oh, Lord—you don't understand? That's the treatment of disease by chemical means. It's all chemotherapy these days—plus nursing plus plus, where hearts are involved. That's where the path. boys come in. And why John Curtis needed Marcus Everly. With some ailments you can hit back sort of at random. But all these new drugs put a strain on the heart, and you can't risk that to some one whose heart is already in a bad way. They had to be absolutely specific. They are now. She's shown a slight but definite improve—Oh, damn!'

The buzz of the night bell on the duty-room telephone hissed up the ward. 'I thought this quiet was too good to last. There goes our empty bed.' She shot soundless out of the ward. She was back immediately. 'Acute appendix for operation to-night. On the way up now. Go and fill two hotties while I shove in the electric blanket.'

The new patient was a youngish man with dark hair and anxious eyes. His name was Huckle.

'Been in hospital before, Mr Huckle?' asked Nixon.

'Not me, Nurse.' He glanced nervously at the drawn curtains round his bed. 'Never had the knife, neither. Proper turn up for the book, this is.'

Nixon said she was sure it was and held up an operation gown. 'I'm afraid this may seem a bit odd—it ties at the back.'

' 'Streuth.' He grinned suddenly. 'Proper draughty.'

'Not if you're lying down. No—we can manage, thanks—don't try and move or you may bring the pain back. That's it.' She shook out the long, thick woollen stockings I had brought with his theatre pack. 'These'll keep your feet warm.'

The stockings amused him as much as the gown. 'Hand-knitted, eh? You nurses knit 'em? Reckon,' he added, without waiting for an answer, 'you must be quite glad of the job of a night. There can't be much for you to do, seeing as the lads are all asleep.'

Nixon caught my eye momentarily. 'I always enjoy knitting,' she said amicably, and went off to scrub her hands before preparing his skin.

When he was ready she told me to scrub my hands. 'You can give his premedication injection. I'll witness.'

Huckle looked surprised to see us. 'More carry-on?'

'Just a little more. An injection into your arm. It won't hurt.' Nixon rolled up his gown sleeve. 'It won't put you to sleep, either. It'll just make you feel very-nicely-thank-you.'

He smiled up at us. 'Bit of all right, eh?'

She watched me critically, then patted his hand. 'Didn't feel that, did you?'

'Nah.' He raised a finger at me. 'Reckon you're used to bunging in needles, eh, Nurse?'

I had given three injections in Josephine. This was my fourth attempt. 'Oh yes, Mr Huckle.'

Nixon told him I should be going to the theatre with him. 'Now try and sleep a little before the trolley arrives.'

My mouth felt dry as I rinsed that syringe. Nixon had followed me into the sluice. 'Been through with a case yet, Dorland?'

'No, Nurse.'

'Never mind. You have to start some time, and must to-night as I can't leave the ward. Don't look so worried. You won't be expected to know or do anything, apart from holding his hand when he goes under, and have an anæsthetic bowl handy on the return journey, in case he vomits. The theatre staff'll show you where and how to dress up; the theatre porters'll know exactly how to cope if anything goes wrong on the way up or down. Just do what they tell you. Let's see—who's on theatre call to-night?' She thought for a moment. 'Blakelock and Paton are the porters on. Blakelock's wonderful; Paton can be moody, but he knows his stuff. Nurse Howard, the senior staff nurse, is on, too. Pity.'

My heart sank. 'Why, Nurse?'

'She doesn't like ward nurses cluttering up her theatre. Don't feel hurt if she sends you up to the gallery. She's done that before. She's not too bad,' she added, smiling faintly at my expression; 'she just doesn't like ward nurses. Think you'll feel queer?'

'I don't know, Nurse,' I said truthfully.

'If the floor does start coming up at you, keep your head down. Tie your shoelace or pick something off the floor. And don't watch the incision to-night. That's always the worst moment. All right?' She turned to go, then swung round. 'I nearly forgot. I saw this sitting on the sand in the fire bucket by the door about ten minutes ago. It's for you.'

I recognized Bart's handwriting on the envelope she handed me, and pushed it in my apron bib to read later. I forgot all about it until I took off my apron in the theatre changing-room, and it dropped on the floor.

Staff Nurse Howard watched me pick it up. 'Don't you bother to read your post, Nurse?'

I put it in one of my pockets. 'I forgot to read it, Nurse,'

She raised an eyebrow. 'Nurses are supposed to have good memories,' she announced, in a very fine copy of Sister Out-Patients' favourite tone.

'Yes, Nurse,' I agreed, and attempted to tie my turban.

'Nurse,' she drawled, 'you are about to attend an operation, not take a bath. Give it to me and stand still.' She flicked the linen triangle into the correct folds. 'The point goes over your head—so—and the ends tie at the back, then tuck in. Like mine.' She turned her head for my inspection. 'See? You must prevent its riding up—and never fix it with a bow in front.' She looked me over. 'Take one of those gowns on the left; the top one. It should fit you. Now all you need are overboots—that cupboard on your left—and a mask. Take one from the jar just inside the anæsthetic room. Put it on and keep it on until your man comes out of the theatre.'

Huckle looked as pleased to see me as I was to see him when I rejoined him in the anæsthetic room. 'Hallo, Nurse. You do look different. I'm glad you're back. I was feeling on me own, like. Proper strange.'

I could hardly explain that I felt the same, so I smiled. 'I'm back to stay.' I tied on my mask. 'In disguise.'

'You are an' all!' His hands gripped the sides of his stretcher nervously. 'Rare do, this is. Never thought I'd be mixed up in the like, I didn't.'

I touched his right hand. 'Like to hang on to me?'

'Ta, Nurse.' His fingers tightened round mine. 'I know this'll sound real soft, but I'm—well, I'm—not too happy about all this.'

'I don't blame you. You've never been in hospital before. It must be an awful shock for any man. Don't worry about it sounding soft. No one in their senses likes having an operation.'

'You don't say?' He brightened visibly. 'Streuth, I'm dry. I could do with a pint, right now.'

'That's the injection you had in the ward. It makes you dry.'

He sighed drowsily as the effect of his premedication deepened. 'Got to know a lot to be a nurse, ain't you? Queer life, though. Seeing blokes sick and being cut up and the like. Don't worry you nothing?'

'Not at all.' I was glad I wore a mask. 'One gets used to these things.'

He said he reckoned one did. He sounded relieved.

A theatre porter was fiddling with the knobs on the anæsthetic trolley. He caught my eye, jerked a thumb upward, then returned to his fiddling.

Huckle sighed again. ' 'Streuth. I could sleep for a week an' all.'

The anæsthetist had come in. 'Sleepy? Splendid.' He pulled down his mask. 'Remember me? I listened to your chest in Casualty. Just let me have your right arm. That's the form. Get his sleeve up, Nurse—and you make a fist, lad. Right. Now'—he held his syringe poised and swabbed the injection site with spirit—'just a little prick coming.'

The telephone bell jangled in the theatre corridor as Huckle went under. 'Oh, God,' murmured the anæsthetist, continuing his slow injection, 'if that's another surgical emergency I'm getting out. What's the matter with them all to-night? Aren't there other hospitals in London? Eh, Nurse?'

I glanced round before answering in case he was speaking to another nurse. Doctors in large hospitals do not as a rule address unnecessary remarks to junior nurses. I was the only nurse in the room, so I said I had heard there were other hospitals.

'Then why can't they take their acute abdos. there?' demanded the anæsthetist, laying aside the syringe and picking up a laryngeal tube. 'What'—he readjusted the angled mirror on a head band and slipped it on his head—'is wrong with Thomas's, Guy's, and Bart's? Good hospitals? Of course. So why don't the customers use them and give poor old Martha's a rest?'

The porter who had answered the telephone returned at that moment. 'Not an admission, sir. The Night Sister just wants a word with Nurse Howard.'

'Thank God for that,' said the anæsthetist piously. 'Let's have that gag, Blakelock. I want to get this tube in.'

We heard Nurse Howard's voice clearly as the corridor phone was only a couple of feet from the open anæsthetic room door. She sounded annoyed. 'Actually, we are just about to start, Sister. Mr Fraser's scrubbing now.' She paused. Then: 'We've only got one, Sister. Sister Theatre likes us to keep a spare. I suppose,' she added, with obvious reluctance, 'he'll have to have it, if he wants it. Right away? Oh.' There was a second long pause. 'I see. May I just—that is, would you mind holding on one moment, please, Sister?' She came into the anæsthetic room. 'Nearly ready, Dr Elks?'

'Not nearly. I'm ready.' The anæsthetist did not look up. 'Stand by to shift that trolley, Blakelock.'

Nurse Howard turned to the porter. 'How heavy is he, Blakelock? Can nurse and my dirty nurse lift him?'

The porter shook his head gloomily. 'Not unless we want him on the floor, Nurse. He's all of fourteen stone.'

'I see.' She looked at me. 'Dr Elks, do you need the ward nurse? Can I borrow her?'

'Take her. I don't want her.' He glanced up suddenly and nodded at me. 'You'll appreciate that I'm speaking professionally, Nurse.'

Howard ignored his rider, and returned to the phone. 'Sister, can I send it up with the ward nurse? She's very junior and will only be in the way. I know he doesn't like—' She stopped speaking as Sister apparently interrupted her. 'I don't know. From William MacPherson. Oh? It'll be all right? Thanks, Sister. I'll send her up now.'

'I don't know where you're going, Nurse,' said the anæsthetist, 'but before you go would you tighten the top strings of my mask. I haven't got a hand.'

Howard joined us. 'Is your name Dorland, Nurse?'

'Yes, Nurse.'

The anæsthetist glanced round sharply, nearly causing me to break one of the mask strings I was retieing. His eyes were amused and curious. Howard's eyes over her mask were equally curious.

'When you've done,' she said politely, 'would you come with me, please, Nurse?'

I followed her into the theatre duty-room. She took a sealed test-tube from the large refrigerator in the far corner. 'Take that up to Sir Marcus, please. You'll know how to get to his office, of course.'

'Yes, Nurse. Should I change first?'

She hesitated. 'Not at this hour of the night. Take off those over-boots and go as you are. When you get back, change your gown and come straight in to the theatre.' She gave me the tube. 'Be careful with that. It's precious. If you drop it Night Sister'll have to open the main dispensary.'

I wondered what the tube contained. I did not like to ask her. She would probably tell me to read the label on it. I had already done that, and was no wiser. Certainly she seemed to have mellowed in the last few minutes, but experience had made me wary with staff nurses. She might be another Naylor—an angel of sweetness one moment, the reverse the next. Nixon had not warned me about her for nothing.

The main corridor was empty and silent. Night Sister was sitting in the outer office of Matron's office as I went by. She glanced up. 'That's right, Nurse Dorland. Take it up quickly.'

I was very glad Garret had sent me up to the top floor lab. previously. Night Sister and Howard clearly assumed that every night junior knew the way there, and I should not have enjoyed confessing ignorance to either.

The Dean's office was in darkness. Only one light was in the alcove, another in the private lift. The top floor was blazing with light and very quiet. I hitched under the top of my gown for my watch. It was five past twelve. I wondered why the pathologists were working late, then instantly decided Estelle was worse. Luckily, before I got in a complete dither, I remembered there were other patients in the world—and if Estelle was keeping them up surely Marcus Everly would be over at the fever hospital as he had been last night, and not sitting here on the other side of London.

There was no one in the lab. with the plate-glass wall. The glass was uncurtained, and, as before, I wished I had time to stop and look at the view. Instead, I looked round for a notice to tell me what to do next. I found one on the door on my left. 'Pathologists' offices. Private.'

I knocked on that door. Nothing happened. I knocked again. With the same result. I looked at the door and wondered if the old man was deaf. He had certainly heard that incubator bell last time. Perhaps he only heard bells?

I looked about for something to ring, or a label to tell me what to do. I found neither. I could not risk putting the tube in the fridge by the incubator, since Howard had told me to deliver it in person, or waste much time as, from her conversation with Night Sister, I had gathered there was some urgency about its delivery. I knocked very loudly and more than a little apprehensively. I had come up on a perfectly legitimate errand at his request, but the prospect of interrupting a man who was reputed to scare the living daylights out of Matron was not a pleasant one. I stood back slightly, expecting him to bounce out in fury. As nothing happened at all I wondered quite seriously if he had dropped dead.

So I opened the door and found myself in yet another lab. It was smaller than the previous one and equally empty. There were three doors off that lab.; a light shown through the fanlight of the door on the extreme right.

Once again I knocked. He was neither deaf nor dead. 'Come in, Nurse.'

The small office was plainly furnished, and, apart from the flat-topped desk in one corner, another lab. The inevitable waist-high china shelf ran the length of one wall; the remaining walls were lined with two elbow-tapped sinks, several bookcases, and three large glass-fronted cupboards filled with stone jars, bottles, test-tubes, and instruments. In the centre of the room was a rather worn zinc-covered table holding a microscope and angled lamp. A man in a white shirt with sleeves rolled above the elbows sat with his back to me looking into the microscope. A thin man with fair hair.

He did not look round or pay any attention to me. He wrote something on the open pad by his right hand, and went on looking into his instrument. He had his back to me, but when he wrote that note he altered his position slightly, and gave me a brief but clear view of his right profile.

I stood stock still. I should have recognized, and been happy to recognize, that profile anywhere in the world until that moment. But that office was the last place in the world in which I had expected to recognize it, and the shock made a mockery of happiness.

'Excuse me, Nurse,' said the Professor, 'I just want to finish what I'm doing.' He did not even glance up. 'I presume you're from the general theatre. Would you leave that tube in the holder on my desk. Thank you for bringing it up.'

I could not have moved if the hospital had been on fire and filled with patients having major arterial hæmorrhages. I clutched the tube and stared at him speechlessly.

He looked round briefly. 'On my desk, please, Nurse.' He returned to his microscope.

My scalp pricked under my turban, my hands turned coldly damp, the mask it had not occurred to me to remove felt heavier than lead. I had never fainted in my life, but I knew quite well what those symptoms meant. I thought, Oh, God, I'm going to pass out.

Somehow I managed to get that wretched tube in the wooden holder on the desk. The floor came up at me as Nixon had warned in a different context. I did not dare risk bending to retie a shoelace. It was too late. If

I bent over I should go over. The room was revolving round me; at least three men were sitting at that table ignoring me. I rested both hands flat on the desk to steady myself, then instinctively pulled down my mask, forgetting everything but my desire to breathe without restriction.

He must have looked round again. I was too muzzy to notice anything beyond that fact that he was on his feet.

'Sit down in that chair behind you, and get your head over your knees. I've got to wash before I can touch anything.'

I obeyed and closed my eyes. A few seconds, minutes, or it could have been hours, later I felt a hand pressing on the back of my head. 'Right down. That's better. Stay there for a little while.'

The hand moved; I heard him walk away. His footsteps sounded a long, long way off. Somewhere nearer a drum was beating loudly.

Something cold touched my right hand. I blinked. A medicine glass came into focus. 'Can you hold it?' he asked.

I sat up slowly. 'Yes. Thank you.'

'Ammon. Aromat.' He put the glass in my hand. 'Sip it.'

His using that name added the final touch of nightmare. My friend the Professor would have called it sal volatile. My hand shook badly, spilling some of the liquid on to my gown. I drank the rest far too quickly, so as not to spill more. It burnt my throat and momentarily choked me. I coughed and spluttered; the drum went mad; and then suddenly the room stopped revolving; I was able to breathe and identify the drum as my temporal pulse.

He brought me a glass of water. 'You'll need this.'

'Thank you.' I knew I ought to look at him. I did so. 'I'm sorry to be such a nuisance.'

He was watching me closely. His face was expressionless. 'I'm sorry you should have had this shock.'

It was a relief to discover there was going to be no more pretence. 'I thought that other pathologist was you. I didn't think you had anything to do with Martha's—apart from playing chess.'

'I know.' A muscle twitched high in his left cheek, but his tone was as unemotional as his expression. 'You must have seen either Dr Eastwood or Dr Carruthers—my colleagues up here.' He took both glasses from me, rinsed and dried them, and replaced them in one of the glass-fronted cupboards. 'Slane's one of my Christian names.' He returned and leant against his desk. 'I didn't realize you were on nights in the theatre.'

'I'm not. I'm in William MacPherson.'

'Why are you in theatre clothes?'

I looked at him, and wondered if I had passed out in the theatre. This had to be a dream. There was no alternative. You do not have to talk in dreams, so I did not answer.

'Jobbing in the theatre?' he prompted.

I woke up then. 'Jobbing' was hospital slang for a nurse on loan. He had walked our wards once. He would know our slang. Our? It belonged to him. But not to my Professor.

I explained.

'I see.' He reached for the telepone on his desk. 'I'll let Night Sister know you aren't fit to go back.'

I stood up without knowing or caring if my legs would support me. 'Please, don't. I'm quite all right now. I must go back. My senior's alone in William MacPherson, and we're busy to-night.'

His hand closed over the receiver without lifting it. 'I'm afraid I can't agree that you're fit to work. I don't doubt that your ward is busy, but no one will expect you to keep going when you're obviously unwell.'

I had loved him very much; I still did. Love is not something you can turn off like a tap at will. Because I loved him he could hurt me more than any other human being; to-night he had done that. He probably had never meant to hurt me. He probably began our friendship for a joke, and kept it on as another joke. Just a good laugh. A riot of fun. The great man had come down from his ivory tower, amused himself being avuncular to a junior pro., but had wisely not trusted her with his real name. That would have been so indiscreet, and he had in every way been the soul of discretion. If I had known who he was I might have had ideas about his money, been tempted to step out of the clearly marked hospital line because a man in his position had bothered about me. Of course it would have gone straight to my head. And he might have lost consequence if anyone had known he had been mixed up with me. Every houseman in Martha's ignored the first-year nurses. A senior member of the hospital staff could not even admit to knowing such creatures existed.

My jeering brain no longer had room for shock or pain. This would really hurt later, when my icy anger thawed.

'It's very kind of you to be so considerate, Sir Marcus'—I used his title intentionally—'but I really have quite recovered.'

He straightened from the desk. 'You have?'

His eyes were infinitely weary. I noticed the fact academically. 'Yes, thank you.'

'Good.' He walked to the door, and held it open. 'Thank you for bringing up that culture. Good night.'

'Good night.'

I heard his door close as I let myself out of the main laboratory. I looked back then. There was something I wanted to see. It was there all right, pinned to the outer door. 'It' was a smallish typed list of all the pathologists in Martha's. There were a good many names on that list;

Tom Neal's came half-way down. The first name ran, 'M. J. S. S. Everly, M.C., M.D., F.R.C.P., Director, Pathological Department, St Martha's Hospital, London.'

I looked at it for several seconds. And then in the absurd way in which you do wonder about inessentials in moments of emotional stress I wondered how he had won his M.C. If it was not for service rendered to MI5, it ought to be. I got into the lift, slammed the gates, and went back to the theatre.

11. A Long, Empty Evening

I should, I thought, have guessed if not the incredible truth—at least, some of the truth. I should have realized he was a Martha's man, and not just blindly accepted all he told me about himself. Yet it had never occurred to me to doubt him or want to doubt him.

My thoughts chased each other round in an unhappy circle as I finished cutting the bread-and-butter; laid the breakfast trays and trolley; set the sluice for the morning washings; folded linen in the tiled bathroom.

Just before dawn Nixon told me Night Sister had been talking on the telephone to the Night Sister in the fever hospital. 'Dexter's having a good night so far.' She looked at me keenly. 'You don't look too good. I don't think nights suits you. Go on the balcony for a few minutes' air.'

The pre-dawn air was cool, clean, and pale grey. London was a drifting dark grey shadow as mobile as the parchment-coloured river. The world was very quiet, and belonged to me. I did not want it. I went back into the warm, slightly airless ward.

Home Sister looked triumphant when I met her in our lift that morning. 'Nurse Dexter has had her best night for over a week. Most satisfactory, dear. Most satisfactory.'

I was too braced against bad news to be able to accept the reverse easily. Slowly, in the privacy of my room, the relief I felt about Estelle began to trickle through my defences. Then, quite suddenly, they all collapsed, and I knew that, although everything had changed, nothing had altered as far as I was concerned.

I sat in my armchair, kicked off my shoes, and relaxed physically, while my mind, unasked, occupied itself fitting together a mental jig-saw puzzle. His presence on the hill in that storm; his letters; his being on those steps the night Lily died; Home Sister's willing permission for me to come in late; all these made good sense. The only things that did not yet make sense were why he had bothered to write any letters, or walked into the Home to see Home Sister. My instant reaction last night hit me like a boomerang. For a good laugh? An Everly version of the Kinsey report?

I winced inwardly, but could not stop. I had to finish that puzzle. Home Sister was on another piece. Now I knew why she treated me as she did. The knowledge made me feel slightly sick.

I wondered who shared Home Sister's specific bit of knowledge about him and me. There was no point in hoping she would have kept it to herself. He was a Martha's legend in his own lifetime, and anything he did would set the grapevine humming. Was that why Night Sister had given me permission to approach the unapproachable last night? Why Howard had mellowed so strangely? And that anæsthetist nearly snapped a mask string?

I did not bother to answer the obvious. Instead, I thought about Vickers. And at last I saw the point in her cracks.

My God, I thought, he probably owns a foreign car, too. Some one in a hospital always sees everything. Home Sister apart, some one must have seen him drive me out that night. The light inside his car was off, but we had had to drive through the well-lit gateway. It only needed one person. Home Sister's version plus our being seen together was more than enough to hit the hospital with the biggest story for a decade. And my being a junior only added to its gossip value. No wonder Simpson talked about a wretched top secret! And I had blithely filled in the gap with the Dexter Block! I ought to have my head examined!

I could not sit still. I roamed round my room in a bitter fury, and all the thoughts I had had about my Professor twisted and taunted and jeered. I thought him so wonderful—was so sorry for him because he worked so hard—looked so tired—lived on snacks. I had lectured him on his health, told him to eat proper meals and stop living on sandwiches.

And then I thought; but he does work too hard, look tired, and apparently seldom troubles to eat the sandwiches.

That thought sobered me. I pushed my hand through my hair, discovered I was still wearing a cap, removed my cap pins, and put them on the dressing-table as if they were made of gold. A long way back I heard my voice talking to Bart: 'If she wanted the bright lights and expensive meals, she could have them any time. Why can't you forget her cash, and just treat her as a human being?'

Perhaps he wanted to be treated as a human being? If I had known who he was I probably should never have been able to treat him as one. Perhaps no one did. He had so much; if he wanted more he could buy it, without two thoughts about the price.

Buy—what? If there was a price tag on love, affection, friends, then none were worth having. Estelle had taught me that was not just a soothing bromide for the poor but a plain truth. I might not know much about men; I knew a great deal about young women. The poor-little-rich-girl line might be suitable with some people; not with her. She never asked for pity, but she was the loneliest girl I had ever known. She wore her loneliness like a cloak of dignity. She had shed that cloak with me. And so had he.

Estelle had often helped me in Josephine, and with my lectures, but never as much as she helped me that morning. Because I knew her, neither anger not damaged pride could blind me indefinitely. Now I knew the truth, I had to face all the truth; I had to try to look through his eyes, to realize there was scarcely a door in the civilized world he could not open with his money and title. He had a freedom of choice granted to few people, but the only door he had bothered to open he had opened with his brains.

I emptied my dress pockets on to my bed, intending to throw my dress into the laundry basket. Only when I saw it did I recollect Bart's unopened letter. I slit it incuriously. My body might be holding his letter, but my mind was a long way from Bart More at that moment.

After a long paragraph on Estelle's paracentesis and much more hopeful prognosis he discussed his nervous system:

> Nervous system is not what it was, angel. It took one hell of a bashing this evening. Hamilton Dexter sent round his chauffeur with a formal but civil note asking yours truly to lunch with him at his club to-morrow. Says he wants to talk to me. I'm not sure what's in his mind; I know what's in mine. I hope she won't mind, but there's nothing I'd like better than to have a straight talk with the old man. I'll let you know what gives.

Remembering what Estelle had told me, I had a fair notion of what lay in her grandfather's mind. He might be old-fashioned, but he was clearly very wise to keep such a strict eye on Estelle while she was so young. She was not an ordinary young woman, and it was foolish to pretend she was.

I smiled slightly, wondering how Hannah was going to react when she heard about Bart and Estelle. Her 'honest to God' would echo round our floor. I took up the letter again, thinking, Dear old Hannah! It would be pleasant to have her back. I doubted if Estelle would ever be able to nurse again; I was going to miss her badly, but so long as she recovered from her illness, that would not matter.

Bart's letter ended with some very generous thanks to me. Something had obviously cropped up when he had signed it. A P.T.O. was heavily underlined. I turned the page over. His writing on that side was an utter scrawl:

Nervous system finally shot to pieces after talking to Joe Carver—brother of Maggie C. in O.P.'s. Frances, you devil! How dare you hold out on me! It's the best story I've heard in years, and, angel, have you rocked Martha's! Never mind. I'll forgive you, and am now basking in the reflected glory, having stood the future Lady E. a hamburger on a park bench. No wonder you've known all the answers. Dead crafty, you country girls—that's what!

I put away the letter. So I knew all the answers, did I? I hadn't even heard the questions. Every one else had heard—not me. Then I realized it was not every one, it was the senior half of the hospital, and the story was only just trickling downwards. It would reach my set soon.

No wonder the poor man had to retire to his lab., if this was what happened when he merely admitted to being acquainted with a nurse and possibly was seen driving her in his car. No one knew he had been writing to me. If they had they would probably have fixed the date by now.

I no longer blamed him for not telling me his full name; I was merely amazed he had risked talking to me. The talk and publicity that must inevitably have followed him all his life must have been agony for some one with his quiet, reticent nature.

I sighed. It had been so much simpler when I was angry. Now I kept seeing his point it was growing more and more complicated. Now I knew what was being said, I should have to do something to stop it. The difficulty was—what?

A vague idea instantly rose to my mind. I should have to get hold of Bart, tell him the truth, get him to help. I could leave him to circulate anything we wanted to circulate. He knew the hospital. Perhaps we could work out something along the lines of Marcus Everly's being an old pal of my father's. He having used much the same line to Home Sister—just why he had taken that risk I still could not fathom, but I should have to think it out later—he had used that line, so we should have to rub it in. We could laugh and laugh and keep on laughing at the idea of any romance. I could invent a mythical young man—even borrow a ring from my mother.

That stopped me again. The Professor had met the parents and told them he was Slane. Why?

It was useless. I did not know any answers, I was growing into the question-mark, and was far too exhausted to think another thought. I felt too tired to sleep until I got into bed. I was not.

Fay Kinsley shook me in Sylvia's stead that night. 'Frances, you can't go on sleeping. You've got to be in the dining-room in ten minutes.' She removed all the bed-clothes over me and hauled on the bottom sheet. 'If you don't get out I'll topple you out.'

'For God's sake go away! I'm in no mood for dormitory pranks ...' I got out of what remained of my bed and shivered. 'What time did you say it was?'

'Twenty past.'

'Eight?' My voice cracked.

'That's what I'm trying to tell you. Sylvia warned me you might oversleep.' She threw me my face flannel and turned on the hand-basin taps. 'Wash your face in cold water.' She sounded exactly like Sister P.T.S. 'And brace up. I've got news for you.'

'Estelle?'

'Yes. Off the D.L. and on the S.I.' She took a clean apron from my drawer. 'Where's your dress?'

I need a clean one. Bottom left.' I was not used to this helpfulness from her. 'Thanks, Fay. I never knew you cared.'

When Fay patted you on the head she had to do it with her knuckles. 'A set ought to stick together, Frances. And you're so irresponsible, if we don't see you get on at night, you'd never bother.'

I said I did not know what we should do without her. 'Thanks for the good news. Seriously ill isn't much, but it's not to be compared with the D.I.'

She polished my shoes with an old apron from my laundry basket. 'I've got another bit of news. You know the new block. It's going to be called the Dexter block.' She smiled knowingly. 'Yes—he's paying for it. The opening's been postponed.'

I was hurrying too much to have to do more than look wide-eyed.

'I heard Home Sister discussing it with Nurse Charles when I was reading the notice-board outside her office just now. I couldn't help hearing.'

Having done my own eavesdropping on occasions, I had to agree with her. 'I suppose they'll wait until Estelle's up?'

She hesitated. 'As a matter of fact, they were talking about that too. They—er—don't expect her back, I'm afraid.'

'She hasn't a hope in hell of nursing again with her heart.'

'You knew?'

'Guessed it.' I fixed my cap on quickly.

She said slowly, 'Don't you mind?'

I put down my comb. 'Very much. On all counts. She loved nursing. I liked her.' I reached for the door with one hand and my cloak with the other. 'Bless you, Fay. Do the same for you some time.'

I left her standing in my room looking as if she had expected me to weep on her shoulder. If I had had time I might have wept, not only for Estelle, but for life in general. As usual, there was no time.

I slipped into the empty place beside Ames as Night Sister arrived in the dining-room to say grace.

'Nice timing,' said Ames, as we sat down. 'Oversleep again?'

'Yes. I don't know how I'm going to wake up on nights. I never hear the bells.'

'Lucky you! I even hear the clock in the hall.' She produced two envelopes from her apron bib and opened them in her lap. 'Keep an eye on Night Sister while I read. Then I'll do it for you. Or didn't you have time to get your post?'

'No.' I poured myself a glass of water I did not want. 'Doesn't matter. I'm not expecting any. Go ahead and read. I'll watch Night Sister.'

Night Sister always rose for the final grace ten minutes before we were due on duty. Consequently I had plenty of time to walk to the office and look for any post. I did not bother. I had heard from my mother yesterday, and expected no letter from home for a week. I knew I had now had my last letter from the Professor. I had avoided my letter pigeon-hole this morning, and did not want to look at it again just yet. It reminded me too much of the past. I walked slowly towards William MacPherson and for the first time in my nursing career arrived on duty a good five minutes early.

Nixon joined me four minutes later. 'You're an eager beaver to-night, Dorland.'

Huckle waved to me directly Sister William MacPherson left the ward. 'How's my Nurse Dorland to-night? I been looking out for you, Nurse. Had a good rest?'

I said I was fine, and how was he?

'Mustn't grumble, Nurse.'

Nixon came into the sluice when I was rinsing the mouthwash mugs. 'I gather you're Huckle's private property?'

'I got that impression too, Nurse.'

She considered me with an expression that would have puzzled me twenty-four hours back. Incredulity and respect were equally mixed in that expression. 'So we can all breathe again? Dexter's on the S.I. ....'

'Yes. I'm so pleased.'

She nodded, looked as if she wanted to say something else, but was not sure of her ground, then went off quickly.

I finished the mouthwash mugs, rinsed some stained sheets, put them in a covered bucket, and took them along to the wet-linen bin that stood on the balcony.

It was a dark night, and the air was cold on my bare, wet arms. I

lingered for a few moments and leant over the stone balustrade, looking
down at the darkened grounds.

The Theatre Block ran parallel with William MacPherson. The
general theatre on the third floor was fully lighted. I glanced over to
those lights, and wondered what would have happened if Huckle had not
come in last night, or if Sister Theatre and not Howard had been on call.
Would he have gone on letting me believe he was Slane indefinitely?

One of the theatre corridor doors was opened as I watched. The
corridor was lined with a row of black oxygen cylinders. The cylinders
against the white wall looked like nightmare teeth grinning wickedly. I
turned, picked up my empty bucket, and went inside.

Bart was sitting on the steps at the foot of Miss Nightingale's statue
when I came out of breakfast next morning. A scarlet and white rugger
club scarf was draped round his neck; his hair was standing on end. He
practically exploded to his feet when he saw me.

'Angel, I've been waiting hours—'

'Sssh.' I held up a cautioning hand and looked round. 'Night Sister
hasn't come out yet.'

'Would I have given you that big hallo if there'd been any blue
dresses around? And what the devil do you care about blue dresses now,
anyway?'

'We'll go into that in a minute. Heard the early-morning bulletin?'

He beamed. 'Best night to date. I got it out of old Sam, who was
listening in.'

'How did you get on with Grandpapa?'

He shrugged hugely. 'He didn't exactly pat me on the head and call
me son, but in a positively hellish way he was pretty decent.'

'What's he like?'

'Granite, until he got going on her. The sun rises and sets on her head
for him. Which made two of us.' He coloured. 'Tell you something,
Frances. You know that letter you wanted me to write? He read it to
her.'

'Oh, no! Did he mind?'

'He said, quote, under the circumstances he considered I was fully
justified in acting as I had. Then he gave me the works.'

'Did you mind?' I asked curiously, noticing how he seemed to have
changed in the past few days.

'I didn't enjoy it, but in his place I'd have done the same.'

'Can I ask—what did you say to him?'

'I love women,' he replied dreamily. 'Can I, you ask so sweetly, and
don't even wait for an answer. If you want to know I told him what I
once told you—maybe in rather better English.'

'How did he take it?'

'In silence. He was doing his granite act then. When I finished he just grunted. I thought, This is where you make tracks, chum, and was on my two feet when he said, "Sit down, boy!" I sat. Then out of the blue he upped and told me his old man was a G.P. Did you know that?'

I shook my head. 'Think that's where Estelle gets her passion for medicine?'

'He thinks so. Know something else? His old man was a Martha's man. Which is why he has a soft spot for the old firm.'

'She never told me.'

'I don't believe she knows. H.D. certainly gave me that impression. He said his old man was a fine character who died when he was a kid. Some uncle educated him, and put him into his own firm. Uncle knew how to do business, nephew knew even better. He went on and up and up.'

'And after his life-history?'

'We had lunch. He showed no sign of softening until the brandy arrived. Then—again quote—he gave me his permission to pursue my acquaintance with his granddaughter, providing there is no talk of any official engagement or marriage until *(a)* she comes of age and *(b)* I am in an established position. Fair enough, eh?'

'Very. Bart, I'm so pleased.'

'Wait.' His voice shook suddenly. 'There's a little more. He said she had asked him to say she would like to see me. I can go along just as soon as Curtis gives the word.'

'My dear, this really is something.'

'You're a good girl.' He slapped my arm gently. 'Very good. And it seems you're going to get your reward. Now we've finished with my angle, tell me all.'

I stopped smiling. 'Yes, I must,' I said urgently. 'I've simply got to tell you—'

'Nurse Dorland.' Night Sister was beside us. 'No doubt you have a great deal to tell Mr More'—she looked him over coolly—'but may I ask you to choose some other place for these confidences? I cannot have my night nurses standing idly chatting with students in the main corridor.'

Bart apologized instantly. 'It was my fault, Sister. I stopped Nurse.'

'It takes two to make a conversation, Mr More,' she informed him primly. 'Nurse should not have allowed herself to be stopped.' She gave us both an old-fashioned nod and walked on.

Bart was contrite. 'I was so sure they'd overlook—'

I cut him short. 'Never mind that. Look, I must talk to you—obviously not here. Can you meet me somewhere soon as I change?'

He hesitated. 'I'd like to—but I'm dressing in the general theatre at nine. Will to-morrow do?'

I thought quickly. Another twenty-four hours would not make any real difference; they might even give me time to work out a more concrete solution. 'Yes. In the morning?'

'Nine, outside. Why? Something amiss?'

I nodded. 'Keep it to yourself till then.'

'I'll be there. You going for your post, I expect? I'll make tracks in the opposite direction.'

I had not meant to go along to look for the post, but as Night Sister was still visible at the far end of the corridor from Matron's office, I walked to the office to get out of her sight.

Ames was rootling through her pigeon-hole. She glanced up. 'You've got one. I saw it when I collected Joanna Dawson's.'

I flipped over the small pile of envelopes in the 'D' compartment, wondering how long it would be before I was able to do that without wincing. One of the envelopes was unstamped. It was addressed to me in the Professor's handwriting.

Ames was talking. I did not hear a word she said. I took up that envelope as if it was brittle as glass, backed unthinkingly to the nearest windowsill, and slit the envelope with my scissors.

It was a longer letter than any he had written previously. He had used Martha's paper, added the time as well as the date. The time was 1.30 A.M. yesterday. I had left his office at about a quarter-past twelve. He might had given it to a porter to deliver, or, more likely, put it in my pigeon-hole on his way out that night. Between 1.30 and 3 A.M., Night Sister and her assistants were always out of the office on rounds. He would know that. He had been a Martha's houseman.

I looked at his signature before reading the letter. It was there in full, for the first time. M. J. S. S. Everly.

'Nurse! Nurse Dorland!' An Office Sister stood in front of me. She looked very peeved. 'Nurse, I have already called your name twice. You paid no attention.'

'I'm so sorry, Sister.' Fortunately, apologizing to a Sister was a reflex action to me. 'I'm afraid I didn't hear you. I was reading my post.'

'That,' she retorted icily, 'I could scarcely fail to observe. Will you in future kindly remember that this alcove is not an extension of the junior nurses' sitting-room? And never let me see you lounging in that unseemly fashion against a windowsill in this hospital again! Please put away your letter and come into the office. The Assistant Matron wishes to see you. I was about to ring over to the Home for you, when I noticed you through my open door.'

'Yes, Sister. I'm so sorry, Sister,' I repeated mechanically, and pushed the letter into my apron bib. Then I realized what she had said. 'The Assistant Matron, Sister?'

I did not know her name, or recollect having seen her before. Our Office Sisters were constantly changing. She was tall and slim, with pale red hair and pale, thin lips. 'I am gratified to have your attention at last, Nurse. Yes. Sister Black wishes to see you now. Come along.'

Sister Black, our Assistant Matron, was the most popular sister in Martha's. She was very plump, surprisingly young, not pretty, but very pleasant-looking. I liked what I had seen and heard of her, but if I had not had that letter in my bib, I should have been very shaken by this summons. The nicest Assistant Matron was still the Assistant Matron.

The pale Sister ushered me in. 'Nurse Dorland, Sister.'

Sister Black told me to come in and close the door.

That did worry me a little. A closed door in Martha's was always an ominous sign.

'Tell me, Nurse,' went on the Assistant Matron chattily, 'have you had a heavy night? Are you very tired?'

Half an hour ago I had been exhausted. I said truthfully, 'We were quite busy, Sister, but I'm not at all tired.'

She said she was very happy to hear that. 'You look very fresh. Good. I fear you have a busy day ahead of you. You may have to-night off, naturally, but must report for duty in Catherine Ward to-morrow night.'

'Catherine Ward, Sister?' I wondered if I had heard right. I did not know of any Catherine in London.

'Catherine, Nurse. At St Martha's-in-the-country. Sister Illingworth, the Sister-in-charge down there, requires another night junior immediately. We cannot supply a nurse for to-night, but will be able to spare you from to-morrow.' She smiled pleasantly. 'I am sorry to have to move you at such short notice, and send you ahead of your set, but for various reasons'—she glanced down at an open book on her desk—'Matron considers you would be the most suitable junior to fill the gap. You had scarlet fever as a child?' she added, without looking up.

'Yes, Sister.' I squinted at her book and read my own name upside down.

'I see you had diphtheria when you were eight. Did you have it badly?'

'Moderately, I believe, Sister.' I tried not to sound too surprised or curious. 'I can't remember much about it.'

She closed the book. 'Diphtheria is always serious, Nurse. Your parents must have been very worried. How fortunate to have it safely behind you! Now go over and see Home Sister. I have already spoken to her about you. Sister will tell you of the arrangements for your luggage and which train you must take. That will be all, Nurse. Good morning.'

Home Sister was in a positive dither when I reached the Home. 'I am sorry we are losing you so soon, Nurse. Dear, dear, dear. So unfortunate.

Hurry up and get your packing done. Leave your cases outside your door, and take only your night things with you. The rest will go down in the hospital van at twelve. You must take the twelve-thirty train. Come into my office when you are ready and I will give you your ticket. So unfortunate'—she clucked again—'so unfortunate.' And she bustled off to find Nurse Charles, muttering something to herself about it all being so upsetting for dear Matron, poor Sister Illingworth, and the already over-burdened Dr Sympson.

Nurse Charles arrived in the hall by one door as Sister vanished through another. 'Get on, Nurse Dorland. Don't dawdle around waiting for the lift. You have a lot to do.'

I had a lot to do, but, instead of doing it, directly I reached my room I stretched out on my bed and took out my letter. Fay Kinsley burst in on me before I was halfway through the second reading.

'Frances, I hear you're leaving us because you're the one pro. in the whole first year who's had dip.'

I lowered the letter and gazed at her. 'How on earth do you know that? I didn't.'

She was very pleased by this. 'It's obvious. One of the pros. in the country is a query dip. I heard Sister Mayhew telling Sister Robert when I collected my post this morning. She even mentioned you by name.'

I had to take things in easy stages. 'Who's Sister Mayhew? I never heard of her.'

'The new red-haired Office Sister. She won a gold medal.'

'Now how do you know that?'

'Every one knows that! Really, Frances! You ought to keep your ears open. You miss just everything.'

I was so enchanted by the realization that there was one thing she had still missed that I very nearly told her what it was. Luckily, she had too much to tell me.

'Nurse Charles was talking to Home Sister about it in the hall just now. I was waiting to make a phone call and couldn't help ...'

I smiled at her. 'I know, dear. What did Charles say?'

'That you having both dip. and scarlet made you the ideal choice. Matron doesn't want to pass on scarlet, or risk sending down an unimmunized junior. Dip.'s a foul illness, and one junior on the D.I. in the last month is one too many. If this girl has got dip. we'll all be immunized.'

'Except me,' I corrected smugly.

'That's what I've been trying to tell you.'

I got off my bed. 'Think this means a second epidemic?' I yawned. 'How long's the incubation?'

Inevitably she had overheard this too. 'Usually two to three days,' Mayhew said.'

'Very jolly. Take up nursing and get the plague.'

Sylvia flung open the door. 'What's all this about your leaving us, Frances?'

I left Fay to explain, put my letter in my handbag, and lifted one of the empty suitcases Home Sister had had sent up on my bed. Sylvia opened my wardrobe and handed me the contents absently while she listened to Fay.

'How do you feel about shifting?' she asked finally.

'Punch-drunk.' I rolled a skirt. 'Life's got clean out of hand lately. Every time I stop to draw breath something happens.'

Fay pulled open all my drawers, and said I would have plenty of time for drawing breath in the country. 'The wards may be busy, but you'll be very much on your own off-duty. The junior set down there are an up-stage lot. They won't speak to you.'

Sylvia said I should have to be upstage too and keep myself to myself. Neither of us bothered to ask Fay how she had come by this knowledge; nor did we bother to doubt her.

Sylvia thought it tough my having to travel after a night on. Fay said I must take a nap in the train. 'Are you going to wear those shoes? If not, let's have 'em. They'll need to go at the bottom.'

They organized my packing and me. Sylvia promised to let Bart know I had left London. 'I'm writing to Alice to-day. I'll ask her to get one of the nurses to pass it on to Estelle. Hannah'll hear direct from Alice as they're in the same ward.'

'Anyone else we should contact?' asked Fay. 'Your family?'

'I'll ring them this evening.' I glanced at my handbag. 'No one else, thanks.'

Fay was on duty at 1 P.M., Sylvia until 1.30. She came with me to the station. 'Did you give Fay that turkey?'

I smiled faintly. 'No. I don't know what's come over her.'

'Sylvia said she didn't either. 'Something's got her all shook-up. You've been dear, sweet, muddle-headed Frances since tea-time yesterday. She even went so far as to admit that she had always been mistaken about you.'

'Where was she working yesterday?' I had to raise my voice to beat the hiss of the incoming train.

'Jobbing somewhere—we're all doing that all the time. I think it was Josephine—yes, of course. Your old pal Monica Player's back there pro tem. Fay mentioned her too. Why?'

'I just wondered.' I did not explain further as the train was still. I did not need to wonder any longer at Fay's altered attitude towards me. The fact that she had managed to keep her news to herself proved how important she considered it—and I—might be.

I did not attempt to sleep in the train. I had the carriage to myself; privacy was too precious to be wasted in sleep. I read and reread the Professor's letter until I came close to believing it was only from my Professor.

He did not ignore the past. He reminded me of it constantly. 'You know my views on explanations. I'm not going to insult your intelligence by launching into one.'

Inevitably his letter was more formal than usual. But the apology which he hoped, but did not expect me to be able to accept, was patently sincere. He wrote at length on our friendship, and the words he used seemed to me the most wonderful ever to have been written. He ended:

I have given you no cause to believe anything I write, so I am not going to ask you to believe the truth in this letter. However, as it is more than probably the last letter I shall write to you, I should like to thank you. You have given me a great deal, Frances. I am very grateful.

I knew that final paragraph by heart long before I arrived at Pine Halt. If only his name had just been Slane. If only. Those two words, I thought wearily, must be the most futile—and the saddest—in the English language.

It was raining lightly at the Halt. A thin wind was blowing down from the hills, and the small station looked bare, cold, and very different from the way it had looked last May when I first met Estelle and Hannah.

The station-master was as helpful as before. 'Would you be Nurse Dorland, miss? They rang from the hospital to say would I ask you to wait for the students' bus. It'll be along soon.'

The rain stopped when the bus arrived. It was empty. The driver asked me to sit in the seat just behind his as he liked a bit of company. 'Real chilly this afternoon, Nurse. Had it cold in town?'

'Not as cold as this. You had any snow yet?'

He chatted contentedly about the weather, the number of patients in the hospital, the number of students he would carry on his return journey. 'Packed in like sardines, they'll be. Talk of the overloaded ark!'

I made a series of exclamations, I hoped in the right places, but did not really hear him at all. I was watching the country around. It had settled for the winter, the trees were brown and bleak, only the evergreens bore leaves, and the rain dripped from these like slow tears. The bleakness soothed me. It reminded me of the winter at home. The pale afternoon sun held no warmth when it came out, the sky remained grey, the land the colour of deep pewter, with only the brown lace of the empty trees and dark green stabbing fingers of the firs to lighten the grey world. Then, as we reached the foot of the long hospital hill, a scarlet tractor bounded out of a side lane, swung dangerously, and perched half on one bank of the narrow road to let us pass. The tractor-driver was young, and dressed in the old Army greatcoat and leather over-jacket the tractor-drivers wore at home. He even had on the same type of tea-cosy hat with a large blue pom-pom. I noticed every detail about that unknown young man deliberately. I had to do that to keep my mind off the original owner of the hill and my own future. I even wondered, as again I had at home, what landworkers wore in winter before the last world war provided a generation and their sons with old Army clothes.

Sister Illingworth was too busy to see me when I reported at her office. A Staff Nurse wearing a sister's belt took me to the Night Home, and handed me over to the Home Sister.

The Home was a long, one-storey, brick building, divided into a rabbit-warren of minute rooms. The Home Sister told me all the rooms had french windows and gave me a key. 'You may come and go through your window, Nurse, but remember always to lock it and remove the key when you leave your room empty.'

My luggage had arrived before me. The suitcases were in my room, my bicycle, according to that Sister, was in the rack. 'Unpack quietly. All the nurses in here are sleeping. Go to bed early to-night, after this busy day. Be in bed again by three to-morrow afternoon and report to Night Sister when you go in to supper.' She looked at her watch. 'If you hurry you should be unpacked by second tea. The dining-room is directly opposite to Sister Illingworth's office.'

I felt far stranger than on my first day in the P.T.S. when I went into tea. A voluntary helper presiding behind the tea-urn poured me a cup of tea, and told me which was the junior table. There were several girls at that table.

I ate in silence while they continued with their apparently fascinating and very technical conversation, in which Klebs-Loeffler, Hoffman's something or other, and something called the *B. xerosis* kept cropping up. They all sounded alarmingly knowledgeable and were obviously as upstage as Fay had forecast. They reminded me very much of Simpson and her colleagues on my first morning in O.P.'s. I had survived that; I would survive this; survival did not mean enjoyment.

When I left the dining-room I wondered what to do. The silent solitude of my room was not very attractive. I had had all the privacy I needed in the train. I was tired, but far too restless to think of sleep.

It was still light, and would be so for roughly another hour. I decided to use the time taking myself on a tour of the hospital. My months in London had shown me how useful it was to acquire a pro's eye view of a hospital.

I quite enjoyed my self-conducted tour. I found the dispensary hidden behind Casualty; the X-Ray department, Path. Lab., and Almoner's offices were a neat trio of Nissen huts disguised by clean white paint and red window-boxes; the surgical stores, repairs and works, chapel, and morgue were straight out of Hans Andersen. Each was housed in a small, weather-boarded hut, and they were clustered together and half hidden by the infringing pines.

The hospital was like a toy in comparison with the parent building in London, and my tour took me less time than it would take me to walk down the main corridor of Martha's proper. I had noticed the names of the wards, but could not go near then as I was out of uniform. I drifted back towards the night nurses' home, but the thought of that silence oppressed me. I turned away and left the hospital by the main gate. Without thinking where I was going, I wandered up the hill to the P.T.S. house.

I paused when I reached it and looked at the building curiously. It was not really long since we had left it, yet it seemed to belong to another lifetime. I thought about my set in general and Estelle in particular. I had to move on. That wretched house reminded me too vividly of her. If ever a girl had a vocation for nursing she had. And because she had gone to a free film show one morning she would never be a nurse again. I wondered if Bart realized how much this was going to upset her. I guessed her grandfather did, and that was one of his reasons for allowing Bart to visit her. I hoped they would let me visit her soon. I would ask for permission just as soon as I had a proper night off. There was so much I wanted to tell her, and one of those things, I realized without forethought, was that as she could not nurse she ought to read medicine. The idea pleased me so much that I nearly went back to write to her at once. The watery sun was disappearing fast. If I wanted to reach the top of the hill I should have to hurry. There was plenty of time. I had a long, empty evening ahead.

It was darker and very slippery under the wet trees. Above tree-level the light returned. I glanced at it only once, then had to pay attention to my hands and feet as the going was exceptionally rough after the rain and I was mostly on all fours.

I reached the plateau, and recovered my breath as the rim of the sun disappeared. I was glad I had made that climb. It was good to be back here, even if I was alone.

And then I heard that footstep behind me.

12. I take the Professor's Advice

I looked round at the shelter quickly, hoping I had been mistaken. I did not want to share the next half-hour with any itinerant nurse or student. When I saw who was behind me I remained momentarily transfixed with my head twisted over my left shoulder.

That afternoon in the park I had thought I was imagining his presence. I knew at once I was imagining nothing. He was there all right. His suit proved that. Having only seen him previously in an ordinary grey lounge suit, a mackintosh, or his shirt-sleeves, I had never visualized him wearing the insignia of a senior member of Martha's. His black jacket and pinstriped trousers made him seem an elegant stranger. His expression was strange, too. He looked as if he doubted the evidence of his eyes.

'Frances?' He came towards me. 'You? What are you doing here?'

My heart was beating so loudly that I thought he must hear it. 'I've been transferred. They're short of a night junior. Some one seems to have diphtheria. I got sent down.'

He stopped a foot or so from me. 'Come away from that edge—you're much too close.' I stepped back, and so did he. 'Did you say diphtheria?'

'Yes. One of the nurses has it—I think.' I wondered how he did not know this, since the pathologists must have to deal with the diagnostic swab.

'Oh, that girl. No. She hasn't got it. She's got an acute streptococcal tonsillitis, plus a query Vincent's angina. A nasty throat. Not diphtheric.'

'Is that why you're here?'

'Roughly.' He spoke with unusual deliberation, as if he was talking in one language and thinking in another. 'Why did they pick on you?'

'I'm the only first-year who's had diphtheria.'

'You have?' He looked at me, then at the trees below. 'When?'

I told him. 'I suppose I'm immune?'

He told the trees that nothing was medically impossible, but it was unlikely that I should get it again. 'When did they send you down?'

'By the twelve-thirty express.' As it was safe to watch him I did so. The other night in his office I had been able to accept that he was not my Professor. Now I had had his letter, even though he was dressed up like a pundit, I could not think of him as anyone else.

'You're not going to have to work to-night?' he asked sharply.

'No. To-morrow night. In Catherine.'

He looked at me again. 'Have you slept at all to-day?'

'Not yet. There hasn't been much time. I only heard this morning.' I paused, to nerve myself to say what I wanted to say. 'I got your letter this morning. Thank you for writing it.'

He inclined his head, but made no comment.

The silence that followed deafened me. I had to break it. 'May I ask you something?'

'Of course.' His tone did not match the invitation in his words.'

'What is—are—Klebs-Loeffler, Hoffman's something, and another thing that sounds like the *B. xerosis*? Are they bugs—I mean, germs?'

He did not answer immediately. He just went on looking at me. Then he smiled. 'I call 'em bugs too. Let's go and sit down while I tell you. You've spent far too many of the last twenty-four hours on your feet.'

I sat on one end of the long wooden seat against the back wall of the shelter, and held my hands tightly in my lap in an attempt to stop them from shaking too obviously. He leant against the side-wall opposite to me. 'The Klebs-Loeffler is a bacillus—also Hoffman's—and the *B. xerosis*. All three are members of a group of the Corynebacterium, with a few others thrown in. You find the Klebs-Loeffler in the false membrane that's characteristic of diphtheria.' His smile reappeared. 'Want any more?'

'Yes, please,' I replied as if he was offering me a plate of bread-and-butter.

'Right. Let's see. Well, the organism is a non-motile, gram-positive, non-sporing aerobe, which produces a soluble exotoxin. Does any of that makes sense?'

'the first part—sort of. The last bit—no.'

The light was fading, but there was still enough for me to see the expression in his eyes. His smile was not reaching his eyes. 'It's a shade complicated. I'll explain if you like, but won't it be more to the point if I just tell you that if you spot the Klebs-Loeffler you know you're dealing with diphtheria? If it's not there you have another look, and rule out dip.'

'No Klebs-Loeffler no dip.?' I echoed, as if his words were the most important I had ever heard. 'Thank you.'

He took out his cigarette-case. 'How did you come by all this confused learning? Young More?'

'No. The girls at tea to-day.'

'You'd better bring the conversation back to diphtheria at tea to-morrow and throw out a few light remarks about non-motile, gram-positive, non-sporing aerobes.'

'I'll have to be in bed, then. I'll save them until I get back to my set. That'll shake 'em. Bart too,' I added absently, thinking how reality differed from imagination. Although I had tried to be strong-minded in the train, I had inevitably drifted into a glorious day-dream in which he and I met again. I had not got around to working out our conversation. But if I had never in a hundred years would I have imagined it including a fascinating discussion on the Klebs-Loeffler, Hoffman's bacillus, and the *B. xerosis.* 'Like all medical students, he doesn't believe nurses know anything.'

'He'll grow out of that.' He considered his open case gravely as if it was important that he found the right cigarette. 'Your leaving town so suddenly must have been a blow to him. Mind if I smoke?'

'Please do.' It was a relief to be able to be honest about Bart if nothing else. 'He won't mind my being away. He's got quite enough on his mind without having to bother if I'm around. You remember what I told you about him?'

'Yes. And?'

'Well—it's all working out fairly well.' I hesitated. 'I think it's going to work very well, in the long run.'

'In the long run?' he echoed doubtfully.

'Perhaps I should apologize. I told you the truth, but not quite all the truth about him. It's all right to do that now, as it's quite official.'

'I realize I am being exceedingly dense, but what is official?'

I explained in detail. Apparently I did not explain clearly. When I had finished he took me back over each point.

'Your anonymous friend was Estelle Dexter?'

'Yes.'

'More was merely in the habit of confiding in you as a mutual friend?'

I smiled briefly. 'He didn't honestly make a habit of it. He only really let down his hair in the park one evening. Before we went to the ballet with your tickets.'

'I remember.' At last he had found the cigarette he wanted. 'I saw you in the park that evening.'

'You did?' Then I remembered too. 'Oh, yes. Bart said you had gone by. I didn't look round. I—er—didn't know you were you.'

'No.' He glanced at me expectantly, as if he was waiting for me to enlarge on that remark. There was a lot I wanted to ask him, and had wanted since I discovered who he was. Originally I had thought I should never dare question him; now we were together, daring did not come into it. He was a highly intelligent man; he knew very well that I was curious about him. If he had wanted to satisfy my curiosity he would have done so. His silence kept me silent. I loved him. I did not want him to do anything he did not want to do.

He struck a match. The wind had blown inland, the air in the shelter was quite still. The match flame flickered dangerously. 'So you were just a disinterested third party?'

I shrugged. 'I can't honestly remain disinterested when two people I'm fond of behave like a couple of ostriches. I had to try to pull their heads out of the sand, if only to bang them together. I know there are a good many snags still in the way for them, and Estelle's still on the S.I.—'

'She's not.' He cut me short. 'She came off at two this afternoon.'

'She did? Oh, that's wonderful!'

'It's very good.' He sounded as pleased as I was. 'I can tell you something more, as it's official. Dr Curtis is bringing her back to Martha's at the end of this week.'

'That's splendid!' I sighed pleasurably. 'Couldn't be better. Bart'll be on top of the world.'

'I'm glad.' He sat down on the bench. 'One more problem we can tick off. A satisfactory, if, to me, rather surprising solution.'

'That Hamilton Dexter should come round?'

'I didn't know Hamilton Dexter was involved until a few moments ago. I had previously thought you were talking about yourself.'

'About me? Me and Bart?' My voice cracked slightly. 'Heavens, no! Besides, if it had been me, there wouldn't have been any problem.'

'No? Oh, yes, I see what you mean.'

I looked at him curiously. I should not have said he was being exceedingly dense, but he was taking an extraordinarily long time—for him—to grasp what I was saying. That fact surprised me far more than his presence on the seat beside me in smooth pundit's suiting. It only seemed natural that he should be there. With the exception of that night in his office, I had never been able to remain on edge when with him. I might be as taut as an over-strung fiddle-string when we met. Ten minutes after meeting it was as if I was at home.

Again we were silent. This time the silence was without strain. I was content to listen to it until eternity.

He said nothing until he finished the first and lit a second cigarette. 'Frances, have you ever lost a friend?'

I did not know what I had been expecting. I only knew it was not that. 'I don't know. Expect so.'

'I don't. I expect your friends hang on to you like leeches. No one,' he added slowly, 'in his right mind would let you go out of his life. You're not only a remarkably attractive young woman, you are—in my experience—unique.'

'Me?' I couldn't believe my ears.

'Yes. You.' He stood up, walked to the entrance, turned to face me. 'We both know I owe you a considerable explanation. You've every right to demand one now we've met. You haven't.' He paused. 'That night in my office, you might have been too shocked, then too angry, to bother. You're neither, now. But all you've asked of me is—Klebs-Loeffler. And I don't believe you intend asking anything more personal. Do you?'

I shook my head.

'Why not?'

I had to answer then. I used his letter as an ally. 'I share your views on explanations.'

'I'll have to be honest. If our positions were reversed I shouldn't hold those views.' He paused again. 'I should never have written that letter. I wish I hadn't.'

'You do?' I could not follow him now. I loved that letter.

'Yes. It was a mistake. A great mistake. If I had known then what I know now, I should not have written as I did. I expect you can understand why?'

There was no point in polite pretence. 'No. I can't.'

'I'd like to explain,' he said. 'Would you mind?'

'No,' I said carefully, 'no.'

'Thank you.' He sat down and folded one arm on the other. 'It won't take long. Are you cold?'

I said I was not at all cold, thank you.

He took his time. 'I've told you I've been under the impression that you were very fond of More. I could well understand his feeling the same about you. I was convinced he did. But for that, you would never have had that shock the other night. And I would certainly,' he added, with unusual urgency, 'never have written what amounted to a final letter from an old—in every sense of the word—friend.'

'You didn't tell me who you were, because of Bart? But,' it had to be said, 'I hadn't met him when I first met you.'

'I know. Now. I didn't previously. I got the impression he was very much in the picture from the first evening I rang you, ostensibly to tell you I had visited your home, in actual fact to ask you to dine with me. You've no reason to believe this, but I dislike deception, and had decided to tell you the truth that night. I told your parents I intended doing that on the first occasion on which I was able to persuade you to come out with me. As I have not been able to do that,' he said drily, 'I have at least kept my word on that. I'm not counting the night Lily Ellis died. I didn't ask you out that night. I took you for a drive without giving you a chance to refuse.'

I could only take this in very, very slowly. And one astounding fact at a time. 'You told my parents? They knew? They've always called you—'

'Slane? That was good of them. I asked them if they would until they heard from you.'

'Why?'

He said, 'May I answer that in a moment? Have you told them what you've found out?'

'No. No one.'

'My God,' he said softly, 'that tells me how much it hurt. I'm sorry. Very sorry.'

I ignored that because I had to. It was a long time since I had had any sleep, my armour of detached interest was wearing thin. Gentleness could shatter it far more easily than anything else. 'I know Dr Anderson took you to visit my parents, but how did you get hold of my name originally?'

He turned to me. It was too dark to see anything now but the outline of his face. 'Why have you taken so long to ask that?'

I told him the truth. 'Either I forgot or, when I remembered, didn't think you liked being questioned.'

'I see.' He was silent for several seconds. 'To be strictly accurate, I traced you through the British Museum.'

'The—what?' I demanded incredulously.

'The British Museum. It was quite simple. You had given me the name of your village. When I looked it up in the A.A. book I found there were four villages with that name in England, two of them in Kent. That's why I went to the Museum. It was a safe bet that in only one there'd been a Mithraic temple. You mentioned it. I found it.'

'I knew there were two in Kent. Ours has a "cum," the other an "in." But that doesn't explain—me.'

'Doesn't it? Frances, you're used to village life. You should know how simple it is to find out anyone's name. I merely drove down there the following week, and spent a long while in your post office sending myself a telegram.'

'Oh. Of course.' I smiled weakly. 'Mrs Mercer.'

'Is that your postmistress's name? A pleasant woman. She said she was quite used to having strangers in her sub-post-office, and told me all the local sights I must see. When she saw my hospital address she was most interested. She told me Mr Dorland's eldest daughter Frances was at St Martha's—said I must be sure to look out for you, and went so far as to describe you very well. If I had any lingering doubts over your identity she dispelled them by telling me your father kept turkeys.'

'How did she know you were at Martha's, if you were sending a telegram to yourself?'

'I explained that I worked there too. Having got that settled, I came down here the following week-end to photograph those hobbys. You know most of the rest. What you don't know you can probably guess.'

I did not know anything; my brain was too stunned for guessing. 'Dr Anderson?' I asked carefully. 'You said you met him by chance?'

'Chance hasn't figured much in our relationship. I just tried to make it appear that way. I looked at the list of local G.P.'s in your post office, noticed Luke Anderson's name, checked in the *Medical Register* to see if he was the man I knew, then made a point of running into him, and getting an invitation out of him. He told me about your father's tape-recordings, and took me round to your home, as I hoped.'

I was beyond surprise, even beyond wonder. 'Why did you take all that trouble?'

'Wasn't much trouble. It was just a case of following a few leads. I wanted your name, and to meet your parents.'

'What would you have done if Dr Anderson hadn't been at Cambridge with you?'

He said that would not have made much difference. 'You had to have a G.P. The medical world's a smaller world than most. Once in it you can generally contact any given person. Some one always knows him. If the unlikely had happened, and I had drawn a medical blank, there was another line open to me. Your father uses the machinery made by my firm. I could have got some man to take me round on some pretext.'

'I—I forgot about that.'

'I'm sorry to have to remind you of it,' he said a little grimly. 'If you're to know the truth you may as well know all.'

'But why—why any of it?'

'Briefly, because I'm old enough to be your father. And happen to share certain views with Hamilton Dexter.' He got to his feet, and, as before, walked to the entrance. This time he did not turn round. 'I wanted to get to know you, and, circumstances being what they are, felt I ought to talk to your parents as well as to you. We talked at length that day I spent with them. I haven't mentioned this to you until now, because only now have I learnt how mistaken I've been all these months. I've been tempted to do so often. It seemed better to leave it unsaid.'

I watched the dark outline of his figure against the early night sky. Below us the pines were a black fringed carpet; there was no moon; the first stars were out.

I said slowly, 'If it had been Bart and me, instead of Bart and Estelle, perhaps if I had known who you were, and told Bart, it might have rocked the boat.'

He faced me. 'You do believe me?'

I could believe without understanding. 'Yes. It makes sense.'

'Then can you also believe why, in the first place, I gave you only half my name and continued to do that in the letters I wrote, before I knew of More's existence?'

'I'd like to. I can't because you haven't told me why.'

'That's true.' He put both his hands in his pockets. 'Surely you've guessed the answer to both?'

I was about to deny that, untruthfully, when I remembered Estelle. In some incredible and wonderful fashion it seemed he and I were going to be able to go on where we had left off on the morning before Howard sent me up to the top-floor lab. But we could only go on if I was as honest as he was now being with me. I said, 'I suppose you have to be careful when you've got a lot of money. And being'—I took a deep breath and plunged on—'a senior member of Martha's, as well as anything else, you possibly felt it might embarrass me if I had known that I was pouring out my life-story and problems to a pundit, and, in another way, it might have embarrassed you to know I knew.'

'You aren't offended by that?' he asked oddly.

'Not now. I was—very angry.'

'I saw that. And deserved it. What stopped your anger?'

'I thought it over, and it made sense too. I shouldn't have got so cross. No,' I added quickly, as he was obviously about to interrupt, 'no—it wasn't fair to fly off at a tangent without knowing the whole set-up. It was particularly wrong to do that to some one who's been so consistently kind to me, and helped me as much as you have.'

He stood very still. 'Frances,' he said, 'you are a very sweet young woman, and I love you beyond expression. But every man has his limits. If you say I have been so kind and helpful to you again, I am not sure I can answer for the consequences.'

I just stared at him. Slowly, very slowly, I realized what he had said. He waited for me to speak, but I was speechless with wonder. Then wonder changed to overwhelming happiness that grew and grew inside me, like a rising fountain of stars.

'I'm sorry if that annoyed you,' he said at last. 'I didn't want to do that. I shouldn't have told you yet. Possibly never. I keep doing the wrong thing where you are concerned, probably because I'm so anxious to do the reverse.'

'Please! Don't say that ...'

'My dear'—his voice was weary—'you may as well let me finish. I've said too much to go back. So I may as well tell you that I want to marry you, and that, absurd though it may sound to hear a supposedly adult man say that he wanted that after meeting you once, the fact remains that it's true. The situation is not without a certain ironic humour—though I must admit for the present the humour escapes me. Having at last met a young woman whom I love and trust in every respect—the one person I have ever known to be genuinely uninterested in my material angle—I find I have met her twenty years too late. She's kind, gentle, and very generous. But to her I can never be anything else but her old friend the Professor.'

His patent unhappiness would have made me jump up, even had he not used that name. 'How did you know I called you that?'

'My dear girl, you've called me that unconsciously, on and off, since the night Lily Ellis died. You used it several times that night. I didn't take you up on it then; you were too upset to know what you were saying. Later it came out again and again. You're a very talkative person. You probably don't realize how much you've told me about yourself, your family, your friends. You certainly can't have realized how much I've enjoyed listening to you. For a little while I quite enjoyed being your Professor. Incidentally, how did you come to hit the nail on the head?'

I explained absently, trying to think of some way to break through his defences.

'I reminded you of an uncle? That's reasonable.' He lit a cigarette. 'Now we've straightened everything out, I think it's time I took you back to the hospital.' He threw away a dead match, and out of the blue began to talk about smoking. 'I miss tobacco in the lab.'

'Can't you smoke there?' I asked to gain time. I had no intention of letting him go yet, but had still to find the right words.

'It's not a good idea if one wants to stay alive.' He held out a hand as if I was a child. 'Come along. You must be exhausted. I'm going to take you back.'

I could not waste any more time in searching for words. 'Before we go—there's something I want to say.'

'There's nothing more to be said. I've talked far too much and for too long, as it is. Shall we go?'

I stood in front of him. 'I was only going to say you have been so kind and helpful to tell me what you have.'

He stiffened perceptibly. 'You've possibly forgotten that I asked you to dispense with all that.'

'No, I haven't forgotten.'

He got rid of his cigarette. 'I don't think I understand.'

'I don't think you do,' I said, and explained.

I might as well have made the explanation to the stone walls of the shelter. He refused to believe me. 'You hate hurting people, Frances. You don't want to hurt my feelings. You're only a child, a weary child— you're tired—don't know what you're saying. You're fond of me—your attitude this evening has shown me that. I'll not pretend I wouldn't give everything I possess to take you at your word. But I refuse to take advantage of your kind heart.' He reached for my hand. 'Come. We're going.'

'Oh, no, we're not.' I pulled my hand out of his. My movements were quite instinctive. I put a hand on each of his shoulders, and looked up at his face. 'You may be an adult man—old enough to be my father if you married in the schoolroom—a Director of our Path. Lab.—a fourth or fifth Bart. (I still don't know which)—and own a firm that manufactures half the farm machinery in England, but you don't know one thing about women. I could willingly shake you hard here and now. I love you very much and have loved you for a long time. You're my dear, dearest Professor—and always will be. So will you please stop talking utter rubbish about my being a kind, generous child'—my voice broke, but I kept on in sheer desperation—'and realize that I mean what I'm saying—or I won't be able to answer for the consequences, either ...'

His arms had tightened round me before I finished speaking. 'Oh, my darling Frances,' he murmured, and kissed me hard. It was some time later that he raised his head. 'Sweetheart, are you sure you don't mind my being so much older?'

'Are you sure you don't mind my having no money?'

He kissed me again, and there was no more talk about age or money.

We went back to the shelter and sat on the bench. He drew my head on his shoulder and played with my hair. 'I've always wanted to do this. I've never seen such wonderful curls.'

'There's not a Sister in Martha's who would agree with you. I've collected hair rockets all over the old firm.'

'You aren't going to be able to collect many more. I hope you don't mind, dearest, but I hope to marry you very soon. I'll write to your parents to-night. Can we go and see them on your next night off? Any idea when?'

'I'll be due for a couple some time in the next week. I'd like to see Estelle, too. Think they'll let me?'

'I'll ask John Curtis. I expect it'll be all right.'

I smiled at him. 'Does anyone ever refuse you anything?'

'Yes. You did. To-night. Anyway, I'll ask John and let you know what he says. I'll be down here at the week-end.'

'That's good.' I stroked his hair, then suddenly realized everything. 'Oh, God! I'm so junior here that not even the juniors'll talk to me! And you're you!'

'I've just been thinking over that angle. It won't hurt me, but is it going to hurt you? I'd be only too happy to go down and announce everything to-night, but will that mean you have to put up with the kind of things you got from that girl Vickers in Out-Patients? I suppose you've now realized what all that was about?'

'Yes. Don't let it worry you. It doesn't worry me at all now. But there's one thing I'd like to know. Why did you risk going to Home Sister that night?'

His arms closed round me. 'You needed help. I wanted to be there to help you. But what about this place? Do we make it public? Or keep it quiet until the last minute?'

I looked down the hill. A sickle moon had risen out of the trees, the clouds had all vanished, the stars were all over the sky. Far below the hospital lights shone through the trees, as if a giant had cast down hundreds of surplus stars.

'I don't suppose I'll have to put up with much. I don't particularly mind if I do. And if I run into any serious problems I can always run to my Professor for advice. He's never disappointed me yet. He always tells me what to do.'

'Did he tell you to go round threatening to shake respectable pathologists?' he asked softly.

'More or less. He once told me that on certain occasions it's essential to be absolutely honest. Which just shows. He always knows what to do in any given circumstance.'

'I believe you're right, sweetheart,' said the Professor. 'He does indeed.' And he kissed me again.

LUCILLA ANDREWS

Highland Interlude

1. To Glasgow as Children's Escort

I was on theatre call with Sister Orthopaedic that Thursday night. Normally Thursday was the quietest night of our theatre week, but the start of the Easter school holidays and the sudden arrival of spring in the last few days had doubled the London traffic and our intake of accident admissions. Our first emergency operation that night started at ten. It was twenty to three and five operations later before the theatre was cleared and reset with the basic emergency setting always left in readiness.

Sister came out of the duty-room as I switched off the theatre lights. 'What remains to be done, Nurse Wade?'

'Just a final check round the outhouses, Sister.' I yawned behind my mask. 'Unless we start up again.'

'For everyone's sake,' she replied wearily, buttoning her cuffs, 'God forbid. Those men still have their night rounds to do. Incidentally, did I hear them all moving off when I was changing?'

'Yes, Sister. Mr Dawkins [the Senior Orthopaedic Registrar] looked in to ask me to say goodnight to you.'

She pursed her pale lips. 'It's a pity Mr Dawkins' manners don't equal his surgery, but I suppose one can't have everything. Right. I'm off to the Office to report to Night Super., and then I hope we can both get to bed. You look ready for yours after this long stint.'

'Just as long for you, Sister.'

'But after ten years in this job, Staff Nurse, I'm more accustomed to long stints.'

The department was very quiet after she had gone, and the air-conditioner hummed to itself like an overworked bee. I checked, then switched off lights in the anaesthetic room, the glove room, the tin room, the autoclave room. As Sister had a fixation about sleeping students on the gallery benches, having once caught one sleeping off a hangover there years ago, I went up to double-check, even though I had already had a good look up from the theatre floor. Sister hadn't many fixations, but the few she had could send her blood-pressure shooting up. As she was, on the whole, an amiable and hard-working woman, her theatre nurses and most of the men working with her were perfectly willing to indulge her little ways. But not Mr Dawkins. He refused to indulge any but his own little ways. Consequently, though once Sister Orthopaedic's speciality had been tea and soothing words between cases, since Mick Dawkins became S.O.R. tea was only served in the surgeons' room at the end of a list, and according to Joe Fenton, the Junior Orthopaedic Houseman, no member of the Orthopaedic Unit now dared taste the tea before trying it out first on a junior dresser.

Though the men had gone, I left their room until last and, from old habit, knocked loudly before going in. It was an accepted, if unproven, fact in our hospital, St Martha's, that any nurse straying into the surgeons' room whilst still occupied was not only risking her theatre sister's fury, but seriously considering changing to an older profession. I was half-way up the room before I saw Joe Fenton sleeping on the desk. 'Hey, Joe! Wake up!'

The desk was tucked between changing alcoves, sinks, and file cupboards. He had been writing notes. His fair head was on his arms, and he did not stir at my voice or when I shook him. Quickly I soaked a towel in cold water. 'Sorry, love, but you can't sleep here!' I slapped the towel on his face. 'Sister won't approve.'

'Oh, Christ! Liz, you bitch!' He pushed me off and stood up, shaking himself like a puppy. 'Oh, God, why can't I die, peacefully? The others gone?'

'Ages ago.' I retrieved the scattered notes as he stuck his head under the nearest cold tap. 'So must you. Sister's gone to the Office, but there'll be murder if she gets back and finds you still here. Mick Dawkins didn't say goodnight to her, nicely.'

'Silly sod with his right little touch of the God Almighty. But handy with his knife.'

'And so'll Sister be if you don't get moving.' I threw him his white coat, pushed his notes under his arm, and propelled him to the door. 'Off, stat!'

'Not yet.' He propped his long, thin body against the wall between the fire appliances and buttoned his shirt. 'I've just remembered why I hung on after the others. I've got to talk to you, Liz. I'm in one bloody hell of a spot.'

'As we'll both be if Sister gets back now. Can't this wait?'

He said simply, 'No. Too serious. Aren't you off this week-end?'

I glanced at the corridor clock. With luck we might have five minutes. 'One-thirty Friday to seven-thirty Monday. Why?'

He hesitated. 'You know it's all fixed for me to take the kids up to Glasgow as Dad's got to take this business trip to Italy?'

'Yes. And—'

'And you know Jadley-Grey rang Dawkins between those first two tonight?' I nodded. 'Guess what, sweetie! Our Mr Jadley-Grey is going to do a demonstration list here on Saturday morning for the benefit of a posse of V.I.P. orthopods. M.D. was almost human. He said he was dead sorry to bugger up my week-end, but as Jadley-Grey is our pundit, that's the way it'll be. So I sort of thought of you, Liz. Will you take 'em up for me?'

I leant against the opposite wall. 'To Glasgow?'

He said, 'I know it's asking a hell of a lot and means spending most of the week-end in trains, but could you face it? Dad won't hear of them going alone, though I think they'd be fine, but he's our old man and he says no.'

'And what happens in Glasgow?'

'You just hand 'em over to Uncle Dougal at Glasgow Central Saturday morning, soon as your train gets in. He can't come down for them as he's lecturing in Glasgow tomorrow night. He's paying all expenses up for the kids and mine both ways, and Dad's paying for the kids' return. It's all laid on—reservations made—the lot. Oh, no!' He slapped his forehead. 'Just remembered! You're going down to some woman in Sussex for some party Saturday night.' He was not the weeping type, but he was very tired. He looked about to burst into tears. 'What do I do, Liz? I can't think of anyone else to ask.'

'Relax, love. If it's all right with your father I'll take 'em.'

'What about your party?'

'There'll be other parties—and anyway, you know my views on blind dates.'

'What about this woman?'

'We were at school together. She's just married. I can meet her husband some other time. She's a nice soul. She'll understand.'

'You're sure?' He beamed at me. 'Liz, I could kiss you!'

'Not here you can't, chum. Out, now! Give me the details in the morning.'

He blew me a kiss and vanished a couple of minutes before Sister returned. She was rather peeved. 'Really, Nurse Wade, you are a dawdler. You should be changed by now. Do get a move on or we'll never get off.'

I got a move on; we had no more emergency calls that night; I had just time to wonder if I needed to have my head examined before I was asleep.

My school friend asked me the same when I rang her before going on duty next morning. 'And why does it have to be you? This Joe Fenton your steady?'

'No. I just like him.'

'Elizabeth! It's too early for a coy chat.'

'I'm not being coy.' I explained having known and liked Joe for years and, as she had known me even longer, added, 'His mother died two months before my grandfather.'

She said in a different tone, 'Oh. Yes. I'm getting the picture. Go on.'

'I've never met the rest of his family as they live in Cornwall. There's a big gap between him and these kids. His twin brother and sister are nearly twelve, and the older boy's just fourteen.'

'Surely they're old enough to travel alone?'

'I'd have thought so. So does Joe. Their father says no. As he hasn't re-married,' I said thoughtfully, 'he probably feels he has to fuss for both. Like Grandfather.'

'But, Liz dear, he was much older!' She changed the subject, smartly. 'What part of Scotland?'

'You mean where does this uncle live? Somewhere in the Highlands, but that's not my baby, as all I have to do is hand them over to him at Glasgow.'

'Uncle got a family?'

'Not as far as I know, but that's not much. He's in tropical medicine and worked in Africa for World Health for years until last Christmas. Not sure what he's doing now. Joe hasn't said. Probably some job in Scotland.'

'Guess so. You been to Scotland, Liz?'

'No. Think I'll see much from the train?

'If you can see in the dark and the kiddiwinks don't start ripping the seats. Have fun—come down to see us soon.'

I was fond of her and very glad she had taken it so well. I had had to put Joe first for a reason I could not really explain to her, since of all my friends he had been the only one who had properly understood how my grandfather's death had hit me. He was still my only Martha's friend with whom I had been able to discuss my parents' death in an air crash when I was seven. I had then been spending a holiday with my paternal grandfather, a widower and only other close relative. Grandfather's home had remained mine until he died in his sleep. He had been both parents and my whole world to me. Joe's world had fallen apart with his mother's death. At the time we had recognized each other's unspoken grief for the agony it was, and mentally borrowed each other's shoulders. Since then, though we made other friends, other dates, in any problem we turned to each other. We enjoyed our relationship and had long been highly amused by the analyses made on it by our mutual friends. Joe said what really foxed the Orthopaedic Unit was the fact that we'd managed to remain on speaking terms for years without going to bed with each other. 'Are we sick, Liz? Or a pair of Victorian anachronisms?' We had yet to work out the answer. It was not losing either of us any sleep.

The theatre was too busy that morning for us to talk. At lunch-time a large envelope in my post pigeon-hole enclosed my sleeper tickets and a letter written on the back of a blank temperature chart. Joe wrote:

Have had sleepers altered to your name and rung home. Mrs Evans, Dad's housekeeper, will be at Euston plus kids, eleven nocte. Uncle D. at Glasgow Central, mané. Kids know his car. Hope they don't play you up—use strong-arm tactics if necessary. Give my regards and so forth to U.D., and if you want to make him happy chat him up about trop. med. He doesn't talk much, but he's all right—doubt he's bitten a woman in years. Thanks again and love. J.

Having a free afternoon, I went along to the Medical School Library. The librarian was shocked. 'D. R. Grant of Edinburgh, Nurse? Has he written anything on Tropical Medicine? My dear young lady! Professor Grant's work on Trypanosomiasis is now one of the standard textboks on the subject. And only last year he produced an excellent paper on Generalized Leishmaniasis, and I understand is now working on another textbook. Of course, you know that at the start of the next academic year he is taking the Chair of Tropical Medicine at—dear me—is it Oxford or Cambridge? Professor Mullen was discussing this only yesterday.'

I apologized meekly for my ignorance. 'I didn't know Professor Grant was a Professor.'

The librarian offered me a disapproving glance and a selection of erudite literature. By tea-time I was well acquainted with the name D. R. Grant, M.D., F.R.C.P., on fly-leaves and under articles, and fairly well up in the nastier habits of the tsetse-fly.

I rehearsed in the back of my taxi to Euston. 'Tell me, Professor, do you miss the tsetse in the Highlands? Did you lecture on Leishmaniasis last night? Generalized, of course?'

My taxi stopped. Another drew up immediately behind. A long, gangling, very fair boy with a Beatle-cut jumped out and began unloading suitcases. He was so obviously Joe's younger brother that I smiled. He gave me a dirty look and turned his back. Then the plump, elderly woman with him looked me over before advancing briskly. 'Miss Elizabeth Wade? I though so. So kind—so pleased to meet you. I am Mrs Evans, and these are the young people. Robin, Judy, Johnnie, this is your big brother's kind friend, Miss Wade.'

The trio looked me up and down in silence. I said, 'How do you do?' They were not giving anything away, so they didn't tell me.

Mrs Evans was no great help. 'I'm afraid we are all very shy, Miss Wade—though, mind you, not with Auntie Bessie on the journey up! But somehow I have always understood Young People. I often think those of us not blessed with kiddies of our own do understand The Young better. Not that some of us can't be just a little difficult sometimes!' She wagged an arch finger. 'But Auntie Bessie understands. ...'

I listened with one ear and did some looking over for myself. Robin, the older boy, was already roughly an inch taller than me, and I was five eight. He had mild acne and a very sulky mouth, but he was too like Joe for me to hold anything against him—yet. Judy was equally fair, thin, and much taller than her twin. Her long hair looked too heavy for her small-boned and very intelligent face. She was very pale, but whether with travel-fatigue or because she was naturally so I could not tell. She barely opened her mouth before the train left.

Johnnie Fenton could have belonged in another family. He was a sturdy child with curly brown hair, a round, cheerful face, and very well-shaped thickly lashed dark-brown eyes. He had far and away the squarest shoulders and most direct gaze I had seen on any child his age. He was as silent as the others, without looking sullen, and though he gave me the impression he wouldn't much mind if I dropped dead, I doubted he would actually take a hand in the killing.

I had started counting the hours to Glasgow long before the guard began looking at his watch. Then Robin discovered he had left a suitcase on the wrong side of the barrier. Mrs Evans said didn't that just go to show how wise his dear father had been not to allow him to escort the twins to Scotland alone? 'Dear little Robin! We are such an old day-dreamer, aren't we? We'd probably lose our tickets, luggage, and twins before we got to Glasgow, wouldn't we?'

Dear little Robin looked, understandably, as if he would like to throttle her with his bare hands, and disappeared into the train with the twins. I stayed at the window as the train began to move out, then saw a man and a porter racing after us, and opened the door. The man leapt in. The porter flung in the luggage, then very neatly caught the floating pound note.

'Why, thanks a lot!' The newcomer smiled breathlessly. 'I surely cut that pretty fine.'

'But you made it.'

'And what is more, all in the one piece.' He checked his luggage. 'I hope the jolt has not harmed my rods. I am hoping to get in some real good fishing over the week-end. This is the first vacation I have had me in years. Are you on vacation?'

'Just up for the week-end.' I was looking him over as covertly as he was me. It was not the kind of scrutiny I had just exchanged with the younger Fentons.

He looked about thirty. He was slight, with sandy hair, blue eyes, and an attractive and rather shy smile. His suit had been made in London, but his short haircut was as strictly transatlantic as his voice. 'Is that so? I certainly hope it keeps fine for you.' A steward was advancing on us. 'Have I gotten in the right door? I do have a reservation.'

The steward examined his ticket. 'In the next carriage, Mr MacDonald. I'll be giving you a hand with the bags. Will you come this way, sir?'

'Be right with you.' The American offered me his hand. 'Thanks for letting me on. Have a real good trip.'

'Thanks. And you.' I was quite sorry to see him go. I'd enjoyed being reminded of my sex. Then I remembered why I was on that train. Pity, I thought, but nice.

The steward had earlier shown us our berths. The boys had adjoining single sleepers on the far side of Judy's. She and I shared another adjoining pair. When I went into mine the connecting door was closed.

I sat on the bed and looked at it. There was no stop before Crewe, and as we were on the train, presumably my charges would settle for the night, even if they had dispensed with the formality of telling me so. Or should I risk it and check?

Then I heard Judy's voice. 'Yes, come in. She's in there.'

Robin's voice was beginning to break. 'Why the hell did Joe have to lumber us with that drag?'

Johnnie said. 'She doesn't look as draggish as Bitchy Bessie!'

'Huh!' snorted Judy. 'She's got the same name. I'll bet she'll gripe like B.B. once she gets started. They all do! It'd have been different with Joe. He's good fun. I wish he'd come.'

'I'll bet he could've if he wanted to.' It was Robin again. 'He's making like the rest. He doesn't do what he says. None of 'em do.'

Judy was sniffing. 'And he did promise to take us up to Uncle Dougal.'

'Oh, hell, Ju!' wailed Robin. 'You're going to sniffle! Why do girls always have to sniffle?'

'I am NOT! I've just got this stinking cold coming, nit. You know that. You know I couldn't tell Bitchy Bessie as she'd have griped like crazy to Dad, and he'd have done his nut as he's got to be in Italy tomorrow.'

Johnnie said kindly, 'Uncle Dougal'll make your cold better, Ju. Dad says he's jolly clever, and I think he's jolly decent. I think it's going to be smashing in Gairlie. He told me at Christmas he's jolly glad to have his house back now the tenants have gone, and he wants us to stay with him lots of times. He said our Mummy was a jolly nice big sister, and he was jolly sorry when she died.'

The sudden silence next door evoked memories I preferred not to think on even after fifteen years. Though I was now old enough to appreciate there were worse things than being a motherless child, it had not looked that way to me even at Robin's age.

I got off the bed and knocked on the door. 'May I come in, Judy?'

They were all on Judy's bed. Robin's long legs were propped on the covered wash-basin. He did not move them. He scowled. 'Johnnie and I are just going to bed, if that's what you've come to say.'

'No.' I leant against the swaying door. 'I don't know what time you normally go to bed, but you're all old enough to have one late night without harm. I just looked in to say goodnight.'

'Night,' they chanted in dismissal.

'Thanks. Sleep well.' I looked at my watch. 'Nearly midnight. I hope Joe gets to bed earlier tonight. Know what I did to that boy at ten to three this morning?' I did not expect or get an answer. I just told them. Then I told them about Mr Jadley-Grey's demonstration list and Joe's ethical position. 'It's hideously unfair as he should be off, but if he doesn't show up to assist tomorrow Mr Jadley-Grey'll go spare, and what's worse, he won't forget it when Joe's due for his next step up the hospital ladder.'

Johnnie said, 'That's jolly unfair.'

Robin muttered, 'That's what she said.'

I said, 'Yes. That's what it is.' They were silent. 'Ah, well, see you in the morning—and, incidentally, my name's Elizabeth, and I'm a year younger than Joe.'

I closed the door and heard Robin's squeak of a whisper.

'Twenty-two! Blimey, is she past it!'

Johnnie whispered, 'She's got jolly long legs.'

I sat heavily on my bed. In my co-ed. grammar the boys had started at thirteen. I was past it. Then I looked at my legs and thought of that American. Perhaps not.

Judy was still asleep and her early-morning tea untouched when I looked in the next morning. 'Glasgow in forty minutes, Judy. Hi!' She was blinking and her face was flushed. 'Sleep well?'

'Yes, thanks.' She turned her back.

I hesitated. Her voice had a rasp. 'Your throat sore, Judy?'

'No. Thanks. I'm all right.'

I did not believe her, but as there was no point in annoying her with more questions for the moment, I moved on to see if the boys were up. Johnnie came into the corridor, fully dressed. 'Robin's dressing. I'm starving! I hope Uncle Dougal isn't late. He's promised us a right nosh for breakfast.'

I offered him a bar of chocolate. 'If you can eat it at this time of the morning?'

'Oh, gosh,' said Johnnie, 'I can eat chocolate any time. Can't you?'

'No. I have to be in the right mood. The mere idea before breakfast makes me want to throw up. Do take it all. Give some to Robin.'

'I say, Elizabeth, thanks!' He suddenly produced an enchanting smile. 'It's jolly decent of you to give us all this.'

I could have hugged him. 'Just hope it doesn't spoil your breakfast.'

'Oh gosh, no. Nothing stops me noshing!'

Robin appeared in a doorway. 'Come and get the rest of your stuff in, Johnnie. We don't want to be late for Uncle Dougal.'

It was Professor Grant who was late. We waited on the platform, and the children watched me exchange waves and smiles with the American. Johnnie asked who he was. Robin, without bothering to lower his voice, told Judy that the Yank looked another rip-roaring weirdie. Judy looked as if she had a headache as well as a sore throat. Mentally I damned all unpunctual professors, and suggested aloud that we should wait for him in the buffet. 'If we sit by that window there we can watch this platform for Professor Grant whilst we eat.'

Robin muttered, 'You don't have to bother. We're having breakfast with Uncle Dougal.'

Johnnie turned into my open ally. 'I think it's a smashing idea, Elizabeth. We can have one nosh now and another with Uncle Dougal. Come on, you lot!'

I was glad to get Judy out of the cold, but otherwise breakfast was grim. Only Johnnie enjoyed the food or made any attempt to help me with the conversation. Robin looked as if being fed poison. Judy looked as if only capable of keeping down sips of tea.

Grim or not, I spun it out until our table was wanted and I could spin no longer. The sun was warmer, so we moved out to a bench that overlooked the right platform and the station yard. Cars came and went. Taxis unloaded passengers, reloaded, drove off. Hovering porters asked if we wanted a cab. We took turns to say, 'Thanks, we're waiting for someone.' An hour later we were still waiting. Judy's flush had vanished. She was grey rather than white, apart from the nasty whitish circle round her mouth. By then my opinion of Professor Grant was unrepeatable.

Robin returned from another visit to the Information Bureau, shaking his head. Judy rested against my shoulder and made no objection when I took her racing pulse. Johnnie watched anxiously. 'You look dead grotty, Ju.'

Robin sat down. 'Suppose Uncle Dougal's forgotten?'

'He wouldn't do that.' I was revoltingly firm. 'Probably he overslept after his lecture last night and is now stuck in a traffic jam. Glasgow's a big city. I could kick myself for forgetting to ask Joe or Mrs Evans where he was staying last night, as we could ring him up.' I had a belated inspiration. 'We could ring Gairlie! I take it there'll be someone in his house to tell us?'

'He's got a housekeeper,' said Robin gloomily. 'But Gairlie's miles away. Cost a bomb.'

'Still, might be worth a try. We'll wait a little longer, then get on to it.'

Judy sighed. 'That won't be any good if he's stuck in the traffic. Suppose his car's busted? Suppose he can't get it mended for hours and hours? You'll have to get your train back, Elizabeth.'

'No, love.' They all looked at me. 'I'd better break this to you, but you're stuck with me until I can hand you over to your uncle. Sorry and all that, but I promised Joe—and for a start, he's a lot bigger than I am.'

The twins were openly relieved. Robin said peevishly, 'It's a dead bore, but—' Then he yelped with joy. 'That's Uncle Dougal's car!'

Judy said in a small, very adult voice, 'But that's not Uncle Dougal driving it.'

The boys had leapt up and grabbed suitcases as a large grey car turned into the yard. They lowered the cases very carefully as if suddenly so unsure of the ground beneath their feet that they had to avoid even the slightest jolt in case it finally gave way.

I stood up. 'You're sure that's his car? Right. You stay here. I'll see what gives.'

The car was now parked across the yard. The driver was a youngish man with a very tanned face. He glanced uncertainly from the children to myself. 'Will you be waiting on Professor Grant, miss?'

I explained. He looked even more uncertain, then handed me an envelope addressed to Joe. 'My dead brother Charlie's wife, Mary Cameron, was asking me to be giving this to Dr Fenton when I was meeting him with the Professor's car. I am thinking you would be doing well to open it yourself.'

I accepted the envelope and turned it over to give myself time to think. 'I take it Mrs Cameron is a friend of Professor Grant's, Mr Cameron?'

'The Professor's housekeeper, miss.' He had a very soft, very lilting voice. 'She was coming to my house early this morning at the Professor's request. He was aware I'm to return to my ship in Greenock by noon this day, and, being himself still away up the Ben, he'd a word with Mary Cameron yesterday concerning the transport of his dead sister's bairns. Can you be driving a car, Miss Wade?'

I was nearly as confused by his mixed tenses as by what he was saying. 'Then Professor Grant isn't in Glasgow? Didn't he have to lecture here last night?'

'Aye. But that was being cancelled for the search.'

'Search—'

'Up the Ben. There are being two English laddies lost away up the north face,' he added, as if that explained everything.

'Up the—' I caught on. 'You mean they're lost on a mountain?'

He bowed gravely. 'That is being so. Ben Gairlie. They are being lost since the forenoon yesterday. The shocking wee mist in the night will be delaying the searching.'

'Yes. I expect so.' I took a mental breath and opened the letter.

It had been written by Professor Grant before he left home yesterday morning. He explained having no time to ring London, and in any event considered that would be premature as he hoped to be back in time to drive in to Glasgow early today.

> Obviously, if you get this, I am still held up. In which case, will you drive up to Gairlie with the young for me? I will ask Mrs Cameron to book a flight ticket from Inverness for you on Sunday, which will get you back to London on time. Take the main road, as it is well sign-posted. There are maps in the car and the car is in good order. The drive covers approximately one hundred and forty miles. Take it easy, as it is a strange road and any time you arrive will be convenient to us. I am more than sorry to have to land you with this and not to appear on schedule at Glasgow, but the circumstances here being what they are, I have no alternative.

I read the letter twice, then looked at the bench. All three were sitting on the edge, but their patience now was as unnatural as their instant obedience when I told them to stay there. Robin's expression was defiant, Johnnie's puzzled, Judy's downright weary, but all three had in common the wariness in their eyes. They could see something had gone wrong now, but where a more secure teenager and a pair of sub-teens would be now driving my companion and myself crazy with questions the Fentons preferred to wait. Secure children never believe the worst can happen to themselves. The insecure know that anything that's happened once can happen again. I remembered the feeling.

I had another look at the letter in my hand. 'Professor Grant says it's about a hundred and forty miles to Gairlie.'

'That is being so.'

I glanced at Judy, clinically. I hoped she had nothing worse than a strep. throat, but if she was cooking something more infectious no general hospital would want to touch her. If it was only a strep. throat no fever hospital would want her. Any G.P. would almost certainly say. 'Home to bed and watch her.'

I had a driving licence and could read a map. There was no-one to worry if I didn't get back to London until I was due on duty again. It struck me that I had no alternative, either. So I asked Mr Cameron if he could tell me the best route to take out of Glasgow, and then we both walked over to the bench.

2. An Interlude in the Highlands

The only wrong turning we took was in Gairlie itself. I stopped a woman on a bicycle.

'You're wanting Achnagairl House? Och, it's away across the water. There's but two houses that side, and it'll be the second on your road.'

Loch Gairlie was a sea-loch. The water was a smooth silver-grey and stretched towards the sea hidden behind the blue mountains curving round the estuary. The hills encircling the loch seemed very close in the late afternoon light, and a massive black mountain, its crest in cloud, towered over the hills like an adult in a kindergarten.

The boys stuck heads out of the car windows. 'That must be Ben Gairlie. Wonder if Uncle Dougal's still up there?'

I had another look at the sleeping Judy, and left them to chat it out together, as they had been doing most of the way. Judy had spent most of her drive asleep. Before leaving Glasgow I had bought a thermometer, aspirins, and glucose-lemonade, as well as a picnic meal for the boys and myself. An hour ago Judy's temperature had been just over one hundred and one, which wasn't high for her age, but could mean she was either in the middle of nothing very much or at the start of something serious. From her look now her temp. was up. I glanced at the mountain as I turned the car. I sincerely hoped their uncle was down and had some antibiotics in his house. I also hoped we would not find he had returned crippled with rheumatism, bronchitis, or both. I did not know his age, and, while we had some youngish professors at Martha's, none was under forty, which was slap in the coronary group. It hardly seemed sensible to start nipping up damp mountains after years in Africa, but that was his problem. I drove back along the road we had just taken, and turned off and over the stone bridge that ran into the narrow road running along the far side of the loch.

Judy woke as I turned the car into a small front drive. The house was tall, narrow, and made of granite. I said, 'Why not stay put whilst we get the things out and announce ourselves, Judy?'

'All right,' she said, with a meekness that made my professional blood run cold.

Robin had jumped out. He looked up at the house, then went to have another look at the name on the open gate. 'It's the right place. Why aren't there any lights?'

I got out, stiffly. 'Still daylight. Maybe they like the gloaming.' I rang the front-door bell. Nothing happened, so I rang again. 'The housekeeper must be round the back.'

Johnnie was beside me. 'It doesn't look as if Uncle Dougal is back.'

'Mrs Cameron'll tell us.' I put my finger on the bell and kept it there. 'Maybe she's deaf?' I looked over my shoulder at Judy, then tried the front door. It was unlocked. I opened it. The boys hollered with me, 'Mrs Cameron?'

The hall was long, narrow, darkly panelled, and highly polished. Johnnie found the envelope addressed to 'Dr Fenton' on the hall chest and handed it to me as if it were hot. 'You'd better open this too, Elizabeth.' I did so, then passed it to Robin.

Mrs Cameron had written that one. Her daughter had acute appendicitis, her son-in-law was on night-shift, and she had had to leave for Inverness on the midday coach to look after her four small grandchildren. She explained that she had left another letter in the study for her employer. 'The beds are aired and ready,' she wrote, 'and food is waiting in the slow oven. I have set the dining-room table. The room fires only require a match. I am hoping the Professor will be safely down from the Ben before your arrival, but should he be delayed I know he would wish me to ask you to make yourselves at home. I very much regret. ...'

'Oh, God!' Robin sat gloomily on the foot of the stairs. 'How bloody awful!'

Johnnie stood with his legs apart, his shoulders back, sniffing the air. 'I say, Elizabeth! Think this house has got a ghost? Be jolly smashing, wouldn't it?'

'All I need to make my day, chum. Let's get in the bags and find bedrooms for yourselves and Judy, and then I'll get her straight to bed.'

'Can't we nosh first?' protested Robin. 'Can't the bags wait?'

'You can do what you like with yours. Judy's must come in as she must get to bed. Can you get her case, Johnnie, as I'm not sure which is hers, and I'll nip quickly upstairs and find her a room.'

Johnnie shot off obligingly. Robin followed me up to the first landing. 'You don't really have to fuss, Elizabeth. Judy often has sore throats.'

My shoulders were stiff with driving, so I was able to resist the urge to clout him. 'That's useful to know. I still think she must get to bed.'

'You could just be fussing. You're not a doctor.'

'And nor are you, son.' I guessed he'd take the term as a gross insult. He did. 'As your uncle is, when he shows up he can tell me if I'm right or wrong. Till then I'm going to do what I think's right.' I had found a rather attractive little room overlooking the loch. 'I'll put Judy in here.'

I took her temperature again when she was in bed. It was one hundred and three. I crushed two aspirins in a little water. 'Gargle and swallow, Judy.'

'Ugh! How foul!'

'Isn't it just? But it'll ease your throat and that headache.'

After the aspirins she drank warm milk. 'You're right. It doesn't hurt so much to swallow now. But I do feel funny. Sort of all aching.'

She had no sign of any form of rash. I stayed with her for some minutes after she fell asleep, and wished I had had more experience in the ordinary childish ailments. Having trained in a teaching hospital, my pediatric experience had been almost exclusively concerned with the abnormal. Consequently, as I now weighed her signs and symptoms, a nightmarish row of differential diagnoses occurred to me. Rheumatic fever? Meningitis? Polio? And God forbid it, but, having seen too much in children, I couldn't rule it out—leukaemia? A high temp., sore throat, headache, general aches—classic kick-off symptoms for the lot. But so they were, I reminded myself, for measles, chicken-pox, scarlet, acute tonsillitis, and even in more severe attacks of German measles.

Her uncle must be back soon. Surely he couldn't spend another night on that ruddy mountain?

Suppose he did? Could I leave Judy all night without getting hold of some local doctor? The telephone exchange or the local minister or someone could give me a name. Should I stop waiting and ring round now?

I touched Judy's forehead. It was slightly cooler and she was deeply asleep.

I tried looking at her as if she were a patient in Martha's and I was on nights. Would I get a medical registrar out of bed for a child in her condition? She was getting sleep, rest, and warmth, the essential basics for recovery from any complaint. I wouldn't call up any registrar—yet. That was the rub. In Martha's I had only to lift a telephone receiver to have an assortment of physicians and drugs on tap. Achnagairl House was not Martha's, and outside the evening was growing misty.

The mist thickened. Judy slept on. The boys and I ate for supper one of the twin casseroles prepared by Mrs Cameron. Every few minutes one or other boy jumped up. 'That must be Uncle Dougal.' It wasn't.

Johnnie pressed his face against a window. 'I can't see anything. How can anyone find anyone in this, Elizabeth?'

That thought had been in my mind for some time. 'Maybe this mist looks different if one's born to it.'

Robin said, 'Those two English chaps lost on the Ben won't be used to it. I wonder if they're still up there?'

'Why?' asked Johnnie cheerfully. 'Think they've fallen off? Will they be awfully dead if they have, Elizabeth?'

A few minutes later I went up for another look at Judy, leaving the boys enjoying a hideously gory discussion and wondering why people get so worked up about the effects on children of violence in their television programmes. I was all for adults being protected in that context. Though I was a trained nurse, the boys' conversation just now had made me downright queasy, but they looked happier than at any time since we met at Euston.

I had left Judy's bedside lamp on and set it on the floor. The circle of soft light was enough to show me from her doorway that she had not stirred since my last visit. She looked hotter. I went in and took her pulse without waking her. It was up.

Her room was at the front, and the dining-room in which the boys were sitting at the back. They didn't hear the mist-muffled voices outside and then the footsteps. I hurried back to the stairs and was half-way down when the front door opened. 'Professor Grant?' I went on down. 'I'm sorry to startle you, but Joe couldn't come up with the children, so I brought 'em. I'm Elizabeth Wade.'

Momentarily, the man in the doorway just stared at me. Then he stepped slowly into the hall, closed the front door, and shut out the mist before removing his white crash helmet with its still-attached headlamp. He wore a crumpled and stained garish orange anorak, his dark hair was soaked with mist and sweat, his face was grey with fatigue and mountain-dust, and his chin was rough with a day-old beard. He was younger than I had anticipated, though his actual age at that moment was impossible to guess.

'Yes. I'm Dougal Grant. Good evening, Miss Wade.' He removed a glove to shake hands and hung it over the ice-axe fixed through his leather belt. 'You're very welcome to my house.' He unhitched and heaved off the haversack on his shoulders, and his stance showed from whom Johnnie had inherited his square shoulders. 'You drove them from Glasgow?'

Before I could answer the boys exploded into the hall, talking simultaneously.

'Quiet, laddies! Yes, those Englishmen are safe—and you can tell me of Mrs Cameron's daughter later. First things first.' Professor Grant put his belt and ice-axe on the chest and unzipped his anorak. 'So Judy's unwell, Miss Wade?'

'I'm afraid so. She seems to have some kind of chill. She's in bed and asleep.'

'No doubt the best place.' He glanced at the boys, then back to me. 'You're a nurse? Trained?' I nodded. 'That's providential.' He sent Robin to make tea, Johnnie to find Mrs Cameron's letter in his study. 'Now they've gone,' he said quietly, 'could you enlarge on that tactfully brief report?'

I gave him the kind of report I would have given any physician, on-duty. Since Martha's nurses were not, officially, permitted to diagnose, I offered no diagnosis.

He said, 'Sounds like a strep. throat. Fortunately I've antibiotics in the house.'

'Good.'

Johnnie had inherited his eyes as well as his shoulders. His direct gaze took me back to Euston last night. 'You think it may be more complicated than that?'

'Quite honestly, I don't know. I haven't seen enough normal ailments. She does give me the impression she's cooking something, but I may be dramatizing.'

'Aye. The worst of any good teaching hospital is the impression it gives one that every illness has to be a major illness. One tends to forget the legion of minor illnesses that never get inside a teaching ward. You must've had an anxious time. I'll take a look at her now.'

'Shall I come?'

'You've done more than enough on my behalf, thank you.' He opened the dining-room door for me. 'If you'll sit by the fire I'll be down directly.' He threw on more logs. 'When do you have to be back on duty?'

'Seven-thirty, Monday morning.'

'That should present no problem as you'll be flying back. You don't object to flying? Good. Then I'll attend to the details later. Are you comfortable in that chair?'

'Very, thanks. But can't I help? You must be dead tired.'

'Weary, naturally, though I'm accustomed to mountain rescue work.' He looked at me, reflectively. 'I doubt you're accustomed to driving the long road from Glasgow, and with a sick child. I'm much in your debt as it is. I've no wish to add to that by returning you to London exhausted by your wee interlude in the Highlands.'

He was gone about fifteen minutes. On his return he had changed into a dark roll-neck sweater and grey trousers. His hair was neat, but with his unshaven chin he still looked thuggish. 'Possibly just strep., though I'll reserve judgment until I can see her in daylight.' He sat down and made polite conversation about Joe, our journey up my job in the theatre, his local mountaineering club. 'Ah, good!' Will you put that tea down on the table, Robin?'

When I refused a second cup he said he was sure I was more than ready to retire. 'Would you care to use the room on the right of Judy's?'

'Thanks, yes, if you're sure I can't help?'

'Quite sure. Thank you.' He gave me a civil little bow. 'I hope you sleep well. Goodnight, Miss Wade.'

'Goodnight, Professor Grant.'

I went upstairs feeling I had suddenly stepped back a couple of centuries, whilst at the same time realizing there was more than one way of getting an unwanted guest out of the family's hair. But I was tired and he was obviously capable of looking after Judy. I dropped thankfully into bed.

Occasionally I woke and heard him next door. Once I looked at my watch. Ten to five. Did he never use sleep?

It was still dark outside, but the mist had gone and through the darkness the outline of the hills was plain. Ben Gairlie was a giant black shadow in the pre-dawn sky. As I had no head for heights of any description, the idea of climbing for pleasure was beyond my comprehension. Presumably, as my host was a member of the local mountain rescue team, he was an experienced climber. I wished I knew him well enough to ask if 'because it's there' was the whole answer, and then my mind flashed back to my former notions of an elderly, arthritic, and bronchitic professor, limping down from the mountain. I fell asleep again, smiling, and when I woke the sun was on my face.

It seemed only five minutes later, and, forgetting briefly where I was, I raised myself on an elbow to blink at the clock over the Medical School. The present returned directly I saw the loch, steel-grey and flecked with white. The sky was heavy with thick white clouds sweeping inland from the Atlantic and obscuring the upper half of the Ben. A colony of gulls flying over the water in strict formation made grey-white splashes against the tan hills, and the sun was shining on the houses on the opposite side of the loch. They were blue and white and they looked attractive, yet they worried me. I could not think why until I realized the sun was in the wrong place for early morning. I reached for my watch. It was eleven o'clock.

The house was silent as I leapt out of bed. I put my head round Judy's door, and, from her colour and breathing as she slept, her temperature was normal. Relief removed some of my ill-humour at being allowed to oversleep. Having worried over and to a minor extent nursed Judy, I had developed the instant affection for her most nurses developed as quickly for most child patients. It could take days, even weeks, to get close to a sick adult, but after an hour alone with a sick child one could make friends for life. With some children one could do that without their being ill; Johnnie was an example. Robin was one of the other kind, and, in fairness to him, he was at a much more tricky age. Dressing quickly, I mused on what type of patient Robin would make, and decided he would be very good providing he was ill enough. With a minor ailment he'd be sheer murder.

I wished I had more than my blue jersey suit, coat, and one spare sweater with me. Yesterday's drive had done nothing for my suit, and the good Highland air was having a disastrous effect on my hair. Combing made it crackle with electricity and then stand on end. I surveyed my reflection, glumly. All I needed to complete the picture was a flower, a row of beads, and a bell.

I went out on the empty landing and paused by a window overlooking the bare front garden and the solitary Scots pine at the gate. A large white foreign car was parked outside the gate, and a man and woman stood by it, talking. It was a couple of seconds before I recognized my host, and not only because he had had a shave.

In daylight his hair and eyes were darker than Johnnie's, his high cheek-bones were more marked, and his jaw was much more square. He was closer to thirty than forty, and he wore a tweed jacket and a darkish kilt. The kilt suited him as he had good legs, tanned and not bony knees, and he was not too tall. He was about five foot eleven. The young woman with him came up to his shoulder.

She was a brunette with regular features and an exquisite complexion. Her pink tweed suit looked handwoven, very expensive, and worth every penny. She looked wonderful, and from Dougal Grant's smile he thought so too. I thought of Joe's 'hasn't bitten a woman in years'. Joe should see dear old Uncle right now. I went on down.

Johnnie charged into the hall. 'You've slept ages. You're as bad as Judy, but Uncle said we weren't to come up to you until you came down. Judy did wake for breakfast, then she went back to sleep, and Uncle says we mustn't make a row as sleep'll do her more good than any drugs north or south of the Border.' Unconsciously he mimicked the faint lilt in his uncle's voice and then very much more marked accentuation of the 'r's'. 'I thought you'd just never wake up. Mrs Pringle says you must have an affection for your bed. She's been fearfully busy, and she's been keeping your breakfast hot hours and hours!'

'Mrs Pringle? Who's she?'

'Mrs Cameron's sister. She used to be Uncle Dougal and our Mummy's nanny when they were small. She came ever so early after Uncle Dougal sent her a message, and she's staying till Mrs Cameron gets back, only she hasn't moved in properly as she came here after she'd been to church, only she calls it "the kirk", and she says today is the

Sabbath. Uncle Dougal cooked us a fab. breakfast before she came. We noshed and noshed!'

'Jolly good. Sorry I missed it. I hope your uncle didn't mind?'

'Gosh, no! He said it was nice for you to rest, and much more fun for us men to eat in peace. He's been fearfully busy,' he rattled on. 'He's rung Joe and Mrs Evans and the old doctor who lives in that only other house this side of the loch. His name's Dr Sinclair, and he's coming to see Judy this afternoon because Judy's got It. Uncle Dougal asked Joe if Robin and me'd had It. Joe said we had, ages ago, and he's had It and Mrs Pringle's had It, and so has Uncle Dougal, and he's going to ask you if you have.'

So she had been cooking something. Whatever it was, from the way she looked, she had it mildly, 'Johnnie, what's It? Can you remember?'

He frowned in thought. 'No. Sorry. Uncle Dougal knows.' He flung open the front door. 'Uncle Dougal, here's Elizabeth, and she wants to know what It is!'

Dougal Grant came up the path. 'I'll explain, directly, Johnnie. Will you away to Mrs Pringle and ask her to make Miss Wade fresh tea?' He wished me a polite good-morning, expressed deep happiness at my long rest, and introduced me to his companion. She was a Mrs Maureen Valentine. He called her Maury.

She looked me over and smiled very, very sweetly. 'The Good Samaritan I've been hearing so much about!' She clasped her hands to prove life had no more to offer.

'So kind! So sensible! So intrepid! But then you couldn't know Dougal normally refuses to let any woman behind the wheel of his car.'

He said quickly, 'On this occasion, Maury, I'm most grateful to Miss Wade for taking matters into her own hands.'

'My dear, I know that.' She laid a hand on his arm and kept it there. 'I'm sure Joe Fenton will be equally grateful. And you've always said he's such a nice lad.' She smiled on me again. 'Let me guess. You two are engaged?'

I smiled very, very sweetly. 'No.'

'You mean it's still a secret? Say no more. I so understand! I was just the same when I first met my beloved Pete. I couldn't talk about it. Remember that summer, Dougal darling? When Pete came up to see Daddy about filming one of his books and we met and married inside of three months?'

'I've not forgotten.'

I glanced at Dougal Grant. I could have been wrong, but I had the immediate impression that he would have preferred not to have been reminded of that period. I looked thoughtfully at Maury Valentine.

She barely stopped for breath. 'We used to live in old Dr Sinclair's house. My father was a writer and passionate fisherman—wasn't he just, Dougal?—and he came up for the fishing one year when I was ten, and never left Gairlie again until he died. I lived here until I married ten years ago and went out to Kenya. For years,' she assured me, 'I practically lived in Achnagairl. You can imagine the comfort it has been to me, since I lost my husband in a car accident last year and came back to Gairlie, to be amongst old friends again. I've a house up the glen, now. I wish you could come and see it—but you'll be leaving us so soon. Such a pity! You've seen nothing of Gairlie.'

Dougal said, 'As I've explained to you, Maury, Miss Wade's return still remains an open question.' He faced me. 'Judy's got scarlet. Have you had it?'

Oh, God, I thought, no! He wasn't going to like it, and nor would Mrs Valentine. Nor did I. I had to be honest. 'Not as far as I know, but as we had an epidemic amongst the staff at Martha's in my first and I missed it, I can only guess I had it as a small child, or have a natural immunity.'

Mrs Valentine's smooth face tightened, peevishly. 'Why not ring your mother? She'll know, surely.'

'Unfortunately, that's not possible.' From the speed with which Dougal spoke Joe had given him my family history. 'So.' He smiled rather nicely. 'Though that question remains open, it settles another. As a scarlet suspect you can't travel anywhere by public transport, and unless I'm much mistaken you certainly won't be welcome back at Martha's until you're in the clear. I hope you'll have no objection to staying on here with us? You'll be most welcome.'

I felt weak. 'That's very kind of you, Professor Grant. Perhaps if I could ring my Matron first?'

'Of course. I'll have a word with her presently. I'm afraid I know very well what she'll say.'

Unfortunately so did I. I apologized for causing so much trouble. He said it was no trouble at all and any apology was due from him to me. 'As the incubation period for scarlet is so short, you won't have long to wait,' he continued. 'I've known cases develop within twenty-four hours of contact, though more commonly on the second or third day after, and never, in my experience, after the seventh day. To be safe, I think we should allow a clear week from today. You agree?'

It was a civil query, but, as he was well aware, I was in no position to disagree with the medical opinion of a Professor of Tropical Medicine. 'Of course. Thank you.'

Mrs Valentine drawled, 'My, my, aren't you the lucky one? A week's holiday in the Highlands!'

I nearly told her to stop worrying. I thought Dougal Grant looked

great in a kilt, but his olde-worlde good manners were beginning to wear
me down. As he was the first Scottish Highlander I had met on his home
ground, I didn't know whether he was a typical or way-out example of
the race, or whether his Scottish upbringing and years in Africa were
responsible for his seeming so out of touch with the life I was
accustomed to living in London. Obviously he and I belonged in different
centuries as well as different races. I preferred mine. The men I knew in
London might not treat me as if I were made of glass, but they did treat
me like a girl, and not just a female. I was only now discovering there
could be a difference. It was amusing, for a little while. I was equally
amused by Maury Valentine's bothering to give me her life history as a
warning-off. I felt much happier about my blue jersey suit, and the
reverse about the coming week.

I was not alone. The kitchen door was closed, but Robin didn't trouble
to lower his voice. 'We're still lumbered with her? How bloody
sick-making!'

Mrs Pringle was small and thin with grey hair twisted in a tight bun
and a lined, defeated face. I did not hear her reply to Robin, but every
time she saw me she gave the height of my skirt hem a more
disapproving glance.

Judy said, 'Grotty luck—for you, I mean, Elizabeth.'

My host asked me to spare him a few minutes in his study. He had
rung Martha's, arranged to have a suitcase of clothes sent up for me and
collected from Glasgow tomorrow, and fixed with Matron that I would
ring her at two that afternoon. 'I thought it best that I should have a
word with her first. I hope you've no objection?'

'None. Thank you.'

He favoured me with another of his cute little bows. 'With your
Matron's approval I've asked Dr Sinclair to keep an eye on your health
as well as Judy's. May I now make a personal request?'

I was intrigued. 'Of course, Professor Grant.'

With the utmost politeness he asked me to behave like a leper
throughout the coming week. 'Gairlie is such a healthy wee place that we
seldom get infections up here. When we do, having no immunity, half
Gairlie succumbs. This house will be in quarantine until Judy's clear,
but, apart from her and yourself, the rest of us can't carry the bug, as
we've had it. You'll recall scarlet can only be spread by direct contact?'

'Yes. I'll be careful to avoid the village and people.'

'You'll not hand it on in the open, though I'd prefer you to take no
chances with children, even outdoors. They may not take it as mildly as
Judy. And, talking of the lassie, I'd prefer you to keep away from her
room until Dr Sinclair allows her up.' He smiled faintly. 'This may seem

a classic example of locking the stable door, but there's no sense in exposing you unnecessarily to the bug.'

That did irk me. I was a nurse. I enjoyed nursing. Judy did not require much, but she needed a little. 'Must I? I've met scarlet so often without getting it that, while I appreciate that doesn't mean I can't be a carrier, I can't hurt Judy and I'm sure I won't get it from her.'

'If you'll forgive me saying so, on that point no-one on this earth can at present be sure.' He paused to let his displeasure sink in. 'I would be grateful if you could see your way to indulging me in this.'

As I could see a brick wall when I met one, I wasted no more energy in arguing. 'Of course, Professor Grant.'

'Thank you. I hope you won't find the coming week too tedious. It will be a great pleasure to us all to have you with us, and despite the tiresome scarlet restrictions I sincerely hope you'll feel free to treat this house as if it were your own.'

It was a pretty if mechanical little speech. I made one back. It wasn't very good, but from his bow I had just handed him the Crown Jewels. Then he suggested I might feel more at home if we used each other's Christian names.

I had to stifle the urge to simper, 'Lud, Professor! So sudden!' Though there had to be a very good and educated brain behind the rather rigid lines of his face, and there might even be a sense of humour, I was taking no chances. I had his message as clearly as I had Mrs Valentine's. As his guest I was free to treat his house as my house—providing I did as I was told without question and minded my manners. I folded my hands and approved his suggestion with what I hoped was becoming modesty. I hoped like crazy he'd bow again. He did. 'I'm glad, Elizabeth.' He held open the door. 'Shall we away to lunch?'

'Thank you, Dougal.' It took all my self-control not to curtsey.

3. The Corn seems very Alien

That afternoon and the following morning old Dr Sinclair looked down my throat, patted my hand, and said had he more patients like me he'd have more time for his garden. 'Have you observed my daffodils, lassie? Och, you should! The first up in Gairlie.'

He was a great-grandfather and thin as paper. He stooped a little, but his movements were brisk and steady, and his hearing and eyesight were excellent. He had retired to Gairlie after forty years as a G.P., and then found himself in constant demand as 'a permanent locum, lassie'. He said he had no objection to the work, but he wished it left him more time to spend with his wife and in pursuit of his hobbies—gardening and climbing.

I enjoyed his visits, since it was pleasant to be treated like a rational human being by a fellow adult, if only for a few minutes at a time. He was a great talker.

'You'll recall the twins I mentioned yesterday, Miss Wade?'

'Yes, indeed. Arrived yet, Doctor?'

'Not they. It's my rest day tomorrow, so they'll wait until I'm in bed tonight!' He clicked shut his aged Gladstone bag. 'A great place for twins, Gairlie. I've had more here than in twice as many years in Dundee. Maybe it's the water.'

'That's an interesting theory!'

'Is it not? I'm full of fine theories, but I've never yet had the time to weigh their merits academically. One of these days I must discuss this one with your learned host. You'll be aware he was a twin himself?'

'No.' I was curious. 'Twin brothers?'

'Och, no. With the Grants of Gairlie it's invariably the two sexes. He'd a twin sister, and the poor lassie died of pneumonia when she was but twenty-five. Three years later he'd lost both parents and his older sister.'

'I'd no idea. How ghastly! Was this whilst he was in Africa?'

He shook his head. 'He was away there for the elder girl's death and returned too late for more than her funeral. He saw his twin and his parents out of this world. Man is born to grief,' he added simply, 'and time I was away. Good day to you.'

During that morning Johnnie told me Maury Valentine had invited Robin and himself to tea at her house that afternoon. 'Robin talked to her on the 'phone. Uncle says it'll be all right as she's had it, only she'd better not come into this house. She asked him to tea, too, but he says he's got to stay to look after you and Ju.'

I didn't care for the notion of a Johnnie-less afternoon. I thought of retreating to my bedroom, but as it had no fire, though I was perfectly happy to huddle in a coat and blankets, I suspected that would occasion great umbrage on two counts—my southerner's weakness for warm bedrooms and the proof the coats and blankets would provide of my finding Highland hospitality lacking. Having already caused Mrs Pringle to take mortal umbrage by offering to help her with the dishes, I was growing wary. If I stayed by the sitting-room fire Dougal would feel duty-bound to entertain me, and our stilted small-talk would not be improved by Mrs Pringle's increasingly obvious distrust of my intentions towards him. On the rare occasions when he and I happened to be alone together she was in and out like a jack-in-a-box, unless we were in the study, when she brooded—and breathed—heavily outside the closed door.

At lunch I asked if I could take an afternoon walk. Mrs Pringle nearly dropped a soup plate in relief, and even Robin approved. Johnnie wanted to alter his plans and walk with me.

Dougal said, 'I'm sorry, laddie, and I know Elizabeth will understand that since you've already accepted one invitation it would be impolite to back out.'

'But it was Robin who accepted, not me. Must I?'

'I think you should. And you'll get a good tea.'

Johnnie brightened. 'All right.' He turned to me. 'Though I wouldn't mind missing the nosh to come with you.'

Dougal caught my eye and almost smiled. I was just beginning to think that we might have made contact at last, when he launched into a long and pompous lecture on the local walk he considered most suitable for my outing. He did not actually call me a mentally-retarded, bug-carrying female alien, but again I got the message. Later he bowed me off from his front gate. He was training me so well that I bowed back, and we wasted another five minutes thanking each other and wishing each other well.

Dr Sinclair's house was about a mile down the road on the inland side. I stopped to admire his daffodils, then walked on thinking of the spring I had left behind in London, and how busy our theatre always was on Mondays, and how often on a hectic Monday afternoon I had longed to get right away. I took a long look all round. This was certainly right away.

Across the loch and behind the purple and tan hills Ben Gairlie was free of clouds, and beneath the snowline the black rock looked smooth as glass. Though the sun shone, the wind was icy and, those daffodils aside, spring had not yet reached Gairlie. My eyes rested on Achnagairl House. Neither spring nor the twentieth century.

The river I had been told to follow was one of the pair that ran into the loch. It was very narrow and in places very shallow. The topaz water ran fast over flat, multi-coloured stones, and from dozens of miniature whirlpools the white spray rose in small clouds. The river-bank was lined with bare willows, and the grass was last year's and yellow with age and from close-cropping by the grazing black-faced sheep. The sheep fascinated me with their high, curving horns, long, shaggy coats, and absurdly long, thin legs. At my approach they scrambled up the nearest hillside like goats, then dodged down for another mouthful directly I had moved on. I had never seen sheep like them. I watched them and thought of Dougal, and knew just how Ruth felt amongst all that corn. Dead alien.

I had been walking over an hour when I came to a sudden sharp swerve in the river. It was a good place to turn back. I hesitated, then walked on.

Beyond the swerve there was a row of granite boulders across the river-bed. It formed a small, but very fast rapid. I threw in a twig. The water tore it in pieces, and the pieces were flung up in the air. I threw in another, and nearly followed it in when I heard that unexpected voice behind me. 'Pardon me, but you are taking quite a chance getting that close. Those rocks right by the edge are slippery, as I have discovered.'

The voice was male, American, and vaguely familiar. Directly I turned I saw why.

He had recognized me. 'Why, hallo! So you stayed on after the week-end? And right here in Gairlie too!' The sandy-haired American I had last seen in Glasgow now had his left arm in a sling and was beaming on me as if I were his first glimpse of the Statue of Liberty after a ten-year exile. If Dougal and Mrs Pringle were typical Gairlie types I didn't blame him.

I beamed back. 'Life's got a bit out of hand over this week-end. What've you done to your arm?'

'Slipped Saturday, my first time out. The doc. up the hospital fixed it and said no fishing until the tendons have rested up.'

'What wretched luck! I am sorry. How long've you got up here?'

'Couple of weeks, maybe. How about you?'

'A week.'

'Why, that's great!'

I did not seriously believe he meant that, but I liked the way he managed to sound as if he did.

He held out his right hand. 'Archibald A. MacDonald, U.S. citizen, grandson of a Gairlie man.'

'Elizabeth Wade—oh—' I remembered and backed before we touched. 'Have you had scarlet fever?'

'Sure.' He was only mildly surprised. 'And the measles and the nastiest case of chicken-pox in Westchester County. Do I have security clearance?'

I laughed and explained. 'It's all right for me to talk to you in the open,' I added, 'but we'd better not shake hands, just in case I'm a carrier. Dougal wouldn't approve.'

He leant against an upturned boulder. 'Who's this Dougal?'

'The Professor Grant I've been telling you about.' I sat on a boulder. 'Where's Westchester County?'

'New York State.'

'And your home?'

'Most the time. Where are you from, Elizabeth?'

'London, England. Both sides.' I looked at the river. 'Seems a long way from here.'

'But real swinging?'

'God, yes! Naturally, being a normal Londoner, I carry my sugar-lumps in one pocket, pot in the other. Snag is I've got on the wrong jacket today. Sorry. Can't offer you either.'

'I'll forgive you, Elizabeth. The once. And what do you do when you're not swinging?'

'Nurse. Heard of St Martha's Hospital?'

He frowned slightly. 'Right by the river? Sure. I know it. Kind of a good hospital, huh?'

'I think so. What do you do?'

'According to the U.S. taxman, I am an automobile salesman.'

I was watching his expression. 'And what's wrong with that?'

'Strictly a horse-and-buggy man, ma'am. And what is more, I detest driving.'

'Do you sell many cars, then?'

'When they twist my arm.' He offered me a cigarette and when I refused lit one for himself. 'So you've not yet seen right round Gairlie?'

'Only across the loch. What's it like?' He was silent. 'Your first visit?'

'Yes. Last time I had a vacation over here I got as far as Edinburgh. This was way back when I was fresh out of college. Grandma MacDonald has kinfolk there. I kind of stayed put. You know how it is.'

In the train we had given each other the quick approving once-over. Now we were doing the job much more thoroughly. I had the impression he found the chore no more unpleasant than myself. I liked that, just as I liked the amiable lines of his face and uninhibited warmth in his manner. I liked the way he managed to look easy-going but not weak. He might be a pushover for a pick-up, but not on anything that really mattered to him.

'You asked how do I like Gairlie? It's this way; what I have seen I like a lot. I guess I am going to get to like the folks.'

'Only guess?'

'Elizabeth, I am the new boy in town. So Grandpa MacDonald came from Gairlie? So that's great—but what are a few generations up here? Not that the folks back at my hotel are not real civil and the guy who owns the joint is—wait for it—one Davie MacDonald. He told me himself he does not usually hand out reservations to strangers as he has regulars returning year after year, but he got checking, and it seems he and I are fourth, or maybe fifth, cousins. So Archie was in—but, kinfolk or no kinfolk, it is still the good old Mister MacDonald.'

'That I believe!' I described Dougal's way-out formality, briefly. 'Was your grandfather another Archie MacDonald?'

It could have been my imagination, but he seemed hesitant. 'Calum Angus.' He sat on a boulder nearer mine. 'Can I ask you something, Elizabeth?'

'Go ahead.'

'Married?'

'No. you?'

'I was. Didn't work out.'

I said, 'I'm sorry.'

'Thanks,' he said, 'but you don't have to be. No hearts were broken. We should not have gotten married, and we were both glad to call it off. She is now married to a real good friend of mine, and I mean just that.'

I believed him. I had not met enough ex-husbands to separate at sight the relieved from the still-sore. The latter were the real menaces.

We went on talking for some while before I remembered the time. He walked back with me and asked if I would take another walk with him tomorrow.

'Sure, if I can get out. I'm not a free agent.'

'Can I call you to fix it up later?'

Dougal had said his house was mine, so I said that would be fine, thanks.

Maury's car passed us on the loch road. Johnnie, in the back, waved wildly. When we reached the gate of Achnagairl House the car had gone. We parted there as the house was in quarantine.

Dougal came out of his study as I let myself in. 'Pleasant walk?'

The study overlooked the front garden. He must have seen Archie MacDonald at the gate. He did not mention the fact, and I was on the point of explaining when Mrs Pringle emerged from the kitchen. In a voice of doom she informed Dougal, 'Miss Wade's tea is waiting on her in the lounge.'

I said, 'I hope I wasn't out too long?'

'Not at all,' said Dougal. 'I hope you'll forgive my already having had tea with Judy.'

Mrs Pringle was still there. She was taking no chances. Directly she had set eyes on my wholly exposed knees she had known exactly what to think. She had seen it all on television. She knew it was only a question of time before I enticed her respected Professor into joining my psychedelic rave-up in the front parlour.

Dougal had letters to write. 'You'll excuse me?'

I knew my place. 'Of course, Dougal.' I went up and took off my coat. Mrs Pringle was still in the hall when I came down. She reminded me my tea would be getting cold and shut me firmly in the sitting-room.

Her step showed she knew she had done her duty. She would defend him with her life—and she would, at that.

Johnnie thundered down the stairs, flopped on the sofa beside me, and helped himself to a scone. As we had the room to ourselves he said the tea-party had been a bit of a drag and Robin had gone soft on Mrs Valentine.

I said, 'Robin's got good taste. She's very pretty.'

He grimaced. 'Sort of. I say, Elizabeth, do you think she's Uncle Dougal's girl-friend? Robin does. I say he's much too old—and so is she. Aged! Much older than you.'

'Not all that much, love. A few years.'

He took another scone. 'Is that Mr MacDonald you were with just now your boy-friend?'

I put down my cup, quickly. 'No. How on earth do you know his name?'

'Mrs Valentine told us. She says he's up for the fishing and she told Uncle Dougal and he said Gairlie was a popular place for tourists and they both laughed. Robin says that Mr MacDonald was the man you saw at Glasgow station, but I wasn't sure. Was he? Has he had It?'

'Yes, to both.'

'Did you know he was coming to Gairlie?'

I shook my head.

'Robin thinks that's why you came up with us. He told Uncle Dougal and Mrs Valentine, and she thought it awfully funny, but Uncle Dougal didn't laugh that time and he said, "That's enough, laddie," so Robin had to belt up. Please can I have some fruit cake?'

I offered him the plate. Charming, I thought. Charming.

'I say, Elizabeth—you won't tell about her being Uncle's girl-friend? Cross-your-heart-and-hope-to-die-in-a-cellar-of-rats?'

I did so. I also did some thinking, and later that evening told Dougal the exact truth about Archie.

'A pleasant coincidence for you. More coffee, Elizabeth?'

I hoped he had believed me. I didn't think he had.

It rained all next day. Through the rain the grey loch rippled with tiny waves, and the broad patch of gorse that on our side divided the bank from the sandy shore glistened like sprinkled gold. The gorse and Archie MacDonald's 'phone call were the only bright spots of my day. Dr Sinclair didn't call, Robin sulked because Maury Valentine hadn't asked him to tea again until tomorrow, Judy was well enough to be bored and need Johnnie's company in her room, and from Dougal's sombre manner towards me I was personally responsible for the Act of Union, 1707.

The rain stopped at noon the following day. I asked permission to take another afternoon walk. Dougal hoped it would keep fine for me.

Archie was waiting at the Sinclairs' house as we had arranged yesterday. We walked by the river, not talking of anything in particular, but laughing a good deal at the same jokes. I began to like him enough to be slightly on edge until he asked me for another date.

Dougal was out when I returned. He had driven up the glen to collect Robin. Johnnie had backed out of the second tea-party. He had spent all morning taking to pieces an old clock, and just had to get it working again. He was showing the partially finished result to Mrs Pringle when I let myself in. 'My penknife isn't thin enough. I want something to go right in here.'

Mrs Pringle fetched a lethal-looking kitchen knife. 'Will this do ye, laddie? Och, but ye're the wee spit of the Professor when he was a bairn no older than yeself!'

'Och, away!' retorted Johnnie. 'Is tha' a fact?'

Mrs Pringle recollected my presence and sniffed. 'Will ye take ye tea now, miss, or wait on the Professor?'

I said I was happy to wait, and they both went up to show Judy the clock. I was rather worried about that knife, but as Mrs Pringle had produced it and Johnnie was a neat-handed child, I told myself to stop fussing and tried to concentrate on *The Scotsman*. There were shouts of laughter above and then Judy's voice was demanding, 'Tell us again, Mrs Pringle. Did Uncle Dougal really fall into the loch in his Sabbath suit and come out covered in mud? Tell us again!'

Edinburgh had a traffic problem. Archie thought Edinburgh the most beautiful city he had ever seen, yet he had no plans to stop off there on his present trip. I was casually wondering why not when a scream jolted me to my feet. A child's scream of terror.

I was on the stairs when Judy screamed again. 'Stop it, Mrs Pringle—stop it—Johnnie—Mrs Pringle—do something!'

It took me only a few seconds to reach her room, but in those seconds the blood from the artery Johnnie had cut in his left hand had hit the bedroom ceiling, soaked his face and hair and Mrs Pringle's white apron. 'Let me take a wee look, laddie,' she was saying shakily, dabbing ineffectually at his hand with her apron skirt.

'I'll do that, Mrs Pringle.' I grasped Johnnie's left wrist, clamping my fingers against the radial artery. 'Sit down, love. This'll soon stop.' I held his arm high over his head. 'It looks messy, but blood's like spilt milk. Always looks worse than it really is. Can you pass me that small hand-towel over there, Judy? Thanks.' I wound this round Johnnie's wrist with my free hand and gave him one end to hold. 'Hang on, Johnnie. This may hurt a bit as I'm going to pull it tight. Good boy. That's stopped it.' I used both hands to tighten the knot. Chuck me that pencil, Judy.' I used this to increase the tension. 'Stay sitting, Johnnie, and I'll clean you up.'

He sat quietly watching me with grave brown eyes. He was dead scared, but he wasn't going to admit it and he kept his head. When I washed his face, he said, 'Thank you,' very politely.

Judy stopped crying. 'You stopped it bleeding, Elizabeth. It was like turning off a tap. Did you know you could?'

'Yes.' I smiled at her, then saw Mrs Pringle was pale green. 'Do sit down, Mrs Pringle. Come on, my dear.' I switched on my most professional manner as she seemed about to protest and was certainly about to pass out. 'That's right. Now, bend you head right forward on to your lap. You've had a bit of a shock. It'll pass.' I took her pulse with one hand and reached for an open box of assorted candies with the other. 'Have a sweetie, kids. You too, Mrs Pringle. It'll help.'

She raised her head. 'Is tha' a fact?'

'It is. Glucose works wonders. Try it. No, don't sit up yet, but when you do, do it slowly.' They were all chewing, so I looked round for something to use as a sling for Johnnie.

Judy gave me a headscarf. 'Will Johnnie have to have his arm stitched, Elizabeth?'

'I'm not a doctor, love, so I can't say for sure. I should think so.'

Johnnie asked, 'Are you going to ring Dr Sinclair? Suppose he's out?'

'If he is and and your uncle's not back I'll ring Gairlie Hospital and ask the doctor on duty for advice.'

Mrs Pringle muttered, 'I canna' put my mind to the number.'

'Don't worry. I'll find it. Keep those sweets circulating, Judy. I'll be quick as I can.' I closed the door quietly behind me, then ran down the landing as Dougal appeared at the head of the stairs.

He glanced over my head. 'I wondered where you all were.'

'With Judy. Dougal, I'm glad you're back—'

'It would seem high time. Have you forgotten my request that you stay away from Judy—'

An arterial haemorrhage always shook me. I had yet to meet the person it didn't. 'I'm not that bloody silly, chum! Johnnie's nicked an artery.'

Five minutes later he drove Johnnie, with Robin for company, to the Casualty Department of Gairlie Hospital. Mrs Pringle was still greenish, so I made tea for her, Judy, and myself. She voiced no objection to my using her kitchen, and when I found a step-ladder, bucket, and cloth and washed off the blood on Judy's ceiling Mrs Pringle, unasked, steadied the foot of the ladder.

'You're not using hot water, miss?'

'Not for blood. Cold works much better, providing you do it at once.'

Judy lay back to look up. 'I expect you're used to sloshing about in oodles of blood, Elizabeth?'

'We don't actually slosh in the stuff, love, but we have enough scattered around for me to be an old hand at shifting bloodstains.' I came down the ladder. 'I think that patch should dry clean.'

Mrs Pringle studied the patch in silence. She followed me down with the bucket when I took the ladder back and removed the stained apron she had left soaking in a basin of hot water and began rinsing it under the cold tap. 'You're right,' she remarked without looking round. 'It's coming away well with the cold.' Then she turned slowly. 'It's a mercy you were in this house just now. You've a sensible head on your shoulders, and that was required. I'm willing, but I've no skill and I'm growing old, miss. I canna' now be taking shocks the way I could as a young lassie.' Her face twisted. 'And to think it was myself gave wee Johnnie that knife! The bairn could maybe have bled to his death.'

She began to weep the helpless, exhausted tears of the old. She wept on my shoulder, and I patted her back and reminded her small boys had been cutting themselves with knives ever since knives were invented. 'Before that they probably cut chinks out of themselves with sharp flints.'

'Is tha' a fact?' she asked pathetically.

'My dear, you know it is. Now, didn't the Professor chop himself up as a small boy?'

'Aye. Maybe.'

When she was calmer I went into the dining-room for Dougal's whisky.

'Och, no, lassie! I canna' take a wee dram without the Professor's permission.'

'Nonsense! I'm sure he won't mind. If he does we can blame me.'

'I'd not have that!'

I said gently, 'Mrs Pringle, I was only joking. Come on. Knock it back. That's it.'

She handed me the empty glass. 'You're a strange lassie, Miss Elizabeth, but sensible—aye—and kind.'

4. *Highland Hospitality and Highland Rain*

From that evening Mrs Pringle never again addressed me as 'Miss Wade'. I became 'Miss Elizabeth' or 'lassie'.

She said, 'I was not aware it was at the Professor's request you were avoiding wee Judy.'

I took her point. 'He's very anxious the scarlet germ shouldn't spread to Gairlie.'

'He's aye been a man thoughtful for others, but never one to communicate his thoughts to others, not even as a wee bairn.'

As far as I was concerned, not only his thoughts. We were living in the same house and I had tried, but I had yet to make any real communication with the man at all.

I tried again that night when the boys had gone up. I was describing Johnnie's admirable calm when Mrs Pringle came in with our coffee. 'Aye,' she agreed, 'a stout-hearted laddie! And that attached to his clever wee sister.'

It was the first time she had joined in a mealtime conversation in my presence. He glanced from her to me without comment. I said, 'Judy strikes me as very bright.'

'Her father tells me her school are much impressed by her I.Q.'

Mrs Pringle paused on her way out. 'And the same affection for her books as poor Miss Catriona.'

'That's so, Rose.' Dougal waited till the door closed. 'Catriona was my twin. She died ten years ago. Pneumonia. B. virulens.' His face took on an extra rigidity. 'You've met it?'

I hesitated, momentarily. 'Only in textbooks.' I watched his expression as he was looking at his coffee-cup. 'I'm very sorry.'

'It was a great grief to us all,' he said, and changed the subject. Knowing grief to be one of the rarities that increase when shared, particularly with strangers, that change I understood. For the same reason I had not told him Dr Sinclair had already put me in the general picture. Nor did I mention the occasion, two years ago, when for a few hours I had set Martha's Thoracic Unit and Inpatient Path. Lab. in a tiz, as during those hours I had been suspected of harbouring the same bacillus. I had gone on duty one night with a pain in my chest and come off with acute bronchitis. A couple of hours later it was double-pneumonia. For that brief period every senior physician and pathologist in Martha's seemed to brood round my oxygen tent, but as the suspected diagnosis had been wrong, I was still alive, and though I had later had pleurisy, eventually I recovered so well that I was still one of the Thoracic Unit's pin-ups. Our chest pundit never saw me round the hospital without pointing me out to the nearest student as an example of what good medicine, good nursing, and a good constitution could do. But during that brief period I had known enough to be very frightened. It is was reasonable to hope Catriona Grant had been spared that part, though inevitably Dougal could not have missed one turn of the screw. I hoped he now realized I understood and sympathized; if he did he didn't show it.

He was talking about Robin. 'As he's so keen to climb, he should learn properly. He's going to attend Charlie Urquhart's holiday climbing school up the glen, from Monday. You've heard of Charlie Urquhart?'

'I don't think so. Sorry. Should I have?'

'No, since this clearly illustrates your lack of interest in climbing.' And without giving me the chance to explain that in this case ignorance was not synonymous with lack of interest, he moved on to a telephone conversation he had with Dr Sinclair that afternoon. 'He considers Judy'll be clear on Saturday, and you on Sunday.'

'Then I'll go back Sunday night?' I hoped I did not sound too eager.

Apparently it would not have mattered if I had. 'I rang up about it this afternoon while you were out. Unfortunately there's no available sleeper until Monday. I've booked you one for that night. I'll drive you in.'

'That's kind of you, but do you really want to do the double journey?'

'I enjoy driving, and it so happens that I want to be in Glasgow on Monday. The twins can come with us. They'll maybe enjoy the outing.'

'It's a beautiful drive—I think. To be honest, I didn't see much more than the road ahead.'

'One doesn't, particularly on a strange road. Talking of things unseen'—he refilled our cups—'it would be a pity for you to leave Gairlie without one trip up the hills. I mentioned that to Maury Valentine this afternoon, and she kindly suggested we all join her for an all-day picnic on Saturday. There's a plateau fairly near with one of the finest views in Scotland. We thought we'd take you up. Would you care for that?'

I was too much of a moral coward and making too little headway for the truth. I hedged. 'Perhaps I should warn you, I've never climbed more than a fire-escape.'

'Understandable,' he said flatly, 'since this is your first visit to the Highlands.' He sat back and folded his arms. 'I doubt you're any better acquainted with the Alps?'

'No. Ben Gairlie's the first mountain I've even come this close to.'

'Indeed? It's a pity you'll have no opportunity to get even closer. The Ben's a fine mountain and as near to Alpine standards as any in the British Isles.'

I thought of my weak head for heights and thanked God. 'Great pity.'

The conversation remained on Scotland in general and the Highlands in particular. Just for a little while he shed a fraction of his reserve and talked more freely than I had yet heard him. He was very interesting, but what interested and astounded me most of all was his almost pathological nostalgia for the past. Thoughtlessly, I mentioned Culloden. He froze visibly. He said very politely, 'I hope you'll forgive a Highlander for changing the subject now, Elizabeth.'

After that I gave up. There was a sticky little silence whilst we finished our coffee, then we both agreed there was nothing like an occasional early night.

He came upstairs with me as he wanted something from his own room, and escorted me to my bedroom door. Mrs Pringle had taken herself off watch, but we needed no chaperon. Dougal thanked me again for my first-aid to Johnnie, produced his usual nightly spiel on the subject of my sleep, with the utmost civility managed to impress me with the conviction that I was not just unattractive, but sexless. Seeing him standing there in my bedroom door, I was suddenly quite wildly grateful to Archie, since without his uninhibited approach these few days with Dougal would have reduced my morale to sub-zero. As it was, it was taking quite a beating.

It was pelting again next morning. Johnnie and I were playing two-handed whist in the sitting-room when Dougal came in at noon. 'There's a personal call coming through for you from London, Elizabeth. If you'll take it in my study I'll play your hand here.'

'Thanks.' I gave him my cards. 'Who's ringing me at this hour? One of my friends come into money?'

He frowned at the cards. 'I can only apologize for being in no position to enlighten you on that score.'

I was growing accustomed to his bout of pomposity, but that one stuck in my throat for some odd reason. 'And I can only apologize for being unable to present you with a better hand, Dougal. Unfortunately I've no talent for card games.'

He glanced at me, but whether or not he realized I was sending him up I couldn't tell. 'Even Homer sometimes nods.' He held open the door. 'Whose bid, Johnnie?'

Maury Valentine might not believe it, but at that moment she had all my sympathy.

The telephone was ringing as I reached the study. 'Hi, there, Elizabeth! Kind of a surprise?'

'Archie! What are you doing in London?'

'I have just had to fly in from Inverness, honey. Seems there's this deal I have to put through, but I'll be right back, Saturday. Can I see you then? You'll be through with the bugs Sunday? Great! So we'll make it Sunday. Can I call round your place Sunday, and maybe you can come round to my hotel?'

'I'd like that. Thanks. Come round and meet Dougal and the kids.'

'I'd be happy to do that—and I guess this Dougal Grant'll like to take one good look at me at that!'

I was curious. 'Why do you say that?'

He laughed. 'Last night I had a few drinks with Davie MacDonald, and from what he let out I have the impression Dougal Grant has been doing one real keen security check on me. So who blames him,' he added good-naturedly, 'seeing he has one mighty pretty English girl as a house-guest?'

'It's the kind of thing he would do, but I think it very big of you not to take umbrage.'

'You figure I should?'

'I would. Bloody cheek!'

He was amused. 'Don't be too mad at the poor guy. So he's an egghead and a stuffed-shirt? So who cares?'

I said, 'Archie, you are very sensible and I am very stupid. But it's this docile little woman act. Getting me down, as I am just not one.'

'And you know what is getting me down, honey? Already I am missing you like crazy. See you Sunday and call you Saturday night to say hallo, the man is right back!'

Dougal was alone in the sitting-room when I got back, as Johnnie had taken Judy up a fresh supply of books and apples. I told Dougal Archie was in London.

'Indeed? You'll miss his company on your walks.'

'Yes. He's amusing.' I asked if my Sunday date would be all right.

'He's hoping to meet you.'

'I shall look forward to meeting your American friend.'

'Perhaps your grandfather knew the Gairlie grandfather of whom he's so proud?'

'Possibly. Certainly,' he added drily, 'Calum MacDonald proved a man his grandson must be proud to acknowledge. You'll forgive me if I return to my study? Johnnie'll be down directly.'

Johnnie took some time, and I spent it trying to fathom why Dougal found it right and proper to hallow the tragic past, but not a crofter grandfather who had had the guts to up and out. Archie had never mentioned his grandfather's job in the States, but from the various remarks he had let fall about his family background Calum MacDonald seemed to have been one more example of successful Scottish enterprise in exile. Then why didn't Dougal approve? Or had I merely imagined his disapproval because I was feeling thoroughly bloody-minded over the immediate prospect of life without Archie?

That set me wondering how much I really liked Archie, whether 'like' was the right word, if I would see him after Sunday, or whether ours would go the usual way of holiday affairs. I started hoping it would not, then realized what I was doing and, from old habit, instinctively clamped down on the hope. If one didn't hope hard one couldn't be hurt hard. That had been my angle for years. Of course, I knew why now, but I had only acquired that bit of self-insight in the last year, and I was not yet ready to do more than acknowledge my weakness to myself. In Martha's I had always avoided 'steadies' like the plague. That way no-one got hurt. Joe Fenton played by the same rules, which was another reason why he and I got along so well. I suspected Archie did the same. I hoped he did, and as that was a safe hope, I didn't clamp down on it.

The rain continued all Friday. I felt like Judas Iscariot over my personal delight in the downpour every time the twins groaned at the prospect of a cancelled picnic. Johnnie's bellow of joy woke me on a Saturday morning. It was the most perfect morning since our arrival in Gairlie.

Mrs Pringle had been offered the day off and chosen to spend the day baking. Her husband was away on his trawler, none of her married children lived locally, and though her husband was related to half Gairlie, she told me after breakfast she aye found it easier to maintain a strong affection for her man's kin when she kept herself to herself.

'Then you're not from Gairlie, Mrs P?

'Och, no. Oban.' She studied my skirt hem, but not as previously. 'I'm not saying you've not a bonnie pair of legs, lassie, but with that expanse you'll take it awful cold up the hills.' She scuttled off and returned with a pair of hand-knitted stockings. 'Do you fancy these?'

'Do I not! Dead kinky!'

We were travelling in two cars, Judy and I with Dougal, the boys with Maury. Dougal suggested this, 'on the grounds of medical prudence'. From his expression when he put it to me it pleased him as little as it was going to please Mrs Valentine.

She was late, and Robin went into the front garden to watch for her. He rushed in squeaking, 'Here's her car!'

Judy drew me aside. 'His voice always comes out a squeak when he's gone on a bird. Makes him right spare! He's been practising all morning to get it low as Uncle's.'

'Poor old Robin! He often go for the birds?'

'Oh, blimey,' said Judy, 'he's sex mad. Boys get so grotty. Johnnie's starting. He's gone on you, though he's not such a drag about you as Robin about Mrs Valentine. Of course, Johnnie's younger.'

'Makes a difference.'

Dougal had gone out to meet Maury. Judy watched him through the open front door. 'Do you suppose he is going to marry her, Elizabeth?'

'Your uncle?' I shrugged. 'Don't ask me.' I was watching Maury making like Stanley should have greeted Livingstone. 'What do you think?'

'Don't sort of know her yet, but Johnnie says she's dead grotty. Johnnie's quite bright—for a boy,' she added, not unkindly, as an afterthought.

Maury wore a tan trouser suit and a blue suède car coat. The outfit suited her. She advanced on me with outstretched hands. 'I'm so glad Dougal was able to persuade you to join our little party, Elizabeth. Haven't you been lucky! No sign of scarlet fever. It does rather look, doesn't it, as if you must have had it ages ago?'

'Not necessarily.' Dougal answered for me. 'Elizabeth may have a natural immunity, but let us not tempt providence until after tomorrow.'

I had spent most of that morning giving myself a 'Let's starting loving Maury' pep-talk. I told myself I had imagined her earlier instant antipathy. I hadn't. Dougal might fox me, but I knew my own sex. I made a few trite remarks and waited in unkind anticipation for her reaction to our travelling order.

'Dougal darling, must we? I thought we'd all go together.' She widened her eyes. They were lovely eyes, even if slightly lacking in expression. 'With you driving, of course!'

'I think we should play it safe for one more day.'

'Then we shall.' She nearly purred to prove she was a docile kitten. 'Naturally, you know best! You'll lead?'

'If you've no objection?'

'Dougal, you know me. I'm the old-fashioned type.' She smiled at me through her very good eyelashes. 'I expect Elizabeth finds that amusing. English girls are so strong-minded and, well—modern—these days.'

Elizabeth was finding her hysterical. She was very good-looking, but if she was really what Dougal wanted as a wife, then he deserved her.

Dougal thought we should be on our way. The master had spoken, and we scattered to the cars like so many obedient chattels.

We left Gairlie by a road new to me and began to climb at once. Within a few minutes Achnagairl House became a grey matchbox and the village a shrinking set of blue-and-white toy houses. Then we were high enough to see over the hills round the loch to the mountain range on the northern horizon, and oddly the twin blue mountains in the east seemed much closer. Oddly, as we were travelling west. We could just glimpse the sea, and a very long way out a handful of minute wispy clouds moving down the coast.

Judy was sitting in front. Dougal's head turned seawards a couple of times. 'I hope the wind doesn't change and bring those clouds inland.'

'Will that matter, Uncle? They're so small.'

'They only look that way because they're so far out. If the wind brings them inland and then drops those clouds could cover these hills like a blanket. So, if the wind changes, I'm afraid we go straight down.'

'How dead grotty! Ouch! Uncle, my ears are popping!'

'Already? We're not high yet. Swallow, lassie. That'll fix your ears. All right in the back, Elizabeth?'

'Yes, thanks.'

Occasionally we passed small crofts built of granite slabs; some had thatched roofs with the thatching repaired with string or held down with heavy stones; others were roofed with corrugated iron. They were all well away from the road and looked picturesque in the sunshine. I wondered how they looked in a blizzard in winter, then accidentally glanced over the ravine edge as we took another hairpin bend and shut my eyes, fast.

'Sleepy, Elizabeth?' asked Dougal.

I had forgotten the driving mirror. 'Just drowsy. Unaccustomed altitude, I expect.'

'It can have that effect.' He produced chocolate from the dashboard shelf. 'Help yourself, and Judy. It'll step-up your blood sugar.'

Judy said, 'That's why Elizabeth gave us all sweets when Johnnie cut himself. Mrs Pringle said they made her feel much better. Elizabeth said they would. Elizabeth's dead clever, isn't she, Uncle?'

'She is, indeed,' he agreed, very drily.

Only Judy thought he was paying me a compliment.

5. A Picnic on a High Plateau

Dougal tightened the straps of Robin's haversack. 'We'll go up by the main burn, Maury, then use the sheep track for the last lap.' He hitched the picnic basket on to his back. 'Twins, stay by me. Robin, look after Elizabeth.'

Robin grimaced. 'What about Mrs Valentine?'

'Darling Robin, so gallant!' exclaimed Maury. 'But you don't have to worry about me. Your uncle knows I'm quite at home here, and poor Elizabeth must feel a bit awkward—not being used to our hills, I mean.'

Dougal glanced at Robin, but so effectively that the boy even lent me an occasional hand. We followed a few yards behind the others, and though the gradient was very steep, the turf was springy and the going pleasant as we took it very slowly.

Maury swung herself round to lean against the slope and look down. 'Ever see such a view, Elizabeth?'

I looked over my shoulder and upwards. 'Never!'

'Bloody hell,' muttered Robin, 'if you're going to keep stopping we'll never get up to the top.'

We moved on up. Dougal's outstretched hands hauled me up the final few feet of sheer rock. 'How do the sheep manage this bit?' I demanded breathlessly.

'They've four feet, not two.' He was suddenly looking at me clinically. 'You're very breathless. You're not cyanosed, but have you ever had any cardiac trouble?'

'Never. Altitude, I guess. How high are we?'

'Just under one thousand feet. Turn round and take a look, and you'll see why we're here.'

We were away from the edge, so I could look out. I inhaled sharply. 'It's like standing on the edge of the sky.'

The plateau topped the highest hill in the district. On every side the hills rolled like petrified giant brown waves that lapped that greater giant, Ben Gairlie, and then rolled on to the snow-crested mountain range in the north. Here and there the brown was broken with vivid blue slits of lochs and black velvet patches of glens. The beauty was genuinely breath-taking.

Dougal said, 'A view worth seeing.'

Maury slid a hand through his arm. 'Not so fine, though, as the view must be from the top of the Ben?'

'Possibly not, if one could see clearly from the top. Every time I've been up the Ben's crest there've been clouds in the way.'

'Every time?' I turned to him. 'Dougal, do you make a habit of nipping up to the top of Ben Gairlie?'

He smiled. 'We all have our odd habits.'

Maury was not amused. 'Really, Elizabeth, before you drop any more bricks I think I ought to warn you you are talking to one of the best rock-climbers in Scotland! No, Dougal, you can't deny that,' she insisted, as he was about to interrupt. 'Charlie Urquhart always says so. He should know. And, surely, even you must've heard of Charlie Urquhart, Elizabeth?'

'Only since Dougal mentioned his name to me the other evening.'

She raised her eyes in horror. 'Only then?'

Dougal said there was no occasion for her to be so surprised, since London was a long way from Gairlie.

She brightened. 'One forgets it's another world.'

I hadn't forgotten. Three days, I thought, and the thought so cheered me that I beamed on them both and went off to talk to the twins.

The plateau covered about two-thirds of an acre. It was criss-crossed with burns, and some of the ground between was boggy, but there were enough dry patches to make the final selection of our picnic spot a lengthy business. Eventually we settled on rugs on the southern side of a heap of granite boulders that provided us with back-rests and shelter from the stiffish north wind.

Maury gave us an excellent lunch, and throughout the meal talked exclusively to Dougal and Robin. Dougal did his best to keep me in the conversation, but he had a tough job, as whenever he produced a subject that could include me she produced another that shut me out. That didn't bother me, seriously, nor did it make me feel a welcome guest. After a while I kept as silent as the twins. Unfortunately, being an adult, I couldn't disappear as they did, directly we finished eating.

Robin wanted to sketch. 'Can I go down to that shelf over the edge there? It's only about thirty feet down.'

'Providing you stay put on that shelf. It's good and wide, but the drop beneath is steep enough for real experience or ropes.' Dougal got to his feet. 'I'll see you down.'

Maury decided her legs needed stretching. 'Wait for me!'

'With pleasure.' Dougal turned, smiling. The breeze lifted his hair and gave him a faint colour. Outlined against the sky at that moment, he looked younger and more alive than I had ever seen him. I could well understand, if not share, Maury's point of view. 'Will you join us, Elizabeth?'

I used laziness as an excuse. He did not press the point. Directly they disappeared over the edge ahead the twins rejoined me. Judy sat on my rug, and Johnnie pottered round examining the picnic basket and haversack. 'I say! Aren't we here for tea?'

'Uncle told Mrs Pringle we wouldn't be back till nearly six.' Judy twisted round. 'Why?'

'There's nothing left to nosh here.'

I said, 'Probably the tea-basket's still in Mrs Valentine's car.'

Johnnie looked worried. 'I only saw one basket.' The moment Dougal and Maury returned Johnnie tackled his uncle. 'Is it in the boot? Can I go down and fetch it?'

'Tea! Oh, my goodness!' Maury was shocked beyond belief by her absent-mindedness. So was Johnnie. The tea-basket was still in the front hall of her house. 'I'll drive back at once. Silly me!'

'No.' Dougal looked at the twins, then at the sky. 'I don't like leaving you girls up here, but this weather does look set, if only for the next hour or so. I'll go for the basket. Well, twins? Coming for the ride?'

'Gosh, yes! A picnic without tea—' Johnnie was too shaken to put the full horror into words.

'Grotty,' said Judy, looking at Maury. 'Dead grotty.'

Dougal had gone to call some instructions down to Robin. He returned and reminded Maury how swiftly hill weather could change. 'Get down to the road at the first sign of any change. Don't hang around. Start walking. Keep on the road and going down, and you'll not get lost.'

Maury crossed the plateau to see them down the sheep-track, then came back and wrapped herself in a rug. 'I feel so guilty about giving poor Dougal this extra chore, but I must admit it's much more peaceful without the prattle of the very young. Aren't you exhausted after a week in their company? My poor Dougal looks positively jaded! Or do you feel'—she studied her hands—'that what with one thing and another it's all been worth while?'

I looked at her before answering. 'I'm not quite sure what you mean. That it's been worth while to get to know the twins? If so, yes. They're sweet kids. I like them a lot.'

'How touching! And clever. Dougal told me you're clever.' She looked up. There was a queer little smile in her eyes. 'Though one can't help feeling rather sorry for Joe Fenton.'

'Joe?' I was beginning to wonder if I was hearing right. 'Sorry, Maury, but I'm lost.'

'Darling,' she drawled, 'spare me the injured innocent, please. I'm another woman, remember? That sweet-angel-of-mercy line may fool some men, but it doesn't wash with me. Nor, I think you ought to know, has it with Dougal. He's seen through you.'

I was hearing all right. 'He has?' I asked softly.

'Do you seriously imagine a man of his intelligence wouldn't? Though, of course, he's far too polite to tell you so himself. But since I happen to dislike seeing scheming young women taking advantage of my friends, I feel it's up to me to do the job for him.'

'That I believe.'

She flushed. 'Don't you take that tone to me, my girl! I won't stand for it!'

'Then I suggest we change the subject, smartly.'

'Oh, no! No! I'm not letting you wriggle out of it like that! Someone ought to tell you just what all Dougal's friends think of you before you leave Gairlie. I suppose you think no-one's noticed the way you've been using him to suit your own ends?'

This unexpected and unimaginable onslaught now had me as breathless as the climb up. 'I—have?'

'Don't pretend you haven't imposed on his hospitality to suit yourself. It's too obvious! You knew no-one could prove you've had scarlet fever. You knew Dougal would have to ask you to stay. He told me himself— his hands were tied. Very clever,' she jeered, 'and very understandable! What's a young doctor like Joe Fenton up against a man who's already inherited one of the largest motor corporations in the United States?'

'Archie MacDonald?' I queried incredulously.

'You never drop the act, do you? But I'd better warn you not to set your hopes too high. As Dougal says, to run his business as well as he apparently does, Archie MacDonald must have inherited some good Scottish common sense in addition to a few million dollars from his Gairlie grandfather. He won't be easily hooked—and one's not too surprised that he's suddenly had to fly back to London on business. One won't be surprised if he suddenly finds he can fly back—after you've left on Monday. So I thought I'd tell you not to count your chickens—just yet.'

I was too angry to think straight. I voiced the first thought in my head. 'You forgot that tea-basket intentionally.'

That so increased her anger that it was obviously true. 'Just because you've everything all worked out you assume everyone else indulges in crafty little schemes! No wonder Dougal's so keen to get you on that train on Monday that he's going to drive you to Glasgow himself! He told me, himself, he gave you the impression he's got business there that day, but he hasn't. He just wants to make good and sure you don't miss that train.' She jumped up, shedding her rug. 'I'm going to talk to Robin. I don't suppose you want to come?'

'No,' I said, 'I don't.'

I felt slightly and physically sick as she disappeared over the edge ahead. I had been weighed-into by ward sisters when I was a junior, but I had never experienced anything quite like this. I lay flat and dropped an arm over my eyes as I had to think things out and could always do that better with my eyes closed. If she returned I hoped she would think me asleep, and if that was cowardly I didn't give a damn. I'd had as much as I could stand of Maury Valentine and fine old Highland hospitality, but I wanted to get things under control before the others returned with the tea-basket, as I did not want to upset the twins. As for Dougal, had he appeared alone at that moment, I'd have sat up and informed him my favourite day for celebration was the anniversary of Flodden Field.

Slowly, I calmed down. I realized that since Maury had resented me on sight, I could write off a certain amount of what she had said as sheer bitchiness. But only a certain amount.

I remembered Archie's reticence about his job and how very little he had actually told me of Calum MacDonald. I remembered how puzzled I had been by Dougal's reaction to Archie's pride in his grandfather. Presumably Dougal assumed Archie had bragged to me of his grandfather's millions. I smiled humourlessly. Had Dougal known the truth he'd have approved vastly of Archie MacDonald's canny streak.

Somewhere I heard a stone chinking as it rolled downwards. I didn't move my arm. I was as soundly asleep as any ward patient at the sight of an unwelcome visitor waiting behind the screen across the open door just before visiting time.

I had liked Archie. I had believed all he said about flying down on business and returning today. But as he hadn't trusted me enough for the truth, earlier, how could I now believe a word he said? And Dougal? My charming courteous host who had made such a song and dance about being eternally indebted to me for my kindness to Judy and later Johnnie! Did he imagine I'd infected Judy with scarlet and then stabbed Johnnie to prove my sterling value as a guest—and hook Archie? Or was most of that just Maury's pathological jealousy? Having run into a quota of people with that same affliction, I did not know that the fact that she had no cause to be jealous of me was neither here nor there. And though she was much better-looking than myself, I was younger. But she had not been in Dougal's car on the drive up. I remembered the edge in his voice when he agreed with Judy that I was clever.

God, I thought wearily, how do I get through the rest of today, tomorrow, and that long drive on Monday? I didn't know, and as I noticed absently that the sun and the wind seemed warmer, I let it ride, temporarily. A brief snooze wouldn't improve my situation, but it should make me feel better able to deal with it. Inside of a few minutes I was asleep.

I woke shortly to find myself shivering and still alone. I sat up, blinking, to clear my eyes before looking at my watch. Only ten to two— and the mist was not in my eyes. A faint haze hung between the sun and the plateau. The sun looked very distant and much smaller.

It was a very faint haze, and being so ignorant of hill weather and having so much to preoccupy me, I did my hair and face. I hadn't forgotten Dougal's parting advice to Maury, but as her handbag was still on the rug she had shed, plus all the remains of our picnic, I guessed she was with Robin. Probably it was warmer on the shelf. The air on the plateau was getting increasingly cold, and though the wind had slackened, it was present. Presumably Maury realized this haze was very temporary, or she would have whisked us down to the road. She might hate my guts, but Dougal's word was her law—if only until she was sure she had him.

I waited some minutes, then got up to investigate. Once away from the sheltering boulders I discovered why the breeze was puzzling me. The wind had changed and was coming in from the west, bringing with it heavy white low clouds that seemed only to skim over the neighbouring hills.

I looked up, thoughtfully. Surely Maury could see the sky as well as myself?

In those few seconds I spent looking up the sun vanished and the clouds turned the plateau into an island. Despite Dougal's frequent remarks on the subject, the swiftness of the change astonished me. Yet, as the clouds had moved so fast, wouldn't they move on as fast? Unless the wind dropped.

It seemed a time for a little strong-minded efficiency. I crossed back to the southern edge, knelt, and peered over. I could not even see the width of the little shelf through the rising whiteness below. There was no sign of Maury, but I could just glimpse Robin's hunched shoulders in his dark-blue donkey-jacket. God alone knew where Maury was, but the boy had obviously dropped off, as I had. Only he was sleeping on a ledge jutting out from the side of a high hill.

I called his name quietly not to shock him into sudden movement. He didn't hear me. I shouted, without effect. I stood up and yelled for Maury, and my yells fell flatly on the thickening air. Robin slept on.

The drop to the ledge seemed to me sheer as a precipice. I got down by slithering most of the way, and only because I had to. Getting back up was going to be another problem, but at least I would then have Robin to help me. I could have wept with relief when my feet touched the ledge, and I groped my way towards Robin. The cloud was so thick that it was only when in reaching distance that I realized what I had taken for his hunched shoulders was a rounded boulder over which he had draped his donkey-jacket. His open sketching pad and pencil lay beside it.

That was when I had my first wave of panic. I remembered hearing that stone falling. It could have been dislodged by Maury returning with Robin to take a walk, but it could have been Robin, falling.

The ledge there was about six feet wide. I lay on my face to look over, but could see only a few feet. For those feet the hill dropped like a wall into a white, wet, silent world. Silent and still. The wind had dropped. I shouted myself hoarse. There was no answer, no movement.

The sensible thing to do was to get back up to the plateau. It would be safer up there, and if, as I prayed, Robin was with Maury, up there I would have a better chance of meeting up with them. If I got back up.

I was very cold and very frightened, being much too conscious of the narrowness of that shelf and the drop beyond. For every upward step I slipped back two, and twice nearly lost my balance when I hit the shelf. After one of the worst half-hours of my life common sense, and I had not much of it left, forced me to accept defeat. I must sit this out on the ledge with my back to the hill. There were hours of daylight ahead. The wind would return and shift the clouds and give one and all a good giggle when they found me.

I buttoned on the donkey-jacket over my coat and turned up both collars. The air was so thick I had to hold my watch to my face to see the time. Twenty to three. Robin must be with Maury. For Dougal's sake, surely she must have kept an eye on Robin when she saw the weather was changing? I was perfectly safe. All I needed was patience. Hours of daylight ahead, I reminded myself repeatedly as the hours dragged by and took me that much closer to the thought I was trying to avoid. The night ahead.

At first, imperceptibly, the cotton-wool air darkened. Then it was all black. A soaking, icy blackness that seeped through my clothes, drenched my face and hair, stung my eyes, and made breathing such an effort that my lungs ached.

I grew cramped with sitting, but dared not do more than stand on one spot holding on to the hill face whilst I stamped my feet and swung my arms. Though it was my first hill mist, having been in countless London smogs, I knew how easy it was to lose all sense of direction. If I lost physical contact with the hill against which I had been leaning I might never find it again. A few steps in the wrong direction, and I'd fall off the shelf.

Between the darkness and the knowledge of that drop I was often very close to blind panic. I recited aloud to stave it off. I went through all the muscles and the bones, and then all the poems I could remember. Once at school, for a bet, I had memorized all *The Ancient Mariner.* I chanted all I could recall until I had hardly any voice left.

The hill face became my friend. I kept reaching back as I sat, touching it for comfort. My fingers left a jutting fragment of rock and clung to it as if it were a human hand.

Time ceased to matter. Unless the mist cleared no-one could find me until daylight. I knew that from my conversation with the seaman at Glasgow Central. He had said the mist had delayed the search on the Ben. What was his name? Cameron. Had Mrs Pringle been a Cameron? No—her sister was his sister-in-law—or was it the other way round? I couldn't remember. I couldn't remember any other existence. I had sat on that ledge for a lifetime.

Then I heard a sound. I sat forward, holding my breath to listen. The silence was absolute. I tried shouting, 'Anyone there?' My shout came out as a croak, and the mist echoed it back as a cracked whisper.

Immediately, 'Elizabeth!' whispered a voice. 'Elizabeth, where are you?'

I neither recognized the whisper nor was able to tell if it came from above or below. I had to resist an overwhelming urge to leap up, in case, after sitting so long, I properly lost balance. 'I'm on the ledge. Who is it?'

'Dougal.' The whisper was louder and now recognizable. 'I'm on the plateau above. Now, listen well and do exactly what I say. I want you to stay very still where you are. Understand?'

'Yes.'

'Are you hurt? Did you fall?'

'No.' Relief was making my head curiously light. 'I've lost Robin!'

'He's safe with Maury. I'm coming down, so keep calling, and I'll make for your voice. You'll not see my headlamp until I'm very close, but just keep calling—my name—anything—and don't move! Right?'

'Yes. Be careful—'

'I will. Keep calling.'

I was still calling when a beam of light blinded me and Dougal grasped my shoulders. 'What possessed you to come down here, lassie? If you didn't fall, why the devil didn't you get straight back up whilst it was still light? How long have you been—' His voice stopped abruptly. His hand had reached my left radial pulse under the two coat-sleeves.

6. The Mist lasts All Night

The mist was in my brain and bones. I was limp as a rag doll and frantically chatty. I told him about Robin's jacket and losing my nerve. Some of my words were slurred. I said, 'I'm not tight, Dougal.'

'I know.' Something touched my lips. 'Have a nice wee drink of condensed milk.'

'Ugh—sickly! Must I?'

'Aye come on, Elizabeth.' He poured it down me. 'That's a good girl.'

I giggled foolishly. 'Thank you, Doctor.'

'You're welcome.' His headlamp illuminated the lower half of his face, and his lips were smiling. His shoulders were pale orange. 'I'm now going to lay you down for a few moments whilst I get off this haversack. Then I'll have you warmer.'

'How? Going to light a fire?'

'Not just now. I've a rug or two with me.'

He wrapped me in two rugs and a polythene ground-sheet that zipped up. He gave me chocolate and then more milk. I was only mildly interested in events, as most of the time I still seemed to be floating over our heads. It was an extraordinary but not unpleasant sensation. I could talk and even co-operate, so long as the minimum physical effort was required of me. I had no memory and no judgment. Had Dougal suggested pushing me off the hill it wouldn't have worried me. I could float.

He was moving around, and his headlamp alternated between a faint amber glow and a pin-point. Then it blinded me again. 'I'm going to move you closer to the hill face, Elizabeth.'

'Why?' (It didn't matter, but seemed polite to ask.)

'You'll be warmer parallel with it. No, don't try and help yourself. I'll lift you as you are in your wee plastic bag.'

'Not so wee as I'm—how tall am I?'

'Between five seven and five eight.' He carried me a few steps, then put me down gently. 'Don't throw your head back, as there's a largish boulder just behind it. I'll have you more comfortable directly.' He cradled my head with his right arm and lay on his side, jamming me between his body and the hill. I had begun to warm up before the move. I was now in a cocoon of warmth.

He laid a hand on my forehead. 'That's more like it. Time for a nice mug of lukewarm tea.'

'Lukewarm? I don't wish to be rude, but what a nauseating suggestion!'

'Aye, isn't it?' he retorted cheerfully. 'No, stay still. I can manage, as I've the vacuum flask ready beside me.' He raised my head and held my mug as I drank, and some tea went down my neck. 'Och, sorry. Let me just get inside my anorak for something to mop you up. Dry?'

'Yes, thanks. Dougal—'

'Yes?'

'You'd make a good nurse.'

'Drenching my patients with tea?'

'What's a few drops? I once dropped a full basin of washing water over a gynae lady.'

'Unfortunate,' he agreed mildly. 'She get pneumonia?'

'No ill effects at all, and it made her my mate for life. She still sends

me Christmas cards. Sister Gynae never forgave me. Whenever she saw
me she said, "Don't drop that, Nurse Wade!" So I just did. She thought
I was being bloody-minded. I wasn't. It had become a reflex action. Like
your good manners.'

'They're a reflex action?'

'Aren't they such a fundamental part of your make-up as to be that? I
mean, if I upped and clouted you now, wouldn't you say, "I do beg your
pardon, Elizabeth," before clouting me back?'

'You're convinced I'd clout you back?'

'Not in your house. Here,' I mused, 'yes, probably. Here, you're
different.'

'Is that so?'

'Yes. Here you're quite human.'

'So?'

'So. Not that you're not a model host, but you're much nicer when
you slop tea down my neck. Oh, God!' Suddenly I realized what I was
saying. 'I shouldn't be telling you all this. Have you taken great
umbrage?'

'Tremendous umbrage. Next time you want tea you'll hold the mug
yourself.'

My brain was working again, but in very slow motion. 'Dougal Grant,
you are humouring me—and I've rumbled why and why the lukewarm
and not hot tea. No sudden heat or harsh words for an exposure case.'

'Diagnosing yourself?' He sounded amused. 'A typical nurse's
reaction.'

'And a doctor's!'

'That's true.'

'Aren't I right? About me?'

'Aye. You've a mild touch of exposure. Only mild as it's not a cold
night and you've your age and sex in your favour.'

'The biological advantage of my subcutaneous fat?'

'No small advantage that, when it comes to combating exposure. Even
without that, as you'll know as well as myself, though women may be
weaker in muscle power, physically they're by far the stronger sex, and
better equipped mentally for survival.'

I said, 'Now you sound like our Prof. Medicine. His lectures are like a
shot in the arm. But I never realized you thought like that. I've kept
forgetting you're in medicine. I suppose you lecture. Are you good at it?'

'Unfortunately not.' From his voice he was smiling. 'Too often I'm
nervous, and when nervous I turn pompous and boring. Then, if a subject
really interests me, I can forget my nervousness, but I go too fast. Also,
I've no patience with fools, which is a great disadvantage in the medical
world.'

'I wouldn't have thought you at all impatient, but I can sympathize. Martha's is a good hospital, but even Martha's produces some right morons in white coats. God only knows how some of 'em managed to qualify. Was that why you opted out of the main stream?'

'It was possibly a subconscious reason. Consciously, I chose to specialize in tropical bugs because they fascinate me. I like research, and I enjoy the field-work.'

'And writing textbooks?' I told him how I had checked up on the tsetse-fly. 'Very impressive, Professor.'

'I'm glad you found it so.'

'But you should have a beard and a few eccentricities. Have you any?'

'Several. Being a canny Scotsman. I keep 'em dark. Let's have some more chocolate.'

'You cold?' I raised my head, and my hair brushed his chin. 'Dougal, how awful of me! I've only just realized you're using yourself as a human windbreak and haven't a plastic bag. You must be frozen.'

'I'm not. Feel my hand on your face.' It was surprisingly warm. 'These clothes are exposure-proof.'

My memory of the distant past was still much clearer than that of the immediate few hours. After the chocolate he altered our positions slightly, and, using the haversack as a cushion for his head against the boulder, raised me enough to rest against his chest and folded both arms across mine. Having grown so accustomed to our present situation, it did not even strike me as faintly peculiar to be in his arms. It seemed as natural as it was sensible, not to waste our mutual warmth.

My private mist of the last few hours began partially to lift. 'You did say Robin and Maury were safe?'

'Aye.'

'What happened to them?'

'Maury ran out of cigarettes and thought she'd some in her car. Robin went with her to fetch them. Apparently they left you asleep, and as the weather seemed set assumed it safe.'

'Yes. I think I did drop off. I think it got warmer about then.'

'That was the wind changing. Unfortunately Maury didn't notice it had until it was too late. Very unwisely, she and Robin had decided to stroll a little way down the road to meet my returning car. They were on the road when the wind dropped. Though not a Highlander, Maury knew enough about the hill to appreciate that to turn back and try and climb the plateau to find you with only an inexperienced boy to help her would almost certainly mean three, not just one, lost. She's never had any sense of direction, but as anyone can follow a road running downhill in any mist she made the only sensible decision and kept on down. They were about half-way down when I met them. There was little mist in Gairlie when I left, and there's unlikely to be more now. They should've reached Maury's house some time back.'

'I didn't realize Maury's not a Highlander.'

'Her father was English, her mother Irish.'

'Really?' The thought of Maury bothered me though I couldn't think why. I let it go. 'Dougal, when did you get into your climbing clobber?'

'When I took the twins back to Achnagairl after noticing the wind had changed. I then drove up, but was less than a third of the way when the wind dropped and driving was impossible. I kept on the road until I met the other two, which, being longer, wasted a lot of time. After leaving them I came on across the hills. Though much shorter, that still took time. It was dark when I searched the plateau the first time. Then I went over the side we came up this morning. Then back all round the plateau. I never expected to find you down here, but, having exhausted the probables, I was working through the improbables. That's why I was so long in finding you. Did you hear none of my earlier shouts?'

'No, but I wasn't listening, as I didn't think anyone could be looking for me in a night mist. Didn't it hold up that last search on Ben Gairlie?'

'Yes. But this isn't the Ben.'

'Could be, as far as I'm concerned!'

'Why didn't you tell me you're scared of heights?'

'Too much of a moral coward.'

'So?' He was silent for several seconds. 'Bad, coming up this morning?'

'In parts. Worth it for the view, though I wish it hadn't resulted in our being stuck out here.'

'Had you not come down we'd still have had to sit this out up top. In point of fact, this shelf, being more sheltered, is more suitable in many ways.'

I said, 'It's nice of you to say so, but—'

'Not nice. True.'

'But why couldn't we have walked back? You walked up.'

'Aye, but mostly in daylight and over hills with which I'm well acquainted. Consequently, I've a healthy respect for them in a night mist. I'll take an occasional calculated risk, but to take an unnecessary one on a night like this is asking for trouble. In the hills as on a mountain, there's a time for action and a time for waiting. This is the latter. Does that bother you?'

'Not now. I didn't fancy the prospect alone.' I could now smile at myself in a pleasantly detached manner. 'I've never known real fear before. Literally, it was throttling.'

'I know exactly what you mean,' he said, as if he did.

I brooded on that for a few minutes. Then I asked why he climbed. 'Is "because it's there" the real reason?'

'That's why some climbers climb, though in my experience not many. It's certainly not my reason.' He hesitated, and when he continued his voice was so soft he might have been singing. 'The hills are my great pleasure—or maybe the better word is love. In the quiet of the hills one can think. Climbers seldom talk much, and some don't care to talk at all. I suppose I climb because I love the quiet and every other aspect of the hills—the sky, the birds, the changing weather, the constant beauty. I won't say I look for danger, but I'd be a liar if I pretended the constant awareness of danger didn't add to one's appreciation of the whole.' He was quiet for some moments. 'I started as a rock-climber.'

'Aren't you still?'

'Aye. But I'm no longer a rock purist.'

'What's that?'

'A rock-climber who wants only to climb bigger and better rocks. If the going's too easy a true rock purist becomes impatient. I've outgrown that stage, but that's nothing to do with age. Some do, some don't.'

'Were you very young when you started?'

'Younger than Johnnie. I was Robin's age when my father took Charlie Urquhart and myself on our first real climb. I've never forgotten the excitement and satisfaction it gave me. I had to go on and tackle bigger and bigger climbs until fit for the north face of the Ben herself.'

I heard the affection in his voice. 'You love that mountain?'

'Maybe—no—yes, I do. The Ben was my first mountain, and one feels about one's first mountain much as one does about one's first girl-friend. Others may be as good or even better, but the memory of the very first lingers and grows more faultless with every passing year.'

'Then you don't climb a mountain out of your system?'

'Not personally, though I've met climbers with that attitude. In my view that's very dangerous. I think one should only climb for pleasure— and by that I don't mean for kicks. Once one stops feeling happy one should come down and stay down; once a mountain becomes an enemy to be defeated, trouble starts. Trouble a few thousand or even hundred feet up is very easily fatal. Charlie Urquhart feels so strongly about this,' he added, 'that if he even suspects any of his novice climbers of trying to climb something out of their systems he refuses to take them up and advises them to chuck the whole idea if they want to stay alive. He knows what he's about, does Charlie. I rate him as currently the best rock-climber in Scotland, and up in the first three in the world. I'm sorry you've had no opportunity to meet him. He's a good man.' He noticed I was stifling a yawn. 'I shouldn't be keeping you awake with all this talk.

You should've stopped me. There's nothing so boring as being forced to listen to an enthusiast in a hobby one doesn't share.'

'I've enjoyed listening.' I was honest. 'Only now I'm so warm and comfortable—' I yawned again. 'Dougal, I am sorry.'

'Don't talk so daft, lassie, and go to sleep.'

I wanted him to go on talking, but was too sleepy to say so. I was asleep before I got around to it.

It was light when I woke. The mist was pearly-grey and clung to Dougal's hair, eyelashes, and rough chin. He was still holding me and smiling. 'You've had a fine sleep.'

I blinked. 'Have you had any?'

'Enough, thanks.' He propped me against the hill face and stood up, stretching as he peered through the mist. 'The sun's going to lift this. We'll have some tea and chocolate and then think about moving. How do you feel this morning?'

'Great, thanks!'

That was a hideous lie, but I hoped the tea and chocolate would do the trick. My chest was too tight, and an ugly little pain was stabbing at my right side. Had I not been ill two years ago I might have blamed the altitude, cramp, or both. Had my memory been less refreshed by sleep I would have told Dougal. But though last night I had slept in his arms, this morning I remembered yesterday. Even if I reached London with double pneumonia I was leaving Gairlie on schedule tomorrow.

Within minutes the sun rose over the still invisible blue mountains in the east. As the rays broke through, the mist was instantly transformed into a series of translucent rainbows, and then, as instantly, the colours vanished from the sky, but not from the suddenly exposed hills. The heather was a brilliant purple, the bracken pure gold, and the dew glittered like topaz.

Dougal heard my sudden gasp, and as that one was in wonder I didn't try to conceal it. 'A sight worth remembering, Elizabeth.'

'Unbelievable!'

'Aye.' He smiled down at me, flexing his shoulders and then extending his arms above his head as if greeting the sun. It was an instinctively primitive and rather splendid gesture, and though his hair was untidy, his chin blue, his clothes crumpled, in that moment there was a touch of splendour about him. I thought of last night and then of his alter ego as my host. Certainly unbelievable, but worth remembering? I took a long breath to think that over, and that was such a mistake that I stopped thinking about anything but the pain in my side.

Dougal was packing. 'We must start off now, as I asked Rose to let Sergeant Cameron at the police station know if we weren't back last night, and told Maury to ring him directly she and Robin reached her house. If we're not down shortly Alec Cameron'll have Charlie out of his bed to pick up the pieces.' He glanced at me as he collected the empty vacuum mug, then did a double-take. 'Are you having difficulty breathing?'

As a direct lie wouldn't fool him, I used a half-truth. 'God, yes! Fear has me by the throat, so be a chum and look the other way.' I jerked my thumb upwards. 'Fear of that cliff you call a wee stretch.'

'Is that it?' He knelt by me. 'Wrist, please.'

'If the rate's not up, it should be. My adrenalin's pumping overtime.'

'So?' His expression was professionally blank. He touched my forehead with the back of his hand, then told me to stay where I was whilst he went up and fixed up a rope. 'Keep in your wrappings, pro tem. It's chilly this early.'

He went up so quickly and smoothly it looked—almost—easy. He threw down both ends of the fixed rope and returned without using either. 'You'll be stiff after sitting,' he said, and helped me stand. My legs felt stuffed with cotton-wool, and my head was at the same time too light and too heavy. I was as glad of his steadying hands as for his ready-made excuse. I said I'd be fine once my circulation got the message.

'No doubt.' He tied the end of one rope round my waist and gave the rope a tug. 'See? Fixed above round solid granite. It's nylon, new, can stand a strain of treble your weight without breaking, and you can't drop further than this length. Clear?'

'Yes. Thanks.'

'And this one round your waist is just a safety rope. Ignore it. This is the operative one.' He tied the second above the first and tested both knots. 'All you've to do is hang on to this and walk up as I pull you up from above. Don't look down or bother if your feet slip, as I'll be manipulating both ropes and won't let you fall.' He put both hands on my shoulders in what could have been merely a reassuring gesture. Or he could have been testing the rise and fall of my respirations. 'All set?'

I nodded. It saved breath.

'It won't take long.' He flung the rugs and ground-sheet over his shoulders and went back up.

It did not take long. It just seemed so to me. When I flopped on the grass above, he unwound the top rope round my waist, then sat back on his heels. 'Stay where you are, Elizabeth, get your breath, then tell me the truth about that pain in your chest.'

'Dougal, don't fuss! It's just the altitude.'

He said evenly, 'You weren't cyanosed at this altitude yesterday. Where's the pain catching you? How long have you had it? Have you

ever known anything like it before?' Again he put both hands on my
shoulders. 'Breathe in. Can you hold it?'

'Oh, God, do stop!' I snapped peevishly. 'So I'm a bit breathless. So
who wouldn't be after being hauled up on a bit of string. You know I'm
not a bloody Highlander by birth or adoption. But you don't have to
keep knocking the fact down with my back teeth. And though I'm very
grateful for all you've just done for me, I do wish you'd stop pushing me
around. I know you mean well—and I have tried to play along—but I
can't keep it up any longer.'

He was watching me without a flicker of emotion. 'I am very sorry
you should feel—'

'Do lay off! I'm feeling lousy enough without being made to feel worse
by your apologizing for my bad manners.'

'You don't have to tell me you're feeling lousy. I'd just like to know,
specifically, why?'

I was too irritable for caution. 'Probably only my old adhesions. They
play up sometimes.'

He winced. 'Adhesions? From—what?'

I realized I had gone too far to go back, so I told him the truth.

'Good God Almighty! Why the devil didn't you tell me this earlier?
You're a nurse. Didn't you realize—' He cut himself short, took a grip,
and smiled a reassuring professional smile. 'Never mind, lassie. What's
done is done, and no doubt you didn't tell me so as not to spoil the
picnic. Don't worry. A few days in bed and a course of antibiotics, and
you'll be fine.'

I had moved from irritability to belligerence. 'I don't want a few days
in bed! I want to go back to Martha's. I'll be fine soon as we get back to
ground-level, and then—' I broke off as we heard a shout.

Four men were running towards us across the plateau. I did not
recognize three of them, but the man out front was Archie. I leapt up,
forgetting the still untied safety rope and the state of my legs. I pitched
into Archie's outstretched arms.

'Archie, am I glad to see you!'

'And am I glad to see you, honey! Baby, you have given me a real
nasty night. Are you okay now?'

I opened my mouth to insist I was fine and instead began coughing,
and for a couple of minutes could not stop. Archie patted my shoulder,
told me to take it nice and easy while he unhitched me from the rope.
But he couldn't manage the knot.

Dougal stepped closer. 'I'll do that, Mr MacDonald.' He did it
quickly, then began methodically to wind the length of rope. He was
looking rigid again and introduced himself very formally to Archie. He
turned to me. 'I'm sorry, Elizabeth, but I'm sure Mr MacDonald will

agree that at present you're only fit to go straight to bed. You're obviously running a temperature.' He glanced round as the other three joined us. 'Good morning, Charlie, Andrew, Tam. You're out early.'

Charlie Urquhart was a sturdy, shortish fair man with a weather-beaten face and the shoulders of an ox. 'Aye, Dougal. It's a fine morning for a stroll in the hills.'

'It is,' agreed Dougal. 'I see you've a stretcher. Many thanks.'

'Man, you're welcome.' Charlie Urquhart considered me with experienced eyes. 'We've the estate car below.'

The other two men opened out like a deck-chair the metal-and-canvas stretcher Charlie Urquhart had carried on his back. 'You can sit down now, miss.'

'Thanks, but I don't need to be carried down. I can walk.'

'No,' said Dougal. 'Get on it, Elizabeth.'

His fellow Scots studied their feet in silence.

Archie shrugged apologetically. 'Professor Grant is a doc., honey. I guess he knows what's best for you.'

I went down strapped on that canvas stretcher. An hour later I was in a single-bedded ward in Gairlie Hospital and back in an oxygen tent.

7. Life in an Oxygen Tent

I found life in that tent very peaceful. This was partly owing to my having been in one before, partly my job, and partly an advantage that arose from the disadvantage of having no close relatives.

In that small, cut-off, oxygenated world life could be very lonely for any patient suddenly removed from a family circle. The plastic walls, though transparent, were a tangible barrier. I was spared the mental hell of watching those I loved watching me with tense, anxious faces unable to do more than put an occasional hand through one of the valve-sleeves. In my lucid moments, for the second time in my life, I was grateful my grandfather was dead. We had loved each other.

During those lucid moments, inevitably, I recognized I was very ill, but the prospect of dying never occurred to me. I had come out of a tent before. In time I'd come out again. I could tell those around me knew their stuff, so I relaxed and left it to them.

Another agony I was spared was the not uncommon lay fear that someone would accidentally turn off the oxygen, or a cylinder run out unnoticed, leaving me to gasp to death in sleep like a goldfish in a bowl without water. Though any accident could happen in any hospital, the chances of that one were roughly the same as the chances of an engine-driver's having a coronary on any train journey.

Strange faces watched me constantly through the plastic walls. Strange voices asked me to swallow tablets, drink this, turn my head there, let my arm go limp, 'for just another wee prick, dearie'. Strange faces and voices, yet vaguely familiar uniforms. The sisters' white dog-collars were too narrow; the staff nurses' dresses looked more blue than dark grey; the youngish woman in a Matron's navy dress had starched instead of organdie cuffs; the huge middle-aged man with close-cropped grey hair wore a pundit's dark suit, but under a long white coat. The discrepancies didn't disturb me. I just observed them.

During those first few days there was one familiar face. It belonged to Dougal, and he looked odd, as he too was in a dark suit. Sometimes I guessed he was visiting me in Gairlie Hospital; sometimes I was too muzzy to remember I was in any hospital; sometimes I thought myself back in Martha's. Once I beckoned Dougal and asked if he had come to London to visit Joe. He pressed his face against the tent roof for me to hear his reply. 'I've had a word with him, and he sends his good wishes. How goes it now?'

'Bit dopey. Otherwise, fine.' His appearance was puzzling me. He looked older and needed a shave. No mountains in London. I closed my eyes to brood on this and slid back under the surface. Later Nurse Craig told me I had asked that question on my second morning. I remembered asking, but not even if it had been day or night.

In those first days neither made any difference to me. Then, slowly, I began to sort things out, whilst still accepting, without question, every element of my strange existence, including Dougal's apparent omni-presence. He was part of the scene along with the injections, the dozens of tablets, the regular arrival of the portable X-ray machine and fresh oxygen cylinders. All the trundling in and out was done by the same two porters. One was a small ginger-haired youth who always winked and jerked up a thumb when he caught my eye. His colleague could have been his grandfather. He was a tall, spare man with thick white hair, a grave, high-cheekboned face, and the haunted, mournful expression of a chronic gastric. When he caught my eye he favoured me with a deep bow and a tragic smile. As far as he was concerned we'd both be better off dead. His name, I later learnt, was Mr Cameron, and he was Head Porter. Ginger-hair was Wee Gordon.

Officially I was a patient in the only Women's Medical Ward in Gairlie Hospital. But my room was one of the two single-bedded small wards that constituted the Isolation Unit and were divided from Women's Medical and the other wards by a long corridor. This made life exceedingly inconvenient for the Women's Med. staff and was why, directly I began to pick up, the person of whom I saw least was my ward sister. No conscientious ward sister will contemplate leaving her busy ward for more than the briefest period on a less than urgent occasion. Mrs Kilsyth, Sister Women's Medical, was a very conscientious woman. She came from Yorkshire, had lived in Gairlie for some years, and was married to a local man. After raising three daughters she had returned to full-time nursing four years before. She was a stout, grey-haired woman with a severe expression, brisk manner, and sensible shoes. She had strong and rather heavy hands. When she wielded a hypodermic needle it felt like a harpoon, but one never had to worry about her giving one the wrong dose or drug. And when she washed one's face and hands she got them clean even at the cost of the odd layer of skin. Her ward, since she took over, had an exceptionally good total recovery record. Having been her patient, I understood why. No patient of Sister Kilsyth would dare die.

Having met other formidable ward sisters, once I was up to registering her type. I found her as reassuring as she was awe-inspiring. She seldom talked, but her silence was restful. She approved of Martha's as a nursing training school. 'Maybe you get too used to a load of fancy gadgets, but I'll say this for the London teaching hospitals, lass—they teach you how to work. How's that? Back to sleep, and don't let me find you awake when I come round in half an hour.'

'No, Sister,' I said obediently, and went to sleep.

I slept most of the time. The huge, portly middle-aged physician I had now identified as Dr MacAlistair, the Medical Superintendent, never listened to my chest without announcing I was the finest wee dormouse to cross the Border. Often I woke to find him sitting on my locker, watching me through the transparent walls with his small, very deep-set grey eyes. When he smiled, as he did frequently, his eyes nearly disappeared. 'Don't stir yourself, lassie. I'm just taking the weight off my poor feet. Would you like to come up the bed a wee bit? Ach, I'll not bother the nurses. Just let me get my arms in the sleeves—there.' He heaved me up the bed very gently and as easily as a child. 'No, you're no weight, Miss Wade! We'll have to be feeding you up shortly. You put me in mind of my daughter, Isobel. She's another skinny, long-legged lassie and training as a nurse in Edinburgh. I'll be showing you her photo another time.'

'I'd like that, Doctor.'

'Watch yourself before you make a statement of that nature, Miss Wade, or I'll be back in here with a three-hour supply of family photos. My wife says I'm a terrible bore about our four bairns. A fine doctor I'll be to cure your chest and then kill you with boredom!'

He was a good doctor as well as a very kind man, and I was ready to run a Dr MacAlistair fan-club long before I was out of my tent. I liked everything about him, and particularly his voice. It had the depth of gentle thunder, and he attacked every word with throat and tongue and roared out the 'r's' like machine-gun bullets. On another occasion I asked if he came from Gairlie.

'Ach, no, lassie. Glasgow. You've heard of Glasgow? The Gorbals, of course?'

'Yes, but also Celtic and Rangers.'

'You're not telling me you're a football fan?'

'Frankly, Doctor, no. I once had a boy-friend who was.'

He frowned hideously. 'And which team did he fancy?'

'I honestly can't remember, Dr MacAlistair.'

He heaved his bulk off my locker, smiling. 'If there's one thing I like to see it's a lassie with tact! You'll do, Miss Wade. You're doing very nicely.' He turned as the door opened. 'Ach, not more flowers, Staff Nurse! What have we in here? A trained nurse, or a pop singer in disguise?'

Nurse Craig had come in with the daffodils and mimosa.

'Wee Gordon's just asked me the same, Doctor. He's thinking to ask Miss Wade for her autograph.' She added another envelope to the small stack on the top shelf of my locker. 'These'll be from Mr MacDonald again.'

Archie was still in Gairlie, and when not sending me flowers and chocolates was writing me notes. According to Craig, he was daily badgering Dr MacAlistair to be allowed to visit me, but Dr MacAlistair was badger-proof. That suited me, as though I was grateful to Archie, I was still in no hurry to pick up the threads. It suited me even more when Maury's flowers arrived. Craig said, 'She wanted to see you, but Dr MacAlistair does not want you tired, so I'd to send Mrs Valentine away. I hope you don't mind?'

'No. Thanks.'

Dougal provided me with another supply of flowers, fruit, and shortbread from Mrs Pringle. He remained my one visitor for a couple of days after my tent was removed. Dr MacAlistair knew his job. It was not until my third day out that I bothered to wonder precisely why Dougal alone was allowed to ignore the 'No Visitors' notice I had seen hanging on the outside of my door when it was pushed open too wide. As Craig had become my mate, I asked her.

Craig was one of the two day staff nurses in Women's Medical, and for a period had been my day special nurse. She was a local girl, and had returned to Gairlie last year after training in Dundee. She was very chubby, and though not exactly pretty, her colouring was glorious. She had auburn hair, dark-blue eyes, a wide sexy mouth, and a highly complicated love-life. She was also a very good nurse.

I had never seen her look embarrassed until I asked that question. 'Have you forgotten Professor Grant's occupation, Elizabeth?'

'What's that got to do with it? I'm not suffering from a tropical bug.' Then I caught on. 'Of course! As I've no relative to be next-of-kin, since Grandfather died the Matron of Martha's has always acted as that for me. As I was Dougal's guest and he's up here, she must have fixed with him to act proxy. Poor old Dougal! Talk about being right lumbered.'

Craig was still pink in the face over my lack of relations. 'I'd not say the Professor regards it in that light.'

'Come off it, love! Though he'll be far too polite to admit it, he must be finding this bedside vigil ploy one hell of a bloody bore. You ever met the medic. who didn't shudder at the prospect of a busman's holiday? I haven't.'

'Elizabeth! Don't forget you were not only a guest in his house when you became ill, but came up to Gairlie to do him a personal favour. I'll not pretend Professor Grant has enjoyed seeing you ill, but naturally he must feel responsible for you. He is. You were his guest.'

I groaned loudly. 'Until death us do part! Honestly, Craig, if you're going to jump on this honour band-wagon I'll start longing for the night and Little Miss N. herself!'

She laughed, then looked primly down her nose. 'You wouldn't be referring to Staff Nurse Smith?'

'You mean her name isn't Nightingale?'

'Och, Elizabeth! You're a wicked girl!' She looked round as someone knocked on the door. 'That sounds like the Professor. And your bed's all untidy—'

'Relax.' I straightened the top whilst she did the bottom. 'He's seen me in bed before.'

'He has? Oh, you mean in here!' She opened the door. 'Sorry to keep you waiting—it's you, Mr MacDonald! Has Dr MacAlistair given permission?'

'He has.' It was Dr MacAlistair's voice from the corridor. 'For ten minutes, and not one minute more!'

Archie came in slowly. 'Elizabeth, honey! Don't do these things to me!' He kissed me warmly, which gave Craig nearly as much pleasure as it did me. 'How are you? Just tell me that. How are you?'

'Much better now, thanks. Thanks for all those wonderful flowers and sweets—now, tell me all. How about you?'

Craig had pushed forward the armchair before vanishing. Archie preferred the locker seat. 'Real cosy.' He held my hand in both of his. 'Elizabeth, I have so much to say to you, but as I have promised Doc.

MacAlistair to take this nice and easy, I guess most will have to keep. Okay?'

I was relieved. Those threads could wait. 'Fine. I'm enjoying being a fragile flower. What've you been doing?'

'Walking. Fishing. I now ask for a dram when I want a Scotch, and never, repeat never, ask for it on the rocks.'

'Time you get back to London you'll enjoy warm beer. By the way, your notes never said, did you have to fly back or did you get that business finished?'

'I stayed right up here.' His smile had grown guarded. 'Any idea how long they'll keep you here?'

'None. That's the worst about being a patient. No-one ever tells one anything.'

I had used that cliché unintentionally, but from its effect on Archie it was obviously a Freudian slip. He turned deep purple, but did not try to avoid the issue. 'Maybe I had that coming. Mad at me?'

'I was.'

'Not now?'

'God,' I said wearily, 'I dunno. Right now I honestly don't know much about anything, apart from being glad to see you. If you think that means I'm after your lolly you'd better get the first fast plane down from Inverness.' He was silent. 'Are you really a millionaire? A proper one?'

'Sure. Loaded.'

'Bully for you, chum.'

He played with my fingers. 'Aren't you going to ask why I held out on you?'

'Why bother? Obvious.'

'That so?'

'Well, isn't it?'

'I would not say that, Elizabeth.' He looked up. 'Honey, we should not be talking this way. You have gone so white, and I promised that doc., and then I make you all tuckered out—I am truly sorry.' He stood up, anxiously. 'Shall I call the nurse?'

'Archie, don't be a moron! Of course I'm white. I've been in a tent. It's a flaming wonder I'm not growing a fungus all over me. Sit down and stop acting as if I'm about to have the vapours.'

'You are mad at me!' He was sunk in gloom. 'You figure I did not trust you.'

I was too tired to figure anything. I didn't tell him since he would probably have bellowed for Sister if I had. 'It's all right, Archie. Forget it.'

He said he could not do that. He was still beating his breast when

Craig removed him and insisted I either had an immediate snooze or she'd summon MacAlistair.

Dougal paid his morning call whilst I was asleep. He asked Craig to tell me he was spending the day in Inverness with the twins and would be in some time during the evening. The night staff were on when he arrived.

Staff Nurse Smith stood at the foot of my bed and sniffed. 'Anyone would think this place was an hotel. Professor Grant's in the corridor. I suppose you want to see him?'

'Thanks, if it's all right with you.'

'Huh! Nothing to do with me! I'm just the night staff nurse in charge of the women's side. I suppose you want me to bring him some coffee when you have your milk?'

'I'm sure he won't expect that, Staff Nurse. He'll understand this is a busy time of the night for you.'

'A doctor'll understand how hard nurses actually work? That'll be the day!'

Nurse Smith was a slight young woman with pale brown hair, too sharp features, and a thin mouth. Another few years and she wouldn't have any lips at all. She had trained in a large London non-teaching hospital, and providing one was ill enough her nursing was fairly good. She didn't like nursing women, the teaching hospitals, or trained nurses as patients, and had told me so herself. Since I couldn't win with her, I didn't try it.

She said, 'I suppose you don't want your pillows done?'

'No, thanks.'

'Then I'd better let your—' She paused deliberately. 'I've been meaning to ask, Wade. Is Professor Grant some sort of a relation?'

'No.'

'But isn't he your next-of-kin?'

'Acting.'

'Why only acting?'

She had been off duty for my first four nights, so it was possible she really didn't know. I told her the truth briefly.

'How picturesque!'

I had had a good many varying reactions, but not that one. It amused me in a macabre way. 'One way of putting it.'

'You are a cool customer! I suppose some people don't feel things like others.'

'Quite.'

She shrugged. 'Better let him in, then.'

'Thanks,' I said.

Dougal glanced back after she ushered him in. 'Have I upset that girl by coming so late?'

I said I thought Smith was merely suffering from an attack of night nurse's haemadementia and changed the subject to Inverness. He took the hint, sat in the armchair, and talked about his day, the twins, and Robin's prowess at the climbing school for the next ten minutes. He had risen to leave when I thanked him for taking me on as next-of-kin. 'Your idea, or my Matron at Martha's?'

'Actually, mine, though I did consult with her. I hope you've no objections?'

'None, apart from wishing this hadn't had to involve you in so much extra on my account.'

'I'd have been no less involved without the official sanction this provides. Surely you appreciate that?'

'Yes.' I also appreciated his present sensible, but not insensitive attitude to the subject in hand. 'As this is too far from London for one of my old friends to fly up and I've no handy relative, temporarily, you've no alternative. No'—he looked about to interrupt—'you haven't. Another type might try and wriggle out from under. Not a responsible citizen—which you are.' I shifted my shoulders, as my pillows felt like sandbags. 'Responsible citizens always get lumbered.'

He came up to the bed and stood over me, his arms folded. 'Though grateful for those kind words, honesty forces me to remind you that if responsible citizens are responsible it is because they basically enjoy responsibility. Or call it by the less attractive word, power.'

I smiled. 'Got a power-complex, Dougal?'

'I prefer your former euphemism.' His smile was self-derisive. 'Whichever is used, there's no doubt that I'm attending to my own ego as well as to your affairs.' He looked over his shoulder at the door, then back at me. 'And since I now have your official approval of my temporary status and you look exceedingly uncomfortable in that position, but I suspect would prefer me not to ring for that young woman with a chip the size of the Ben, I'm going to do something about those pillows.'

'There's no need, honestly. But how did you know she's got a chip?

'Och, Elizabeth! Have you forgotten I'm even more accustomed to hospitals and nurses than yourself? And I've seen one or two medical patients in my time. I've even made a few beds, particularly in Africa, when very often the only nurse was the witch-doctor's untrained second cousin twice removed, and a laddie at that. Come on. Stop trying to argue with the doctor, dearie.' He slid a hand under my arm and sat me forward carefully, then correctly supported me with the back of his shoulders whilst fixing the pillows. 'That's better. Dig your heels in. Up you go.' He smoothed the pillow directly behind my head. 'How's that?'

'Splendid, thanks. I mean that. You'd make a good nurse—But didn't I tell you that when I was in my plastic bag?'

'So you did.' He straightened and tucked in the top bedclothes, but left the turn-down of the top sheet loose.

I flicked the sheet with a finger. 'A very professional touch, Professor.'

He smiled down at me. 'A man of many talents.'

Momentarily I thought back to my week in his house, that night on the hill, and then that sunrise. Many talents and many sides. It seemed a pity one had to be struck down with exposure or serious illness to discover the pleasant ones. Yet whichever side he had yet shown me, one element remained unchanged. He still made me feel sexless, and though that no longer irritated me as much as previously, that was only because I still felt too weak to be really human. That was why Archie's brief visit had so exhausted me. But, breast-beating and all, I wanted to see Archie again, and soon. I quite enjoyed Dougal's visits, but I wouldn't mind overmuch if he didn't turn up. I realized that was selfish and ungrateful, but since there is nothing like a bad illness for bringing both those qualities to the surface, neither seriously disturbed me yet.

Nurse Smith did. Half an hour after Dougal had gone she woke me from a deep sleep to give me my hot milk and sleeping tablets. The tablets took some time to work. I watched the darkness and thought about Dougal and Maury, and then of all she had said that afternoon on the plateau. After that I was very glad Staff Nurse Smith was such an eager Little Miss Nightingale.

8. *A Patient's-eye View of Hospital*

The 'No Visitors' sign came off my door, and my fellow patients from Women's Surgical, as well as Women's Medical, started paying me visits. They said I'd been on their minds since admission, and they feared it must be terribly lonely for a stranger from England to be shut in a wee room away down the corridor, but they hoped I appreciated poor Dr MacAlistair had had no alternative. 'There was not an empty ward bed the day you came in, and with no hospital nearer than Inverness it was either in here or on the floor. And you could maybe have carried in the scarlet fever.'

I assured them I liked my room, did not consider myself the victim of racial discrimination, was delighted to meet them, and offered them Archie's candies and Mrs Pringle's shortbread. We exchanged brief life and detailed medical histories. It did not surprise me at all to discover they knew very much more about my pleural rib than I did. They advised me not to waste my breath trying to persuade MacAlistair to let me up. 'Until it's quite clear he'll do no more than let you sit out of bed whilst it's made. But you're doing well. Maybe you'll be up for a wee stroll down the corridor in a week.'

They were right.

The early mornings between six and eight were particularly sociable. My room became the recognized meeting-point for the bath queue, second-cup-of-tea drinkers, and refugees from Nurse Smith. My fellows were more charitable than myself. 'There's no denying she's a hard worker,' said young Mrs Ferguson, of Bed 2, Women's Surgical, 'and she could be a lot worse. She knows her job, even if she's no time at all for a body that's not dying. What she needs is a man.'

'Aye,' agreed the two other dressing-gowned ladies present. 'That's a fact.'

I asked, 'Is Gairlie short of men?'

'Och, no!'

We were in the middle of a delightfully coarse conversation when Miss Donald tapped gently on the half-open door. 'Room for a small one, ladies?'

Miss Donald was sixty-eight and a retired school-teacher. She had specialized in the seven-to-eleven age-group, and still tended to treat the whole world as if in those age-groups. She was a quiet, rather shy woman, with a gentle voice and even more gentle air of habitual authority. Her arrival automatically cleaned up any conversation, and as she had the ardent curiosity of the very lonely, that sometimes made things difficult.

She came in smiling. 'And how is our little English visitor this morning? Have we had a good rest?'

Mrs Ferguson's place had come up in the bath queue. The two others ambled off, and Miss Donald sat on my locker and accepted a piece of shortbread.

I asked after her night, and then if she was beginning to feel her stitches.

'Pricking a little, dear. But we have to expect a little discomfort, don't we?'

She had been operated on for what she described as 'a small stoppage'. From the few details she had given me and her general appearance she had an advanced carcinoma of the bowel. I did not tell her so, and was very sure she did not need telling. She lived alone, as the aged female friend with whom she had shared the last forty years had died a few months ago. She always referred to her with deep affection as 'Miss Christie'.

She admired my flowers. 'We have some very generous admirers—and quite right, too! I saw our Mr MacDonald in the hall yesterday. Such a charming young man, and, well—he can't really help being American, can he?

I wished I could share that with someone. Dougal was the only possible person, and even though he and I had established a new, improved relationship, I doubted it was not yet strong enough to take my being amused by the apparent Scottish passion for things Scottish. Also Archie was one of the people Dougal never mentioned. Robin and Maury were two others. It had taken me some time to notice that, but now it struck me as more obvious at every visit.

That particular morning I had an unexpected visitor. Mrs Pringle arrived wearing her Sabbath best, clutching a basket of fruit, yet another tin of shortbread, and a sponge-cake. She came in tentatively, took one look at me, and burst into tears. 'Och, lassie! You're that pale and thin! They canna' be feeding you well!'

It took some minutes to calm and convince her I was neither starved nor on my death-bed. 'What's going on at Archnagairl? Tell me all!'

She dried her eyes. 'Robbie's still up at Mr Urquhart's and liking it fine. The wee twins'—she sniffed pathetically—'are up the glen with the Professor. He's some business to attend to for Mrs Valentine, seeing she's away to Inverness herself and was aye a good friend to poor Miss Catriona. Aye, lassie'—the tears rolled down her lined face again—'how you put me in mind of that poor lassie! The Professor says you've been spared—but are you really better?'

'Much!' (I was beginning to doubt it.) 'I'm glad Robin likes the climbing school.'

'Aye, but much more than the foolish laddie deserves after neglecting his uncle's words and helping to cause the terrible sadness that came to Achnagairl House. The twins were that distressed! Johnnie was quiet as a wee mousie, and Judy'd not touch one apple. Not even the one!'

That nearly had me in tears myself. 'Poor little things! I'm so sorry—'

'It was no fault of yours, Miss Elizabeth. I'm well aware of the facts! It's not my place to speak my mind, or, I'll tell ye—I'd be saying plenty!' She was bristling with indignation. 'That a guest of the house should have been neglected in such a way as to endanger her life—as the Professor says, it doesna bear thinking, and matters not that the neglect was unintentional! That Mrs Valentine!' She pressed her lips together. 'It would not be fitting for me to say more.'

'So she liked Maury no more than I did. Interesting. Mrs Pringle, I
probably shouldn't ask, but is the sound of wedding-bells really in the
air? Or just in her and my imagination?'

She looked at me thoughtfully. 'Och, I've not the Professor's
confidence on such matters. I'll not say you're wrong. I'll not say I'll be
surprised. When a wise man loses his head over a bonnie face he can act
as daft as any foolish laddie in love for the first time.' She sighed. 'Sex.
That'll be the trouble.'

I was as startled as if Miss Donald had come out with a four-letter
word. 'It is?'

'Aye,' said Mrs Pringle. 'Not that I ever had any use for it myself,
mind—but the trouble I've seen it cause! Terrible!'

She left a little later, promising to come again and just managing not
to add, 'If you're still spared to us.' Craig saw her out, then returned.
'What do you think you're doing, Elizabeth?'

I had closed my eyes and crossed my hands on my chest. I opened one
eye. 'Oak or elm?'

'Had she got you measured?'

'Has she not! The poor old dear's off to order the wreath. And,
incidentally, she's ag'in sex. Root of all evil.'

'Is that a fact? Remind me to tell my boy-friend. He'll not like it at
all. What do you want for your sweet? Creamed rice or fruit salad?'

Smith was on nights off and the alternative night staff nurse, Mrs
Lewis, was her opposite in more ways than one. Mrs Lewis had returned
to nursing after a thirty-year break, surviving two husbands, bring up
and seeing married five children. She was a stout, amiable woman, with
a fixed belief in the therapeutic qualities of hot, strong tea and hot-water
bottles; a tendency to regard the antibiotics as new-fangled and still
largely unproven nonsense; and a strong antipathy to using any drug
stronger than aspirin. Directly Dr MacAlistair or Mr Stewart, the one
resident surgeon, had done their night rounds she donned pink wool
bedroom slippers, which she often forgot to remove before the day staff
came on in the morning. Since slippers of any nature were not only
against hospital rules, but anathema to Sister Kilsyth, the necessity to
remind Mrs Lewis to get back into shoes was one of the farewell
instructions passed on from up-patient to up-patient on discharge.

Mrs Lewis was a superb and very kind, if old-fashioned, nurse. She
shared with Dr MacAlistair the ability to inspire genuine love in
patients. And even if occasionally at night it sounded as if she were
going berserk in the nearest sluice, not one of her suddenly disturbed
patients minded. On the contrary. Smith was a very quiet night nurse, so
the uproar proved God was in His Heaven and all was well with the

world as old Mother Lewis was on the job. Like contented children, contented patients sleep better than the other sort.

Being a patient in a strange hospital in what I had finally come to accept as a strange country was an interesting experience. And novel, since I now realized that previously as a sick nurse in my own hospital, to the staff, as well as myself, I had remained one of 'us'. In Gairlie Hospital I was one of 'them'. Though the staff and most of the patients knew my job, my home background was sufficiently distant for all to accept me simply as 'the English lassie with the chest in Isol. One'.

For the first time in five years I really learnt how patients talked amongst themselves; the full strength of the inter-patient bond; and why every patient I had come across anywhere rated kindness the most important qualification any doctor or nurse could possess. Personally, I would not have exchanged Mrs Lewis in her bedroom slippers for any one of Martha's high-powered ward sisters. And whilst I respected and quite liked Martha's thoracic specialist with his M.D. and F.R.C.P., given the necessity and choice, I'd take my chest to Hamish MacAlistair, M.R.C.P. and sole resident physician in a hospital that could have been lost without trace in one of Martha's smaller blocks. Every Martha's main ward held thirty-two beds.

In all, Gairlie Hospital had thirty-two surgical beds, twenty-two medical, ten maternity, and two isolation. Dr and Mrs MacAlistair lived in a house on hospital property, but just across the road from the main gates; Mr Stewart, a bachelor, had a two-bedroomed flat above the administration offices.

I had these details from Dougal on one of his evening visits. Mrs Lewis was on, and we were both drinking tea. He asked, 'Tea doesn't keep you awake?'

'Never.'

'The advantage of being a nurse?'

'No. Nothing to do with that, and don't ask me why, as I know tea's a stimulant, but Mrs Lewis can get the entire female side to sleep on one teapot. Her technique may seem out of the ark, but it does work! She's the best nurse I've ever come up against.'

'I agree—' He hesitated for no good reason, then rephrased, 'Hamish MacAlistair would agree with you. She was on when you were first in. You don't remember?'

'Not really. Just a vague recollection of great kindness.' I put my empty cup on my locker seat. He was my one visitor who seldom, if ever, used it. 'Dougal, I've never liked to ask the others. Just how big is this place?'

That was when he gave me the details. 'A toy.'

'But a highly efficient toy. What area does it cover?'

'Most of the Western Highlands and the islands. They fly the patients down by helicopter. As the strip's on the other side of this wing, maybe you've not heard them landing?'

'Once or twice, when the wind's right. Craig calls them the "wee choppers" and regards them exactly as we do ambulances in Martha's. Dead trendy and space-age this toy!'

'Aye. Trendy, moddy, fab., gear, and not to mention grotty.'

I smiled. 'Judy has been educating you.'

'Not only Judy.' He returned my smile. 'I'm grateful. It's always useful to enlarge one's vocabulary, and the knowledge may prove invaluable when I get down to England in October.'

'Afraid you'll have problems about understanding the natives?'

'Not afraid, convinced. I'd no idea how out-of-touch my years abroad had left me until you and the children came up here. The boys, particularly Robin, may look very changed, but fundamentally they don't strike me as very different to myself and my contemporaries at their ages. Maybe they're a bit more open about liking girls. When I was fourteen I liked girls, though it'd have taken a gun to my head to make me admit the fact. But you and Judy'—he shook his head, still smiling— 'if you're typical of your generation of English girls you're not merely a new generation, you're a new race.'

'Hey, Dougal! I'm not Judy's age, and you're not all that much older.' As I spoke I recollected my thoughts on this subject whilst in his house. In an odd way it was rather disconcerting to discover he had shared them.

'At this moment you don't look more than a couple of years Judy's senior, and I feel about a hundred. Do you know what those twin fiends have had me doing today?'

I was still laughing at his description of a quiet afternoon's fishing with the twins when Mrs Lewis showed him out, beaming approvingly. 'The Professor's a fine bedside man,' she said later as she settled me for the night. 'He leaves you looking better than when he came, as a good visitor should.'

He certainly left me feeling better, as he never burdened me with any type of problem, or let fall a remark that could upset me even indirectly. He was pleasant without being hearty, and never overstayed his welcome. A model visitor, I thought, and unfairly grimaced in the darkness. I was growing mildly attached to him, but I would have liked him so much better if only he occasionally slipped up, or at least stopped humouring me.

I thought again of that row with Maury, and as I was now much stronger, the follow-on, if not the row itself, gave me an ironic pleasure. Her unintentional neglect had proved one nasty boomerang for her. Mrs

Pringle was up in arms. Dougal's stern Calvinistic sense of duty had forced him to appoint himself my official source of support and comfort. Archie, far from avoiding me as she had forecast, was continuing to inundate me with visits, flowers, and candies. Even Smith approved of Archie, and helped herself freely to his candies, since, as she said every time, he could afford to be generous.

From the little I had seen of Dougal and Maury together, so could she. I did not expect she would be, even if she had sent me flowers and a get-well card. But if Dougal hadn't used a gun at her head to get both out of her, then it must have been a damned close-run thing.

But Maury, Robin, Vietnam, and what exactly I was going to do between leaving hospital and being fit enough to return to work were external and still very remote problems. I was far more interested in Miss Donald's future; the path. lab. report on Mrs Ferguson's biopsy; and to hear what kind of night Christine in Bed 4, Women's Medical, had had. Christine was thirteen. She had acute rheumatism and was on the D.I.L. I had not yet seen her, but I knew as much about her progress as my fellows had known about mine when I was on the D.I.L. Probably Dr MacAlistair and Sister Kilsyth knew more. Only probably.

My first early callers next morning were medical. 'The poor wee lassie looks that poorly. Her parents've not left her bedside the whole night.'

'And she's their only child, isn't she?'

'Aye. And a wee frail lassie, she is.'

I said slowly, 'That could be an advantage, Mrs Burns. Small, wiry kids are generally the toughest. Has she been ill before?'

'Her mother says not—apart from the measles and the mumps—the usual—you'll ken.' Mrs Burns turned to her companion. 'Did you manage to get a wee look at the chart on the desk, Mrs Mackenzie? I could not read it without my glasses.'

'I observed it well.' Mrs Mackenzie gave us the latest four-hourly reading. It was not good, but it was no worse than this time yesterday.

Mrs Burns sighed and drained her tea. 'She's not picking up.'

Mrs Lewis bustled in. 'If the Mothers' Meeting's about to commence I'd best get you tidied first, Miss Wade.' She looked at us all as she pushed back her white front curls. 'And why are you all wearing long faces? It's not the Sabbath!'

Mrs Mackenzie said, 'It's that wee Christine. It saddens the heart to see a bairn that poorly.'

'That's a fact,' agreed Mrs Lewis, throwing me my dressing-gown with one hand and setting a chair at the foot of the bed with the other. 'She's an ill bairn, but God willing, she's on the mend.'

'She is?' Mesdames Burns, Mackenzie, and I chorused.

'She's no worse this morn than she was yesterday, and if she's no worse she must be better. Once a bairn starts to improve, there's no holding her. A bairn can be nigh gone the one moment and sitting up demanding jelly and ice-cream the next. I'm not saying wee Christine'll be on the jelly today—but it'll not be long. Will you watch yourself, Miss Wade! Sit you down in that chair and leave that side of the bed to me. If Mrs Mackenzie cares to give me a hand that'll be fine, but you must away to your bath, Mrs Burns. You're returning to your home this day, and you'll have a busy day ahead. Aye, I'm aware your man's getting the dinner, but I ken well you'll be back in your kitchen getting the tea before the day's out. Rest whiles you can, woman. Or you'll be back in here with that wee ulcer bleeding again, and it'll not be so wee the next time!'

When Mrs Burns came to say goodbye to me at noon the cardiac specialist had arrived from Inverness, examined Christine, and was taking coffee with Dr MacAlistair in Matron's office. Mrs Burns had a chronic gastric ulcer that at intervals turned acute, and was an old hospital hand. 'There was not a smile from the pair of them, which was a great weight off my mind. It's when a specialist is awful cheerful that a body has cause to fret. But time I was away.' We shook hands. 'Take care of yourself, lassie, and be sure you let me have a card when you get back to England.'

I had already promised cards to rows of ladies, and we had all asked each other to take care of ourselves. None of them seriously expected to get my cards or see me again, but in that moment, just before discharge, we were even more closely bonded than passengers after a long or short journey in the same ship. Few shipboard passengers genuinely contemplate the prospect of the ship's sinking. Fewer still were the patients who survived a period in hospital without once facing the sometimes, but by no means always, irrational fear of not getting out alive. That communal fear was one of the toughest threads in our bond, and one that remained unbroken until the hospital, or private car, carried the discharged patient through the main gates. Every hospital patient sooner or later hears the apocryphal story of the patient who collapsed and died whilst shaking hands in farewell with the ward sister. Sooner or later most nurses have seen that happen.

'Twice,' I told Archie that afternoon. 'I know I'll see a third, and every time anyone says goodbye I'm on edge until I hear they've got right away. I know that must sound like a load of old codswollop and that superstitions are stupid. So what? I'm stupid.'

'I would not say that, Elizabeth, though I am interested that you do not appear to object to facing up to what is, maybe, a weakness.'

'Why? Do you object to doing that?'

'Depends on the context, honey. On the job, no. Outside of my office'—he shrugged—'maybe I do prefer to side-step. I like to take life easy, maybe as mostly I have had life real easy. So, whereas on the job when I have to do something I do not like I just go ahead and do it, when I am on vacation, or merely off for the week-end, I like to relax all along the way.'

'Dead sensible. Keep that up, and you'll never get ulcers or a coronary.'

'Sensible, maybe, but egotistical.' He walked over to the window and looked out. I looked at his back. I sensed he wanted me to wait until he was ready to go on, and while I was prepared to do that for his sake, for my own I very much hoped he was not bracing himself to utter words that would in any way alter our very pleasant and—at least to me— purely superficial relationship.

He turned with patent reluctance. 'I've been side-stepping all afternoon, Elizabeth. There is something I have to tell you.'

I braced myself. 'Good or bad?'

He smiled faintly. 'You surely like to lead with your chin! Not all that bad, maybe, but not too good. I have to leave you again. I have to fly down to London right after leaving you now. I do not want to go, but I have to do that.'

He looked so upset now that I was almost ashamed at my own relief. 'Problems in the motor industry?' He nodded. 'There doesn't seem much percentage in being your own boss if you can't leave yourself alone to enjoy a holiday.'

'I don't object to having my vacation interrupted. I just do not care to leave you.' He came back, sat on my locker-seat, and took one of my hands in both of his. 'Do you recall that talk we did not finish my first visit with you in here?'

'Yes, but does it have to be finished? Does it even matter?'

'I would say it does.' He brushed his face against the back of my hand. 'I would say I owe it to you. Care to hear me out?'

'If that's really what you want?'

He said simply, 'What I want right now, honey, is you. It's all right— it's all right—' he added quickly, 'you do not have to tell me that is not what you want right now. I can figure that each time I touch you. Maybe before you took sick—maybe after, when you are well—maybe. Not right now. Right now one chaste kiss, and, as you would say, that is your lot!'

'Yes. Thanks. I'd guessed you understood. I just hoped you felt the same.'

His eyes laughed. 'Baby, I have not been poorly sick, and though you may not know it, you surely look cute in bed. But this does not explain why I first held out on you, though, obviously, it was why I wanted to get acquainted with you. I didn't tell you'—he hesitated—'I guess because I was scared.'

'Scared I'd be after your money?'

He met my eyes. 'It's happened before. I hoped it wouldn't happen with you. I didn't figure it would, but I had to be careful for a reason that may sound crazy.'

'I'll tell you if it does.'

'You do that.' He was now looking at me as if I were a painting. 'Do you also recall my telling you last time I was over I stopped in Edinburgh?'

'Yes.'

'I met a girl there. You look so like her she could have been your sister. You even talk the same way and have the same cute accent. And she was a nurse. Quite a coincidence?'

'Yes.' I was very interested. 'Go on.'

'I was all of twenty then, and she was one year older. I didn't just fall for her, Elizabeth. I loved that girl, I surely did.' He stopped speaking for several seconds and went on staring at me. He was not seeing me at all. 'I was a brash, spoilt kid who thought he knew all the answers. Back home I was the cute kid they all loved to love. So she had to love me back.'

'She didn't?'

'Just the bank-roll, honey. Just that.'

'Oh. Yes. You're sure?'

'Sure I'm sure. She told me herself. One night I took her to some party and she was real loaded. I was off the liquor that night, I'd picked up some kind of an intestinal germ and wasn't feeling too good. You know what it's like when you're the only one at the party who isn't stoned. It was one good party,' he said bitterly, 'if not for little Archie. It was way out of Edinburgh, and I stopped on the road home to have it out with her. We had quite a talk, and then I got real mad, and drove on. It was raining hard. I drove too fast.' Suddenly, he shuddered. 'I did not even see the truck until I hit it. Then I blacked out. I woke up in hospital. They did not tell me until the next day.'

My throat was tight. 'She was dead?' I asked unnecessarily in view of the expression on his face.

'Her neck broke when she hit the windshield.'

'My dear. I'm so sorry.'

He nodded, absently. 'They were all real nice to me. Wet road, raining, darkness, and maybe I'd been driving too fast, but there was no alcohol in my blood, no speed limit on the road, anyone could have a blow-out—which made me the poor kid in the clear.'

'Court case?'

'Just a formality.' He paused. 'My old man flew over. He went to see her folks. They were as good to him as they'd been to me when they came up for the court case.'

'They must've known you loved her.'

'Holy Christ, Elizabeth, I did! I surely did.' He let go of my hand and looked at his own. 'So now you know why I don't care to drive.'

He left a few minutes later. Craig came in directly he had gone, looked at me hard, then rehung the 'No Visitors' sign on the outside of my door without exchanging a single word with me. I was delighted, though it took me some time to stop feeling like the ghost of a girl whose name I still didn't know. I wondered how long it would take Archie to stop seeing in that light—and if he ever would.

9. A Very Gentle Ghost

Archie's business affairs kept him in London very much longer than he had anticipated. He rang me regularly and bemoaned the fact at such length that it occasionally occurred to me to wonder if he were not protesting a little too much. Then I felt ungenerous in the extreme, since from one of Craig's many boy-friends I learnt Archie's hotel room remained reserved and he had left behind his fishing tackle.

But whatever the real cause of his absence, the more I thought on it, the more convinced I was that the breathing-space was a mutual godsend. Though, in theory, I was perfectly happy to lend Archie a mental shoulder, in practice I still hadn't the energy. And as he had now opened up his emotional flood-gates, had he continued to see me daily as previously, it was unlikely that he would have found it easy to close them again. I hoped this break would help him to do that. He was now so emotionally involved with me that he had to be right away before he could begin to see me in anything like the proper perspective. My resemblance to his former girl-friend could have confused him enough on its own, but on top of that, though he might not know it yet, he was still being pressured by the emotional stress of my illness. That such stress could temporarily distort the outlook, and even the entire personality of a relative, friend, or any member of the staff concerned with a very ill patient, was now taken so seriously at Martha's that for the last few years the student nurses had been given special courses of lectures on the subject.

I remembered our psychiatrist saying: 'This lecture won't save more of you nurses from becoming temporarily over-emotionally involved with some patient at some time or other. But by helping you to recognize the condition exists I hope that may help it to prove a less traumatic experience. Without help it can be exceedingly traumatic. And if you should recognize it in yourselves, whatever else you feel don't feel guilty. I say that, not merely as there are few greater emotional spurs than guilt, though that fact is worth bearing in mind, but because there is no cause for guilt in this context. I'm not a nurse, but observation and experience have convinced me that on some occasions it must be as impossible to maintain an emotional detachment and nurse successfully as it is to remain unemotionally involved during a successful sexual intercourse.'

There my class had exchanged one of those 'here we go back to sex' glances and stopped listening. Most of us had been exchanging those glances in other classes since we were sixth-formers, and particularly at Sixth Form Conferences. At every conference I had been to, whatever the official subject, every speaker had talked sex at us. Once my form complained in a body to our headmistress. She said mildly, 'I'm sorry you feel sex is being thrust down your throats, my dears, but it is rather important.'

Mrs Pringle would agree. After reflecting on Dougal and Maury, then Archie and my own earlier reactions to him, I wished I had paid more attention to those lectures. Without my family history first and then my illness to act as emotional brakes, had I seen much more of Archie I could very easily have mistaken a great physical attraction for love. Unless I was very wrong, before Archie left Gairlie he had been on the brink of the same error, and even now, though possibly keeping away intentionally, given any real encouragement, I was fairly sure he'd kid himself he wanted to marry me.

Would that be such a mistake? We did like each other. He said he wanted me, in return he'd give me undreamed-of security. Yet, having had to rely on myself for these past four years had resulted in my being much less scared of insecurity than my friends with large families. In ten years' time I might be tempted to marry for it; in twenty years I'd probably bitterly regret I hadn't. But I was not marrying a man I didn't love and who didn't love me at twenty-two to provide myself with a financial cushion when I hit the menopause.

It took me a few days to think all this out. I had finally renounced Archie as a future husband and was feeling smugly noble one evening when Miss Donald pottered in to my room to say she was being discharged next day.

I was sitting in my armchair.

'No, no, dear. We mustn't disturb you. Let me tuck that blanket round you again. There.' She sat on the locker and folded her hands in her lap. 'Did we enjoy our stroll along to the ward?'

'Loved it. I feel fine now. I just wished Sister Kilsyth would let me do more than amble round gently nattering to one and all. They're so hectic along there.'

'I've yet to see our good sister off her feet. But she is too wise to overtax your strength. Ah!' Wee Gordon had knocked and was pushing in the portable telephone trolley. 'If our young man is due to make his nightly call I'll be on my way.'

Gordon plugged in the portable. 'I doubt Mr MacDonald'll be through before another thirty minutes, Miss Donald.'

I said, 'Thanks for shoving that in, Gordon, but I'm not even sure I'll get a call tonight. It's not fixed.'

'Och, he'll be through.' Gordon winked. 'Money to burn has Mr MacDonald.'

Miss Donald said she thought that was just as it should be as poor Mr MacDonald must be missing dear Miss Wade sadly in London. 'A fine city. I was there years ago with my dear Miss Christie. You'll be anxious to be back.'

With Miss Donald I could be honest. 'I'll be glad to get back to work. Strictly between ourselves, I'm not all that keen on my next step.'

'It's been arranged?'

'Yes. I had a letter from my Matron at Martha's this morning. She's booked me a room in some guest-house-cum-convalescent home at Hove. It's run by an old Martha's nurse and caters mainly for sick nurses and doctors. I expect it'll be fine, just as I'm sure the one you're off to tomorrow'll be fine. But, like you, being used to being independent, the prospect of being fussed over when I'm not ill doesn't exactly entrance.'

She smiled very sweetly. 'We have much in common, dear, so you'll not mind a little advice?' She laid one thin hand on mine. 'Don't be too independent. The years go so fast and the courage of youth wears thin when one is not as young as one was. But I'm fretting you to no purpose. You'll be marrying shortly, and marriage, I've often observed, is not an independent state for a woman. May I ask'—her eyes shone—'is it really right he's Calum MacDonald's grandson?'

I hadn't the heart to disillusion her. She had so little, as well as so little time left. 'Yes.'

She sighed pleasurably. 'It's like a fairy-story!'

I let her dream a few seconds, then talked about Christine. 'Isn't it splendid she's doing so well?'

'My dear, the joy of seeing the relief and thankfulness in her parents' faces! So much joy!' She looked round my room. 'I'll tell you in confidence, dearie, that when I heard I'd to come to this hospital for my small operation I was a little frightened. All my life I've enjoyed such good health, and dear Miss Christie was only ill at home two days before she passed away from that stroke. Not having been in hospital before, I thought to find here only sadness and pain and ugliness. It's but one wee side of the picture, all that. Is it the same in St Martha's?'

I nodded. 'There's an old hospital maxim: "The mud and the stars are present in every hospital ward. Which one sees depends on oneself." Of course it's true. What's equally true, but seldom remarked on, is the laughter. Haven't you noticed how much laughter there is in any ward?'

'So frequently that it's occurred to me I've not laughed so much since I was a young girl. I am so grateful for all the kindness I have received here. I don't mind telling you, dear, I've no wish to leave—' The telephone began ringing. 'The faithful Mr MacDonald! I must let you have your nice little talk in private. See you in the morning.'

Archie was too glum for any nice little talk. His business deal had gotten itself loused up; it was pouring with rain in London; he had just spent fifty minutes sitting in a taxi in a traffic jam; he thought he was starting one of his real nasty head colds; if he was starting one he did not know when he would shake the darned thing off.

I made sympathetic noises, suggested vitamin tablets, oranges, a hot bath, hot toddy, aspirins, and an early night. He said he would try the lot, but did not expect anything to work, as when he took cold he surely suffered. 'What's news with you, Elizabeth—and make it good!'

So I gave him the latest Gairlie Hospital gossip, but did not mention Hove. The thought of that project was like lead in the pit of my stomach. Mention it, and I'd start wailing too. Archie had been very good to me and, for quite a while, for me. Lending a shoulder at long range was far less exhausting than in person, but all the same I was so relieved when he rang off that I wondered if I needed vitamin tablets. Or perhaps I was short of iron? Or just guts?

The portable telephone was wanted in one of the wards. Gordon escorted in Dougal when he came to collect it. 'The Professor's been waiting on you these last ten minutes, Miss Wade.'

I apologized to Dougal. He said the delay had given him the opportunity to catch a word with Hamish MacAlistair, as well as enjoy a talk with my friend Miss Donald. 'I gather MacAlistair's told you that you'll fly back to London only over his dead body?'

I smiled faintly. 'Yes. As I have to have his consent to satisfy Martha's, that's out.'

'But, as I think you are also aware, he's not too happy at the thought of your taking that long journey directly you leave hospital. Why don't you delay your return for a few days and spend them at Achnagairl House? You'll be most welcome, and though the children will be gone, as Mrs Cameron is now back with us and Mrs Pringle remaining for the time being to help her sister get the house straight after the exodus, that'll take care of the local conventions. What do you say?'

I had been rehearsing my answer to this invitation he had no alternative to making ever since MacAlistair stomped round my room muttering darkly about the long car and train journey. Dougal never burdened me with problems, but every visit he paid me added to the debt I owed him. If I added much more to it the weight would be crushing. 'It's very kind of you, Dougal, but I think I should go straight back to London. And I'll be going from hospital to hospital, as my Matron wants me to stay a day or so in Martha's before going to Brighton. If I know her she'll have our S.M.O. lined up to listen to my chest directly I get out of the taxi. I think I should get straight back. After all, I only came up for one week-end.'

For once he gave in, instantly. 'I can appreciate how you feel, but should you change your mind at any time the offer remains open.'

'Thank you very much.'

'Not at all.'

We were silent, and the silence was as strained as those first silences in my first week in Gairlie. Then we both started talking about the children. Tomorrow was the last day of their holiday. I asked if he was doing anything special with them?

'If this weather holds we're all going a little way up the west face of the Ben to watch the Trials Charlie Urquhart always holds on the final day of his holiday school. The twins are in a fever of excitement. Robin's strongly tipped for the Beginners' Medal. Then, after the Trials, Charlie throws a farewell party for his students and their families. As the fun and games starts early and goes on all day, I'm afraid it'll be rather late before I look in here tomorrow evening.'

'My dear man, don't bother to do that. You're going to have more than enough on your plate tomorrow, from the sound of it.'

'It'll be no bother,' he replied politely. 'Just rather late.'

I glanced at him, reflectively. He was looking rigid for the first time since my admission. 'What time does the party end?'

'Nine. Early the following morning the whole camp packs up and moves off. I'll be taking the children down that night. Their father is meeting us in London and there already. I'll be coming straight back.' He got off the locker seat he now used, as I was in the armchair. 'How's Archie MacDonald faring in London?'

I was more than faintly startled. 'He was a bit gloomy just now, but I think, on the whole, pretty well. His firm are involved in some massive takeover bid, but just who's taking over what I don't follow.'

'There've been several very clear hints on the matter in the financial columns recently. You don't read them?'

'Never. Perhaps,' I added, purely for something to say, 'I should start?'

'All knowledge is useful,' he agreed tritely.

We hadn't talked small talk since my admission, either. It was my turn. 'How's Maury?'

'Well, thank you.'

'Still in Inverness?'

'She returns tomorrow.'

''For the Trials?'

'Possibly. Along with half Gairlie.'

'I hope it keeps fine for you.'

'Thank you. I'll be off now. I hope you've a good night and good day tomorrow.'

'I'm sure I will. Thanks for coming in.'

'It's been my pleasure.' He sounded his old formal self, and he bowed his old formal bow. I did not then know my discharge date, but I knew from that moment that I was cured.

Being cured, I felt restless. The small commotion in the corridor some minutes after he had gone was a welcome interruption. I opened my door. A few yards away Sister and Craig were speedily loading a trolley with blankets and clean linen from the ward linen-cupboard in the corridor. I noted the amount. 'Three admissions? But your ward's full, Sister.'

'It is. So we are putting up two emergency beds and transferring Mrs Spearn into Isol. Two as she's our most convalescent medical.' Sister looked at her watch. 'Nurse Craig, you should have been off duty forty minutes ago. Just help Mrs MacInnis [the nursing orderly] put up the two beds and be off. She can wheel Mrs Spearn along in a chair, and I'll manage the beds alone.'

Bed-making alone took more than twice as long as in pairs. 'Can't I help, Sister?' I suggested. 'I'd like the exercise.'

For one moment I thought she was going to let me. 'Not without Dr MacAlistair's permission, lass. Thanks.' Sister whisked the trolley so quickly back to the ward that the plump Craig panted after her. I waited until they disappeared, then went along the corridor to Dr MacAlistair's office and knocked on the closed door.

'Come on in!'

I opened the door. He was writing at the desk. 'Ach, it's you, lassie. And what's caused you to wander so far abroad from your room?'

'Please can I help Sister make three beds?'

He studied me. 'Restless?'

'Yes.'

'A healthy sign. You may. Only the three for tonight, understand.'

'Thanks.' I hurried back to the ward and handed this on to Sister.

Sister said, 'Then let's get on with t'job, lass.'

Early next morning I did the ward beds all round with Smith. When I joined the tea-drinkers in my room Miss Donald said we looked as if we really were enjoying our little busman's holiday. 'No. No more shortbread, thank you, dear. It is delicious, but I shouldn't have taken this first piece. As I used to tell my dear children, sometimes our eyes are bigger than our tummies.' She touched her middle gingerly. 'A few twinges. The thought of moving.'

Mrs MacPherson, a middle-aged post-op. appendix, said she too had only to move to twinge. 'And do I get any sympathy from my family? Och, no! "Only an appendix!" they tell me. I'm telling you, ladies, the next time anyone says to me "only an appendix" there'll be murder done! The agony!' she assured us, smiling serenely over a large slice of fruit cake. 'Terrible! And what does that Mr Stewart say? "Och, Mrs MacPherson, it's not so bad as that, and why don't you straighten up when you walk, woman?" And how the hell does he know how bad it is, seeing as he's still his own appendix tucked away in his belly? And how is a body with my shape to straighten up the more? Flat as a board fore and aft have I always been—and a terrible grief it's been to my man these last twenty years. Having a—' She glanced at Miss Donald and hesitated, then corrected herself, ' "Going to bed with you, woman," he says, "is taking my life in my hands. It's a wonder I've not done myself a terrible mischief cutting myself." Not that that's stopped me bearing six bairns, and each one born as easily as shelling wee peas from a pod. I'd as soon produce another bairn than have that wee monster out again— though what my Alec would say if I did, seeing as I'm turned forty, wouldn't bear thinking! Och, he's some shocking ideas has my Alec—but he doesn't remember them when he gets to bed at night, so I'll not be surprised if I've to book up in maternity again. Is that my bath ready?' She clasped her stomach with both hands as she got out of the armchair. 'Ouch! There goes another of that laddie Stewart's wee stitches. He's not a bad laddie, but what wouldn't I give to get busy with my needle on him!'

Miss Donald on the locker-seat went on smiling to herself after Mrs MacPherson had gone. A Mrs Jamieson, a youngish and still mild mitral stenosis, took the armchair. I was on the edge of my bed. Mrs Jamieson asked in her slightly breathless cardiac's voice if Mrs MacPherson ever stopped talking.

Miss Donald said, 'I believe only when under the anaesthetic or asleep, but she has made us all laugh so much in Surgical that I doubt anyone could object. Despite her comments, even Staff Nurse Smith admits she's an excellent—' Her voice stopped abruptly, and she caught her breath.

Mrs Jamieson sat forward. 'Miss Donald, are you well? You're that pale!'

Miss Donald was more than pale. She was colourless. She pitched forward as I leapt off the bed, caught her shoulders with one hand, and reached for my bell with the other. 'Mrs Jamieson, could I have the armchair?' As I spoke I got I got both hands under Miss Donald's armpits, and as Mrs Jamieson pushed forward the chair I managed to lift the unconscious old lady from the locker and lower her into the chair. I took her pulse, very briefly, then hauled forward the spare oxygen clylinder that still lived in my room. I had the attached mask over Miss Donald's face and the oxygen turned up high when Smith rushed in looking pink in the face.

'What the hell do you think you're doing ringing that bell like that—' She broke off and bent over Miss Donald. She looked at me and then at Mrs Jamieson. She said briskly, 'You've been up long, Mrs J. Back to bed.'

'Can I not help you with Miss Donald?'

'I can cope. Wade can help if she likes. Off you go, and slowly. I'll get the hypo. tray, Wade.' She rushed off, and was back before I had time to pull a second blanket off my bed and tuck it round Miss Donald. 'Get up her sleeve—oh—you've done it.' She gave the injection swiftly. 'I'll get MacAlistair. That stuff touching her?'

'No.' I was taking Miss Donald's pulse. Or, rather, I was trying to take it. 'She's stopped.'

'Thought she had already when I first saw her. Help me get her on your bed, then get MacAlistair for me. As we've only got three minutes, I can't waste any before trying to get her back. Not that I think we will, as she looks typical of a bloody great pulmonary embolus.' We were both breathless after laying Miss Donald's body on my bed. I left Smith giving her the kiss of life and applying external cardiac massage and ran to the duty-room.

Mrs MacAlistair answered the telephone. 'I'll tell my husband; he'll be over instantly. Who is that speaking for the Staff Nurse? Miss Wade. Yes.'

Dr MacAlistair arrived in the final minute. He had his white coat over his pyjamas. He took over from Smith, but with no more success.

Later, when my room had been cleared and my bed stripped of everything, including the mattress, MacAlistair came back alone. He now wore a sweater and grey trousers over his pyjamas and under a clean white coat. 'Sit down in that chair, lassie. I want to talk to you.'

I moved from the window. He sat facing me on the locker seat. He said simply, 'As you must be well aware, the Lord has just shown great mercy to a sick and lonely old woman. That growth was only partially removed. She'd secondaries starting up everywhere. We'd to move her out, as we need surgical beds too badly to keep in one surgical patient one strictly unnecessary moment. To let her stay might have cost the life of someone who could be saved. But both Mr Stewart and I have long been aware of the veritable hell that lay ahead for her.' He paused heavily. 'Maybe I shouldn't say this, but I will; I'm glad we didn't succeed in bringing her back. It was our job to try. I'm glad we failed.'

'So am I. I think she would have been too. She didn't want to leave. She was happy here. She told me.'

'Aye. She'd formed a great affection for you, lassie. She'd no-one of her own left to love, and we all need to love. Your presence at her death will have been a comfort to her, if not to yourself.' He looked at the empty bedstead. 'You'll know we've no empty beds in which to move you. You'll not know, but maybe you can guess, that there's not one bed in this hospital that has not been a death-bed many times over, including this one. If I move you out now I'll have to move some other patient in. But if you honestly feel it will upset you too much to remain, though there's not much room next door, maybe we can double you up with Mrs Spearn, temporarily. I'm not too happy about that, as with your chest you need as much air space to yourself as we can provide. Maybe for a day or so, it'll not hurt.'

The moment Miss Donald had died I had wanted to rush from my room and never return. But I had been fond of her, and her death had been so kind. I had seen death too often to fear death itself. 'I'll stay, Doctor.'

'But will you have to force yourself to do that?'

I looked round the small ward as if seeing it for the first time. 'No. This room's got a peaceful atmosphere. Miss Donald's death hasn't altered that. It couldn't. She was so gentle.'

'A gentle ghost won't worry you?'

'I don't think so.'

'Good gurrrl.' He patted my hand. 'You'll take your breakfast in the ward today, but once this bed's made up again you get back in it and stay there until well into this afternoon. I'll listen to your chest later and see what damage all this has done you.'

'I don't feel as if it's done any.'

He stood up. 'I've no doubt at all you're right. There's nothing like an emergency for speeding a cure. Come. I'll walk with you to the ward, and if you're up to it Sister Kilsyth'll be glad to have you lend a hand to help wee Christine with her breakfast. I wish that lassie's appetite would improve as well as her heart. She needs all the coaxing she can get, and that takes time. Time, as you'll know well, is always in short supply in a busy ward.'

I helped Christine with her breakfast before I had my own. Consequently, as MacAlistair and Sister appreciated, I was able to face mine.

The whole women's side was subdued that day, but more from respect than sorrow. Woman after woman came along to Isol. One. All, with one exception, said the same thing: 'A terrible shock, but a great mercy she went so quickly. Maybe she'd not have been able to fend for herself much longer. It's a sad fate to be old and alone in this world.'

The exception was Mrs MacPherson. 'Is it right she was taken with a smile on her face?'

'Yes. It was you that put it there.'

'Is that a fact? Aye, but it'll be pleasant to remember. No doubt it was a great mercy, but I'm grieved she's gone for my own sake. She was a good woman, and there are not so many of those that one less makes no matter.' She clasped her stomach automatically as she lowered herself carefully into the armchair. She did not open her mouth again for a full ten minutes. Miss Donald would have been very touched. In her absence I was for her. As Miss Donald had said, she and I had much in common.

10. Goodbye to So Much

I was watching the clock before Gordon pushed in the telephone trolley that evening. I felt haunted by twin ghosts, but neither was the ghost of Miss Donald, dead. They were Miss Donald in life and myself in the future. Had Archie, Joe Fenton, even Dougal, asked me to marry him that night I'd probably have accepted. For the first time in my life that night the future really frightened me. It was probably as well that Archie didn't ring.

Gordon was nearly as on edge as myself. Several times the portable was wanted elsewhere. Each time he returned it. 'The lines from London may be busy, Miss Wade.'

'Or Mr MacDonald. He's a busy man.'

The 'phone rang at nine-thirty. 'It's not Mr MacDonald but Professor Grant,' announced Gordon's voice sadly, 'from Mr Urquhart's establishment.'

Hell, I thought, hell! Even if we talked small talk again, Dougal's presence would be preferable to my own bleak company and the silent telephone. 'Thanks, Gordon.' I was too glum to bother to hide the dejection in my voice. 'Put him through.'

'I am through,' said Dougal's voice. 'Good evening, Elizabeth. Are you still expecting your London call?'

'Yes, but—'

'Just excuse me, one moment. You there, Gordon?'

'Aye, sir?'

'Don't hesitate to break in if that call comes through while I'm on this line. Elizabeth?'

'Yes, Dougal?'

'How are you today, and will you forgive me if I take you up on your last night's suggestion and skip tonight's visit? The party's been extended another hour, and I'd rather not drag the kids away.'

'Of course not. Thanks for ringing.'

'And what kind of a day have you had?'

Gordon was almost certainly listening-in and in Dougal's background I could hear pop music, shouts, and laughter. It was no occasion for the whole truth, but I kept to the truth. 'A routine hospital day. How's the party going? As it's running overtime, I guess well.'

'I'm reliably informed it's a right groovy rave. No doubt you can hear the uproar. I'm afraid it's stopping me hearing you well. How do you feel tonight?'

'All right, thanks. How about the Trials? Did Robin win anything?'

'He got the Beginners' Medal. As you'll appreciate, great is the rejoicing in the Fenton clan, and I'm trying—but not too hard—not to look smug. He did very well. He went up the test stretch like a natural.'

'That's splendid. Do give him my congratulations, unless'—I was too glum for pretence, either—'you think it'll spoil things for him.'

'I very much doubt that. I'll pass them on with pleasure.' There was a slight pause. 'Did Hamish listen-in today?'

'Yes. Quite clear.'

'That is good news.'

'Yes.'

'Been doing too much in the ward in celebration? Is that why you sound tired, or is it just this line?'

'Could be the line.'

'Then I'll get off it and give you a breather before your next call comes through. I'll be in in the morning before we leave. Sleep well. Good night.'

'Dougal, before you hang up, could you tell the twins—'

'I'm sorry, miss.' It was Gordon. 'He's already hung up. Shall I get him again?'

'No, thanks. Not important. I can tell him what I wanted to say tomorrow.'

I replaced the receiver very slowly. For a man with Dougal's impeccable manners to hang up on me was tantamount to his having slapped my face. It had the same effect. I felt ghastly when my crying jag wore itself out, but it did me a lot of good. I was too exhausted to do anything but sleep very well. Next morning my temperature and chest were normal, and stayed that way for the remainder of my time in Gairlie Hospital.

Again I helped Smith with the ward beds. Since yesterday our mutual attitude had changed. We were not, and never would be, mates, but we now knew we not only made beds at the same speed and in the same way—there are roughly six different ways of making an approved hospital bed—but had discovered that, in a crisis, we could work on the same side and in unison. That did not alter my fundamental conviction that she was in the wrong job, or hers that I'd been grossly over-pampered as a patient and unfairly enjoyed an over-privileged professional position as a Martha's-trained nurse. But we were now prepared to accept each other professionally, warts and all. It was like the switch from cold war to co-existence. No real joy, but a considerable relief.

She offered me a saucerless cup of tea in the ward kitchen before the day staff came on. 'How much theatre time have you had?'

'Eight months orthopod; six general surgical in my fourth year.'

She raised her eyebrows. 'Bloody great slice out of your fourth year. I thought Martha's prided itself on the variety of its training, as well as on being THE snob hospital in the British Isles.'

I ignored her second crack and answered the first. 'Usually we are switched round every three months in training. It just happened that when I'd worked my way up to head student nurse in the G.S.T. [General Surgical Theatre] three of the five staff nurses got married within two months. I was kept on as acting-staff until the honeymoons were over.'

'H'mm.' She sniffed. 'Does Archie MacDonald want to marry you?'

'Not knowing, can't say.' I helped myself to more tea. 'You going steady?'

'With a Scotsman? Do you mind! Women are worse than fourth-class citizens up here!'

'Perhaps a bit olde-worlde—but the manners are good.'

'Good! Huh! A load of bloody insincere buggers, if you ask me!'

'Don't we have a few of those back home?'

'At least back home one's right to earn one's own living and live one's own life is taken for granted. Here they think one's touched or something. They think all one wants is a man. Of course, they're all sex-mad!'

'They are?' I queried, thinking of Dougal. 'Maybe that's why they wear kilts?'

Like so many women who like using four-letter words, she had a very prim streak. 'Don't be disgusting! If you must know, I think men in kilts are downright obscene!'

'Smith, you can't! They look so cute. I love 'em.'

'You would! You upper-classes are all the same. Only one thought in your heads. Probably just as well in your case, as after this second go you haven't much future in nursing, have you?'

I emptied the remains of my tea in the sink and rinsed my cup whilst I got my mental breath. 'Is that just your idea, Smith, or unofficial official?'

She realized she had let out a trade secret, and tried to conceal the fact by battering me over the head with her bruised ego. 'You're joking, of course! I'm just the bloody night staff nurse on the women's side, I'm just responsible for every bed in both wards for eleven hours every night I'm on, but as I don't entertain Matron and Kilsyth to tea like Lewis, I'm not a bonnie local lassie like Craig, and I didn't train in St Martha's Hospital, nobody ever bothers to tell me anything—unless I've slipped up. Then even God Almighty MacAlistair deigns to talk to me. But as it so happens that I do know some medicine, sometimes I get ideas. Of course, I'm probably wrong.'

'I said, 'Not as wrong as all that with my medical history to date.'

She was frowning. 'You really mind like hell.' She was not asking a question, she was stating a fact. 'How extraordinary!'

'Why?'

'I wouldn't lose any sleep over it if I had Archie MacDonald in my pocket. Even if he hasn't proposed yet, you lift a finger and he will. The whole hospital knows that.'

'Bully for the hospital,' I said drily.

She went pink with impatience. 'Even if you obviously don't love him you can't be fool enough to turn down all that money. Think what an insurance it'll be for your old age.'

'Sickness benefit, too. Can't lose, can I?'

'Your type always comes out on top!'

I recognized she was genuinely trying to comfort me, and it was not her fault she was incapable of giving an encouraging pat on the head without using her knuckles.

'I hope you're right. Thanks for the tea.'

'If you hadn't drunk it I'd only have chucked it away.'

I went back to my room and stood at the window looking out at the loch and the blue-and-white houses directly below the hospital. The sun was still behind Ben Gairlie, and the shadow of the mountain lay across the calm water. On the far shore Achnagairl House was small and grey. I watched it unseeingly, my mind back in the theatre on the night Joe asked me to take a trip to Glasgow. Just a normal Thursday night. No warning bells had sounded. Not even one uneasy instinct.

Smith could be mistaken.

The night staff nurse? When every night she was on, in Sister or Craig's day report she was given the inside story on every patient's prognosis—as we had both known.

I took out the various letters I had had from Martha's. I sorted them carefully. Matron's; Sister Orthopaedic's; my nursing friends'. They contained a great deal of concern for my health, good advice on how to be a model patient, masses of Martha's gossip. There was not one 'looking forward to having you back in the theatre'.

I should have noticed that earlier—had I been looking.

I had to have official confirmation. I waited until Sister's first round. I said, 'It's just occurred to me—'

Sister said bluntly, 'You can relax, lass. Staff Nurse Smith has already shopped herself. So she let it out? Well, you're a sensible lass, so you'll realize she's only jumped the gun by a day or two. We'd have had to tell you before we let you out, as you'd got to prepare yourself. Best do that now.'

After she had finished I was really grateful to Smith. The verdict wasn't as bad as I had been expecting. It still entailed leaving Martha's.

Sister said, 'Anyone can get pleurisy once. After second go only a fool'll take chances on a third. No fool gets to be Matron of a large city hospital. You'll have to watch that chest of yours for the next couple of years, and your own Matron'll know that. The killing pace, the dirt in city air, is not for you. After a decent sick leave you'll have to fix yourself up with a quiet job in a small country hospital. That'll not be hard. Whole country's short of trained nurses. You've enough theatre experience to run a theatre like the one here. With but thirty-two surgical beds our Sister Theatre seldom has more than a morning or an afternoon list. She has the odd rush, perhaps once a month, perhaps less. Happens she doesn't fancy the easy life and wants to get back to a city. She's asked Matron to find her replacement. So that's one job for you going here for a start. You might brood on it. Unless you've other plans?'

My mood had altered from last night. Instead of being frightened by life, I was flaming mad with the bloody thing. 'No.'

'Oh, aye?' She eyed me shrewdly. 'Then you'd best do right brood, hadn't you, lass? Take your time, and you'll not take wrong road.'

'Yes. Thanks, Sister.'

'You don't have to thank me for doing m'job. That's what I'm paid for.' She produced a large card from the file under her arm. 'As Nurse Craig's off, I'm on "ups" menu. What do you want for your lunch? Baked cod, boiled beef, or Irish stew?'

'Oh—fish, please.'

'Roast or mashed?'

'Roast, please.'

'Creamed rice, sago, or apple tart?'

The thought of food made me want to throw up, but I chose apple tart. Sister moved on to Mrs Spearn. Sister would not have altered her morning routine one iota even if convinced the world was due to end that afternoon. 'Routine's got to be done,' she'd say, 'and no patient of mine's facing Almighty on an empty stomach.'

As a junior student nurse I had regarded ward routine as an unnecessary evil forced on reluctant patients and nurses by unimaginative and tradition-ridden authority. I had often been as infuriated by some ward sister as she with me for spending too long with an ill patient and being late with some mundane chore like the menu, screen sheet, or mouth-wash round. I had listened, dumbly mutinous, to endless 'You have a duty to the living as well as the dying, Nurse Wade! A ward has to be run as a whole, and to do that successfully requires strict attention to ward routine. That routine is the framework into which the ward day and night must fit, and the very regularity of the routine is a comfort to all. Next time I tell you to take round the menu at 10 A.M. I want it done at 10 A.M. That is the time my patients expect the menu round, and I will not have their peace of mind disturbed by your unpunctuality! Is that quite clear?'

It was now. Though the thought of the menu choked me, the very normality of its regular morning appearance was a comfort. In ten minutes the first medical round would start with Mrs Spearn. In half an hour the mid-morning drinks trolley would trundle down the corridor. On this particular morning it would be followed almost immediately by the library trolley. Then Matron's round; lunch; afternoon rest hour; tea; visitors; baths and bed-making; evening medicines; temperatures; supper; more drinks; sedatives. No need to watch the clock in any ward. One look at what the ward staff were up to told one the exact hour of the day. Deadly dull, perhaps. Deadly soothing, certainly.

The two elderly ladies who presided over the library trolley had just moved on when the nursing orderly came in. 'A visitor with Dr MacAlistair's permission as it's early.' She held open the door. 'You may come in, laddie.'

My book slipped off my bed and on to the floor. 'Robin! How very nice to see you!'

He picked up the book, which gave him an excuse for being scarlet in the face. He was much more tanned, his fair hair was more bleached, and he looked even more like Joe. 'I came to say goodbye. I've just been across to say it to George MacAlistair. He asked his dad for me.'

'How kind of you both! Er—which MacAlistair boy is George?'

'Middle. He's fourteen, like me. We met at the climbing school. He's good value.'

I said that was nice for them both, asked him to sit down, and congratulated him on his medal.

He perched on the arm of the chair looking hideously uncomfortable in every sense. He stared at the floor. 'George had to chuck climbing. He gets giddy. Mr Urquhart said that was nothing to be ashamed of. George is a right nut.'

'Oh?'

'Ummm. He was—well—sort of ashamed. But he doesn't have to be, as he's bloody brave and he's got a medal to prove it.'

'That's impressive. What did he do?'

'Dived into the loch last year,' he mumbled to the floor, 'and pulled out an English visitor who'd fallen in and couldn't swim. It was bloody rough, and the loch currents are bloody strong. Uncle Dougal said the man would've been swept out towards the estuary.' He looked up then. 'Did you know the loch currents are strong?' I shook my head. 'You know our Aunt Catriona, who's dead. Did you know Mrs Valentine once saved her like that?'

'No.' I was curious. 'When?'

'Ages ago, when they were kids. Aunt Catriona got cramp. Uncle Dougal says she'd have drowned for sure if Mrs Valentine hadn't got her out, but Mrs Valentine didn't get a medal as they didn't tell anyone till long after, as it was rough that day and they weren't supposed to have gone swimming. Aunt Catriona wrote it to Uncle Dougal. He was away at school then. He told us the night you got ill.' He was scarlet again. 'He told us why you were down on the shelf. I thought he'd go spare about my leaving you. He was dead decent.' He grimaced. 'I felt awful. But I didn't mean you to get ill. I just didn't think.'

I hoped I said the right things. Since he showed me his medal a few minutes later, it was possible that I had. He did not stay much longer, and his whole visit was clearly hell for the poor child, but as clearly, from his sudden cheerfulness on leaving, a necessary hell. In parting I was honest. 'I'm very glad and grateful to you for coming, Robin. See you around, I hope.'

His stay in the Highlands had left its mark. 'My pleasure.' He copied Dougal's bow as well as words.

Sister swept in. 'You'd think this was Piccadilly Circus this morning! Off you go, lad, to make room for two more. Special consent from Matron and Dr MacAlistair, as they're under age.'

The twins came in slowly, then flung themselves at me, talking simultaneously, directly Sister vanished. When Dougal came in to collect them both were sitting on my bed. Judy was on her third apple from my fruit-bowl. Johnnie was keeping up his strength with shortbread.

Dougal wore a dark suit and an avuncular expression. He bundled the twins out to wait with Robin and leant both hands on my footrail.

'Matron's just told me you can leave on Saturday. You been told?'

'No.'

'The patient's always the last person to hear. Don't worry. I'll either ring or call in on your Matron at Martha's between trains, and there's plenty of time to fix up your return arrangements when I get back.'

'I can do that—'

'Of course. If you had to. But as you came up here on my behalf, getting you back to London is my responsibility.' He smiled. 'Indulge my power-complex, if only for the last time.'

'What with one thing and another I was too punch-drunk for strong feelings. 'Right. Thanks. Let us now hope, third time lucky.'

'Let us, indeed.' He came round to the side of my bed. 'I've just heard about Miss Donald. You're probably up to the back teeth with being told it was the kindest thing that could happen to her.'

His insight was a relief. 'Just about.'

'I can imagine. Not that that makes it any less true, or less painful for you, and not only as you were so involved in her death. Are you still thinking—there but for the Grace of God—'

I smiled bleakly. 'You should be in psychiatry, not trop. med., Dougal.'

He sat on my locker-seat. 'It requires no special knowledge to appreciate that. Are you?'

'Not this morning.'

'Last night? I wish,' he said, 'I'd known.'

'Hardly small-talk for a teenage rave-up.'

'I realized that when Matron told me. She also told me,' he added slowly, 'Sister Kilsyth has spoken to you about your nursing future. I'd been hoping that one could wait until I returned and you were that much stronger.'

'I'm quite glad to have it over. How long've you known? The start??'

He looked straight at me with troubled eyes. 'Yes. I'm more sorry than I can express, and particularly so that you should have had to face it today, after yesterday. Is there anything I can do for you in London that might help?'

I was not sure if by that he meant chat-up Archie on my behalf, or bulldoze Martha's into finding me a cosy sinecure. 'Like what? Pull a string? You got strings?'

'A few. The medical world's pretty small, and I've old friends or colleagues fairly well scattered.'

'Well, thanks.' Carefully, I smoothed the unwrinkled turn-down of my top sheet, and thought of the job going here. 'I rather think I may have the answer already, but I want to think on it more before I decide. It's very nice of you to offer.'

'Nice!' he echoed abruptly. 'Elizabeth, you must surely appreciate how responsible I feel—and am—for this turn of events—'

'Responsible?' I cut him short. 'Dougal, you're not seriously suggesting you're responsible for the fact that I'm prone to pleurisy?'

'Possibly not for that specific fact. There are others involved for which I'm incontrovertibly responsible!'

I looked at his set face. Had it done any good I'd have shaken him, physically. It wouldn't. He would merely pat my hand, say 'There, there, little woman,' or something similar, and continue to wear my pleural weakness as a hair shirt for the rest of his life. I couldn't have that, and not only because one man around with one guilt-complex was more than enough for any girl. I owed Dougal too much, and, as I now realized, I liked him too much to let this hurt him unnecessarily and unfairly.

I said, 'On second thoughts, you were right to settle for trop. med.'

He raised an eyebrow. 'So?'

'Yes. No trained pyschiatrist would base his arguement on such purely superficial facts. He'd dig up the lot. "To rock bottom, nurses," as the tame head-shrinker who lectured us at Martha's always says.'

'Indeed?' His expression was no more forthcoming, but I had too much to bother me with that.

'Indeed. So if we're going to dig—let's! Sure I came up to bring you the kids, but you didn't ask me. Joe did. But it wasn't his fault his boss decided to do a demonstration list that Saturday, which lets Joe out. One can hardly blame his boss, as Saturday's the only possible free morning for such a list, so he's in the clear. But not me. I said yes. I could've said no.'

'If I might refresh your memory on a remark you made to me in a rather similar context—'

'Not just yet, Dougal. I'm still digging. Where was I? Oh, yes, those two lost English lads who prevented your getting to Glasgow—' He was about to interrupt again, so I waved him down. 'Relax! I'm not going to

hang my pleural cavity round their necks. I'm far too well trained by old
S.I.'

'Old whom?'

'Our tame head psychiatrist. He's known throughout Martha's as Dr
Sexual Implications.'

He smiled a small reluctant smile. 'Gets some analysts that way.' He
stood up, glancing at his watch. 'Nevertheless—'

'Dougal, I know you're in a hurry, so be a dear and just this once let
the little woman have her say. As we were—I can hear old S.I., "Why
did they seek to climb a mountain, nurses? Obviously to fulfil some basic
need. And what is the fundamental need and driving force of the human
race, nurses?"' I spread my hands. 'See, Dougal? You weren't at first
base! You're not responsible. I'm not responsible. But I've been ailing
sick, you've had to brood over me like a Dutch Uncle, Craig had to
bust-off with a boy-friend two back because he took umbrage at her
standing him up to stay on and special me, and the rest of the staff here
have worn out a fortune in shoe-leather pounding up and down that
corridor outside—because a couple of stray lads happen to have
unsatisfactory sex lives. But old S.I. wouldn't let them carry the can.
Not him! He'd get busy on their parents' sex lives, and if he couldn't pin
an Oedipus on one lad, or both, he'd regard himself as a sad disgrace to
the Freudian school. Then he'd work on the parents' parents.' I smiled
up at him. 'Stick to your tropical bugs, Professor. You can't win against
Freud.'

He didn't answer that with words. He dropped a hand on my head
and lightly ruffled my hair, as if I were one of the twins. As I was not,
his gesture had a singular, but not unpleasant, effect on me.

He said then, 'I have to leave now. Keep well whilst I'm away.'

'I will. Have a good trip both ways.'

About an hour later I was still wondering if Smith might not be right
about my one-track mind, when Gordon practically exploded into my
room with the portable. 'A personal call to you from Mr MacDonald,
and he's waiting on the line now. He's calling from London Airport.' He
plugged in, feverishly. 'No doubt he's on his way back here.' He picked
up the receiver. 'Will you be putting Mr MacDonald through now, Mr
Cameron? Here's Miss Wade.'

After my eagerness last night my immediate reaction now astonished
me. I could only hope the enthusiasm in my voice did not sound as false
to Archie as it did to me. 'Hallo, Archie! So you're coming back to
Gairlie? How splendid!'

There was a faint and deafening silence, during which Gordon
vanished. Then Archie said uneasily, 'I'm sorry, honey, but that's not
why I'm calling you. I have to be back Stateside. We take off in a

half-hour. I should've called you night, but I was talking half the night, and it seems I now have to talk to Washington. Maybe I'll be back in three, four weeks, but who knows when you have to deal with Washington.' He hesitated. 'Sore, Elizabeth?'

It was a time for truth. 'No. Naturally a little surprised, a little sad. I hate saying goodbye to my friends.'

His sigh of relief travelled clearly across England and Scotland. 'I've kept telling myself that's how it would be for you, but knowing how it was for me up in Gairlie—and with you so like that other poor kid—'

'I realized that. But, Archie, I'm not her.'

'That I have now figured. I still don't like to leave you. Elizabeth. I aim to come back and finish my vacation some time. Can I see you, then?'

I said he could. He said he would contact me directly he returned to England. I asked after his cold; he asked after my chest; we said we'd enjoyed meeting each other. Then, as we had nothing left to say each other, he rang off. I thought it possible we might meet again, but not probable. Who liked being reminded of the one thing he wanted to forget? But I had liked Archie, so for a little while I did feel a little sad. Only for a very little while.

11. Clouds across the Moon

I helped Sister with the beds that evening, then roamed the ward for more jobs until she turned me out. Dr MacAlistair came out of his office as I was returning to my room.

'Am I right in diagnosing an acute attack of the terrible tedium of true convalescence, Miss Wade?'

'Perfectly, Doctor.'

'A good sign.' He opened my door for me. 'May the Lord preserve us! Roses in April! Where did these come from? Glasgow?'

'London.'

'By air and the evening coach from Inverness?'

I smiled faintly. 'Not the coach. Special delivery.'

Gordon had been as shocked by the extravagance, but much more delighted. 'Ach, what it is to have money to burn to impress a bonnie lassie!' said Dr MacAlistair gravely. 'Now, about your discharge on Saturday—' and he went on to tell me I could be up and dressed from midday tomorrow and all day Friday. 'We can't pitch you out before you've got the feeling of your clothes again and take some fresh air. It'd be different if we were sending you home a few miles in a hospital car. I take it you're still determined to make the long road and rail journey straight off?'

'I'd rather do that.' He was regarding me in silence. 'Is it too stupid?'

'If I thought that I'd keep you in another week. I'd prefer you to build up more strength first, as all that travelling's bound to tire you, but if your mind's set on returning to England, at your present stage it'll do you less harm to let you go. A restless mind is not conducive to total recovery. But don't look so stricken, lassie. Naturally you're anxious to get back to your own circle.' He looked at the roses. 'I hear Mr MacDonald's up to his ears with his takeover bid in London.'

'It seems to be giving him problems. Actually, he should now be either in Washington or nearly there.'

As Mr Cameron had been on the switchboard when Archie called and I had not mentioned this to anyone else, Dr MacAlistair was surprised. 'When'll he be back?'

'He's not sure. Perhaps in a few weeks. Perhaps not.'

'So.' He hunched his heavy shoulders, dropped his chin on his chest, and studied me clinically and kindly. 'These wealthy Americans think less of crossing the Atlantic in a jet than I think of driving to Inverness. They must find the world an odd wee place.'

'Exhaustingly odd.'

'To my way of thinking, too. I prefer to stay put, to take my time with places as well as people. I'd say that was a sign of approaching old age, had I not always been the same and produced our two youngest laddies with the same outlook. The eldest and Isobel have the opposite temperament. They have to see over the next hill. Do you?'

'The hill, yes. I like seeing new places, doing new things, and generally I make up my mind in a hurry, but about things, not people. I like to take my time about people. I don't always manage that, but I do try to stand back before I get too involved in case I don't really want to be involved.'

'Is that a fact?' Again he looked at the roses. 'There are many worse maxims for a young lass to follow, and particularly one who's to fend for herself.' He slapped my shoulder. 'You should've been born north of the Border, lassie. You'll do, but this won't, as I've a job of work to do! It's a hard life for a hard-working man with my feet,' he growled, and stomped off.

The evening dragged on. Next morning was as bad. A lifetime passed before I was able to get dressed, in clothes over a size too big, which vastly improved my morale.

Craig enthusiastically produced a tape-measure. 'Twenty-two, and if you breathe in more I'm sure I can make it twenty-one!'

'Lay off!' I breathed out. 'Want me to look like a pouter pigeon?'

'Think the man's been born who'd object?'

'Yes. Old MacAlistair. His blood-pressure'll shoot if he catches me trying to constrict my breathing apparatus.'

'But think what it'll do to Archie MacDonald's blood-pressure when you get to London!'

I surveyed myself sideways in the small mirror she had brought in. 'As you were off yesterday, I haven't had a chance to tell you—'

Her reaction to my news amused me. She was livid. 'The sod! To fly out on you just when you'll need him!'

'Don't blame the poor man. Business is business. He doesn't owe me anything.'

'Elizabeth, are you out of your wee mind? After the fuss he's made of you and about you ever since you came in here there's hardly a body in Gairlie not convinced he's spoken for you. If he hasn't I'd say it was high time he did!'

'Oh, God!' I groaned. 'Here we go, back a couple of centuries. Really, Craig, I thought you'd more sense. What about your Ian? Your Tam? Your Alec? Have all three spoken for you, and if so, how in hell are you managing to keep them from each other's throats?'

'They're different! They're laddies I've known most of my life, and none of them can afford a wife yet any more than I've a wish to be a wife yet. Archie MacDonald can afford a harem!'

'Have a heart, love. From the little I know of him his business leaves him hardly enough time to deal with one woman, much less a couple of dozen. Though he talked a lot about being glad to get away from it all, there's obviously nothing he enjoys more than making bigger and better automobile deals. What's so wrong with that? I thought of all races you Scots like people to take their work seriously.'

'Maybe. But also their personal responsibilities.'

'I'm not Archie's.'

'You really mean that?'

'Look,' I said, 'look. We met on holiday, we clicked, I got ill, he sent me flowers and candies. To send those to a woman to any American male I've ever met is as natural as breathing. For a time he thought I was his dolly baby. Illness makes people emotional, he's an emotional type, so he got emotional, plus, plus. But he's no fool. Once he got right away he began sorting things out. He now knows what happened to him up here.'

'And what about what happened to you?'

'Do stop making like the avenging angel. Nothing's happened to me!

Oh, sure, I was gone on him for a while, but I was through that before he left here, and he knew it. And if you say "Is tha' a fact?" I'll start chucking things!'

'Don't you dare when I've tidied your room! Talking of rooms, what about his reservation at the hotel and all the fishing tackle he left behind? I'd a date with Ian last night. He'd have told me had Davie MacDonald had any instructions to cancel the room and forward the tackle.' We looked at each other, and the same thought passed through both our minds. She said, 'You could find out by ringing his London hotel.'

'And shock the living daylights out of poor Gordon? Anyway, I honestly think he's now in Washington.'

'And forgotten his tackle? A fisherman?'

I shrugged as Sister arrived to see I was sufficiently wrapped up. 'Just round the hospital, and that's your lot.'

I had thought my legs back to normal after my ward exercise. They felt very odd in the open air. I walked round the small building, exchanged waves, and collected a couple of wolf-whistles on passing the male wards, peered into the minute Casualty Department, went twice round the exterior of the dolls'-size theatre block. I was wondering if I had the energy to cross the helicopter landing strip when Craig came out of a side-door. 'Mrs Valentine is on the line. She'd like a chat with you. Do you want me to find you?'

'Hell!' I had to think of Dougal's angle. 'I guess I'll have to be polite.'

'Och, why bother? You certainly owe her nothing. I'll get rid of her for you. She's that rude to nurses it'll be a pleasure!'

'No. I'd a hunch this was something I'd have to get over before leaving Gairlie. May as well face it now.'

'I still don't see why.'

We went indoors. I said, 'Because her intended has been very good to me.'

'Is that a fact?'

Scotland was leaving its mark on me, too. 'Och, away, don't be so bloody thick, Craig! You know it is!'

The portable was back in my room, and Maury was back in her old gushing routine. She just wished—how she wished—she could get in to see me, but she simply hadn't one teensy-weensy moment between rushing to and fro from Inverness and all the tedious business that selling a house involved. But she had promised darling Dougal to keep an eye on me in his absence, and she was not going to get a wink's sleep if I didn't reassure her in person.

I reassured her. 'What's this about selling a house?'

'Dougal hasn't told you? Darling, he's advised me to sell my house up the glen. I mean, as he says, who wants two houses?'

'Who, indeed?' I was only surprised by the new intensity of my own dislike at the thought of her moving into Achnagairl House. 'I hope you're getting a good price.'

'Dougal says it's very fair. It's some friend of his who has made the offer and he's dealing with most of it for me. I'm such a helpless sort of female. He's such a comfort to me.'

'I'm sure he is.'

There was a faint silence. As there was a limit to how saintly I was prepared to be for Dougal, I left her to break it.

'Elizabeth, I just have to tell you how terribly—how desperately upset I've been about your illness. I just thought we'd nip down for more cigas—of course, I didn't like to disturb you as you were asleep, and I never dreamed the weather would change, and poor little Robin was so keen to explore. I'm just so impulsive—I suppose that's because I've always been so artistic—and sometimes I—well, I suppose you could say I fly off the handle. But, as Dougal says, don't we all on some occasions say and do things we don't mean—if you see what I mean?'

I saw amongst other things that Dougal must have put the fear of God in her to produce that apology. I told her I quite understood, we all had our human frailties, all was forgiven and forgotten, and every cloud had a silver lining, as I had grown so attached to Gairlie Hospital. She enchanted by replying it was an ill wind and she was SO happy to hear me sound so happy. 'You really are better? When exactly do you leave us? And how is Archie MacDonald?'

I said Archie and I were fine, and I was leaving on Saturday. Having then had a surfeit, I invented a medical round as an excuse to ring off.

'Isn't that typical of hospitals! They just give me the shudders. But I did force myself to visit you, and some wretched girl wouldn't let me. Dougal said she had to say no.'

'He was right, but thanks for trying.'

'He's always right. What would I do without him?'

I could have told her. 'Lucky you don't have to.'

'How sweet of you to say that, darling!'

I pulled a face, which was childish, but some relief.

There was a general post in Women's Medical that afternoon. During rest-hour an elderly woman was admitted in coma after a cerebral haemorrhage. Thirty minutes later Mrs Burns was re-admitted in a collapsed condition after a severe haematemesis. It was Sister's half-day, but as she had not gone when the elderly woman arrived, she was still working behind one set of drawn curtains when Mrs Spearn and I took round the tea-trolley. Craig was running her feet off between the other set of drawn curtains and the bed-patients.

Mrs Burns's voice was weak, apologetic, and audible to the entire ward. 'Aye, I ken well, Doctor, you said no alcohol—but it was just the one wee dram—or maybe it was more than the one—but I'd had words with my man—and I'm awful sick with this diet!'

'No doubt you are, woman,' said Dr MacAlistair, not ungently, 'but it's a sight better than being awful sick with the blood the way you've been this day. Will you stay quiet now! How do you expect a man to get this wee needle into your vein and put back some of the blood you've lost if you keep thrashing about?'

Sister whisked the used transfusion trolley into the sluice later, and had to leave it uncleared, to rush back as Mrs Burns started vomiting again. Mrs Spearn and I looked at the trolley as we returned with our own from the ward kitchen to start second cups. I said, 'Think Sister'll create if I clear that?'

'Maybe. But you'll know how to do it, and she's that busy.'

I rinsed the various dishes and instruments, helped myself to a mask, and pushed the trolley on to the sterilizing room. Dr MacAlistair passed the door as I swung over the large wooden-and-glass timer. 'So! A new nurse on the staff? Make yourself too useful, and I'll be changing my mind about your leaving us tomorrow.'

'How's Mrs Burns, Doctor?'

He said dourly, 'As well as any gastric patient with a chronic ulcer can be after downing half a pint of good whisky. She's a strong woman. Had she as strong a will we could cure her.'

Craig cannoned out of the ward as he disappeared. 'Elizabeth, can you make me a kaolin poultice for Miss Henderson?'

'Sure. How big?'

'Four by two.'

The kaolin lived in the stock cupboard in the duty-room. Sister was at her desk. She said I could do the poultice and no more. 'You're not on the staff yet. I'm not letting you wear yourself out.'

'I'm not tired, Sister.'

'And I wasn't born yesterday, lass.'

Craig was looking for me when I went to find her to say the poultice was ready and sitting between kidney dishes on the lid of the bowl sterilizer. 'The Professor's waiting on you in your room.'

I was sorry for the stroke patient, Mrs Burns, and the hard-working staff, but I had really enjoyed being busy again, and the thought that Dougal was back. Until that moment, I had not properly realized how much I had been looking forward to his return. I bounced into my room. 'Hallo! Sorry to keep you waiting. How did it go?'

'Well, thank you. I've not had a chance to see Hamish MacAlistair, but I don't need him to tell me you've maintained your improvement. You look a different girl.'

'I feel it, thanks.' I jerked a thumb. 'Poor things, they're all hectic in the ward. Sister's just chucked me out, but do they need help!' I sat down, hoping he would do the same. He looked extraordinarily travel-weary. 'Did you get to Martha's?'

'Yes. I saw your Matron and Joe.' He gave me a civil message from Matron and a letter from Joe, which I put aside to read later. 'I've booked your sleeper for tomorrow night. I'll call for you at one o'clock. That'll allow time for hold-ups on the road or by the weather. The forecast isn't too good, and the glass is dropping, but even if we've snow they'll keep the main road to Glasgow open after any fall short of a blizzard.'

'Snow? This late in the year?'

'Not late for the Highlands.' He was still standing and beside my roses. 'Though high summer here.'

'Aren't they lovely?'

'Very.'

I told him about Mrs Burns. 'Poor woman—but can you imagine anyone being so foolish?'

'Is there a limit to human folly? I wouldn't have said so.'

I opened my mouth to tell him about Archie and changed my mind. He was more than travel-weary. He had done enough hospital visiting, and now I was having to stand on the professional sidelines myself I realized just how frustrating his visits must have been for him. I told him Maury had rung me.

'So she told me.'

'I thought, very sweet of her,' I lied.

He bowed.

I said, 'It was sweet of Robin to come.' He said nothing, so I took a chance. 'I'm grateful to both, but shouldn't I also thank you?'

'If you wish.' He sounded tired and more than slightly bored. 'Its unnecessary, but if that's what you want to do you do it.' He backed to the door. 'Before I left home I asked Mrs Pringle to pack the possessions you left in my house. I'll bring your suitcase with me tomorrow. I expect Mrs Pringle'll be in later, or early tomorrow, to say goodbye to you.'

'Thank you.'

I felt deflated after he had gone. I thought of all the questions I had wanted to ask him about the job here. The more I thought of that, the more I liked it—just so long as it did not entail seeing anything of Maury Valentine. But to rule her out would automatically rule out Dougal. Would that matter, even though at present Dougal and Gairlie were practically synonymous terms in my mind? I thought over the last forty-eight hours, then didn't know what to think, and opened Joe's letter as a kind of counter-irritant.

It proved just that. Joe wrote:

Wish you were here, Liz, to treat me for acute shock. I am a nervous wreck after the blast I have just had from dear old U.D., wearing his best pundit's suiting and with every 'r' vibrating as always when he blows all fuses. God help us—and me! For your information I am one bloody selfish, feckless, thoughtless, careless laddie. (Tautologous? Sure! I did not tell him. I am also one coward.)

A. I asked a gurrl to do a man's job. (He never heard of female emancipation?)

. I neglected to inform him you had once had pleurisy. (What in hell did he expect me to do? Send up your bloody medical-history sheet? How was I to know he was going to nip you up the bloody airy mountain? Or that you would be fool enough to risk your neck for that silly bugger Robin?)

C. You'd made no mention (quote) of getting so much as a postcard or pressed flower from me. Why not? I told him. Ergo, *D, E,* and *F* are unrepeatable.

Liz, my love, for Christ's sake don't risk your bloody neck again, or you'll be risking mine. Never known the old boy so steamed-up. Still, thanks a lot, and I'm dead sorry to hear the latest turn-up, though hellish bucked to hear from certain post-blast dark hints that all may not be black as night when your lamp goes out. The best of British with this well-heeled Yank. I may join the Brain Drain yet. Always liked the Yanks. Remember Della-Lou from Texas? On second thoughts, forget her, as I am now dating Daisy Dawson in the face of stiff opposition. She says my hair is too long. Tell me if it is when you stop off en route for darkest Hove.

My love,
JOE

I closed my eyes to concentrate. Clearly Craig had not been exaggerating about the local attitude on Archie and myself. I wished I had straightened Dougal out just now, then realized it was probably better that I had not. Until he had me off his back, with his way-out sense of duty he might have felt he had to reach for a shot-gun. Or would he use a dirk?

'Asleep, Elizabeth?' One Mrs Sinclair, from Women's Surgical, had put her head round the door. She was being discharged that evening, and we exchanged addresses, promises, and goodbyes. She asked me to say goodbye for her to Women's Medical, as she did not like to intrude with the ward so busy. 'Your turn tomorrow!'

Mrs Lewis was on that night. She showed in Mrs Pringle before taking the day report. Mrs Pringle was armed with more shortbread and another fruit cake. 'Don't thank me, lassie! It was a pleasure to be baking! The emptiness of Achnagairl House these last few days and the terrible silence tonight with the Professor shut in his study working!'

'I can imagine. But you'll be glad to have him back.'

'Och, but he's away again tomorrow for the rest of the week-end.'

'Is he now? He's staying in Glasgow?'

'I've no doubt he'll do that, though he's not yet informed my sister Mary of the fact. But Mary was meeting Mrs Valentine when she was out shopping this morning.' She looked disapprovingly down her nose. 'Mrs Valentine was asking what time the Professor'd be leaving with you in the morning. It appears she's invited to some house-party in Glasgow this week-end, and there's something wrong with her car. I expect she'll be asking for a lift.'

'Reasonably, as he's driving me in.'

'Maybe so. Mary told the Professor, and he was away up the glen to see her directly he returned from London and before he came on here. I'll not be surprised at all to hear he's taking her along with you.'

Nor would I, even though the idea vastly depressed me. To cheer myself up I said, 'One thing, as it's such a lovely moonlit night, tomorrow should be a beautiful day.'

'I doubt it.' She sighed sadly. 'The moon'll soon be hidden. There's a nasty wee breeze getting up.'

Inside of an hour the wee breeze was strong enough to sweep huge clouds over the moon and whisk up black waves on the loch. Across the water Achnagairl House was a dark smudge lit by pin-points. I stood for some time at my window, looking at the house, after I had switched off my light and before getting into bed, and only then realized that to do that had become my nightly habit ever since allowed up. Last night, I thought, and the thought was curiously saddening.

I was wide awake when Mrs Lewis pattered along in her bedroom slippers at eleven-thirty. 'Is the wind disturbing you, Elizabeth?'

'It's a bit rowdy, but it's not bothering me. Is it the others?'

'They're all sleeping now.' She went over to the window. 'I hope it drops.'

'The noise worries you?'

'Not for myself, but it could signify a change to worse weather, and I'd not care for that with the hospital so full.'

I sat up and hugged my knees. 'Why should that affect the hospital?'

'It's the week-end, dearie, and the time of the year when the tourists come up to climb. Once here, they'll be determined to climb, whatever the weather.'

'But are there many here now the school holidays are over?'

She sat on my bed. She was not only the best nurse I had come across, she was the only one I had known dare do that. 'The universities are not yet back. Earlier tonight Sister Kilsyth was saying she'd heard from her husband that a large party of English students arrived yesterday and are camped on the far side of the Ben till Tuesday. And Staff Nurse in Men's Surgical was just telling me last night she was dancing with some of the laddies here in Gairlie. They've come to climb the Ben, so, as Sister was saying, it's to be hoped their party leader has a good understanding of Highland weather. This may blow out before morning, or blow up into a blizzard.' She glanced again at the window. 'Sister'll be anxious. You'll know Andrew Kilsyth works with Mr Urquhart?'

'Sister's husband? I didn't know.'

'And he was one of the men to carry you in here!'

'How awful of me! I never guessed or thanked her.'

'Och, she'll understand.' She tilted her head. 'This wail puts me in mind of your second night. It was worse at dawn. The Professor said it sounded as if the wind was trying to move the Ben.'

'He was here that late?'

'He was here all your first two nights, and sitting on that locker. You don't recall? You were poorly—but he was greatly concerned and no trouble to the staff. There's not many a doctor who'd have behaved as well. Doctors can be as difficult as visitors as they are as patients. But the Professor's a good man—aye—and he's been a good friend to you.'

'Yes.' I looked at my locker-seat. 'Very.'

12. *'The Lost English Laddies'*

I woke for a short time at first light. The wind had dropped, the loch was the colour of gunmetal, the waves had subsided, and the heavy under-swell made the water heave like oil. The sky was a queer crimson-mauve, and despite the radiators the air in my room was icy.

Mrs Lewis arrived with another steaming cup of tea. 'There's snow on the way.'

I repeated Dougal's words about the road to Glasgow.

'He's right,' said Mrs Lewis. 'It'll be different on the wee roads over the hills. The snow may lay there all week, but they'll start clearing the main directly it falls.'

I thought of those students. 'And on the Ben?'

'There's snow on the Ben throughout the year and ice on the slopes. Another fall'll only add to what's there already.' She warmed her hands on the radiator by the window. 'I do not like the look of that sky at all.'

'But it's so clear, and isn't that crimson the sign of a good day?'

'Maybe in your part of England it might be a good sign. Not here. Do you see those sea-birds lining the loch shore? In fine weather they're away out to sea at dawn. They've come in for sanctuary. But the wind's gone. Maybe it'll stay fine.'

'You think it'll get up again?'

'It can do that before you've finished your tea.'

The wind had not returned when she moved my cup, refilled my hot-water bottle, and tucked me down. The sky had turned yellow and the blue mountains in the east purple, but there was no sign of a cloud. When Craig's voice in the corridor woke me later the sun was shining from a clear sky and starting to melt the fine carpet of snow. It had all disappreared before I finished breakfast.

As the hospital was so full my room was needed for a patient coming in at lunch-time. I finished my packing, stripped the bed, carbolized the furniture and bedsprings, and then remade the bed with the nursing orderly before nine. Gordon arrived to carry my case into Sister's office and the orderly and I added all my still-fresh flowers to the collection in the ward.

The elderly lady was still in coma. Mrs Burns, after three pints of whole blood, was back on form.

'Could I not get my teeth into more than sops, Sister? I'm famished!'

'Are you daft as a brush?' retorted Sister sharply. 'Do you want to bleed again?'

Mrs Burns's beam was undaunted. When Sister retired to her office Mrs Burns informed the ward it was no wonder to her the Sister should be in a wee fret. 'Her mind's on her man. You'll ken he works for Mr Urquhart. This looks no day to be up the hills.'

I was so preoccupied by my coming drive that I had forgotten the student party. 'Surely, Mrs Burns, if there's any element of risk Mr Urquhart won't take anyone up?'

Half the ward assured me there was no climb without risk even in the best weather. 'It'll be that party of English students that's fretting the Sister,' put in Mrs Jamieson in her breathless voice. 'Have you not heard they were seen starting up the north face just after dawn this morning? A large party, so the paper-boy said. He watched them through glasses. It's to be hoped they're experienced and have had the good sense to come down with that first snow. Here's another wee fall.'

The snow fell finely past the ward windows and, as previously, swiftly began to melt. I walked over to one and looked at Ben Gairlie. It was nearly hidden in cloud, and the clouds were moving in from the sea more rapidly than even a few minutes ago.

The patients said, 'Maybe you'll have to postpone your journey, Elizabeth.'

I felt that should have upset me. I was ashamed by my own selfishness, and much shaken that it did not.

Shortly after Dr MacAlistair stopped me in the corridor. 'This weather is only local. I've just been having a word with Sergeant Cameron at the police station. There's no snow to the south and the roads are clear, so you can stop looking so anxious.'

'That's not all that's on my mind, Doctor.'

'Oh? And what else?'

'I was wondering if that party on the Ben has come down?'

'Sergeant Cameron has no information.'

'Is that good or bad?'

He said, 'It could be either.'

'If there should be any kind of problem, would you hear?'

'I take it you mean the kind of problem that might involve a rescue operation. Yes. I'd hear. On such occasions the police are the first to be informed. They promptly get in touch with Charlie Urquhart, the leader of the Gairlie Mountain Rescue Organization, and nearly as promptly inform us to expect whatever the number of casualties or exposure cases it may be.' He patted my shoulder. 'Stop fretting, Miss Wade. With any luck those English laddies are sheltering somewhere safely at this very moment.'

'And without luck, Dr MacAlistair?'

He shrugged heavily. 'I'll get a call from Sergeant Cameron.'

The snow stopped, but the wind increased. When we lunched at twelve the loch was nearly as rough as last night. I said goodbye to Matron, my physiotherapist, the women in both wards, the staff. Craig was specialing the woman in coma, whose condition had suddenly deteriorated, and was only able to wave at me over the top of the curtains. I mouthed, 'Can't thank you enough—I'll write.'

Sister escorted me into the hall to wait for Dougal. Dr MacAlistair joined us. 'So this is where we lose our oldest inhabitant! Ach, I've an aversion to farewells, so I'll do no more than wish you godspeed and good health and fortune.'

We shook hands. I said, 'Doctor, I don't know how to thank you and Sister and all the nurses for all you've done for me.'

'My dear gurrrl, we've but done our jobs, and as you'll well know there's no greater satisfaction in our profession than seeing a patient who was carried into here in a bad way walking out with a bonnie colour in her face and a healthy impatience to get back to her normal life. Though

I'll tell you this, my dear—had I not given my consent to all these arrangements before the temperature started falling last night, I'd have picked another day for your discharge, badly though we need your bed. But, if necessary, we could have fitted you into an emergency in the middle of the ward for a night or two. However, as you'll be driving in a warm car and will have Professor Grant to take good care of you down to London, you'll be in safe hands. The weather's warmer in the south of England. From there on you should take no chill.'

'Professor Grant isn't taking me to London. He's staying in Glasgow—' I looked from one to the other. 'Isn't he?'

Both were shaking their heads. MacAlistair said, 'I'd a word with him only an hour ago. He repeated the intention he'd had from the start of seeing you safely to St Martha's.'

'Why didn't he tell me?' I demanded almost peevishly.

Sister remained silent. Dr MacAlistair suggested it might have slipped Dougal's mind. 'Or possibly, being a man who has always preferred to let his actions speak for themselves, he considered such a communication unnecessary. I'm not saying that's wrong, but, having a wife and daughter, I'm aware any high-spirited lassie prefers to be consulted on matters that concern herself. Would you not agree, Sister—' He broke off as Gordon suddenly pushed up the lodge window.

Gordon called, 'Sergeant Cameron for you, sir. Will I put him through to your office?'

Dr MacAlistair vanished. Sister folded her arms without comment. Gordon pulled out and pushed in plugs at the switchboard. A bell rang in Matron's office across the hall and was muffled by the closed door.

Another bell was ringing in my mind. It was unexpected, unwanted, and as tangible as the bell in Matron's office. It was also, without question, an alarm bell.

Gordon called again: 'Miss Wade! Professor Grant. Will you take it in Box 2?'

I shot into the second of the two public booths in the hall. I knew what Dougal was going to say before I raised the receiver. I said it for him. 'This is where I came in. You've got to join the search party?'

I heard his quick intake of breath. 'You know already?'

'Guessed from the signs and symptoms.' My voice astonished me by sounding so normal. I didn't feel normal. 'Many involved?'

'Eighteen.'

'Not all eighteen lost?'

'I hope to God not,' he retorted, 'but it's a possibility. They started up in a party of twenty. Two have now managed to get down for help. Their deputy-leader is still up and injured, and they've lost touch with the other seventeen and fear they may all be in difficulty. Charlie's just had the alarm call from the police. He's just rung me. As I'm here, I have to go up with the others, even though it entails letting you down. Those students have to be got down before the weather gets worse, as it almost certainly will from the look of things. I've no words, or time, to describe how much I dislike having to do this to you, but I can't pretend I've any bloody choice. I'm in Charlie's team, and I've got to go up. I'm sorry.'

I was suddenly very, very frightened. 'It's not your fault. Of course, I understand—'

'Elizabeth, let me do the talking. I should have left already. Just listen. Davie MacDonald is going to drive you to Glasgow with one of his hotel guests, an Englishwoman, a Mrs Sumner. Davie says she's a sensible, kindly woman and very willing to keep an eye on you. ...'

I was listening mechanically without taking it in. When he finished I said, 'Thank you, Dougal. That's very kind of you, Dougal. I'm sorry about this, too.' Never in my live before had I been so conscious of the inadequacy of English, or, come to that, any other language. 'I've never thanked you properly. Take care on the Ben. Good luck.'

'And to you. I shall be coming south shortly, so we may meet again. I hope so. Goodbye, and a good journey now, and, as we say up here, haste ye back.' He rang off.

Sister Kilsyth waited blank-faced. 'Lost your escort?'

'He's fixed me up with another.' I did not bother to explain. I was not clear just when I had made up my mind, but I was dead clear I had no bloody choice either, if not precisely why. I had a rough idea. 'Sister, I want to stay and help.'

She said calmly, 'Oh, aye? Ask the Doctor.'

I waited till MacAlistair reappeared and tackled him. 'Are you expecting all eighteen as possible emergency admissions?'

He was grave. 'Aye.'

'Couldn't you use an extra pair of trained hands? Even in a hospital with a staff as big as Martha's that number coming in together would present a major problem. This is so much smaller and you've a full hospital. How'll you manage?'

His eyes smiled. 'We've cured the lassie, and she's now going to take over the hospital! What have we done, Sister? And you ask how we'll manage, Miss Wade? As we've done previously. Do you recall Easter last year, Sister,' he added, 'when we admitted thirty over the one week-end? And there was not a spare bed in all Gairlie with the number of English relatives up and needing accommodation.'

'I've not forgotten,' said Sister. 'The wards were so packed with emergency beds it was hard to get round and take a pulse.'

'Hard! This whole wee hospital was an obstacle course! But they all did well—and so did the nursing staff. All off-duty went by the board,

Miss Wade, and one was hard put to differentiate between the day and night staff, the hours the nurses worked. It was the Easter holiday week-end—but not for Gairlie Hospital. We managed. We'll manage again.'

I felt flattened. 'You don't need my help?'

'I did not say that, but since it is a nursing point, it must wait on Matron's decision. You wish me to ask her for you?'

'Dr MacAlistair—would you? Oh! Davie MacDonald.' Having taken in more than I realized whilst Dougal was speaking, I explained that bit. 'Can I ring him to say I'm staying?'

'Do you want to stay so much?' Dr MacAlistair studied me searchingly. 'Aye. You do. Then I'll put you out of your anxiety and tell you the last thing I wish to see any ex-patient do is set off for a long journey with an anxious mind in this weather. I'll have a word with Davie MacDonald for you, and another with my wife. She'll be happy to offer you hospitality, as we cannot keep you in this hospital since we're likely to require every emergency bed we possess. Ach! Here's Davie for you now. Don't step out in the cold. I'll speak with him.'

'Doctor, thank you. Thank you very much.'

'It's no trouble. But I'm warning you that as your ex-physician I shall advise Matron that if she permits you to work it'll not be for long. Now, to Davie MacDonald!'

The snow was falling again and more heavily. In the few minutes Dr MacAlistair spent outside the world turned white. He stamped and shook himself free of snow before coming back into the hall. 'Don't look so worried, lassie. As you're aware, Davie has to be away to Glasgow on his own business. I've left your train ticket with him, as he's obligingly offered to attend to the cancelling of your reservation. He'd already agreed to do the same for Professor Grant, when the Professor rang him directly he heard the English party had started up the Ben earlier this morning. Realizing the weather was deteriorating and what could happen, and knowing Davie had to be in Glasgow, apparently Professor Grant thought fit to make provisional alternative arrangements for you. After he was called out one wee word to Davie was enough. But he said nothing of this when he rang me.' He paused. 'Are you going to take new offence at the lack of consultation?'

'No. Thank you, Doctor.'

He had to see Matron. Sister took me back to her office to remove my outdoor clothes. 'Sister, how long can this take?'

She watched her ward from the doorway. 'A few hours, all night, or longer. A big operation takes time, and this is big.' She flicked her watch over her apron-bib. 'The whole search-party'll be mustering now at the police station. They keep all their heavy, communal equipment in the shed next door.'

'They'll need a lot?'

'Stretchers, first-aid kits, blankets, tools, ropes, spot lamps, and the heavy batteries and gas cylinders to supply the lamps. Like I said, lass. A big job.'

'They'll carry all that up Ben Gairlie?'

'Oh, aye. On their backs.' She looked at me, but I didn't feel she saw me. 'The stretchers alone weigh fifty pounds each. In good weather it can take between three or four hours to get up to their rest-hut. This snow and the weights will slow 'em down.'

I had never known her so talkative. I said I hoped she did not mind my questions.

'No. What else do you want to know?'

'How many searchers?'

'Around twenty-five between the first and second teams. More if the reserves have been called. I reckon they will as they'll be needed to search round the rest-hut, or some to stay at base camp to get the victims away fast. As it takes about four hours to carry an injured man down the Ben,' she said drily, 'happen they'll have a long wait.'

'Yes. I suppose the first team has the best men?'

'The best climbers,' she corrected. 'They're all good men. Obviously, it takes experience and skill to be capable of, and willing to, climb anything, anytime, in any weather. The pick are in the first. They'll be first up, last down. If necessary, they go up again and again. My husband's in that lot. Aye.' She answered my unspoken question. 'And Professor Grant.'

I found I could not comment on that. 'The lost are always found?'

'They'll not return, and never have, empty-handed. They'll stick on the job until they've found the lot. They'll bring 'em down to us here, alive or dead. Till then there's nowt for it but to wait and hope.' A spasm of anxiety flickered over her set face. 'That'll not be easy. Happen it never is.'

It was not easy. All that long afternoon every face, sick and well, was haunted by the thought of the lost Englishmen. As the afternoon wore on items of news trickled in. Nearly all the lost were university students, and the whole party was from the West of England. We learned that the students had been saving for their week-end for the past year. Most were paying their first visit to the Highlands, some to climb, a few to ski. On their journey up their official party leader had developed violent food poisoning and been carried off the train at Carlisle. His son was one of the lost. The deputy leader, a Mr Morgan, was a twenty-six-year-old reader in ancient history, an experienced rock-climber who had gained his experience in Wales and the Lake District. He had never climbed in Scotland before.

I was having tea in Matron's office with Matron, Sister Kilsyth, and Dr MacAlistair when Matron's telephone rang. It made me jump. The others sat very still. Then Matron reached, almost casually, for the receiver. 'Yes, Sergeant? Yes. I'll tell him, as he's here with me. Thank you.' She put it down. 'They've left the rest-hut. Soon we may have real news.'

Sister asked to be excused to help Staff Nurse Craig get ahead with the routine. Officially Sister was off duty till six. She had only stopped working ten minutes ago.

'A good plan, Sister.' Matron waited for the door to close. 'Poor Sister! She'll be on edge until she hears her husband is safely back, but never once on these occasions have I heard her utter one word of complaint.'

'Andrew Kilsyth is a good man. His wife wouldn't wish to change him. He loves the hills.' Dr MacAlistair glanced at me. 'Take that from him and he'd be another man.'

I didn't mind his guessing. I merely wondered when he had. Probably long before I knew myself. It was that first fear that had cracked it wide open. I was still so frightened for Dougal that there was room for little else in my mind. Maury, Dougal's reaction when he found I was still in Gairlie, my expected arrival at Martha's, never even occurred to me.

Matron and MacAlistair were discussing Mr Morgan. Matron said, 'It will help Mr Urquhart to know the lost are being led by an experienced rock-climber, even though now injured. Surely he'd not have taken wholly inexperienced laddies up the north face? Then she answered herself. 'If he has it'll not be the first time we've known that happen.'

Dr MacAlistair nodded grimly. 'He's young to lead so large a party, and being a rock-climber'll be ambitious to tackle the stiffest route. We've to remember it's his first time in charge—as Charlie'll not overlook.' He went on to explain to me why it was so vital for the searchers to learn as much as possible about the characters, as well as the actual climbing experience, of those lost. 'There are never enough men to cover a mountain like the Ben, so the searchers have to try and think themselves into the minds of those they're searching. Naturally, the more they know of those minds, the better they can do that. Then as time is all-essential and as much ground as possible must be covered before dark, they make first for the places they would have chosen for shelter for themselves, had they been the lost. If in vain they report back and start again.'

'How do they report? Short-wave radio?'

'Unfortunately when that's most required the mountains render it useless. They do have a short-wave set at the rest hut, another at base, a third back here at the police station.' He looked at the window. The snow had changed to driving rain. 'This'll freeze solid directly it hits the Ben. Ach, the poor, thoughtless laddies! Little did they think when they set out to climb their mountain how their day might end! But when did any normal laddie on holiday give a thought to danger?' He sighed. 'Let's hope they're dressed for this.'

'They might not be? People'll climb Ben Gairlie without proper climbing clothes?' I demanded.

My companions exchanged resigned glances. 'My dear,' said Matron, 'we've had them carried down from the Ben without proper climbing boots, with clothing only suitable for a country walk, with often not one wind or waterproof garment. They've come up here on holiday and regarded the Ben as no more than a high hill. We've had students who've never climbed anything starting straight off on the north face, as I said earlier.'

'You look as if you find it hard to credit that, Miss Wade,' added Dr MacAlistair, 'but it's the truth. We've had victims of the Ben who've tackled her not only in the wrong clothes, but without maps, compasses, or even a whistle or a torch in their pockets. Those last two alone have often made the difference between life and death to the lost. No climber should set foot on a mountain without them. Do you know what every expert'll tell you is the greatest single danger to any climber?' I shook my head. 'His or her own inexperience.'

'I'm beginning to understand that.' Then, as I had to be reassured, I had to ask, 'Do the searchers ever get lost?'

Again they looked at each other. Dr MacAlistair took his time. 'They're not irresponsible laddies, lassie. They're all local men who know and have trained on their mountain and understand their weather and have their eyes wide open to all the risks involved. As most are married men, they'll have personal as well as professional responsibilities to steady their foot- and hand-holds. Though they come from assorted backgrounds, they're accustomed to working as a team under Charlie Urquhart.'

He had not answered my question, and we all knew it. 'What kind of backgrounds?'

'Ach—doctors—there's another besides Dougal Grant—artisans, council officials, railwaymen, crofters, fishermen—and maybe others. Can you call them to mind, Matron?'

'Not off-hand, Doctor.'

They were being kind. It was no help. So I was blunt. 'I've read of rescuers being killed. Has it happened here?'

'From time to time.' Dr MacAlistair stopped avoiding my eyes. 'I've known more than one Gairlie man fall to his death searching for a stranger he'd never seen and whose name he never learnt. But that's never stopped the searchers from continuing, and there's never any shortage of volunteers to fill the empty place. Naturally, they're all volunteers.'

'Naturally,' echoed Matron.

Naturally, I thought, and remembered my original impression that the twentieth century had not yet reached Gairlie. It hadn't.

I thought of London. I thought of Easter Monday last year. For the third year running, with one of my nursing friends, I had marched the last fourteen miles and sat in Trafalgar Square and sung 'We shall not be moved' and chanted 'Hands off Vietnam.' I thought of hippies and junkies and pop maniacs and rave-ups and freak-outs and love-ins. We were a dead trendy lot. We were going to show the world how to make love, not war. We were going to find out all the answers. Up here in Gairlie they were so antiquated, they didn't even bother with the questions. They thought the Act of Union had been passed the day before yesterday; Culloden was yesterday; the words first uttered nearly two thousand years ago were new enough to condition men's actions. Naturally one man should be willing to lay down his life for another.

No-one, throughout that afternoon and evening, mentioned the word 'love' to me. No-one asked me, 'Why must our men risk their lives for your idiotically, if not downright criminally, careless fellow-countrymen?'

They all said, 'Those poor English laddies! They must be brought down safely.'

I learnt a lot about Scottish Highlanders and about love that long afternoon in Gairlie. I learnt even more about myself. It was an afternoon to remember, and not only because that was the afternoon I grew up.

13. A 'Routine' Mountain Rescue

The telephone in the MacAlistairs' front hall rang again. Mrs MacAlistair went to answer it, leaving me by her sitting-room fire. We had spent the last two hours and had our supper on trays by that fire. We were alone in the house, as the three boys had gone back to their boarding-school yesterday. Mrs MacAlistair said she invariably flapped round like a frustrated old hen for the first few days of every school term, and if anyone was doing anyone a kindness it was me. 'Normally Hamish is very good and comes over as much as possible, but how could I expect him to leave his beloved hospital, even for five minutes, tonight? You'll take coffee? Or would you prefer tea? Or hot chocolate?'

She was a tall, handsome, gay woman, and, being even more of an extrovert than her husband, she seldom stopped talking. She said her children talked as much, having long learnt that their only hope of getting a word in was to shout both parents down. 'Perforated eardrums all round when the MacAlistairs get together.'

In her house I felt neither an outsider nor an honoured guest. I just felt she was glad of my company, that she did not object to my jumping like a scalded cat whenever the 'phone rang, and considered my staying on perfectly normal in these circumstances. 'If they only let you hand round tea; someone has to do the job, and being trained you'll not produce it at the wrong time, or give it to the wrong person.'

Her caller that time was another anxious wife unwilling to disturb police or hospital. 'Helen Innes. Bob's in the second team—oh, again!'

She was away several minutes and returned looking ready to spit. 'Some women never learn! Do you know what I've just been asked? If you and I would care to join Maury Valentine and some English friends she's just discovered are staying in the hotel. She's just heard you're still here, and thinks a wee party will do us all good. Tonight! With Gairlie holding its breath! Of all the feckless, insensitive creatures! Hamish may say it's not her fault she was ruined by doting parents and then a besotted husband old enough to be her father—but I've never had any time for her. I'm sure you'll forgive my refusing for us both without bothering to consult you first.'

I heard her husband's voice behind that last remark, and wondered, without any embarrassment, how much he had told her. Embarrassment was a superficial emotion. I was now dealing in the basics. 'Thanks a lot for doing that. A party! I don't get it—or do I? Is this her antidote to anxiety? She was off to some house-party in Glasgow, I suppose she could've gone with Davie MacDonald. She's scrapped that for the search.'

'Maury Valentine let that come between her and her precious social life? Are we talking of the same woman? The search has occasioned her no anxiety! All that's now bothering her—and I quote—is the tedious blight these little escapades cast on the local atmosphere.'

'She said that?' But—she's crazy about Dougal Grant! She must realize'—I had to be careful for Dougal's sake, if not my own—'it's dodgy on the Ben right now.'

'There's but one person that woman's crazy about, dearie, and that's herself. As for scrapping any week-end plans—she said nothing to me of that, and she's not the type to hide a sacrifice, or, come to that, make one! I was very short with her. I've not my husband's endless patience and I'm not forced to act gently towards her like Dougal Grant, since she never saved my twin sister's life. And has she taken full advantage of that debt! I doubt there'll be a man more relieved than Dougal when she shortly removes to this new house she's buying on the other side of Inverness. I expect you've heard she's selling up here?'

'Yes, but'—I swallowed—'she's moving out?'

'You're not surprised? Of course, having been hospitalized, you'll not know how much time she's spent away recently. I gather the new attraction is some film man who used to work with her husband. He's been in Inverness this last month making preparations for some picture he plans to make there this summer. It's common Gairlie knowledge she now has her eye on him.' She smiled wickedly. 'She's a fine-looking woman, so if he's no hard-headed Scotsman maybe she'll have a hope!'

I said, 'I'm sorry, but I'm lost.'

'Now, why, Elizabeth?'

I told her of all I knew and had been given to understand, by Maury.

'And being a stranger you took her word for it? Elizabeth! How could you be so daft? Have you met no possessive wee bitches in London? Couldn't you've guessed by trying to get rid of you so plainly she was indirectly paying you a great compliment?'

'There was more to it than that. She always seemed around Achnagairl House. Part of the family.'

'As she once saved the life of one of his family, knowing Dougal, does that really suprise you?'

'No. Not now. But, Mrs Pringle—'

'Told you Maury Valentine was setting her cap at her beloved Professor? Well, for once, dear old Rose Pringle was right. Not that Maury ever had any hope in that quarter. Dougal may fall over backwards to repay a debt, but he's far too canny to allow himself to be entangled into marriage by a feckless creature who continues to behave like a spoilt bairn even though well turned thirty! But dear old Rosie'd not think of that. She's always been convinced any girl who so much as exchanges the time of day with a man is after his name. Didn't she even suspect you of that?'

'Yes. I thought it was just me. She was so scared I'd seduce him she got in a tiz every time she'd to leave us alone together during my first week.'

Mrs MacAlistair laughed. 'Without disrespect to your charms, dearie, you'd have a job! Life changes slowly in the Highlands, and though you might occasionally find the Highland gentleman who'd allow himself to be seduced by, or to seduce, a guest under his own roof, you'd not find

him under the roof of Achnagairl House! Poor old Rosie! No wonder she
made such an unhappy marriage since she knows so little about men,
even now. Does she seriously believe there's a match in the making
between those two?'

'Yes.' I didn't hesitate. 'So did I.'

She was a heavy smoker. She lit another cigarette and inhaled
thoughtfully. 'Maybe it's something in the Gairlie air. Would you like to
know why you really got that invitation tonight?' I nodded. 'Maury
Valentine is now of the opinion there's a match in the making between
you and Archie MacDonald. The future Mrs Archie is worth knowing.'

'No!'

'Obviously, dearie.' She smiled very pleasantly. 'So I'll tell you
something I certainly shouldn't. It occurred your first night in hospital.
Dougal was with you when Maury rang him and he took the call in
Hamish's office. Hamish had no wish to overhear, but he was waiting in
the corridor and he did. Maury had asked in friends and wanted Dougal
to join the party. Hamish said the roof nearly came off Gairlie Hospital!'
She rubbed her hands together. 'I wish I'd been a fly on the wall!
Hamish said he'd never heard a man so angry—and after that it was no
surprise to us when we heard she was selling up and moving on. Not that
that stopped her demanding or getting further assistance from Dougal,
since he'd never let his personal feelings intrude on an old debt—oh,
'phone!' She vanished, and was back before I had properly taken any of
this in. 'The first is down. Matron says you may go over now.'

'God bless her!' I jumped up. 'You don't mind?'

'I just wish I could join you, but doctors' wives disturb the staff, and
I'm so out of date I'd probably even make the tea wrong. Away with
you—and good luck!'

The student strapped to the canvas and metal stretcher was
semi-conscious. He was suffering from exposure, a broken ankle, and
multiple grazes. Two other young men came in with him. They had not
been in the climbing party, as they had come up to ski. They were about
twenty but looked younger as they were scared. Their anoraks were
strung round with ropes, climbing irons, and ice-axes, all new and
unused. They told me they had grabbed everything they thought might
be useful in their main camp and gone with the eight other skiers to
offer their services to the leader of the rescue-party. 'Some little fair
chap called Charlie. Decent little chap, but he said his lot could cope and
told us all to wait at base. The others are still there with Dick Evans, our
ski-ing boss, but as John, Tom, and me are the only three from Taunton,
as John was down we thought we'd better stick with him. He looks dead
dodgy. He's going to be all right, isn't he, Nurse?' The speaker looked at

the white physiotherapist's overall Matron had lent me. 'Or are you a doctor?'

'Nurse.' We were then in Dr MacAlistair's office. My main job was note-taking. I gave them more tea, then sat at the desk. 'What's John's full name and address? Age? Does he live with his parents? Have they a telephone? Good.' I handed the answers over the telephone to Matron after filling in John's admission card, and asking for their own personal details.

They waited until I had put them down. 'Why us?' asked the one called Tom. 'We're not patients.'

'Your families'll be glad to know that.'

'My God, I never thought of that! Poor old Mum and Dad! Will this be on the news?'

'Been. B.B.C. and I.T.V. at six. No-one can take any pictures yet, but weren't there reporters at base?'

They said only God knew who hadn't been at base. 'It's been snowing like hell there the whole bloody time. That chap running the show seemed to know his stuff. Does he?'

I said, 'His name's Charlie Urquhart.'

'THE Charlie Urquhart?' they chorused.

'Aye, laddies.' Dr MacAlistair was in the doorway. 'Were you not aware he's a Gairlie man?'

'No. Sorry, Doctor,' apologized Tom. 'We haven't been to Scotland before, of course, we've heard of him! We're from England.'

'A country I've heard of. Now then—your friend is on his way to a ward. As he'll be happier to see faces he knows near his bed, you may sit with him a while, if you sit quietly. If not, out you go. That clear?'

'Fair enough, sir.' The second student had spoken. 'This exposure— everyone keeps talking about exposure—what exactly is it?'

'Exposure is a severe chilling of the body surfaces leading to a progressive fall in the body temperature. Unhalted'—MacAlistair looked from one student to the other—'it leads to death.'

The speaker swallowed. 'Can it happen any time? In the open?'

'It can happen any time to any person exposed to cold, or high wind, or fatigue, or a combination of all three, in the open air. Tell me, were you laddies out dancing again last night?'

'Only a few of us. Only till midnight.'

MacAlistair nodded to himself. 'Come and sit with your friend John.'

On his return he sat on the desk-edge. 'In bed at midnight. Up again at four-thirty. What kind of a preparation for a long climb was that?'

I said, 'But even though it's his first time in charge, surely their leader realized the climbers had to get to bed early?'

'I've no doubt he did. I've no doubt he checked them in their bedrolls before retiring himself. So he'd not have seen them later sneaking out the back and away to the dancing. No healthy laddie thinks to waste a holiday week-end in sleep—as I well remember from my own student days. An experienced leader will always sleep with one eye open for such pranks. A young man suddenly taking over his first party has much to learn. Ah!' He lifted the jangling receiver. 'Aye, Matron. Good.' He replaced it. 'Three more on the way. Exposure and multiple grazes, but no other visible injuries.'

It was dark when the next three arrived, and much colder. One of the ambulance men told me there was now a blizzard round the Ben. From that moment my fear reached saturation point.

I did my note-taking in Casualty. Dr MacAlistair, young Mr Stewart, Sister Casualty, and Staff Nurse Smith were working in pairs. Smith was as surprised to see me as I was to see her.

She sniffed. 'Why haven't you gone?'

I asked, 'Why aren't you? You've got nights off.'

We didn't trouble to answer each other.

'Miss Wade.' MacAlistair beckoned me. 'After you've handed on their names take a stool and a feeder of tea and feed yon laddie lying on his face.'

The student's name was Michael. He came from Bristol. He said he had slipped so far on his back that he had felt he'd travelled the entire face of the mountain. 'The men who found me had seen where I came off. They said I'd gone about five hundred feet.' He twisted his head to try to see over his shoulder. 'It hurt like stink until they gave me that shot. Have I bashed myself up much?'

Beneath the dressings the skin was hanging in ribbons from the entire surface of his back. 'Quite a bit, but you'll mend. Have some more tea.'

'Thanks. I'm thirsty as hell.' He had an attractive fair face and did not look much older than Robin. He was nineteen. 'English, aren't you?' I nodded. 'Worked here long?'

'Not long.'

When he had been moved to a ward and Casualty was empty again I asked MacAlistair, 'Could he have slid five hundred feet and survived?'

'It's possible. Only last month we'd a man actually drop that distance and sustain no more than a twisted thumb. In the same week we'd another fall thirty feet and to his death.' His head jerked round as Sister Casualty answered the telephone. 'Only one? Well, one is one.'

A posse of anxious friends accompanied the next admission. Charlie Urquhart had sent a message to base insisting that only Dick Evans, the skiers' leader, and one student of his choosing should remain with the reserve rescuers.

'A wise move from a wise mountain man,' MacAlistair told me

privately. 'Charlie wants them well away before the night sets in and they take it into their well-meaning but foolish young heads to creep off in the darkness, lend a hand themselves, and add to the number still missing.'

That admission was seriously injured. He had a fractured skull and was growing spastic from brain damage. At each of his incoherent mutters and twitches the posse winced in unison. The warm air of the little Casualty Department was heavy with a mixture of wet clothes, wet bodies, wet ropes, wet irons, wet wood, and the faint but unmistakable smell of fear.

MacAlistair looked up over his mask. 'The lot into my office, Miss Wade,' he muttered. 'Off you go, laddies, away with the nurse! We'll attend to your friend.'

They trailed after me, looking back as they did so. Mechanically they accepted mugs of hot tea, gave me their names and addresses, parents' telephone numbers, and, when possible, addresses of parents themselves on holiday. They did not talk amongst themselves as I dealt with each in turn. They watched what I was doing intently, and when I suggested they remove their anoraks, gloves, and scarves and drape them on the radiators to dry I had to repeat myself before they slowly started unzipping.

One had very dark and very long side-boards and a blue chin. He looked a little older than the others. I had taken down too many names and ages to identify him yet. I learnt later he was the oldest student. He was twenty-one, reading economics, and his name was Nicholas Hawkins. His home was in Exmouth.

He roused himself with a visible effort. 'Nurse, I've just remembered—George Tucker's parents aren't home this week-end. They've gone down to Cornwall.'

George Tucker was the head injury.

'Any idea where in Cornwall?'

He shook his head. I asked the others. They shook their heads.

I asked, 'Any idea what kind of a car his parents have? Or, better still, the number?'

'No. Sorry. I say, Nurse—how bad is he?'

'Quite honestly, I can't answer that as I don't know the answer. Dr MacAlistair—he's the big one—will be along soon, I'm sure. He'll tell you.'

'He won't mind us asking? You know what doctors are.'

'Yes,' I said. 'But this one won't. He's good.'

Matron's line was busy, so I took my notes along to her office. In the lodge Mr Cameron and the night porter were side-by-side at the switchboard dealing with the non-stop stream of incoming English calls.

Gordon, in a theatre gown and white plimsolls, was whisking an empty
stretcher trolley away from the men's wards and back to Casualty as I
crossed the hall.

The secretary of a local welfare organization was in the office with
Matron. He was saying, '... beds offered and waiting will accommodate
all eighteen sets of parents—' when Matron saw me waiting in the
doorway and held out a hand for my notes.

I told her about George Tucker's parents.

'They should come up if they can. We need them. I'll ask the police.'
Matron picked up her receiver. 'Sergeant Cameron, please.'

Recrossing the hall, I met Craig. She said Sister Kilsyth was running
her ward single-handed, Lewis was doubling between Women's Surgical
and Men's Medical, and she herself was in Men's Surgical.

'How's your old lady?'

'She began to rally about six. Still in coma, but still very much with
us. Sister's coping.' We turned quickly as Mr Cameron tapped on his
glass window and held up two fingers. 'I'm muddled, Elizabeth. How
many's that?'

'Seven down, eleven to come.'

'God willing,' said Craig, hurrying on.

The waiting students were sitting on the floor and leaning against
the walls when I took them in fresh tea and sandwiches about an hour
later. A couple got up to make room for the tray on the desk. One was
Nicholas Hawkins. 'Is George any better?'

'He's sleeping.' Dr MacAlistair had come in. 'If he's not much better,
laddie, at least he's no worse. But I've good news for you. Six more
coming in in two ambulances, and one of the six is your deputy leader,
Mr Morgan.'

They were all on their feet. 'How are they all?'

Dr MacAlistair shrugged. 'Ask me after I've examined them. In the
meantime you eat those fine sandwiches the nurse has made for you, or
you'll be hurting a bonnie lassie's feelings.' He caught my eye. 'A word
with you, Nurse.'

I followed him into the corridor. He closed the door. 'You've had just
about enough. Time you were away to your bed.'

'Doctor, no, please! I'm not tired.'

'You're not a good liar, either. Ach, the red light is flickering. The
ambulances are turning in. I'll see what we've got, then deal with you.'

Mr Morgan was unconscious from exposure and a blow on the head
from falling rock. His skull was intact, but his right tibia and fibula were
fractured in two places.

The official leader's son was amongst the six. He had a more moderate degree of exposure and a broken ankle. His voice was husky, but he couldn't stop talking.

'Give him some lukewarm tea, Miss Wade,' said Sister Casualty, 'and let him talk himself out. It takes some that way.'

For one very brief moment I remembered how much I had talked myself. I wasn't sure which hurt more—the thought of Dougal then or my own blindness. Then I thought of Dougal now, knew the answer, and stopped thinking.

Between sips of tea the boy told me he was eighteen and had been climbing with his father for three years. 'I climbed in Wales last summer with Bill Morgan. He's good. It was hellish bad luck his slipping in that first snow this morning. He'd told us earlier we must all stick together, and we meant to, but suddenly the whole bloody world was driving white. My goggles weren't any good. I couldn't see a thing even when I took 'em off. No kidding, Nurse, I couldn't even see the bloody mountain more than a yard up or down. Then it stopped a bit, and the only person I could see anywhere was the man hitched to me. Then'—he shuddered—'he slipped. I felt the rope pulling me after him, but the belay held. Then I saw John in a sort of heap on a ledge below. He was out cold when I got down to him, and I couldn't get him round. I stuck with him until it started snowing again. Then I thought I'd better get down for help. I stuck an ice-axe in the snow to mark him, unhitched myself from the rope, and spread that out to use it as well. Then I fell.' He stopped for breath. 'Have they found him yet? His name's John French. I tried to ask when they found me, but I hadn't any voice.'

'He was first in. He's doing all right.'

'Good.' He sighed. 'Poor old Dad! He's going to be even sicker over this than he was at Carlisle. Tough on old Bill Morgan. Not his fault. How is he?'

'Coming along nicely. Have another drink.'

'Thanks. Helps my throat. Bloody sore.' He smiled painfully. 'I yelled for hours. I couldn't shift as my foot was jammed. I'd smashed my torch when I fell and my whistle'—he produced the frayed end of his lanyard—'don't know when it came off. So I just lay there and shouted till my voice ran out. I couldn't even croak when I heard them looking for me. I saw their signal flashes. I couldn't signal back. That was the worst. I thought I'd be left out to die.' He gripped my hand. 'I nearly died then from sheer bloody funk. I was praying like crazy. They seemed to be moving away, and then they came back. I wanted to tell 'em about John, but I couldn't. I heard someone say something about finding a glove. It wasn't mine, but they came back and searched near me, and that time they found me. Funny that, isn't it?' Then he asked the question all those who were conscious had asked, 'How many still up there, Nurse?'

Again Casualty was cleared. Men's Surgical could take no more emergency beds. The emergency row down the centre of Men's Medical was half filled. Mrs Spearn and the new patient in my room had been moved into emergency positions in Women's Medical. Isol. One and Two were now small double wards. When I asked to help in the wards Dr MacAlistair said if I so much as put my head into one he would send me straight back to his wife. 'I'm not joking, lassie.'

I knew he wasn't, so I removed myself to make more tea for the Cas. Staff.

Mr Stewart and Smith had vanished to the theatre to deal with those requiring immediate surgery. In the lulls Dr MacAlistair did his night round. During one a middle-aged woman was admitted with acute appendicitis. A consultant physician attached to the hospital, who had arrived earlier to offer his services as anything from house physician to porter, was now giving the anaesthetics for Mr Stewart. 'As routine an occurrence,' remarked Dr MacAlistair to me, 'as the arrival of an acute abdomen in any hospital crisis. She'll have to be done tonight.' He sat on a bench. 'In any wee hospital the staff learn to resemble a stage crowd. It's a hard life, though I doubt we'd change it.' He patted the seat beside him. 'Rest your feet whilst we're empty and quiet.'

The quiet applied only to Casualty. Outside the wind was screaming and the loch waves were thundering. 'Such a ghastly night!'

'It could be worse. There's no mist, and that's the real killer. That stops even the trained teams now working on the Ben.' He sat sideways to look at me beside him. 'That was why Dougal Grant had to sit out that night with you. No mist, and he'd have had you up that wee climb on his back in no time.' He paused, briefly. 'You'll no doubt be aware that had he not been with you that night, ill though you've been in here, you'd not have got here in the first place.'

'I realized—no—I didn't. I knew I owed him a lot. Not my life. I do?'

'Aye.' He got up and walked over to a window, then faced me. 'No easy position for any man to find himself.'

'Not easy—because he saved my life?'

He nodded. 'Since that's the greatest debt any man or woman can owe another, the burden of your gratitude will weigh heavily on any man of honour and pride.' He came and stood over me. 'He's never referred to that debt to my knowledge, but naturally his medical experience will long have informed him of the fact.'

'I wish to God I'd realized this sooner!'

'If you'll forgive an elderly physician with a daughter your age talking to you as he would to his daughter, I'd say it may not prove such a bad thing that your decision to stay was made before you did. Gratitude can as easily force the hand of a generous recipient as it can tie the hands of a generous donor. Of course, there are some men who would not be averse to taking advantage of a lassie's gratitude. I would never include Dougal Grant in that breed—' He lunged for the suddenly ringing 'phone. 'Aye, Matron?' His eyes lit up. 'I will. Yes. Grand news!'

I jumped up. 'All down?'

'At the rest-hut. As that was the final call it came from there and not base, as the others. All exposure cases, but they're getting them under control, and no other injuries. The "recall to base" is going out now. In a few minutes the searchers still on the mountain will be making their own way down.'

Relief numbed me. 'How will they hear any signal in this gale?'

'You think they've not been keeping one eye cocked all this time for the wee firework display?'

'Fireworks?'

'A series of greens followed by thunderflashes and whistle signals as well. Ach, that's a weight off my mind!' He stretched his shoulders. 'A pack of bairns, the lot! They could've been my own sons. The Tucker laddie's not too good, but given time he should do. Thank God I'll not now have to face any English parents tomorrow with the words that've been lurking at the back of my mind since that alarm call came in. I've had to say them too often, and it's made worse by the laddie being healthy and on holiday.' He sat on the bench, his heavy body sagging with relief. 'It'll be hours before they get 'em to base and here. I'm not letting you wait on that, and nor is Matron. She's just asked me to thank you kindly and pack you off.'

'Doctor, please, I don't want to go.'

He looked up at me. 'Lassie, you've learnt fast, but you've still a lot to learn. Listen. After the victims are down and away the search-party has to re-muster, record individual reports, bring back, clean, check, and replenish the communal equipment before stacking it away ready for immediate use. There's no saying how soon it may be required again. All that'll take time, and weary men need to take their time. The searchers'll most literally need to get their feet back on the ground again. They'll need a wee chat together, a wash, a fag, a cup of tea, maybe a dram or two. They'll not have touched a drop whilst they've been up, but who'll deny their right to a few once down?'

'I see.'

'I thought you would. It'll be morning,' he continued, 'before Charlie Urquhart walks in here to take a look at the rescued for himself, as is his custom before returning to his home after a search. So away with you to my good wife and tell her to expect me when she sees me, which may be for my breakfast.'

'I'll tell her. Thanks for letting me stay around. I just wish I could've done more to help.'

'You've done all you could, and a lot more than you should.'

I looked all round the empty Casualty. It still smelt of wetness and ether and sweat. 'If you hadn't let me, by now I'd be up the wall.'

'Aye,' said Dr MacAlistair, 'some such idea did cross my mind. Just the once or twice, you'll understand.'

14. Dougal stays for Breakfast

'A cup of tea, Elizabeth?'

I opened one eye. Mrs MacAlistair wore a blue tweed dress and was holding a small tea-tray. Isobel MacAlistair's bedroom was flooded with light. 'Good morning.' I sat up. 'Any more news?'

'All safely down, and though the boy with the fractured skull's not too well, Hamish said on the 'phone just now that he could be a lot worse. His parents are on their way up, along with about fourteen others and Mr Morgan's young wife. As for reporters! You can't move in Gairlie without knocking one down this morning, and if they don't stop pestering my long-suffering husband, that may yet happen! Did you sleep well? I wish you looked it, dearie. Stay where you are, and I'll bring up your breakfast.'

'Thanks, but I'd rather get up.' I looked at the window. 'The storm's gone.'

'It went out with the tide at dawn.' She walked over to the window. The room was on the first floor and at the front of the house. 'There's Sister Kilsyth returning after a couple of hours off and looking as if she could use a month's sleep. Ah! There's Charlie's car leaving.' She leant out to wave, then closed the window. 'Do you really want to get up? Or are you merely being polite?'

I hesitated, recollecting my first morning in Achnagairl. Possibly the MacAlistairs preferred breakfast to themselves. 'I wasn't, but I haven't really any strong feelings. Which'll be easier?'

'To have you down. We both enjoy company at breakfast.' She smiled at me. 'Maybe I'm being unfair, but I've generally found it a more English characteristic to be a bear with a sore head in the early morning. Take your tea quietly, and then come down—and don't be surprised if

Hamish sends you back to bed for the morning. Oh, I'd forgotten, I've a message for you from him.' She stopped in the doorway. 'He's seen Dougal Grant around the hospital, but he's had no opportunity to tell him you're here with us. You'd best ring Achnagairl and explain directly you're up.'

Suddenly, I remembered everything. I lost my nerve. 'Won't he have gone to bed? I don't want to disturb him. Perhaps later?'

'I doubt he'll catch up on lost sleep until tonight. As it's fortunately the Sabbath, most of the searchers'll be able to take today easily, but were it a working day they'd be straight off to their jobs after a hot bath and change.'

'They don't get given extra time off?'

'My dear, it's only very recently they stopped losing their pay on searches. They get given no time off for recovery, but at least now, where necessary, they do get their pay made up to them.'

'I'd no idea!'

'How could you? But you should ring Dougal as soon as possible. You were previously his guest, and it would be most impolite to let him hear from others that you're here with us—and there's no doubt he will, very shortly. Gairlie's a small place, and we're all interested in the affairs of our neighbours, but not only because we're busy-bodies. Being so isolated, we're all greatly dependent on each other, so the concern of one concerns all.'

I knew she was right. I just wished I hadn't made such a fuss about getting up. 'I'll ring as soon as I'm dressed.'

I started rehearsing over my tea.

'Dougal, this is Elizabeth. I'm still here because—' and there I dried up.

I leapt out of bed and dressed at the double. That occupied my hands, but was no help to inspiration.

The weather had not stopped Davie MacDonald from getting to Glasgow. During one of the lulls last night Sister Casualty had remarked on hearing he was back at his hotel. But Dougal's being in medicine stopped my spinning a splendid tale about Gairlie Hospital grinding to a halt without my help last night. I could have fooled Archie, but no doctor, that it took an S.R.N. to make tea, write notes, and handle the odd feeding-cup.

I roamed my borrowed room. Tell him the truth? Oh, sure! 'Dougal, this is Elizabeth. I couldn't leave until I knew you were safe, because I suddenly discovered that if anything happened to you I'd want to die.' Why not go over and ring from the hospital? Then Gordon as well as Dougal would need acute shock therapy.

The front-door bell rang. I looked out, but the porch roof was in the way. Mrs MacAlistair called, 'Can you get that? It'll be Hamish without his key, and if I leave my bacon it'll burn to a frizzle!'

'Sure!' I ran down and unlocked the front door. 'Good morning, Doc—' I swallowed fast. 'Hallo, Dougal!'

He was still in climbing clothes and as transfixed on that doorstep as on his own at our first meeting. His orange anorak with the huge black L.G.M.C. across the chest was as wet and crumpled as on that former occasion; his boots were as scuffed; his ice-axe was fixed through the same leather belt; the white Eiger climbing helmet in his hand still had its attached headlamp; he was still wearing the medical kit on his back, and the haversack had a large red cross on a white ground. The white was as grey as his unshaven face. Everything was the same, apart from his immediate expression. For one unguarded moment when I opened the door he had looked at me as he had looked at the sun that morning we saw it rise over the hills.

Then he was smiling politely. 'Good morning, Elizabeth. This is a nice surprise. Hamish, didn't tell me you were a guest in his house. I should've guessed he'd persuade you to change your mind what with yesterday's weather.'

'Wasn't it shocking?' Mrs MacAlistair had joined us. 'Dougal, how good to see you safely back! Come in, come in! What's that? Your boots? My dear man, with three growing laddies and Hamish to tramp all over them, my floors have learnt to thrive on heavy boots! You'll join us for breakfast, of course.'

Dougal stepped just over the threshold. 'It's very kind of you, Margaret, but I'm not fit for human society in these clothes or with this beard. I called as Hamish put his head out of a window just now and said if I was passing would I tell you he hopes to be over in about twenty minutes.' He glanced at me, then back at her. 'May I return when I'm more presentable?'

Mrs MacAlistair said that with due respect she had never heard such nonsense! 'How else would you be dressed after twenty-odd hours on the Ben? You'll be weary and hungry, and I refuse to consider your leaving my house without a hot meal. I can imagine what Hamish would say if I did! Have you dry sweaters under that anorak? Then take it off, man! What's that I smell? Oh, my precious porridge! Hamish's day'll be ruined—' She backed kitchenwards. 'Elizabeth, look after him for me! There's a fire in the front room—close the windows—forgive me—' and she vanished.

Dougal and I looked at each other. We could have been total strangers suddenly left to entertain each other in a strange house. Dead polite strangers. I offered to help him with his haversack. He said, thank you, he could manage. He deposited his helmet on the hall table, unhitched the haversack, unzipped his anorak, folded it carefully outside in so as not to dampen the table polish, and smoothed his hair with both hands. 'Fortunately, I'd a wash at the police station, but'—he fingered his chin—'sorry about this. One night and I look as if I've been on the meths.'

'It's being so dark,' I told him brightly and tritely.

The log fire in the sitting-room was going well. I took rather a long time to close the windows. The early-morning air was tangy and unused, the sky pale blue, and the loch smooth as blue silk. The few lights still on in the hospital looked old and pale.

Dougal was behind me. 'Grand morning.'

I turned, and he backed. 'Lovely. Incredible after yesterday.'

'Often the way of it.'

That took care of the weather.

'Dougal, do sit down. You must be exhausted.'

'Just weary. I'd rather stand.' He surveyed the comfortable and slightly battered room as if playing Pelmanism. 'I'm glad you let yourself be persuaded to stay on. Has any time-limit been settled?'

'Not yet.' I sat on the arm of a chair.

'No doubt Hamish was too busy to get round to it yesterday. Did Davie MacDonald cancel your reservation?'

'I imagine so. He told Dr MacAlistair he would.' I then thanked him for that arrangement and asked why he had not told me he was taking me to London. 'I thought you were staying in Glasgow.'

'Why should I want to do that?'

I said carefully, 'It seemed a reasonable idea. Clearly, it wasn't. Why didn't you tell me?' I repeated.

'I intended doing so on our drive. I said nothing earlier as I thought it might worry you health-wise, or make you feel forced to remain up here until there could be no question of your being fit enough to travel alone.'

'You were just going to do another round trip?'

'Aye.'

I smiled slightly. 'Keep this up, and you'll be British Railways' pin-up.'

'Maybe they'll name a train after me.' He had been holding his hands behind his back. He let them now hang at his sides. 'Of course, you've let Martha's know?'

'Sorrow and grief! I forgot!' I looked at the clock on the mantelpiece. 'Matron'll be expecting me any minute now.'

'No. Not for at least another hour. When I saw her I told her we'd have breakfast somewhere first.'

'That's a break—though God knows what she'll say this time.'

'Since you've been detained under your doctor's orders, there's not very much she can say.'

It was not moral cowardice alone that made me let that one ride. I had noticed the condition of the inside of his left hand. 'How did you get all those cuts and grazes on your left palm?'

He gave it a cursory glance. 'Just carelessness. I lost a glove.'

'It was your glove!'

'What do you mean?'

I explained, then added, 'Even if it was someone else's wasn't it fantastically lucky it dropped where it did?'

He didn't answer at once. He just looked at me in silence for some seconds. Then he asked very quietly, 'Elizabeth, were you working in the hospital last night?'

'Pottering would be the better word.'

'So? And until what time did you potter?'

His 'r's' now would have done credit to Dr MacAlistair. Recollecting Joe's letter, I hedged. 'I'm not sure, exactly. Not very late.'

He frowned, and his eyes suddenly looked much darker and his chin more blue. 'Didn't the leader's son go down in that batch of six?'

'Yes.'

'As I recall, it was eleven before they were away from base, according to Charlie's records. Obviously you were still working when they arrived—'

'Dougal, not working!'

He ignored my interruption. 'Were you there when the final call was put through from the rest-hut?'

'Only just. They slung me out directly after.'

'Good God Almighty! So I should bloody well hope! Small wonder you're so white and exhausted this morning! And here I've been mentally congratulating Hamish MacAlistair on his professional wisdom in keeping you here under his eye even though he's temporarily no hospital bed for you! Wisdom! The kindest thing I can now say is that the man must've taken leave of his senses.'

Despite Joe's letter, Mrs MacAlistair last evening, and the obvious fact that there was nothing like physical fatigue for taking the temper to flash-point, I was dumbfounded. His self-control had always seemed to me so absolute; even that moment on the doorstep had been only one moment; until now nothing would have persuaded me he would ever really let rip.

'Dougal,' I said, 'you don't understand—'

'Och, too bloody right I don't!' His voice shook with rage. 'How do you expect me to understand how an experienced physician came to allow a girl straight out of a hospital bed after a serious illness to have any part in the kind of work such an avalanche of emergency admissions must've occasioned over the road last night? There's but one element in this I do understand—and it's one I find singularly unpleasant! But I well understand that had you had any family, or even friends, with you yesterday to protect you from the consequences of your own generous nature, there's not one person in Gairlie Hospital who'd have dared suggest you lend a hand—'

'No-one suggested. I offered.'

'That I can believe!' He all but spat the words. 'Being well acquainted with your sweet, daft way of plunging in to help others regardless of the cost to yourself! But that's immaterial. What's not is the plain fact that you weren't strong enough to be allowed to work last night—as your appearance this morning provides incontrovertible proof. To have taken such an advantage of you was bloody monstrous—as I shall certainly tell Hamish and Matron at the earliest opportunity!'

'Dougal, for God's sake, cool off!' I got off the chair-arm, and my legs felt as peculiar as on my first day out of bed. 'Mrs MacAlistair'll be in any minute—you must let me explain. You've got this all wrong. No-one took any advantage of me—and if I look like the wrath of God this morning, that's not because of any work I did—'

'For God's sake, girl! Do you take me for an inexperienced student laddie incapable of assessing the clinical evidence presented to me by my own eyes? Do you imagine the fact that I've been ham-strung by ethics has spared me from observing every single sign and symptom you've produced throughout the course of your illness? You've no more need to explain you were fighting for your life as well as your breath when I'd to sit there, helpless, and watch you in that oxygen tent!'

I had not wept in another person's presence since my grandfather died. That particular wall had remained intact, even with Joe. It was the thought of my first two nights in that tent that knocked away the wall's foundations. Without warning, tears poured down my face, and I could not stop them. I flopped on to the chair-arm and wept over the back of the chair.

'No, Elizabeth, no! I shouldn't have spoken like that—but I never thought to hurt you.' Dougal's voice was urgent and wholly altered. 'But you don't have to turn away and hide your tears from me, lassie. Come.' He half pulled, half lifted me into his arms and stroked my hair as I wept into the curve of his neck and shoulder. 'It's all right, lassie,' he said over and over again. Then, 'I'm sorry I lost my temper, but you know it was not with you, even though you bore the brunt, and for that alone I can't forgive myself—but to distress you like this doesn't bear thinking! But it'll be all right—we'll sort this out the way you wish—it'll be all right.'

I knew it would. I just couldn't stop crying to tell him. The comfort of his arms had unleashed years of unshed tears. I had had occasional crying jags before, but nothing like this, and so utterly beyond my immediate control.

His hold tightened as I shook with great gasping sobs. 'Calm down, lassie, calm down.' His voice was very gentle, and he laid his face against my hair. 'You must calm down for your own sake. Your reserves are much lower than you realize. Go on tearing yourself apart like this and you'll put yourself back in a hospital bed. Do you hear me, lassie?'

'Uh-huh. Sorry—' I gasped, 'so sorry.'

He caught his breath, and as his lips were so close to my ear I caught his barely audible, 'My dearest love, don't say that to me after what I've just done to you.'

I stopped weeping as abruptly as I had started. I was still gasping, but I no more bothered with that than with the disastrous effect the deluge must have had on my face. I raised my head to look at him. 'Am I that, Dougal?'

Suddenly he looked much older and very tired, and his eyes were guarded. 'That's something else I shouldn't have said. It's of no consequence.' He smiled with his lips. 'Just add it, along with my earlier lamentable display, to the clinical picture you must now be forming of a post-climbing syndrome.'

'Did you mean it?'

He nodded briefly.

Momentarily I was too happy for speech. I just relaxed against him, and if he hadn't gripped me I would have hit the floor. I said, 'Thanks,' and smiled at him.

'Elizabeth, why are you thanking me?'

'Dougal,' I said, 'dear Dougal. I realize you're nearly out on your two feet, and I've just given you hell throwing that attack of the vapours—'

'You mustn't say that—'

'Dougal, listen!' I managed to free a hand and put it lightly over his lips. 'I know you weren't here yesterday, so you can't know the hell I went through for you—and though you may have been suffering from the chronic and dead-wrong Gairlie fixation about Archie and me, I still can't believe any post-climbing syndrome can make you that thick! Why do you think I've been drenching you? What do you think I'm doing in your arms?' I moved my hand, and his expression now nearly made me weep again. 'That's right,' I said as if he had spoken. 'That why I had to stay yesterday. No-one persuaded me. I just refused to go—and that was just because I couldn't leave you. That wasn't because of all you'd done for me—quite apart from saving my life. I didn't even realize you'd done that, till late last night when Dr MacAlistair told me. Yes, it was late, but if I hadn't badgered them into letting me hang around across the road I probably would've been back in some hospital bed somewhere by today.'

He shook his head in astonished wonder, and he flushed, dully. 'You were so anxious for me?'

'Hollow with fear.' I told him exactly how I had felt yesterday about Gairlie as well as himself. 'I was ashamed to be so selfishly concerned mainly for you, but that didn't stop my thinking each time we heard more were down, thank God, he's that much nearer to coming back. I'd no idea then you'd be coming back—to me. I just wanted you back in one piece. I don't know if that makes sense?'

'If not in one way, certainly in another. You'll recall you were on the D.I.L., and I, my darling, was in hell.' His eyes searched my face. 'Even though I thought you if not actually in love, as near as made no matter, with Archie MacDonald.'

'No. For a bit, a bit fixated, as he was with me. I snapped out of it some time back, and he's well over it now. I expect you've heard he's now in Washington?'

'No. Though Davie did tell me when I first rang him yesterday morning that he'd a letter in the morning's post saying some friend of Archie MacDonald's would be coming up from Monday to use his room and tackle for a couple of weeks. Davie was not best pleased, as he likes to vet his guests. I assumed Archie MacDonald was remaining in England to be near you.'

'He flew to Washington the day you took the kids down.' His expression tightened. 'No, Dougal! Like I said—all over by mutual consent.'

His expression relaxed. 'The man must be daft, but if this was so— and, of course, I believe you—why were you so anxious to return to England?'

'Various reasons.' I thought of mentioning Maury, and instantly dismissed the thought as too unimportant. 'The two main ones were my impression that you'd had a surfeit of me and my own desire not to add more to the staggering bill I already owed you.'

'You didn't realize I was only too willing to do anything I could for you? Och, lassie, if I've been thick you've been plain daft!'

'I know that now. But it was only yesterday I began to see myself clearly. You took until just now. Previously, I've been certain you did all you did purely out of your stern Calvinistic sense of duty.'

'You were not only wrong about myself, you were confusing the Highlands with the Lowlands. Calvin's theories didn't penetrate the Highlands to anything like the same extent.'

'That so?' I smiled. 'That's what comes of doing only modern history from the third form up—and of being an ignorant foreigner, and also,' I added quickly, as he looked about to protest and there was something I had to say, 'of being me, personally. Being me, it was far easier to think you just hide-bound by duty, rather than recognize the disturbing truth about you and myself. I discovered yesterday that I'd loved you for some time—my subconscious knew that—but consciously I didn't want to love you or any other man yet. Love hurts. I didn't want to be hurt. Yesterday taught me not only is there no way round that one, but if there should be I wouldn't now take it.'

He took a long breath. 'Knowing how much life has already hurt you, and at such a tragically early and impressionable age, I'd find your courage now incredible, did I not know you so well.' He drew me closer. 'You'd the impression I'd had a surfeit of you? You'd no idea the thought of your leaving Gairlie seemed to tear the heart from my body? Or that I wanted to take you to London not only to look after you, but to be with you that much longer?'

'I didn't guess any of that.'

Not just one sun, but a whole galaxy, was rising for us both.

He said, 'There's something more you couldn't guess. Yesterday, when we were at base, I heard Davie's car had been seen leaving Gairlie. The thought that you'd gone so distracted me that at first I could think of nothing else. Then I found I'd lost my glove and had consciously to thrust you out of my mind. When a climber lets his concentration break he's in trouble. I'd a job to do that didn't include adding to Charlie's problems with another accident. But the effort of pushing you out, mentally, exhausted me far more than any climb I've ever done. When we got down this morning I felt like an old man—and when you opened the door to me—Archie MacDonald or no Archie MacDonald—it took all the control I possess not to grab you—like this.' His arms tightened still more as he spoke. 'And when we first came in here I didn't dare touch you. But seeing you looking so frail and weary and lovely, though I'm not normally a violent man, and though Hamish MacAlistair's over twenty years my senior, had he come back too soon I could willingly have hit him for what I thought he'd done to you.'

'That was one impression I did get right. You looked as if you couldn't wait to set the heather alight.'

'Maybe so, though it was not the heather that was already alight then—and right now.' He kissed me, hard, and having started it seemed as if that was something he couldn't stop. Then suddenly, he raised his face from mine. 'My darling,' he murmured anxiously, 'I'd forgotten this shocking wee beard! Have I left one inch of soft skin on your bonnie face? Why didn't you tell me to stop?'

'I didn't want you to stop. I like your wee beard—even if it does feel like wire wool.'

'So?' His eyes lit with passionate laughter. 'At least you'll know what to expect in the early mornings when we're married. That is—will you have me, sweetheart?'

'Thank you, I'd love to.'

He sighed contentedly. 'That's a mercy, as you've got me, lassie. You've had me since I first saw you standing on my own staircase, though the love I'd for you then was but a shadow of the substance it is now.' He kissed me again. 'Now I can properly take care of you the way I've long wished. Now I'll never let you leave me. Will you mind not returning to England until after we're married?'

'Not in the slightest, though I've no idea what I'll do till then, and my Matron may object.'

'I'll attend to her, presently—if you leave her to me?'

'Gladly!'

'And the other wee details?'

'Of course.'

He grinned like Johnnie. 'Naturally, when we're married, you'll continue to indulge my every wish with this enchanting docility?'

'What else? You know me, love—the most docile of little women.'

'A fact I'd observed within two minutes of first meeting you. Obviously, only a meek, helpless girl could've decided to drive those kids up from Glasgow in a strange car, over strange roads, to a stranger's house, and then dealt so intelligently with Judy. And your natural submissiveness was even more apparent that time Johnnie nicked his artery and I put in an ill-timed remark, but I was made very aware of it on many other occasions. Not that you weren't politeness itself with your "Yes of course, Professor," or "Certainly, Dougal," but it was the charming expression in your beautiful eyes that told me so clearly the gentle thoughts passing through your truly docile mind.'

'Really?'

'Aye. Every time I made some arbitrary remark your look said plainly, "Drop dead, you despotic bastard!" '

'I wasn't bad as that! But you were so formal!'

'Don't you mean, bloody pompous?'

'Well, yes. But only in your own house. You were quite different that night on the hill—nearly always—in hospital.'

'On the hill I was able to hold you in my arms. Certainly, the wee plastic bag made a difference, but not all that difference at that stage of our relationship. In hospital you were ill. Back in my house you were my reluctant guest whom I could see to your bedroom door—and then had to close the bloody thing between us.'

'It was that?' I stroked his hair. 'But you made me feel sexless.'

'That's not the effect you've had constantly on me. When I'm on the defensive I always turn pompous—but there's one thing more I want to ask you. If it wasn't for Archie MacDonald or his roses, why did you seem so happy when I returned on Friday?'

'I'd enjoyed working again, I'd missed you, I was delighted to see you back. I wanted to ask if you thought I should apply for a theatre job at the hospital here. It's going shortly. That's why I didn't take up your offer to pull a string for me.'

'Is that a fact?'

'Aye. It is that, Professor.'

'And for that, my sweet, gay, brave, lovely Elizabeth, you can kiss me—and quickly now, as that sounds like Hamish returning up the path.'

'I didn't waste any time.

Nor did Dougal. Before that day was out, our wedding day was fixed for six weeks later.

15. The Bells are really ringing

I spent those six weeks with the MacAlistairs. They were good weeks.

Joe's telegram was the first reaction I had from Martha's. 'Can't wait call you auntie love Joe.'

My Matron wrote: '... delighted. As you will understand, I have been dreading having to tell you there could be no question of your returning to work in St Martha's for at least two years. ...'

Judy wrote: 'Fragmentingly fab! Can I be bridesmaid?'

Since the great majority of my fellow ex-patients lived locally, they called to give me their good wishes and not-so-small tokens in person. Young Mrs Ferguson said, 'Though that poor soul Miss Donald was convinced your Yankie laddie was the man of your choice—and I've nothing against the Yanks, you'll understand—it was no surprise to me to hear you'd chosen Professor Grant. It's not that I'm prejudiced—but there's no denying you can't beat a braw upstanding Scotsman in his prime!'

Archie answered my letter by return. He wasn't surprised either. 'Once I got back here, I figured it near as dammit, and I am real glad for you both.'

My grandfather had considered young women incapable of managing

their own business affairs, and so tied up the money he had left me that
I was unable to touch the capital until I was thirty. It was no fortune,
but handy. The income tax was one hundred and fifty a year. But in
Grandfather's will a special clause had set aside two hundred pounds to
pay for my wedding and trousseau.

Grandfather's solicitor wrote: 'Send me the bills.'

The MacAlistairs having as good as adopted me, I showed them as
well as Dougal that letter, to end the argument I had had with all three.

Isobel MacAlistair came home to meet me, and later joined her
mother, Craig, and myself in Edinburgh when we bought my
wedding-dress. Craig and I had coffee together whilst the others called
on some distant MacAlistair relative.

'My God,' she said, 'you English are a crafty lot! Did you fool us all!
Not that anyone's been surprised by your man. As Mrs Lewis says, one
look at his face when you were on the D.I.L. was enough for a blind
man! But you with your blether about imagining him promised to Mrs
Valentine! Had we not turned so hectic just then, I'd probably have seen
through your low English cunning from that alone, seeing that I've lived
in Gairlie most of my life and never heard one word of that from any
other body! Mind you, I'm not saying she's not cast for him in her
time—but she's cast for half the men in Gairlie, including my Ian at the
hotel. But they're an awful slippery lot to land, having learnt a trick or
two from the salmon—and I'm not that sure she actually wants to land
them. I'm of the opinion she gets her kicks just trying to take them away
from other women.'

'We all have our hobbies.'

'That's a fact! I hear her latest is another film man. Is it right she's
now in Spain with him?'

'Yes. Plus a whole film company. He wants to make his Highland
picture there to be sure of enough sun.'

'Och, Gordon'll be sad! He's hoping for a job as an extra. He fancied
himself as an actor, but does he ham!'

'Poor Gordon! How does he fancy Dougal and me?'

'Thrilled to bits by your spurning the flesh-pots for a hard-working
Highlander! How's the latest trop. bug opus progressing?'

'Surprisingly well, it seems, despite interruptions. He's doing a lot of
work at night.'

Mrs Pringle had called and wept on and for me. 'I was that
astonished, lassie! I'd be that satisfied—but are you strong enough to
wed? There's a wee bit of colour to your face, but you're awful frail about
the body! You'll not be thinking of bearing yet awhile?'

Later she baked and iced a magnificent three-tiered wedding-cake.

'Nine pounds of currants, Miss Elizabeth, and not one that I didna pick over myself to be sure there was no wee seed!'

All four Fentons were flying up with their father. Gairlie Grants were expected from all over Scotland. 'It'll be as bad as Celtic playing Rangers at Hampden,' grumbled Dr MacAlistair, 'but I'll get you up that aisle, Elizabeth! With my weight, I'm grand at getting through a crowd.'

On the afternoon before our wedding I was waiting with Dougal at Achnagairl for the Fentons' arrival from Inverness, when Charlie Urquhart arrived to settle some guest-ferrying problem. As Mrs Cameron wanted my advice on her wedding hat, I left the men together. When I got back to them Charlie was leaving and saying, 'We'll miss you, man, but—' He broke off. 'Festive bonnet settled, Elizabeth?'

I waited until Dougal and I were alone again in the study. 'Mind if I ask, why's Charlie going to miss you? Is the L.G.M.C. planning its next training climb whilst we're away?'

'Apparently.'

'Can't we get back for it? You haven't been up since that last search, and though I don't know exactly how much training an old climbing hand like yourself needs, presumably, like any other sport, if you're keeping it up you have to keep in training.'

'It's thoughtful of you to suggest that, Elizabeth, but it'll not be necessary to curtail our honeymoon. Charlie and I have already settled the matter between us, and in any event the precise date of the next training climb's not yet settled.'

'Then why on earth was he crying "woe, woe" just now? Suddenly I looked at him much more closely. He was standing with his back to the window, the loch, the hills, and the Ben. I glanced at the mountain over his shoulder, then back at his face. 'And why are you looking rigid? I suppose it could be pre-wedding nerves—'

'No such thing!'

'Then why?' He didn't answer. 'Dougal, you wouldn't be thinking of doing anything crazy like resigning from the L.G.M.C.?'

He was now pretending he was solid wood, which answered my question long before he did that with words. 'Why crazy? I'll have to opt out some time; now's as good as any. Naturally, pro tem, I'll have to go up on emergencies, but that'll be my lot.'

'If you lay off training and climbing for pleasure you could be right.' I walked up to him. 'Have you suddenly gone stark raving nuts? Or just got a death-wish?'

'Neither. But if you want it spelt out, I'm not putting you through hell again for my pleasure.'

I was very, very touched and very, very worried. 'My darling man, you're not doing this for me. I won't have it!'

'My darling girl, I'm sorry, but you've no say in the matter. It's my decision made of my own free will.'

I could still recognize a brick wall when I saw one, but this was no time for retreat. 'Your last word?'

'Aye.'

'Because you want to spare me from being hurt?'

'As I've said.'

I said slowly. 'Bully for you, chum! But if this is how you're going to run our married life I don't see how we can have much of a life together. We obviously can't have any kids, according to your rules—'

'Elizabeth, you're being ridiculous—'

'Oh no, I'm not! Forgotten I've done Part One midder? I've seen rows of normal deliveries. I haven't seen one in which the mother didn't go through hell for some, if not all, her labour. Since you're so determined to keep me in the cotton-wool wrappings, I'm damned if I see how you're going to get round that one. Come to that, hadn't you better get working on another self-denying ordinance before you consider getting into bed with me? You've never asked me, so I've never told you, but I happen to be a virgin.'

He coloured. 'I hate to say this, sweetheart, but this is emotional blackmail, not reasoned argument.'

'But haven't you just given me to understand reasoned argument is out? Who can argue with a man who's said his last word on a subject?'

'I'm sorry you should feel that way.'

'So am I! I want to marry you, tomorrow, but you, the man I said I'd marry, mountains, wire wool, and all! I don't want you with bits hacked off—and that's what I'll get if you chuck climbing until you're around Old Sinclair's age, and maybe not even then, as he still potters up in his own time, as he told me. I don't expect his wife enjoys it any more than Sister Kilsyth or any of the other wives—but who expects to enjoy everything and have it all for free? And what makes you think those other women can take it, but I can't?'

He said quickly, 'That question never entered into my mind—'

'Then it bloody well should've done! I know you acted with the best of intentions, but for a man who wants to spare me from being hurt you're doing a dead grotty job right now. Obviously, you don't think I love you enough to give as well as to take.'

'Elizabeth, that's not true! As if you haven't shown me—and are showing me even more now—how much I mean to you.' He reached for me with both hands. 'Have I really hurt you with this?'

'Yes. I don't like being shut out by you. Would you, by me?'

'No. I'm sorry.'

I said nothing.

He looked at me, very thoughtfully. 'Not even you can persuade me to shorten our honeymoon, but I'll be seeing Charlie again tonight. I expect he'll be able to fix the training climb for after our return.'

I knew I'd won. I knew that part would always be hell. But worth it.

Mrs Cameron's voice called, 'Here they are!'

Judy was my one bridesmaid and waiting in the MacAlistairs' hall when I came downstairs next morning. Her dress was powder blue, and she wore a wreath of blue velvet daisies on her long blonde hair. 'Elizabeth! Wowie!' She walked round me. 'You look an absolutely fab., trendy dolly! Dig that for a maxi! Uncle Dougal won't know you!'

'Never fear, lassie. I'll whisper a wee word of introduction in your uncle's ear.' Dr MacAlistair patted his portly waist. 'Here am I looking so fine in my morning coat, but not once has anyone happened to remark that I resemble a fab., trendy dolly! It's a hard life for a poor man.'

Mrs MacAlistair was in a stone-coloured outfit and matching straw sombrero. She swept Judy back into the waiting car, then returned to fiddle with my veil. 'That's perfect, dearie! Where's your posy—ah—you've it there! Are you sure you've remembered your grandfather's signet ring on that chain round your neck? That takes care of the old—your dress is new—but where's the blue? Mercy me! You must have something blue!'

'I have! my petticoat frills—look.'

'Of course! But borrowed? You'll have to borrow—Hamish—lend her something!'

I said, 'Mrs MacAlistair, you've lent me that lace handkerchief—see? You gave it to me upstairs.'

'So I did! I'd forgotten!'

'My dear,' said her husband, 'will you away to the kirk before you forget your head? We're late as it is. If we delay more the anxious bridegroom will be convinced I've absconded with his bride. Away, now!'

Mrs MacAlistair kissed me. 'Don't be nervous, dearie—you look so pretty—there's nothing to be nervous about—' She dropped her handbag and gloves. 'Just keep calm and enjoy your own wedding.' She looked round wildly. 'Where's Isobel? She should be down—'

'She's waiting in the car with Judy and the laddies, my dear.' Dr MacAlistair pushed her handbag under one arm, her gloves into her hands, and propelled her through the front door and down the path. He returned mopping his brow. 'Wives at weddings! May the good Lord have mercy on the poor husbands who've to deal with them! Now, let's have a look at you, lassie.' Carefully he lifted my veil. 'Ach, but you're a

lovely picture this day. I'm as proud to walk with you up the aisle as
your own father would've been, could he have been spared for this
happiness. Come, come, no greeting! Well, perhaps the one tear or two.
All brides are allowed that. That's better. Ready?'

Craig's boy-friend Ian had arrived to drive us to the church in the
hotel car that should have taken me to Glasgow. He was a large
red-haired young man, wearing a spruce dark suit, wide smile, and huge
floral buttonhole. The car shone with polish and was festooned with
white nylon ribbons.

The caterers gathered behind us in the porch to see us off. The cluster
of nurses, up-patients, lay staff, and porters waiting in the hospital gates
surged forward, smiling. Gordon rushed up to the car with his camera.
Mr Cameron was standing just outside the main entrance. He smiled his
sad, sad smile and bowed from the waist.

'It is to be devoutly hoped,' murmured Dr MacAlistair, 'that no
urgent caller is attempting to contact the hospital at this moment.'

In the car he told me every member of the hospital staff who could
get off duty was now waiting at the church. 'And there's not one who
doesn't take personal credit for this match, myself included.'

I was too moved for speech.

'So you are nervous? Again, a bride's prerogative, but I much doubt
you've cause to be. You've got a good man, and he's got a good lass. I
think you'll do well together.'

I couldn't think of the future. I couldn't even accept the present. The
girl in the white lace dress couldn't be me. Those bells ringing couldn't
be ringing for me.

The taxi had stopped. Craig's Ian rushed round to open the door with
a flourish. Dr MacAlistair helped me out and settled the fall of my veil
at the back. A man's voice called 'Will you please hold it there just one
minute, Doctor!' A woman's voice exclaimed. 'Och! Now there's a bonnie
bride!' And I actually looked round to see who was getting married.

Through a haze that had nothing to do with my veil I saw the little
posse of women in headscarves and carrying shopping-baskets waiting by
the lych-gate; the photographer backing with his camera poised; then Joe
looking unrecognizable in a morning suit and flanked by Robin and
Johnnie, and all three with buttonholes to rival Ian's. I saw Dougal turn
and the way his whole face lit up as he saw me. I didn't really see
anything else until we were back in the MacAlistairs' emptied and
transformed sitting-room, with the caterers hovering tactfully in the hall
as we waited for the others to join us. Then I properly registered
Dougal's ceremonial kilt, superbly cut black jacket, and glorious lace
jabot.

'Dougal, you look out of this world!'

His bow surpassed Mr Cameron's, but there was no sadness in his smile. 'Having just married you, my darling, that doesn't suprise me at all, as that's precisely how I feel. I told you how incredibly lovely you look in the car. Or didn't you hear a word I said?'

'Not really. I'm only just beginning to surface, and seeing you now in that wonderful get-up—I'm going under again. This can't be for real!'

He kissed my ring finger, then brushed the back of my left hand against his chin. 'Just give it a little time, sweetheart, just give it a little time.' His eyes caressed me. 'It'll sort itself out.'

'Yes. Thanks, love.'

'Not at all,' said Dougal politely, as Mrs MacAlistair rushed back up the front path. 'My pleasure.'

LUCILLA ANDREWS

Ring O'Roses

For
Alison and Hector

Chapter One

The Cross of St George was flying from the square tower of the old grey church that afternoon. The lilac bushes by the church were purple, white and blue-mauve; and in the banks of the lane running up from the village, there were bluebells, buttercups and early cow parsley. I had remembered the wild flowers, but forgotten the grass was so green.

'Young Ruth can't grumble for her wedding.' Bert Mercer pushed up the peak of the tweed cap he had worn during the seven years Ruth and I travelled in his school taxi. 'Bridesmaid, aren't you? You'll be on time. The ringers are still down the Lamb.' He turned into the vicarage drive. 'Been on your holidays, have you?'

'I'm just finishing one. Back to work on Monday.'

His blue eyes considered me calmly as he braked. 'London?' I nodded. 'Didn't fancy Canada same as your mum and brother, then?'

I avoided looking at the house next door. The two houses stood alone on the hilltop and opposite the church. 'I enjoyed working there this last year. A beautiful country.'

'That's nice.' He glanced at that other house. 'Could've done with your dad last winter. Me chest was playing up again. This new young chap gives me these tablets and says to stay off the spirits. Won't mix, he says. Tablets!' He snorted. 'That's all these young doctors know, seemly. Your dad wouldn't have given me no tablets. He'd have fetched me down a bottle of his linctus, told the wife to tuck me off with a hot toddy, I'd have sweated it out and been back on the school run in the week! Three weeks I had on the club with them tablets! How was I to know as he meant to stay off the beer? Didn't say, did he? Missed your dad, I can tell you! You didn't catch him telling a working man to stay off his beer.' He heaved himself out and lunged into the back for my bags. 'When did you get back from Canada, then?'

I smiled. 'Just over two hours ago. I was due yesterday but our flight was delayed by a snowstorm in Montreal.'

Bert Mercer and his ancestors came from the village at the foot of that hill. The village had seen the Romans arrive and leave; the Jutes burn it down; the Normans take it over; the Battle of Britain overhead and a fair selection of World War II bombs fall on and around it. The village could show emotion, when very drunk. 'Snow, eh?' Bert shoved up his cap another inch. 'Wouldn't fancy it this time of the year meself, neither.'

'Cathy, dear! Welcome back!' Mrs Desmond exploded through her front door, kissed me warmly and re-skewered her hat. 'Bert, will you kindly leave those bags just inside the door and go back to the next train—splendid!' She ushered me into the transformed vicarage hall, round caterers and trestle tables, to the foot of the main stairs. 'You'll find everything waiting in the guest-room—next to the old school-room—remember? You won't mind if I leave you to find your own way, dear? Ruth's having a little trouble with her veil—she's a bit edgy—bride's prerogative, as I've told her! But she was quite relieved when you rang from the airport as she did find yesterday a little trying. Of course, the best man's slipping a disc was rather unfortunate—'

'Nigel Jarvis?' I exclaimed. 'Ruth didn't tell me on the—'

'As I've said, dear—we are a bit edgy! The poor boy came off his tractor, but as he's not badly hurt and the tractor skidded on alone into a half-empty dyke and was quite undamaged, really we can only be thankful. Tractors are so precious at this season! Not too travel-worn? Good! Off you go! The Vicar and Danny have already gone across to the church and we mustn't be too long.' She waved me up the stairs as if it were five minutes, not over three years, since I had last been in her house. Nor, despite a new cream straw sombrero and navy silk outfit, did she look in any way altered. She had always been a large handsome woman with a weakness for huge hats and the engrained air of being about to declare the bazaar open.

I was very fond of Mrs Desmond. She was so genuinely kind and had a lack of imagination I had found restful as a child. Being incapable of visualizing the worst, Mrs Desmond had waited until one fell out of a tree before putting it out of bounds. My mother had only to see a child glance at a tree to see a broken back. In Mrs Desmond's place now, my mother would be convinced the dress made to measurements exchanged across the Atlantic would never fit me; she would take the best man's accident as a bad omen that must inevitably herald the bridegroom's breaking his neck before he reached the church, or the Vicar's suffering a stroke from the emotional strain of marrying his favourite child to a man taking her to Australia for two years directly after the honeymoon.

My brother had mother's temperament. 'How can you stand going back? It'll be agony!' both had assured me constantly for the last month. Being even less sure now than then that I could stand it, once the anaesthetizing effect of my post-flying hangover wore off, I was very grateful to have been sent up to get changed alone before even seeing Ruth. The mental breathing space was such perfect therapy that for the first time in my life I wondered if Mrs Desmond was as unimaginative as we had all assumed, or if thirty years of marriage to a theological scholar with a dry sense of humour and very High Church leanings in a country living where, irrespective of social backgrounds, all three qualities were regarded with deep suspicion, was responsible for her reputation for seeing only the silver linings. She was a very popular as well as very good Vicar's wife.

The long powder-blue velvet dress, matching shoes and gloves fitted exactly. The hair ribbon was the right length. I studied the result in the long mirror and tried unsuccessfully to accept the pallid blonde zombie staring back as myself. Her ability to stand still was no help as I was now back to feeling the sway of the 'plane. It was like being suspended on the end of a piece of string held by eternity with a childish streak. Just as one grew accustomed to the sway, eternity twitched it up or dropped it down.

A knock on the door startled me disproportionally. I opened it carefully as a drunk and blinked at the man in a morning suit holding a posy of cornflowers and pink roses. 'You look different, Joss,' I said.

He was Ruth's elder brother and was smiling rather nicely. 'So do you, Cathy. Very charming but not yet with us. Why don't you sit down?'

I backed and sat on the bed. 'It isn't lack of food. They fed us all night.'

'Just time-lag.' He gave me the posy, explained he had taken over as best man and driven up with it as it had been accidentally delivered to the bridegroom's home. 'The ringers were staggering out of the Lamb as I came by. I must get back before they start or poor Tom'll blow another gasket.'

'Poor Tom. Poor Nigel. Your mother says he's not too bad.'

'Just cursing his guts out at doing this at this time of year.' He asked after my mother, brother and sister-in-law but tactfully omitted my step-father.

I said, 'He's a very nice man, Joss. I didn't expect to like him, but I do, very much.'

'I'm glad on all counts,' he said, as if he meant it.

Ruth and I were the same age, twenty-four. Joss was five years older, Danny a year younger. As kids the five-year gap had been enough to cause Ruth and me irritation, without being sufficient to make us respect his being able to tie his own shoelaces, or buy himself a beer at the Lamb while we had to sit outside eating crisps and ducking behind parked cars when any member of the P.C.C. or Mothers' Union went by. All our childhood, Joss and I had accepted each other, partly as we had no alternative and partly as we had managed to achieve a kind of undemanding but solid understanding that was firmly based on shared roots and mutual indifference.

The young Desmonds all had their father's dark hair and eyes, but only Joss their mother's heavier features and build. As a boy he had been all jaw, nose and triangular eyebrows, with bones that looked too big for him. We had last met at my father's funeral, but I could not now remember what he had then looked like. I had a dim recollection of his saying that if I ever wanted to look round another hospital, to give him a ring, he would show me round Benedict's and buy me a meal. I had not taken that up and nor had he done more about it. During the remaining years of my general training in St Martha's, London, I had seen Ruth regularly but neither of her brothers. I noticed absently Joss's bones no longer seemed too big and that my face seemed to be puzzling him. I asked what was wrong with it. 'Do I need more lipstick? Or have I forgotten to make up both eyes?'

'Turn to the light.' He came nearer, and being considerably taller than myself and standing, bent for a closer look. 'You'll do, as you are.' He stepped back rather quickly. 'See you.' He went out and closed the door. I got up quickly and looked at myself in the mirror. I was still wondering if I had imagined the expression I had seen flickering through Joss's eyes just now, when I chanced to look out of the window and forgot everything else. The window overlooked the back garden next door. The new owners had replaced my father's cherished rose beds with turf. I had just enough time to re-do my eyes before the bells started and Mrs Desmond called me to Ruth's room.

Ruth's Victorian-styled dress was of broderie anglaise and her long dark hair was piled up under a short lace veil. She was a very pretty, slim girl and she looked dreamy. We walked round each other in silence then began to laugh, wildly. Mrs Desmond beamed on us. 'There's nothing like a good laugh to settle the nerves,' she said.

Tom Everett, Ruth's bridegroom, had been in the fifth at our co-ed grammar when Ruth and I were first-formers. His father was owner-editor of the local paper and around that time had bought a house in the village. As Tom had fed us with some of the pastry from the meat pies he bought to eat on the journey home, with unusual charity we had named him Acne-Chops. One morning in his 'A' Level year he had appeared in Bert's taxi with a pipe. After we told him we thought a pipe did something for an older man, he had sucked it constantly in the taxi until he left school. He never lit it.

Ruth spluttered, 'He still doesn't smoke.'

'So wise,' said Mrs Desmond. 'I wish Danny would give it up.'

The pealing bells cascaded over the hill, the village below and the flat green farmland beyond when Mrs Desmond and I crossed the lane a few minutes later. ·The little group of women waiting by the lych-gate stepped aside. 'It's the old Doctor's girl! You remember poor Dr Maitland—took bad just after evening surgery—gone he was, gone— before his poor wife could get a hand to the 'phone for the ambulance— cruel shock—and how are you then, dear? And your mum? So young Paul's got hisself a wife, eh? There! Your turn next, dear! Lovely day you got for your Ruth, eh, Mrs Desmond?'

The bells faded away but the birds went on singing. The sunshine filtering through the stained-glass windows sent shafts of red, blue and yellow onto white-washed walls that had been five hundred years old when Tudor England was middle-aged. Suddenly the faces swung round, some familiar, some strange, some appraising, some envying, some smiling. I only properly noticed Tom Everett's face. He looked quite incredibly happy.

This time: 'Dearly beloved we are gathered together ...'

Last time: 'Man that is born of woman ...' Was that the last time? Hadn't I been here in the months before our house sold? If I had, I couldn't remember. I couldn't even remember the two family weddings I had attended in this last year.

'We're on the move, Cathy,' murmured Joss.

In the vestry he drew my hand through his arm as we formed up behind the parents and asked very quietly if I thought the final hymn had been a strictly tactful choice.

'What was it?'

'Now thank we all our God.' His eyes smiled into mine. 'Take it easy. You sang the official version, not the bawdy variation you wrote after 'O' Levels.'

'I'd forgotten that.' I smiled back as we followed the little procession down the aisle.

A battery of professional and amateur photographers was waiting outside the church. We were grouped and regrouped. 'Bride and her mother alone, please ... bride and bridesmaid ... cheese, ladies, cheese, please ... bride and groom again. ...'

The front gate of our old house looked naked without the brass plate. The flowering currant bushes in the front garden had been replaced by ailing rhododendrons. They wouldn't do well in that soil. Too much lime. 'Nothing'll do well in the wrong soil,' my father said.

Canada had been wrong for me. I had not been able to say that to my family as it would have hurt them too much. With the enthusiasm of converts and the self-exiled's need for justification, they saw in black and white. Canada was their Promised Land, England all strikes, scruffy students, drugs. 'Why go back?'

Simply, I had missed England. When my training ended, I had taken a year's job in a Canadian hospital to see if my mother was as content as she seemed from her letters. She was more than that, she was happy. After her re-marriage three months ago I wrote to the Chief Nursing Officer at Martha's. She had answered by return, offering me the job of Senior Staff Nurse in Luke Ward. 'After so much departmental surgery,' she wrote, 'I think you will enjoy a return to medical nursing.'

Tomorrow I was due back at my old digs in London. Yesterday I had been sorry my weekend with the Desmonds would be cut short. I liked them all, but I wasn't sorry now my flying hangover was wearing much thinner. It was too early yet to tell whether or not coming back was a mistake, but not that parts of it hurt like hell.

Particularly the reception. At first.

'Cathy, I want all your news! My dear, it seems so strange not having the Maitlands on this hill. I expect you're quite sad to see the old house again?'

'Drink up, girl,' said Joss. 'I'm tired of toting this full bottle.'

'So your dear mother has re-married, Cathy? I always thought she was so devoted—but they say he's a wealthy man? Not that he can take your father's place in your heart—I know just how you feel, dear—'

'Cathy, you can't imagine how we miss your father! He was such a good doctor—he'd come out in any weather at any hour—I expect you miss him still?'

'Let's have your glass, Cathy,' said Joss.

'Cathy, I can't wait to hear all your news! But, darling—have you heard about our railway? They're trying to take it away, so we've formed an Action Group. ...'

Suddenly, it was over. Slowly, the cars disgorged from the Glebe Field; the caterers began stacking glasses, folding cloths; the parents and elder relatives retreated to the Vicar's study before their dinner with the Everett seniors; Danny started organizing our party. Danny was now taller and thinner than Joss, with his better-looking face hidden by a thick black beard.

I had to have quiet. I drifted out to the vegetable garden and sat on the bench against a wall. It was too far from the house for the voices on the front lawn to be more than a distant babble weaving into the background hum of tractors. On any fine Saturday at this time of the year, that hum lasted as long as the light. The air smelt as it always had; of new-cut grass, new-turned earth, diesel, lilac, and faintly of salt from the sea eleven miles away. My travel fatigue had gone, but thanks to the champagne I looked at our old house with nothing more than an affectionate incredulity that it should still be there, without us.

Joss joined me so silently that I was unaware of the fact until he sat down. We exchanged smiles in a silence that picked up old threads far more tangibly than words. It had the unstrained quality only possible between old friends on the same wavelength and was as soothing as my former solitude. But watching him staring at nothing, I was amused to find myself thinking that had we only met today, this particular silence would have been the last thing I would have expected, or maybe even wanted from him. For the first time I understood why my local girl-friends used to envy my treating the vicarage as a second home and grumble at the waste of the best bit of local talent, when Joss brought home his dates from Cambridge, and later as a medic. student from Benedict's. The stream stopped once he was a houseman as then he seldom got home and when he did, he slept. When our house was sold he had been a junior surgical registrar at Benedict's, with even less free time. Occasionally, in London, Ruth had mentioned him in connection with some girl, but in her letters this last year, only under the general 'the family are all flourishing'. I wondered vaguely about his present sex life, and then with more interest why every old friend over thirty-five this afternoon had asked when I was going to find myself a husband and been so annoyed by my truthful reply that I was in no hurry to marry.

'So many of you girls say that these days! You know your trouble? Too much freedom, too much money, and you mustn't mind my adding, too irresponsible!'

I had let that go with a weak smile since none of the speakers had worked in a hospital and someone, generally Joss, kept refilling my glass.

He roused himself to ask how I felt about Danny's rave. 'Too tired to face it?'

'No, but when I helped Ruth into her going-away gear she told me you only got down this morning. On call last night?' He nodded, watching me thoughtfully. 'Are you?'

'Not too tired, but too old. I'd much prefer us to opt out for a civilized meal somewhere on our own. How about it?'

I hesitated, though I was in no mood for another party. 'Joss, I know you're officially lumbered with me—'

'And you with me, darling. If you can stand the strain a bit longer, I'll continue to enjoy it.' His expression was surprisingly kind. 'Been very hellish?'

I shook my head. 'Mainly thanks to all the champagne you've been pouring into me. Anyway, I realized people meant to be kind—'

'Dear old chums.' He grimaced. 'Theirs is "the loving kindness that is pity's kin—and is most pitiless." What's the verdict?'

'I'd much rather dine with you. Thanks for the invitation and kind thought.'

He stood up and held out a hand. 'Darling, you've been living too long amongst the primitive colonials if you can now kid yourself any

Englishman is ever prompted by kindness when he puts this proposition to a very pretty little dolly.'

I laughed and stood up. 'And will there be etchings on your lugger?'

'On home territory? Only a chastely framed copy of the Vicar's eldest lad's Union Rules. Hence all afternoon, one miserable glass of champagne.'

'Joshua! Such nobility!'

'Such craftiness! I hoped I'd be driving the lugger.'

We drove miles across the marsh to a newish road-house he said was good value. When the sun went down, the wide, empty sky was scarlet and gold; the wild roses in the low hedges were pale, ghostly; the cow parsley edged the flat green fields with white lace; and the dykes pointed long topaz fingers, seawards. The fat, omnipresent lambs were old enough to risk drowning as they slithered up and down the dyke banks, and everywhere the curlew rose in flapping black and white clouds.

I thought aloud. 'This was the kind of English evening that had the brain-drainers over the other side weeping into their Scotch or Bourbon.'

'I'd miss it.'

'I did.'

He slowed, then glanced at me. 'Would've had me back too. Many want to return?'

'Around sixty per cent of those I met would be back tomorrow if they weren't hooked on the lolly.'

'Understandable.' He drove on in silence for a little while. 'What was working and living over there really like, Cathy?'

We had finished dinner before I finished telling him and asked his news. 'The last I heard, you'd both parts of Fellowship and were running Benedict's Accident Unit. I remember, as that was when I went to ours. Still there?'

'No.' The way he was watching me through his thick dark lashes struck a forgotten chord. Half-closing his eyes when shy or nervous had been one of his mannerisms as a boy. 'I've crossed the river.'

'To Martha's'? I smiled widely. 'How? When? Why?'

'I answered an advert for Hoadley East's senior registrar. Six months ago. I wanted to work with him.'

'Joss, I'm impressed! You must be very good!' That was true. Sir Hoadley East was our senior consultant orthopaedic surgeon. Martha's Establishment was notoriously addicted to appointing Martha's men to Martha's jobs, no matter how well advertised. Any outsider who beat the system had to be demonstrably better than Martha's best. 'Congratulations,' I added.

'Thanks.' He pushed back his chair as the record player switched from ten-year-old pop to a Glenn Miller Album. 'Come and dance to this soothing syrup before the good impression wears off—or are your feet killing you?'

I stood up. 'My feet are fine, thanks.'

'Good.' He held out his arms. 'We'll do a nice decorous turn around the floor.'

A few minutes later, he asked, 'When did we last dance together?'

I had to think. 'Before—before you went to Cambridge. You wanted to practise in the schoolroom. Didn't work out. You said I was too short for you.'

He brushed his chin over the top of my head. 'Not now. You've grown.'

I looked up. 'Not since I was thirteen, but you have.'

He smiled. 'A very young and foolish lad. I like your scent. Handsome present from a well-heeled brain-drainer?'

'From my step-father.'

His hold tightened slightly. 'Very generous of you to wear it, Cathy.'

'I felt I should. He's being so good to Mum—and he insisted on paying my fare home. He's generous, plus.'

'Sounds a good chap.' He was briefly silent. 'Meet many Canadian good chaps?'

'Quite a few.'

'Husky, well-scrubbed, manly characters?'

'To a man.'

'Yet you came back?' He held me a little off to look at my face. 'Does this mean you prefer decadent Englishmen?'

I opened my eyes wide. 'I have this weakness for crumbling civilization.'

He drew me closer and rested his face on my hair. 'Rule Britannia.'

We danced in silence and extraordinarily well together until the record ended. ' "Come Dancing",' said Joss, 'must see us.' He breathed as if he had been running and we went back to our table without touching each other again, and tried to pretend that the dance had altered nothing. But the new tension between us was tangible as the dinner-table. As always when that happens, we were having two simultaneous conversations. Neither of us paid much attention to the one we put into words. Our silences grew more frequent and were as strained as that earlier one had been easy, for much the same basic reason.

The vicarage lights were on when we drove round to the garage behind the vegetable garden. Being so far from the house, once the garage light was off, momentarily the country darkness blinded my now unaccustomed eyes. A few hours back I would have grabbed for Joss. I grabbed for the garage door.

'Want a hand, Cathy?' He could have been a polite stranger, only had this been our first date a stranger would not now have had to ask that.

'Thanks.' I felt his hand reaching for mine, but very slowly. 'And for splendid dinner, Joss.'

'Thank you. Can we *rep. mist.* some time? I'd like that very much.'

'I would, too.'

'Good.' He kissed my hand. 'How's the champagne?'

'Wedding or dinner?'

'Both.'

'Nicely assimilated by all that good food and coffee. How's yours?'

'Did you lace mine with vodka?'

'No.'

'Must be this moonlight,' he said and lightly kissed my lips.

I looked at the dark moonless sky as somewhere an owl hooted. 'How many times did you get called up last night?'

'I dunno.' His arms were round me and he began kissing me properly. 'Serendipity,' he murmured, 'that's the word I want.'

I was having even more difficulty in touching down than after the flight. 'For what?'

'The faculty of making happy and unexpected discoveries by accident. Cathy, this is bloody absurd—'

'Crazy. We should go in.'

'We should, but that's not what I meant.' His deep voice was unsteady. 'You've hit me so hard I can't think straight. All I can think is that I—hell—I think I bloody love you. Mind?'

I hadn't any breath for speech. I shook my head. He did not say anything or move for about two minutes. Then he said conversationally, 'You're right. Time to go in.'

The Vicar came out of the kitchen with a glass of milk on a tray as we went in by the back door. 'Ah, there you are! Pleasant evening? Good, good. Your mother's rather tired so I'm just taking this up—oh yes, Joss—your hospital rang about an hour ago. Your Senior Surgical Officer asked if you would be good enough to ring him directly you got home. I hope this doesn't mean you'll have to leave us prematurely? I'll just take this up and be with you both, shortly.'

Joss and I had exchanged similar glances. After the Vicar vanished up the back stairs, I asked, 'This your free weekend?' He nodded dreamily. 'He can't want you to drive back tonight?'

'Your hospital, darling. Like to bet?'

I looked at the time. It was a quarter to one on Sunday morning and fifty miles from London. 'No.'

Joss raised both arms from his sides then let them fall in a gesture that was both triumphant and defeated. 'If it's not union rules, it's suffering humanity. Come and comfort me whilst I find out what's bugging Michael Roth, but I warn you—don't offer me an apple or a flagon as I don't fancy either!'

I took his offered hand. 'I won't.'

He rang from the Vicar's study. He had to drive back that night, as a man called Stan Lawson had a temperature of one hundred and three.

Chapter Two

Stan Lawson was Senior Accident Officer in our newish Accident Unit. In Martha's the job had the same status as the deputy Senior Surgical Officer, and was a yearly appointment open only to Fellows of the Royal College of Surgeons with at least six months full-time accident experience. It appealed only to a minority of individualists, owing to the irregular and generally very long hours, the necessity for making and acting on their own immediate decisions, and the professional vulnerability consequent on constant contact with a litigious general public.

Stan Lawson had been Junior Accident Officer when I worked in our A.U. up to leaving for Canada. When we said goodbye, he told me he intended applying for the job when the then S.A.O.'s contact ended. 'I'm thirty and I've been someone's stooge long enough. I want the buck.'

I wished him luck and said I hoped he would not collect the ulcers that seemed to go with that buck. He'd shrugged. 'There's no interesting job without massive problems, but at least, in the A.U., we're spared the super bloody problem bugging most of the human race—why am I in this business? Here we're in business to save healthy lives. I think that'll keep me off the tranquillizers.'

It was his weekend on and he had worked all day feeling terrible but was too busy to do anything about it. When he got back to his flat, his wife, a junior ward sister, had taken his temperature, then rung the S.S.O. The latter told Joss Stan was the sixteenth member of the staff to go down with the new 'flu virus since Joss left that morning. 'Yesterday—two. Today—this! The S.M.O.'s being revoltingly smug. For the last two or three weeks, every time he's heard of the odd case in London he's said once it got a hold it would rip round like bloody dynamite. This is the new bug that hit the States a few months ago and as none of us here have met it, my learned opposite number says it won't surprise him if even the immunized pick it up. When not slapping himself on the back tonight, he's forecasting closed wards before the month's out. Ghoulish

bastards, physicians. I'm sorry to do this to you, but I can't get hold of
George Charlesworth [the J.A.O.] as he's spending his weekend touring.
In any event, he hasn't enough experience yet to take over for more than
a day or so. Can you make it tonight to move in first thing tomorrow?
Today was a bloody shambles. If this weather lasts, tomorrow'll be
worse.'

Joss rang off and linked his hands behind my waist. 'You get this bug
across the water?'

'Me and two-thirds of the hospital. If it's the same, it's dynamite all
right. Makes one feel like death before, during, and after.'

'Bundle of sunshine, aren't you, darling?' He kissed my neck.
'Wonder how many people Stan Lawson's handed it on to today.'

'I was wondering that. The invasion's very short. Poor Stan. This'll
worry him a lot.'

'Chum of yours?'

'Just to work with. He's sweet—so's his wife. She's three years senior
to me.' I held his face away. 'You met her?'

'No. I'm the new boy, remember? I've met old Stan. Decent chap.
So's George Charlesworth.'

I smiled. 'There you're one up on me. I know his name, but I don't
think I've ever seen him.'

'Quiet little man with glasses. I've heard he doesn't know much but
learns fast.' He frowned to himself. 'I've also heard one of the three Unit
staff nurses is particularly good but can't remember which.'

'How come you're such a mine of information on the A.U.? And
who's Sister there now? Know that too?'

He grinned. 'Yep. A girl called Naomi Butler. Benedict's girl. We
worked together in our Unit.'

'A Benedict's—' I laughed with him at my reaction. 'Just fancy!'

'And knowing your own hospital, how do you think they'll fancy this
Benedict's take-over?'

'Oh—maybe just a complaint to the Race Relations Board.'

His triangular eyebrows shot up. 'Only that? No tar and feathers?'

I stopped smiling. 'Joss, have you had much of that?'

'The occasional dirty crack's inevitable if one muscles in on any
enclosed community.'

'Do you dirty crack back?'

He laughed quietly. 'I just wear my Benedict's tie.'

'My dear man! Why haven't you been lynched? Got a death wish?'

'Oh no, my love,' he said in a different voice, 'oh, no. So don't look at
me like that, Cathy, or I'll be in danger of losing my job tonight.'

I backed rather breathlessly. 'I'll make you some tea whilst you
change.'

'Tea?' The Vicar had joined us. 'I must say I'd enjoy a cup myself. You'll find your way round, Cathy? Splendid!'

Joss followed me into the hall. 'Thank God,' he said piously, 'there'll always be an England—just as long as there's a tea-leaf left.'

After he had gone the Vicar and I finished the pot in the kitchen. Mr Desmond looked round the huge Victorian room as if seeing it for the first time. He was a slight, neat man with fine-drawn, very regular features and thick grey hair. He looked ten years older than he had in church that afternoon. My father had been his great friend. We had exchanged general family news, but neither of us had mentioned either my father or Ruth. Danny was still out and the big house was very quiet.

He took off his glasses to rub his tired eyes. 'Parenthood, Cathy, is a blessed but disorientating experience.' He sighed. 'For around twenty years the uproar created by one's children frequently causes one to fear for one's sanity and eardrums—and then the silence becomes even more disturbing. Come and see us whenever you can spare the time.'

'Vicar, I'd love to. Thank you.'

'That will give Margaret great pleasure. She is going to miss—our daughter. And if, when you visit us, you'll kindly turn that lamentable record-player in the schoolroom to full volume and cause Margaret to protest you're disturbing my sermon, you'll be doing more than one act of charity.' His dark eyes smiled like Joss's. 'The Lord has given to me greatly, but in His wisdom omitted a talent for sermon-writing. Disturbed concentration has long provided an equally cogent excuse for my unfortunate parishioners and my ego.'

It was the longest conversation we had ever had, possibly as Ruth had always been around formerly and she talked as much as her mother. I was too tired that night to work out whether her marriage, or absence, had been the catalyst with him, or even what had happened between Joss and myself. I was merely conscious of a new and wholly unexpected joy simmering inside me exactly like water coming to boil in a kettle. The sensation lasted all weekend. Before I left Mrs Desmond echoed her husband's invitation and said how delighted she was that Joss and I were working in the same hospital. 'Naturally, I realize St Martha's is a big place and you may not see much of each other, but I expect you'll manage to keep in touch, won't you?'

'I think we will,' I said, feeling a hideous—and enchanted—fraud.

My landlady gave me a tremendous welcome and the inside story on the new ground-floor lodgers. 'God knows they're quiet enough girls and I've nothing against all-girlie parties, but I do wish they weren't always so miserable and intense. You don't think they'll start burning their bras in my hall? I can't stick the smell of scorching.'

Roxanne Alder, the girl with whom I shared the attic flat, was temporarily away on a modelling job. She had left welcoming messages strung all round the place and enough food in the fridge on the landing beside the cooker to keep me for a month.

In Martha's at seven-fifteen on Monday morning, the Night Superintendent reminded me of Bert Mercer. 'Have you been away, Nurse Maitland?'

I explained myself.

'Luke? Oh—yes—I've a note about you from Miss Evans.' The Chief Nursing Officer. 'Here we are—yes—well, Staff Nurse, you'll get to Luke eventually, but as we appear to have a minor influenza epidemic on our hands, you're presently needed elsewhere.' She looked up over her glasses. 'Thirty-four staff and students nurses down since Friday. Most inconvenient as this is the holiday season. So you've been doing some more accident work in Canada?'

I hoped she did not notice the effect that had on my adrenals. 'Yes, Sister. Though technically in acute surgery, more often than not I was in reception.'

'Did their methods vary greatly from those used during your six months in our Accident Unit?'

'Apart from the terms and administrative details, there was very little difference, Sister. Most of the surgeons and anaesthetists with whom I worked were British and had qualified here.'

'At the British taxpayer's expense,' she observed coldly. 'Presumably, that causes them no discomfort, but one wonders how comfortable they would be, were they, or their relatives, admitted as emergencies to one of the many smaller hospitals in this country chronically short of medical staff. However—to return to your immediate future. Miss Evans wants you temporarily in the Accident Unit, as first staff nurse. Both first and second are on the sick-list this morning. Sister Accidents will come on at eight and with you early—' she rootled for another note—'you will have Nurse Jones, the junior staff nurse. I'll try and catch Sister on her way in, but if I fail, when you report to her as her temporary deputy, will you explain I regret having no replacement at present for her second staff nurse, but one will be sent just as soon as a nurse with the necessary accident training can be spared from the wards.' She sat back and straightened the lace bow under her chin. 'Enjoy your break?'

'Very much, thank you, Sister.'

She was a Londoner. In the twenty years since her general training ended, she had only left Martha's to train as a midwife in Oxford. 'Provincial experience is always useful,' she said, 'but you'll be glad to be back.' Simultaneously, her tone dismissed any question of any doubt in my mind, all other hospitals as second-rate, the existence of the Atlantic Ocean, and myself. It amused me, but explained why nine out of ten nurses in the outside world reacted with an instant snarl to the name Martha's, why so many Canadians had anti-English chips, and why Joss occasionally walked Martha's wards in a Benedict's tie.

The prospect of seeing him so soon, plus working with him, was such a glorious bonus that I was almost scared to dwell on it. Fortunately the problem of being temp. dep. to a Sister who neither knew nor was expecting me proved life needn't be suspected of being too perfect. I had yet to meet the Sister, anywhere, who didn't detest sudden senior staff changes, and above all having to hand over to an unknown deputy. Yet even here Joss being a Benedict's man was another bonus. If Sister Accidents in two days had to cope with an unknown acting S.A.O. and myself, on past showing, God help us all.

Five years ago our old Casualty Department had been rehoused in the ground floors of the new and adjoining General Surgical and Orthopaedic Blocks and renamed Emergencies and Accidents. The twin departments remained under the overall charge of the former Sister Casualty, Miss Mackenzie. She now presided in Emergencies, which infinitely the larger department. Every non-accident patient admitted to any of the two thousand beds came in through Emergencies. This was staffed by a posse of junior sisters, staff nurses, student nurses, medical orderlies and medic. students acting as dressers. The S.M.O. and S.S.O. had their own offices and examination rooms in the department and all the non-A.U. residents worked there on rota. The A.U. men—and Martha's had yet to appoint a woman doctor to Accidents even as anaesthetist—were the only residents in the hospital with no responsibilities outside the curved and windowless walls of the Accident Unit. And owing to the highly specialized and high-powered first aid that is modern immediate post-accident therapy, though hers was a junior sister's post, inside the A.U. Sister Accidents ruled as absolutely as any Sister Theatre in her own theatre. Only once, and after a series of mutinous murmurs from the A.U. staff had vibrated on the grapevines, had Miss Mackenzie been known to exert her superior authority. Shortly after, there had been a new Sister Accidents. The grapevines never discovered if the previous one had resigned in fury or been sacked, but the day the new girl took over, every wire in the hospital was red hot with the news that Miss Mackenzie had smiled. Miss Mackenzie was a trim, pale, white-haired Edinburgh lady and in her thirty years as a sister had never been known to suffer fatigue, hunger, emotion, or fools. She could make senior consultants dither like nervous housemen, reduce the S.M.O. and S.S.O. to apologetic medic. students. Lesser ranks became jellies or lost weight, depending on their temperaments. In the last month I spent in the A.U., I shed ten pounds. A gastric 'flu bug had caused another massive staff crisis and shot me from junior to first staff nurse overnight, and then for my final terrifying week to acting Sister, with Miss Mackenzie brooding over my every move.

On my last evening, etiquette insisted I call at her office to say goodbye. She had wished me good fortune in a voice of doom. 'Miss Evans,' she added, 'has informed me of your domestic obligations. But should your mother's welfare be to your satisfaction, and some young man not persuade you otherwise—which I fear is very possible—I hope we will see you back in your training hospital.' She almost smiled. 'You may appear but a wee-bit lassie, Nurse, but you know how to work. You managed quite well, just now.'

I had reeled to the Staff Nurses' Home where my set had revived me with cooking sherry as everything stronger had been taken to our flat for the farewell party Roxanne and I were giving that night. There were now only four of my old set left; three were junior sisters and one a staff-midwife. I liked them all, but none had been amongst my particular friends. It was through one of these, Peter Anthony, that I knew what the girls were doing. Peter I had known years. When I left he had been a senior house-physician and his last letter some time in January said he had ended all with Sue—or it could have been Carol—was uncertain about his future but thinking of trying anaesthetics. Peter Anthony's uncertainty was one of the few certainties in an uncertain world. As long as I had known him, when he ended all with the pre-Sue-Carol legion, he had spent hours flat on the floor of our living-room bleating about his uncertain future and why no one ever liked him. Roxanne and I only objected on one count. Our room was small and Peter was six three and weighed fifteen stone. When not bleating, he was good fun, being very easy-going, generous with his car, and invaluable as a chucker-out at our parties. He had never made a serious pass at either of us and only once a mild one at me when he brought me back from a rather bad party. He had turned up the following morning, a Sunday, smitten with guilt and a crashing hangover. After two pots of black coffee he said it must've been the vodka as he'd never fancied me and did I fancy him? I said sorry, no. He said that figured as he knew no one ever fancied him. He knew he was a sexual failure. He knew he would never make it in general medicine, he wasn't sure whether he should try pathology and did I know the name of the dolly with red hair and legs last night and better still her 'phone number. I had forgotten her name now, but not her keeping him off our carpet for a good two months. As I had also forgotten to answer his last letter, I wondered if anyone had told him I was coming back, or if he had left Martha's. Someone in the A.U. would know. There was always someone in every department who knew everything about everyone.

The junior staff nurse was alone in the nurses' changing-room. She had her back to me but I recognized her instantly though I had never before seen her in a staff nurse's uniform. 'You're this Jones! Hi!'

Her real name was Helen Jones, but her set had nicknamed her Dolly long before they were out of the P.T.S. She had the smooth dark fringe, wide long-lashed blue eyes, chubby cheeks and dimpled chin of a Victorian china doll. When we last worked together on the same day and night shift in Albert two years ago, she had been the best junior I ever came across. I was delighted to see her and certain she was the girl whose name Joss hadn't remembered. Behind that china doll's face, Dolly Jones had a very good brain and five good 'A' Levels to prove it. Martha's only insisted on two for student nurses.

She literally fell on my neck. 'Staff, forgive the corn, but you're corn in Egypt! When I got back from my days off yesterday, heard Chalmers had gone home with a temp. Saturday night and White was ailing sick in the Home, I nearly threw a full-blown *crise de neufs* only I couldn't as we were too something busy! But, really—a girl can take so much! Morning, noon, and night—"At St Benedict's we did it this way—" ' she broke off. 'Hey! You have heard the ugly news?' I nodded, smiling. 'But the whole soul-searing story? Not only Sister but also our acting S.A.O. from that place over the river? As Peter Anthony said last night, yesterday was a black day for Martha's. Our cherished A.U., the newest and most expensively equipped department in the hospital, taken over by a brace of Benedict's throw-outs. Peter said he was very sorry he'd switched to anaesthetics, though actually he's making a rather good R.A. [Resident Anaesthetist] here. Come to that,' she added without letting me say anything, 'and though it goes against the grain to admit it, our new boy knows his accident therapy. Yesterday was nightmarish. All London took to the roads and half ended up in mangled messes in here. The new boy coped as well as Stan L.' She flapped her long eyelashes. 'Wonder why Benedict's chucked him out?'

I had intended asking how long Peter had been A.U. R.A., but was too incensed on Joss's behalf to remember. 'Couldn't he have chosen? For the chance to work with Hoadley East? Even Benedict's must know Hoadley's one of the best orthopod surgeons in the world.'

'I guess so—' she did a double-take. 'How do you know this? Don't say you know Joss Desmond too! Is there a woman either side of the river who's not on first names with the man? Top of the pin-up pops is our Mr D.—and they do say as hot off the job as he is on—only for God's sake don't let Butler hear you say that as he's her private property! How do you know him?'

I was about to explain my family had lived next door to his for the first nineteen years of my life when I properly registered all she had said. I didn't believe it all, but it was a useful reminder of the efficiency of our grapevine. I said I had been at school with Ruth Desmond, his only sister, and asked about Peter.

'He came to us just after me—ten weeks back. He took a course earlier this year, then had a short spell in the General Theatre—didn't you know? He knew last night you were coming to us today. He got it from one of the Office Sisters. That's how I knew. He said he was going to ring you—didn't he?' I shook my head. 'He was fearfully pleased. Biggest erotic thrill he's had since you left from the way he was carrying on. I haven't known him so chatty since he used to haunt you in Albert—I say, did you say Ruth Desmond?'

'Yes.' Suddenly I felt much happier. Her thinking me capable of giving Peter an erotic thrill showed how much salt the rest needed. 'Why?'

'You weren't by any chance at the wedding on Saturday? You were? Oh my Gawd, Staff—don't mention it! Please! He ditched a date with Butler for it, or went off without her, or something, and the atmosphere between them first thing yesterday morning was sheer ruddy murder for the poor ruddy staff. Luckily, he made with the charm and softened her up,' she smiled, 'which didn't surprise me one bit. Dead sexy, that man. He could soften me up any day of the week and twice on Sundays, if I weren't allergic to queues. I must say, it's going to be quite amusing having something sexy around the joint for once. Maybe I should cross the river?'

The student nurses were arriving from their breakfast. 'Maybe,' I suggested, 'we should get started? And as you know Sister's form, will you start them off?'

'Sure. Oh—by the way—how were the States?'

'United, I believe. I've been in Canada.'

She gave me one of her innocent dolly stares. 'Golly gosh, Staff, I wouldn't know the difference. I dropped geography before 'O's.' She held open the door for me. 'Sister likes us to muster in the Receiving Room. She calls it "the R.R." and the A.U. "the Unit".'

'Fair enough, I suppose.'

Dolly said meekly, 'She calls Miss Mackenzie "Sister Emergencies".'

That did shake me. 'Oh, no!' Miss Mackenzie answered with composure to 'Sister', 'Sister Casualty', or 'Miss Mackenzie'. 'Sister Emergencies' evoked a look that could fragment a diamond. 'Why hasn't someone tactfully warned Butler?'

'So who wants a shelf in a morgue fridge?'

'That bitchy?' I suddenly remembered how very little Joss had said about Butler. 'She know her stuff?'

Dolly nodded gloomily. 'She's got a gold medal. That's why Miss Evans gave her the job.'

I said slowly, 'Hospitals don't throw out their gold medals. Why on earth did she cross the river?'

'Seeing you know Joss Desmond—if he were yours would you let him off the hook without a fight? Not that he showed any inclination to put up one, yesterday. Maybe she did the right thing following him over. Maybe he'll achieve the impossible and turn this back into a happy department.'

'It isn't?'

She shook her head. 'Chalmers and Stan L. get along with Butler pretty well as they've just got to, since they work in each other's pockets. White can't stick her guts, and vice versa. She makes George Charlesworth nervous—he's J.A.O. and rather sweet. Peter Anthony says he and she simply don't communicate.'

'How about you?'

She hesitated. 'I like the way she works and I like the work here. It's the atmosphere and the constant "at St. Benedict's" that makes me want to throw up. This last month the atmosphere's been so thick I think Miss Mackenzie's caught on to it. One of my set's staffing in Emergencies. She says old Mother Mack wasn't at all pleased by all the staff changes in here during Butler's first two months.'

'Who went?'

'The last R.A. didn't take up the option on his second six months—that's how Peter got here. One staff nurse and two student nurses asked Matron for transfers. One had to be put under sedation. Didn't do the A.U. any good and everyone knows it's the Sister who makes or louses up every department.'

I was trying to be detached. It wasn't easy, but I was trying. 'Accident work isn't everybody's baby but you have to get here to find that out.'

'Oh well,' said Dolly under her breath as we joined the waiting nurses, 'if you're determined to spread Christian charity, you've come to a joint that can use it.'

I suspended thought till I waited in Sister's empty office at five to eight. It was one of a row of small offices lying off one side of the narrow corridor leading from the staff exit from the Receiving Room and ending in our changing-room. I opened the large log-book on the desk and looked through the long list of yesterday's admissions. In every case the 'seen and examined on admission' column was signed 'J. R. Desmond, F.R.C.S., Acting S.A.O.'

I thought about Dolly. She enjoyed a good gossip and improving on a good story, but she was neither a liar nor a fool. I thought about Joss on Saturday. Then, simply, I didn't know what to think. I closed the book with a snap as quick steps came down the corridor. The next thing I knew was Peter Anthony lifting me up by the waist to kiss me as I was a foot shorter than himself.

'Peter, off! Down, boy!' I freed myself and dodged round the desk. 'Want to get us both slung out first thing on a Monday morning?'

He backed smiling to block the doorway as he smoothed his slightly curly and very yellow hair. It was shorter than when I had last seen him and cleared his collar by about half an inch but his sideboards were longer and thicker. I had forgotten he was so good-looking as he was one of those people I invariably forgot in their absence and was delighted to see in person. 'Hell, Cath,' he protested, 'we're alone so what better start to a Monday morning? You don't know how I've missed you! Why didn't you answer your 'phone last night? I'd have come straight round if I hadn't been on call.'

'Didn't hear the 'phone. Probably with my landlady—'

'I'll forgive you.' He lunged at me again.

'Peter, watch it! Sister's due!'

'My God, so she is! I don't know if you've been warned, but—' he glanced cautiously over his shoulder and turned puce. 'Oh, sorry—want to come in?' He stepped aside and my heart seemed to lurch with joy. Joss came in slowly, wearing a clean long white coat, dark suit, Benedict's tie and a polite expression. 'Good morning,' he said, 'I'm waiting for Sister.'

Peter waved vaguely. 'You won't know each other. Mr Desmond from St Benedict's, our temp. S.A.O., Staff Nurse Maitland back home from the colonies.'

Sister had arrived, so, correctly, Joss ignored me and smiled at her. ' 'Morning, Sister!'

I was not too happy about his tie, but in any circumstances in a British hospital the safest way to play it is to stick to etiquette. I did the same. When Miss Butler had finished apologizing for delaying Joss's breakfast, I wished her a good morning as if the two men were invisible. She did not bother to answer or even look my way. 'Do you want Mr Desmond or myself, Dr Anthony?'

Joss looked at the floor and Peter as if he had been caught having a fix at the Dangerous Drug Cupboard. 'Er—neither, Sister, thanks. Just—er—collecting some notes from my office to read over breakfast.' He vanished down the corridor.

Naomi Butler was about twenty-seven. She was tallish and very slim, with light brown hair and a delicate-featured face that was much too pale. She looked to me not just grossly over-tired but ill. I wondered if she had an anaemia problem, and then as I knew I had never seen her before, why something about her seemed familiar. I had plenty of time to wonder, as she was still ignoring me and explaining why she had sent a message asking Joss to call in on his way to breakfast. 'There appears to be some industrial injuries query about the man Francis Albert Ayer we admitted to Intensive Care last evening and I thought you'd prefer to sort it out quietly before we're officially opened as you used to in St Benedict's—' She paused, frowning, as Dolly arrived. 'Well, Staff?'

'Excuse me, Sister, but a mechanic from Repairs and Works is here and would like to see you about the oxygen piping in the Shock Room.'

Joss said, 'I can wait, Sister.'

'If you wouldn't mind?' Her smile was very attractive. It disappeared when she finally turned to me. 'Staff Nurse Maitland?'

'Yes, Sister. The Night Superintendent—'

'I've seen her. I'll deal with you, directly. Wait.' She went off with Dolly.

Joss and I looked at each other. And I smiled. 'I didn't expect this, Joss.'

He didn't smile. 'Quite a turn-up for the book. Tell me something, Cathy—' he took a deep breath. 'How much accident time have you actually had on this side of the Atlantic?'

I had not expected the lunatic, the lover, or the poet in the A.U. at this hour on a Monday, but nor had I expected this. I answered his question then added what I had said to Night Super.

'Uh-huh,' he grunted.

'Have a good drive back?'

'Yep. Thanks. Get to your digs all right?'

'Fine, thanks. Just fine.' He saw my glance at his tie, so i smiled again. 'I didn't realize you always wore your battle colours.'

He glanced downwards. 'I don't.'

The silence was stifling. I remembered he hadn't had breakfast. 'Busy night?'

'Not particularly.'

'From the log, yesterday seems to have been nightmarish.'

'Just the usual fine summer Sunday holocaust.' He looked at me through his lashes. 'One doesn't expect to play ring o' roses on the job. Not that one's anything against the game—when one's nothing better to do.'

For a few seconds I was too angry to answer and half my anger was directed at myself. He wasn't the first man to regret Saturday night on Monday morning, but he was the first I had taken seriously. 'Can't say it's ever really sent me. How's Stan Lawson this morning? I haven't heard.'

He said very gravely, 'Not too well, I'm afraid. This seems a very nasty bug.'

'Very nasty,' I agreed as Sister came back.

Chapter Three

'And another police call coming your way, Staff.' The Head Porter rustled some notes at his end of the line. 'One male, one female. Youngish. Minor lacerations, bruises, shock. Driver and front seat passenger, in private car A. Head on, private car B—not going too fast, am I?'

'Just getting that, thanks, Mr Jarvis.' I wrote swiftly on the huge memo pad on the standing desk fixed to the wall at the far end of the Receiving Room. The remainder of the wall was occupied by a line of scrubbing-up sinks.

The three telephones on the desk were red, yellow and green. Set above and on either side of every door in the department were three similarly coloured bulbs. All incoming calls were announced by flashing lights and the only bell ever sounded was the fire alarm. The red was only used to herald admissions; yellow, for outside calls coming through the main switchboard; green, was the inter-hospital line. There was a red telephone in every room and office in the A.U.., including our changing-room.

'Car B, Mr Jarvis?'

'Haven't got 'em out yet. Two involved and up front. Both unconscious, seemly, and in a right mess. One male, one female. Small car, no belts visible. They've got the firemen out.'

'Car A wearing belts, I take it?'

'That's right. Some,' he added laconically, 'never learn, do they? Should be here in about ten minutes.'

Sister glanced through my notes then passed them to Joss. There was a temporary lull on and they were in Cubicle 1 with the four final year medic. students working as accident dressers for that week. The only girl medic. asked, 'Why the fire brigade, Mr Desmond?'

'They've the right type of tin-openers for this type of job.' As the room was empty of patients, all the cubicle curtains were drawn back. Joss looked the five accident tables over. '4 and 5 for these two, Sister? Right. Eccles—' he nodded at one student, '5 with Mr Palmer [the houseman] Huntly, 4 with Mr Charlesworth. Miss—er—'

'Dawson,' said Sister before the girl could open her mouth.

'Thanks.' He told the girl to shadow Dr Anthony and the final student to stick by him. 'MacDonald, isn't it?'

'That's right,' echoed Sister and the student together.

The A.U. trained staff always worked in pairs that were arranged by Sister at the start of each day. At present, Sister was paired with Joss, Dolly with Mr Charlesworth, Nurse Henty, the senior student nurse, with Mr Palmer, and Nurse Fisher, a third-year with more A.U. time than all the other student nurses with the exception of Henty, was with Peter. The most junior houseman, Mr Geddes, was in our plaster theatre for the day, and officially assisted by Mr Kovac, the plaster technician. Mr Kovac, a middle-aged and highly competent Pole, had run the plaster theatre since the A.U. opened. He was a good and tactful teacher.

As necessary the pairs became a team of four, six, or eight, working simultaneously on the same patient. When possible, 1 and 2 were reserved for the most injured, being technically the senior cubicles, but they were all identically equipped and had enough floor space for a team of ten to work, uncramped. Each had its own anaesthetic machine, sucker and respirator, piped oxygen supply, trolleys set with sealed sterile dressing and instrument packs for anything from removing a splinter to the amputation of a limb. The trolleys with metal stands painted red instead of the ubiquitous white held the settings for emergency tracheotomy and cardiac arrest.

The tables looked rather like operating tables but were far more comfortable to lie on. A battery of buttons raised or lowered transfusion and drip stands, altered any part or the whole table to any position wanted. The previous Sister Accidents said the only thing her tables could not do was walk, but give the designers time and they would get that taped. In the rare temporary lull on a Monday morning, she had always demonstrated their uses to the new medic. students starting their weekly rota. I had not yet seen Miss Butler address a direct word to any of them. She gave the impression of regarding them as a necessary evil she was prepared to suffer but under no circumstances enjoy. She wasn't unique in that, nor in the cold glances she had given Miss Dawson's heels and hemline when she first appeared. I could think without difficulty of a dozen sisters with the same reaction. The student girl's hemline was now hidden by her gown and from the way she was standing, the sooner she could get her feet into flatties the happier she'd be.

My job for the morning was 'lights and messages'. 'You won't be any use to me till you've had a refresher,' Sister's tone dismissed my Canadian job as a sinecure best forgotten. 'A year off's a long time.'

The A.U. was officially open from 8 a.m. to 10 p.m. seven days a week and when closed could open at any hour for major emergencies, minor accidents at night being dealt with in Emergencies. The large night staff there always included at least one staff nurse with accident training. When necessary she worked in the A.U. at night with the other nurses from Emergencies, but as Martha's had no shift system for residents, with the A.U. men. These had a weekly rota which gave them—on paper—every other night off-call, one weekly half-day, one free evening, and every other weekend off. The 'weekend' began at noon on Saturday and ended at midnight on Sunday. I could remember the one week when Stan Lawson, as J.A.O., had all his official time off, on time. It had happened in my first month and was still an unbeaten record when I left.

Long before the A.U. first opened, time and motion experts worked out in detail the nurses' shifts. The result was impressive. Every night at ten, all we had to do was hand over to the Emergencies girls and go home. The time and motion experts had done their homework, but they had never worked in an A.U., as hospitals with such units were still rare and hadn't existed when most of them qualified, or trained. It was hard enough to hand over a ward on time when a patient has just had a coronary, or is having a major haemorrhage. It was impossible to remember the clock, much less hand over, when attending to a human being soaked in blood, grime, oil, and with the ends of broken bones visible through a business suit, or dance dress.

Miss Evans understood this, She insisted the student nurses work only their allotted shifts, but left Sister Accidents free to arrange the hours of her staff nurses and herself, providing we somehow got the right number of hours off every week. But the only fixed free time on which we could depend were our two weekly days off. The uncertainty obviously affected our social lives and this was why Miss Evans still refused to appoint any married nurse as Sister Accidents. Stan Lawson was the only married S.A.O. we had so far had, but as his wife worked in the hospital and they had a hospital flat just across the road, in their case it was working out pretty well. Any married man with a family living out was unlikely to have more than three nights a month at home. The tiny hospital flats, originally for bachelors, were now rented to married staff without children. This was another of the many reasons why the S.A.O.'s job appealed only to that handful of individualists.

The red light flashed again. As I reached for the red 'phone, Sister called down the room, 'Lights, Nurses!'

Again, Mr Jarvis: 'Elderly gent. for you, Staff. Seventy-odd. Query fractured left femur. Shock. Stepped in front of a double-decker without looking—bit hard of hearing, I shouldn't wonder. On his way in—hold it, Staff! And another! Little lad. Query greenstick fracture right forearm, minor lacerations, shock. Come off his bike—day off for half-term, I reckon. Parents not yet contacted—got that?'

'Nearly.' The occupants of car A were being wheeled in on low accident stretcher-trolleys. I asked if he knew more of car B?

'Seems they're having a bit of trouble still. The roof's caved down like a sardine tin that's been stamped on, they say.' He rang off and I winced.

The small boy, Mark Alan Langley, arrived before the elderly man, a Mr William Henry Pears. Mark was eight, fair, skinny, and it was his first visit to a hospital. Though without his parents and surrounded by masked and gowned strangers, he was as sensible and co-operative as the most intelligent adult. But unlike an adult on finding himself a patient for the first time, Mark was totally unimpressed by all he saw.

Mr Palmer and Nurse Henty were attending to him. Joss had seen him and ordered his treatment on admission, as he did for every patient, then returned to Mr Pears in C2. He took another look at Mark as the technician was adjusting the angle of the portable X-ray machine. The Langley parents had been contacted, 'phoned their consent for treatment and were on their way up. 'Comfortable, Mark?' asked Joss.

Mark said he was O.K. but unless they were all right nuts he didn't see how the bloke could get a picture of his arm from underneath the bed thing. 'This metal'll cut out the rays.'

'It won't.' Joss explained the bed and mattress were specially constructed to let the rays pass through. He used 'constructed', not 'made'.

Mark remained unimpressed. 'Colour pictures?'

The technician apologized. 'No.'

'Am I on closed-circuit t.v.? Don't you even have closed-circuit t.v.?'

'I'm afraid not,' said Joss.

'I say,' said Mark, 'this is a rather grotty old hospital, isn't it?'

Mr Palmer drawled apologetically, 'We have been going six hundred years.'

'Cor, that's older than my grandad! No wonder it's creaky.'

Dolly was washing at the sink next to the desk when Sister paused by me. 'Nurse Maitland, will you inform me directly the Langleys arrive, but put them in the relatives' rest-room and offer them tea.'

Dolly waited till Sister moved away. 'What does she think you are? A first-year?'

'Maybe Benedict's first-years don't answer 'phones and make the tea.'

She pulled a face behind her mask. 'Maybe Benedict's haven't sent us the rightest little megalomaniac in the business.'

A few minutes later, Mr Palmer re-scrubbed beside me. He was a tallish, willowy young man with a very trendy hair-cut and a languid air. He was nearly as dark as Joss but had blue not brown eyes. I had seen him around at parties as a student, but this was the first time we had worked together. 'Great place this for crushing the ego into the ground,' he murmured behind his mask. 'Do you suppose that revoltingly erudite little monster's mama was once a Miss Butler?'

I caught his eye. Joss was only a yard away. 'I've no more details yet, Mr Palmer, as Mark's parents haven't arrived.' He glanced round and then winked at me without saying more.

Peter was next to use that sink. 'How much longer are they going to be getting those poor sods out of car B?'

I told him what Mr Jarvis had said and he winced. 'How are the Gamlins?' The couple in Car A.

'Desmond says she can go home once she's rested-up, and he shouldn't be warded more than overnight.'

I smiled voluntarily. 'That's something.'

His eyes smiled over his mask. 'I'm glad you're with us. Every this morning I've felt the gods have it in for me I've looked at you and changed my mind. Know what I mean?'

I knew exactly. Being a small blonde with curves if under-developed, in the right places, I had long come to terms with the fact that to most men I wasn't a sex symbol, I was a teddy-bear substitute. I got cuddled, but seldom embraced. Joss on Saturday night had been a new experience for me as well as one I now wanted to forget as fast I could—if I could. Angry as he had made me, seeing him all morning wasn't making things easier.

He had moved to the sink beside Peter's. Soaping his hands and arms, he looked my way as casually as Stan Lawson or any other S.A.O. would have done. 'Taking them the hell of a time getting that car open. Much longer and the poor bastards'll come in as B.I.D.s.' Brought In Dead.

Peter said he was thinking that. 'Anyone with them?'

'Mr Jarvis hasn't said, but presumably they've got some medic. there as our Crash Team hasn't been called out.'

Sister caught my eyes and beckoned. 'Staff, I wouldn't have thought it necessary to say this to a nurse of your seniority, but possibly you've acquired some different professional standards in the past year. In future, please remember, I do not like my staff to gossip on-duty.'

She was Sister, so I apologized meekly, though I thought she was mistaken. I thought that again in the next temporary lull. Car B was now on everyone's mind. The men and medic. students were standing around or sitting on high stools, staring into space. The nurses were silently dealing with the clearing, checking and re-stocking that went on constantly between cases. I thought the silence unhealthy. Formerly, here even more than in the theatres, when patientless, the staff had used casual, crazy, even heated discussions, as a safety-valve. The whole staff, as all the nurses were senior students, since only third and fourth years worked in the A.U. The present atmosphere reminded me of my first ward ex-P.T.S. and how much my set as well as myself had resented being treated by our nursing and medical seniors as moronic machines the year after we'd grown accustomed to being accepted as intelligent young adults in our sixth forms. At the end of that year Miss Evans had become our first C.N.O., instead of Matron. She was still in her thirties. Her revolutionary ideas on the treatment of student nurses had horrified many, but not all, our older sisters, but inside of two years had cut the Martha's drop-out rate amongst student nurses by twenty per cent. Looking around it struck me as time St Benedict's had a Miss Evans, and then I noticed Joss surveying the room in much the same way as myself.

Mr Palmer had been strolling round aimlessly. He stopped to watch some adjustments Peter was making to the anaesthetic machine in C1 and obviously absently, after fiddling with a pair of scissors lying on a shelf by his hand, put them in his pocket. Sister rounded on him as if he had been caught shop-lifting. 'Mr Palmer, those scissors you're secreting happen to be my private property!'

It was a very little thing. In any department the wrong scissors got picked up by the wrong owners a dozen times a day. But as everyone was on edge, it united the home staff into an outraged band of brothers and sisters. Mr Palmer's reactions enhanced the unity.

'Sister, I'm stricken with remorse—but stricken!' Bowing affectedly, he returned her scissors at arm's length. 'Pray accept my most humble— nay—profound apologies and assurances that to take your personal property is the last thing I would ever desire to do. How can I make amends?'

Joss said, 'Just ask Mr Jarvis for a couple of sacks, nip down to the basement for some ashes from the boilerhouse, get off those shoes and get started for Canterbury. It's only sixty odd miles.'

Sister had looked ready to hit Mr Palmer, but as Joss had spoken, she smiled weakly. The staff had its first, and only, communal laugh of the morning.

The red light jerked every head towards me. I shook mine as Mr Jarvis dictated: 'Male, 21, burns to face, head, arms. Motor mechanic. Minor explosion in garage workshop. No others involved.'

The red light continued to flash with the monotony of traffic signals. At last: 'Got 'em out, Staff. Car B. Both on their way—'

'Thank God for that, Mr Jarvis.'

'That's as maybe, Staff. Ready?'

I braced myself. Mr Jarvis was an experienced and humane man. 'Sure.'

The police had discovered the couple's names and address. They were a Mr and Mrs Yates and in their forties. Mr Yates had visible multiple injuries to his head, chest and both legs. Mrs Yates' visible injuries were worse. 'Nasty,' added Mr Jarvis.

'God,' I muttered, 'yes.'

Joss grimaced as he read my notes over Sister's shoulder. He gave them to the medic. students. 'Take a look so you'll know what to expect. And remember what I told you earlier. No one'll mind if you feel queasy, providing you get yourselves out before you pass out. No bloody heroics, please.' He turned to Sister. 'We'll start with four on each.'

Sister nodded. 'Nurse Maitland, as I'll probably be held up, will you see Mrs Gamlin gets a lunch-tray in the S.R. [Shock Room] and make her some fresh tea.'

'Yes, Sister.'

Dolly and Henty exchanged mutinous glances. I was tempted to mutiny with them, but I had to see Sister's angle, now, if I hadn't earlier. I had never worked in the present accident team. For any team of any nature to work well takes regular practice together as well as skill. Practice takes time; there was none to spare in the present situation. It was an A.U. maxim that the longer a dangerously injured patient took to reach us, the less time there was to save his or her life. Once the Yates's arrived and Joss decided what had to be done, and done first, for them, the team had to know without more talk, not only their own but everyone else's job.

In these cases, the S.A.O. never had more than minutes for his decisions. There was no time for consulting the opinions of pundits, taking X-rays, or pathological tests. In time the last two would be taken probably by the dozen, providing the S.A.O. had correctly judged which was the most serious injury or clincal condition requiring the most immediate treatment. A snap decision would have been difficult enough when examining an unknown patient in a clean nightgown in a ward bed for the first time. Accident victims were generally fully dressed, but no matter how they started out, no one stays clean after being involved in a bad road smash. The diagnosis of visible injuries could be complicated by clotted blood and road dirt, but brain and internal damage did not always show up at once in a patient already in coma from shock. The last Sister Accidents once said that in her view to be a good S.A.O. took experience, skill and guts in equal parts.

Joss, Sister, Peter, the pathologist on A.U. call for the day, went out to meet the ambulance, and up into it when it arrived. It seemed a long time before the stretcher trolleys were wheeled in. It was less than five minutes.

The green flashed. 'S.S.O.,' announced Mr Roth's rather harsh voice.

'Mr Desmond free? Oh—? Right. I'll ring back, later. What's that—message? No. Purely domestic issue. Can wait.'

The pale green and opaque fibre glass curtains were closed round C1 and on either side of C2. Mrs Yates was in 1. She had been in there about twenty minutes when Miss Dawson came through the curtains and slowly towards me. She was an attractive girl with a naturally high colour and auburn hair. Her face was pale green before she began to sway.

'Here.' 5 was empty. I switched shut the curtains with one hand, pushed her onto the table with the other. 'Stretch out, love, or you'll pass out.' I pressed the button that raised her feet about her head. 'Stay put whilst I answer that yellow. I'll be back.'

Her face was damp and she closed her eyes. 'Thanks.'

'Is the S.A.O. available to take an outside call, Staff? He's not—oh, don't tell me!' The switchboard girl sighed. 'I've got a caller hanging on that's not going to like this. A Mr Hall. Grandad of a kid called Mark Alan Langley.'

'He doesn't want us, he wants Charity. We sent him up there over an hour ago.'

'Staff, do you mind? I'd a word with Mr Jarvis soon as Mr Hall was on the line and put him onto Sister Charity. And a right barny they had! I only got the finish—he's going to be writing his M.P., the Health Minister, the Prime Minister—the lot! Don't ask me why, nor why he says he insists on getting an official report for his record—don't ask me what record. Sounds dead spare, he does, and he's not going to like this wait! Shall I put him on to you?'

I damned Sister Charity, mentally. Her tactlessness with relatives was only beaten by her excellence at nursing sick children. 'Sure. See what I can do.'

'And the best of British to you, mate,' she said in one voice, and in another, 'The Staff Nurse in the Accident Unit is on the line to you now, sir.'

Mr Hall had an educated voice and was in a flaming temper that was probably two-thirds delayed-action anxiety. He had had, he said, as much nonsense as he could stand from domineering women and he did not propose to take any more from me. He was not asking for the moon, he was merely asking for the simple courtesy that was incidentally his right as a tax-payer. 'Whom do you imagine pays your salary, young woman? My fellow tax-paying citizens and myself! Be good enough to ask the surgeon who attended my grandson, Mark Langley, on admission, to spare me three minutes of his time. I'll wait.'

I watched the drawn curtains round 1 and 2. He sounded the type to bombard Miss Evans, the Dean, and the Editor of *The Times* with irate letters, though on what grounds only God and Sister Charity knew. In these circumstances, that should not do Joss and Sister any harm, but as anyone with any experience of hospital life would understand, unfairly, it would not do them any good. Sister Charity was in a different situation, being a long-established law unto herself. Every paediatrician in Martha's knew she was tactless with relatives, but would go to the stake rather than lose her nursing talents.

Then I remembered Butler's remark about different professional standards and an elderly Canadian nurse with whom I had worked. On similar occasions, she'd mutter to herself, 'You want the truth, huh? Buster, you will surely get a load of it!' Her technique worked superbly on English-Canadians, Scots-Canadians, French-Canadians, British-British.

And Mr Hall.

'Is that so? Dear, dear, dear! How most distressing! Naturally, you can't consider disturbing the surgeon's concentration—Mr Desmond, did you say? When would you suggest I call him back? Three-thirty? Before the evening rush-hour starts? I quite understand—thank you—if you would tell him to expect my call then? You will? Most obliged—may I ask your name? Ah! Tell me, Staff Nurse Maitland, did you by any chance see my grandson when he was admitted to your department? Very shaken, I've no doubt, without his parents—I beg your pardon—oh!' His voice was now oozing pride. 'Well, well! I'm delighted to hear he behaved himself. He's not a bad little fellow, really, but being my only grandchild—yes, I thought you'd understand. Good day to you!'

Miss Dawson had lowered her feet and was sitting up. 'Someone giving you his life's history?'

I nodded and wrote a note telling Joss to expect the call and why, then pinned it to the baize board above the desk. I took her pulse. 'Your colour's better but I shouldn't go back yet.'

She shuddered. 'Must I? At all?' She read the answer in my expression. 'Or switch subjects?'

I nodded again to save our voices disturbing the others and beckoned her to follow me into the Shock Room. The fourth-year student nurse working in there was trying an assortment of slippers on a youth who had cracked his left tibia falling off his scooter and was waiting for his plaster to dry before going home. Our Shock Room was in actual fact less dramatic than it sounded, being where our patients rested until going home. The only other patient there now was Mrs Gamlin. She was asleep behind drawn curtains.

Miss Dawson took a look round them, then came and sat on a stool by the standing desk that was a twin with the one in the Receiving Room. 'I can't believe they were in the same accident.'

'The Gamlins' car was much bigger and heavier—and they had on belts.'

'That's what Mr Desmond said. He's good, isn't he?'

'I've only worked with him this morning, but I've heard he is.'

'He must be or Hoadley East wouldn't have shoved him in over our own men's heads—and even the orthopod boys admit Desmond knows his orthopaedics. But that woman—' She was shuddering again. 'Did you see what she looks like? No hair—no face—she didn't even look human. I was all right, till I suddenly realized she was a woman—I don't know why that did it?'

I said, 'There but for the Grace of God ...' I got her some tea from the urn. 'This is a bit stewed. I'll make fresh soon, if you'd like to wait.'

'This is bliss, thanks.' She looked at the Martha's badge on my apron bib. 'How long've you been a staff nurse?'

I had to think. 'It's over two years since I finished midder.'

'That long! Why on earth are you making the tea and answering the 'phone?'

'Someone has to.' The green was on. 'Accident Unit. Staff Nurse Maitland speaking.'

'Canteen here, Staff,' said an aggrieved female voice. 'That lunch you ordered for a patient. It's ready, but you'll have to send someone to fetch it. Lunches have started. We're much too busy to run your errands.'

'We'll collect it, thanks.' I rang off and asked Miss Dawson if she would get the tray. 'Just take off that gown and mask. I'll explain to Sister, later.'

'Thanks,' she said, 'thanks a lot.' Then she said, 'Staff, does one get used to this?' I shook my head. 'That why Sister looks so ill? Being at it all the time?' She looked upwards as I suddenly reached for the green 'phone. 'What's happened to that green? It's gone red and it's not flashing.'

The nurse across the room caught my eye. I said, 'Yes, Sister,' rang off, and took Miss Dawson into the corridor. I closed the door, picked up the green receiver on the wall shelf. 'Lodge, please. Mr Jarvis? Accident Unit, Nurse Maitland. Morgue trolley, please. Yes. Mrs Yates.'

Miss Dawson leant against the wall. 'I—I suppose you still want that tray?'

'Please.'

In the Receiving Room, Joss was washing at the sink by the desk. We exchanged bleak glances. I told him the trolley was coming.

'Thanks, Staff,' he said mechanically, and went on soaping his hands and arms to above the elbows.

Chapter Four

By Thursday in that week the 'flu epidemic in south-east England was making front-page headlines; the London hospitals were only admitting emergencies to medical beds; Florence and Stephen, our sick-staff wards, had overspilled into the Private Wing, our S.M.O., Dr Gray, was daily risking violent injury from his juniors by his reiteration that the worst was yet to come; and I was still on 'lights and messages'.

There were some minor changes in the U.A. One of the medics., Mr Eccles, and a fourth-year student nurse had caught 'flu. The latter had been replaced by a girl in Henty's set who only finished her A.U. time last month. Her name was Rosalind Roberts and the Office appointed her to Henty's job, and moved Henty and Dolly up to acting third and second staff nurse. This seemed to please Sister, even if it did not stop her brooding over us like a short-tempered if highly efficient ghost, or encourage her to take more than a fraction of her official daily off-duty.

Having worked with a few other sisters equally determined to work themselves into the ground, though I enjoyed the attitude no more than most senior staff nurses, it only worried me now as it looked to me as if that was precisely what Butler was going to do. Neither Dolly nor Peter agreed. Dolly said she couldn't recall Sister looking anything but ready for a shelf in a morgue fridge. 'She always hung around when Chalmers and White were on.'

'As much as now?'

'Not quite—but she hadn't her very own dashing white surgeon running the shop then. Can't say I blame her.' She flapped her china-doll eyelashes. 'I fancy Sister's D.W.S.'

'I thought you didn't fancy queues?'

'So where does it say a girl can't change her mind?'

Peter was convinced all that ailed Sister could be put right with a few shots of iron. 'Half the women in England are only over-tired because they're short of iron.' He reached out a hand and hitched down my lower eyelids. 'You could use some, Cath.'

We were in the canteen just then. My feet were hurting after standing around all morning watching others working under pressure and my temper was unimproved by the chat Joss was having with a pale, willowy brunette physiotherapist in the coffee queue. She was of the same physical type as Miss Butler and I suddenly realized why the latter had struck me as familiar when we first met. All the girls Joss had brought home in the past could also have been painted by Burne-Jones.

'Don't maul, Pete! I loathe it!'

He looked ready to burst into tears. He had had a bad morning. Sister had snapped at him for breaking a large glass funnel, his mother had written him a stern postcard for forgetting his father's birthday and he had had a letter from his bank manager about his overdraft. He insisted he hadn't meant to maul as he knew no one liked being mauled by him and if I was going to be like that he'd just settle for the fact he hadn't a friend in the world. He glowered at Joss's back. 'Why do some chaps have it made? What's he got that I haven't—as if I didn't know?'

'Well, if you fancy Butler—?'

That cheered him. 'Rather settle for my bank manager. What am I going to say to the sod, Cath?'

We drafted a placating letter for the rest of our break. When we left, Joss and the physio were at a table by the door. He didn't turn his head. Nor did I, but I've always had excellent sideways vision.

Had Joss and I only met again in Martha's, he would have been the obvious, and first, person I'd have asked about Butler's health. Last Saturday had altered our relationship more than I would have believed possible until it happened. Previously, after some other man and I stopped dating each other, we had always stayed on amicable terms, and I had never known any of those dates as long, and well, as I knew Joss. It took me a couple of days to realize that was the basic problem. Making a fool of oneself to a semi-stranger mattered only as long as one remembered the stranger's name—if it mattered at all. But who enjoys looking a fool to a life-long friend, or easily forgives that friend for witnessing the folly? Yet oddly, and disturbingly, when watching Joss in the A.U., it never once occurred to me to think of him as Ruth's brother. I did frequently wonder if I had dreamed up Saturday night.

Thursday was invariably the quietest day of the A.U. week and that one was typical. I was off from two to five; Sister, officially, from five-thirty. When Miss Mackenzie appeared in the Receiving Room just after eight, Henty and I were alone. Sister was still in her office working on the day's notes with Joss, it being a hospital rule that all accident notes had to be entered in full in the A.U. log on the day, or night, on which they were made. After any rush of admissions, this could literally take hours and needed the S.A.O.'s co-operation owing to the complicated treatments given and the fact that his signature stood against each entry. If the S.A.O. was taking his rare time off, the J.A.O. acted for him, just as her deputy was permitted to do for Sister. I had not yet been allowed to write even the date in our log.

Henty was mending gowns and I was tidying the blank forms filing

cabinet by the X-ray screens. Miss Mackenzie's advent made Henty leap
off her high stool and I shut the metal filing drawer so fast it nearly took
off my fingers. 'Good evening, Sister. Can I help you?'

Miss Mackenzie's grey eyes X-rayed the room, Henty and myself.
'Good evening, Staff. Are you on, is Sister still here?' And when I
explained, 'I will not disturb Miss Butler as she's busy. Kindly ask her to
step into my office on her way off.' She had another look round. 'Very
quiet, just now.'

'Yes, Sister. No admissions for an hour.'

'Thursday,' she said. 'Low pay packets. And whilst that is regrettable,
there's no doubt in my mind the situation had saved many a life. I'll see
myself out. Thank you, Staff.'

'Thank you, Sister.'

Henty and I stared at each other in silence until the airtight doors
sealed themselves.

'Staff, why didn't she just pick up a 'phone?'

I did not answer at once. Henty was a quiet, trim, likeable girl and
fast worker, but I didn't yet know her well enough to know if she could
keep her mouth shut. 'Maybe she was just passing.'

Henty blinked thoughtfully through her steel-rimmed granny glasses.
'Do you think Sister's getting the bug?'

'I've wondered that, but as the invasion's so short, I don't think she
can be. She certainly looks very tired.'

She picked up her sewing. 'She has for the last month. Could Miss
Mackenzie have noticed?'

'Very little Miss Mackenzie doesn't notice.'

We exchanged another meaning stare. As she was obviously wondering how much she could trust me, she tested the ice again. 'I suppose
all Sister Accidents do a lot of overtime.'

'Occupational hazard in their job.' I glanced at the wall clock. Sister
objected strongly to being interrupted for non-essential reasons when
writing up the log, but if she took Miss Mackenzie's visitation as that, I
didn't and nor did Henty. I asked her to watch the lights whilst I went
along to Sister's office.

'Hold it, Staff, hold it!' Mr Palmer swept in beaming with the
eagerness of the bearer of bad news. 'My dears—my very dears—
lamentable tidings! Our Stanley has right lobar pneumonia. The
physicians are in a positive tiz-woz! They've got him in a tent—giving
him the whole works!'

'Oh no!' Henty and I exchanged 'that's why' glances as we spoke
together. 'How utterly miserable!'

'I'm very sorry to hear this, Dave.' Joss had come in, unnoticed.
'Where've they got him?'

'Stephen Small Ward One. The S.M.O.'s just said he won't be back inside of a month. And guess what else our own dear Cassandra said—'

I left them to it and went along to Sister. She was still writing at her desk, but with her head propped on her left hand as if the weight was too much for her neck. She took both my items of news with a weary sigh. 'This seems a particularly virulent virus.'

'It caused a lot of bad chests in Canada.'

'Did you get it, Staff? Not that that'll prevent your getting it again. Pity about Mr Lawson, but with antibiotic therapy he should soon clear up. I only hope Mr Desmond keeps healthy for us.'

'Yes.' She looked so ghastly that I added, 'Sister, forgive me, but are you feeling all right? You look rather tired.'

She smiled at me for the first time. 'I'm always this colour without make-up. My grandmother used to say I should eat more carrots. She pinned her faith in the human race on carrots. Fed me so many, I now can't look at 'em.'

I had never known her so human. I was almost sorry. If I was going to start liking her, my life in the A.U. was going to become even more complicated than it was already. Peter underlined this when he drove me home that night, being off-call. He nearly hit a bus when I suggested Butler might be human underneath.

'Scrub that! The woman's impossible! God alone knows why Joss Desmond fancies her.'

'He's fancied highly strung neuros since he was in hot pants at prep. school.'

'How do you know that?'

I pretended I had forgotten to tell him. 'Didn't Dolly Jones tell you I was at school with Ruth Desmond?'

He shook his head, gloomily. 'She's not on speaking terms with me now as I'm a chum of old George. He and Dolly've had another of their out-fallings.'

'Dolly and George Charlesworth? A pair? Since when?'

'Last few months. Haven't you noticed they've been at each other's throats all week?'

'No.' I was surprised and intrigued. 'Are they serious?'

'Don't know that she is. Poor old George has got it badly. He's dead glum now. He says Dolly fancies Joss Desmond. Seems every woman in Martha's fancies the guy. Do you?'

'I have this anti-thing to crowds.'

He laughed and drew up outside my landlady's house. 'I didn't think you would. For starters, you couldn't push him around. You've never gone for guys you can't push around—or with dark hair.' He smoothed his blond hair smugly. 'It's the Nordic charm that sends you. Going to ask me for coffee?'

'If you want some and you make it.'

He got out of the car. 'Know what sends me about you? The gracious warmth of your invitations.'

I smiled peevishly. 'Come off it, Pete! You know I make lousy coffee and Roxanne's still away making a telly commercial somewhere in the Italian Alps.'

My landlady was in the hall. She had always liked Peter and greeted him as if he were back from Canada. Over the coffee he made very well I asked why he had not contacted Roxanne whilst I was away.

'With my overdraft?'

'I'll bet Roxanne's is bigger. She earns a lot when she's working, but she isn't always in work.'

'She seems to do all right without.' He got off the sofa for a closer look at the full length photo on the bookshelf of Roxanne modelling a lace trouser suit. In common with most of the men who were my friends he had never been able to believe Roxanne's highly decorative exterior hid an ardent and very hard-working career girl. 'Why hasn't she yet managed to land one of the well-heeled legion she runs around with?'

'She doesn't want to. She likes working.'

'I suppose being a champagne girlie is working—of a sort.'

'Peter,' I said, 'don't be bitchy.'

He turned, smiling. 'I just hate the idle rich. Any more coffee in that pot?'

I investigated. 'Sorry, no. Be an angel and make some more.'

He picked up the pot, then stood looking down at me, reflectively. 'Why do I let you push me around?'

'Because you and I, lovey, have a beautiful relationship.'

There was a new and very serious expression on his face. 'I can think of worse,' he said shortly, and went out to make the coffee on the cooker on the landing. I wondered absently what was on his mind, then remembered what he had said about Joss. I was in a very bad temper when he got back, but as he had relapsed into one of his 'the gods have it in for me' moods, our mutual gloom was downright companionable.

Normally, my gloom wore off overnight. Not that night. When I joined the other living-out day staff nurses waiting at the dais end of the dining-room for Night Super to read the day register in the morning, I decided leaving Canada had been the greatest mistake of my life.

Dolly Jones squeezed in beside me a minute before one of the Night Sisters arrived instead of the Super. 'Think the old girl's got the bug?' she murmured without moving her lips.

I shrugged in answer as the Night Sister was looking directly at us.

'Good morning, Nurses. As the Night Superintendent has been unavoidably detained, I'll start for her. Nurse A. L. Adams ...'

The ward changes came after the register. The Night Sister closed the book and produced a list. 'Several changes today, Nurses. Departments first. Emergencies and Accidents. Nurse J. Smithers from Emergencies to the Accident Unit as extra fourth-year nurse. Nurse Donkin from Mark Ward to the Accident Unit as extra third-year nurse.' She looked up and at me. 'Staff Nurse Maitland, the Night Superintendent will ring you directly she is free. In the meantime will you carry on as usual with the early routine. You will find the Accident Unit already open. Now— Ear, Nose and Throat Department, Nurse M. Francis ...'

Dolly's eyes were closed. 'Please God, please God *not* another school bus. I can take most things,' she muttered, 'but not mangled kids.'

My stomach heaved. 'Too early.'

She breathed out. 'So it is. Forgot.'

Henty joined us as we left the dining-room. 'There was nothing about a train crash on the seven o'clock news.'

'Whatever it is,' gasped Dolly as we shot towards the A.U. 'it has to be big. Another eighteen down with the bug this morning, but we've got two extras. I'll bet we find every cubicle occupied.'

Neither Henty not I took her up. If we had, Dolly would have lost. Our Receiving Room was empty, though looking as if someone had let off a bomb in it. The Emergencies night staff were grey with fatigue and the empty vaco-litres of blood waiting to be returned to the Path. Lab. needed a stretcher-trolley of the usual basket.

'Sorry about the mess, Maitland.' The senior night staff nurse swallowed a yawn as she gave me our log, dangerous drug and medicine cupboard keys. 'Been one of those nights.'

'Won't take long to clear. Non-stop admissions?'

'No one in between three and five, which was a break as we were still clearing up the seven involved in a three-car pile-up around midnight. Four men to Albert, two girls to Catherine, one to I.C. [Intensive Care] and all still with us, *pro tem.* But the balloon really went up at ten past five. Twenty-two workmen.' She yawned hugely. 'The coach taking the early shift to some all-night building job tangled with a jack-knifing lorry loaded with steel girders.' She nodded at my expression. 'Yes. Messy.'

'Where've they gone?'

'Ten home after treatment. Six to Albert, three to Arthur, three to I.C. The last lad was only fit to shift a few minutes ago. We had to get all your men, apart from the S.A.O., out of their beds again. He was still up in his office doing the notes of the three-car job. He's still there working on the new lot, but the rest have gone back to their rooms. I was about to raise the poor man some tea. Can I leave that?'

'Sure. Sorry you've had it so rough. Sleep well.'

She smiled slightly. 'I won't sleep when I get to bed. I'll just bloody die of tiredness. Thanks.'

In the Receiving Room the girls had the floor and walls clean. After my explanation, Dolly demanded, 'If we've no patients, why extra staff?'

'God knows.' I pulled off my cuffs and unbottoned my sleeves. 'As we don't know how long we've got, I'll do the work-list verbally. Nurse Jones and Henty, cubicles for immediate admissions, please—don't wait. Nurse Smithers, follow Nurse Jones. Nurse Fisher, show Nurse Donkin how to set the Shock Room. Nurse Fraser, Hedges and Black, re-stocking and testing all round, starting in here. I'll do laundry, desks, dispensary and outhouses.'

Donkin whispered to Fisher, 'How many immediate admissions are we expecting?'

'We aren't,' retorted Fisher, 'but we could have 'em any time. Watch the red bulbs over the doors. When they flash, we're in business.'

It was fifteen minutes before we had the room ready and I was free to check the outhouses—i.e. the offices, stock, linen, and other equipment rooms off our corridor. Sister's office was tidy. Peter's looked as though hit by a hurricane rather than a bomb as there were no blood stains. I put on a kettle while I straightened it up, made tea, knocked on Joss's closed door and went into his office without waiting for an answer.

'Good morning,' I said. 'Tea.'

He looked up from his writing with bloodshot eyes and the deliberation of old age. Even the condition of his uncharacteristically untidy hair had aged. It was dulled, lifeless. The front of his crumpled white coat was speckled with blood and there were ink stains on the right cuff. The mask round his throat was a limp paper frill. 'Thanks. I'm just finishing these notes. Then I hope to God the customers will let me get a bath, shave and some breakfast.' He fingered his blue chin very slowly. 'If not, I'll probably drop off over the next one in.'

'I can imagine.' I found a space for the tray and poured his tea. Seeing him like this had shaken me even more, if in another way, than Monday morning. He not only looked so much older and exhausted, he looked so vulnerable. 'I know you don't take sugar, but couldn't you use some?'

He smiled faintly, 'If you say so, Nursie—and don't mind my promptly throwing up on this carpet.'

I smiled and put down the tongs. 'Maybe you're right. You never did fancy sweeties.' I put the cup by his right hand. 'Sorry you had such a ghastly night, though I gather it's been pretty successful.'

He stiffened. 'We got 'em out of this Unit alive, but whether two of the chaps now in I.C. or their relatives'll thank us for saving them is an open question. One had two inches of driving mirror sticking out of his frontal lobe and the rest inside. The other poor bastard had his skull sliced open like a boiled egg. If I.C. do another great job on them,' he added bitterly, 'two nice human vegetables from here to eternity.'

I held on to the edge of the desk. 'Joss. I'm sorry. I didn't know.'

'Nor will the backroom boys if I don't finish these something notes for them. Shove me the log some time and I'll put 'em in.' The green light flashed. He reached the green receiver before me. 'Accident Unit, Desmond—oh? Yes, Sister, she's here.' He nodded to me to wait but did not hand over. 'Sorry, Sister, what was that? Oh!' His voice altered and his face clouded with anxiety. 'She is? I'm very sorry. Very.' He listened, frowning. 'Yes, I've thought so, too. Yes. Of course. We all will. Yes, right now.' He passed me the receiver. 'The Night Superintendent.'

'Bad news?' I mouthed, taking it.

'Bloody awful.' He picked up his pen and went back to his notes.

Miss Butler was warded in the Sisters' Home with query glandular fever. 'In Dr Gray's opinion,' said Night Super, 'no question of influenza, but this is only his provisional diagnosis.' She talked for quite a time. She did not mention leukaemia, but from what she said it was as omnipresent in Dr Gray's, Miss Evans,' and her own mind as in mine. I watched Joss as I listened. Not only mine. I thought of Butler's colour, perpetual tiredness, thinness and snappy temper. All four did not have to be the forerunners of serious illness, but few were the serious illnesses without those early symptoms.

'Now, to deal with the Accident Unit, Nurse Maitland. I have just come from Miss Evans and have been asked to tell you she wishes you to take over temporarily as acting Sister Accidents. Do you feel you can manage?'

I felt paralytic with guilt and fear. 'Er—yes, Sister. That is, I hope so.'

'I'm sure you'll do nicely. Miss Mackenzie and the Office will, of course, give you every assistance. Mr Desmond has just promised every help from the residents—but our residents never let us down! Miss Evans will ring you when she is free to see you during the morning to discuss administrative details. All right?'

There was only one answer. 'Yes, thank you, Sister.'

'Thank you—Sister.'

I put down the receiver slowly. 'How old is she, Joss?'

He went on writing. 'Twenty-six.'

'I thought she looked much too tired. Has she always?'

'Not as much as recently.' He glanced up, briefly. 'So we're running the shop now?'

'Yes.' I was too shaken to be warned-off. 'Joss, I really am very sorry she's ill.'

He sighed, blotted the page, sat back and looked at me wearily. 'Stuff the placebos, Cathy, as I'm too bloody tired to swop 'em.'

'It wasn't a placebo, but if that's how you want to take it—'

'Christ, woman! I don't want to take anything or anyone—I just want to sleep for a week! As I can't, do me a favour—and don't say do I mean 'get lost' or I'll probably hit you.'

I believed him. 'What?'

'Do something about the atmosphere in the something Unit, or we'll all be queuing for beds in Florence and Stephen. I'm not a psychiatrist, so don't ask me why happy departments stay healthy. I just know they do. Get happiness-spreading. Get this dive an oasis of brotherly bloody love, before some patient gets bumped off because the team's too short-handed and bloody-minded to do the job properly. And as this has to start at the top, you and I'll have to love each other. Get me?'

'Yes.'

'Good.' He took up his pen. 'With the news under your belt your happiness-spreading should be off to a head start.'

I turned at the door. 'I thought we had to love each other?'

He raised his triangular eyebrows. 'Passionately,' he said flatly, 'but even a decadent Englishman has his limits. Never before breakfast.'

I looked from his haggard face to his stained coat and the notes piled on his desk. 'That tea'll be stone cold if you don't drink it soon.' I went out and closed the door quietly.

Chapter Five

'I'm glad this repulsive weather is doing someone good.' Roxanne hitched her chair nearer the electric fire in our living room. 'When the camera crew and I got out of the 'plane yesterday and saw snow, we blamed the gin.'

Peter draped an arm along the sofa behind my shoulders and watched the hail hitting the window. 'One of the few patients we had in today swore blind his grandad had seen the Derby run in a snowstorm. Personally, I go along with Joss. Straight case of the Lord tempering the wind to the shorn lambs.'

'Lamb,' I said, 'singular.'

Roxanne glanced at me as she flicked back her long dark hair with both hands. We had talked most of last night, but Joss's name had only come up since Peter brought me home tonight. 'What's the latest on the sick Sister?'

Peter answered. 'Almost certainly glandular fever, though her blood count still isn't adding up as Charlie Gray'd like it. Time'll tell.'

I groaned. 'Leave the corn to the S.M.O., please!'

He flushed. 'You mean your middle name isn't Cassandra too, Cath?'

We had had a tremendous row over Butler. And as few things can beat a guilt complex for putting people in bad tempers, initially, every member of the A.U. home staff had blamed everyone else for missing the diagnosis. This had consequently relaxed tension all round without any help from me, and given Joss an overwhelming psychological advance. In one of our note-writing sessions he said he didn't know whether he was more amused or sickened to find himself currently top of the A.U. pops.

Miss Butler was now in Florence Small Ward. Joss visited her for a few minutes at least twice a day and made a particular point of telling us so. When we sent her flowers from the A.U., he had passed on her grateful thanks to the whole staff. The same evening doing the notes he told me that had he been Naomi, we'd have had our flowers back, stat, with a note telling us what we could do with them. 'Naomi was quite touched, but, of course, she had a temp. of 104 when they arrived.'

'Her temp.'s still swinging?'

'Yep. Was that chap Colin Arthur Morris driving the sports job or the estate car?'

'Sports. Thomas John Chester drove the estate.'

'Thanks.' He added the word then glanced across the desk I still thought of as 'Sister's.' 'Stan Lawson's doing all right. He hopes to be discharged in the next week, and have three weeks sick leave. He sent you his regards.'

'Good. Thanks for telling me.'

'As my old man and St Paul would say, faith, hope and charity—and the greatest of these is charity.' He smiled faintly. 'Strain killing you?'

'Not nearly so much,' I lied, 'as having Miss Mackenzie constantly on my neck.'

I thought over those note sessions whilst Peter explained to Roxanne why the cold snap had sent road accidents down and home accidents up. 'Long cold hours of daylight, so the weekend motorists stay home, get down to do-it-yourselves, fall off faulty step-ladders, dig chunks out of themselves with rusty chisels, or slice off their fingers with saws.'

'But you said you'd had a very slack weekend!'

'Compared to the normal holocaust of a normal July weekend, we have.' He saw her surreptitious check on the time. 'Sorry. Should've remembered nothing's so boring as other people's shop.'

'But I love hospital shop! I was only looking at the time as my agent said if she didn't ring by eleven tomorrow's job's on for sure. Do go on, please!' Roxanne turned to me. 'I wish he would, Cathy.'

'Go on, Pete. The girl needs a nice bedtime story seeing she's got to be up at four-thirty.'

'Four-thirty? You're not serious?'

Roxanne and I exchanged resigned glances. In the past we had both told Peter more times than we could remember that more often than not her job entailed getting up in the small hours as so many photographers preferred working by early morning light, or wanted a London setting when the streets were empty. I said, 'She's always creeping out between four and five. That's why she likes having early nights.'

'She doesn't like 'em,' corrected Roxanne, 'she just has to have 'em. If the camera doesn't lie, the swine accentuates. Unless I get enough sleep, the client'll take one look at the rushes and bellow "Get me another girl! I want my goods advertised, not the fact that some stupid cow needs pep pills!" Oh, hell!' Our telephone was ringing. It was in my bedroom, having been put there by a previous tenant. 'I'll bet that's my agent! I'll get it, Cathy.'

'I hope it isn't,' I said when she had gone. 'She's dead keen on tomorrow's job.'

Peter lit a cigarette. 'What's his name?'

'Why,' I said, 'why are men incapable of understanding that a girl can be dead keen on her job and just her job?'

'Hell—with her looks? There must be some man in her life.'

'Sure, rows, but none mean a thing to her—apart from her father. As he raised her alone after her mother died when she was ten, that's hardly surprising.'

'I'd forgotten him. Didn't you say he was an actor, or something?'

'Yes. He acted till his wife died, then started a drama school to stay put. Up north. He's doing very well. He was playing Cyrano when she was born—hence her name, and looks. I met him once. He's still staggeringly good-looking, tall as you but about half your width.' Roxanne was back, smiling. 'Still on?'

'Not my agent. For you. Mrs Desmond from darkest Kent. We had a nice chat about how glad we are you're back.'

'Mrs Desmond at this hour?' I shot into the bedroom convinced disaster had struck either my own or the Desmond family. Mrs Desmond only wanted me to spend my next free weekend at the vicarage. She had just been talking to Joss. 'He said this would be a good time to contact you. I wish he could come down too, but he says the residents are still only getting half-days. Such a worry for you all, this wretched 'flu. It's in every house in the village, but we've missed it so far—touch wood—oh dear—I know that's pagan but I must. And poor Naomi! But what a relief it is nothing worse than glandular fever. Such a nice child—very quiet—but very sweet. Joss brought her home several times last winter— I do enjoy it when the boys bring their girls down, though between ourselves, with Danny I do have difficulty keeping track of their names. I call them all "dearie"—so much safer. Can we expect you next weekend, Cathy? I do hope so as we'd love to see you and there is a little health matter I'd like your advice on. Not a word to Joss,' she added briskly, 'just between you and me.'

Knowing her age it was not hard to guess what that was. I said I would love to get down for the day if I was not free all weekend, but it was possible I might be. One of the junior orthopaedic sisters was due to take over as Sister Accidents when she got back from holiday on Thursday. 'I've a couple of days off owing,' I added.

'So darling Joss said.'

Darling Joss had been a mine of information. She knew all about Stan Lawson's progress, Miss Kenton, the orthopaedic sister's name, and that Joss thought her a very nice and most efficient young woman—which was more than I knew.

'How nice,' I said.

'Isn't it, dear? I'm so pleased you two children are working together. Ruth will be amused! Must ring off now. See you soon!'

Roxanne went to bed a few minutes later. Peter left at midnight as that was one of the few rules on which our landlady had strong feelings. I was undressed and brushing my hair when Roxanne came in wearing her thickest winter housecoat and half a pound of cold cream on her face. 'The lad's changed a lot since I last saw him.'

I was surprised. 'I wouldn't have said so.'

'He has.' She was adamant. 'He's turned into a man. Want some tea?'

'Love some, but how about your rushes?'

'Not sleepy and I'm sick of staring at the ceiling. I can't take a sleeping pill this late or I'll look even worse.'

I swung round to face her. 'How long've you been taking sleeping pills?'

She had to think. 'I had a miserable bout of insomnia just after Christmas. A tame medic. I know gave me some. They've been a lot of help.'

'Sure. That's why you can't now sleep without 'em.'

'Cathy, I'm not hooked! I haven't asked him for another lot. I don't think they're particularly strong.' She went for the bottle. 'Are they?'

I shook out a couple. 'Yes. How many did he give you? Sixty, from the size of this bottle?' She nodded and I replaced the capsules. 'He warn you to mix these with alcohol?'

'Yes. And that they'd make me a bit muzzy till they wore off. He said not to drive—things like that. He was very sensible—and so am I—so stop looking at me like that! I know what I'm doing!'

I lay on my bed. 'Sure, you do! You're twenty-three. If you want to die at thirty, why shouldn't you?'

'One bottle of sleeping pills doesn't make me a junkie!'

'I didn't say it did. Yet. But if you now don't sleep so good unless you have said these little knockouts, if I were you, I'd watch it. Did your tame medic. give you anything to counteract the muzziness?' Her expression answered me. 'Do I know him?'

'No. He's not from a London hospital.'

'Pity. I'd like him to drop in on our own friendly neighbourhood junkies at Martha's. Two jolly wards and a clinic open twenty-four hours a day that never lacks for customers. And every one of the poor kids originally started convinced they'd never get hooked—they could handle it. "Takes you into another world, see, Nurse. Releases like all the creative energies." ' I paused, thinking back to my fourth year. 'Takes 'em into another world, all right. Only how do you create when you're dead?'

'Do stop talking about death!'

'You can't, if you're talking about drugs. Two go together. Like bacon-and-eggs.'

'Only if you're hooked on hard drugs.'

'Sure,' I said, 'but it's a proven fact that every addict, every single addict on the hard stuff, first started on the soft. And once you get on the hard drugs, lovey, you are going to die in about seven years. Maybe much less. Very occasionally, just a little longer.' I paused again, but she was silent. 'Those poor kids used to say "No worse than tobacco or alcohol." Being an alcoholic doesn't do anyone any good, but it's a curable condition. Dying of carcinoma of the lung isn't much fun, but I've seen a good many die of it who've never smoked in their lives—though more who have. But I've never had to sit on the chest of a boy who's chucked smoking, to prevent his bashing his brains out against his headrail as he wants another cigarette.' I locked my hands behind my head. 'Some of the girls were my age. Lots from good homes—on paper. They didn't look like girls. Dirty old women until we cleaned them up. Then just emaciated old women.'

Her brown eyes stood out blackly against the white cream. She jiggled the capsules in their bottle. 'Honestly, knockouts?' I nodded. 'I'd better show you my pep pills. I've only taken about three of them. They make me feel odd.'

When I saw them, that did not surprise me. 'Did your tame medic. qualify in the U.K.?'

'Yes. He's English.' She hesitated. 'Shove both lots down the bog?'

'And your tame medic. with them.'

We had first met when she had her appendix out in Catherine during my second year. A year later we met again by chance at a party. Roxanne had just found our present flat, and I wanted to live out but couldn't get digs I could afford near enough to Martha's. Our flat was a fifteen-minute walk away.

We gave it three months on trial as we barely knew each other and our jobs were so different. We found we got along very well, possibly as we both insisted on going our separate ways, but also as our jobs turned out to have a surprising amount in common. Odd and often long hours; irregular days off; no automatic right to free weekends; and in both unpunctuality on the job was a major crime. In consequence, it suited us equally to keep the flat reasonably tidy and unavoidable chores up to date. We never borrowed each other's clothes or men, if only, as we agreed, because Roxanne was six inches taller than me and we liked totally opposite types. When one of us was entertaining the other kept out of the living-room unless the guest was someone like Peter and part of the establishment. But if either had an unwelcome guest, we did one of the best sister acts in the business. That only once failed; I had rung Peter and he had rushed round as chucker-out. It had made his week, as the limpet had been an ex-steady of Roxanne's who had once been very rude to him.

The temperature shot up that night. Next day summer was back to normal and so was our Monday admission rate. By early afternoon the four new medic. students were wilting visibly. They asked Mr Palmer if it was always like this?

'No, no, dear boys!' He pulled down his mask to mop his face. 'They're only coming in one at a time, today. We only call ourselves busy when they come in by the half-dozen. Not today.'

'Mr Palmer,' I said, 'please, please, don't tempt providence!'

'Not providence, Sister—' he leered amiably as he scrubbed at the sink besides me—'but how about you?'

Joss was washing at my other side. 'Not a chance, Dave. "Unmoved, cold, and to temptation slow." Goes with the job. Right, Sister?'

'Handed out with the Sister's belt, Mr Desmond. You going to get some lunch now we've actually stopped?'

'Seems like a good idea—oh Gawd!' The red light flashing. 'Open your big mouth like that again, Dave, and I'll take you apart with the nearest scalpel and chuck the pieces to Miss Mackenzie for closer grinding.' He dried his hands and read over my shoulder the memo sheet handed me by Nurse Smithers. 'This poor old girl's been lying on the floor since Saturday night, Nurse?'

'That's what the ambulance men told Mr Jarvis, Mr Desmond. In a very neglected condition, they said. The police broke in after the postman saw her lying in the hall when he was pushing a thick circular through her letter-box. She lives alone and the neighbours hadn't noticed she hadn't got her milk in.'

I caught Dolly's eye. 'In C2, please.' I glanced at Joss. 'Sorry about your lunch.'

'Doesn't matter. Lost my appetite.'

The old lady was a Mrs Jennings. She was seventy-nine, very overweight, with arthritis in both legs. She had caught 'flu last week and as she had not called any doctor, it had turned to pneumonia. Her fall down the stairs had fractured her left femur. She had sewn herself into three sets of underclothes and was so infested that even her eyebrows were affected.

Miss Mackenzie paid one of her now habitual visits to the room as Dolly and Nurse Fisher in special gowns were sealing Mrs Jennings' clothing in the large, sturdy brown paper bags provided for this purpose. Mrs Jennings had been moved to a side ward in Intensive Care, Joss had gone to his belated lunch, and I was carbolizing C2's table.

'Don't let me disturb you, Sister.' Miss Mackenzie stood at the foot of the table. She looked at the row of buttons and the rest of the high-powered equipment. 'We pride ourselves on our progress, but Lord Lister would feel at home, just now, in more ways than one. I doubt he was confronted by a more distressingly neglected patient when he first used the carbolic spray in Glasgow Royal Infirmary over one hundred years ago. 1867 as I recall. 1971. Men can be placed on the moon, but in this city old folk can be found in this condition. Progress? H'mmm.' She waited till I had finished then came with me whilst I changed gowns and washed my hands. I was growing so accustomed to her at my elbow that I only dropped the soap once. 'I was sorry to send a patient in that condition to this department,' she said very quietly, 'but as Dr Gray was forced to admit, officially we should not have accepted her. She should have been transferred to a geriatric hospital. Did Mr Desmond object?'

'Only on her account, Sister.' I did not repeat his private comments to me as they were unrepeatable. 'Directly he examined her he insisted she go straight to Intensive Care.'

'You warned Sister Intensive Care?'

'That she was dirty? Yes, Sister.'

'Good.' Her stern face relaxed slightly. 'It is most fortunate that our

Senior Accident Officer is officially permitted to share the Senior Medical and Surgical Officers' privilege of admitting patients on his own authority, but unlike the two senior residents has no overall responsibility for the total bedstate. I have observed Mr Desmond to be a humane as well as sound surgeon. I assured Dr Gray Mrs Jennings would be admitted without question. I'm much relieved.'

I was torn between fascination and disgust by this insight into the works of bureaucracy. 'Sister, otherwise, we couldn't have taken her in?'

'St Martha's has only one geriatic ward and that is full, Sister.'

'I see.' I didn't, but I had to say it. 'In Mr Desmond's opinion she should do quite well. Sister, what'll happen when she goes out as she seems to have no living relatives?'

'I have already contacted our senior social worker. That will be attended to, Sister. Very well.' She nodded to herself, 'Thank you.'

Later, I handed this on to Joss. 'Did you guess we were being used as a side door?'

'Yep.'

'You didn't say!'

'Not my job to teach you yours. Anyway, she had to come in.' He scratched his neck. 'I ate most of my lunch under a shower, but I'm still itching.'

'I feel I'm crawling.'

His eyes danced for the first time since that Saturday night. 'Togetherness, at last!'

I could have kicked myself had my knees not suddenly felt so weak. 'Can Mr Geddes take over the plaster room? Mr Kovak should've been off an hour ago. He'll never go if I don't push him out and he is looking awfully tired.'

'I'm tell Geddes. You don't think Kovac's getting the bug?'

'His temp. was normal when I took it this morning. I think it's just middle age.'

'I hope you're right. I like our elegant Pole and the only man I've seen slap on a better plaster is Hoadley East.'

I handed that one on. 'Don't let on that I have, Mr Kovac.'

The plaster technician's lined leathery faced creased into one of his rare smiles. 'I enjoy my work, Sister, but appreciation is always pleasant.' He managed to bow elegantly in a flapping gown, long white plastic apron and white tennis shoes. 'It will remain our secret—but I am in no hurry to go. I finish that young man's plaster.'

'Mr Geddes is just coming and he'll do it. You must go off, Mr Kovac, or you'll be ill. And what will the A.U. do without you?'

Mr Geddes was small, fair, willing, but nervous. So he bustled in, importantly. 'Right! What's to do?'

Joss had arrived. 'Wheel in that chap on the right, lad.' He took off his white coat. 'Mind if I keep my hand in, Mr Kovac? Once, long long ago, it was rumoured that I crossed the river to be an orthopaedic registrar.'

'Sister, sorry—' Nurse Fisher cantered in. 'Mrs Hicks is in a tiz. She's suddenly discovered she must've left her handbag in the ambulance as she remembers them picking it up when they put her on the stretcher, but not bringing it in here. It hasn't much money in it, but her brother's telephone number at work is in her diary. She's just remembered he asked her to collect his kids from school and they'll be out in a few minutes.'

Mrs Hicks had mild concussion and shock after being knocked down by a girl parking a scooter and was behind drawn curtains in Bed 4 in the Shock Room. The scooter-driver was resting in 5 after having her right clavicle replaced. Both women were later going home in hospital cars.

The handbag had slipped down between Mrs Hicks' mattress and headrail. I rang the head teacher first. He said I could rest assured he would attend to the matter forthwith, and with every respect, Sister, if anything frightened him more than a woman behind a steering-wheel, it was a woman on a mechanically operated two-wheeler. Mrs Hicks' brother was glad his sister was not badly hurt but he couldn't say he was surprised as she never would wear her glasses. 'That's you ladies, all over! All you think of is looking pretty for us mere males and God bless you for it, say I, for one!'

I wondered momentarily with whom Women's Lib would have the tougher struggle and decided on Mrs Hicks' brother as it takes imagination and maturity to feel and admit fear.

The rush hour had began when the Receiving Room red light next flashed. Joss, Peter and Mr Geddes came in together almost immediately, and bringing with them the faint and rather sickly smell of wet plaster. They had listened-in on the Smithers-Jarvis conversation on the plaster room red 'phone. Messrs Charlesworth and Palmer who arrived a minute later had caught it in the rest room.

'Seven, eh?' Mr Charlesworth gloomily studied the huge off-duty rota pinned to the green baize board against the wall above the standing desk. 'Why do the morons have to try and overtake in the rush hour? There goes my early evening. Yours too, Sister?'

'Looks that way, Mr Charlesworth.'

I was down as off at six, but Dolly and I had already arranged that I would stay on till she got back at seven. It was Henty's day off, and though Roberts was a good senior student, she wasn't even an acting staff nurse and it was Monday. Smithers was still too new and the other girls too junior to help Roberts run the department alone. I paired Roberts with Mr Charlesworth, asked Smithers to stay on 'lights and messages' and felt a new sympathy for Butler as I saw the look the girls exchanged.

Joss was watching me. Just after, waiting for the ambulances, he asked, 'Roses or carnations?'

'Roses, please.'

By half past eight all seven men had been moved to the wards. I left Dolly to do the notes with Joss when he got back from supper. On my way out I met Dr Gray in Emergencies' hall. As always now, he enquired mournfully after my own and the A.U. staff's health and advised me to see we all kept up the extra vitamin tablets and took at least a ten-minute brisk walk in the fresh air every day. 'Don't forget, Sister, sensible prevention can well prevent the necessity for cure!'

'I won't forget, Doctor. And how are you?'

He was a dapper little man with the face of a highly intelligent and kindly rat. 'I think I'm well, thank you, Sister. Can't say I've had time to reflect on the matter. Do I look well?'

I smiled. 'Yes, Doctor.'

'Good, good,' he said sadly. 'I haven't a spare male medical bed tonight.'

Chapter Six

I was late off, but Miss Mackenzie was later. 'In and out till we closed,' said Dolly.

'Like this morning.'

'And when you were off this morning. She hung till we suddenly emptied ten minutes ago. We can't be doing things wrong or she'd have said so. Maybe she's just decided she likes the A.U. better than Emergencies?'

I shook my head, thoughtfully. This was beginning seriously to worry me. It had made sense in my first week, but being well into my second with only one more full day in charge, I would have expected—and hoped—Miss Mackenzie's visits would have decreased. The reverse had happened. 'She doesn't like accident work. She told me the other night she's too old for it now. She said it took the stamina of youth as well as training to withstand the pressure. She thinks that's why we haven't an Accident Consultant on the Staff. All our present pundits qualified before this place was opened and though she didn't say it, I gathered they wouldn't touch the job if you gave it to them with a plastic rose. If Michael Roth makes the Staff maybe he'd take it on, having been an S.A.O., but having been one—why ask for his coronary in the late thirties instead of the usual late forties?'

'Mother Mack tell you all that?' I nodded. She propped her elbow on my desk, her chin on her hand and flapped her eyelashes. 'Ooh duckie! She fancies you!'

I smiled. 'Oh no! If she has a weakness—which could be denied—it's for a braw laddie in a white coat. She once told Hill [Butler's predecessor] that at the risk of seeming prejudiced she was forced to admit there was no nicer laddie than a nice young Scots doctor.'

'I know why she's haunting us! She fancies Mr Geddes! Our Hamish! Wait till I tell him!'

'Don't you dare! The poor boy's terrified enough of her as it is! He was so ham-strung by her watching him cut off a leg plaster this morning, the ends of his tie somehow got caught in the shears and he had to cut half of it off to save himself from strangulation.'

She slapped a hand over her mouth to stifle her shouts of laughter. 'What did Mother Mack say?'

I mopped my eyes. 'She didn't. She just looked at him.'

Peter ambled through the open doorway. 'What's happened to the customers? And why the unseemly levity?'

I caught Dolly's eye. 'Just having a jolly handing over report.'

Joss was back from tea. 'What've you done with them all?' He peered round my office as if expecting to see patients stacked on the filing cabinets. 'Tuesday and the rush hour's started. Damned unhealthy.'

I jerked my head at the sudden red flashing above the door and listened-in on the red receiver. Dolly whispered, 'Health restored, Mr D.,' and he gave her a thumbs down sign.

The evening was busy and Miss Mackenzie was with us for most of it. Next morning was busier. She did not come in once. By lunch time, Mr Geddes and I were equally unnerved.

Dolly and George Charlesworth were back on dating terms. Later, Dolly vowed she had told him to keep it quiet and he'd only let it out to Dave Palmer who swore he'd just mentioned it to only one of the medic. students. In the event, before the first patient came in that morning, the entire A.U. staff knew for a fact Hamish Geddes was the dead spit of the great and long-gone love of Miss Mackenzie's life, a gallant and little Highland M.O. last seen playing his bagpipes when not operating single-handed on the beaches at Dunkirk. Poor little Mr Geddes went puce behind his mask every time the double doors swung open. He only relaxed after lunch when Joss sent him to work in the plaster room. His relief was short-lived as we promptly had an in-rush and had to get him back.

A girl who had broken her left arm falling down some narrow, stone basement steps and a hefty young Irishman in semi-coma and with a badly slashed face came in together. The Irishman had been carried to the hospital by five of his mates. They sat red-faced, anxious and exuding beer funes in our relatives' rest-room. They said the patient was a Michael Joseph Murphy, aged thirty-one, and wouldn't hurt a baby unless he'd the drink taken. 'One jar and there's no holding him back at all.'

Mr Palmer asked how many jars Murphy had had before the fight started?

The mates were appalled. 'Mother of God, Doctor would a decent man be counting?'

Mr Geddes and Nurse Smithers were with the girl in C3, Mr Charlesworth and Nurse Henty with a West Indian railwayman in C4. He had a hairline skull fracture and some very bad bruises, but had been incredibly lucky. A car with faulty brakes had run straight into him as he was correctly crossing a light-controlled pedestrian crossing. He had been flung right over the car and landed head down on the opposite pavement. He was twenty-one and a keen amateur boxer. He probably owed his luck equally to both.

Murphy was in C5, as C1 and C2 were awaiting seriously injured men on their way in. After his initial examination, Joss beckoned Mr Palmer. 'Dead drunk and no other damage I can find, but get a picture of his head and let me see it. Fix that face. All yours, Dave.'

Mr Palmer crossed himself. 'Sir, ever so dear sir, can I have danger money, please?'

'Leave it to me. I'll see your next-of-kin gets it. Get a medic. to help you.'

I said, 'And Nurse Fisher, Mr Desmond? Nurse Hedges can run the Shock Room.'

Joss hesitated, then smiled. 'Yep. Good idea.'

Fisher was my size, red-haired and the prettiest girl in the A.U. Mr Palmer said he was lost, but lost. 'It's not that I'm anti-feminist, Sister—nay, I'm all for the burning of bras—they do get in the way—but I just think a pretty little dolly doesn't look her best without her teeth.'

Joss said, 'If Murphy surfaces to find a pretty little dolly holding his hand, chances are no one'll lose their teeth. Use force on a surfacing drunk his size and his won't be the only face that needs about fifteen stiches. Also there's over a thousand quid's worth of equipment in this cubicle.'

I went for Fisher. Joss came out of 4 as she disappeared round the drawn side curtain of 5. The only innovation I had made was to return to the former Sister Accident's custom of always keeping the end curtains of occupied cubicles open as I shared her view that this made supervision and movement easier. Etiquette insisted I ask Joss if he objected. He hadn't. 'We closed them at Benedict's, but when in Rome ...' was all he said. He had shown the same adaptability from the morning I took over. He never now referred to the A.U. as 'the Unit', used any but Martha's jargon, or wore his Benedict's tie. This made my job a lot easier, even if it underlined with a new clarity his earlier belligerence on Butler's behalf. I hadn't much time to let this bother me, but I remained aware that I had shoved it to to the back of some mental cupboard, just as I did with clothes to which I had suddenly taken a dislike. I could then forget the things existed. I hoped it would work as well with Joss, but as I didn't dislike him realized I was giving hope a tough job.

The expected patients again arrived simultaneously in separate ambulances. One, a bricklayer's mate, had fallen thirty feet onto rough ground, and had a fractured pelvis and some ugly lacerations, but his head was unhurt. The second man had been driving a heavy lorry that had hit the side of a road bridge and then overturned. He had multiple injuries and his condition was dangerous. He went into C1.

Joss had about two minutes in which to tell Mr Charlesworth what he wanted done for the bricklayer's mate. I caught Nurse Black's eye, mouthed 'Medic.' and nodded at C5 then C2. She nodded back and swiftly collected Mr Palmer's assistant and joined Henty and the J.A.O. in C2.

Eight of us worked together on the man in C1: Joss, Peter, a pathologist, radiographer, Mr Geddes, Smithers, two medic. students, and myself. The only person who spoke at all, and only very occasionally, was Joss. He and I were working on the man's ripped open abdomen. Peter had him anaesthetized. The pathologist and one student were setting up a blood transfusion in his left ankle. The second student was cutting off the left, and apparently less damaged, side of his clothes. Smithers was very carefully cutting the right trouser leg as shafts of bone were glinting through the sodden thick material. Mr Geddes was cleaning surgically the right leg. The radiographer, a girl, was swinging the heavy portable around for the necessary X-rays as if working a box camera.

Someone lightly touched my shoulder. 'Just to say, please ignore us, Sister. Forgive the interruption, Mr Desmond.' Miss Evans, our Chief Nursing Officer, stepped back to Miss Mackenzie waiting about a yard from the table. Neither spoke to us again and I had no idea how long they stood there. Afterwards Fisher said for about ten minutes. Joss did not recall seeing them at all.

I had thought Fisher good, but I had not realized how good until that afternoon. Nurse Donkin, the new third year, was 'lights and messages'. Fisher was the same set, but while Henty and I were tied up, Fisher took over as well as a good senior staff nurse. The porters arrived and removed the West Indian and the girl in C3 to wards. Murphy surfaced and began muttering angrily.

'There, there,' said Fisher's voice, 'there, there. You're all right, dear. No, don't try and sit up. You had a little accident, you're in a hospital, I'm a nurse—the doctor's just stitching a little cut on your face—quietly now—just hold onto my hand. ...'

Mr Charlesworth appeared beside Joss. 'I'd say mine's ready to shift to I.C. Shall I carry on here whilst you look?'

'Yes.' Both men stripped off their gloves and put on clean. When Joss returned from C2 they did so again. After a heavy day our used-gloves count often ran into three figures. 'Go with him, George,' said Joss.

Donkin was hovering. I nodded twice. She vanished to ring the lodge for porters and the special I.C. trolley and the ward to say a patient was on the way. Shortly after she was back with a memo sheet. She held it out for me to read without altering my position.

I said, 'Mr Desmond, female, seventy-one, fractured right tib. and fib. on the way in. Home accident.'

'Palmer. I want the J.A.O. here.' And when Mr Charlesworth returned. 'He can use another drip. High in that left arm, George.'

A little later the drips and blood were running in well and the internal haemorrhage had stopped. Joss asked, 'Sister, do we know anything about this chap beyond the name on his driving licence?'

'His home's in Manchester. The police have contacted his wife and she's coming down as soon as some relative arrives to look after their three children.'

'Hold it!' Peter spoke sharply. 'Foot's going up to top.'

We all froze as if playing grandmother's footsteps, and watched Peter. 'Stopped.' He pulled off his stethoscope with one hand, pulled forward the scarlet-framed 'crash' trolley with the other. Joss had come to life, had his gloves off and started cardiac massage.

Giving cardiac massage is very exhausting. Whilst the qualified men took it in turns, Henty and I kept the man's injuries at blood-heat and Smithers kept the sterile saline we were using at the right temperature. That entailed constant topping up and changing of the bowls in the double-bowl stands. Once, a medic. student asked, 'Will you have to open up his chest wall?'

'If necessary,' Joss grunted, 'but it shouldn't be as he's started again. He should be able to manage on his own soon.'

He was right. 'Good.' He stood back, pulled off his sodden mask, dried his face with it, and chucked it away, breathing as if he had run a mile in two minutes. 'How's he your end, Peter?'

'Nicely.'

Another pint of blood had run in before Joss murmured, 'Do we know their ages, Sister?'

'All under five. Two boys, one girl.'

He didn't say more. We worked on in silence till the man was fit to move to I.C. Peter, George Charlesworth and Henty went with him. The rest of us removed gloves, masks and stained gowns in that same silence. It held an element that was hard to define and was present in all the faces when the masks came off. It was one I had noticed before, on both sides of the Atlantic, after what went down in the notes as 'successful therapy for cardiac arrest.' It wasn't triumph, satisfaction, or even relief, as most of us knew death too well to underestimate the strength of the opposition. It was not unconnected with the fact that the name Lazarus made instant sense to anyone with the sketchiest Christian upbringing, and particularly so now. Lazarus had been a young man when he was raised from the dead.

Miss Evans sent for me that night. The day report from Intensive Care was uppermost on her desk when the Office Sister ushered me in and ominously closed the door on her way out. I had been too tired to be overshaken by Miss Evans' summons, but when she asked me to sit down, the combination shattered me. In Martha's it could mean one of two things: bad personal news, or a professional bouquet.

Miss Evans was smiling. 'I gather you had a little trouble with that man in Cubicle 1 after Miss Mackenzie and I left you this afternoon. But Sister Intensive Care says he seems to have settled down quite nicely tonight.'

I breathed more naturally. 'I'm so glad.'

'Of course.' She went on to ask me to stay in Butler's job until she was fit to return. 'Possibly two or three months, possibly more. Glandular fever can take a long time to clear up. No objections? Good. I admit I can ill spare Miss Kenton from the Orthopaedic Block and, on reflection, see no occasion to alter present arrangements in the Accident Unit. But one point must be made clear, Sister!' She then lectured me sternly on the subject of off-duty, said I must have this Saturday off and Miss Kenton would relieve me for the day and next week, when Staff Nurse White returned, from midday Friday to midday Monday. 'All right, Sister? Good girl.' As I stood up, she added with the lack of formality that was one of the many reasons for her popularity, 'Now I'll tell you something that'll make you forget your poor feet, Sister. You may share it with your staff. It is Miss Mackenzie's considered opinion that our present Accident Unit is a credit to St Martha's. Thank you, my dear. Goodnight.'

I tottered back to my office and since we were finally empty, into my chair. A mountain of notes was waiting. I just stared at them. Joss was at supper. I wondered how he would like being a credit to St Martha's and smiled foolishly.

Peter put his head round the door. 'What did she want?'

We were still oozing smugness when Joss returned and infuriated me by saying he had known I was stayin on for the last two days. 'How can you be so mean? Why didn't you tell me?'

'Union rules, dearie.' He began sorting notes. 'Why don't you go home? Nurse Henty can manage these.'

I hesitated. 'Take hours.'

'She's a bright girl. Good experience for her.'

Peter said Joss was right and he'd get a porter to get me a taxi as he was on-call. 'All you look fit for now is bed, Cath. Just wish I could take you there myself.'

'There, there, dear boy, ever so there, there.' Joss had Dave Palmer's voice perfectly. 'Keep it cool. Get going, woman!' He looked up at Peter then back at me. 'Don't worry. If necessary, I'll get Nurse Fisher to hold his hand.'

Chapter Seven

'There's no need for you to stay as long as myself, dear.' Mrs Desmond adjusted the angle of her ginger straw in the hall mirror. It was less than a yard wide. 'The Vicar has to see Tom Mercer about the guttering on the Lady Chapel roof and will run you back. I must stay till the end or umbrage will be taken as they stay for ours.' She glanced at the closed study door, then added quietly, 'I'm sure the old ticker's fine and it's just indigestion, but as your father always said—when in doubt, see an expert. You're certain this won't get you into any trouble?'

'Positive! I'll have to do it through Miss Evans, but both she and Dr Lincoln Browne will understand you want to be reassured without worrying your family.'

She put a hand on my shoulder. 'Darling, am I fussing about nothing? Is it just my age and because my children have grown up and gone?'

I suddenly felt very old. 'I think you're being very sensible. If you

were Mum, I'd have said exactly what I did this morning.' The study
door was opening. 'Feeling strong, Vicar?'

We were going to the annual summer church fête in the next parish.
Mr Desmond's aversion to fêtes was an old family joke and on his own
admission the reason why his own was always successful. He left it
entirely to his P.C.C. and his wife.

'Strengthened by a sense of duty and sublime sensation of
self-righteousness, Cathy. Ready, my dear?'

The road ran through fields of young green hops climbing forests of
poles, and corn now golden but in places still flattened by last week's
hail and heavy rain. The sun was warm without being hot and all the
elders were in flower. The parish lay away from the marsh and the last
stretch of road had originally been laid by the Romans along the crest of
a wooded hill. The wood was still there, too. The overhanging branches
cut out the sun and the light was cool and green as in the depths of the
sea.

The fête was in the vicarage garden and two Special Constables were
directing the traffic coming and going from the car park in the field
opposite. One was Bert Mercer. 'Back again are you, then?'

'Bert, why are you supporting the rival firm? Peace been declared?'

He smiled slowly and mopped his broad face with a glaringly white
handkerchief. Mrs Bert once worked in a laundry. 'You'd not reckon
that if you was along the Lamb, tonight. Still, they said did I mind?
Well, it seemed right.'

The two villages had fought each other on Saturday nights and Bank
Holidays for as long as anyone could remember. No one knew why. It
had never prevented inter-marriages. The same surnames were listed on
the war memorials in both churchyards.

'The same names,' mused Mr Desmond, 'would've been listed after
Agincourt and Crécy, had any man bothered to make such a list. And
when not fighting the French, they'd still have belted the daylights out of
each other.' He surveyed the back lawn crowded with the inhabitants of
both villages. 'The English have a deep affection for their old tribal
customs. But one aspect invariably puzzles me on these occasions. From
whence do all these worthy ladies wearing coloured meringues on their
heads come and to where do they disappear, between fêtes? I never see
them in church.'

'Oh, yes, Vicar! Think of Harvest Festival. They all come. There's
barely standing room.'

He smiled over his glasses. '*Mea culpa.* I have overlooked that most
cherished old tribal—or to be accurate pagan—custom.'

The cake stall was under a chestnut bowed with white candles; the
fancy goods, under an ash; the pick-the-right-card-and-win-a-bottle stall

discreetly arranged by the hedge at the bottom of the garden. The hard-working tea ladies coping with the insatiable demand for nourishment from within two minutes of the official opening raced round their tent growing redder as their urns grew emptier and the butter in the bridge rolls turned to oil.

Mr Desmond savoured his. 'Butter. From George Mercer's herd.'

One of about fifteen Mercers sitting near overheard. He was a tall, fair teenager who could have been Bert's son, had Bert had sons and not only daughters. 'That's right, Vicar. Me Dad sent it up. How'd you reckon?'

Mr Desmond nodded at a distant farmhouse just visible through the trees. 'What's that farm there called, lad?'

The boy looked superior and his elder relatives amused. 'Martin's, 'course. Didn't you know that, then?'

'Yes, and I should, seeing I was born there. Old Mr Martin, whom your grandad'll remember, was my grandad. Your grandad was the best young stockman he ever had, and he taught me the taste of a good butter. Brigadier Bell bought the farm twenty years ago from the man who bought it after my grandad died.'

The clan chuckled appreciatively. 'Walked into that one, didn't you, young Trev? He knows, does the Vicar.' They eyed the host vicar, an incomer, much as the A.U. staff had Naomi Butler. 'Makes a difference.'

The shooting gallery, an innovation to me, was tucked round the side of the front garden and doing the best business of the day. Brigadier Bell was loading the guns, his wife organizing the queues of men, boys and a few girls, with crisp firmness. The size of her pink linen hat was rivalled only by Mrs Desmond's. They were old patients and friends of my parents. We exchanged glad cries as they were too busy for more.

'The Established Church,' observed Mr Desmond as we strolled on, 'has always been gifted with a very practical sense of priorities.'

We had agreed to leave before the official entertainment began, but the middle of the lawn had been cleared and the little children started country dancing while he was still shaking the necessary hands. For years, the three Desmonds, my brother and I had danced on the Desmonds' lawn. The parental bribery rate had risen as we approached nine, the maximum age. At eight, Ruth and I had collected two choc-ices from my father, two lollies from the vicar, half a pound of jelly babies from my mother, and a pound of apples to salvage our teeth from Mrs Desmond.

In the car, I said, 'We'd eaten the lot before you'd announced who got the most points bowling for the turkey. We weren't sick, but I can't think why not.'

He smiled. 'Your father used to say about the only thing a healthy child's stomach can't digest is cast-iron.' He paused, shortly. 'I still miss him, sadly, Cathy, as of course you do. He was a good man who did much good with his life. And he was my friend. God willing, we shall meet again.' He glanced sideways and answered my thoughts. 'Yes. I do, though perhaps not at your age. Youth has so much faith in itself, that it often seems to feel the need of no other. Once youth's brief glory has burnt out, if one has the blessed good fortune to be given the gift of Faith, one does not underestimate its necessity. Ah—Tom's van waiting!' He slowed to a stop and gave me his front door key. 'Leave it on the latch. You'll be all right on your own?'

'Fine, thank you. And for the outing.'

His older, thinner, more aesthetic face, smiled Joss's smile. 'Thanks to your pleasant companionship I enjoyed it much more than I anticipated, and many would add, deserved. With you shortly!'

I looked at our old house at I let myself in. It did not hurt as much as I expected, but the empty vicarage hurt much more. I could see Joss standing in the study on that other Saturday night and myself drifting round all the next day, like some naïve teenager in a fantasy world where Love was Real and nothing to do with sex. Sex was something the biology mistress shoved down one's throat in those constant 'straight from the shoulder' chats that embarrassed her as much as it bored the class. I remembered Ruth and myself moaning, 'Sex, again! Oh, God— that drag!'

I found a rug and cushions and went out into the garden. Just beyond the pond, between the willows and the apple trees, there was a patch of rough grass that under one of the unwritten laws children observe amongst themselves had been 'the girls' patch'. It was invisible from both houses and had the new advantage of being free of associations with Joss.

I kicked off my shoes, watched the sky filtering through the apple leaves and thought about the fête. That was a mistake, as Mr Desmond's behaviour reminded me of Joss's at Ruth's reception. I switched to the A.U. and wondered how Miss Kenton was getting on. She had come in yesterday for a few hours to get into the routine. She was a tall, rather striking girl in her mid-twenties with very dark hair and the slightly hearty, slightly insensitive air of a good head girl. 'Right,' she'd said, 'what's to do? You name it, m'dear. You're boss!'

The 'flu epidemic was beginning to subside, but the senior registrars were still down to one day and one night off, instead of their alternate free weekends. On paper this was Joss's. Mr Roth's deputy, Mr Carr, was standing in for him tomorrow. One of the registrar anaesthetists was taking over for Peter today. Peter had wanted me to go home with him

to soothe his mother as she thought it was time he married. When he
didn't bring a girl home, she always produced some daughter of one of
her friends.

A moorhen rustled across the pond. The blackbird in the nearest
apple tree was singing like a nightingale. One summer evening in my
first year I had got home for the evening before my days off to find Joss
with my father in the garden. Joss had looked in to say goodbye before
going back to Benedict's after a holiday. A patient had arrived, Joss and
I had stayed in the garden and counted seven nightingales singing in
chorus.

I had had a surfeit. I closed my eyes to shut out thought and was
asleep almost immediately. I woke when someone gently touched my
face. I smiled, stretched out my arms and blinked, expecting to see Mrs
Desmond. Joss's face was a few inches from mine.

For about five seconds I wasn't sure if I was awake or asleep. We
stared at each other with an equal kind of incredulity. I had to touch
him to be certain and put my hands on his shoulder. 'It's you?'

He kissed me so wonderfully that at first I was incapable of coherent
thought. Then I got my face free. 'If you're that hungry, go and make
yourself a meal!'

He raised himself a little and his colour altered. 'If you don't want it,
don't set it up!'

'I did *not*! I thought you were your mother!' I pushed him off without
difficulty as he was standing up. 'You should be in the A.U.! Why aren't
you?'

He had propped himself against an apple tree and was now equally
angry, though he controlled it better. 'Worked out easier for John Carr
to take over this afternoon and tomorrow morning.'

'How was I suppose to know that?' I slung the rug over my shoulder
and glared at him. 'Your parents didn't say you were coming.'

'They didn't know till I turned up. Didn't know myself till lunch. The
parents don't expect a warning. This happens to be their—and my—
home.'

'Where I thought vicar's lad's Union Rules obtained. Oh, sure I
know—what are old pals for but to help out? Tell you what, Joss—I'll
buy you your very own teddy bear.'

He flushed. 'You've made your point, duckie.'

'So I should hope!' I was shaking with rage. 'Providing you with a
therapeutic release doesn't give me one single frisson!'

He looked me over. 'Snap, darling.'

'Children, there you are!' Mrs Desmond joined us, beaming. 'Isn't this
a lovely surprise, Cathy? Such a pity Joss has to go back tonight, but as
he's promised, of course, he must and he can give you a lift—'

'I've got a cheap day return—'

'A bit of a waste, darling, but so much nicer to drive back on this lovely evening. Such a long drive alone. He'll love to take you. Won't you, Joss?'

He looked at me. 'Always happy to help out an old pal.'

'That's settled! Come along. Supper's ready!'

'Supper?' I looked at my watch. It was seven. 'I've slept hours! I'm so sorry, Mrs Desmond—'

'Now, why? You needed the rest. Joss and his father had a nice quiet tea, then Joss fetched me. Gervase said you were still sleeping when we got back, but we had to wake you now as Joss has to be back by ten.'

I asked, 'Not on call tonight, Joss?'

'No, but I've got a heavy date.'

At supper, after the P.M. on the fête, the subject was Naomi Butler. Mr Desmond was glad to hear that nice young woman was progressing well. 'How much longer should she be warded, Joss?'

'Week or so. Then a very long sick leave.'

'Malta?' Mrs Desmond turned to me. 'Did you know Naomi's parents have retired out there? Such a beautiful island, I believe. Joss was out there for his last summer's holiday.'

'How nice,' I said.

'It was,' said Joss. 'Naomi and I did our best to miss the return flight. Mum, I hate to rush off, but as we've got over fifty miles ...'

Mrs Desmond saw us off as someone had called to see her husband. 'Don't forget, Joss, if Naomi would like a quiet week with us before she flies off, we'll love to have her.'

'Thanks, Mum, I'll tell her.' He kissed her and got into his car.

Mrs Desmond kissed me. 'You'll let me know?' she whispered.

'Soon as it's fixed,' I answered as quietly. 'Don't worry too much. He's a very nice and quite brilliant man. I'd take my heart across the world to him. You'll like him.'

She kissed me again. 'Come back soon.'

Joss had the engine on and was fiddling with his safety-belt. He could not have overheard us, but he watched his mother very thoughtfully in the driving mirror as he drove off. 'She's looking much too tired. You notice?'

'Yes. Missing Ruth.'

'Typical! Typical trained nurse's reaction! Fatigue must have a psychosomatic origin! No question of the cause being organic, or very possibly just physiological, occurs to your clever little mind!'

'Cause such as glandular fever?'

'Not in this case, though it's a diagnosis I've heard dismissed as bloody-mindedness by the bloody-minded.'

'And one I've known even high-powered and conscientious physicians find difficult to diagnose in the early stages.' I thought Mrs Desmond's secrecy unnecessary, but having promised to maintain it, took refuge in platitudes. 'No matter how pleasing, the marriage of one's only daughter can be a traumatic experience, Australia's a long way off, and commonest things are the most common.'

'And the menopause is a difficult time for women and I've an Oedipus! What's your other little problem?'

I didn't answer. We drove out of the village and along the first of the many side lanes that were a short-cut to the motorway in a blazing silence. Being on edge I played with the nearest buckle, a habit my mother said had started in my pram. Suddenly, he drew up in a passing place.

'Why've we stopped?' I demanded more sharply than I could have wished.

He switched off the engine. 'If you haven't seen enough sliced-off faces, I have. You've worked that something strap so slack, first jolt and you'll be out of it and through the windscreen.' He tilted my seat to release the length of strap I had somehow managed to jam underneath. 'Try that for size—and don't be so bloody neurotic, woman!' He brushed my hands aside, then reached forward and opened my door. 'Or get out! Only five miles to Asden and you'll be safer even if these lanes are lonely. Or have you forgotten the high percentage of accidents caused by the driver's mental irritation?'

'No.'

'Then sit still and stop messing about with that bloody buckle! Touch it once more and you walk! And you can stop nerving yourself to repel boarders. All I want right now is to get us both back to London intact.'

I nearly got out, but my feet were hurting. I held my hands in my lap and looked at him. 'This allowed?'

He slammed the door. It was over twenty miles before we spoke again, or far as I knew, looked at each other.

He had avoided the motorway and we were climbing the long, three-lane road running over the Downs. Pre-motorway it had been the main London road, and with the heavy traffic now siphoned off was nearly as quick as the motorway. Once anyone worked in an Accident Unit, fast driving lost its charm. If speed of itself is no killer, accidents at high speeds kill. Nastily.

That bit of road ran up the side of one of the highest hills in the county. It was edged by wide grass verges backed, on our right, by the hill. The far side of the left verge was fenced for its entire length by sturdy iron railings. A few yards from these, the hill fell sharply for hundreds of feet. The view was a local 'must' for tourists.

Spread out below and reaching to the horizon were miles of apple and cherry orchards, deep green hop gardens, acres of yellow corn. The black and white woodwork of the half-timbered farms and one-time yeomen's houses took on a pristine freshness in the evening sun. The pink-fawn bricks of the houses glowed a soft orange and the cottages really did have roses growing round their doors. The cottage gardens were tiny, patchwork quilts, and the printed cones of the white oasts dotted the landscape like pepper-pots. It was the England of U.S. travel posters and the fact that it actually existed and belonged to me—along with fifty-five million others—suddenly gave me such unexpected and unashamedly possessive pleasure that I regretted our row still more. I wanted to share it with Joss and to tell him I had just belatedly understood something my father once said. In the last war he had been an RAF M.O. He had said that while convinced the outcome of the Battle of Britain would have been the same had it been fought over any other part of the country, he had always thought the Germans had loaded the dice against themselves by attacking over one of the loveliest corners of England. 'No man fights harder,' he said, 'than the man defending his own backyard. That summer the Garden of England was living up to its name.'

Joss's urgent, 'Christ! Watch it, mate!' jerked me back to the present. I looked round and did a double-take.

A large silver car had come round the curve of the hill and was swaying drunkenly from one lane to another. 'Driver had a blackout? Or steering gone, Joss?'

'Seems to be trying to get it under control—' he steered us onto the left verge and stopped. 'He's trying to get it into the hill—oh God!'

The car had hit and reared up the side of the hill. Momentarily it had stayed poised on the two back wheels, then it did a complete backwards somersault. Now, on four wheels but facing uphill, it shot sideways right over the road and grass, then swivelled leftwards and bonnet first pitched into the rails.

I closed my eyes just before the ghastly clatter of metal on metal. 'Joss, has it gone over?'

'No.' He drove on with his foot right down then braked so abruptly only our belts held us in our seats. 'Three inside.' He lunged into the back for his medical bag and ran for the wrecked car. I tore after him. I was dimly aware a white mini had drawn up behind us but on oath couldn't have said who was in it.

The crumpled bonnet was jammed by bent but unbroken railings. The car roof was dented and crinkled as screwed up silver paper. Every inch of glass was opaque but apparently unsplintered. The engine was dead. The smell of leaking petrol was nauseating.

The right hand doors were either locked or jammed, and so was the left rear door. The front opened. Joss was lifting out a girl as I joined him. A youngish man was slumped over the wheel and an old man with white hair was in a heap on the floor at the back.

The girl's eyes were open and had the glaze of acute shock, but otherwise she seemed unhurt. When Joss set her on her feet, she stood unaided. 'She shouldn't walk.' muttered Joss, 'but she's got to get the hell out of here. Take her. I'll get the others.' He dried his hands on the seat of his pants and dived inside.

His hands and the girl were drenched in petrol. She was tallish and fairly slim, but too stunned to move herself. 'Never mind, duckie,' I said, 'I'll carry you.' I hadn't used a fireman's lift since I was a child. She was heavy, but it was easier than I expected.

Joss had laid the old man on the opposite grass verge before I got there. 'Stay with 'em. I'll get the driver.' He vanished again.

I was straightening from depositing the girl, when an elderly lady suddenly appeared from nowhere beside me. She held two rugs. 'Will these help?' she asked unsteadily.

'Thanks.' I covered both figures. 'Were you in the mini? Where's it gone?'

'My husband's gone for help—I insisted—he's nearly eighty—can I help?'

'Could you hold the girl's hand? She's conscious—and for God's sake, don't smoke! Spilt petrol.' I ran back across the road.

Joss had the driver's head and shoulders out. He was roughly Peter's size, a dead weight, and Joss's face was streaming with sweat. 'I said I'd manage! Get out! That engine smells hotter than hell!'

'don't be such a ruddy hero!' I grabbed the man's legs. 'I've got him. Move!'

'Why do you have to be such a bloody-minded little bitch?'

I didn't answer as I needed my breath.

We had just put down the driver when the old man came round, tried to sit up and fell back with a whimper of pain. As Joss crouched by him, I remembered his medical bag. It was still lying on the grass by the silver car. I had gone before Joss saw me. 'Leave that!' He bellowed. 'Come back!'

I had the case and was running back when, it seemed to me simultaneously, the hill exploded and Joss pulled me down with a rugger tackle. When he hauled us both up, the grass around was on fire, the car was hidden in a sheet of flame, the back of his jacket, hem of my skirt, and some of my hair-ends were singed, The case had been jammed between us when we went down and was intact.

The elderly lady was sitting on the grass looking as stunned as the girl. 'You should've left it—you should've left it—where's my husband—these poor souls need a doctor—oh, dear—I'm too old for this.'

Joss had his jacket off and was kneeling by the old man. I jerked my head his way as I had one hand on the girl's and the other on the driver's pulse. 'He's a doctor.'

She was too shaken to believe me until she saw Joss take his spare stethoscope out of his bag.

The driver looked in his late thirties. He was still unconscious. There was an ugly bump and a quite deep but already clotted gash high on his forehead. I could not find any other visible injuries, but did not attempt to move him at all. His pulse was good. 'Bleeding?' asked Joss without looking round.

I knelt by him. 'No. From his pulse more like concussion than a fracture.'

'Hope you're right. Don't touch him more. Girl?'

'Just shock, I'd say.'

'Uh-huh.' He pulled the wrapping off a syringe. 'This poor old boy's got a bump at the base I don't like. His left tib. and fib's snapped and I suspect his femur.' He frowned at the fine-boned too blue face under the heavy white hair. 'His heart isn't liking this at all. I don't like pumping stuff in in the dark, but if the ambulance takes much longer—what do you think?'

I took the old man's pulse. Or rather, I tried to take it. 'Joss, you must. He's going.'

'Yep. I know.' He looked round at the empty road, then took the necessary phial from his bag. 'Hell of a way from Asden,' he said as he gave the injection.

The old man sighed deeply, once, then again, and then his breathing altered to that deeper rhythm. Joss and I breathed out with our hands on wrists thin as paper. 'That's better, Doctor,' I said, and we both smiled.

The elderly lady was watching. 'He really is a doctor. A real doctor.'

I went back to the other two. 'Yes.'

'And you? Another doctor?'

'Trained nurse.'

The girl had opened her eyes again. She had short, thick, light brown hair and a sensible face. I explained for the third time what was happening. This time she understood and tried to smile. 'Thank you,' she whispered.

The driver had not stirred and his heart was magnificent. I returned to Joss and told him.

'That's a break.' He sat back on his heels watching the thin, closed, old face and the slight rise and fall of the rug over the man's chest. He looked very tall and had wide shoulders, but being so thin his body was barely visible under the rug. 'His shape's helping him, but his age isn't.' Joss looked at me. His face was filthy and the cleared patches round his eyes and mouth stood out, whitely. 'If he has to hang on much longer without oxygen—' He looked over my head. 'God bless all ambulance crews!'

So many times, so many patients, so many relatives, had said, 'I don't mind telling you, Nurse, when I saw that ambulance draw up outside, I could've wept with relief.' If I hadn't known precisely what they meant before, I did then.

A police car and motor-cyclist arrived with the ambulance. A second police car and the white mini followed a few minutes later.

The elderly lady and her older husband were a Mr and Mrs Frayling and lived in Asden. They sat together on the grass watching the stretchers being lifted out and into the ambulances. They did not talk. They just watched.

Joss beckoned me from the ambulance. He was going with them to Asden General Hospital. 'You'll bring the car for me?'

The policeman who had taken our names and addresses came up to say they would be in touch with Joss later about his statement.

'Right. Cathy—'

'Yes?'

'Don't push the car or yourself.' He mopped his forehead with the back of his wrist and left another white streak as the ambulance man shut the doors.

I watched it disappear, then looked over at the still smouldering wreck. And then I had to sit down, fast.

Chapter Eight

The occupants of the silver car were Norwegian tourists. The old man was a retired marine biologist, a Professor Ulvik. The girl was his daughter, Nina, the driver her husband, Arne Alesund. They all lived in Bergen.

'She'll be out tomorrow.' Joss took the motorway turning from the roundabout. 'Alesund probably in forty-eight hours. He was round before I left. No sign of any fracture in his first pictures.'

'Pity that car hadn't belts on the back seat.'

'Yep. It was the roof that clobbered Alesund.' He shook his head at his thoughts. 'They've got the old boy in their pint-sized I.C. He didn't look too good when they let me look in again on my way out.'

'Think he'll do?'

He shrugged unhappily. 'The Night Super seemed an intelligent and efficient woman. The one registrar apparently running the whole bloody shop tonight seemed to know his stuff, though his English wasn't half as good as the Alesunds'. They've one hundred and ten beds, and according to the Night Super without the 'flu bug hitting them as hard as us, they've a chronic staff shortage. The junior night sister running I.C. impressed me, but she only had a couple of teenage kids to help her. I'm dead sure they'll all do their best, and their best can't be bad as Asden General has a very good reputation. But as nursing a patient with intensive care takes several pairs of skilled hands, it won't be their fault if sometimes their best just isn't bloody good enough. We think we have staff problems! Huh!' He was silent. Then he said, 'I felt an utter bastard walking out, just now.'

'Joss. You had to.'

'I know my medical something ethics! That doesn't mean I've to love them, or myself!'

I looked at his tense profile. He had had a wash and his hair was neat, but I found his appearance as disturbing as that early morning in the office. The crash had given me more than a physical jolt. 'Go ahead and hate yourself, but don't expect me to join the hate-in.'

We were in the slow lane. He checked in the mirror then slowed more. 'Why the other cheek?'

'I have this weakness for living. If you hadn't flung me clear, quite probably I'd now be dead. And as I doubt I could've lugged those men out alone—and anyway wouldn't have been there alone—but for you, those three'd be dead. Would you fancy ending up burnt to a crisp?'

He shuddered. 'Lay off! My stomach's not strong enough!' He smiled faintly, reluctantly. 'This mean the war's over?'

'Until the next one.'

His smile deepened. 'You had me worried. For an ugly moment I thought I must've clobbered your head when I brought you down. Were you hurt?'

'Don't think so. I don't remember. Hey—something else I've forgotten! Your date!'

'Taken care of. I rang from the hospital. That reminds me—' but he stopped as if he had suddenly decided not to share whatever he had remembered. His 'What did you say the old girl's name was?' was an obvious after-thought.

'Frayling. Husband's a retired bank manager,' I added absently, wondering what he wouldn't tell me.

'Retired, where?'

'Asden. She told the cops you ought to get a medal.'

'Not you?'

'Well, yes.'

He was amused. 'Togetherness does something deep down to a guy.' We had gone another five miles in silence before he asked abruptly, 'Do you think he'll do?'

I thought of the old man's face as he lay on the grass after that injection. 'Yes.'

'Why?'

That took more time. He didn't hurry me. 'I don't know. Could be wishful thinking, but I don't think it is. Sort of in my bones. You know?'

'Yes. I hope to God you're right. He looked a nice old boy. At his age, he'd want to die in his own home.'

'How about your bones?'

'Go along with yours, but my judgement doesn't. Only one bright spot there; I know I'm too emotionally involved for a balanced judgement.' He smiled at me as we stopped before another roundabout. 'You used to call them your inkstinks when you always won pinning on that repulsive pig's tail.'

'By cheating. I used to squint under the blindfold.'

We continued swopping childhood horror-stories till we crossed the river. 'Second or third left from here, Cathy?'

'Third, and last house but one on the right.'

When he drew up, as our relationship had taken a great leap backwards I asked him up for coffee and to meet Roxanne. 'Our landlady doesn't object this side of midnight.'

'So Peter says.' He seemed to be having a problem making up his mind. 'Yes—I'd like to see Roxanne. I gather she's worth looking at. What'll she be doing home on a Saturday night?'

'She has a date with a camera outside the Tate Gallery at six tomorrow morning.'

'That figures.'

'It does?' We were out of the car. 'Hasn't got through to Peter in years.'

'Simple soul, Peter, but a decent bloke.' My real brother couldn't have sounded more fraternal.

'Even Homer sometimes nods. Will Roxanne be entertaining?'

I unlocked the front door. 'Doubt it. Why?'

He closed the door first. 'Just remembered something I've been meaning to tell you all afternoon. The bug's taken a new lease in the Orthopod Unit. The wandering boy's wanted back from tomorrow

afternoon. John Carr's staying in the A.U. till Stan Lawson gets back at
the end of the week.'

I turned from the stairs and faced him very slowly. 'I've never worked
with John Carr.'

He was looking at his feet. 'He was J.A.O. a couple of years back, I
think.'

'Yes. Just before I got there. Do you mind?'

He looked up. 'Why should I? I crossed the river to be Hoadley East's
registrar.'

'So you did.' I had to look away as he was watching me too closely.
'One of these fine days I may even reach Luke. Let's get on up.' I went
ahead up the stairs and quickly. I felt as if I had suddenly lost one of my
limbs.

Mr Carr was good at the job and pleasant to work with. I did not
suspect till his last night that neither of us had enjoyed the week. 'I
never knew how I lasted out as J.A.O., Sister. This factory-belt isn't for
me. No time to know the patients, follow them through, even remember
their names. I'm not surprised Desmond's pleased as hell to be back
amongst his orthopods. I can't imagine how Lawson enjoys it—but even
he got pneumonia, and Miss Butler got glandular.' He gave me a clinical
glance. 'You going to last? You're looking damned peaky tonight.'

That took care of what remained of my morale. 'Just ready for my
long weekend, Mr Carr.'

I rang the Night Super at Asden General again before going off. We
were now chums. Professor Ulvik had been moved yesterday to a general
ward. Mrs Alesund was staying in an Asden hotel to be near him, and
her husband had had to return to his job and the three children they had
left with his parents in Norway. 'He's beginning to pick up nicely, but
not too nicely.' The Night Super's West Indian voice had an attractive
lilt. 'As I've just told Mr Desmond, I think we can all be very pleased
with ourselves. He is seventy-six.'

I thought of ringing Joss, thought again, and told Dolly as we locked
up. She had heard of the crash from George Charlesworth, before I
arrived on duty on Sunday morning. On Tuesday, I had heard from
Peter that the police had proved the steering column of the car had
snapped before it burnt. On Wednesday, thanks to Mrs Frayling, the
Asden Gazette made its weekly appearance with a front-page story that
included potted biographies of my father, the Vicar, Joss and myself,
and an interview with the head teacher of Asden Grammar School.
'Catherine was a reliable and popular prefect and a valued member of
our First Hockey Eleven.'

My copy from Mrs Desmond arrived on Friday. Dave Palmer had one on Thursday from grandparents living near Asden. Had Joss not already made it public property, the grapevine would have had the hottest story in weeks. In the event, aside from being wished a good game of hockey by the A.U. staff every time I went off duty, being old history it caused no comment.

From Dolly and via a friend she had staffing in Florence, the A.U. knew of every visit Joss paid Miss Butler, how often he sent her flowers—and the variety, his choice of soothing books, and the size and price of the boxes of Edinburgh rock on her bedtable, the sweet being one for which she appeared to have an insatiable taste. When Dolly announced Joss was taking her home next weekend before she flew to Malta for a minimum of two months sick leave, Dave Palmer suggested we must, but must, have a whip round for the wedding present. 'And shouldn't we spare a few teensy-weensy new pence towards the wreath for the many ever-so-dear girlish hopes those wedding bells'll kill stone dead? But woe!'

That night, after I had given her the latest on Professor Ulvik, we found Dave's watch on a shelf in the plaster room. George Charlesworth was on call. Dolly said he was bound to waylay her on her way out and she would give him the watch for Dave. 'A nice child, Dave, but it's time he grew up.'

I was curious. 'Why do you say that?'

'Sister, dear Sister! Malta's a long way off. Our Mr D. is dead sexy, dead human and so are les girls.'

I smiled over-brightly. 'You don't reckon much to fidelity!'

'No.' Her smooth, chubby, dolly-face both hardened and saddened. 'Nor would you, if your dad had walked out on your mum when you were seven, just because the child he'd given her turned out to be a hydrocephalic.'

We were alone in the department. I leant against the plaster table, appalled. 'Dolly, I didn't know—'

She shook her head, but she didn't hear me. She stared at the blank X-ray screen and the pictures she saw evoked a blazing bitterness in her huge eyes. 'He was a cute baby. He smiled and smiled, but he could never sit up. He died when he was three. My mum's never got over him, or my father. She's loved the selfish sod. God knows how—but women are such bloody fools!' She paused and I kept quiet, partly as I was too moved, partly as she needed to say more. 'Women are so brainwashed into a fear of insecurity, they swallow all the blurb about love and marriage being the only answer, whole. Then they discover marriage is the second biggest con-trick ever pulled on women. Maternity has first place.' She faced me. 'My mum was twenty-seven when she was lumbered with the baby and me. She'd no training and couldn't leave us to get one. Dear old dad paid maintenance just often enough to keep him out of jug. Not that mum would've put him there. I would! She's forty-two now and looks sixty.'

'Dolly,' I said, 'to say I'm sorry is almost an insult. I just wish I'd known—'

'Apart from Miss Evans, you're only the second person I've told in Martha's. The other—guess who—' she smiled very faintly '—our Mr D. My father rang one night we were doing notes late. The switchboard meant to be helpful and put him through. He started creating when I wouldn't talk to him. Mr D. fixed him. I'd had to tell him a little. Then I told him the lot. He was perfectly sweet. Know what he said?'

'Tell me.'

She blushed. 'This'll sound rather awful, but he said he thought this probably explained why I was such an outstandingly good accident nurse.'

'I think he's right on both counts.' I was nearly as appalled by my own blindness. Neither in Albert nor here had it ever struck me she had one serious personal problem. 'I'll tell you something I shouldn't. Miss Evans and Miss Mackenzie want you in Butler's job when she finishes her contract. Like it?'

Her face lit up. 'Give my soul for it!' The light went out. 'Think Mr D.'ll have told Butler? Men blab worse than girls when they think they're in love. George tells me everything—silly yobbo!'

'I don't think Joss will.' I reminded her how long I had known him. 'Even as a boy he knew how to keep his mouth shut and all the Desmonds have a very kind streak. Incidentally,' I added slowly, 'so has George Charlesworth. He's a gentle, steady lad. I now understand you're dead scared of getting involved, but do me a favour. Give him—and yourself—time. Just time. Don't push him out of your life too fast. Take ten years. I'll bet George is still waiting.'

She said simply, 'Duckie, I hope not. I like George, and it won't do him any good with me.'

I was uncomfortably certain she was right.

Peter was waiting to drive me home. He was annoyed by my delay, peeved to hear Roxanne was in Portugal with her father, as it was a place he had always wanted to visit and could never afford. I was relieved when he decided not to come up for coffee. It had been a heavy day and Peter's bleatings after the patients' and Dolly's genuine problems had irritated instead of mildly amusing me. When I let myself in to our flat I was glad to be alone with my thoughts. Then I started thinking. That was not my favourite night of the year.

Mrs Desmond came up to see Dr Lincoln Browne on the following Wednesday afternoon. She arrived nearly as apprehensive about meeting

Joss as about her check-up. 'How can you be so sure we won't run into him, dear?'

I explained Sir Hoadley had started his Wednesday theatre list at one P.M. for the last twenty years. It was then two. 'They're doing eleven this afternoon. This first two are bone-grafts and'll take hours. They'll be in the theatre till nearly seven.'

'Eleven operations? In one afternoon?'

The number wasn't exceptional, but to soothe her I blamed the heatwave.

She turned into an elderly woman when the consultant's secretary ushered her in. Half an hour later she had shed twenty years. 'Darling, such a relief! He wired me up to his machine, showed me the graph I didn't understand at all, but he says my heart is splendid! Can I take you out to tea?'

Being due back in the A.U. in forty minutes, I took her to the Sisters' dining-room. 'Don't worry. Even if the orthopaedic theatre goes mad and stops work, Joss won't come in here. Our residents need a gun at their heads to come through that door.'

Mrs Desmond glanced at the few, mostly elderly Home Sisters, delicately consuming cucumber sandwiches at Miss Evans' table. Miss Evans was not present. The Sisters were not talking and from the gravity of their expressions had unanimously agreed a little nourishment was in order as one always had to wait the hour before performing Last Offices.

'Not that I'd mind seeing Joss now—' Mrs Desmond hushed her voice in sympathy—'but he might. Even one's unpossessive children can be extraordinarily so, at times. And no matter how well one knows them— or thinks one does—one can never be quite sure what will hurt them and what won't—or I can't. So, as that nice man says no one has to be told anything, can we leave it between us? And, dearie, do advise me further. I'm sure I should pay someone something. His secretary said, no. Yet he saw me as a private patient!'

'No. As the mother of one of the staff. Some of our pundits might have charged you. Not Lincoln Browne. It's an old Martha's tradition that the hospital looks after its own and he's nuts on traditions. Wasn't this so at Benedict's?'

'Mercifully, I never had occasion to find out. Can I write and thank him?'

'Probably make his week if you do.'

She was puzzled. 'Patients don't thank specialists?'

'Generally,' I said, 'and oddly, only when everything's gone wrong. Then the pundits are inundated with letters from grateful relatives.'

'Now I come to think of it, Joss once said that!' She adjusted the set of her small (for her) cream boater. 'I suppose you don't see so much of him, now?'

I had not seen him since the night he left our flat. 'Martha's is a big place.'

The temperature went on rising. Saturday was the hottest day in London since the summer of '59. That evening the flags on our terrace were still steaming, little bubbles of liquid tar were dotting the hospital yard, and the oil from the turning and parked ambulances gave it a surface like ice.

The A.U. was air-conditioned, but all day every cubicle, every bed, had been re-occupied as soon as it was emptied. It was well after ten when Stan Lawson limped into my office, flopped onto one chair, arranged another for his feet, and pushed his glasses up on his high forehead. 'Cath,' he said, 'I know just how Canute felt. But he only had to deal with a mighty ocean of water.' His long, thin, humorous face was made longer by the very short haircut he had acquired since we last worked together. Otherwise, we had picked up where we left off. 'This is one of those times when I despair for the human race. When they aren't trying to kill each other on the roads, they're on the job with broken bottles, knives, razors, chair-legs. How many fights in so far?'

'Twenty-one.'

'Forty, last night. At this going we'll top that by midnight.'

Peter had come in. He sat on a hard chair against the wall, leant back and closed his eyes. 'Why can't the sods live in peace?'

'We'd be out of a job Friday and Saturday nights if they did.' Stan loosened his tie, uncapped his pen. 'Cath, remind me to write the brewers a note of thanks for keeping us off the dole queues.' He read my first entry in the log. 'Sylvia Mary Eccles, Mrs, 34 C. of E. What in the name of God did I do for Sylvia Mary?'

I passed him her accident card. 'You told Mr Palmer to put five stitches in her left wrist.'

'So I did! The cat jumped in from the garden, knocked the empty milk bottles into the sink, bust half the breakfast china and what her hubby said she wouldn't like to tell me, doctor, she was sure. Sylvia Mary was damned lucky.' He wrote as he spoke. 'Another millimetre and she'd have sliced her radial artery—and what would hubby have said then? Damned lucky to have a garden, this weather. Wish I had one.'

I said, 'I didn't know you liked gardening.'

'Detest it! But if I had a garden I'd have a lawn. Then I could paddle my poor feet in the early morning dew.' He glanced at Peter. 'He asleep?'

'I think so. Peter?' Peter didn't react. 'Flat out.'

'Some people have it easy.' He wrote on. 'Did I tell you I ran into Desmond and Miss Butler leaving for the country after lunch? She looks like a new girl. Wouldn't mind being down in Kent with them tonight.'

'Should be cooler there. Ready to sign?' The red light was flashing. 'Oh, no!'

He took the red receiver from me. 'You, Sister, are off! Unless this is a major, it's going to Emergencies.'

I still heard Harry, the senior night porter, clearly. 'Got a kicks in the face coming in for you, Mr Lawson. Male. Young. Five teeth gone. Query fractured jaw. What do you want me to do with him when he arrives?'

'Harry, Sister is present so I will refrain from specifying more than—keep him in Emergencies. I'll be in.'

Peter had woken. 'God, how I hate Saturday nights!'

I said, 'This heat can't last.'

'Nothing,' said Stan, 'even lasts. It may look that way, but in this life, my friends, it doesn't. Not even these notes, Cath. We'll finish 'em by midnight—if we're bloody lucky.'

It was exactly midnight when Harry got me a taxi. The taximan said, 'Working the late shift, eh?'

I didn't tell him the truth as he wouldn't believe it. I didn't hold that against him as there were some truths I did not want to face, myself. 'Yes. Happens, sometimes.'

Chapter Nine

Roxanne was back from Portugal and spent three days modelling furs. By the third evening she looked as if she had been put through a mangle. 'Those lights in this heat! If any man offers me a mink after this, I'll strangle him with it!'

'I wouldn't.' I kicked off my shoes, hung my legs over the arm of a chair and closed my eyes. 'I'd flog it and use the lolly on getting this flat air-conditioned.' I opened one eye. 'I thought there was some knees-up your agent said you mustn't miss tonight?'

'That's tomorrow. Got a light?'

I chucked her matches. 'Who're you going with?'

'Joe.'

'Doesn't he always end up sloshed blind?'

'Yes, but he can be darned amusing till he passes out, so long as he keeps off the subject of his ex-wife. He knows I'll take myself home when I've had enough. And drunk or sober,' she added, 'he's a very good photographer.'

There was a tremendous thunderstorm during the following afternoon. The A.U. had its quietest evening in weeks. Stan and I had finished the notes and were doing a newspaper crossword, when Peter put his head round the door and said he'd drive me home for a cup of Roxanne's coffee. She made superb coffee.

I explained why she would be out. 'Lift off?'

'Don't be so bloody silly! Of course not!' He stomped on down the corridor.

Stan glanced up. 'What's got him?'

I shrugged. 'Storm's still in the air. I'm surprised more people haven't been edgy during this heat.'

'I'm not. To be edgy, one needs time in which to feel hard-done-by. No time, no edges, and no insomnia. Been sleeping like a log?' I nodded. 'Same here and I'll bet throughout the A.U.' He filled in another word. 'Finland—and it fits. Didn't Peter go there last year?'

'Forgotten—no—yes—he sent me a postcard.'

'Time he had another holiday. He got one fixed up?'

'Dunno. What's a voracious sea-bird? Nine, down.'

He blinked at me owlishly, a sign his quick brain was in action. 'Cormorant.' He reached for the green receiver as the green light flashed. 'Probably me.'

It was. He wrote in 'cormorant' as he listened to a long spiel from Harry. 'I'll bet she is. Right, I'll be in, now.' He stood up, smiling. 'We do get 'em!'

Two foreign seamen, each with a black eye, had walked unannounced into Emergencies and sat themselves in wheelchairs. 'Seems they don't understand English, Spanish, Maltese, Italian, French, German, or Polish. Harry's been rounding up night orderlies as interpreters and the Night Super is out for his blood.'

I smiled. 'You off to transfuse him?'

'Harry'll survive, but he's not so sure about his young ladies. He's got them lads under his eye, Mr Lawson, sir, as he doesn't reckon much to the looks they're giving his nurses and though that young Mr Smith's doing his best, he's only a slip of a lad as don't need a shave more than once a fortnight and he reckons the senior night staff nurse is a bit worried, like. And seeing we're quiet and I'm a married man, meself, he thought, did Harry, he'd best have a word with me.' He polished and replaced his glasses. 'Forgive me if I go and prevent multiple rape?'

'Any time. Stan, might they be Norwegians?'

He blinked again. 'That's a thought.'

Peter was delighted Stan thought he needed a holiday. 'Understanding chap, Stan. Sensitive.'

'He should've been a physician.'

'Come off it, Cath! All surgeons may just be bloody technicians but
that doesn't make them all insensitive butchers.'

I allowed he had a point and did not pursue mine as there were some
things I preferred to keep to myself. I had been back long enough to
realize Roxanne had been right about Peter. Even if he still bleated, he
had grown up. He had never had, and probably never would have, Stan
and Joss's intuitive faculty of perception, but once he caught on he
considered every facet of a situation with the plodding thoroughness that
solves difficult diagnoses and great crimes. He was mildly enjoying
anaesthetics, if not enough to want to specialize. Latterly, he had begun
speculating about general practice. I told him I thought this the best idea
he had ever had. Despite his occasional conviction he was unloved and
unwanted, he was one of the few people I knew whom everyone liked.
My father thought it more important for a G.P. to like, and be liked, by
humanity, than to have a burning zeal to heal. 'The most useful qualities
are stamina and patience. If he's got patience, his practice'll flourish and
his patients forgive him any number of mistaken diagnoses. Nine out of
ten patients don't come to surgery for a diagnosis, they come because
they've got to talk to someone, or crack. Mind you, if you don't listen,
back they come with their ulcers, dermatitis, asthma, urticaria—the lot!'
Peter was normally very patient, which was why he had just surprised
Stan. His constitution was as strong as his build. I now thought him
made for a G.P., though before I went to Canada I would have said he
was far too immature. Recently, I had realized that could merely have
been because the same applied to myself.

He was making coffee and I was doing my hair when Stan rang to
ask if Peter had a Finnish phrase book. 'We've decided our lecherous,
black-eyed mariners may be Finns. If he can't oblige, ask if he knows a
good Finnish brush-off. The night staff nurse—and Harry—are on the
verge of acute anxiety states.'

I called Peter. 'Stan wants some Finnish four-letter words.'

'Stan wants—what?' Peter charged in, pushing his hand through his
hair. Stan's comments made him flop backwards onto my bed and shout
with laughter. 'Yes. In my room. Help yourself.' He rang off and smiled
up at me. 'How much of that did you get?'

'Only your bawdy splutters.'

'Just as well, when Stan's on form.' He undid his tie. 'That storm
hasn't made it any cooler.'

'Still hanging around.' My shoes were full of feet so I removed them.
'I've never heard Stan on form.'

'Nor will you.' He stretched out his arms, contentedly. 'Take more than Women's Lib to crack our Stanley's solid non-conformist upbringing.' He raised his head. 'Isn't that your living-room door?'

I went out to investigate and forgot the comb in my hand till the sight of Joss following Roxanne in made me drop it. 'Hi!' I said weakly, and ran out of conversation.

Joss was in a dinner-jacket that had been cut by a good London tailor this year. Roxanne's long blue-grey printed voile was edged with layers of lace. The dress had a very high lace collar, long graceful sleeves and could have been worn by her great-grandmother, had the skirt in front not been split from hem to thigh. The opening was edged with more lace and he tights matched the blue in the material. They could both have stepped out of one of Roxanne's magazine photographs. I felt like Little Orphan Annie after a particularly tough stint with my begging bowl.

Roxanne was explaining her joy at recognizing a human face at the worst party of the year, when Peter ambled through my bedroom door slowly replacing his tie. Roxanne stopped in mid-sentence. 'Didn't see your car, Peter!'

Peter exchanged amiable waves with Joss. 'Had to leave it round the corner. Joss rescued you from a fate worse than death? Bad champagne?' He was watching her with such open hostility that I almost forgot Joss was watching us both. 'How come you were there, Joss?'

'I've been dining with my old boss from Benedict's. He had to look in and asked me along to give him an excuse to get away, fast. I introduced him to Roxanne.' He smiled at her. 'That's taken care of my next job.'

Roxanne blew him a kiss. 'Why don't we all have a drink?'

Joss said if it was all the same to her after all the bad champagne he'd as soon have some of the coffee they had just turned off.

'My coffee!' Peter slapped his forehead. 'Had it boiled over?'

'The plate was red-hot.' From Roxanne's tone, Peter was clearly trying to bankrupt us through our electricity bills and, failing that, to burn the house down. 'I suppose we should be thankful it wasn't gas.'

'Oh, I don't know,' said Joss. 'Isn't gas cheaper?'

I was about to explain Stan's call, but Peter had caught my eye. 'If it had been gas,' he remarked with uncharacteristic smoothness, 'what a wonderful way to go.'

I thought of Dolly Jones for several reasons. 'Let's all have some coffee.'

Roxanne and Joss sat entwined on the sofa. Peter sat on the arm of my chair and when not playing with my hair, dutifully nibbled my ear. As Roxanne always looked especially good when she was angry and had to hide it, the only person I wasn't sorry for was Joss. The atmosphere reminded me very much of my first week in the A.U.

It eased, briefly, when Joss said he had seen Professor Ulvik and Mrs Alesund in Asden last weekend. The Professor's slow progress was continuing and his daughter had asked for my private address. 'She wants to see you again. All right my handing it out?'

'Sure.'

Peter slid into the chair behind me, lifted me onto his lap and wrapped his arms round my waist. 'Much more comfortable,' he murmured as if we were alone.

Roxanne ignored us and nibbled Joss's ear. I asked if the Norwegians intended claiming damages from the hire-car firm. Joss shook his head, which couldn't have been easy as Roxanne had very good teeth.

'Why not?' demanded Peter. 'Surely, the firm'll be only too happy to settle out of court?'

'They've offered. The Alesunds won't touch it. She said her father'd blow all fuses at the mere suggestion, and they think he's right.' He was suddenly embarrassed. 'They think they owe England too much.'

'Good God! Why?' Peter, Roxanne and I spoke together.

'Something to do with the last World War.' He looked directly at me for the first time since he came in. 'Seems they've long memories in Norway.'

'Rule Britannia.' I met his eyes and nearly said that again when he had to look away first.

But for our landlady's rule we would probably have sat there all night as very obviously neither man intended making the first move. At two minutes to twelve, Joss kissed Roxanne and Peter kissed me. They went down the top flight side by side and looking straight ahead.

I closed the door and leant against it. 'If there's one thing I enjoy, it's a jolly evening with chums.'

Roxanne was stretched on the sofa with her eyes shut. 'Cathy, I'm terribly sorry. Just because my party was a drag was no reason for busting up yours—'

'Don't be a moron, Roxanne—'

'Don't be so bloody charitable!' She sat up. 'Think I don't know why Peter was in such a filthy temper when we walked in? Think Joss didn't catch on? Long before Peter spelt it out?'

I said, 'No. We weren't. We haven't. We won't.'

She went scarlet. 'For God's sake! Which century do you think I'm living in?'

I had never known her so angry. I was so fascinated. I forgot my own. 'I'll tell you what you interrupted—'

'Thanks, but I can go to an X movie—'

'This one kicks off with two Finnish sex-maniacs in wheelchairs—' I smiled at her expression. 'True. Listen.' And when I finished, 'Don't ask me why Peter took your turning up with Joss as a slur to his virility. Could be Joss makes him feel inferior, but I'm not asking. I like my beautiful relationship with Peter and asking dodgy questions is the second best way of killing any beautiful relationship stone cold dead. Do you want the bath first?'

'No.' She had stopped looking angry and in self-defence had fallen into one of her professional poses. We privately called this one 'Nobody knows the trouble I've seen but stick around, buster, and you'll find out.' I did not say so, now. 'Cathy—'

'Yes?'

'This—umm—Martha's Foundation Ball in September. Hasn't Peter asked you?'

'Yes. Joss—you?'

'Yes. When he drove me back. Think we'll—umm—join up?'

'And which century do you think you're living in, Roxanne?'

I did not discuss that evening with her again, or with Peter in the A.U. It was getting on for three weeks before I next saw Joss and by then I had other things on my mind.

The temperature had returned to normal for late summer and as August ended our admission rate rose to its normal Bank Holiday climax. In one of the three momentary lulls we had that Monday, Dave Palmer said he didn't think he would ever be able to eat food his hands had touched again. 'But useless, utterly useless, to tell me I've been wearing gloves. They reek of blood, positively reek!' He groaned at another red flash. 'Dear lemmings. Go home.'

'Brace up, lad,' said Stan. 'Holocaust season closes after today till Christmas. Well, Sister?'

I read aloud Nurse Hedges' memo sheet. 'Six. Two adults, four children. One family. Estate car ...'

Five minutes later Hedges was back. 'Both sets of parents of that honeymoon couple are here, Sister.'

'Waiting-room and tea, Nurse. Mr Lawson'll see them soon as he's free.'

Another memo sheet. 'Elderly pedestrian. Male. Knocked down by van. Multiple injuries. Name, address, unknown.'

Message after message. Accident-trolley after accident-trolley. The same anguished mutters, the same whimpers of pain, the same sickly sour smell of fresh-spilled blood. Relative after relative, sitting in rows in our waiting-room in the same incongruously garish holiday clothes, with the same stunned expression on their faces.

The estate car had belts fitted to the front and back seats. The youngest child had been in a safety-harness and the other three wearing their belts. The parents had left theirs undone. The father had been doing around seventy when he had a front off-side blow-out. Both parents were sent to I.C. on the Dangerously Ill List. The children were shocked and cut by flying glass, but none seriously.

The youngest had come off best as she had been asleep. She was four, very chubby and articulate, and her name was Jeanie. The precautionary X-ray showed her skull to be so perfect and intact that George Charlesworth breathed in sharply as it was illuminated on the X-ray screen. 'My God,' he muttered to Stan. 'Come and look at this.'

Jeanie looked seriously at the two men, then plucked my gown sleeve. 'Is that really him?' she whispered.

I bent over her. 'Sorry, lovey, I don't understand. Really who?'

Her round baby face was alight with excitement. 'God. That tall gentleman with the glasses. That's what the small gentleman with the glasses called him. I didn't know God wore glasses though I know He wears a long white dress as I've seen pictures of him.' Stan had overheard and moved to her other side. 'Please, are you God?'

Stan flushed to the roots of his short hair. 'No, love, sorry. I'm just same as your Daddy, only I'm a doctor. Know what a doctor is?'

'Doctors mend people. Mummy told me.' She gave George Charlesworth an accusing glare. 'Why did that small gentleman with the glasses call you God?'

George Charlesworth was pink. Stan answered for him. 'He wasn't really talking to me, Jeanie. He was—he was sort of saying a little prayer.'

With the total unselfconsciousness of the very young, she flattened her fat little hands together under her chin. 'Like "Gentle Jesus meek and mild"?'

For a moment the two men and I were silent.

'That's right, love,' said Stan. 'Like that.'

On that same table, that morning, the three of us had stood and watched a slightly older child die.

Later, Stan said, 'I wish I could have the buggers here.'

I was punch-drunk from the day. 'Which buggers, Stan?'

'The buggers who were in too much of a hurry to get to the sea—to Auntie May's—to the pub—the best picnic spot. I wish I had them here. And you know what I'd do?' I shook my head at his tired, grim face. 'I'd not take 'em to I.C., the kids' wards, the bloody shambles the girls are now turning back into a clean Receiving Room. I'd not bother showing 'em the relatives, or let 'em listen to that "We never thought this could happen to us, Doctor!" I've had over and over all day. None of that!' His voice shook with the dreadful anger of a peaceful man. 'I'd just take the buggers to the morgue. I'd stand 'em there, a bit, to listen to the ticking of the fridges. Then I'd pull out just the one shelf. The one with that little lad with half his head missing. And I'd say, "Take a look, mates. You've got the time. Saved it on the roads today, didn't you? And this is what those few minutes bloody cost. Take a good look. Then—*off* home and sleep easy." '

I did not say anything. I left him in the office and went along to the relatives' waiting-room. It had finally emptied, the tea-urn was only lukewarm, but there was enough left for one cup. I took it back, put it by him and sat down again. After he had drunk the tea we did the notes.

Chapter Ten

I had a letter from Mr Alesund next day and we met for lunch in the following week. She was waiting in the foyer, but I did not immediately recognize her as the young woman in a tan jersey suit and tan velvet beret.

She was amused. 'My face is clean!'

'Mine, too, but you recognized me.'

She had unusually wide-set eyes with an even more unusual quality of innocence in their expression. 'Miss Maitland, Arne and I have three children. Our boy is eight, our girls seven and five. I shall never forget either your face or Mr Desmond's. Now, sherry?' Her fluent English was only slightly accented. 'Or something else?'

I had rather dreaded that lunch, having recently discovered how uncomfortable a burden was gratitude. I was now finding it as hard to dismiss Joss as not worth bothering over, as to meet him without feeling irritated and vaguely guilty, because I probably owed him my life. I had expected much the same reaction to myself from my hostess. It was not all that uncommon in patients after a successful recovery from dangerous illness. My father had said that was because few people cared to recall their black periods of those connected with them. 'It is so much easier to be a generous giver. To be a generous taker requires real, and rare, generosity of spirit.'

Mrs Alesund possessed it. Her friendliness was uneffusive, but she made it very plain she was my friend for life. She talked as an old friend, of her family, and father. He was now up on crutches and hoping to leave hospital, shortly. 'He's so enjoyed his regular visits from Mr and Mrs Frayling, and the Vicar and Mrs Desmond. With the Vicar he's got on very well as both men are scholars and served in your Royal Navy during the last World War.'

'I knew the Vicar had been a Naval padre.' I did not add that the rest was news to me.

'An interesting and amusing man. Coffee?'

'Thank you.' She had not mentioned Joss again. I did, and learnt he had driven her over to tea at the vicarage on his half-day last week.

'It was a lovely afternoon and we had tea on the lawn. It was a very pleasant and very English occasion.'

'With wasps in the raspberry jam and suicidal flies in your tea?'

She laughed. 'Having lived next door for so long, those wasps will be your old friends. I had hoped young Mr Desmond could join us today, but unfortunately he's working. Of course, you'll know that.'

'No.' I explained our different jobs.

She seemed surprised. 'Not your young man?'

I smiled. 'Boy next door.'

She agreed that was often an insuperable barrier later and asked if I had ever visited Norway. 'You must! It is a beautiful country. Do you ski?'

'I did some in Canada. I loved it, though I'm no good as I started too old. Your children ski?'

'Indeed! Norwegians are on skis as soon as they can walk. You must spend a winter holiday with us sometime. When do you next have a holiday?'

I took her invitation as a charming gesture, but not to be taken seriously. 'Thanks, I'd love to.' I went on to tell her my immediate future remained problematical owing to Butler's health. Miss Evans had said I must have two weeks off before the end of the year, possibly late October or early November and would that suit me? Since the last thing I presently wanted was the thinking-time a holiday would provide, I said, very well, thank you. Miss Evans had then given me a long look and asked how many days off I had owing. My answer evoked a deep sigh. 'Not blaming you, my dear. I haven't a sister who escaped the 'flu who doesn't now need a rest-cure. Now let me see—' she studied a rota. 'Yes. By the last weekend of this month, Nurse Chalmers'll be back—her father's much better—and Nurse Jones from her holiday. Take from Thursday to Tuesday, inclusive.'

Mrs Alesund asked if I would spend my break at the vicarage. I said I thought not as there was so much I wanted to do in London. We agreed London was a fascinating city, though the traffic was terrifying. She was returning to Asden that afternoon and to Norway tomorrow. Before I left, she asked me to call her Nina. 'I think of you as Cathy, having heard your old friends use the name so often. I won't say goodbye, as we will meet again. Till then.'

I wrote that off as another, charming gesture. I said as much to Joss

when I met him by chance on my nightly visit to the Office with the
A.U. report that evening. He was in a hurry, too. He said I could be
right, that he had been sorry to miss our lunch but I knew how it was. I
said I did and we went our separate ways. When I looked back he had
disappeared.

'You're very grave, Sister. Disturbing evening?'

'Er—no, Miss Evans, Quite quiet.'

Back in the Receiving Room, one of the medic. students was trying to
unload the last four unsold ball tickets in his book. 'Best knees-up of the
year status-wise! Come on, Mr Lawson! Make the in scene!'

'Dance, lad? Me? When I've flat feet and am tone deaf? What are
you trying to do? Deprive me at a stroke of my job and my lovely wife?
Take a look at next week's off-duty rota on that board! Mr Charlesworth's just told you he's got his tickets. How long'd I draw my pay if
I left the shop to run itself? And how'd I persuade my wife not to fulfil
her promise to divorce me if I risk crippling her on a dance floor the
once more? Away, wretched youth! Flog 'em elsewhere!' He glanced at
the lights. 'Thought this peace was too good. And the next one is—
Sister?'

Nurse Black was 'light and messages.' We were patientless, so she
read aloud: Youth, name, address, unknown. Minor burns, shock,
semi-drowned. Clothes set alight when removing paints from house-boat
with blow-lamp. Jumped in river, can't swim. River police witnessed
event, bringing him in.'

'Makes a change.' Stan washed his hands. 'If there's one thing I like,
it's a bit of variety.'

Peter waved off the ticket-seller like a fly. 'If you ask me, the chap
was flogging tickets. My blow-lamp still handy, Sister?'

'On the anaesthetic machine in C2, Dr Anthony.' There was a roar of
laughter as the medic in question glanced into C2 instinctively. 'It's all
right, Mr Dennis. Dr Anthony only chucks medics in the river when
there's no R in the month.'

'Only snag there, I can never remember the date.' Peter smiled at me
over his mask as the red light reappeared. 'We're in business again.'

The youth was a Barry Steven Thomas. He was twenty, very skinny,
with long, dank, dark hair and a sharp-featured, intelligent face. He
worked in a television-cum-radio shop and though semi-conscious on
admission, responded so well that initially he refused to be admitted to a
ward. 'Only got me clobber burnt and a bit of a soaking, didn't I, then?
Said yourselves I been dead lucky only to get them small burns. You've
fixed me. I'm not stopping.'

Stan had called in a thoracic registrar as some water had penetrated

Barry's lungs. The registrar said we'd feel much happier if he would come in for a day or two. 'The Thames isn't precisely crystal clear.'

'Can't be that mucky, Doc, seeing as the fish come back.'

I said, 'You just don't fancy hospitals, Barry?'

'S'not that, darlin'.' He grimaced to himself. 'I'm not fussy, but it's this bird, see? Always meet her down the disco Wednesdays, don't I? Go right spare she will, if she reckons I've turned her in. Have to get meself a new bird, won't I? Don't want no new bird. Proper little darlin', she is. I'm getting out of here, see?'

I said, 'Wouldn't your bird understand if we got a message to her? What's her name? And the disco? Better still, know the number?'

He gave all three. Peter joined us as I was noting the lot on the upturned hem of my gown. Barry said I'd best ask for Big Sid. 'He's all right, is Big Sid. He'll not reckon her name, just say as she's the small blonde job, third table back, right. He'll fetch her, you tell her and I'll sign in.' He winked at the two men. 'Sister's a proper little darlin', ain't she, then?'

Joss stopped by my table in the canteen next day. Peter was in the queue for our coffee. Joss had had a letter from Ruth and she sent me her love. 'She feels marriage is an institution with a great future.'

'I've heard it well spoken of.'

His smile wasn't fraternal, it was downright avuncular. 'Hence the successful Lonely Hearts' Bureau Doug Pearson says you're running in the A.U.?'

Doug was the thoracic registrar. 'All part of the N.H.S.' Since we were so nauseatingly chummy, I asked about the holiday he was starting some time next week. 'Foreign parts?'

'I think so, though it's not quite settled.' He looked ostentatiously at the canteen clock as Peter approached with two cups of coffee. 'If that's right, I'm late. Hi, Pete—see you, Cathy!'

Roxanne was booked to make a television commercial in Venice two days after the ball. At the moment, she was doing so well professionally that we barely saw each other. 'Always the same,' she said. 'Either every fashion editor in London wants you at once, or no one remembers your name.'

She was reorganizing the two-foot-long carpet-bag she used for her modelling gear some nights later when I got back by taxi at eleven. 'Peter on call?'

'No. Something late he wanted to see on telly.' I sat on her bed. 'Where's tomorrow's?'

'Brighton, at eight-thirty.' She muttered to herself as she repacked. 'Shoes—light—dark—high—flat—boots—where the hell are my boots?' I picked them off the floor. 'Thanks. Joss rang me just now to fix up

times for Friday. Going to Malta, he said. Isn't that where his regular
woman is?'

'Yes. What about sandals?'

'God, yes!' She dived into her shoe-rack. 'Tights. Tights—plain—
coloured—body stockings—socks—strapless bras—bra slips—' she
looked up. 'These taxis must be costing you a fortune.'

'They are. If you keep on working at this rate, I shall end up
bankrupt.'

'Thought you said he was watching telly?'

'Every man needs a hobby, dear.'

She smiled slightly as she intoned over her hair accessories. 'Wigs—
hair pieces—heated rollers—spray—where's my blasted setting lotion?' I
was sitting on it. 'The client wants a simple day dress, possibly striped.
I've got in one striped horizontal, one vertical, one floral, three plain
coloureds. Think that's enough?'

'I'd say.' I waited a moment. 'Did you know you make him feel
inferior?'

'Me *and* Joss?'

'Yes. In different ways.'

She flung herself into the pose we called 'One step nearer, Mr Hands,
and I'll blow your brains out.' 'He knows there's a difference?'

I said soberly, 'I think he's serious, Roxanne. I've never thought so
before, but I do now. Of course, I could be wrong.' She said nothing.
'Decided you're not interested?'

'Decided I need time to think. I was so sure eventually you two would
drift into marriage. I can now see that's not on, but—' she zipped up the
bag '—nor is my chucking away good lolly I can only earn for a year or
two more, to boost any man's ego. And even when the public get sick of
my face, as they will, I'll never settle for being the doctor's wife. I'll turn
agent and I'll make a lot of lolly. I like lolly and I like working. How
about his ego, then?'

I thought it over and had to be honest. 'I think it might work
providing you were hellish tactful. Is he worth it, to you?'

'I don't know. I've got to think.'

I said, 'He's only soft-centred. He's not all mushy.'

'I like soft-centres.' She lit a cigarette. 'I'm just not sure the time's
right. My dad says everything depends on timing. He says if you can get
your timing right, you can be the biggest ham in the business and stil
have 'em queuing in the rain for a mid-week matinee in Wigan. Get it
wrong, and no matter how talented, you'll lay an egg. He says it's the
same off-stage, and that lots of people mess up their opportunities not
because they don't recognize 'em, but because they grab 'em at the

wrong moment.' She gazed at the bag. 'Maybe I should take the dog-tooth check. Yes, I will.'

She was still dressing when Peter came for me on Friday night. We didn't wait as we were joining separate parties, if for no other reason than convention. The tables round the floor always were booked months in advance by the various Units. Comparatively, the A.U. staff was small and we had a single table for six. The Orthopaedic Unit needed two tables pushed together and fourteen chairs. Being the social event of the hospital year, the residents always drew lots before buying tickets. The losers stayed on either in their own jobs, or on loan. Stan had kept out of the draw, which automatically freed George Charlesworth. He was with Dolly, and Dave Palmer, smirking with his luck in the draw, had brought the very pretty Nurse Fisher.

Stan was running the A.U. with Hamish Geddes, a locum anaesthetist from Swansea, and Mr Smith from Emergencies. Stan sent us a message on a memo sheet via one of Harry's night porters. 'Minorities appeased. Smith's home, Ulster. Have requested precautionary peace-keeping force from U.N. Enjoy *dolce vita*, but kindly refrain from bringing pieces for repair to A.U. as scuppers already awash with blood and beer from regular customers.'

The lace frills on Dave's shirt provided universal joy and attention until Joss walked in with Roxanne. Her tight-fitting, apparently seamless, sleeveless black velvet dress had a high halter neckline and was split up the left side to mid-thigh. She wore no jewellery and had taken off her watch. The effect hit Peter, as well as every other woman in the room, like a bomb.

Dolly said without rancour, 'I feel like a Christmas tree.'

Peter was breathing carefully. 'That's her job. Have to switch yours, Dolly, if you want to afford fifty quid on a dress.'

I said, 'That dress didn't cost Roxanne fifty quid. Cost her five sixty including the zip. I was there when she bought the material. She made it herself. She likes sewing.'

Fisher was intrigued. 'I've seen her on telly commercials. You actually know her, Sister?'

'Been sharing a flat with her for years.'

'So that's how our dear Mr D. drew the jackpot! Just because you and he were kiddiwinks together? Why don't any of my dear old kiddiwink chums introduce me to birds that look like that?' Dave was so concerned with his woes he did not notice another houseman removing Fisher until they were on the floor. 'Oh, villain! I have been robbed—but robbed!'

Peter tritely observed that would teach him a bird in the hand was worth two in the bush—even if poured into black velvet.

George Charlesworth reluctantly took his eyes off Dolly. 'Who's everyone going on about? That bird with Joss Desmond? Oh—yes—not bad. Dance, Dolly?'

Dancing with Peter, I said George revived my faith in human nature. Peter was glad I had any faith left to be revived. 'Let's get some air.'

The ball was in the Medical School's largest ground floor lecture room. The building stood away from the wards and as it was a fine night, all the french windows were open. We went out on the terrace and leant on the stone balustrade overlooking the river. The water was black and smooth as oil. The lights on the embankments and the bridges lined and strung the blackness with yellow diamonds. The empty office blocks on the far bank were towers of white diamonds, and the skyline of the City was charcoal petrified lace against the pink-black London sky.

Peter propped his chin on his hands. 'When I was a student, I thought I'd never be able to leave this. Not that I seriously thought I ever would, if I thought at all. Don't believe I did. I just had a vague idea that if I hung around long enough Membership—' he smiled at himself '—and M.D., the lot—would somehow drop into my lap. S.M.O., the Staff, Dr Anthony, sir, Sir Peter Anthony. Lord Anthony. All I needed was patience.'

'Patience you've got, Pete.'

'No. You're mixing it up with laziness. But I don't just want to move off now, as I can't be bothered to make the effort to stay. I now know that if I sweated my guts out, I'd never make the top grade here. Martha's may turn out specialists by the dozen, but I'm not specialist material.' He turned to watch the dancers passing the open windows. 'Not in a million years would it have struck me to risk offending our top brass and getting out of step here, by demonstrating my conviction that some Benedict's man knew more about my line than our own pundits. You don't get to the top without taking chances. I don't like taking chances. Thought I did. I don't.'

I had turned and we were both watching Joss and Roxanne. 'Nor did my father. He loved being a G.P. I think he was a very good one.'

'Joss says he was first-rate.'

'Do you think his gamble'll pay off?'

He nodded gloomily. 'Hoadley's sold on him. Fair enough. He's a bloody good surgeon and he works bloody hard. Everyone at the top in medicine knows everyone else, so they'll have heard across the river. If he'd mucked things up here, Benedict's would never have forgiven him for opting out for Martha's, but if they aren't already cooking the fatted calf, I'll bet it's ordered.' The music stopped. Roxanne, smiling, stretched out both hands to Joss. 'Nothing succeeds like success. Nothing at all.' He swung round to face the water. 'Roxanne's doing very well too, isn't she?'

'Very, though a model's life at the top is generally very short-lived. Have you done anything tangible about G.P.ing?'

'There may be an opening in Leeds in the New Year. A joint practice. Don't suppose I'll get it, but I've applied.'

'Roxanne's home town. You must tell her. She'll be very interested.'

'For God's sake—why?'

'Aren't you interested in anything concerning your own home town? And she may know some of the partners. Her father lives there. I know it's a big city, but most cities break down into villages and everyone in a village knows everyone else's business and more than somewhat about the nearby villages. Got an interview? Then ask her tonight when you dance with her. She's leaving for a job in Venice on Sunday and she might be able to give you some helpful hints if only about which football team not to support.'

He said, 'You're still a lousy liar, Cath. So you think I should dance with her?'

'I'm thinking of Stan. He'll be hellish narked when the river police fish you out of the river.'

He hesitated, then laughed. 'Almost worth it to see Stan's face when they wheel me in. Come on. Let's participate.'

Sir Hoadley was sitting by Roxanne at the O.R. tables when we returned to our own. In common with the many pundits present, he was in tails. Since there was no Accidents' consultant, we all agreed champagne was the only possible antidote to our deprivation symptoms. The popping of Sir Hoadley's shirt-front and the redness of his face provided additional consolation, but we had to avert our eyes from Dr Lincoln Browne. At any Martha's function for the last quarter of a century, the tall, elegant cardiologist had been, and remained, amongst the top three most attractive men present. His grey streaks had altered to white since I last saw him and he had a few more lines and no longer danced since he had had his first coronary. I did not expect him to remember me as it was years since I worked in Cardiacs, but he bowed from across the floor. Dave asked if I shared a flat with him, too?

'Unfortunately, no.'

Miss Evans was impressive in grey lace, Miss Mackenzie terrifying in what appeared to be a black shroud. Sister Florence, the oldest and stoutest sister in the hospital, was draped in purple satin. She loved dancing and stood no nonsense about waiting to be asked. 'Come along, boy! We'll dance!' Having on some occasion in the last twenty years had every member of the nursing staff present as a patient, she toured the tables methodically, checking up on her ex-patients' health, husbands, babies, teenagers' prospects of getting into university, and future nursing careers. 'Can't expect you gals to stay single these days.' She lowered herself into Dave's chair and we all sat down again. 'Too many young men about. First time in history you gals are in a minority group. Enjoying it, eh? Sure you are! I would've loved it!' She peered at Fisher. 'How's that throat, child? Behaving itself? Good. No more trouble with that back, Nurse Jones? Thought it would clear up.' It was my turn. 'No more of that bronchitis you had in your first year? Always said you'd grow out of it.' She noticed Dave's stance. 'Straighten up, boy! Remember your vertebrae! Want a curvature before you're my age?' She suddenly beckoned Joss from the edge of the floor. 'Well, Mr Desmond? Missed you in my ward, lately. Good news from Malta, eh? And who's this pretty gal? Why don't I know you, Nurse? You're not a nurse? Pity. You know how to carry yourself, child. Take my chair—I want a word with Mrs de Winter.' She moved on to the next table.

The second, and olde-tyme group, started up again as I introduced Roxanne to the A.U. party. Joss stood watching in silence with his shoulders back and eyebrows up. Peter dithered until Roxanne smiled straight at him. Two minutes later, Joss and I were alone. He had sat in a chair on the other side of the table before he remembered he was not my brother. 'Or do you feel strong enough for a schmaltzy waltz?'

'My feet,' I said truthfully, 'are killing me.'

He smiled politely. 'Then I can give you the message I should've handed on earlier. Arne Alesund rang me this evening. They've both flown over for a fleeting visit and want us to meet them for lunch up here tomorrow. He rang from Asden.'

'Tomorrow I'm on at one—'

'I said that was on the cards. He suggested coffee, a drink before lunch, or both. Seems they've some specific reason for wanting to see us. Nina would've written you but she's somehow sprained her right hand.'

'I can make anything up to twelve-thirty. How about you?'

He grinned. 'Free man. Holiday started this afternoon.' He stood up as Dr Lincoln Browne was suddenly at my elbow. 'Evening, sir.'

'Good evening, Doctor—and to you, Miss Maitland.' The pundit smiled on us both as he shook my hand. As Joss was a surgeon and had never been one of his students, he obviously did not recognize him. Martha's had roughly ninety residents and even more post-graduates around, and when in doubt all strange men were addressed by the title 'Doctor', and more often than not, correctly.

Dr Lincoln Browne refused a chair as he was leaving and had already said goodnight to Miss Evans. 'Seeing you having this brief rest, I couldn't waste the delightful opportunity. I know you'll be glad to hear I've had a most charming letter from our mutual friend, Mrs Desmond. I was very glad you sent her to me,' he added seriously. 'It's a rare pleasure to be able to remove a genuine anxiety from an intelligent patient. Wish it happened more often. Well! I must just have a final word with my old friend Sister Florence. Very nice to see you back in our midst, Miss Maitland. Goodnight to you both.' He bowed himself off to the next table. Joss bowed back.

I glanced from the next table to Joss. 'Listen—'

'While we indulge in a little therapeutic schmaltz.' He came round and offered his hand. He said nothing until we were dancing. 'Do tell me,' he murmured in my ear, 'to whom have you sent my old man? And Danny? One does rather like to know these things when they concern one's own family.'

My head knocked his chin as I tilted it back to look at his face. 'She didn't want to worry you.'

He gave an equivocal little grimace. 'When did this come up? That Saturday at home?'

'Yes.' I remembered our conversation as we left the vicarage.

So did he. 'Crafty little bitch, aren't you, darling.'

'Joss, I didn't think it necessary—'

'To encourage the lad's Oedipus? Dead right. Can't be too careful with these unnatural emotions. Think where it got Oedipus. Still— thanks.'

I gave up. 'Forget it. Did Arne Alesund give you any idea why they particularly want to see us?'

'He said they'd rather do that *vis-à-vis*. My guess is, they want us to lean on the Prof.' He smiled. 'He's just cracked another new walking-plaster, bouncing on it when no one was looking. His ward sister told me last week she'd be whiter than him before he left. The only way they can get him to rest at all is to hide his crutches. Obviously, takes more than that to restrain the tough old Viking, but he is seventy-six and he has been bloody ill. The Alesunds had hoped to fly him home tomorrow, but he said this afternoon he's quite happy to hang on a few more days and ta-very-much but he hates flying and when he goes home he's going as a good Norwegian should, by sea. And he will—if he doesn't bust his neck testing the next new plaster.'

I was smiling. 'Or telling the Captain how to steer across the North Sea.'

'That's for sure.' He held me closer and we finished the dance in an apparently companionable silence. Being, as we later discovered, the penultimate dance, it was longer than usual. I found it so long I was very glad when it ended. Joss then said he would ring me in the morning after ringing Arne Alesund and took Roxanne back to his own table. Peter collected me.

Next morning Arne Alesund handed me a sherry and Joss a beer. He raised his own beer. 'Skål!' His accent was much stronger and his English less perfect than his wife's. 'Good practice for next weekend, no?'

Joss looked as bemused as I felt. 'Skål!' we said.

Chapter Eleven

The mountains were growing higher and changing colour. They ranged the length of the northern horizon, sepia and charcoal, black and navy blue, all streaked with white and patches of dark green velvet. The long vivid blue slits of the fjords ran softly inwards, like venous blood returning to an invisible, gigantic heart. Beyond the coastal range were more mountains, and beyond those, more mountains, rising up and up to the end of the world. The farthest mountains were half-hidden in mist.

As we sailed closer, the pale grey sea was broken by innumerable rocky islets speckled with moss and scrub bushes and lined with patient rows of sea-birds. The sea was smooth and the morning sun gentle in a cloudless sky.

Joss folded his arms on the rail beside me. 'Pebbles plopped on the water by some absent-minded giant. Incredible,' he mused, 'to think we're so far north in autumn. This could be the Med. in spring.'

'No Force Ten gale,' I murmured, and felt rather than saw him look at me, curiously. Having woken with the type of crashing headache that fills the brain with painful cotton-wool and seals off the world behind a thinner layer, it was some seconds before I recalled never having seen the Mediterranean and tuned in to his train of thought. 'Pity your Malta project had to be cancelled.'

'I'm not all that sold on the sun and I do like Scotland. I hope this weather lasts when I get to Edinburgh next week.'

'This chum Naomi flew back with one of your old chums?'

'Yep. From Benedict's.'

I made no comment, partially owing to my headache, partially as I was wondering if he would now tell me Naomi had seen Miss Evans on Wednesday afternoon. When he didn't, I did not tell him I knew she was not returning to Martha's, or that my five days were now tacked on to a two-week holiday. This was our first real conversation alone, since our brief chat over travel arrangements yesterday between Asden station and Asden General. Professor Ulvik had regretted even more volubly than the Alesunds that I was not free to spend longer in Bergen. Since I hadn't known this could be possible till Wednesday night, by which time the Alesunds, at their own expense, had fixed our shipping tickets and the project was already cutting a large enough chunk out of Joss's holiday, it had seemed only tactful to keep it quiet.

I only learnt on the morning after the ball that Joss's previous arrangements had been turned upside down, as Naomi had suddenly decided she wanted to join him in the U.K. Joss said he had already cancelled his flight ticket, but offered no other explanations to the Alesunds or myself. The former had been delighted. 'Speaking frankly,' said Arne, 'we are much pleased and much relieved. The Professor is tall and with his plaster, very heavy. A man is necessary to support and— maybe—keep him a little quiet, no? But Thursday, business forces me to Oslo. I would not be content for Nina, or any other girl, to come with him alone on the sea. Last weekend we had a hurricane. Speaking frankly, next weekend—who knows?'

When Joss drove me back to the flat, I said I was surprised Norway sounded as much a man's world as England. 'I thought the Scandinavians were too civilized for that kind of nonsense.'

He frowned at the car ahead. 'Not knowing, can't say. But as the Prof. standing just clears six five, even though he hasn't an ounce of spare flesh, isn't it just possible Arne's argument has a practical rather than prejudiced basis? Almost certainly, you'll outlive me, but the fact remains my muscles are stronger than yours.'

'And trained nurses don't learn how to lift?'

'Cool off, Cathy!' We could have been back in the vicarage schoolroom. 'Only one weekend. They know we're free, we don't want to upset 'em, so we're hooked. As the Chinese so wisely say—relax, and enjoy it!' He drew up and said he would be in touch. He sent me a postcard from the vicarage saying the weather was good, Naomi had guessed the correct weight of the cake at the W.I. 'bring-and-buy', he would meet the 11 A.M. at Asden on Thursday morning and whatever else I forgot, to remember my passport.

Miss Evans had been off duty on Wednesday night. If had been a heavy day in the A.U. Monday and Tuesday had been worse. We now had the full staff back, but when the Office rang to say Miss Evans wanted to see me in her flat, as Miss Evans always did her own dirty work, I was convinced my five days were about to be written off, but was too busy to work out whether I was glad or sorry.

Miss Evans offered me an armchair, a cup of coffee and profound apologies for having to make a request she normally tried to avoid. Then she asked me to add my holiday onto my weekend. 'It won't be too short notice? You're sure? My dear girl, that is a relief! I'll tell you why.'

Naomi Butler had called on her that afternoon and asked to be released from her contract for purely domestic reasons. Miss Evans did not say what these were and etiquette prevented my asking. 'In the circumstances, naturally, I agreed, though I am exceedingly sorry to lose such an excellent nurse. Inevitably, this leaves me with a staff problem and is why I want your holiday over, immediately.' She refilled our cups. 'Nurse Chalmers leaves to marry her parson in November. In December, Nurse White takes her new post in Australia. Had you not already told me you want to return to the wards, I would now be offering you a permanent contract as Sister Accidents. Nurse Jones is not yet sufficiently experienced, but I would say, possibly by January? You agree? Good! So does Miss Mackenzie. And you're willing to remain in the Accident Unit until then? Thank you. Now—what are your views on your present fourth-years?'

Having given them, I said, 'Though still a third, Nurse Fisher is exceptionally good.'

'That pretty little thing? Is she, indeed! I'll bear this in mind when her training ends.' She made a note in the large diary on the coffee table, then glanced up with a wry smile. 'I suppose she's not engaged to young Mr Palmer, as that could be a complication, later. According to Mr Roth, once that young man has his Fellowship, he could make a good future J. and S.A.O. I've nothing against inter-staff—what shall I call 'em?—good friendships, and wouldn't have a hope of stopping them if I had, but I will never knowingly allow an engaged pair, any more than husband and wife, to work in the same department. It isn't fair to impose the inevitable strain on either—and, above all, unless they have rare self-control, it must affect the quality of their work. Consequently, without wishing to pry into my nurses' private lives, I do like to know who is going steady with whom.' My expression amused her. 'Running a large hospital is a complex occupation, and particularly a teaching hospital. The overwhelming majority of my staff are under thirty and—to begin with—single. With our inter-hospital marriage rate, I often wonder if I'm running a hospital or the most successful marriage bureau in London. Do you mind telling me—are those two children thinking of an engagement?'

'Not that I've heard, Miss Evans. I wouldn't even have said they were going steady.' I was fascinated by this latest insight into the life of a high-powered hospital administrator. 'They're both—well—'

'Playing the field?' she queried briskly. 'Good. Good. At their age that's a sign of maturity. I've long observed it's invariably my most immature children who leap into marriage in their first or second years. Sadly, more often than not, inside of five years they want to leap out again. But I've kept you long enough! Enjoy your break, and I have to say, you look ready for it, my dear. Let's hope you return refreshed and not to another 'flu epidemic. Dr Gray tells me the odd case is still appearing around the country.' She saw me to the door. 'I will announce this news after I've spoken to Mr Lawson and Nurse Chalmers over the weekend. For the present—I think we've just decided you need more than a weekend's rest. Have a good time—and thank you very much!'

No one in the A.U. had time to ask questions when I got back. It was also Mrs Lawson's birthday. At ten, George Charlesworth and I pushed Stan off and got on with the notes. Peter was on call. He said he would be in to say goodbye, but had not returned when I was ready to go. George said he would explain. 'He'll miss you. One does—miss people.'

Dolly's holiday ended tomorrow. She had only returned temporarily for the ball. Suddenly I not only felt very sorry, but a new respect for George. Even after working with him and Dolly, I had not guessed their one-sided relationship until Peter told me. Obviously, Miss Evans had not heard, and only Peter and Dolly had mentioned it to me. I wondered if unselfishness failed to make news because it was unspectacular, or so rare that nine out of ten people didn't believe it when they saw it. Then I wondered how long it would take Dolly to believe it, or if her early background was going to leave her a permanent emotional cripple. That left me feeling so dispirited when I got back to the flat that I was very glad Roxanne was at a party. I wept over my packing as I had not wept in ages and when I let the little woman in me have her head, I never had cared for an audience.

Roxanne was free next morning and only woke about ten minutes before I left. 'Say that again, Cathy! What domestic issues?'

'God alone knows!'

She unwound a few dozen curlers. 'You are fierce! All this hard work. Very bad for the soul. A jolly jaunt is just what you need—'

'Jolly? Prof. Ulvik's four years off eighty and St Peter held those gates open for about a fortnight.'

'Joss said it was a damned close-run thing and the only two people who thought he'd make it were the old boy himself, and you. Joss says he's good value. So's Joss. And he keeps his hands to himself. I wouldn't mind an orge in Norge with him, even if his heart is in the Highlands.'

'Edinburgh is in Midlothian. The Lowlands.'

She laughed. 'Never mind, dear. With any luck you'll hit a Force Ten gale and all be revoltingly sick before the ship goes down.' My taxi had arrived. 'Any last message for your next-of-kin?'

I smiled reluctantly. 'Yes. Peter's interview for this Leeds job is now this Monday. I forgot to wish him luck. Ring him for me and don't be surprised if he sounds incoherent. Interviews and exams always reduce him to a pea-green jelly.'

The Alesunds had hired a chauffeur-driven car to take us from Asden General to the ship's berth at Newcastle. The Professor was escorted down the front steps of the hospital and into the car by the Matron, Assistant Matron, a registrar, houseman, two sisters, and a posse of nurses. Though on elbow crutches, he towered over everyone present and his white, blue-veined hands looked far too frail to lift a walking-stick, much less support him. He did allow his ward sister to lift his plastered leg into the back of the car while a nurse held his crutches. All other offers of help were dismissed with polite firmness. 'Many thanks. I manage!'

'Don't crack that plaster before you get home, Professor! See you in Bergen!'

Joss was in front. He turned round to us as we drove off waving like royalty. 'Invited them all to stay, sir?'

'Yoss, of course, of course!' The old man's face was as white as his hair and withered by illness as well as age. His very blue eyes seemed to belong to another man. They were vivid with intelligence and humour and were decades younger than the face from which they looked on the world. 'One of the few advantages of becoming a monument—and to become one it is necessary to pass three score years and ten—is that one can encourage pretty women to visit the monument in his home, without causing offence to any.' He studied me, thoughtfully, 'So. You are Miss Catherine Maitland? How do you do, Miss Catherine Maitland?'

We had already shaken hands. We did so again. 'How do you do, Professor?'

'Ah, ha!' He clapped his hands. 'I love the English! A pretty girl helps to save my life—I break my old bones—I am in hospital many weeks—but do we discuss this? No, no. no! We ask each other how we do, and neither must give the answer. Not on! That is the correct idiom, now? And, is it—on—to presume to call you Cathy? As Yoss?' He wrinkled his nose. 'That terrible English J! Not for my aged Norwegian tongue, or I would do—as the good sister frequently assured me—myself a great mischief.'

He slept some of the long drive. Awake, he did not talk a great deal, but when he did he was very amusing. And astute. 'So, Cathy? You are surprised at such levity from the aged Professor? I tell you something! The Norwegian is the Scandinavian Irishman. Did you ever meet the Irishman too old to enjoy a good joke in good company? Now I have made the poor child blush! Yoss, discuss the weather! In moments of embarrassment the English always discuss the weather. This I have observed many times in many years.'

I changed my mind about Arne Alesund's remark before the ship was out of the Tyne. The Professor treated newly scrubbed decks, polished floors, stairs and companionways as trivial hazards to be ignored. After Joss had saved him from slipping for the third time by taking his weight whilst I collected the dropped crutches, I said quietly, 'He needs more muscle-power than I've got.'

Joss looked at me, hard. 'If you're feeling sick, ask the stewardess for those pills she's doling out.'

We had three single cabins in a row. The Professor was in the middle. He rested after we sailed, but refused dinner in bed. 'I have eaten too many meals alone. Tonight, I give a little party.'

I caught Joss's eye and shook my head, doubtfully. He gave me an ugly look in return and when we left to freshen up told me to stop being a bloody wet blanket. 'So he's putting the pressure on himself. How in hell would he've survived what he just has, if he hadn't? He's going home, not improbably for the last time, and he wants to celebrate. Sulk as much as you like on the way back, but tonight we're going to bloody celebrate. Or are you feeling sick? You're a filthy colour.'

I reminded him I was never sea-sick and had not spent the last week on holiday. 'Or have you forgotten what the A.U. can be like?'

'No. Nor one hideous moment I spent in the damned Unit!' He went into his cabin and closed the door. He hadn't called it 'the Unit' since Butler left it. I wished I hadn't noticed, and then, as pointlessly, that the last rush had not left me so extraordinarily tired. Dinner was a nightmarish thought as I wasn't hungry, but when it came, I enjoyed it. The Professor was in tremendous form and the food and wine were excellent. 'Now, another toast. Skål, Cathy! No, no, Yoss, not so! When you say "skål" you must look into the eyes of the one you toast whilst you finish your drink. I watch you! Better! I think now I will retire and you must join the dancing, eh?'

We did not argue then, or later, when he was settled for the night. I said, 'Joss, I'm too sleepy.'

'You look it. 'Night.'

I slept ten hours which probably accounted for my waking with such a headache. Despite dark glasses, the glare hurt my eyes. I turned my back on the sea and the Professor lowered his newspaper. He was lying in a cane deckchair against the sun-deck bulkhead behind us. 'Is the North Sea often this calm in late September, Professor?'

'Sometimes, yes. Sometimes, all month she rages and roars. The North Sea, as every sea, being as unpredictable as woman is to man.' He threw aside his rug as the ship altered speed to turn into the fjord. 'Stavanger! Good. I join you. And this afternoon—Bergen.'

We steadied him between us at the rail as we glided into the blue mirror of the fjord and the mountains curved behind us, shutting out the sea. As we neared the green arm of the harbour, a small fleet of fishing boats chugged by seawards, and countless little black and white ferries pottered around us like water beetles. 'Buses,' said the Professor. 'You go by road. We go by water.'

The tiny white wooden box houses with red, green, blue and grey roofs covering the steep slopes surrounding the harbour stopped looking like toys. We were close enough to see the colours of the curtains and in practically every window, rows of potted plants blooming in contented domestic jungles.

'Good!' The old man's sigh was contented as the engines stopped. 'Now, no delay as there is little time. I'll stay in my cabin whilst you two go ashore.' He waved aside our instant objections. 'So you will see Stavanger on your return? I will tell you something! No man can foresee or promise tomorrow. Tomorrow is either a hope or a dream. Today, and only today, we live. Today, a new land is waiting for you. But life does not wait, happiness does not wait, and nor, alas, does youth, or this ship! You have only two hours. Off! Off!'

Ten minutes later Joss knocked on my door with our landing passes. He raised his eyebrows at my coat. 'Chilly?'

I had just taken my temperature and a couple of anti-cold tablets. I did not feel strong enough for the truth, or another crack about wet blankets. 'Thought I might need it ashore after this central heating. Shouldn't we look in on the Prof. to say we're off?

'I've just told him and our stewardess.' He walked off leaving me to trail after him like an Arab wife. He did wait at the foot of the gangway. 'What do you want to do? Drift? Or make for anywhere special?'

I wanted to lie down and die. 'Drift. You?'

He had a look round. 'Same.' He smiled. 'Not another country. Another world. These are docks!'

I pushed up my dark glasses for a better look and thought of the grime and noise in the docks round Martha's. The little harbour was busy, but the quiet and the cleanliness were as soothing as they were incredible to our alien eyes. We drifted at first in a rather tense silence, and then in a kind of dream, stopping and moving on, without words.

We stopped some time to watch the water slapping like oil against the little boats tied up to the edge. Boats piled with green vegetable, potatoes, fresh fruit, baskets and baskets of crabs.

I jumped back. 'Joss, those crabs! They're walking out!'

He laughed. A long thin fisherman in a yellow jersey, jeans and red pom-pom hat waved at us. 'You wish to buy my crabs? Best crabs,' he said in English, 'only from me!'

'Not today, thanks!' We waved and moved on.

A little way on, a small boy was fishing with a bit of herring fixed to a bent pin on a piece of string. 'God,' muttered Joss, 'this takes me back.

The hours I fished the dykes at home and hardly ever caught anything—
which reminds me. Mother says it's a long time since you were down for
a weekend. I explained you wouldn't have one for a couple of weeks but
if you can make that one it'll suit her, as Dan'll be away and I'll be back
on the job. Plenty of room.'
    It was an ideal moment for explaining about my holiday. I did not
take it. I might have done, had the previous moments not been so
tranquil. I said I would write to his mother, simply must see the
fishmarket and charged across the cobbles with the eagerness of the
many housewives choosing with experienced eyes the live fish from the
open tanks. 'Ever seen so many fish?' I was talking to myself. Joss did
not reappear until I reached a sealskin slippers stall several minutes
later. 'Come and see what I've found, Cathy.'
    He took me across the road to the small and glorious mosaic of colour
that was the flower-market. He vanished again between the banks of
bronze, orange, yellow and white chrysanthemums and I ambled past the
azaleas and cyclamen to the roses. Roses red, pink, yellow, near-mauve,
and all exquisitely scented. The long-stemmed yellow tea-roses reminded
me of my father's pleasure when he took a First at the county show with
either the identical or a very similar variety. I touched one unthinkingly
as I tried to recall the name. The stout lady behind the stall lifted it
from the bunch. 'You wish?'
    'Yes, please.' Joss's voice answered. I glanced round and he thrust a
huge bunch of chrysanthemums at me. 'For Nina. Prof. says she fancies
them.' He paid for the rose. 'What are these called? Didn't your father
get his First with them?'
    'Yes. And couldn't have been more thrilled if he'd won the pools. I
can't remember the name. Isn't that awful?'
    'You were only about eleven.' He retrieved the chrysanthemums and
held on to the rose. 'I had a chat with my old mum about you and L.B.
Both very sweet, she said.' He looked round the flowers, then offered me
the rose. 'Couldn't find an olive branch. In lieu of—from me to you.' He
flushed slightly. 'Dead sloppy I am this morning. All this foreign travel
is disorientating for an English lad.'
    I wanted to cry, gently. So I laughed. 'Thanks.'
    'My pleasure! Now, for God's sake, woman, move, or we'll miss the
bloody ship!'
    We made it within minutes of their unhitching the gangway. Our
gallop had done strange things to my legs, but I put the rose in water
before I registered the fact. Later, I wrapped it in wet tissues and zipped
it in my sponge-bag. I felt remarkably like a deprived Victorian maiden
and not only because I hadn't with me an album in which to press it.
    It was evening, not afternoon, when we sailed into the Professor's

home port. The towering outlines of the seven mountains of Bergen
merged gently into the slowly darkening sky. The fir forests on the lower
slopes were black, not green, velvet and the snow above tree level
gleamed whitely in the light from the already high three-quarter moon.
The water in the fjord could have been navy blue silk and as our ship
moved towards her berth, she split the water with the sound of tearing
silk. There were only a few stars in the sky, but the land blazed with
millions stretching upwards from the harbour to what appeared to be
half-way up the mountains. 'If we have one thing in Norway,' said the
Professor, 'we have water. So, cheap electricity. So, we leave our lights
on. Electricity is much cheaper than the new switches.'

He was again at the rail between us, but this time when the engine
stopped, he did not say a word. Joss and I kept quiet. The expression on
the old man's face said all that needed to be said. No aged and frail
professor, but a tough old Viking, had sailed safely home.

The Alesunds, their son, the Professor's elder widowed daughter, her
two teenagers, Arne's brother with his wife and sub-teen sons were all
waiting. The reunion was affectionate, dignified and infinitely moving.
Very little was said as we drove in four cars to the Alesunds' house. The
Professor had lived with them since his wife's death some years ago.

The front door was open. The two little girls in dressing-gowns were
waiting in the hall with Arne's parents. By unspoken consent, everyone
stood aside to let the Professor walk alone through the front door, and
then, with a tidal wave of emotion, the entire family engulfed him.

Joss handed me a clean handkerchief. 'Haven't seen you weep since
you got measles on your eighth birthday.'

'Ninth,' I wailed. 'And what's wrong with my fancying a bit of slop?'

'Nothing's wrong, dearie. There, there—' He patted then gripped my
hand and his manner changed. 'You're running a temp,' he said very
quietly.

Nina had remembered us. 'Come in! Come in!' My face caused no
comment as every woman present was now happily mopping her eyes.
After one, and dynamic, drink to the Professor's return and a fresh orgy
of handshaking and congratulations, we were taken to our rooms to
change for the massive dinner party due directly the smaller children
were in bed. 'Late for them,' said Nina, 'but a great family occasion they
had to share.'

Arne put down my suitcase. 'Speaking frankly, we are a family-
minded people. You join us soon, no? We will have a great celebration!'

I smiled till they closed the door then flopped on the bed. The
aquavite had finished me off. Incapable of thought, I lay with my eyes
closed listening to Arne explaining to Joss the finer points of the new
bathroom they had installed between the guest rooms that were later to

be the girls' bedrooms. Then Joss said something about remembering he needed something I had for him in my case and had knocked on my door and come in before I was off the bed. He shut the door and leant against it. 'Second time round?'

I flopped back. 'I've been hoping not all afternoon, but I'm horribly afraid so. I could kill myself for bringing it here. What am I going to do?'

He did not answer, at first. He came and sat on the side of the bed, took my pulse, felt my forehead with the back of his hand, looked down my throat, then fingered the glands in my neck. He produced a thermometer, shook it down and smiled very kindly. 'Speaking frankly, darling, I suggest your best bet is to call me Sister Florence.'

Chapter Twelve

The house had been built on a small plateau blasted out of the side of a mountain. The window of my room overlooked the roofs of tower flats and box houses similarly perched and a fjord below. Across the water were high green hills and then mountains rising one behind the other as they had from the sea, and their colour kept changing. Black, blue, sepia, purple; each time I looked a different shade, each time the same impression of continuing to eternity.

From Friday night to Tuesday morning that was my only view of Norway. By mutual consent, since the elderly and very young are particularly susceptible to 'flu and its complications and the household included both age groups, Joss was my only human contact. The very little nursing I needed, he did very well. And he never came in without a message of regret and sympathy from one of the family. On Sunday evening he delivered another from the Professor with my supper-tray. I said I was sorry to be in purdah, but even yesterday when I had felt like death, it had been a tremendous relief that the family had the intelligence to realize that this was the only way to cut down the risk.

'That doesn't so much need intelligence as imagination. Much rarer, but they've got it.' He put the tray on the dressing stool he had turned into a bed-table. 'Not hungry? Don't let it bug you. What you can't eat I'll get rid of before anyone sees it when I wash up.' He sat on the foot of my bed. He was wearing a white drip-dry, scarlet cravat and black cords and looked very nice. He tanned easily and after the sea and northern air he could have been in the sun weeks. 'Nina's given me a fish-kettle as my crockery sterilizer. I now know why nurses have asbestos hands. Two days on the job, and I can pluck anything from boiling water.'

My temperature an hour ago had been normal for the first time since I took it in Stavanger. We hoped that was because I had the forty-eight-hour type, but as I was packed with aspirin and prophylactic antibiotics it was too early to tell. Joss, like every other doctor I knew of, never travelled without his private emergency supply of the latter. That saved us bothering Nina's doctor, and as I had started coughing on Friday night, very probably saved me from having bronchitis. I now had no trace of a cough and was feeling sufficiently better to be conscious I looked a wreck and thoroughly peevish. 'Your halo, Joss, is blinding me.'

He laughed. 'Thank God, yours has slipped! Your unnerving docility has had me wondering if I should ring Canada. Did I tell you Arne's contacted the shipping company? Sorry, thought I had—' he added before I could raise an objection. 'Obviously, you can't travel tomorrow—'

'Joss, if it's the forty-eight hour—can't I!?'

'Over my dead body, dearie,' he said pleasantly, 'and Arne's, and Nina's, and the Prof.'s—may I go on?' I nodded, glumly. 'The company have been very decent. If you're clear, they can fix us up on Wednesday, if not on the next ship back, which'll be Saturday. The Alesunds are hoping that's what it'll be—my God!'

'Wednesday you're due in Edinburgh?'

'No. I've written to Naomi and chums. But I haven't written to Miss Evans. Could be time, but to be safe I had better cable. What time are you due on on Wednesday?'

'I'm not.' I fiddled with my salmon mousse and explained.

There was a short silence. Then, 'That's handy.'

I looked up and he looked out of the window. 'Miss Evans didn't tell me what domestic reasons.'

'She wouldn't, as they're strictly personal. Not that I feel the cloak and dagger are necessary, but I'm not Naomi.' He faced me, slowly. 'Handy, but the hell of a waste of a holiday.'

'Not exactly fun for you, home-nursing in foreign parts. Dead bore.'

'That what you think?' He winced extravagantly. 'There goes my ego! I've been fancying myself with my lamp!'

'Joss, to be fair—'

'For God's sake, don't now tell me I've got a vocation, or I'll know you're having a relapse. Oak or elm? As you were—wrong country— pine? And do you positively insist on brass handles?'

I smiled weakly. 'You are a fool! No. You do lay a real cool hand on a fevered brow.'

'Watch it, or you'll get my cool hands round your fevered throat.' He stood up, smiling. 'We ministering angels have our feelings. I shall now go and soothe mine by having the remains of my ego hammered by the Prof.'

'More chess? But you're very good.'

He shook his head. 'Not in his league. Whatever ails his leg, his brain's first-rate.'

'Is his leg playing up?'

'No more than one would expect seeing what he does with it. He's scaring the daylights out of us all with the chances he takes, but as he says, plenty of time to rest when he's dead.' He nodded at my tray. 'You eat all that up and you'll grow into a big strong girl and be able to go home on Wednesday.'

I did a Dolly with my eyelashes. 'Yes, Sister Florence.'

'Wait.' he said, 'wait until you see me in my purple satin. That'll really send you.' He blew me a kiss and went off smiling. I went right off my food, but forced it down. He was being so damned kind, I had to co-operate. For the same reason, when he tentatively suggested next day ringing his mother and my going straight to the vicarage to convalesce until the weekend when he presumed I would want to be back in London, I agreed. I would have done so had he suggested I convalesced on the next moonshot. He promptly took my temperature. 'I thought so. Subnormal. Depression setting in nicely. Whose throat do you want to cut first? Yours or mine?'

My temperature stayed down and none of the family showed any signs of catching my 'flu, or went down with it later. At the farewell dinner-party on Tuesday night, Arne's brother Olaf suggested I had picked up an indigenous variety from some fellow-traveller and that could account for them all having some immunity. Olaf, a lawyer, was the elder and better-looking brother, though neither could be described as anything but plain. They were both large men with powerful shoulders, egg-shaped heads with scrubbing-brush hair-cuts and pale blue eyes that in repose had the same strange innocence I had first noticed in Nina's, but seemed even stranger in obviously successful professional men in their mid-thirties. I had never seen that innocence in the face of any adult Englishman of any age or background.

Joss said, 'This is quite possible, Cathy, and why it hit you so hard, though it's obviously a milder, shorter variety.'

'Then why didn't you get it?'

'I just don't get 'flu now.'

There was a universal groan. 'Joss,' I exclaimed, 'how can you so smugly ask for trouble?'

'I wasn't being smug. Just stating a fact.' He looked round the candle-lit table. Being a gala occasion, the cheap electricity was turned off. 'English hospitals have some kind of 'flu epidemic every year. Don't ask me how I've missed out, year after year. I just have.'

Nina said, 'I know why! There is an English poet—what is it—a pure heart?'

'His strength,' observed the Professor drily, 'is as the strength of ten because his heart is pure. Alfred Lord Tennyson.'

Joss raised his glass. 'Skål, Nina.'

The Professor's blue eyes had seen too much for innocence. He glanced from me to Joss. 'I have known learned pyschiatrists who would say you owed your good health not to any immunity from any virus, but from an immunity to the desire to escape into illness. Is that so? Ah, no!' He answered himself. 'That is a foolish question since such desires are too deep in the sub-conscious to be—to be—fished up, at will. Or even for us to be aware of their presence. The layers of the sub-conscious go deeper than the depth of the Atlantic and are as crowded with blind, unknown shapes as are the deep waters. But, I tell you something! Something less serious but of great interest. Have you looked upon an octopus, eh?'

'Octopus?' Joss echoed as the entire family bellowed with laughter.

The Professor said they could laugh, but only because the octopus had not climbed out of the sea before the man. 'I tell you! Such is the intelligence of that marine creature—nothing in the sea can compare. Such grace, such delicacy, has the suckered arms of that mollusc—such wisdom in that head—' He turned to me. 'You have not seen our Aquarium. Next time, I take you. Next time, we will have a great party. In Bergen we know how to give great parties, no?'

'Speaking frankly,' said Arne, 'yes! Bring Cathy back soon, Joss!'

'Very soon,' added Nina.

'You understand, Yoss? We will not wait too long for this next party. No waiting.' The Professor raised his glass. 'Now we drink a little toast to our English guests.' He hauled himself up on the arms of his high-backed chair and balanced on his good leg and one hand on the table. Joss and I alone remained seated and staring at our plates. 'To Cathy and Yoss, but for whom three of us would not be here tonight. Skål.'

'Skål,' chorused the family.

We thanked them and rose with our own glasses.

'One minute, Yoss.' The old man looked at us with an odd little smile. 'One more, then you may make a pretty speech, eh? First, I ask you two something. At Christmas, you've seen the tree from Norway in London?'

'Every year.'

'You know why it is there?'

We both flushed. Joss said. 'Well—er—nice gesture after the war.'

'A nice gesture?' The Professor nodded to himself. 'Very English. So, I tell you something, my young, very English, friends.' He looked slowly at the faces of his family. 'It is my belief and one I share with all here old enough to remember, that we are in this room tonight, because of your country.' He paused as the elders nodded, then went on in an unemotional tone that heightened the emotional moment. 'We saw our world collapse. We heard the world say England must collapse and our hearts were sick with the despair men only know when hope is dying. But England did not collapse. And we could hope again. Without hope, man is finished. With hope, the impossible is possible. Your country—do not forget—your country alone—gave back hope to Europe and maybe, the world. So, we send you a tree.' He lifted his glass. 'The toast is England.'

Leaning on the rail as the ship inched from the land next morning, Joss said, 'Follow that, he said.'

'You did all right.' I borrowed a handkerchief to wave back at the farewell party on the quay. The turn-out was even larger than on our arrival, as it now included the elder Alesunds and two little girls. Arne's mother had kissed us both. 'Such a heavy boy for you to carry. Such a heavy boy! Not goodbye. Until next time!'

Every adult repeated those last five words. The children echoed them parrot-wise, shouting them over and over through the fine rain as they waved wild, macaroni arms. The Professor was doing his stork act on his good leg and had his second crutch tucked under his arm like a walking stick to free his hand waving a red-spotted handkerchief. Joss said we had better get behind the sun-lounge glass before the old man finally broke his back slipping, or I got pneumonia. 'Feeling like chewed string? Sit down and I'll get us a drink. Or are you too wet?' He seemed about to touch my coat then changed his mind and put his hand in his pocket.

'Hasn't gone through.'

I sat on the arm of a chair, watching the tugs pulling and pushing our ship right across the harbour to turn us round. The rain turned much heavier, the fjord was gunmetal, and the greyness matched my mood. And Joss's. When he came back with our drinks, he stood fairly near, but we did not talk.

The huge warehouses on the waterside shrank to match-boxes; the yellow, the blue, the green, the tan, the white box houses changed back into toys; the seven mountains of Bergen receded behind the curtain of water and the ship's screws began to throb. The dark mountains round the entrance to the fjord were ominously close and their crests were hidden in the low sky. Just there, the fjord turned a dramatic emerald green, and the alteration of the ship's motion was as dramatic when we moved into the cold grey and impatient sea.

I steadied myself against the gentle roll as I got off the chair. 'Would you mind if I go and get things organized in my cabin?'

Joss shot me a rather peculiar look but only said that was a good idea and he'd do the same.

We were returning by another ship, but being from the same company our single berth upper deck cabins were almost identical with those on the outward voyage, though now side by side. This had vastly amused our hosts. 'Boy and girl next door again, eh?' I had laughed dutifully, but felt if I heard that corny joke again I would probably scream. When we reached our doors, Joss unlocked mine for me, handed me back the key and unlocked his own. 'I'll give you a shout for second lunch,' he said as the occupant of the third in the trio came into the narrow corridor.

She was a solid lady in sensible tweeds with short iron-grey hair battened down with a black velvet bandeau. 'Fellow Brits homeward bound? Miss Bilson!' Her handshake hurt. 'Just down from the Arctic Circle. Been up there? You should! Wonderful skies, wonderful sunsets. D.V., I'll go back! Always return when possible. First—look-see; second—get the feel. Used to tell my girls—taught forty years for my sins—you can't get the feel of a poem, picture, or place at first sight. Get the taste second time and never gulp. No taste when you gulp.' Her small eyes appraised us and my ungloved hands with interest rather than curiosity. 'Only done this crossing once? Mind some advice from an old salt? They say the sea may be choppy, which means roughly a Force 7 to 8 gale. Take a couple of anti-seasick tablets before we leave Stavanger and you'll enjoy your dinner tonight—particularly you, young woman! Bit green round the gills, already—but forgive me! First sitting! I must rendezvous with the cold table!' She bounded off.

I leant against my doorway. 'Never have I felt so inadequate.'

Joss smiled politely and suggested I put my feet up until lunch. After lunch he suggested I had an afternoon snooze. Whilst the ship was in Stavanger we drank coffee in the lounge and read good books. He provided me with a social history of England and himself with one on Scotland. 'I thought you only read history before and during exams, Joss?'

'No.' He didn't look up. 'To each his own form of escapism.'

I watched covertly his intent, unguarded face. With his present tan he could be a southern Italian until he opened his mouth. Not really good-looking, but the type of looks that turned every female head in the dining-room and this lounge. I thought of a remark some woman made to Byron. 'I shall long remember the gentleness of your manner and the wild originality of your countenance.' I knew what she meant.

He glanced up. I looked quickly at my book until my ears stopped drumming. We continued reading till the ship sailed. Watching the whole process while we were at supper, Joss switched back to the fraternal heartiness he had brought to a fine art over the weekend. As we knew each other too well, I knew we were equally relieved when I went to bed early.

One of the things that weekend underlined for me was the effect of early childhood on adult character. Being the eldest child in our two families, 'looking after the girls' had been bred into Joss before he lost his milk teeth. Also, consideration. As children we had known—as children invariably do—that while his parents loved him, his father had preferred Ruth, and his mother Danny. They were a singularly devoted couple and possibly when Joss had been born had unconsciously resented his intrusion. My father frequently said the odd child out in any family generally ended up the pick of the bunch if only because he or she early learnt the necessities of adaptability and unselfishness. 'Providing the child's character is strong enough to shrug off the inevitable chip.' Having been the apple of his eye and Paul of my mother's, in his lifetime I had not properly understood that. I had begun to do so in Canada, and, as I only clearly saw now, that was mainly why I had returned to England. Finding oneself for the first time in one's life as an outsider in one's own family was a disturbing experience. In my case, so disturbing that I had not dared face it until I got right away. As my bunk pitched and rolled, not unpleasantly as I had taken Miss Bilson's advice, I wondered uneasily how far I would have to get away from Joss, before I could view him as dispassionately. Then I wondered about Naomi's problem and Joss's burying himself in Scottish history. If the past was any guide to the present, all three of us had our problems, right now.

England had appeared on the horizon when Miss Bilson bounded into the lounge next morning. I was ready to go ashore and obediently waiting with my dressing-case and handbag, while Joss dealt with our other luggage and tips. 'How's the invalid this morning? Miserable complaint, *la grippe!* Rather break a leg. Broke one last year on Kilimanjaro—second time up, fortunately. Sleep well? Yes, indeed, thanks! Sleep like a top rocked in the cradle of the deep—sleep like a top, anywhere, D.G.! Had a very pleasant bridge game with your young man last night—plays a good hand—said he didn't care for dancing— still, thought it very decent of him to make up a fourth with three old fogies—and here he is and the good old U.K.!' She wrecked my knuckles for the day. '*Bon voyage*, ashore! No, thanks you, Mr Desmond, I'll manage my own bags—always travel light. Toodle pip, if I don't see you on the train!'

Joss surprised me by saying we should have a self-drive hired car waiting and offering her a lift.

'How kind! How very kind! But one of my Old Girls is meeting me in London and then I'm Devonshire-bound. Enjoy your drive, south-east. What time do you expect to be home?'

'With luck, six to seven.'

I waited till we were alone. 'Why didn't you tell me the Alesunds had fixed this up?'

'Assumed you knew. Sorry. Ready?'

'Hang on a moment.' I sat down. 'There'll be the usual queue at customs and immigration and there's something I want to sort out.' I looked up as he remained standing and watching me with his eyelids lowered and eyebrows up. 'Joss, I haven't asked your immediate plans as, well, none of my business, but, obviously, between us, the Alesunds and I've messed them up, good. When does your holiday end?'

'Next Friday. I can still have a clear week in Scotland.'

'But we're two-thirds of the way up.'

'And my car is in Asden. This set-up suits me fine. The Newcastle firm supplying today's car have a reciprocal arrangement with the garage where I've left mine. We'll change cars at Asden, I'll drop you off at home and after a meal and a bath get back to London as I've a heavy date there tonight, but not until tennish so I should make it easily. Tomorrow I'll drive north.'

It was absurd to feel so deflated. 'Good thing you like driving.'

'Isn't it?' He picked up my dressing case. 'Come on.'

'After he had signed for and we were in the waiting car, I said there was something else I had to say and thanked him for looking after me like a Dutch Uncle.

He smiled quietly. 'Thanks, darling. Nice to be appreciated. Too bad these docks don't run to a flower market or you could buy me a rose— which reminds me! On the 'phone mother said if you don't feel up to London on Saturday, ask Peter down as she and the old man'll be delighted to meet him. He is off, isn't he?'

'Yes.' I glanced at my dressing-case in the back. The rose was still in my sponge-bag. 'He only had Monday as an extra for this interview.'

'What interview?'

I explained as he drove off. He thought it a splendid idea. 'Peter'll enjoy being a G.P. and he should do a good job, though as your father would say, he won't get much of a chance till he gets himself a wife. Oh—Gawd!' He sighed. 'This traffic is bloody awful and I don't know my Newcastle. Mind if the lad concentrates till we're clear?'

'Of course not. Sorry I forgot what hell driving is when one doesn't know the roads.'

He slowed to glance at me. 'Yep. Death would be a happy release. Sooner I get you home to dear old mum, the better. This unnerving docility is wrecking my vibrations. Much more, and I'll have to start taking my own temperature.'

'Sorry—or is that the wrong thing to say?'

He smiled in answer. We did not talk again till we stopped for an early lunch in York.

He rang his home after our early tea in Cambridge. His mother had a W.I. and his father an Organ Fund meeting that evening but both hoped to be home by eight. We made such good time that we could only have missed their departure by a few minutes. The ground-floor hall light had been left on when he drew up in the vicarage drive. Momentarily, after switching off, he rested both arms on the wheel and his shoulders sagged.

'What was that you said about my liking driving?'

'Shoulders seized-up?'

'Uh-huh. They'll unseize in a bath. Let's get in.' He heaved himself out and unloaded the luggage from the boot of his own and smaller car. 'Stiff?'

'Bit.' I felt more limp than my first day out of bed. I knew as surely as I knew my own name, this was the end of the road. We had been alone since noon yesterday. He had not even touched my hand, accidentally. Why should he? What normal man wanted to touch his sister's hand?

He unlocked the front door. 'Supper'll be eight-thirtyish. Mother said don't wait up if you want to go straight to bed and anyway there'll be tea and sandwiches waiting in the school-room.'

I was trailed in behind him. 'Your mother's a remarkable woman. She thinks of everything.'

'She does.' He sorted the post on the hall table. 'One for you.'

'Me?' I took the envelope curiously. 'Peter! How does he know I'm here?'

He shoved his post unread in his pocket. 'Naomi said she'd be writing to Stan. He'll have told him.'

'How did she know? Didn't you say you wrote her on Saturday? This wasn't fixed till Monday.'

'No, dearie. But there is such a thing as the international telephone service.' He picked up my bags. 'Your usual room.' He went on up with them.

I followed very slowly. There was nothing to hurry for now.

Chapter Thirteen

He waited in the school-room till the electric kettle boiled, made tea, called to me to help myself and went on to his room. I heard the bath running as I poured my cup. I took it and Peter's unopened letter to one of the aged cane armchairs on either side of the heavily guarded electric convector in the hearth.

That room evoked such an attack of nostalgia that for some minutes I just sat, stared, and rode with the punch. The solid table at which, for years, Ruth and I had done our homework was covered with the old red baize cloth with a bobble fringe that went back to the years when this had been a communal nursery. The lower shelves of the white-painted bookcases were still jammed with Noddy, Big Ears, Mary Mouse; higher up the battered sagas of the March girls and Katy were crowded between William, Jennings, Jim Hawkins, rows of Percy F. Westerman, Black Beauty and the smug Swiss Robinsons. Jane Austen, Charlotte Brontë, Mrs Gaskell and Charles Dickens shared the top shelves with science fiction, Dorothy L. Sayers, Agatha Christie and Ellery Queen. And the tatty grey carpet shared with the blue hearth-rug the same fading ink stains. The room as always smelt faintly of lead, Plasticine, carbolic soap, and for some reason we had never been able to trace, burnt toast.

I dragged myself back to the present, opened Peter's letter without enthusiasm, but for once was relieved and not appalled by its length. Peter either communicated on paper with three words on a postcard, or not less than six closely written case-history sheets. He never used normal writing-paper, even for airmail.

The first two sheets concerned his interview. I read slowly, as it gave me something else to think about. Though convinced he had made a hideous impression, he thought it would have been much worse had Roxanne not decided to visit her father and hold his, Peter's, hand. She had been very sweet, he wrote, and took him to tea with her father, but he wished I had warned him Mr Alder looked exactly like a middle-aged Hamlet. He wished I hadn't got 'flu, as he wanted to talk to me about Roxanne. Mr Alder had suggested they both spend this coming weekend with him in Leeds. Roxanne seemed to think it a good idea. Peter thought it a good idea. Did I? And if so could I ring him before Saturday? Stan said I would be at the Desmonds. 'Stan—' but the sheets were in the wrong order. I searched smiling hugely for the correct follow-on. '—had a letter from our Naomi yesterday and is being hellish smug whilst the A.U. reels as Joss had tipped him off. Expect you know all from him now, but in case you don't, get this!'

I had to read the next item three times before it got through. It left me gasping, not smiling.

Two weeks ago in Malta, Naomi Butler had married quietly a Benedict's man called Ian MacDonald to whom she had previously been twice engaged. 'Seems after the last great out-falling, she shook the dust of Benedict's from her apron and crossed the river, and didn't see him again till he visited her in Florence. (And why weren't we told? Someone has blundered—though Stan says he reckons folk never see what they don't want to see.) Anyway, chap then followed her to Malta. Stan says sun either opened her eyes or blinded her, but she sounds dead chuffed and her new in-laws likewise. She said she'd waited to write until after she had met them as they weren't at or warned about the wedding and she felt it would be incorrect to make it public before meeting them. I said what was wrong with a joyful cable? Stan says nothing unless you have a fixation for doing the correct thing the correct way and that's the way that wins gold medals. I still think she slipped up when she opted for our A.U. to give herself time to think. Who has time to think in any A.U.—or wants it? Get this next—'

I could not, for the moment. I put down the letter, drank some tea, and breathed very, very carefully. Joss knew and had known some time. Joss was driving to London tonight, Scotland tomorrow. The question was—since her name wasn't Naomi, what was it? Fiona? Catriona? How the hell could I know? I just knew Joss and young men in general. When one was determined, come what may to get from A to B, commonest things being the most common, the girl he most wanted was at B. I picked up the last page.

'—this morning George, Dolly and I had to go out in a Crash Call ambulance. First time in months and I don't fancy a repeat. Spot on the clearway just beyond the fly-over. When we arrived, all we could see at first was twisted tin flung all round the road and a bloody great red pool in the middle. George stopped to pick up what we thought was some poor sod's false teeth. Cath, they were not false. We found the chap who owned them in five separate pieces. ...'

'God, no!' I dropped the sheet and buried my face in my hands as my stomach contracted.

'What the devil has that fool written to do this to you?' Joss's urgent voice was very close. I lowered my hands to find him bending over me.

'Read this.' The page shook as I held it out. 'That last paragraph.'

He backed as if offered a ticking bomb. 'Don't be so bloody silly! I'm not reading another man's letter to his girl!'

'Don't *you* be bloody silly!' Even my voice was shaking. 'Would I be handing it to you if it were—I was—oh hell—you know what I mean! Read it!'

His X-ray glance couldn't have been improved by Miss Mackenzie, but he did as I said. His face twisted. 'Christ!' he muttered. 'The impact must've been around one hundred and forty.'

'Joss, please—skip it. I know it's my job—I'll go back to it—but just now I haven't the guts to take it. Do something for me?' He gave me another X-ray as he nodded. 'See if there's anything more than will I ring him about Leeds and love, as I can't face the rest. Is that all?'

Again, he hesitated, then obliged. 'Apart from saying Roxanne'll ring you over the weekend.' He folded the sheet. 'She off on another telly commercial in foreign parts? And want this back?'

'No, thanks,' I pushed the other sheets into the envelope and handed it to him. 'Shove it in there and then put it—oh—the back of the toy cupboard'll do. The closed one. I'll get around to shifting it some time, but I don't want to think about it now.'

He said oddly, 'Yes. You always used to sling things you wanted to forget in here.' He closed the cupboard doors. 'How did Leeds go?'

'I think, very hopeful.' With the letter hidden I was glad of a cheering subject. After telling him Peter's personal news, I smiled slightly. 'With any luck, this is my swan-song as his favourite teddy bear. Incidentally, you were right. Stan told him I'd be here and has heard from Naomi. In—some detail.'

'You mean she's told him she's finally had the sense to marry Ian MacDonald. If the Archangel Gabriel isn't a Scot he should be, seeing that chap's patience. God knows I wouldn't have put up with what he has, though there's a lot I like about Naomi.' He refilled my cup and poured himself one. I'm glad she's written to Stan. He's such a nice chap even she likes him—and she never has taken kindly to the human race—or not until she knows said race well. That takes her a good three years. Doesn't mix easily. Some don't.'

He had sounded as if talking in one language and thinking in another, but being preoccupied, it took me a little time to notice both that and his changed appearance. He had on his best dark suit, clean white shirt, Benedict's tie and had had a shave. He looked incongruously smooth in this setting, disturbingly attractive, and, I realized belatedly, very angry.

That tie always had worried me. I had to test the untested ice. 'Your date tonight at Benedict's?'

'Yep.' He glanced at the closed toy cupboard. 'You're all for Roxanne taking Peter off your back?'

'I'll say! I'm very fond of old Pete, and he's one of my best friends, but to be thoroughly corny, there comes a time when the best of friends must part and I think that time has come if only as life in the A.U. provides me with enough problems. Once I used to enjoy collecting all my friends. Not any more. Haven't the energy. Maybe I'm getting old.'

'Everyone feels that way after 'flu.'

'This isn't post-'flu. This has been coming on for some time, but I didn't knowe how to break the habit without hurting his feelings. That I didn't and wouldn't want to do.'

'A touchingly faithful teddy bear.'

I stiffened. 'Why so superior? Isn't this—isn't this very much the set-up between you and Naomi?'

'Oh, no. Oh, no.' He walked to the bookshelves and stood briefly withi his back to me. 'As a teddy bear, sweetie—' he faced me slowly '—I'm not in your league. Far too immature. That's my trouble.'

I stood up. 'What do you mean—in my league?'

He put his hands in his pockets ·and looked me over as that first morning in the A.U. 'In my infantile league,' he drawled, 'the only teddy bears that get taken to bed have brown mock fur all over them and growl when you punch their stomachs.'

I blushed more with amusement than anything else. 'You don't seriously think—'

'Serious thought on holiday, darling, is something I avoid like the plague!' He looked at the table cover. 'Strange to remember I once had. to stop you from chewing off those bobbles. And how you'd then beat it under the table and glare at me accusingly as a puppy denied the privilege of eating the new rug.' He looked back at me. 'But those days are long gone. You do as you like, since that's what you like to do—and I do likewise. And that, as of now, is to get moving and see my old boss at Benedict's tonight as he's tentatively offered me a job when I finish with Hoadley and I want to clinch the deal before I join with the cohorts of MacDonalds I've promised to look up across the Border. Once my holiday ends, the year and my contract'll have ended before I next draw breath—and that can't be too bloody soon for me! I won't hang on for the parents. I'll stop by at the village hall and explain to mother. Why don't you go to bed? You look terrible.' He smiled sardonically. 'Recently, I wouldn't have said our mutual roots had many advantages, but at least it means I know I don't now have to offer you a shoulder. Poor old Peter. I'm almost sorry for him. I hope he gets a better deal from Roxanne.'

'Hold on, Joss!' I spoke between my teeth and got between him and the door. 'I don't want to wreck your future, but there are some things up with which I'm not prepared to put! So who told you I'd been to bed with Peter?'

'For God's sake, don't be tedious, darling! I'm not digging dirt in this suit.'

'Then let me tell you something!' I told him the truth. 'Of course, if you've been fool enough to believe the grapevine, you won't believe me.'

His eyebrows rose languidly. 'Maybe that would impress me, had I only been put in the picture in strict confidence by no more than ten of your old chums the night before you turned up in the A.U. I'll admit after that I lost count as well as interest. But—er—as you may remember—more than once you kindly provided me with the type of evidence that does tend to lend an air of verisimilitude to an otherwise bald and unconvincing narrative. So stop pretending you're an outraged Victorian maiden since we both know only one of those epithets is applicable.'

I leant against the door. 'Are you talking about the night you brought Roxanne home from some ghastly party?'

'That could be called the highlight, though it wasn't the first or last time I've seen you in Peter's arms.' His colour had risen, too. 'The first Monday morning's reunion was touching beyond belief.'

'Don't be so moronic, Joss—he was just pleased to see me! As for that night—just bloody listen!' Again I told him the truth and this time threw in my comments to Roxanne on that occasion. 'This teddy bear doesn't much mind being cuddled by her friends,' I added, 'but she minds very much being called a liar to her face.'

He walked in silence to the far side of the table and folded his arms. His colour had so drained even his lips were white. 'Obviously I had my lines crossed. I'm sorry. I apologize.'

My anger evaporated. I had not seen him so white since the day my brother smashed his new watch and my mother—unfairly, since Paul started the fight—made Joss, the bigger and older boy, apologize first. The next time Paul started a fight, my father had been watching and had had to break it up. Back in our house, when mother complained of Joss's savage temper, my father reminded her all boys were little savages under the skin, but he had never known Joss hit first. *Cet animal est très méchant. Quand on l'attaque il se défend.*'

'Joss. Did you mind?'

'Mind?' He winced visibly. 'Cathy, have you an amnesial blank over Ruth's wedding day? Or—' he jerked his head at the toy cupboard '—have you just shoved it out of sight?'

'No, but—'

'So you remember what I said to you?' His tone was much calmer than my altered heart rhythm. 'Just didn't believe it?'

'Joss, I—'

'Yes, or no?'

'Well—yes—at first. Not after.'

'Why not? Come on! Naomi?'

'Yes, but not just her.' I needed a long breath. 'You weren't exactly forthcoming that first morning in the A.U.'

'Did you expect me to be? Having heard *ad nauseam* Cathy Maitland was returning from Canada to Peter Anthony's waiting arms, I walk in and—surprise, surprise—clinch just breaking up. What was I supposed to do? Tap him on the shoulder and say, mate, you don't know what you missed on Saturday night? As I didn't—you just wrote me off?'

'No—oh, hell, Joss! I thought—well—after the wedding, the soft lights, sweet music—you know what I mean!'

'Do I?' He flushed, darkly. 'You're damned right, I do! As the Prof. would say, Cathy. I will tell you something! I never thought my ego could take more of a bashing than you gave it that afternoon here before that smash, but I was so wrong!'

'Listen, please, listen! I know that wasn't fair—'

'On the something contrary, since you thought I was having it on with one woman and making passionate passes at another, your reaction was fair bloody comment! Twenty-four years!' He slapped the table with one hand. 'You've had twenty-four years to add me up and that's what you figure? Thanks very much!'

'Joss, cool it! You don't have to be hurt—'

'Don't have to be? God Almighty!' Suddenly, the lid came off. 'You stupid, insensitive little bitch, what do you think I'm made of? Expect me to enjoy being thought not merely a liar, but a lecherous bastard so short on small-talk and self-preservation that I tell all my dates I bloody love 'em and kiss 'em as I've kissed you, as a variation on chatting 'em up about the weather? And wouldn't let the fact that the woman I'm supposed to be hitched to is some place else or ill, stop me? Right little sex-maniac, am I?' He slammed the table with both hands. 'Am I? Then it's bloody lucky for you I've been off-colour this last weekend and specifically these last twenty-four hours. Right next door and all I had to do was walk in and there you'd be in another of those prim little nighties you fancy—which, incidentally, are a damn sight more seductive than anything you can see through. And did I mind having to keep my hands off? For your information, Cathy, I minded like bloody hell! As I minded having to watch you and Peter in and out of the A.U.! And having to walk out on you that night after the wedding. Have you forgotten your set-up then?' He only gave me time to shake my head. 'So you've remembered you were punch-drunk from the flight, homecoming, and the champagne. Did you realize your resistance was so

low you could probably have been had for the taking? God only knows
why you think I didn't. By your reckoning, no time'd suit me better than
the time when circumstances have already obligingly lowered the girl's
defences—'

'This isn't true—'

'Stuff that hypocritical docility! It was tough enough to take when I
thought you were using it as a civilized way of holding me off, for
Peter's sake! It's a damned effective defence, as only a sadist fancies
swiping that other cheek! I never thought I was a sadist, but right now, I
wouldn't bet on it! Did I mind?' He caught his breath. 'Yes! So bloody
much that though you've had 'flu and I'm still fool enough to love
you—nothing—nothing would give me greater pleasure than to clout you
now into the middle of next week! Take my advice and stay that side of
the table till I've cooled off!'

I was flattened against the door by shock and joy. I had to lick my
lips to speak. 'Is it all right if I get something from my room?'

'Better still, stay there! You'll be safe! As I've told you, we
sex-maniacs can go off-colour!'

I didn't risk smiling. Not yet. I opened the door, then spun round.
'You won't vanish in your car?'

'I'm not that much of a fool. If I got behind a wheel at this moment
I'd be in five pieces before I was a mile out of the village.' He saw my
grimace. 'I warned you, Cathy.'

'Yes.' I met his angry, hurt, and infinitely vulnerable, eyes. 'Back in a
moment.' I rushed into my room, flung open my dressing-case, and then
went very slowly back to the schoolroom with my sponge-bag. He had
not moved. I stood at the other end of the table. 'By—er—a strange
coincidence I just happen to have an olive branch in here.' I flicked the
sponge-bag to him. 'As I love it quite disproportionately, I'd rather you
didn't shove it down with my back teeth, but won't hold it against you if
you do. But if you laugh,' I added quietly, 'I shall probably kill you with
my bare hands.'

For a second time I could have offered him a ticking bomb. Then he
picked up and unzipped the bag and emptied the contents into the palm
of his left hand. He stared at the dead rose and soggy brown tissues for
about thirty seconds. At last, he looked over to me with an expression
that held more than a hint of a resemblance to the Professor's as we
sailed into Bergen. 'Have you got an album in which to press this,
Cathy?' he asked unsteadily.

'No.'

'Can I give you one?'

'Yes, please.'

His face tensed, but not with anger. 'What kind do you want?'

'Huge and white with gilt edges—' my voice was uneven '—and—and a red velvet heart and lots of lovely slushy flowers on the cover.'

The tension vanished. 'It'll bore the kids—but the grandchildren'll love it.'

'That's what I thought.'

'Did you? When?'

'Well, actually, it's been in one of those cupboards since Ruth's wedding.' I smiled shyly. 'I—sort of took it out for a better look while you were pounding me to a jelly.'

'Pounding didn't worry you?'

'Shook me, but I knew you wouldn't clout me. You've threatened to clout Ruth and me, long as I can remember, but you never would and we knew it. That's why I only beat it under this table when you wouldn't let me eat the bobbles. Had you been Paul or Danny, I'd have beat it fast for one of the parents. That's why—' I spread my hands '—this weekend I thought—just old Joss doing his usual big-hearted stuff. And now knowing how it was with you and Naomi—hell—she was your type and—and only last week she got the weight of the cake right!'

'She did.' His eyes smiled wonderfully. 'Made a nice extra wedding present. She'd brought Ian down to meet the parents for the afternoon.'

'You didn't put that on your postcard!'

'It didn't seem a good idea, quite apart from the fact that she didn't want it publicized, as I suspected the Alesunds and the Prof. were determined to throw us together. To each his own defence mechanism.' He swung himself over the table as he used to as a boy and landed beside me. He did not touch me. 'Why didn't you tell me you were feeling ill at Stavanger? And on holiday? Not to lumber me?'

'Yes.' I touched his tie. 'Do you really have to leave tonight?'

'No.' He held my hand against his thudding chest. 'I can see the man any time this week. The job he's offering is good and has a flat, rather like Stan's, thrown in. Can we talk about it, later?'

'I'd like that.'

We smiled the same smiles. He said, 'I don't have to be in Scotland. Didn't have to be in Malta. It was just somewhere to go when they shoved this holiday at me to get the books straight—out of range.'

'Of me—and Peter?'

'Yep.' He patted my flattened hand. 'You can feel what you do to me. And you, my darling, have done it since Ruth's wedding. Absurd state of affairs. Touch you and my rate goes up around one hundred and sixty, stat. Do you wonder working with you in the A.U. nearly turned me into an old man? As for this weekend—' He drew me into his arms and buried his face in my hair. 'I gathered around the house that Olaf and wife had offered to fetch the Prof. by sea, but our trio weren't having any.' He tightened his arms. 'Nor were we.'

I kissed his chin. 'The Prof. would say, very English.'

'Speaking frankly, darling, no wonder the world thinks us mad.' He raised his head to look into my face. 'Know something, Cathy? I adore you.'

'Know something, Joss? I do, you.'

He kissed me then as if it were years, not months, since Ruth's wedding and we have to make up for all the missing years. And then we heard his mother calling from the hall. 'Children! I'm back! Where are you?'

He gave a kind of stifled yelp that was a mixture of happiness, laughter and impatience and suddenly lifted me high in his arms. 'Up here aboard the lugger!' he yelled back.

Chapter Fourteen

The last Thursday of the year was our last working day in Martha's. We fixed to stay that night in town as the Lawsons were giving us a farewell party and we would drive down to the vicarage on Friday morning. Joss was spending Friday night with Ruth's in-laws as our wedding was on Saturday. I was marrying from the vicarage and the Vicar's brother was giving me away as he had Ruth.

The Alesunds were flying over. Professor Ulvik bombarded us with cables. 'Did I not say we would have a great celebration?'

Mrs Frayling wrote: 'How very kind of you to invite us. Yes, indeed, we remember you both. ...'

Miss Evans said, 'Oh, dear! Oh, dear! But—how delightful!'

Being not only Thursday, but the day before New Year's Eve, we had one of the quietest as well as coldest afternoons of the winter in the A.U. The party was due to start at seven; Stan, Peter, Dave Palmer and I were off at six. Joss finished in the Orthopaedic Unit at five-forty-five. Apart from Naomi, her husband and Roxanne, all the other guests were from Martha's. 'Going to bankrupt me,' said Stan, 'so the next happy couple from the A.U. gets seen off on canteen coffee.'

George, Dolly, Henty, now an official staff nurse, Hamish Geddes and an R.A. on loan from the General Theatres were staying on to run the department with the student nurses and medics. Our two newish staff nurses were off that day to be back to support Dolly over what, in all probability, would be one of the heaviest weekends of the year. Miss Evans had firmly dismissed my tentative offer to alter the date. 'Miss Mackenzie is as satisfied as I am that Miss Jones will manage—and Miss Mackenzie is on for the weekend.'

Everyone, including the S.S.O., had co-operated over the Lawson's party. Peter's replacement joined us at five. By half-past, we were empty.

Stan surveyed the staff-packed Receiving Room. 'Anyone for hockey? We can play it seven-a-side.' He smiled at me. 'You'll not know yourself with real work to do when you get to your new medical ward across the river, Sister.'

'Ever-so-dear sir, spare us the reminder of such treachery! A betrayal, no less!' Dave swept imaginary tears from his eyes. 'To think we took the man to our bosom—cherished him—nay—revered him—and what does he do? Swipes our Sister!' He waved at the wall clock. 'Twenty minutes from now and lost, but lost to us for ever—oh, woe!' The red light was flashing. 'Turn that off! I want to go to a jolly party!'

We all watched the new fourth-year's expression as she wrote swiftly, and at length. Stan murmured, 'Looks as if party's coming to us, lad. But, jolly?'

The accident was less than a mile away. A heavy commercial van had skidded onto a pavement, into a rush-hour 'bus queue and crashed on into a shop window. The driver was killed outright. Thirty-four people were injured, fifteen seriously.

Stan rang his wife while we waited for the first ambulance. It arrived at ten to six. It was twenty to eleven before we were empty again.

Stan crumpled his limp mask into a paper ball. 'And we needed seven-a-side.' He beckoned Peter and Dave. 'You two get off.' And when they said they would rather wait for us to finish the notes, 'Any more ruddy mutiny and I'll pull rank, change the rota, and there'll be no early half-days Saturday for either of you. You'll your lovely lass waiting, Peter, and this'll be toughest on her seeing she's not in the trade, though it'll teach her what to expect once you're wed. Best get over before she changes her mind. You too, young Dave. Out from under my feet! Feet!' He fell into a chair. 'I can stand the blood, the muck, the ruin of me social life, and a diet of bridge rolls and sausages on sticks for the next month—but I can't stand me fallen arches!' He propped an elbow on the desk and smiled, wearily. 'I'd chuck you out, Cath, if I thought I'd get away with it.' He picked up a 'phone. 'Harry? S.A.O. Orthopaedic Theatre finished yet? On the last chap now? Which one's that? Him? No. He'll not take long. Thanks.'

Goerge helped with the notes. Hamish Geddes and medic. students helped Dolly and Henty with the cleaning, clearing and re-stocking as the student nurses had had to be sent off, protesting. The place was straight by half-past eleven and Dolly stayed on and came in with fresh tea and some rather stale biscuits as we finished. 'Sorry, but these are all we've got in our tin.'

Joss knocked on the open office door. 'May I come in?'

Stan offered him a saucerless cup. 'Make yourself at home! You're one of the family.'

'Thanks.' Joss smiled at me as he sat down. He looked as weary as the other men, but there was no weariness in his smile. 'All go, ain't it?'

'If there's one thing I can't abide,' said Stan, 'it's a dull moment. Repair shop packed it in for the night?'

'Quarter of an hour ago.'

'How'd they make out?'

'They should all do,' said Joss slowly, 'but some'll take a bit of time. How was it here?'

I said, 'Bit nasty.'

'That's right,' said Stan, 'but could've been nastier. We packed 'em all off breathing, which is more than I thought we'd do when some came in.'

George said, 'And tomorrow's New Year's Eve.'

'Brace up, lad,' said Stan kindly. 'Comes round every year. So this time next year when you've got my job you'll know what to expect.' George went purple. 'Didn't you know you were in the running for it?'

I looked at Dolly looking at her cup. 'Actually,' muttered George, 'one—hoped.'

'Dead sensible,' said Joss and Stan nodded.

I did not say anything as Miss Mackenzie was in the doorway. I stood up, quickly. 'I'm sorry we're so late, Sister. We are just going.' The others had risen. 'Er—would you like a cup of tea?'

From her expression I was offering her whisky. 'At this hour—yes—I think I would, thank you, Sister.'

Dolly fetched a cup and saucer. I gave Miss Mackenzie my chair, Stan gave me his and sat on the desk when we all sat down again. He asked, 'Emergencies quiet, Miss Mackenzie?'

'Just now, Mr Lawson. Quite a busy night all round. I only stepped in to say goodbye to Sister and'—she was smiling—'Mr Desmond. St Martha's will miss you both.'

I had never been so glad Joss was a Benendict's man, and had not been brainwashed by her as a student. He said the right things for us both whilst the rest of us exchanged shocked glances. He did blush like a schoolboy when, with a return to her habitual gravity, Miss Mackenzie said she had heard the patients in the Orthopaedic Unit had circumnavigated the rule forbidding members of the staff to accept presents. 'A specially printed outsize card bearing the crest of St Martha's which they have all signed, I belive?'

Joss fingered his collar. 'Yes, Sister.'

'A card can scarcely be termed a present, but I would suggest few presents could give greater satisfaction.' She looked at us all. 'One misses the personal touch in departmental work.'

Stan agreed. 'One doesn't like to be impersonal, but often they've moved on before there's time to remember the names on the labels.'

I said, 'Last time; in Canada; and here; it still feels funny not having patients to say goodbye to.'

Miss Mackenzie said, 'I've no doubt. But I know Mr Desmond will agree that had you not moved them on, there would be a great many less names on his card.'

Joss nodded. 'You couldn't be more right, Sister. We repair them in the Orthopaedic Unit, but this is where the lives are saved.'

She turned to Stan. 'How many have you saved, Mr Lawson? This last year? This last six months? Can you count? Stan shook his head. 'No,' she added crisply, 'it would need an accountant to give the figure from the numbers you deal with.' And then she said, 'In an Accident Unit you can't hear the voices of your recovering patients, but if you stop and think for a wee while, you should hear the voices of the living who, but for your work, would be dead. A pleasing sound.' She pushed back her chair and we all stood up. 'If you'll kindly give me your keys, Sister, I'll lock up with Sister Jones.' Dolly's expression made Martha's history by evoking Miss Mackenzie's second smile in half an hour. 'It is after midnight, Sister Jones. You have taken over.' She accepted the keys, shook my hand and then Joss's. 'Bring your wife over to see us when you return to St Benedict's, and take Sister home, now. It's been a long day.'

I collected my cloak and the dressing-case with my things for the party from the changing-room. Joss took the case, we said another round of goodbyes and walked slowly down the A.U. corridor, into Emergencies hall by the staff door, and out of the main entrance. We did not speak and he did not reach for my hand until I slung on my cloak and we crossed the hospital yard. 'Do you mind leaving too much, darling?'

I glanced over my shoulder. 'Not with you.'

He laced his fingers through mine. Our hands were cold, but the clasp warm. 'What do you want to do? Catch the end of the party?'

'Not unless you want to.'

'Not tonight. I just want to be alone with you.'

We walked on to the residents' car park, he put my case on the roof of his car and we both turned instinctively and looked back at the hospital. The theatre blocks were in darkness. The red night lights were on in all the wards, but the corridors and stairwells were brilliantly lit.

Ghostly, white-capped figures flitted by the red windows; white-coated figures walked more slowly past the lighted windows and would walk more slowly still as the night went on. In silence, and again it seemed instinctively, Joss raised his right hand in the old Roman salute, then we got into the car.

In the darkness he kissed me with passionate gentleness. 'Thanks for this, Cathy. Thanks a lot.'

I kissed him back.

Only the main gates were open at that hour of the night. Joss drew up before the small gate lodge and switched on the inside lights briefly for the porter pressing his face to the window to identify us. He waved us on, we waved back, Joss switched off the interior lights and nosed carefully into the always busy main road. The gate porter sat down and picked up his mug of tea. He did not come down to shut the gates as that was the entrace used day and night by the ambulances, so the gates always stayed open.

Big Ben chimed the half-hour as we crossed the river.

'Tomorrow,' said Joss, 'tomorrow. Last one this side of Jordan.'

We drove on, smiling.